Note from Author

Content Warnings

———◆◇◆———

This book contains a lot of heavy themes that might be triggering for many. Please, carefully read the list below before going into the book. As an author, I try to keep my emotional state out of what I write and try to not reflect it into the characters, but unfortunately many of the characters are portrayed as dealing with issues that I and many like me suffer in real life. This book will get heavy at times so please do not skip this list:
Gore, death, mutilation, murder, blood, vulgar language, torture, self harm, violence, child abuse, emotional and physical abuse, loss of loved one, depiction of panic attack, anxiety, depression and PTSD, death of a child, flogging, scars, alcohol abuse, hallucinations, derealisation, war, mention of infertility and stillbirth, mention of genocide, dissociation.

And lastly, explicit content. This series is intended to be read by mature readers (18+) as there are several explicit scenes.

For those living in winter and searching for spring.

PS: Mother, do I really need to say it again? This is as far as you can go in this book. Turn around now.

THE AURA

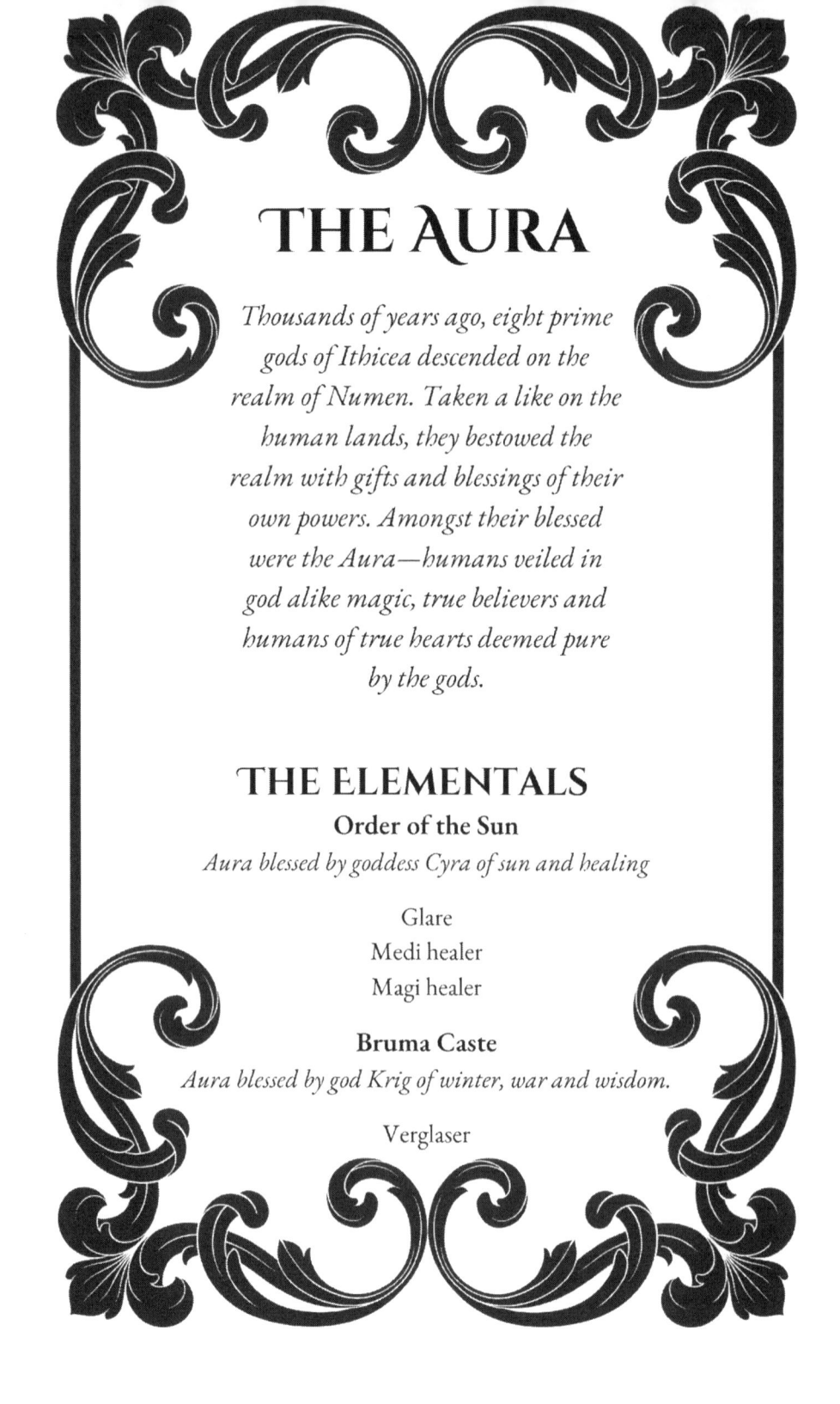

Thousands of years ago, eight prime gods of Ithicea descended on the realm of Numen. Taken a like on the human lands, they bestowed the realm with gifts and blessings of their own powers. Amongst their blessed were the Aura—humans veiled in god alike magic, true believers and humans of true hearts deemed pure by the gods.

THE ELEMENTALS

Order of the Sun
Aura blessed by goddess Cyra of sun and healing

Glare
Medi healer
Magi healer

Bruma Caste
Aura blessed by god Krig of winter, war and wisdom.

Verglaser

Order of Sky and Air
Aura blessed by god Nubil of sky, thunder and clouds

Elding
Nimbus
Zephyr

Order of Life and Soil
Aura blessed by goddess Plantae of earth and rebirth

Senchi
Shinze

THE SPIRITUALS

Order of the Dark
Aura blessed by goddess Henah of moon, darkness, shadows and empathy

Umbra
Empath
Obscur

Order of Fire
Aura blessed by god Adan of fire and truth

Scarlet

Crafter Order
*Magic wielders, different from Aura,
blessed by god Celesteel of magic,
otherworld and spirits*

Dark Crafter

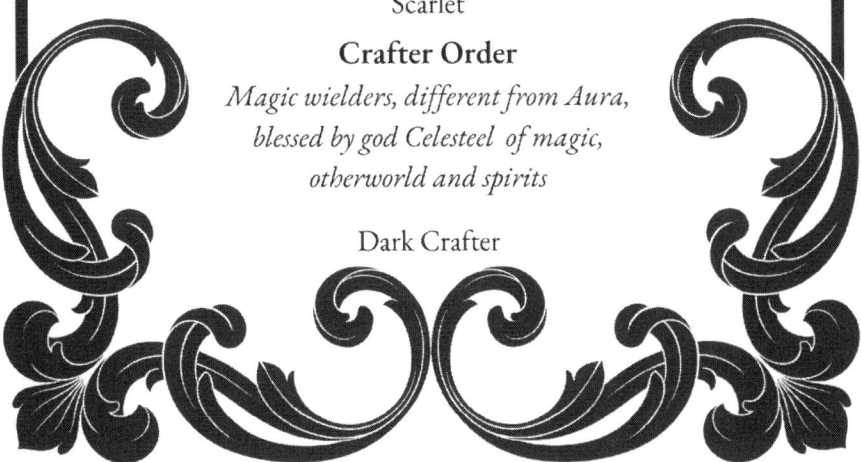

Numengarth

Solarya
Theros
Noor Island

Azar unburnt Isles

Hollow sea

Seraphim
Heyes

Azar unburnt Isles

Mahara Channel

Dravan Isle

Taren
Olympia

Breshall

Moor sea

Vrammethen
Norodoh

The Darmain Island

Comnhall

Lyra

Dardanes

Casmere

Islines

Brogmere

Tenebrose

Venzor

Koy

Grasmere

Sable Abyss

...er sea

Soren Forest

Isjord

Hanai

Fernfoss Village

Aru

The Sayuri

Myrdur

Kirkwall

Arynth

River Nys

Kilmarnock Forest

Asra

Eldmoor

...ris

...riata

Sitara

Sea of the dark

The Boroughwaters

Danics

Heca

Sidra

Isle of Nephthys

OLYMPIA

Soren Forest

Myrdur

Valda Acme

Volant

Llyn

Taren

Kvan

Kilerth

River Taren

Eredyn

Lanner

Saker

Caldayn

Alder

Amur

Drava

Dravan Isle

Hollow sea

Moor sea

Juramentum

Kilian

A little over thirteen years ago.
The heat was not as bad in September, but there was an ember of choking humidity in the air of Sitara. Perhaps it was the swelter coming from the Sea of the Dark that served to keep its cold-blooded creatures alive. Golgotha had settled here hundreds of years ago along with all of his creations after his realm had been destroyed. Times had changed. Realms no longer prayed to monsters, they loathed and torched them. Lack of belief crumbled heavens and demoted gods. It was how Golgotha had landed on our realm. A god amongst humans, yet he was shunned not only by his peers but us lowly creatures of lesser worlds.

The rock I'd sat on overlooked the bay ahead. An empty, creaking and soulless bay, perhaps the only of its kind in the whole of Adriata. Our seas were bright and warm, filled with life and were welcoming to ventures and exploration. Not this one. No one dared venture beyond the shores of Sidra or Sitara. Not because Adriatians were afraid of the eudemons creeping beneath the surface of the black water, but because of a silent treaty our domains had fallen to agreement with. Eudemons remained in their sanctuary and we remained away from theirs, it is how it always was. Peace was a fickle thing amongst humans, but sacred to the old demon god—he'd kept it for hundreds of years.

"You always think too much," a strong male voice called from behind, one that had gone a tone deeper from the last time I'd seen him. He took a seat next to me and pointed at Mal. "Is he still set on testing if he has nine lives like an Aitan sphinx?"

"Malik!" I called loudly, warning my brother who'd taken the opportunity of my distraction to set foot right on the edge of a cliff. "Move back from the cliff or this is the last time I will bring you anywhere with me."

My brother sneered and blew me a raspberry, but did as told.

Sigh.

"Has it gotten worse?" he asked.

I nodded, still tracing the movement of my little brother. He'd bloomed his blessing fully and that meant my father took every opportunity to ruin his innocence of a child and shape him into a man at only ten years of age. Last, I'd caught him strapped to a chair, bleeding from his ears and nose, my father's magic clinging in the air while teaching my brother what pain of the soul was. No one deserved to know that much suffering. No one. And especially not my ten year old brother.

"It will get better," I said. I lied.

"Is your father still sick?"

"If you hope to catch a glimpse of my sorrow, you are mistaken. If you are here to catch me satisfied, more severely so. And if you hope to catch my excitement in becoming a king, I warn you, Eren Jonah Krigborn, I will forever name you a little shit."

He grinned. "I am older than you—you are the little shit."

"Missed my point."

"So," he prodded, taking off his jacket, probably already beaten by the heat of my lands. "You might become king soon."

"That would make her my queen."

He snorted. "Is that all that came at the thought of what I said?"

"She would hate it, no?" I still had not gotten used to how her name rolled on my tongue. *Snowlin.*

"Probably." Eren fiddled with the sword he'd rested on his lap. "Probably little less if my father made her queen of Isjord."

I spun to face him. "You are the heir."

He sighed, but it seemed to be a reaction of relief for some reason. "Heir is chosen, Kilian."

"Why would she be queen?"

"Father, he…he treats and trains her like a ruler is expected to be trained and treated before taking the Isjordian throne."

Something bubbled in me and I shot straight up. Last I'd seen Eren be treated and trained like the heir his father expected him to be, he was covered all inches of his skin in purple, had an arm cast, a limp and two broken ribs. "Has he hurt her?"

"She is stronger than you think."

"It was not what I asked," I tried to say calmly despite the rippling anger surging through my veins.

He reached inside his satchel and pulled a stack of papers out. "What you asked for. This is the last time I do you a favour of this sort. Albius refuses to sneak me into Adriata again."

I took the letters from his hand, still glaring at him for leaving me unanswered, but I was fairly sure I'd gotten my answer. He had hurt her.

The moment I read the title of the papers some of that ire dissipated. "Thank you."

He chuckled. "You are very, very odd. I have no idea why you are in need of those."

"Getting to know my future wife," I said, flicking through birth certificates, midwife notes, tutor notes and many other documents from her growing years.

"The only information those will give you is that she wailed, had a nappy rash and breastfed twice a day."

"As I said, getting to know her." I folded them neatly to my side and turned to him again. "Tell me."

He groaned and dropped his head forward. "This is an obsession, your future Majesty. What makes you think my father will let you marry her?"

"Because I already have the approval of mine."

He shot up. "What? You asked him?"

I nodded.

"And he said yes?"

"Would be good for our kingdoms. He thought of the idea very king-like of me."

His eyes were wide. "Nubil and his blessed crown. You are insane."

"Obeying her order."

"She is a child. You are a child too. You both are children."

"And soon we won't be."

"She...she...she is not an Aura."

"Whatever life she lives, I will too. I won't prolong my life. I will age."

He gaped wildly at me. "You are insane."

"Devoted."

"No, no. Insane," he said, still not blinking and then he laughed. "You think you will like her?"

"I already do. What you have told me, I think I will more than like her. Tell me some more."

"She set the hall on fire last week."

It was then I laughed. Last time I'd laughed was when Eren had told me she'd tied up a soldier and stuffed his mouth with snow for calling her a crow. My brother paused from where he was playing and gaped at me for some reason. Eren too.

"What about heirs?" he asked, narrowing his eyes on me.

"What heirs?"

"Yours. Who will succeed Adriata?"

"Does she not want any?"

"What if she can't give you children? What if it is too dangerous? She is part Olympian and part Isjordian."

"She is still human. It will not be an issue."

"But—"

I raised a brow at his oddness. "Is there something you are not telling me?"

He pursed his lips and shook his head, staring at the dark waters.

"Liar."

He huffed a scoff. "Cheat."

"Rich of you to point that out considering you are lying."

"She would be annoyed if you did that to her—read her emotions that is."

"How would I tell if she is lying? Without my magic, I mean."

His brows almost touched his forehead. "That is the point. You are not supposed to tell, and especially not by using magic. If someone doesn't wish to tell you something then it is better it remains a lie than a bitter truth."

"What is her tell?"

He frowned. "What?"

"The tell when she lies. I won't use my magic on her, but I'd like to know. You told me she often pretends she's not in pain or hurt or sad so she won't worry you. I want to worry, and I can't if I don't know if she is lying or not."

He laughed and shook his head, but silently thought it over for a while. "She usually doesn't bother to lie—she is straight forward like that."

"That I know."

"But," he stopped and stared at his sword for a fifth time in our encounter. Why did he stare at it every time we spoke of her? "She does keep things from us, that would be a lie, too, yes?"

I didn't like how his shadows read of pain—heart wracking pain—but I concentrated on his words.

"She bites the inside of her lip, almost always. I know it seems like the most obvious tell, but that is hers."

"That seems simple."

He sheathed back his sword and stood. "What favour will you owe me if I can tell you where she is?"

My attention shot straight up to my head, making me almost light-headed. "Where is she?"

"Close."

"Any favour."

He sighed and turned to me, his expression almost too severe. "If you complete your mad plan, and she is not what you think she is, don't hate her. That is my one favour."

I blinked slowly. That was a stupid way to waste a favour. "Take me to her."

He scoffed. "Mad. Absolutely mad."

Eren had sat down with Mal in the strip of forest separating Adriata and Arynth while I half hid behind a tall conifer, watching the obsidian haired girl run back and forth, chasing and giggling at the black Aitan morph. The creature had grown from the last time I'd seen it and so had she.

My eyes never left her. "Hello, Snowlin," I whispered to myself and her eyes suddenly rounded from the half-moons and searched her surroundings almost as if she had heard me.

The princess grabbed a small branch and threw it with all the force she had toward the forest where we hid. And the morph rushed after it.

The black cub hissed when she took in my presence and then immediately relaxed when I extended a hand to her little snout. "Hello, Memphis." It was what the princess had named the creature after her mother had gifted it to her and saved it from Silas's punishment. Eren told me her favourite story was that of Memphis the cat and Spaz the rat, the two enemies who tortured one another endlessly. She'd named her uncle's ponytail as Spaz and her morph as Memphis. I'd never laughed harder before.

Memphis indulged in my petting, purring and nudging my hand for more scratches. Dyurin drew inspiration from everything when he created his animals. He had created morphs reminiscent of the night skies. Black fur like the dark night and shiny eyes resembling the northern stars. But that was not all. Not many knew, but morphs were gifted from Henah, too. This is why they could bond with others. They felt everything and everyone. And when they drew a bond with someone, they eased relief into their soul.

My magic to her was warmth and food for her own soul, and I fed her little bits of it till she was no longer hungry.

"Memphis!" the Princess called, her golden eyes searching the thicket of forest for the animal.

With one last belly rub, I whispered to the morph, "Protect her. Protect her with all you have. Protect her for me. Never leave her side. Oath."

The morph's beady stare rose to mine and I heard her small voice echo in my head, *Oath*.

PART I
DAWN

CHAPTER ONE

Pandemonium

Malik

The warning of death hovered in the air as body after body rushed out of the barracks, all donned in thick black armour and heavy weapons. Some of them had never seen a fight outside the training grounds and some had already seen too much—so much that their shadows were shivering from old memories alone without even a thought of the battle ahead.

My brother stood at the gates along with Triad while they recalled orders and battalion numbers as if we stood a chance of fending Isjordians off with numbers. Our army was all over the kingdom, spread along the three cities still struggling to keep their own troubles away. Every single soldier left was already here and the numbers were frightening. We had not prepared for war. What had happened to Olympia was repeating all over again. The only difference is that if Silas wanted to attack under the blanket of night, he'd lose.

Kilian had not said a word. Not to anyone. He nodded from time to time as if to assure people he had not lost it still. And I wished I could be fooled as the rest of them were. I wish I didn't know the pain of his heartbreak that I had absorbed. Or the glaze of his eyes when his attention slipped from the surrounding onto the distance ahead, as if he was waiting and searching for her to return to him—for her to march ahead and tell him that she was not—

That she was not dead.

"Commander," Neo, one of my soldiers asked, the rest of my squadron following behind. "What are our orders?"

My men lined up one after the other, the look of stone and rime on their faces. They'd been prepared all their lives for a moment like this, for the moment their powers were used to kill. One touch. That what would it take an Empath to kill, to inflict so much pain one's heart would stop.

"We move toward the gates and shut them, Umbra and the rest will deal with those advancing toward Amaris. Make the trip short, do not exhaust your strength. Use all you know. Neo, you and Emaya take soldiers to the west and east gate, I will close the central one. Estell you will stay behind," I said to the youngest among us.

They all nodded, but her. "Why? I passed all the training. Please take me."

I didn't need her death in my dirty conscience. "You will protect the castle."

She frowned. "But—"

"It's an order, Estell. If I see you out there, collect your things and be sure to never cross me again."

Her head lowered and she nodded, sulkily backing away.

Kilian caught my attention—my brother was looking straight at me as if he knew what was already simmering inside of my head. The despicable bastard who had to know me to the root of my hair.

When he made toward me, I backed away and turned toward the barracks. Last thing I needed was to have my brain dissected, to be asked to speak my feelings and work through them. I hated how he'd taken the role of my father better than my father ever could. And sometimes anger was better salvaged then worked through—especially in a time of war.

Mist and blood covered my body. Crammed tight between Isjordian forces that had permeated almost past river Nyx and through *alaar*, we hung by a small thread of hope that battalions from the southern cities would near us before ice placated our sacred lands and that my Empaths would make it in time to the gates before all of Silas's soldiers passed through. Highwall had been breached early on, almost too early on. As if soldiers had been there long before Snow's death.

Snow's...death.

A hand went to my chest, feeling remnants of my brother's heartbreak. An Obscur's heartbreak—magnified with much more than anyone other than him could bear. For a heart to carry that much emotion, it had to be excruciating. It was for me.

Body after body fell before my feet as I attempted my way through Isjordian troops to reach the Highwall and shut the gates that poured with Isjordian soldiers like they were mushrooms. Fading wasn't an option between the *alaar* and Highwall—any external interference was impossible so I had to make it there by foot.

"Now or never, Malik," Larg called from behind me. "They are reaching Nyx. Too many for Kilian to hold on his own."

My brother waited across the river for anyone who could reach Amaris, considering the ever-flowing lines of Isjordians, some might have already made it to him.

As if on cue to my thoughts, the skies began cracking with small tears of black. They spread and widened, engulfing the blue of noon to turn to a dark night. Immediately, shadows grew stronger, darker and vibrant with power while Isjordians waved their weapons blindly at us amidst the surrounding dark. Their panicked calls signalled that they had not prepared for this, for my brother's power.

I felt magic rise in my bones, the amplifying strength dark gave me, so I fell to my knees and did what I did best. Raise the dead.

I dug my hands through the warm soil, a touch of magic zapped through my fingers and I pulled on it. Like a puppeteer, I threaded feel onto strings and tied the dead to it. Eldritch Commander. Unfortunately, I'd won that title fair and square.

Bony limbs tore the earth, leaving their graves. One by one, hundreds and thousands of skeletal figures poked out to the surface. My army of the dead. The army I'd fought my father arm and teeth to never raise, and I'd lost. For each soul that rose, a bit of mine got buried. To tamper with the unliving meant tampering with Celesteel. I was a man playing god.

I stood, invisible threads pulling with my steps and the army of dead tackled the living at my command. Viciously tearing through with no worry of death, crumpling and rising, crumpling and rising continuously after each attack—undead and unkillable.

Blistering shards of ice came toward me and before I could duck to evade contact, they crashed against a thin shield of air.

I held my breath and spun round, searching. I'd seen only one man do that before.

Cai stood a few feet behind me, his eyes narrowed, a cold expression marring his face and a strange grey leather armour donning his tall frame. A moment after, Nia poked out of the *alaar* by his side dressed the same as him, fray painted on her, too, as she swung her sword body after body and wielded ghastly shadows to leave a trail of dead Isjordians behind.

They'd lost their friend from the hands of my people. They'd lost their sister. Why were they here? Why were they fighting with us? Had they not found out yet?

"Cai—"

He took off his gloves, revealing what I had never seen before—a map of black tattoos draping all over his limbs. Runes travelled alongside the markings. Crafter magic. "All sorts of travel magic is forbidden within the mist, no?"

"What?"

His jaw tightened. "Answer me, Your Highness. Will the *alaar* allow me to open a portal here?"

"What portal, Cai, what are you talking about?"

He raised his hand to the sky and spoke in Calgnan, "*Ghail.*" *Open.*

One by one, dozens of red round portal runes showed overhead, above the *alaar*, before men and women poured out of them, dropping from miles above onto land. Gusts of wind boomed as they landed with a thud.

I struck still when winged humans began pouring out of the sky, white wings flashing bright despite the cast of night, all donned in the same attire as Nia's and Cai's, a white cloth bearing an eagle insignia draped from their shoulders. They dove into the crowd of Isjordians without hesitation, overwhelming them with magic we'd long thought it lost. Wind howled from all sides, ice splintering against their shields.

Zephyrs.

Winged Zephyrs.

I spun, noting the soldiers and the strays of wind magic pouring out of them. What in the hells?

The skies suddenly cracked. The night sky was packed with thunder that brightened our surroundings as if a second white sun hung over us.

"She is early," Cai said to Nia, and then turned to the soldiers he'd called from the portals. "*Taegha.*" *Shield*, he shouted.

"What is happening?" one of my soldiers asked. Even the Isjordian soldiers seemed to have taken a halt and stood at attention, eyes toward the skies that flashed as if the doors to heavens were opening again.

A thin shield of air rose over our heads as gravel, weapons and bodies began lifting in the air packed with heavy current.

Lighting cracked above once and then right in front of us. Screams tore the screeching silence that the loud blinding bolt emitted as it landed too close to both Adriatian and Isjordian bodies. The sheer amount of magic filling the air was dizzying. All of my senses rose to alert.

My ears still rang from the sound and I blinked away the blurry vision the lightning had caused, focusing where it had struck.

The green floor had frosted over, a light pelt of snow forming for feet along the blast's radius. Air grew cold and our breaths misted white.

Something stood from between the grey smoke burning and charring the land.

No, not something.

Someone.

A gust of wind dispersed the mist and raven hair fluttered in sight, electricity skittering around her body. The air charged with heavy magic and then deafening thunder rained on land when she rose both palms to the sky. Dozens of lightning poured and struck ahead, over the Isjordian troops.

The ground shook. Smell of burnt flesh and agonising screams broke between the heavy whizz of electricity.

Just like it started, it stopped. As if...on command. It took a moment for the haze and smoke to rise from the charred flesh and soil, and when it did, all my senses were assaulted by what laid ahead.

Death. So much of it.

And power...strange power.

The raven-haired woman turned halfway and I stumbled back. Yellow eyes, porcelain skin, rosy scar. The only thing foreign on the face that I knew so well were streaks of black tattoos creeping over her features.

No.

No.

"Snow?"

She was alive?

She was alive.

Snow was alive.

"Keep the ground, I'll shut the gates," she said to Cai before taking the form of a lightning bolt and disappearing from sight. A thud of lightning assured she'd landed somewhere nearby and the smell of char and electricity assured me that I'd not imagined all that had happened.

The thunderbird of lightning risen from the cold white ash.

Impossible. It had to be impossible.

She was alive. She was more than alive.

I looked around. Where was my damned brother? He had to see this. He needed to see this.

No. No. No. The Snow I knew was human.

The Snow I knew could not emit not a gram of magic. I would have felt it. Sensed it. I would have known. That can't be her. It had to be someone else.

A grip tightened around my arm when I tried to move toward the Highwall. "Don't even think about it," Cai growled and then let me go, disappearing into the crowd.

Sounds returned crashing all at once, a battle still ensued around us. The men and women who'd dropped from the skies had joined the fight alongside us, keeping the Isjordians back. Wind howling and ice splintering against their shield of air.

I moved forward, the dead making a circle of protection around me while I hurried for the wall. The more fell dead, the more my army distended. While their battalions shrunk, mine swell.

Once I neared, I climbed the tower stairs to the top. I could hear the humming of lightning and feel the density of the magic she was emitting weighing over the flow of the spiritual that surrounded us.

Then I saw her again. Someone was in her grasp as she slowly moved toward them. Once I got closer, I recognised the man engulfed to his neck in ice, begging and weeping. Prince Aryan.

Something he said made her body seize, the thunder halted too, the air quelled from heavy magic. Her uncle's mouth moved fast and her hold on him dropped all of a sudden, ice crawling away from his body. The voices were muffled as I approached, but I caught the end of the conversation before she swung her sword, impaling his head from the shoulders.

"You cannot find them, not without me. You will have to turn this realm upside down and inside out," her uncle threatened.

She scoffed. "Upside down and inside out it is."

The impaled head rolled to the ground and I could swear that her shoulders rose as if they had been under heavy weight the whole time.

"Snow?" She didn't have the time to fully turn to me because I had her in my arms, holding her tight. Tight enough to feel her slow-paced pulse over my own and then the tip of a blade pushing through the leather over my stomach.

Laughter poured out of me. Gods, it was her.

"Hello to you too, Princeling." It wasn't the threat of the blade that made me pull back, but the cold, molten lava pouring from her voice. One I'd never heard her use before. The same icy stare greeted me, the stare of a carcass that didn't resemble the woman I'd known to wear it before. The smirk that drew up her face from my stunned silence made this new exterior even more terrifying. "I've always liked you. Always wondered how long it would take you to realise just how much you should really fear me." She sheathed her dagger back and threw a glance at the battle beside us. "Eldritch Commander. The prince of night. The man who can raise the dead finally fears me."

"I don't fear you."

"And he lies. You've always been the funny one."

"Why did you save us?"

Her brows rose. "Save you?" She reached into a thigh pocket and made toward me. Taking my palm in her hand she placed something light there. "The things I save, Princeling, are the things that were meant to wither anyway."

I glanced down at my hand and stared at the small branch of white flowers. Lily of the valley.

"Pretty, aren't they?"

The eudemons. The unblessed. The frost. The drought. The floods. The lily had bloomed like a blanket all over the cities each time one of those things had happened. I shook my head. It couldn't be. How?

"What are you saying, Snow?"

"Those hungry for fear will feed on tendrils of faith. And when you are starved of the very thing you are taught to feed on, you people would rather go hungry to death than try doubt. I took a page out of your very own fairy tale book. And who knew, a little flower would help me starve your people of the very thing they live for. Starved out of faith."

"You left the flowers."

"I did."

"How?"

She pointed a finger toward the sky. "The same way I'm not letting Isjord take what is mine to ruin." She huffed a tired sigh and pointed to the gate behind her. "They need their undead commander. I will shut the gates. Let's keep my new toy nice and shiny, shall we?" With that, she backed toward the gates, ice blistering the narrow roof corridors of the Highwall with each step she took. White bolts of electricity skittered behind her, crawling to her back and forming a set of wings that carried her up in the air before she dropped from the wall to the gates.

The prophecy—she stood before me. Fuck.

CHAPTER TWO

Nivalis

Snowlin

Heights have always fascinated me. The higher up, the more clearly you could see what laid beneath you. From the roof of Highwall I could see the signs of my rage, the signs of my father's insanity and the signs of the Adriatian weakness. All three were confirmation of my victory. It shouldn't amuse me, but it did. Destruction always amused me. I was taught to enjoy it—beaten to crave it.

I'd shut the three gates of Highwall. My soldiers lined the long perimeter, Sebastian and Albius on the other side held back anyone attempting to return to Isjord. They had seen too much. My death was leverage. I ought to stay hidden from the world.

Isjordian troops had thawed to lifeless bodies and were being buried by the Adriatians. Though they'd escaped unscathed, they didn't win. The calm after the storm was often louder than the actual storm. Silence was the loudest sound. I ought to make it quiet.

A winged Volantian approached me, bowing his head. "How do you wish for us to proceed, my queen?"

"Man the wall. No one leaves Adriata before I tell them to. The Crafter will be here soon to mend the veil back. Report to Sebastian if there is anything strange roaming around the entrances. No one comes in and no one goes out. No one."

Clutching my uncle's head tight, I dropped from the wall. The land beneath my feet charring from the force of lightning. One of the many gifts of an Elding—bolting. We were the between of a spiritual and an elemental Aura. My magic was a symbiote that fed on my mana and that of the spiritual. It was why there was no monster like me. But there was another reason why there was no monster like me. And they were about to find out.

Snow, my snowflake, mother's voice drifted past me, whispering all sorts in my ear of prayer and plea as it had done relentlessly ever since Aryan had pushed me off that tower.

"Shhh, ma. You will want to hear this well." And for the first time, I blocked her from my mind with more noise—thoughts of how I'd make sure her death was made just.

Adriatian soldiers halted their movement as I made past the field of injured they were tending to. The faces that previously wore disdain were now dressed in fear. I could feel the rapid heart thrumming in their chest, like that of a hummingbird.

Taking a deep breath, I savoured the way tendons of fear latched onto their necks like leashes. All slaves of my power.

Funny. The thing I always forbid myself to use was what served me most well.

My soldiers had clustered by the edge of river Nyx. Cai's irritated scowl was visible from a mile away. He'd not taken well to the new plan I'd forged to aid Adriata. He'd not taken well to the little fiasco with Aryan either. This time I'd properly messed up from the way he refused to even acknowledge me. How many times had I promised him to not do what I did that day.

The general from Highwall, Larg, stepped toward my men. "Do we get an explanation for all this, or are we expected to keep a blind eye that a bunch of Olympian Aura just aided us from Isjord?"

"That would be the least of your worries," Lazarus, the Volantian general, answered boredly in a thick Olympian accent.

The Adriatian general frowned. "What is it that you want?"

Kicking my uncle's head to Lazarus's feet, I crossed my arms behind. If I had them free, I'd be too tempted to wrap them around someone's throat. "I have what I want. Lazarus, would you be a dear and take that to the Crafter? I'd hate for it to rot from all this blessed heat."

Swords were unsheathed, arrows were stringed, shadows darkened, prayers were spoken, yet no one made a single move and gods still remained heedless. I waited, and when all weapons were pulled back from realisation, they all retreated a step back. And all that brought a lovely smile to my face.

"That's right," I said. "A curtsy would have been good. Kneeling, too. Might want to use those legs before I break them all."

Some flinched, others murmured prayers. Didn't they realise that the only god that would ever hear what they said was me?

"Snowlin," Larg called, approaching to inspect his otherwise still breathing queen.

"It's *Your Majesty* to you, Adriatian," Lazarus growled, his wings ruffling in agitation.

Didn't even get to roll my eyes. It was not worth the headache. Volantians and their hot bloodedness made me prone to migraines.

"She is not our queen, never will be," a young man shouted, coming to view. A familiar face, one I'd seen at the trials once before. Brave front from someone whose heart was about to make him a Midworld spirit in a second or two.

Lazarus stood from where he sat and levelled the Adriatian a glare. "She might not be your queen, but she is mine."

Larg took a step closer to me, confusion bunched between his dark brows. "What queen?"

I flicked some ashes from my shoulder. "I am certain you have a guess."

He shook his head, studying my troops one by one and then me, eyes lingering on the insignia on my shoulder. "I have to be wrong. Olympia perished."

"Myrdur perished."

His gaze dropped to the ground, a frustrated hand running through his long curly greyed locks. "The mist is poison. There is nothing beyond"

"The mist is protection and just because you can't see beyond doesn't mean there is nothing beyond. What is it with you Adriatians and short-sightedness?"

"It is not possible."

I leaned in and whispered, "Just how I am not the *Ybris*?"

His attention snapped to me. I waited for it to transform—for confusion to turn to fear. Yet to my disappointment it never came, he looked merely stunned and curious. "How could you control it? Your magic is meant to be chaos, uncontrollable. How?"

Leave it to a man to tell me what my magic is and is not. Pointing my chin to the charred field of death behind us, I gave him a smile. "*I* am chaos, Larg, and *I* navigate it my way, too. I was never going to allow anyone beside me to control it, neither were my siblings."

Shock widened in his face. "Silas never knew?"

"Never even doubted. I have his attempts scarring my body." Taking a step closer to him, I looked up at the cracks of night that hadn't quite covered day. The magic of the Obscur Asteri. "My uncle lied to you all those years ago." He had lied to everyone, including my father. "He never knew either. But you have always wanted for me to be that monster, so here I am, General."

There was a flash of panic somewhere behind all that old armour or age he had. "You showed nothing but kindness today, Snowlin."

"Kindness?" The laugh leaving my mouth took me aback as well. "Who is guarding Amaris while all of you are here? Who is guarding Amaris while your battalions are tending Lyra, Sidra and Sitara? Who is guarding Lyra, Sidra and Sitara while my men are still bringing eudemons, the unblessed, rain and murk to your shores?"

Adriatian faces paled as they exchanged uncomfortable glances among each other. One particular Adriatian was staring at me like he'd never stared at me before. Mal wore his disbelief with anger, something I couldn't understand considering who he was and who he was related to and who he pretended to be and how he lied. I could count the list till the never tomorrows.

The same man I'd seen at the trials stepped forward, anger blazing his eyes and defiance curling in his smile. Grey, was it not? "This is our land and we are under the blanket of night. I'd be afraid to make such threats if I were you."

Blinding white lightning illuminated the dark sky bright at my command. For a few flashing seconds, even the sun wouldn't have outshone this night the way lightning did. "It can thunder at night, too."

Something stirred behind the Adriatian lines. Something cold and warm at the same time. Something threatening to scourge my soul while wanting to blanket me from all harm. Night felt somehow darker. Day somewhat dimmer.

And then I saw him.

Beautiful as ever, he stared at me like no man should ever stare at his death. Full of longing, want, agony and something else. Had he been happy to hear of my death? Had he rejoiced with his people to celebrate that he'd won over me without even lifting a dagger?

Titling my head to the side, I said, simpering, *"Husband."*

His eyes flashed and his chest rose along his heavy breaths. I'd never seen him this struck before. "Tend to our dead and head to Amaris," he ordered his men, his attention never leaving me. "Now."

His men scattered toward the forest and the charred battlefield behind us.

Grey brushed past me, still glaring daggers to my face.

"Boo," I whispered and he flinched back, making me and my people laugh.

I didn't even see him get close till I was in his arms. He pulled me so tight in his embrace, I could feel every dent of his body melt to mine. Everything else seemed to blur away the moment his heat enveloped me. It was easier to breathe, somehow. His scent of spring made parts of me hurt—mostly my heart. And I was torn. Torn between hugging him back, drowning myself in his caress, and pushing him off of me. My body remembered his tar-soaked lies, his bloodied hands on me, the poisoned sugary words he'd whispered, the care he'd faked to trap me. It always did. The tremble permeating every inch of me made my fists clutch tight enough to sting with that pleasuring hurt.

From the corner of my eye, I caught Nia making toward us. "Snow, wait—" But it was entirely too late.

The man embracing me sucked a sharp breath and for several long moments I thought he had forgotten to breathe. "Breathe, Your Majesty, only I can tell you when to die." I shook like a leaf in autumn air, clinging tightly to the dagger I had dug to his side.

Blades were unsheathed, arrows were drawn and magic polluted the air around us. All with me as their aim.

The man holding me breathed fury. But not at me. "Anyone who has a single weapon pointed to my wife will have their head sent to their families on a stick!" Kilian shouted and the shadows vibrated with him.

Wife.

A silent gasp left me as he took my hand and pushed the blade onto his flesh. He held me tight, rocking me with him, his hands raking over my body, between my hair and over my skin, feeling me, holding me and breathing me in. His lips touched my temple, pressing soft kisses on my cold flesh. And all I could feel was a hollowing numbness that was growing shallow—so shallow that what I wanted hidden was surfacing. A simple touch had never made me feel anything before. But there was nothing simple about his touches.

"This was your cruellest game, my love." A rough sob vibrated from his chest, but it hurt me all the same. "You play so cruelly."

I fought back the sob threatening to climb up my throat for this man. "I could say the same, but I am used to your cruelty. Get used to mine," I said, twisting the blade in his flesh.

He only let out a sigh and it was not one of physical pain. "You're alive. Why don't you feel alive?" he asked, kneading his fingers on my back.

"Because I feel like nothing." His blood had begun coating my gloves and soaking through to my skin. "How does it feel, Your Majesty? How does my revenge feel?"

Something wet fell and slid down my cheek. A tear. Not mine. "Better than your death."

Why? Why was I letting it hurt me? "Let go of me."

"Never." His hand slipped behind my neck, he held me so possessively I almost ate my words back. "Mine," he growled in my ear. "You're mine. To have. To hold. To protect. Mark this promise, my love, I will never let you out of my sight."

How dare he? "I will kill you," I whispered harshly, twisting the blade further into his flesh. "I will kill you little by little every day, just like you have killed me every day for the past thirteen years." I took a step closer bringing our bodies even closer together, my dagger pushing further into him.

"Half of me died that day and the rest when I was told you died. Nothing will hurt nearly as much as that." His face nuzzled the crook of my neck. "I already ruined the only thing I have ever wanted to protect."

"We are past pretending, *darling*."

Facing me, he grabbed my chin with his other hand forcing me to stare into those icy eyes that were glazed with tears. I hated how unshaken he looked despite. "I will make it my purpose to remind you of the definition of pretend, wife."

That made me laugh a little. "How did you think this was going to go?" Tilting my head to the side, I gave him a smirk. "Have me fall desperately in love with some poor excuse of guard, forgive you when I realised who you truly were and forget my revenge? Did you not get to know me at all? Come now, you must know better than that?" Leaning in, I whispered, "How hard it must have been for poor you to act like you did. To act like you could ever care for someone like me. Someone who was so against the principles you adored. Someone dirty in your rule books. Someone tainted like me."

"You know it was no act. You know what you meant to me." His jaw was set tight. "You know it."

"I don't think I do. I don't think I care. I don't think I would mind whether it was or not. You lied, but so did I." Unwrapping my hand from the dagger, I stepped back letting go of him. "Keep the dagger," I said, pointing to the blade digging in his flesh. "Now you can make a set with the other one. But touch me again and you will have a whole armoury to supply. Actually, you might need it. This is the last time my men fight to protect this hot hell."

Pulling the dagger out like he was made of hay, not flesh, he cocked a brow up. "Protect? Protect what exactly?"

My jaw tightened at the level of his calm. I had his kingdom by the balls, why was he acting like he had me by my imaginary ones? "What is mine to ruin. And now if you will pardon me, I have a new set of guests to entertain."

My kingdom awaited me grey and thunderous, the skies cried and poured heavy hail and thunder over the tall mountains surrounding the obsidian castle.

The walls were closing in around me and the world swayed while I struggled to make the way to my chambers.

Breathe.

Breathe.

My knees weakened, and I dropped in the middle of the corridor. The white and obsidian marble beneath my hands coated crimson and the murky reflection that stared back at me grew bigger and bigger, splashes of crimson giving the terror looking back at me a horrifying colour.

His blood. It was his blood.

With shaky fingers, I tried to remove my gloves and wipe the blood coating my skin away.

Breathe.

Breathe.

Red blurred my visions and I slammed a fist on the floor and then another and another till the marble cracked, my knuckles splintered and all I could feel was pain—numbing the ache in my heart that was rendering me breathless.

And that is how Cai found me.

Bloodied.

Weak.

Breathless.

Disappointment. Confusion. Worry. All I could read from my council members. None had said a word, not while I explained my findings in Isjord, not when I spoke of the divine weapon no one knew of, not when I told them I married the Adriatian king and was now their queen, not when I told them that Adriata was now my prisoner different to how we'd been planning for years.

I initiated my plan almost two years ago with the majority of the support from my court. Olympia rarely had engaged in armed conflicts in the past, never to initiate war, but this was a new era. My era. The era where my kingdom would get its glory back. The era where my people did not have to live cowering, hiding, haunted and hunted. Instead, we would hunt and haunt all that had closed an eye to our downfall and those that had caused our downfall.

There was one person, however, who kept me footed from advancing my plan sooner.

"We cannot afford to handle Adriata at this time," Alaric spoke right on time. If Alaric had a thought, it was everyone's thought to deal with. "The plan was to attack after we'd dealt with Silas and Isjord. Not while we figure out how to keep Silas from these sceptre pieces."

How very convenient for him. "I need Adriata, Alaric. They will be under my mercy until I am sure their sceptre piece is safe and away from my father."

"You presume they will let you have it?" Alastar, Alaric's father and the Dravan tribe leader, asked.

Let me have it? That was funny. "No presumption, they have no choice."

The old man frowned. "How?"

I shrugged. "Simple diplomacy."

"You mean threats?" Alaric asked.

"Why are you repeating my words?"

He heaved a sigh. "Snow, heavens."

"Their cities are still under my mercy, our troops still guard Highwall, Visha is lifting back the Highwall veil and…their council is in my dungeons."

Gasps and murmurs buzzed at the revelation.

Alaric shook his head with visible disappointment in me. "He is the Night King, Snow. You do not threaten the Night King."

"Not threatening anyone, only getting them to pay their dues. And from what I've gathered, he won't be missing any of the ten I got down there. Adriane, Stregor, Lucian, Adrastos, Zander, Esther, Ambrose, Calliope, Leon, Maya. Those names familiar to you, Alaric? They certainly are getting familiar with the darks of Taren right now." Each and every name I'd read on the signed documents retrieved by the soldiers. The ten signatures approving of the attack.

When his face twisted with surprise, I continued, "You know me well. Well enough to know that I stopped being petty when I found being vindictive more productive." Their council was in my hands for all the right reasons. When Albius brough word of the agreement meeting in Arynth and mentioned head council Adriane Drakos was attending, I was ecstatic. I was ecstatic to know one more person who owed me had not been claimed by early death.

He ran a hand over his thick beard and offered me an apologetic nod. "I had no idea he'd kept the same council, kid."

Ten out of ten signatures that sealed fate that solstice night were in my dungeons. All ten alive. I'd not touched a single other member of his court. Only the ones who owed me.

"As much as I am thrilled to hear that you are finally getting Adriata to pay their dues, I have to ask," Bayrd, Lazarus's father and the Volant tribe leader said. "Will the Night King reprise his position beside you—as our king? Though by law of humans you are married, your marriage was not blessed. The throne you hold has never seen such violation and disrespect."

Alaric choked on a gulp of water. "You are out of line, Bayrd."

To have my nerves played like a violin by the Volantain leader was not new, but he'd chosen an ill time. He was lucky I liked my marble table clean from blood.

Bayrd's white feathered wings twitched just slightly behind him. "We all are owed to know, especially my son. The two were destined to marry."

Smile and blink. Smile and blink. If his tribe didn't adore the ground this man stepped on, I would have fed Memphis his guts long ago.

Cai snorted from beside me. "Easy throwing destiny and greed in a bag, old man Bayrd."

The Volant tribe leader sneered, red creeping up his neck. He had a thing about Cai. Something about him losing to his father for the general position in my grandfather's court. Grudges ran deep in my kind, I suppose.

"How will it be, Snow?" Lazarus asked. From the unusual calm of his tone, he was trying to manhandle me of a sort. "Will you correct this issue? The bargain has been fulfilled, you could have him threatened to annul."

Cai chuckled beside me. "Highly doubt Kilian will take well to threatening less to letting her go."

Bayrd's wings stirred. "And what do you propose, General, since you are so proficient at solving this situation?"

I should stop this. Really, I should, but I missed the entertainment.

Cai mimicked Bayrd's movement, leaning back on his seat. "Leave it be. We are in a situation where respecting tradition should be the least of our worries. Our queen is also more than capable of ruling Olympia as proficiently as she has done it for the past seven years. A king will aid nothing to the throne nor to the situation. Unless you see her rule to be lacking. Is that what you are trying to say?"

Bayrd's eyes shifted uneasily from me to the rest of the council. "You all well know that is not what I meant."

"Then it is settled," Cai said, standing. "With your permission, *my queen*, I'd like to leave for Eredyn."

My queen. He'd only addressed me as that once before, as a joke when I got crowned. Cai was not mad at me, he was furious. Issue was that I didn't know for what reason. For lying to him in Adriata or for lying to him yesterday when he'd tended to my hands after I'd broken several of my knuckles?

"What will we do about the sceptre pieces?" Cori, leader of Kvan and the youngest among us, asked. "Will we have to gather them all?"

"One is all I need," I said. "If I find one, we can place it under craft and father could hunt it down for all of his lifetime if he wishes to do so."

"How would we do that when even our elders have not heard of such a thing?" Leanna, the Llyn tribe leader, pointed.

Craning my neck to the side, I eyed my silent Dark Crafter. Fiddling with one of her beaded bracelets, her attention poked holes on my very expensive marble table. "What is it, Visha? Did they cut your tongue after I went away? You are unusually quiet."

Her sea foam green eyes grew wide as did her red flush of embarrassment over her freckled face that matched the vibrant colour of her hair. "Your father, how did he find out about this? The last time the sceptre was used, all knowledge about it was burned and destroyed. Very few must still know about it, very few that would have already sworn to secrecy."

"You know about the Octa Virga?"

She gave me a small nod. "Before the sceptre was broken in pieces, it was kept in the Isle of Nephthys, guarded by Dark Crafters and eudemons of Golgotha. Celesteel and Golgotha had both been tasked to allow only those worthy of using the sceptre to access it. Nephthys' waters and air are poison, and Golgotha is still a god."

"They did not do a very good job, then," Alaric said with a sigh.

The witch shook her head. "Kegan, king of Seraphim, used his child to retrieve it. He'd studied the sceptre for years before and started to fill his youngest daughter's head with tales of heroes and ridiculous dangers this realm had to fight to survive. He'd faked plagues and wars. Groomed and raised her a hero in the eyes of his people, having her fight sea monsters and evil of all sorts for years before he sent her to retrieve the sceptre. She was of pure heart and clean intentions; Golgotha's truth eudemons and Crafter veils had let her breeze through to the tower of Nephthys where the sceptre was kept."

"Who knew of this, witchling?" I asked.

"Only the Grand Maidens. Ancient knowledge is passed to us from one to another during our training because we are still tasked with the upkeep of Nephthys." Visha, too, was destined to become a Grand Maiden one day. The one day she would never allow to come. And for that, she'd come to seek my help.

"Are you implying Urinthia has sided with Silas?" Alaric asked, leaning in with concern.

The witch straightened in her seat. "If there is one thing my mother enjoys is chaos. But this is not her work. Gods forbid because if it was, Silas would already have the whole Octa Virga completed."

"Melanthe Delcour is a close second," Nia said. "We can presume she is the one to reveal it to him."

Visha jerked her head in disagreement, unruly ruby curls falling over her eyes. "She would not know. My cousin doesn't possess that form of knowledge, nor would she have ever had, and if she did, there is only so much a Summoner can do to work out the location of the pieces. She is trained to lure magic into her, to use it as a centre scent that attracts other magic and creatures to her from this realm and many more. Besides little tricks like that and simple craft like veils and traces, there is not much she can do."

"Nia," I said, turning to my friend. "Head to Eldmoor and enter Red Coven later this week, after the coast is cleared of Isjordian soldiers. Keep an eye on Urinthia. At the first interaction you see with my father, notify me."

She nodded and then reluctantly asked, "Who will mediate Adriata in the meantime?"

"For now, we leave them to stew in their failure. It will season them for what's to come."

Visha hovered above me with a burning garni that smelled like a rotten corpse while I laid sprawled on her cold granite table. My cheek had gone numb and was prickling where it met the cold surface, but I was too bothered to even move. She was the only one who could help me. Sleep was hard to come and when it did, I wished it hadn't. Olympians feared dreams more than reality, and better than anyone I knew why.

Visha's cold hands traced the seal on my back and I jumped a little. "Blessed be Aidan and his flame, warm up your hands a little."

"The seal is intact," was all she said.

Spinning to check her over my shoulder, I gave her a glare. "Check again." Usually, it was the answer to my sleepless nights. If I pushed my magic, or used a bit more than the seal allowed, I'd never be able to rest. That day in battle I had pushed a fraction past my limits.

Instead of obeying, she pulled my shirt down and blew off the red candles around me. "The only thing I can do about your nightmares is take them away, Your Majesty."

Pushing up, I stood and straightened my clothing. "One night, Visha, give me something to blur them away. One night of sleep is all I need."

She blinked slowly, there was no sympathy in her eyes. There was nothing in there actually. Visha was like a coffin. Hollow and filled with a skeleton. She's been the same since the day she crossed the *zgahna* and found me in Taren six years ago. Quiet, observant and loyal. The daughter of Urinthia Delcour was many things, annoyingly quiet was the best way to describe her. "The Midworld is not my ground, I cannot interfere with those that have not passed onto the Otherworld. The only thing I can do is guide them beyond."

I spun on my heels and before exiting her witch cave, I kicked a basket of herbs till they fluttered in the air. "You're useless, witchling."

"Sweet dreams," she murmured, but it was loud enough for me to hear.

Nia waited in the corridor, shaking her head at my action. "Bullying Visha won't be any help."

"No, but maybe a visit to our prisoners might." It was due time, anyway.

Nia faded the two of us into the northern tower's dungeons. The stench of death hit my senses while we made our way to the depths of the corridor, toward the special place I usually called my sanctuary. It was where I spent the spare time most dedicated to a hobby or a night out. The dungeons in

Taren were a different kind of twisted architecture. Its walls were supported by the Taren valley, the space between the two sister mountains where the city of Taren spread. History would tell it differently each time, but it was said that Nubil had buried his lover, a healing guardian of Hemera, on the grounds of the valley. The stone and earth were alive, its touch healed, its presence prolonged life. Sick, healthy, pregnant, barren, young and old went to the valley to seek healing. And healing they received. The valley stone and soil kept the hearts of my victims slow and beating while I had my fill of their pain. Each time I dragged them to death, I'd strap them on a lifeline to keep them alive enough for more taste of death.

Nia shivered as we went past holding cells. "This place still creeps me up."

"Remind me to order a chandelier hung on these halls because the ambience I was aiming for with all the decoration was a family friendly one."

She scoffed and pushed me with her shoulder. "Don't tell me you can't feel the dead still lingering here."

I shrugged. "The living annoys me, at least the dead don't speak. Not loud enough to aggravate me."

Two soldiers stationed at the end of the corridor bowed in holy greeting and pushed a thick key onto the enormous metal doors behind them. The hinges creaked from the weight emitting a loud cry to echo all the way down the corridor we left behind.

Ten forms slumped on the ground, all of their limbs chained to the walls, a rotten smell already filling their air. The two soldiers filtered light inside, lighting all the torches inside the room and all of their terrified faces came into view.

"Missed me? I've been a very bad hostess, look at your poor state," I said, kicking a leg out of my way as I paced toward Adriane. "Head councillor, it suits you—all that dirt and grime. You fit right in."

She lifted her blue-grey eyes to me and suddenly the resemblance to his stare made me bristle. "I thought we were to discuss my death first."

I twisted a bunch of her long, brown locks between my fingers. "I was thinking it to be more of a monologue on my part. Though with not much talking. I am more of an actions matter more than words sort of person."

"Do what you will do," she gritted out, dropping her head back on the wall, almost surrendered.

Gripping her hair tight, I brought her face close to mine. I wanted to see the fear well and clear. "You see, Adriane, I take my tasks slowly, meticulously."

"H-Helenia, is that...is that you?" a slimy voice croaked behind me and I spun fast. "I would recognise your mother's eyes anywhere. You look just like her. It is me. Your father."

My friend had locked in place, tears streamed down her face while her attention had glued to one of the councillors sunk in a dark corner. A whimper pushed past her lips and she began shaking.

The man...it couldn't be.

With two short strides, I pulled her to me and out of the room.

Once the guards shut the gates, I sat her on the ground with me. Panic had seized her and she wheezed like there was not enough air. Once before I had seen her of this sort. Years ago, a couple of nights after we had found her. "Shhh. Nia, come on, sweetheart. Open your eyes." Resting my forehead to hers, I swayed to the two of us back and forth. How could I be so stupid, bringing her down here with me. "Remember what I said, Nia. Remember that there is not a breathing being that will ever hurt you in this realm and all the next. Have I lied to you? Are you calling me a liar, Helenia Drava?"

Slowly, she peeled her wet lids open. So much pain crossed her beautiful bronze eyes, I wanted to take it all away, for her not to hurt anymore. "No."

"Is it him?" Her father. I knew he had been a member of the Moon Court and part of the Adriatian council. Over the years, I just had hoped he had dropped dead or disappeared so he would never be part of Nia's life.

Shutting her eyes tight, she nodded. "Are you going to hurt him?"

"Nia," I said, tipping her chin to look at me. "I am going to kill him and you are not going to ask me to spare him."

Agree with me, damn it. I've never wanted to hurt someone more than that man.

"Alright." she whispered. "Alright."

I nodded and hugged her tight to me. "What do I do, Nia? How can I make it better?"

She hiccupped, hiding her face in the crook of my neck. "I don't know."

CHAPTER THREE

Amarantinum

Snowlin

I'd spent twenty-four hours in the dungeons. By the fortieth finger I'd broken, the crunch wasn't all so crunchy anymore and the blood had turned a shade of pathetic. I was bored out of my brains and a thread of my dress was poking my neck, torturously egging me on.

The sound of nervous breaths in the dim alcove gritted on my nerves. I'd slumped by one of the walls next to a councillor whose face I couldn't make out. As a matter of fact, I couldn't make out any of their faces in the dimly lit room. It was a rule of mine not to discriminate. All would suffer the same anyway. All ten of them.

"Tell me again, Adriane," I spoke, my voice echoing and breaking the dripping noise a leak in the ceiling made. "From the start." No matter how many times I'd heard it from her already, she'd never once stuttered a word or cried or begged or pleaded. She was going to repeat that story till her eyes bled red and her throat scratched with pins of pain and guilt.

Her chains rustled when she straightened herself up. Perhaps I did discriminate. Hurting her had felt almost as good as hurting the king himself. "Four...four days," she stuttered, and my smile became serpentine. "Before the solstice, we received news that all of Silas's *Ybrises* had been seen manifesting their magic. Stregor and I decided to gather Moon court and a full vote was cast for an organised attack the day of the solstice. Considering the distraction of the festivities, it was the perfect time. We'd gathered the Aura, the soldiers and last we got—" Silence filled the room for a little while. "Last we got his Majesty's signature."

My head dropped back to the wall. "How does it feel? To fail."

"We didn't fail," a gravelly voice bit out. And I loved that.

"You did," I said, quietly. "And you all will find out why very soon. Once I get the wolf and the dragon to join this thunderbird." I'd made myself laugh to the brink of tears, yet everyone else shifted to attention, not as amused as I. Their silly heartbeats grew louder, concerned and panicked. "I'm going to make sure to fulfil that prophecy till the last word and show you what true wrath looks like."

Adriane's stare glistened a little. Oh, and there it was. The beautifully dreaded fear. "What do you—"

"Shhh," I whispered and waited till the room grew quiet and anxious again. "Do you know what annoys me?" I asked absently, and the person next to me shivered and muffled a cry. "That sound crickets make on a very hot summer night. All the heat, the tossing, the turning, and the bad dreams, and you still have to hear that gods awful noise. Don't you agree?"

From the light shadows casted by a distant torch, I could make out her jerky nod.

"Your breathing," I said. "It is making the same nerve gritting noise. Don't do it."

She sucked in a sharp breath and held it.

"Hmm," I hummed, closing my eyes for a moment, relishing the quiet. Silence always bothered me before, it was omen for the latter noise. I always tried to find a way to fill it—a scream, a cry, a plea, a song, a rhyme, a story, the sound of blade parting flesh over and over and over. Now, however, I was the latter noise and all I wanted was ruckus to drum while I walked the altar of everyone's demise, not the last puffs of air of rotten carnage I left behind.

It wasn't long till the councillor was coughing and wheezing out of air and ruining my reverie. "I...I'm sorry, I couldn't. Please, please don't hurt me."

I pushed up to my feet and grabbed a fistful of her hair before hoisting her up to her wobbly feet. "What is your name?"

Her hands shot forward as if they were enough to hide from me. "Es...Esther."

"Esther Laveau, daughter of Felix Laveau, priest to the Lyran congregation. You were made councillor after he retired twenty years ago. Like father, like daughter, you both have spread your propaganda far and wide around Numen, even left some bread trail for me to chase you. Fifth name to sign the order of the Solstice attack thirteen years ago. Didn't take you much thinking, did it?" Pulling my dagger from the sheath, I nailed it in her stomach and dragged it up till it met her ribs. Oh, how many times reading and studying her had I wanted to do that.

The woman screamed in pain, enough to give me a proper headache. Fascinating, really. "So, you know of pain, huh? This must be a new revelation because you bore no recognition of it when you signed the death of thousands years ago."

She cried, holding a hand to her stomach while her guts threatened to spill out. "F-Forgive me. Forgive me, please. I have a young boy, please. I have a young boy."

"Don't worry, I'll make sure he follows right after you. I won't separate mother from child," I hissed and leaned to her ear. "I am not cruel like that."

"Have mercy," she pleaded, grabbing hold of my wrist. "Have mercy."

Funny this one. "That was one. Only twelve more to go." Dragging her to the far wall of the dungeon room, I tied an iron chain connected to the healing stone of the valley to her hand and let the ancient magic do its work to heal her. Slowly, it would mend her insides, replacing the lost blood, too. But ever so slow—so slow that you felt each fibre of you knit back just how it tore in the first place. "Perhaps I'll find where I've lost my mercy and forgive you then. Perhaps not." I crossed my fingers before her face. "Best of luck to you."

When I turned back to face the room, everyone gathered themselves tight, hiding their faces from me. Sigh. "You're all boring me." With that, I decide to explore the surface above the dungeons. See if anyone missed me much.

Memphis was waiting for me behind the doors, licking her paws. She looked bored as I was. When she'd been trapped in my father's dungeons her mood had been infectious, her playfulness, too. Even the day I'd broken her cage and sneaked her out she had been vibrant. A creature like her was meant to be surrounded and adored, it was in the nature of a morph. After the night of our bond something had settled in her, making her the creature she was never meant to be. Recluse and distant. Overly protective of me and unforgiving.

I bent down to scratch that spot behind her ears that she liked but stopped when I saw my bare hand in the much brighter light of the corridors. Blood had matted and crusted to my skin, folding between each raised scar on my palm. The only one who could give her pets and scratches was always too bloodied to do so.

She pushed up and rested her snout on the crook of my neck, seeking the affection herself. "Why isn't it enough, M?"

My bonded nudged my head with hers, and for a moment I was her. I could taste the sweet air, feel the breeze around me as she had. My senses tickled as the paradise of vivid juniper and vibrant flowers, a heaven of varicoloured creatures became sharp in my head. It soon murked with smoke and pained shrieks and cries, it blurred with fleeing burnt and terrified animals hurrying towards the Hollow waters where a worst fate found them—my father's army, waiting to capture and imprison them. She'd been afraid at the time—I could feel that too.

Her gentle voice resonated in my head, *Because what we want is gone and we can never get it back.*

Visions of the moment where my father had ruined her home flashed through one last time before it all turned to black.

I basked in the calm she offered me for a little while, the comfort she'd never denied me even before we were bonded. "I need to bathe, I stink."

She huffed in agreement, making me giggle.

The cold bath I took and all the skin damage I'd done attempting to scratch the blood away didn't wake me up as much as colliding with a sturdy body on the way out of my room. Son of a b—

"My queen," Lazarus purred, his eyes raking my dishevelled form with too much relish. Once I'd been flattered by his attention considering he was the crop of his sort. Now, all I felt was an ick. The general was a good lover. The good kind you abandon right after the deed and forget till your next desires strike. Clearly his ears were stuffed with feathers because he still loomed over me like we were divinely fated to be with one another.

He raised a hand to pull up the dress strap that had slipped down my shoulder, and I jerked back. Uhm...why did I do that?

He seemed surprised too, his hand still elated mid-way. "I was on the way to call you. The Hanaian queen is here as is Lord Arynth and Sebastian." He lowered his hand and gave me an assessing look from the tip of my hair to my cold toes.

"Whatever you wish to say, save it."

Lazarus's expression hardened. "You have not seeked me since your return."

"I can entertain myself just as efficiently. Perhaps better sometimes." Yet, I couldn't remember the last time I'd done that. Actually, I could remember my last attempt at that which ended with me tossing and turning in bed unsatisfied and even more bothered than before. All because the only thing I could think with my hand between my legs was him and his touch.

He'd ruined another thing for me. But the last thing I had in mind was this one.

"One truth you ought to tell me. Does it have to do with him?"

I rolled my eyes. "You forget your place, Lazarus."

His wings ruffled and expanded a little as they often did when he used his biceps to think, not his brains. "My place was right beside you."

Heavenly hells. "Keyword being *was*." I pushed past him and climbed the stairway to my chambers.

"Snow," Nia called, meeting me midway in the corridor. She frowned at something behind me. "Why were you with that pigeon?" Nia couldn't stand the man. "Please tell me you didn't—"

"Nia, the only taste I have now for bird is perhaps skewered."

She scrunched her face. "You don't eat meat."

"Exactly, I'd rather eat meat at this moment." The issue with Lazarus was not only that my taste for bird had changed or that the bird had never properly satisfied me, but that he'd grown some form of delusionality from our few...get-togethers.

"Adriatian girl," the Volantian general said in greeting. And there was the reason why Nia Drava had once in her life considered murder by arson.

"Bird boy," she greeted back with a polite bow of her head. "Like for me to show you just how Adriatian I am?" Like that, shadows rose taller around us, and I could swear Lazarus flinched just a little.

Throwing an arm around her neck, I gave her a kiss. "Don't make him soil himself in my corridors, Nia."

The two of us chuckled while the massive man shook his head and strutted away, vexed and with a mildly hurt pride.

After smacking a bunch of kisses on her soft cheek I asked, "How did you leave Eldmoor?"

Her expression looked beaten and marred with tired purple shadows. I'd hate to think it was because of the man who'd sired her. If only I could erase all memory of him from her. Maybe it was too much to send her to Eldmoor with all that was going on. She insisted she went. She said it would be good for her to be far from Taren and Adriata for a while. I was starting to regret letting her convince me.

"Asra is not how I remember it to be." Nia had spent most of her years far from Olympia, studying other kingdoms in my stead, collecting information I needed, making sure their ships and soldiers strayed clear of our shores and their attention and curiosity away from my lands. Nia was the golden asset of my court. Her skills in persuasion and infiltration were immaculate not because of her magic, but because she had trained them to be immaculate without her magic—the same one she'd only grown confident to use after Kilian had taught her.

I frowned. "In what sense?"

"Please don't over panic." She waited for me to settle after that request and then pushed her sleeve up.

My eyes widened at the angry scar stretching on her forearm. My breathing grew furious. "Panic? Nia, you got injured. I got you injured."

She sighed. "The issue is I didn't actually get injured." She reached into her pocket and handed me an amethyst with a black rune engraved in it. "It was one of the hexes I found around the Red Coven veil. It places a curse on everyone that trespasses within miles of it. They know, Snow. They know someone is attempting to enter their lands. They are on high alert in all corners and down to Heca. I'd never felt the presence of so many Dark Crafters gathered in one spot—ever."

I took the stone from her, feeling the strange engraving with my thumb. The rock was warm and whatever it contained triggered something to roar in cautions inside me and black striation of tattoos crawled over my hands in response. "Take it to Visha and have her look at your arm too before you go to a healer."

She nodded.

"Vocalise it, Nia."

She rolled her eyes. "Yes, mother, I will see Visha."

I smacked her bottom.

"May I ask," Moriko's cold voice came from the far end of the corridor. "Why are you inappropriately touching my lover?" Her blunt dark hair was pinned back, revealing the sharp structure of her features and the deadly hooded dark brown stare that suddenly softened when it met Nia.

I pointed a finger in her direction. "To gods you call her that again."

The Autumn Queen raised a brow as she neared us, towering over Nia's shorter form. "You what?" Pinching Nia's chin, she lowered her lips to my friend's and the two shared a loving kiss. Too loving.

"I really didn't need to witness that."

Nia giggled and Moriko gave me a satisfied look before wrapping an arm around her waist. "Why is she keeping you far from me?"

"Eldmoor," Nia said. "We think Urinthia might be helping Silas."

Moriko's deadly earthy gaze slowly narrowed. "She sent you there on your own?"

"I am right here," I said, lifting a hand.

Nia blinked a little confused at Moriko. "Are you saying that I am incapable of defending myself?"

Moriko didn't answer. The smirk she gave Nia was enough of an answer. And so was the kiss that followed.

Though it struck me as odd to see it, I liked this. Nia giggling and enamoured. Right after Moriko had met us in Arynth, Nia served as emissary to Hanai. Fading back and forth, aiding and gathering help. Little did I know that Nia had been brave enough not to hide her infatuation, and Moriko had been smart enough to appreciate it. And I was happy she had chosen someone like the Autumn Queen. If she broke Nia's heart, I would open war to the whole of Hanai and scorch her butterfly filled lands to ashes. And of course, Moriko knew that. Therefore, the chances of that happening were slim.

All too comfortably, her hand began descending lower and lower Nia's back and I sneered. "Are you here to fondle my spy or you're actually bothering me with something useful?"

Moriko gave me an amused look. "Bothering? Is your time down the dungeons so prime?"

"Yes. Unless you volunteer for my cadaver inspection then I'd much rather be up here." My gaze raked over her and a bit of boredom fled from my system at the thought. "I'd like to find out if there is soil in your veins and a stone between your lungs. That is if you have lungs. Do you breathe through leaves and branches?"

Nia giggled a little, but the queen pointed a hand toward the meeting room, not amused by amusement. "After you."

"As always, Mor dearest, as always," I said, strutting towards the doors.

Visha, Sebastian and Albius were waiting for us. The two Lords who were both keeping an eye on Winter court and my father. If it had not been for them capturing any soldier that had managed their way back to the gates after the battle in Adriata, father would have long known my secret.

"Thank you for coming, Albius," I said, taking a seat at the head of the table.

"Of course, Your Majesty," he offered politely. Before, he'd regarded me as a grandfather would, with endearment and adornment, now he stood tall and straight, polite and careful, as he often regarded my father. Oddly, he'd not been surprised to know of my magic, not as much as he'd been to know of Olympian. According to Nia he'd been more impressed and fascinated than worried or afraid.

"Bash," I greeted. "You look eerily pale."

He gave me a crooked smile. The Dravan born was Alaric's nephew and one of my most trusted men. His mother, Alaric's sister, was one of the fallen Skye warriors during the night of *Draugr*, and according to many he'd inherited her sharpness and astuteness. Both qualities that would deceive and please Silas. "You've done a number on your father and now he is doing a number on us. He's got in him that Adriata has been manipulating Isjord just the same. The city walls are all armed to their teeth."

I smiled. "The best thing I've heard today besides all the screams."

"Both our cities are also looming with Aura of all sorts," Albius added. "It seems they are seeking any opportunity to pass through the Highwall into Adriata. Some have even crossed the Arynth mountains, seeking a path through the Sea of the dark. Of course, I've managed to delay them and made Kilian aware, but I am afraid it won't be long before they figure out another path through to Adriata." He cleared his throat, somewhat hesitant to say what he wanted to say. "Your Majesty, will you plan to aid Adriata permanently?"

"Not aiding them, Albius. Keeping Isjordian paws out of my toys." The answer didn't seem to satisfy him because his mouth pursed almost regretfully.

Sebastian tapped his fingers on the marble of the table and the sound pinched my nerves. "Bash, say it before I round your fingers to the knuckle and feed them to my morph. You know how she has been eyeing you for years."

His fingers stopped and he pulled them over his lap instead. "Silas has it in his head that Aryan is alive. Given the silence from Adriata's part after the battle. Considering the past, the winning party usually waved a sign of victory to the enemy. It is thought that perhaps your...uh, the Night King is keeping him prisoner."

"Heavens, spit it out," I sneered.

"I have reason to believe he is trying to infiltrate Adriata to search for him."

That made me laugh. "He can keep searching. Maybe I'll throw him the bones after the crows stop digging for flesh. Anything on the sceptre?"

Albius said, "Freya sent news that more war camps have been raised northwest of her land, near Hanai."

Moriko nodded. "The Brisk Lord has confirmed that he had to let two dozen Umbra toward Hanai. Silas already doubts Ibe, so he didn't risk it."

"It seems they are aiming for your piece next," Sebastian remarked, and I nodded in agreement.

Her expression hardened. "We have tripled our guard on each of our temples. From Koy to Aru, we've secured them all. Hanai is ready for your father."

"Nia," I said, turning to my friend. "Let Cai know to spare soldiers toward Hanai."

My friend blinked a bit surprised. "Why don't *you* tell him?" Her brows furrowed as she looked around. "Actually, why is he not here in the first place?"

Yes, Snow, why is your best friend avoiding you and doing just about anything else besides being near you? I cleared my throat and turned to Sebastian. "Is Grasmere still Lordless?"

He rubbed his temple. Seems like my father was really wearing him out. "Silas has chosen someone to take Lord of Grasmere duties, a hand Malena had under training—Gara. A little vicious thing almost as bad as Malena was," Sebastian said, irritated. "People say she and Reuben Krigborn were planning to announce their engagement this summer."

That got my full attention. "My, how did I miss such news?"

"You will never be able to sway this one," he said, noting my smile.

"Little time to sway when they are on their knees, Bash."

"Not sure what method you will use but we might need to use it fast. Grasmere is the only city we still don't have in our grasp and if I might say, one of the most important ones. Ships have stopped leaving their port for a couple of days now. I don't know if that is a good or bad sign for us."

"Both," I said, running a tired hand over my eyes. "No more ships for us and indicating a possibly a new route for his travels to search for the sceptre pieces in Seraphim and Vrammethen."

Moriko faced Visha who'd quietly observed the whole gathering. "Did you have a look at the trace craft I gave Snow in Arynth?"

She nodded. "It drew a familiar bond with me. The magic definitely belonged to my cousin, but I am certain it was not to trace the sceptre itself. The magic laced to it was pretty simple, something a Crafter in their teens could do. They could be tracing something associated with the sceptre, so it led me nowhere."

The Autumn Queen scowled somewhat doubtfully. "What if your mother truly has a hand in this?"

"That has nothing to do with my witch, Mor," I said. My trust was very limited, but I trusted Visha.

Moriko nodded. "If you believe that, so do I. I trust your judgement."

Sebastian rubbed a hand over his stubble. "So, we have no lead whatsoever on any of the pieces. We have no lead anywhere on this whole situation."

Albius hummed. "We are chasing a spirit. Perhaps we might need to find its grave and dig out the skeletons."

"What are you saying?" Moriko asked.

The old man pursed in thought. "Figure out the guardian before we try to figure out the sceptre. Crafters back then were cunning and wily, they would have thought this to the roots of it, manufactured ways and gears to control the joining of the sceptre. There might be other ways around it, perhaps it is how Silas is leading his hunt. We could be tackling this situation too aggressively by chasing him around."

And it clicked. "Exactly how my father would expect us to deal with it if he knew we all knew," I said, finally piecing together some of my father's strategy. Send us after the pieces, make us chase circles around attempting to locate them and while we are distracted, he is collecting them all. "You're right, Albius."

Not long ago it felt like I had the steering wheel of my father's ship. And I still did, it was just that all my galleys were steering in different directions while I led them aimlessly with a blindfold on. However, there was one who could give me some direction.

I turned to my friend again. "Nia, I need you to bring someone to Taren for me."

"Who?"

My smile grew. "Driada Castemont."

CHAPTER FOUR

Nox

Kilian

A week had passed since the Isjordian attack. A week had passed since Olympia had come to existence again. A week had passed since Snow destroyed the Night court and forced me to appoint a new council. A week had passed since I figured out how all our misfortune had come to be. The lilies, the monster, the unblessed, the tides, the rain, the hale, the frost. Adriata was in shambles. People were scared before. Now they were terrified. Not only had a war instigated between us and Isjord, but the old fear that hunted my lands for years had returned. She had hidden everything so well, one would never even doubt. But I wasn't just anyone. How had the presence of such strong magic never been caught by my senses?

The skies groaned with unshed storms and a strong wind blew in the highest cliff of Lyra, like the sound of a flute it whistled while it passed between the five feet long sarsen stones that once opened the gate to Cynth.

A dire wolf of war and frost, a dragon of wind and clouds, a thunderbird of lightning risen by the cold white ash. Children of two lands, the Elding children. One would spin the sky to the void, the other would freeze the lands and the last would crack the realm in half with lightning. Three Aura born under the sky of Nubil and the lands of Krig, the wrath Ybrises.

The prophecy still swirled in ink black shadows over the fifth stone. Somehow, I was glad it did. It meant that she was still alive. It meant that seeing her again that day had not been a product of my sick heart. She was alive, but why was I aching as if she wasn't?

"I-It is fascinating," Atlas said from beside me, his words drowned by the unnatural storm gurgling above. His attention pinched on the prophecy stone that was meant to carry the fate of our realm. "How she is able to control it. Never have I heard or read about an *Ybris* who can command their power. Controlled by their own magic, not in control of their magic—it is how Astrum liber describes them to be." A strangled laugh left him. "Never have I heard an *Ybris* to have lived to her age either."

"There is craft inked on her back, some patterns from the old language of gods. Nothing I could decipher without looking at an alphabet. I reckon it is how she has managed to control it."

Young Atlas gnawed on his thumb. "W-Whoever would craft something of this sort? Who would even think of creating a craft of this sort?"

I pried his bleeding thumb away from his teeth. A terrible habit of his that I'd tried to help him eliminate for years. "A prime Dark Crafter. Only they can still use the old markings of gods in this realm."

"A prime Dark Crafter?" He blinked wildly. "But there is only one bloodline of prime Dark Crafters."

"The Delcours." The bloodline that founded Red Coven, the same bloodline which the Grand Maiden comes from. There were not many left. Melanthe and her sister, Urinthia and her daughter were the last of them. One of them had to have crafted Snow's seal. And out of the four, only two were really eligible. Urinthia and her daughter. But that would mean both knew what Snow was.

Atlas shivered, his massive lavender robes swaying with the motion. "S-She was terrifying without even knowing she had magic. And now? Terrifying would be an understatement. Not to mention she almost killed you. T-Twice."

I couldn't help but crack a smile. "Atlas, if she had wanted me dead, I would be dead." And for what reason she didn't want me dead I did not know. The way her head worked was a peculiarity I still hadn't managed to fathom.

"My king," a guard called from behind us. "The council has gathered."

Atlas sighed and righted his robes that hung too big for his smaller frame. "F-From one chaos to another."

More than two dozen confused faces stared anxiously in my direction. Beside Larg and Triad, the Umbra Commander, who had fought in the battle with Isjord, all were new to their position. Along with Larg and Atlas, we'd selected the new members of Moon court. From priests to scholars, I'd managed to filter the best of the crop to sit in my court. Nesrin was the only one who had rectified her father's position which belonged to her by blood right. No other heir of the previous Moon court had wanted a hand in the matter, mostly out of fear that a similar fate to their parents would heed them despite knowing their parents were paying the price of a war crime not that of pettiness.

"I'm sure you will learn to mask your fear better from now on," I said, and a few flutters of flush embarrassment joined the ash colour of fear dancing from them.

"The Olympian soldiers man the Highwall along with our own. Are we under invasion, Your Majesty?" a young priest asked, he was probably a few years older than Atlas and chosen by him too.

"No," I simply answered. "But we are under threat." It was no better, but in no era had Adriata surrendered without a fight, we wouldn't do so now.

"Do I presume my father dead?" Nesrin asked.

Mal snorted from his seat beside me, and all attention turned to him. "Had you not already? I did. Thirteen years ago. When he raised a battalion of Aura to kill her mother and siblings."

Her face tightened, more with anger than despair. "He did what was right. What any one of us would have done to protect this kingdom. Didn't she turn out to be the monster he thought her to be?"

I tensed.

Mal leaned on the table, a disdainful smirk twitching in his lips. I knew I should stop this, but after everything I don't think I even wanted to. "Since you bear no regret, bear no bitterness, Nes. And mind you, your queen is no more a monster than your father is a saint."

Her nostrils flared. "She is not my queen."

I leaned back, fully irritated now. "How so? If she is mine, why is she not yours?"

Her mouth parted open in surprise. A reaction I could not grasp as there was not much to be surprised about considering there was an agreement for me to wed Snow. "After all of this, I thought your agreement was undoubtedly broken."

"Agreement or no agreement, I did vow to her as she vowed to me. I am married to her and she is married to me. And that makes her your queen, this kingdom's queen. Mine as well. Not only will you respect her, but you will kneel to her." Turning to Nesrin, I said, "I suggest you correct yourself next time, Councillor, don't waste my breath on obvious matters."

Her mouth parted, shadows of hurt reflected her hurt eyes.

"You might want to reconsider pursuing this argument further," Larg intercepted before she had a chance to speak. "Not only did she marry my godson, but she fought away the Isjordians. Considering they went to such great lengths as to pursue an agreement, call dead their own princess and then attack with pretend to honour her death, I'd say Silas is preparing for something far more sinister. She done us a favour and we ought to not stare a gift horse in the mouth."

I nodded and regarded all the faces of my court. "To end that note, if there are any more issues regarding my wife, I suggest you hand in your seat now because the only other way you will be leaving it will be by death. Issued by my hands."

Shiver of fear crept up in the air and it tickled my nerves.

No one moved, but I knew most disagreed.

"Did they glue you to the chair, Nes? Need a hand or a push?" Mal provoked, but the Lyran born only glowered at an empty spot on the table, not answering and or moving.

After no objection, I nodded and turned to the Umbra Commander. "How is the situation on the Highwall, Triad?"

"Our guards are sharing duties with the Olympians and so far, none have been hostile. Kirkwall and Arynth seem to have received orders of retreat as there is not much movement in the cities and Isjordian guards are littering every corner of their own walls." He sighed. "It seems Silas had not anticipated this outcome."

"Let's hope he is stunned enough to not try a second time," my brother said.

I'd just settled down after issuing guard orders when Nia entered the meeting room looking like a dartboard for an Empath.

"I thought I have taught you better than that," I said, standing to fill a glass with liquor. She was in Adriata now, and here more than anywhere else, emotion could be your biggest weakness and your best defence. And right now, Nia was a walking prey on my soil.

She swallowed nervously, her bloodshot eyes drifting to the floor. "It...it has been like this for a few days now."

Alarm seized me and I went to her side, lowering a glass of water to her. "What is the matter? Are you unwell?"

She shook her head. "Nothing like that." Squaring her shoulders, she straightened and so did her shadows. Good. "Would you call Malik in? This is for the both of you to hear."

Not long after I'd sent word, the doors slammed open, and my very hungover brother dropped to a chair beside Nia. I'd make a note to check on him later, something was up with him, and he was hiding his shadows from me.

"More court dramatics?" he asked, sloppily filling himself a glass of water. "Let me guess. Betrayal? A royal affair? Friend betrays her queen for the enemy conqueror?"

Nia cringed. "You stink of alcohol."

"And you don't. Is the source of that misery your inability to have fun?"

Her expression hardened. "It is a time of war, Malik."

He chuckled. "And pray tell, which side of it do you stand on? The lines are blurring by the second you keep sitting with my brother and I."

"Mal, enough," I warned.

Nia's expression turned cold. "If Snow had decided to attack Adriata there would be no war. When Silas attacks next, there will be no realm to hold up a war."

Once she was done explaining all that had happened, from the Isjordian soldiers they had caught in Myrdur, Snow's already planned return, the change in their plans from destroying Isjord to taking it from Silas, Aryan Krigborn kidnaping Snow and the purposeful attack on Adriata to Silas's plan with the Octa Virga, both Mal and I were stunned into silence.

"How many pieces has Silas found?" Mal asked. "Supposing he has already found the one in Isjord and considering he might have the Solaryan piece with how strained their relationship with the sun kingdom had become. So, two?" he estimated, sobered up all of a sudden. Nia opened her mouth to speak, but my brother beat her to it. "What does Snow want?"

"To find at least one piece, then Silas won't be able to complete the sceptre."

He shot back to his feet, fidgeting back and forth. "How is he locating these in the first place if no one is meant to know their locations?"

"We don't know for sure. Some think that Urinthia might have something to do with it."

I shook my head. "Not the Grand Maiden I know." Urinthia and I had a long history. That woman had no desire to cause chaos though she fed from it. She was a politician. She knew well the inevitable costs of war. All she wanted was to keep her family safe. To keep Red Coven safe. Meddling with Silas would ruin all of those chances.

Nia glanced at the two of us and said, "We have someone who might know her better."

Mal barked out a ridiculous laugh. "Of course you do. Sounds like the Snow I know. Who is it?"

"Her daughter, Visha Delcour. She is Snow's Crafter."

The answer to my equation.

"Snow has her?" Mal asked, sharing a look with me. Was this why Urinthia had hid her daughter away? She had not been hiding her at all. Snow was.

"No, she came to find Snow. Walked through the *zgahna* and travelled the inside region all by foot for gods know how many weeks. To find Snow."

More pieces were beginning to slide into place. Snow had a mighty powerful hand on her side. "Is she the one who put the craft on her?" I asked.

Nia shook her head, lacing her hands nervously. I knew she wasn't supposed to tell us all this and I had probably already gotten her in far enough trouble to earn her friend's anger once again. "No. That was Lysander, an old Crafter and friend of Alaric's, Pen's father. Alaric met him in Myrdur and served under king Jonah before accompanying Serene to Isjord. Snow has had the seal since she was born. Her magic manifested the day she took her first breath."

Some things were not making sense. "She has old markings of gods on her back, Nia. Only a prime Crafter can use them."

"He was the bastard son of Donovan Delcour, Urinthia's father, and someone called the violet witch."

Macaria had a son with Donovan?

"Urinthia's second in command was her father's lover?" Mal asked, narrowing his eyes on Nia.

She nodded. "She abandoned him in an orphanage so she could keep her position in Red Coven, apparently Lysander was a threat to the Delcour lineage. His daughters would be direct heirs to the title of Grand Maiden. And very inconveniently for them he did have a daughter. Though none of them know."

"Penelope." Not only was she a Delcour, but she was an heir for the Grand Maiden title. "And this *seal* is meant to keep her magic in control?"

Nia let out a long, tired sigh. "Not exactly. Not in control. It empties her magic in Celesteel's realm. Like a gate—it pours it out of her and back into Caligo."

"But she uses it."

"She draws back from the gate, like fractions of it. What you saw that day was a fraction of what she can do. At least in control of it."

"What happens if it breaks?"

"It won't break."

"How are you so sure?"

"Because she knows what she can do if it does break, and she knows how much she will hate herself if she lets it break."

"How is she?" I finally asked. I don't know how I resisted without asking first thing. Hells, I missed her terribly.

My brother snickered. "She put a dagger through your gut, and you want to know how she is?" After his outburst, he rubbed a hand over his eyes and took a seat again. "So, how is she then?"

"Having the time of her life in the dungeons. Besides what is down there, no one sees much of her anymore."

I knew my old council's fate, but my blood still grew cold thinking of what she might be doing to them.

"She has Murdoc locked down there, too," Nia said quietly, and a sense of uneasiness rose over me. There was something far more sinister between her and that priest than what she'd told me, I was sure of it.

"Are you supposed to be telling us all this?" Mal asked.

"Yes. Not the last part though." She stood and brushed her grey leathers. "She sent me to get you. For lunch."

I raised my brows. "Are we eating my councillors?"

She scowled. "Don't give her ideas."

"Wait a damn moment," Mal said. "You're just going to go to her?"

I stood and so did Nia. "She could well kill me sitting right here, brother. And I miss her to death, so to answer your question, yes, I am going to see her." The thought made me smile and my smile seemed to make my brother frown with incredulity.

"She actually wants to see both of you," Nia said.

Mal waved a hand in the air. "Not dressed for the occasion of slaughter. If I am to meet the guillotine, I ought to put a pair of pearls around my neck first."

Nia rolled her eyes and grabbed both of our arms with no warning.

Not a fraction of a second later, she'd faded the both of us to Olympia.

My eyes took a minute to adjust. We were standing at the top of the tallest building I'd ever stood on and one so close to the sky I could feel the clouds and electricity between my fingers. Breath-taking, figuratively and literally. The air was thin enough that it took me a few breaths to adjust to its density. Mountains surrounded the dark castle from all sides, tall and towering, creating shadows over the valleys. The full faces of the mountain littered in buildings and movement despite the height and the tilted slope. Olympia was a canvas of green, grey and flashing white.

"Fuck," my brother grunted, shaking his head from the dizziness of our surroundings.

"Taren, the capital of Olympia," Nia explained, taking in on our confusion.

It still felt unbelievable—the old kingdom of skies lived.

The floor beneath our feet was of a glittering obsidian and so were the walls of the high towers surrounding us. "How? I thought this place was extinct after the *zgahna* took over the Volants and Olympians moved to Myrdur."

Nia directed us past the terrace we stood on, toward a pair of spiralling stairs that showed the whole face of the almost glassy black castle. "Olympia has manipulated the realm through millennia, dressing their history in lies to protect their lands. The mist is protection, it gives no harm to the land or the people. It is a layer of protection and life. Taren was rebuilt eighteen years ago. Myrdur was just a tribe, millions more lived inside the mist. Exactly twelve more tribes. Those now form the council of the kingdom, Snow's court."

Mal lingered a few steps behind us, spinning and touching everything that came in his line of sight. "What's with the leathers and the glassy swords?"

Nia pointed to a window framing angry skies. "It's not glass, it's whitestone. A mineral mined in Eredyn, the mountains struck most by lightning. Metal attracts lightning and our skies thunder during the day and night. The only person who wears metal is Snow."

"The thunderbird," Mal murmured, and Nia winced.

Guards loitered every corner of the windowless castle, all staring ahead and not paying mind to anyone passing by them—their attention deadly on their duty.

We halted in front of a dark corridor lit by blue light pointing to a pair of massive black wooden doors.

Nia wrapped a hand around my wrist, stopping me from pulling the knob. "Remember, the Snow you knew from Isjord was a role. All of us were a role. If you thought her cruel then I'd be cautious now."

The moment the doors swung open, my gaze searched for her, and I almost sighed in relief at her sight. She stood by a tall window, staring emptily ahead, obsidian hair plaited to the side, revealing that creamy neck that I once bruised with my mouth. Dressed in a grey floating dress that swirled around her torso and fell loose to her feet, she looked like every dream of mine. Perfect. But so far from my reach no matter how much I ran.

I still couldn't trust my senses. I needed to touch her. Feel her skin over my own. Inhale her. Make sure I hadn't gotten sick enough to imagine all this.

"Son," a groggy male voice called. I'd glued my attention to her so that all around me had become fog. It took me a moment to focus on the faces sitting around the massive dining table. All of them were chained to their seats and wearing the mask of a corpse. "Kilian," Stregor called again, shifting toward me in his chair.

"That is twice that you've spoken without permission," Snow said, taking a seat at the head of the table. "Do it again and it will be without the benefit of a tongue."

Gods, how I'd missed that voice.

"You've come to take us back," Ambrose, one of the councillors said. "Free us, Kilian. Give this *Ybris* bitch what she wants and get us out of here."

"Take a seat, Your Majesty," Snow called to me, pointing to the chair across hers and then to my brother. "Princeling, you too."

"Will you tie us up as well?" My brother sassed taking a seat in his appointed chair.

She cocked her head to the side, some humour flashing in her stare. "No. Unless you want me to."

My brother grinned, flashing his pearly whites. "Kind offer, but I prefer it the other way round." He turned to point his head to me. "My brother, too. But I guess you might already be aware of that."

All humour vanished from her features. "Careful, Princeling."

Mal chuckled and at this point I established he was not hungover. He was downright drunk. "Why, will you kill me?"

Her brows rose. "Actually, yes."

Ambrose spat before her. "Careful how you speak, you animal."

"Shut up, Ambrose," I ordered, the room dressing in the gloom of my spilling magic as I pulled the chair back and took a seat. Snow jerked in her seat a little, her golden stare eyeing my magic with some horror, and I immediately regretted using it.

All of the councillors' heads turned in my direction. This was their mess I was sorting, they at least owed me peace while I did it. Blessed peace which I've had too much off these days. I had tasted chaos—electric chaos. I craved nothing else but. "What am I doing here, love?"

She blinked tiredly, her thick lashes fanning over sombre eyes. Had she not slept? "Did you know Taren has the richest mines in the whole of Dardanes?" She stood, taking a butter knife in her hands while circling around the table. "Our metal is strong. Of course, not as strong as your black steel, but similarly indestructible in a sense. Rocks of metal usually injure the men when it is mined because it is so sharp. It is said that even a dull blade can nick skin." She stopped beside Ambrose, my whole body seizing with unease. "I've never cut a tongue with a dull blade before."

In seconds, she gripped Ambrose's jaw with one hand and pried his tongue out before slashing the butter knife across the soft muscle. In one slow cut and several screams later, she flicked half of my councillor's tongue on the table. Blood coated her black leather gloves as she plucked grapes from the table and shoved them in his mouth. "When I tell you to fucking eat, you fucking eat and keep your trap shut."

Tears and pain marred Ambrose's pale face, blood dripping from the corners of his mouth. He gave her a jerky nod. I thought she'd had her fill of satisfaction, but I was proved wrong once again when she flipped the butter knife between her fingers and dug the blade in his eye. Ambrose's head flopped back, limp and lifeless. Hells.

The stench of sudden death made me dizzy for a moment.

"Eat," Snow said to no one in particular, pulling the knife back and chucking it on the table. The thud reverberated around the room, and few flinched before hurriedly obeying and cautiously beginning to chew the food in front of them.

Mal chuckled and pried an apple from the table. "Meal and a show."

"Your council is as useless as you used to say." She dropped on her chair and cocked her head toward Stregor with a wicked smirk etched on her lips. "Or you're as deceitful as your king and know how to seal a secret. Tell me, how does an Empath see lies?"

Stregor's shadows were all over the place as he spoke, but none were of lies, "I will tell you again, I have not the slightest idea what on the gods or hells an Octa Virga is let alone where to find it."

There it was. The reason why she had brought me here. The reason she had spared Adriata in the first place.

She stood and made toward me, her silk dress swished at every step revealing her lean legs and my eyes couldn't help but drop there. Stopping before me, she lifted herself on the table and leaned close to my face. "I suppose Nia has made you aware of the details surrounding my father and the sceptre."

"What is she talking about?" Stregor pressed.

A vein on her neck twitched and she let out an irritated sigh. Before she got to her feet, I grabbed her wrist to stop her from dragging her blood show. "What is it you want from me?"

She pulled away from my hold and plucked a napkin from the table to wipe the skin I'd touched. "Want?" Her brow rose. "I want nothing from you, because you will give it to me."

Stregor struggled in his bounds. "It will not happen, whatever she is going to ask of you. You will not allow that thing to take over our kingdom. Not when I've spent my life protecting it!"

"Stregor, Stregor, running on a thin line here my friend," Mal crooned, leisurely chewing on his apple.

Snow went still and then slowly turned to my councillor. "Stregor?"

My councillor faltered and began shrinking in his seat. He knew what that name meant to her. "My daughter won't allow you to hurt me."

Nesrin? What did she have to do with this?

"Your daughter?" Snow asked, her mouth curving down in distaste. "Just for that I will make sure to keep you alive enough to feel your eyeballs as I feed them past your throat."

"What does Nesrin have to do with this?" I asked.

Snow's attention snapped to me like a whip. "Nesrin is his daughter?" All of a sudden, she burst out laughing. She laughed and laughed till her body began shaking with remnants of her amusement. "Oh, I am going to have so much fun."

Stregor attempted to stand, chains digging in his skin and holding all of his limbs down. "Do not touch my child!"

Snow kicked to her feet. "I will not touch her, but I will make sure she never touches anyone ever again." Picking another butter knife up, she strode toward him.

Tension filled the room and Stregor turned to look at me full of beseech. I was not a man of mercy, and he knew that. And even if I was, it was not my mercy to give.

She gripped his hand and then struck down on his wrist with the round blade. This was not a storm I could stop from raining. She had waited long for this and she deserved her solace.

"Bloody Cynth," my brother cringed at the sound.

Screams, the crunch of bone and flesh made few of the councillors vomit onto the table. Blood splatters had flown over the furniture and wall, pooling on the table and dribbling down to the floor. Fisting his hair, she pulled his head back. "Do you know how it feels to have two of your hands cut? Hm?" She pulled the blade back and pierced his wrist again. Emotion bled in her previously blank features. "She was so small when I found her, starved, bleeding, terrified. With both her hands cut to the wrist. But no. She does not fear the man who cut her limbs and made her feel half a human, she feared you and that tramp of a daughter of yours. Every night, she screamed of a sister and father who haunted her. Why is that…Stregor?"

Couldn't be. No. This was not what I thought it was. Nia. What she had told me in Isjord. "You are Nia's father?"

Snow pulled the knife and dug once again, his words cut by screams. "Her father's name is Alaric Drava. This man is no father to her." One last time she pulled back and dug the knife again till the limb separated from the arm.

Grabbing a torch from the wall, she placed the flame on his cut flesh, cauterising the wound and Stregor's screams grew hoarse. "Wouldn't want you to die before I have had my fill and you bleed like a little bitch." Pushing from him, she motioned to her guards. "Get him patched up. Next, I'm going to cut the one he signed my mother's death with."

One by one, the room emptied till only her, Mal and I were left. Wiping her hands on the tablecloth, she turned to me with a saccharine smile. "Where were we? Yes, what I want and how you are going to give it to me."

Tilting my head, I took in all of the change my longing for her had masked. The much thinned frame, the dark shadows under her eyes, the slight sway on her walk as if she was dizzy, her slow-moving pulse, the slight tremble of her hands. "Why haven't you been eating?"

"The Adriatian sceptre piece," she said, ignoring me and sitting by a large arched window overlooking the mountain face carrying the city. She closed her eyes at the quiet breeze brushing her. "You are going to get it for me."

I already knew what she wanted from me. And worse, I already knew that not in a million lifetimes would I ever refuse her. "You look like you haven't gotten any sleep at all."

She just stared and stared ahead, and for the first time I felt like I didn't know what went inside her head. "My Crafter will work to get Highwall's veil back. I don't want any of your sort out of their cage and my father out of my sugar pot."

"Something has happened." Many things had happened, but there was something else bothering her. Something more.

Finally, she turned to me, that emptiness in her eyes almost made me flinch. "You have a week. If you can't find it in a week, I will burn the whole of your land to find it myself."

I stood up. "You do that, my love."

"I thought you'd know by now," she said, reaching to a stop just a foot from me. "Just what I am capable of."

"I do know. But I also know that with your father searching the sceptre and whatever else is bothering you, there is only so much of your time and effort you are willing to spend over Adriata. One thing I know for sure is that you are not petty before logical. Normally the pettiness comes after."

A knock sounded at the door and a smirk rose on Snow's lips. "Right on time. The things you make me do, *darling*." The venom dripping from that word I used to long to hear was deadly.

"Kilian, Malik." Driada's voice made Mal and I freeze on the spot.

Snow walked to me until our chests were barely touching. "It came to me after, but there is one vow I forgot during our wedding." Her smirk grew to a wide grin. "I will find all you love and care about to ruin before your very eyes."

From the corner of my eye, I caught Mal's slow sobered up movements. Snow would hurt Driada, that I knew, but this was about me after all.

"Shame, it was rather romantic." Leaning down to her ear, I whispered. "We all lose and ruin those we love and care for at some point in our life, my love. You must be desperate to pull out your big girl threats. When you are willing to bargain for my help, let me know. I am a king, not an idiot. Threaten to burn Adriata and I will entertain you till your soldiers are so burnt out they won't know what direction the wind blows. Threaten to kill my council and I will find a new one, a better one. Hurt Driada and see just how many other sacrifices of the same I've made."

When I pulled back, she wore a satisfied smile. "I don't believe you for a second. I think you're rather scared." She ran a sole finger over the seam of my jacket, stopping just above my heart. She looked up at me so innocently. "I think I like it."

"Is there something the matter?" Driada said, making her way to Snow's side as if she hadn't just been used as a threat against me.

"Ma, stay where you are," Mal ordered roughly, and all movement seemed to stop in the room.

Circling me, Snow went past Mal, giving him a complacent look before cradling my stepmother's hands on her own. "Apologies, Driada, I didn't mean to leave you alone in Taren."

"Oh, no, my *asteri*, don't apologise," Driada offered. "The townsfolk were lovely." My stepmother turned surprised to me. "But why are the two of you here?"

"I could ask the same," I bit out more harshly than I intended and Driada's smile waned.

Confused, Driada's glances bounced between the three of us. She'd always been too naive for her own good. Not seeing past Snow's actions at all. "Snow sent that lovely girl to pick me this morning. We had breakfast in the city, but she was called to the castle."

Nia. Her warning. Gears began clicking in place. She knew I wouldn't give in. Knew to use one of the few people that would make me snap.

Snow reached for the door and Nia came into view. "Would you help Driada back to Amaris, she must be tired."

Nia nodded and extended a hand for my stepmother and gave me a look of warning.

"Thank you, for inviting me," Driada offered.

Snow gave her a small smile but full of intention. "You must come again, hopefully Alaric is here for you to meet." Once Driada left with Nia, she turned to us, that feigned smile completely wiped off her face. "We are in a bit of a quandary here. Were this under the circumstances I'd already planned before, there wouldn't even be a discussion, but we are not. And as you said, I can't afford to play cat and mouse with you while my father plays king of the realm with divine toys. Very fortunately for you, the skills and knowledge you possess are what I need."

"Why the threats?"

She waved a hand. "No threats, only a warning. It was fun, wasn't it? Watching you break in a thousand little pieces of fear. Didn't you already know, toying with catch is a favourite pastime of mine?"

My jaw was locked tight. "I'm very mad at you right now, Snowlin."

She tilted her head to the side and grinned so maliciously it would have made grown men shiver. "You've got three days to think. Meet me in Myrdur in three days. Think of your terms and I will think of mine."

Mal chased a step behind me. I could practically hear all of his questions spoken out loud. And it was almost grating.

"Say it."

"You will do something stupid."

"How very little faith you have in your king."

"The king is a dick. My brother is a bigger dick."

For the first time, I couldn't help but laugh. "How am I two different people?"

He stopped and I had to stop, too. "When your arse is on that shiny chair you can somewhat think rationally when it comes to her. And when you're this," he said, poking my chest with a finger. "Is like all the rules Kilian Castemont has obliged since before he knew how to suck on a tit have all disappeared."

"I was bottle fed."

"I've always known there was something wrong with you. All that powdered milk." He sighed, rubbing an eye intensely. "Don't...don't hold on to her anymore."

"Mal, last time I let go of her they told me she was dead. The next time I let go of her is when I am dead."

"She will hate you. More than she already hates you."

"At least she is feeling something for me, brother. I'd rather have that than nothing at all." I was not going to lose her again. And what I had planned would probably enrage her, but I never claimed to be a good man.

Myrdur lingered with a mist of death. Restless spirits clung to every corner of the massive graveyard Old Olympia had become. I'd never felt this much heavy chaos and pain gathered in one place. From the corner of my eye, I could spot my brother shifting uncomfortably on his feet. Malik's head hung low, twitching repeatedly with whatever it was sensing. The curse of being an Eldritch Empath—to feel not only the living but the dead, too.

Larg rested a comforting hand on its shoulder before meeting my gaze and offering me a nod of reassurance.

"What happens if no bargain is settled?" Larg asked.

"We will go to war," Mal answered. "If the Olympian forces leave the Highwall we are going to war with Snow *and* Silas." My brother turned to me. "Don't be too much of a massive dick and get us all killed."

"Don't think I need to be anything but silent to get on Snow's bad side at the moment."

A red light flickered in the horizon before us and soon a round portal opened. Caiden, a winged male I'd seen in battle and an older man with a great build, scarred face and greyed hair came forward.

It still had not settled with me. Olympia was standing. The kingdom of skies had lived hidden for years. With Snow as its ruler.

"Your Majesty," the older male greeted. "My name is Alaric Drava—"

"Snow's father," I interrupted.

His mouth pulled in a crooked smile, and he nodded. "Snow's father." He turned to Mal. "And you must be Driada's son. No longer the wee thing from twenty-two years ago, are you?"

"You know my mother?"

"Aye, Driada visited Myrdur often with her father. Her and Snow's mother were inseparable."

My brother turned to me. "Did you know this?"

I nodded and witnessed my brother wear hurt in his features for the first time since we were only children.

Cai huffed a sardonic laugh. "It's a sickness then," he said to Mal. "He doesn't only lie to those he sends to have killed, he lies to his brother as well."

The winged male next to him snorted and then ruffled his massive wings before flying over a tall building's terrace.

"What's his issue?" Mal asked, pointing to the glaring winged male.

"Him," Cai said, pointing his chin to me. "Lazarus and Snow had a thing going on before we came to Isjord."

Jealousy poured over me as I met Lazarus's gaze from the distance. *A thing.* What *thing*?

Alaric cleared his throat. "My daughter has married you, and I know you are not only powerful but mighty smart, too, so you must be aware of our tradition and the respect we pay to the holy joining of marriage."

Caiden groaned and looked around. "To gods she hears you and this will end up a blood bath."

"With all due respect to your tradition, Alaric," I offered. "I will not hold Snow to it. Despite what it means on my behalf, to Snow this was solely a trade."

Slowly, his brows rose up. "And what does it mean to you?"

"Ric," Caiden called sternly.

"Cai, my muffin," my brother purred. "Tense, are we?"

The Zephyr angled a deadly look on Mal.

The sky turned strange, angry storm filled clouds hovered almost too close above. Lightning broke the deathly calm, landing close to us. Too close.

Not lightning.

Her.

She was breath-taking. Flimsy black material that covered her figure hung loosely and piled to the floor, her lean legs peeked out with each step she took, the heavy gold jewellery circled and hung around her and did nothing to keep the cloth in place. A crown like no other rested on her head, spiked obsidian almost resembling black glass. Queen. She always carried the might of one, it was because she truly was one. Queen of Olympia. My wife.

"My, my, my," she said, swaying her way to us. "Already cosy and comfortable with the enemy. Hello, Larg."

The massive man bowed his head in greeting. "My queen."

"Ouch," my brother grumbled.

Snow's smirk rose. "Princeling." When her attention turned to me, every bit of her tensed, her mannerisms almost ready to recoil. "Darling husband. What a pleasure to see you again." Those yellow eyes swept my head to my feet and back up again before a disdainful sneer curled her lips.

"Missed me?"

She offered me a saccharine smile, the same she offered to all her enemies. "Rather fondly. Shall we?"

I pointed a hand to the massive building behind us. "After you, my heart."

"I'd rather not give you my back. After you."

"You are not sleeping," I almost hissed out when she swayed a little on her feet. Purple marred her under her blood shot eyes, no tinge of colour on her face beside those striking golden rings.

"There is no time to sleep when you plan war, Your Majesty," she said, moving around the half-battered building facing the Volants. "How can I sleep with that noise piercing my ears?" She'd muttered the words that were probably spoken to herself rather than me.

"How long has it been calling to you?"

Her head jerked in my direction. "What?"

"The ringing, I can hear it as well."

"That is impossible. *Zgahna* is the call of my ancestors. The only other people that would be able to sense it are Thora and Eren. Other than that, perhaps—" Her words got caught in realisation and she stared wide eyed at the fog-covered mountains.

"Your husband," I finished for her. "And that I am."

"Not for long."

Sliding my hands onto my pockets, I leaned against a wall. "You were mine and will remain mine. To joy, to sadness, to live. Remember?"

"Are you pleased?" She perched on a broken window ledge. "To have first lied to me, then trapped me?"

"I didn't trap you. The marriage was set to take place and if I remember correctly," I said, pointing to the visible black ink on her arm, "you couldn't have avoided marrying me because of that bargain. Just like you can't avoid this bargain. Just like you couldn't avoid what happened between us and what you felt for me."

Her stare grew dark, and rootlets of white mist filtered through the cracked walls and open spaces of the ruins around us. The *zgahna* poured out of the Volants onto Myrdur, creeping and blanketing the ruins under till nothing but porcelain clouds were visible.

It slithered below my feet in Snow's aim where it pooled and conjoined till the mass grew tall enough to measure to her height. The mist slowly took the shape of a white serpent, it hissed as it slithered around Snow protectively.

A sense of threat touched the back of my neck, but my magic didn't stir in response. To her, it never would. For her, always.

"Down," Snow ordered, her voice vibrating in the air, turning to a spectral whisper that vibrated all around Myrdur. "I command you."

At those words, the mountains shook, the gravel beneath me shivered and the misty serpent hissed one last time before blasting in a gust of wind and dispersing into thin air.

"I played a game when I was younger," she started, her voice empty and so was her attention. "The first person I killed was a soldier who used to guard me. No older than fifteen. He was like an older brother to me. Father knew what he was doing by choosing him for my first kill. I learned two things that day. Dried blood is hard to get out of your nail beds and that the only thing between me and becoming my purpose was emotion."

She continued, "The game started at dawn when I woke up. I'd rid myself of fear at dawn and learn hate, so every dawn I went to face my fears—Murdoc. I'd let him beat me till I was unconscious, and soon I was numb of fear. By sunrise I'd grown numb of pain, too. Hate grew like an overgrown weed, it didn't even need much encouragement."

My eyes drew shut in pain. I didn't need to see to know the hurt. And I ached all over for her. "Snow."

"Noon was a special time," she said, staring into the distance. "If I wasn't skinning animals in the kitchen, I was skinning traitors and enemies of my father's. So, each noon I'd learn to convince myself that I was rid of feeling disgust, horror and empathy. I thought I was already the perfect soldier, but fear and pain and empathy are not the emotions that make you weak. No, father was right, they often made you stronger. Happiness, trust, care—those were true weaknesses. I spent my dusks, my twilights and my nights fighting them too."

"That is not true."

"Because I loved my mother, my siblings? Because they made me happy?" she asked, turning to me. "Because I cared?"

"I know you did."

"Exactly my point, Your Majesty. I was never the perfect soldier, and I failed my father every day. They were my weakness and *you* got rid of them. *You* made me the perfect soldier, the one my father was never able to create. It took me many dawns, sunrises and noons to train fear, pain and empathy, but it took me one dusk, one twilight and one night to lose joy, trust, care and my happiness. It took me less to lose what I felt for that lie of yours."

Her chest rose fast, and the thrum of her heartbeat matched the thunder that was gurgling above. "Are we to bargain, or do you still have another trick to play?"

"There will be terms," I said.

She scoffed humorlessly. "I've never dealt a hand with you that I haven't had to bargain for the loss of something, Obscur Asteri. Lay your terms and I will lay mine."

"You will hold off your attacks on Adriata. I cannot help you while I have my hands tied in all four corners."

"There is only so long you can keep me away from burning your kingdom. But for now, I will pull them away and you will help me find the Octa Virga pieces."

"We will be civil."

That made her snort and then cackle, a dark sort, and a sound I'd never heard from her before. "Civil? Me and you?"

"No petty games and little threats using my stepmother like the charade of that day."

"You're boring, Adriatian." She sighed, leaning forward on a window overlooking the mist. "Everything is boring me lately."

She'd be rid of that boredom very soon. "You will resume your duties as my queen, attend meetings, rule by my side. Be my equal." That got me a short chesty laugh from her and once she realised that I was serious, her expression tensed. "And you will spend your nights in Adriata, with me."

Her attention snapped to me, for the first time since that day she had given me more than a blank reaction. Fury. "No."

"It is one of the terms I am not willing to negotiate. Your duties to Olympia will have their daylight and the ones to Adriata moonlight. You are the Adriatian queen as much as you're the Olympian one."

"You said with *you*."

"You've heard me correct. You will spend them where I do. Nightfall to dawn, you will be sleeping in my bedroom. Right next to me."

Something like fear flashed in her tired stare while considering my words. *Let it not be of me,* I begged all gods. "Exactly what are you hoping to accomplish by having me do that?"

"That is for me to know and you to oblige. Remember—terms?"

"This is what you do, isn't it? Coerce me into participating in a lie, forcing me to stay by your side. Forcing me to feel for you because you know I would have never even thought anything but disgust for you. You know I would have never let you touch me. I cannot seem to rub off the itch of you out of my skin. I am more disgusted with myself than you. I hate me more than you. I loathe my words more than yours. I still want to hurt myself more than you. Because at the end of the day, it was me being stupid not you. Is this what it is?"

I took a step to her, and she flinched, taking a step back from me. "Snow."

"You will help me find my brother and sister. For that term this is what I offer."

I froze. What? "What brother and sister?" Her hands began curling in a fist and I knew what she was about to do. "Snow, what brother and sister?"

"They are alive." She swallowed. "During the attack, my uncle tried to bargain the truth for his life. He'd hid them from my father the night of the attack and planned to use them as his way to the Isjordian crown."

It took me a moment to process what she had just revealed. "Are you certain?"

"No, not certain and I killed him thinking I'd be able to figure a way to find them myself. It could take me weeks to years, all that time I am not willing to spend away from them if they are truly alive. Time you are able to spare me."

Numengarth was vast, with places not even marked by human touch. The two siblings could be kept somewhere even magic wouldn't be able to find them. But for her, I'd defy all rules of magic—all the rules of this realm. "I will find them."

She gave me a nod. "Then it's a bargain." She took off her glove and extended her hand to me. I slid my warm palm across her soft clammy one and held it tight for a moment before repeating the seal of our bargain. A black band of runes curved around the top of her hand and then mine, a sting in its wake that would not be remembered compared to the sting its end would bring. Once this bargain was severed, there would be nothing tying us together.

"You can let go of me now."

I held her a few heartbeats more, running my thumb across her flesh. "Till now, I thought you were a mirage. A play my sick heart was putting out for me. I refuse to sleep thinking I'll wake to a day where that mirage has ended. But you are real."

"You should have prayed that I wasn't. You should have prayed that my uncle had truly killed me."

I shook my head. "I would have chased after you. Every afterlife, heaven or hell, I would have searched it all."

Her face twisted with emotion all of a sudden, dark brows drooping, and that golden stare rounded with sorrow as she looked up at me. I didn't understand. I couldn't read her. For the first time since I'd met her in Isjord I was confused again, and she'd become that same mystery. "Was that it?" she asked with a small voice that shivered. "How you expected me to react?" She snorted and then blasted in gales of laughter. "Oh, darling, you have no idea who you are dealing a hand with."

Perhaps I didn't.

"See you tonight, at nightfall." Backing away, her body lit bright with electricity. The next second she was gone.

CHAPTER FIVE

NEXILIS

SNOWLIN

The Fogling screams made me cringe in a pain that shot up to my damned brains. The bat-like giant creatures were born out of magic and destruction the night of the *Draugr*. The million-man massacre had generated enough magical havoc to contort the fallen Aura to these creatures that remained to torment Olympia for years after. Despite being created from the darkness of human souls, the Fogling feared darkness and lived in the skies and mountain peaks that tore above the blanket of clouds facing Hemera. They needed light to live. The strange ways of gods and their wicked ways to prove points no one cared about.

About forty large, black, leathery bodies of the talon-armed creatures laid slain on the mountain floor as my soldiers gathered to burn them. We'd never had to kill them before. For twenty-seven years they roamed the skies, but never descended on the land to attack. Now, somehow, they rained down on my lands as if they were a rageful storm—angry at us. Perhaps angry at me for failing to grant their souls the rest they needed. For failing to kill my father when I had the chance. For holding back from claiming Myrdur so I could fulfil my selfish plans.

"That was twice as many as last time," Tristin, the leader of the Skye warriors said, dropping to the stony ground of mount Amur where one of our smallest tribes had built life. Tristin was the woman that trained me in fighting. The one who turned my punches from angry to tactical. The one who strayed my aim from killing to evading. I owed much to her. She was one of my most trusted.

"And thrice as many as I last remembered to hoard in a flock," Cai commented, dragging one of the creatures to a pile that was to be burned.

Tristin nudged my shoulder and pointed her chin to my stern friend. "What's his matter? One of his soldiers ran out of the train grounds weeping the other day."

I wished he would just make me cry too, but that would require him to actually speak to me. The man wouldn't even look at me after the day of the battle. The most reaction he'd given me was when I bargained with Kilian. The disapproval of me meeting him could have withered flowers if there had been any in Myrdur.

"You know men and their mood swings," I said. "Nothing that candy, some ego stroking, and a good barber's visit cannot solve."

She shrugged. "My guess is because you married that Adriatian king."

I narrowed my eyes on her. "This is why I didn't want you to marry Leanna. Poisoning your well polished brain with her deranged fantasies." No doubt the Llyn tribe leader had spoiled Tristin's highly trained mentality with these tales.

She cracked an unusual smile and ruffled her white, short rain drenched hair. "I thought you didn't want me to marry her because you had a crush on me."

"That too." Kicking an innocent rock away, I stood up. "Send a couple more Nimbus to keep Amur under clouds till we figure where the Fogling are hoarding in such masses."

The only way we kept the Fogling out of the cities was by casting darkness over the cities with clouds—dark clouds. Nimbus were stationed almost everywhere, ensuring that the blanket of safety remained above the cities at all times of the day despite the unpredictability of weather. Occasionally, the Nimbus would pull the clouds back to allow light touch land. Unfortunately, much needed sunlight to grow and thrive.

She sighed, surrendered. "It was one hour, Snow, one hour of sunlight for the first time in two weeks. Amur will start to freeze over soon enough. The weather is already shifting here. I'm starting to think there is something else triggering them," Tristin said carefully. "Each time Isjordians breach Myrdur, they triple."

Immediately, I seeked Cai in the crowd of soldiers. His form moved slower than usual, more helpless and hopeless looking. It must be breaking his soul to see his city still be stepped on and soiled by Isjordians. To have the memories of his parents tarnished by their presence.

"When has he slept in his bed for the last time?" Tristin asked, following my line of sight.

Cai had made camp down Myrdur since the first sighting of Isjordians were seen in Fernfoss months ago. Last I'd seen him spend the night in his room was long before we set camp in Fernfoss waiting for Isjord to call on me. "I don't know."

She stood, her massive white wings unfolding behind her. "He listens to you, get him to sleep at home," she said, before launching in the air and disappearing between thunderous clouds.

Home. Had Cai ever considered Taren his home?

"Cai," I called, slowly reaching him.

He cast a short look at me before continuing to arrange the Fogling body neatly atop one another. "Has Her Majesty finally got the time to tell me what happened this morning? Or are we keeping that one a secret too?"

"Portal us to Taren. This Majesty would rather repeat it once."

He huffed, dusting his palms together before peeling his gloves off to reveal intricate black markings and runes on both his hands—craft that Visha had woven into him. Our kingdom was difficult to travel through, it could take days to climb from one tribe to the other and considering the frequency of the Fogling attacks and Isjordians roaming in Myrdur, we could not afford to lose time. So, the witch had worked her craft and sown it to Cai's magic, and now he was able to travel from one location to the other with only a word.

All the way to the meeting room, I dreaded the moment where I'd have to tell Cai of the bargain I struck with Kilian. From time to time, I'd caught his side glances at my wrist and the fresh bargain that still burned, and they were enough to tell that he wouldn't like what I'd exchanged for it.

"Her Majesty seems rather calm after everything," he commented snidely.

"I am."

"Do you think you can get Kilian to play your game by threats alone? Are you underestimating the Night King solely because you exchanged a few kisses and affections when he was in his guise?"

I stopped. Is that what we'd done? Exchanged a few kisses and affections? Is that what he thought we did? Was it all that we'd done? "I think you're underestimating me, Cai."

And as expected, when I sat the three most important people in my life down, Cai was the first one to react. "You will what?" he almost shouted the words in my face, having not taken the terms of the bargain all too well. I could see the steam of rage leaking out of his ears.

"There was a reason," I said.

"As there always is for each of your madnesses," Alaric murmured, pinching the bridge of his nose all frustrated.

"Never do anything without cause for the harm. You taught me that," I said.

"Pinning this on my parenting again?" the old man sighed.

I shrugged and then unravelled the rest.

Isjordian soldier after soldier cleared their path for me, their faces terrified as I made way to my uncle.

His sword hit mine, sending him flying feet away, current and static surrounded my blade. He stood once more and before he could make step forward, I raised my palm releasing my magic once more, half of his body frozen, pinned still by ice and frost.

"How—how did you do it? How is this possible?" *he asked as ice gradually covered his skin.*

"A kingdom cannot be built in a day, and you are foolish to think you can destroy it in one as well. Now the question is, dear uncle, how are you going to do it? I mean, pay for what you have done?" *I asked, lifting my blade to his throat.* "How could your death possibly satisfy me? Maybe I should do more than just kill you. Shall I carve your insides, keep you conscious while I rip your soul piece by piece? Surely no heaven could accept rot like you anyway."

His body trembled. It was not from the frost, it was from me. The wide fear in his eyes fed so much of my hunger. "You cannot...you will not kill me."

And I took offence from the fierceness of that statement. My eyebrows rose in question as I let a wicked grin spread across my face. "Isn't it prophetic, uncle, how my mother was the one to break your black little heart and I to carve it out? How happy you must have been, to see her bleed and die. Now tell me, how will I feel when I do the same to you?" *I said, letting my blade graze his neck until a stream of red chased down his rotten skin.*

"Thora and Eren are alive," *he blurted out as the frost rose to cover his face. My grin turned to a snarl at his ridiculous words.* "They are alive, I have kept them alive. The night of the attack they were not killed!"

"You think me a fool?"

He jerked his head in denial. "This is not a lie. Your father doesn't know. I planned to use them for my own plans, after all Eren is the heir to the throne."

His words settled heavy in my chest. They could not be, he was lying. The world started spinning. The sword clunking faded from the background as mist and fog clouded my reality, my chest was storming, the heartbeat loud on my ears and pulsing around me.

Lies. Lies. It was all lies. "If they are alive, what makes you think I need you?"

"You cannot find them, sweet niece, not without me. You will have to turn this realm upside down and inside out," he said, huffing a long vile laugh, as if he still owned my courage.

Mirroring his smile, I got in his face and said, "Upside down and inside out it is."

His features wide in horror as I swung my sword, impaling his head from his body, dragging it down to pierce his already dead heart.

"Convenient time for all of you to be so silent," I said with a sigh and dropped back on my seat.

Alaric abruptly stood and paced the room. He'd not once uttered the name of my mother or siblings, never had he sat down with me to reminisce their memory because it haunted him every day. "I would know. I would know if they were alive. How could I not know?" And there it was, the blame and the guilt. "The ballroom had burned to the ground, kid, I know. I remember," he insisted, his words stuttering. "I checked every burnt body there. Every. Single. One. One by one. I found your brother's sword next to where he'd burned. And I found Thora's smaller one right next to him. I buried those bodies, Snow, with my own hands. I buried them." He stopped and ran a shaking hand over his mouth. "Who have I buried if not my children?"

"He lied to her," Cai's passive voice began chipping a fragment of my hope. "Saw an opportunity to distract Snow from killing him and took it. Enough thinking this more than it is—a lie."

I frowned.

"Cai," Nia said. "What if he was not?"

"There is a way," Visha said quietly. "To find out if he lied or not. If they are alive or not."

Nia shook her head. "She won't do it."

I leaned on the table. "Do what?"

Visha said, "Let me enter your dreams and let their souls pass onto the Otherworld. If they pass, they are spirits and if they don't, whatever has been hunting your sleep is not the dead. Just your own demons."

"No. He will help me find them. I'll search every corner of this realm if I have to. And with their help, I'll be able to do it ten times as fast." Using my siblings as an excuse was a low blow, but I needed Cai not to hate me right now.

"If you think he can find them," Alaric said. "Let him find them. Anything, we will do anything."

"You do know that your siblings will be hunted down like day one if the Adriatians figure out they are alive. And you do know that the first to hunt on them is your…it's…him," Cai stuttered out, running a hand through his dark locks.

I had gone blind. Why was I seeing the stubble in his usually clean shaved jaw, the half inch longer hair he meticulously kept at a certain length, the dark around his eyes, the shadow of fear curving down his mouth.

"Cai," I stood to approach him, and he took a step back from me.

"I have to get back to Kvan, Cori still needs help to move the *Fogling* bodies out of the village before they rot and attract other wild animals."

"I am sorry." The words still tasted sour in my mouth, but it was somewhat easier than before to drag them out. "For not letting you know. For letting you think something had happened to me."

He halted and gave me a half look behind his shoulder. "So am I, Snow. So am I."

Alaric had pursed his lips in thought. "Bring the boy to Taren. It is tradition that he meets me."

I rolled my eyes, and he pointed a finger in warning like I was five. "He is not a boy," I tried to say calmly.

"Even worse," he bellowed, his thick Dravan accent barely making him comprehensible. "And you're married to him for Nubil's sake. I warned you well, hen. Told you that marrying the boy comes with great trouble. You know our traditions well though you pretend not to. Things changed the moment you let him live and that bargain sealed the deal."

"It's a bargain and I have nine others just the same."

"Well, are you married with the other bargainers, kid? You had a great grandfather down the line who married a few men and women all together. A grand lot that was."

I groaned and turned my attention to the quiet mouse, Nia, holding her laughter by the corner of my room. "Since I am told to bring him home, why haven't you asked Nia here to bring Moriko to meet you?"

Nia's face fell and a red flush climbed almost up to her hairline. "W-what?"

Alaric's bushy brows bunched, his attention bouncing back and forth between Nia and I. "Why would she bring the Autumn Queen to meet me?"

Nia launched at me before I had a chance to answer and tell him how his youngest daughter was spending more than meeting hours her emissary duties concluded, and that the other night she didn't even return from Hanai.

"Alright, that's enough!" Alaric shouted while Nia and I wrestled on the ground.

I started giggling first, overwhelmed with emotion all of the sudden. Nia was panting from our scuffle when she dropped on the ground beside me, laughing too. The door of my room slammed shut alerting Alaric's departure.

"Thank the gods," she whispered. "Sometimes, a lot of times, I think I lose you inside there." She rested a gloved finger on my temple. "The thing with Kilian, finding out about Thora and Eren, Murdoc and the council." A tear slid from her eye. "My...my father. All those things would have made me lose my mind. Just when I think you might, you always return to me. Thank you."

Turning on my side, I gathered her body in my embrace. "That was the cringiest thing I've heard. My toes can't uncurl."

"I think you like a bit of sugar in all the poison," she said.

Silence ran in the room for a short while before I asked, "Are you well, truly?"

"I think I am. Mostly. I think I'll soon get better."

"And Mor, have you told her about him?"

"Yes," she said quietly. "I trust her."

Trust. To Nia that was more important than care or love or anything else. If she trusted Moriko, it meant that she really liked the woman. "That is good."

She shuffled and turned to her side to look at me. "What will you do?"

"For now, I'm going to find my most scandalous night dress and have my fill of his frustration. He might be the Obscur Asteri, but he is just a man after all."

She giggled. "Wear that thing that you bought in Fernfoss and the lacy stuff that the courtesan in Taren gave you." She pushed up on her elbow, looking down at me. "I'm really sorry, for not telling you when I found out who he was."

I shook my head. "I would have killed him then and ruined everything."

"Do you still...care for him?" she asked carefully.

Like a bucket of ice spilling over me, the rush of hate flooded through me. "No, but at times I forget that I hate him. That has to be worse than still caring for him. And he did that to me. Made me feel ashamed of my own self for even daring to feel."

The doors banged open and Pen strutted like she owned the place. "It's the air, I could swear it on Hodr," she said, outraged almost. "The nuts are laying on the ground now."

Nia snorted, but I gave the big mouthed red head a glare. "One day, carrot, I will feed you to a nice little, white rabbit."

Pen stopped all of a sudden and turned to me, tears pooling on her lashes and her adorable freckled face twisted in a cry.

I cringed at the sight. There was something about people and their crying faces. "Calm, Pen. I was just fooling around."

Her lip wobbled and she sniffled between sobs. "It's the first time you've spoken to me since that morning in Adriata." Tears chased a stream down her face. "You sleep down in the dungeons, eat alone, bathe alone, dress alone, don't even speak to me when I pass you through the corridors at all. You don't even let me brush your hair!"

All expression fell from my face. What?

Knowingly, Nia stood and wrapped a hand over her neck. "Alright, let's go get her something to wear."

After a long cold bath washing the stench and black blood of the Foglings, I was already regretting accepting the bargain. At least this one term.

Pen had twisted her head to the side, raking her widened stare all over my body. "But…but…that is so…tiny." She'd not taken well to the Olympian wardrobe, but the slinky ivory satin nightgown that barely brushed past my cheeks and hung up by the sheer will of two hair thin strings on my shoulders was a different story altogether.

"Quick," Nia said, ushering me toward the balcony. "Leave before Cai comes back to see you off. He will not let you leave if he sees you in that."

One the way, I grabbed my trusty pillow and warned, "If I don't return by dawn, presume I've killed the bastard and am raging disaster on Adriata."

"Funny," she mocked. But I was completely serious.

Bolting took me less than a moment, but it was a good means to release some pent-up magic. Usually, I lit the sky in thunder and struck land once or twice to cover flakes of my magic shedding out of me. My seal gathered the ever-flowing magic in my body like a pot tipping with water, and if I didn't tip the water, I'd drown and overflow my surroundings too. I'd lose control and the seal would slip free.

The earth beneath my feet had charred from the hit of lightning, soon all of this land would be littered in soot and bones. Soon. It bothered me how that 'soon' had been postponed—like an itch I couldn't relieve.

His gardens were magical at night. The sweet breeze was infused with the scent of flowers, the soft lulling night sparkled with fireflies and restless flower folk jumping around, and for the first time, the sound of cicadas seemed to form a cohesive melody. What took my breath away, however, was neither the blooming night flower nor the round rosy moon, it was the infinite blanket of night twinkling with the most stars I'd ever seen. The more beauty I found the more I wanted to ruin it. Make it all dirty and paint it red.

A gasp pulled my attention to my surroundings. A young guard had frozen before me, eyes aghast and locked in shock.

"Point me to you king, I am already late."

A scream tore from his throat, and I put a hand over my chest. "Sacred balls of Nubil, that startled me. Your king, you daft thing."

Then he surprised me a third time tonight when he took off in a sprint toward the opposite direction from me. And I was left blinking to myself a couple of times.

"We thought Nia would accompany you," Mal's voice came from the top of the stairs leading to the castle. The prince's dishevelled form was perhaps the handsomest sight of tonight. His brown locks were loose from the usual band and blew in the breeze as did his unbuttoned white shirt. "Should have made our guards aware you might be coming by…other means of transport."

None of us spoke. Just stared at one another for a moment. It was beginning to annoy me. I loved words yet I'd swallowed everything I had to say.

"Hello, Snow."

"Hello, Princeling. I am late."

"So, they are alive," he said, taking a jagged deep breath. "Your brother and sister."

Cai's words flooded my mind and for a moment made me regret having asked for their help. "Not until I find them."

He nodded. "Third floor, left corridor, first room to your right."

I stopped a few steps above him. Something was bothering me. "Why are you looking at me like that?"

He shook his head lightly and barked a short laugh. "Thought I saw something. Had a drink with my brother earlier, but shouldn't have, really."

Just like that he was gone.

The lilac-coloured corridors were void of life yet full of it. Lush candlelight and moonlight pouring from the massive arched windows blurred together, creating a dream haze along my path. The gentle sway of gossamer ivory curtains along the summer breeze almost lulled me to sleep right there.

For a few minutes I waited in front of the beige wooden door before taking a deep breath, squaring my shoulders and pushing the silver handle.

It was just how I had imagined his world to be. Deep mauve and onyx, softwood and silver accents glistened under the melancholy of the dark and strands of lone moonlight. How dark was the dark truly? Perhaps it was because I'd always felt so protected from it—from him—because suddenly…it had muted.

He was so still one would miss him. Sat back on an armchair on the far back of the room, facing the door, his sleeves rolled up revealing the band of our bargain and strong arms that once I'd begged to be held from. He cradled a tumbler with an amber liquid, his whole attention to it even long after I'd entered. I'd never seen him so dishevelled. How did he look so human when I knew he was the furthest from being one?

It wasn't that cold, but when his gaze hit me, I shivered. Like that, he held my raging stare for a little while before his eyes travelled slowly over my body. His jaw tensed when he took the next sip of the amber liquid.

My ridiculous body was starting to betray me again, I felt my nipples pebble under his dark scrutiny. Crossing my arms, I hoped to hide any evidence of my shameful attraction to him.

He hissed and I noticed his gaze over the flimsy bust of the nightgown. "No shoes," his voice broke the cold with more cold. Not what I'd expected him to ask considering he had pinned me with his stare like he was a snap away from devouring me.

Despite being tempted to leave him unanswered, find a spot on the floor and just let this night go by and leave at dawn, I answered, "The earth grounds and expels some magic out of my body. That is why I don't wear shoes."

I knew I'd done right to tell him when his face cracked just the slightest from that stoic mask of solemnity that was itching me for destruction. How dare he be calm when I wanted to be fury.

He lifted the tumbler to his lips, his eyes never leaving me. "You hid it well."

Locking my hands behind me before I did something like wrap them around his throat or trail them over those lips that I longed to feel over mine, I moved toward him, slowly. "No, I didn't hide. It was always there, in a blizzard, a rain cloud, thunder, a raging storm. I never hid. Couldn't even if I wanted to. What I did was lie, mask it." Reaching him, I bent down to his eye level. I wish I didn't have to drown the whimper that rose when his scent suffused me. "Pretend." The grin spread before I could help it. "I know a thing or two about pretending."

He met my stare dead on. He knew a thing or two about pretending himself. I wanted to hurt him. I wanted to hurt him to tears. His pulsing heartbeat mocked me. "I think I'd be able to separate the act from the truth."

"Yeah, I'd think so too. After all, you tried so hard to get under my skin, didn't you? Only to fail."

His silver irises faded just the slightest, I could practically see doubt gather with each twitch of the nerve on his temple. "I am not sure if it is you or me you are trying to convince that there was nothing between us."

"Convince?" I took the tumbler from his hand. "I don't need to convince anyone." The air grew colder at my command. Ice slowly coated and spread over the glass I held. A chuckle escaped me when his attention flinted to it. I hissed when the cold bit onto my skin. One moment of pain and all sensation of cold on my skin vanished. Cold and I never got along, but the pain was bearable and never enough to cause me any harm. I had, after all, spent all my life in it. Trained, beaten, slept in it, too. And sometimes it had comforted me when no one could. The cold eventually burned and turned warm. "The Winter Princess who couldn't bear the cold. You should have seen your expression that day. It was delicious." I took a sip of the chilled burning liquid and sighed when the chestnut taste kissed my throat, and then almost gagged from the strength of the liquor. Hells. "Do you know what was better? Knowing I could catch a few moments of rest at night while knowing you were out there. I knew that day for sure that you wouldn't hurt me. It was enough to convince Nia, too. She wouldn't stop prattling about how you were this mystic being with an ominous presence that threatened to envelope all that was good."

I chugged the whole liquid down and lowered the tumbler back on the table. My sight dizzied for a moment. Of all my vices, why did I have to be lightweight, too? "The moments I hurt seemed to be the moments you were most vulnerable to my prying. Malik told me all about you after we turned from Brogmere. General, he said—you were the king's general." A bitter chuckle left me. "Still, someone who knew more than any spy of mine knew, you were the closest thing to the man I was hunting. I needed you to be vulnerable."

I could see the gears rotate in his head. He was searching for everything he'd told me.

"*Alaar*, reassurance, the council," I said, before it took all night for him to piece together the things I'd done. "I swear that night you would have given me everything if I'd batted my lashes a tad stronger. Anyway, the only thing hindering the king's decisions—your decisions—was the council. I ought to get rid of them first. That is your guilt to bear, you planted that thought in me. And then, I just so happened to find out who was in your council. I knew Adriane for sure and then you mentioned Stregor when we stayed in Arynth. Can you imagine, two of the people who owed me equally as you were both alive. My luck had soared."

He filled the glass with the amber liquor, lifting to sip where my lips had left a mark against the frosted glass. "What else?" he asked, too boredly for my taste. Like he wasn't believing my words. "Tell me."

"You don't seem to understand me," I said, taking the glass from him to take another sip. Perhaps I needed it to make this night bearable. "I wore pretend like it was my second skin, not gloves to take off." Liar. Liar. Liar. Damned liar. I'd never lied this badly in my existence.

"You know I see colour shadows when people go through emotion."

A smirk pulled on my lips. "I'm told you can't see mine."

"Correct." He leaned forward, our faces a hair away from touching. His heat began enveloping me and I melted. The cold dispelled from the room and the glass condensed on my hand, it felt like flowers could bloom from the tip of my fingers. "Your lies have a taste, my love. Not a colour."

All amusement wiped from my expression. "It is so loud," I whispered over his lips, running a finger down his chest and over his roaring heart. "Making fun of me and my pain. Reminding me of how it beats while my mother's has stilled. Beating while my own is comatose." Ice glided over my fingers, extending beyond my nails to form sharp claws. I placed them on his chest, digging them on his skin just slightly. My limbs shook with rage and the outside shook from thunder. "I want to rip it out. What taste fills your tongue now?"

His hand slid over mine, dragging it lower down on his chest. The touch burned my clammy skin. "There. You don't want to hurt your pretty hands on bone."

"Don't touch me." With that, I pulled my hand away and marched to a sofa braced by the corner of the room.

The room was violently spinning, but I could feel his gaze on me when I gave him my back. My traitorous skin zapped with electricity at the attention of the man that did worse things to a few other organs.

Sick. Sick. Sick. He had made me sick. He was my sickness.

The chair he rested on creaked, footsteps left the room and then water ran from an adjoining room.

Giving to the alcohol induced dizziness, I dropped to the sofa. Adjusting the pillow at the hand rest, I laid myself on the uncomfortably small space. The velvet friction against my skin sent my senses on a buzz. I tried to focus on the clapping thunder outside that shook trees and poles, the screeching sound ticking with each blow of wind and a shadow wavering on the ceiling. It was uncomfortably silent otherwise. With a sigh, I turned on my stomach. The flooring was beautiful and dizzying, I liked it. Intricate violet patterns curled and twisted on the tiles like a maze, and I traced a finger over them. How long would I have to spend my nights with him? My heart raced like a silly thing, but my brain raked with solutions to end this situation. *Kill him. Imprison him. Break the bargain. Force him. Take his brother and mother. Threaten him.* Sigh. Why had I not done just that? Why had I allowed him to manipulate me into this ridiculous bargain?

A blanket was thrown over me. "Was there not enough fabric for a proper nightgown?" The edge of his voice was menacing. I'd never heard him like this before.

I looked up at him. "No man has minded seeing me in this before. Actually, they might have minded because if I remember clearly, I never wore this for long before I was naked."

A shadow crossed his face and I swear his silver orbs shone black. No, they really did. Bracing himself on the sofa and over me, he leaned down to my face. "Don't go poking the bear. You have no idea what *you* make me capable of."

I shivered even though the liquor had made my body incredibly warm. "You have no claim over me." His act was tiring me,

"Your lies are starting to stink now, *wife*."

"Whatever helps you sleep at night, Your Majesty. Sleep pretending I won't let any man have their way with me after every night I spent with you just to wash the stench of this nightmare from my thoughts."

He smirked. Actually smirked. "Hmm. No need to taste or smell them anymore. They're falling apart the second they leave your mouth." He straightened and it was only then I noticed he only wore a pair of loose linen trousers that hung low on his hips. The deep V of his muscles pointing my attention right over his bulge pushing the thin fabric. My mouth went dry and then pursed with fury when he said, "Let another man touch you and I will use their carcass to feed the soil of my garden. You are mine."

You are mine.

You are mine.

The words bounced with intent to annoy me. Spinning to lay on my back, I kicked the blanket away, aware the short thing had hiked up enough to show my underwear. "I don't usually stay for the long run, you can do as you wish with their carcass."

He rubbed a frustrated hand over his eyes and left to return shortly with an item of clothing in his hand. Kneeling before me, he grabbed my ankle and attempted to push it through a pant leg.

I began thrashing and then a sharp whack to my bottom stunned me to silence. Did he just—

"Stay still, you brat." He pulled up the trousers all the way to my hips and fastened them with the ties. I let him. I somehow let him. Why did I let him? Gods, the room was spinning so much.

"Fuck," he said, rubbing his jaw in frustration. "I don't know what was worse, seeing you bare or seeing you in my clothes."

My chest rose in staccato—this was too much. I was angry, so angry, but why wasn't I angry at him? This man who had killed my mother. This man who dragged me through hell. It was the same one who'd suddenly made the stars shine at night. "Go away," I whispered harshly, treacherous tears threatening to pour out of my prickling eyes. "Get away from me."

"You're not sleeping there."

"Pray tell, where am I sleeping tonight?"

"Where you will sleep every night." He raised a brow and pointed to the bed behind. "In my bed and right next to me."

I got in his face. "You can't force me to do that, there was nothing mentioned in our bargain about that." I couldn't. Sour betrayal stung my thoughts. Did my mother's heart weep black blood when she had seen what

I'd let him do to me—touch me, kiss me? When I'd touched him back, kissed him back?

"Then you better make some space because we are both sleeping on that sofa tonight and the foreseeable future." Before I made to speak again, he grabbed my chin and brought my face close to his. "Go on. See where defying me will take you."

Defy him? "Fuck. You." For lack of any actual words forming in my mouth.

A smile tugged at his lips. "Not tonight." Without warning, he threw me over the shoulder and went to drop me on his bed. He flipped the cover over me and tucked me tight. "I'd give you a good night kiss too, but I'd rather not be punctured again."

It was too loud. My breathing, my anger, my pulse, my thoughts. On top of that, everything was also spinning and now blurring red.

After he settled on the other side, the room went stark dark. "Move and I will tie you to the post, Snowlin. And it will not be the type of tied up that you or I will like."

"Touch me and all to hell with saving the realm because I will kill you." I swallowed hard, following the movement of shadows in the room. At each flicker of movement, my heart jolted. This was going to be a very long night.

And long the night was. My lids ached from remaining open and aware all night long. Dawn drew along sluggishly as if it loathed me, as if I'd wronged it. From his controlled breaths I knew he had not slept either. Silently watching me. Did he enjoy this? Did he enjoy making me his prey again? Did he enjoy the chase?

At the first sound of a cockatoo and the sight of mauve colouring of the sky, I shot to my feet and left his room.

Dawn. Hate. The two had gone hand in hand since I was a child being trained to show the skill I so proficiently hid. Hate was a food best swallowed early and with an empty stomach because I was a glutton for it—to feel hate. I craved it. Perhaps father had won somehow. *If you hate well enough, nothing else feels strong enough after it. Like sugar after liquor. Regret, sympathy, distress, they all vanish when you hate.* Yet it was dawn and all I felt as I clicked his door open to leave was numbness. A sharp numbness. No hate. And the anger I felt was now pointed at myself—for faltering when it came to hating him.

Colours of dawn had revealed much that night had hidden. Soldiers clad in black leather and their onyx steels lined the outside periphery of the castle. Their attention set and stern. They couldn't see me, but it felt like they could sense me even within the walls because their hand went to their baldrics. Only these people could make me forget what I was capable of.

I didn't turn to look at him, my feet almost carrying me to a jog as if I needed to escape. Corridors bypassed like a warping nightmare with crawling monsters breathing down my neck, reaching for my limbs. I tasted ash on my tongue. I felt blood pour out of my cheek. Hot panic bruised my airways, each breath felt like a punch and rock heavy. Everything was heavy and itchy and constricting, even my own bones.

All over again. It happened all over again. The feel of their oily touch made me whimper and I suddenly couldn't breathe. A cold sensation brushed my neck, like the monster was breathing down close to me. And I was trapped and sentenced to just feel it tear me apart.

Not now. Gods not now. In and out I breathed, attempting to soothe air onto my spasming lungs like Cai had taught me. Focusing my attention ahead like Nia had told me. Steeling strength like Alaric had trained me. Once cool drops of earth scented pattering hit me, my feet stopped on their own. I stood in the drizzle that turned to rain then thunder, basking in it till it perked my senses back to reality. Or maybe it was the feel of new wounds tearing in my palms marking yet another day I had to use one pain over another. Whichever it was, it sent a realisation that snapped me like whiplash.

"Don't run."

I froze. Chills racing along my spine at the nearness of the gravelly cold voice behind me.

I waited. Counted. Counted for too long a while. They normally disappeared by now, but they weren't.

A warm hand slipped over mine, linking fingers with mine. I could recognise this man by touch alone. From his warmth. His scent. "I'll take you to Olympia."

Turning around, I dared to crack my eyes open and look at him, expecting to find the figure of the monster I always saw before these nightmares ended—a scaly creature of dark with hunger only for me. But when I turned, I only saw him. Drenched dark brown locks hung over his beautiful eyes—eyes that looked like they were only ever meant to look at me. No claws, no warping dark. Just him. Him and that damned look he only ever gave me.

Panic stretched in his expression, and he cupped my face as if to search the trouble in my eyes. "What is it, my love?"

I think I'm scared of you for all the wrong reasons. "You reminded me," I lied easily, anger rolling down my tongue. "That I still have to run." Pulling out of his grip, I took steps backward, enjoying how his face began to fall. Then I disappeared with the thunder.

Everyone that passed me along the Taren castle corridors pulled back, giving me a wide berth as I made my way to my bedroom.

I was breathing fire. I had to be. My lungs were burning, my vision steaming.

Slamming the door shut, I paced the distance back and forth the room till I'd worn my soles out and gotten myself dizzy enough to collapse.

The hells was happening to me? The hells was I doing?

The hells.

The hells.

The hells!

My fingers dug in my hair, and I screamed, the outside storm drowning the noise with strident lightning hitting the ground over and over till I decided my vocal cords had done me no wrong and that I was wasting energy I could put elsewhere.

I was losing my mind.

It was like every thought of mine was slipping away.

Grabbing a dressing gown, one of my daggers and plastering a smile on my face, I made my way to the dungeons.

My mother's voice echoed all around me, pleading and begging me as it had been for the past week, but my mind was slowly crawling with a blanket of numbness and soon...her calls disappeared.

CHAPTER SIX

ATTONO

SNOWLIN

It had been barely days since the bargain, and I was exhausted. Not only from lack of sleep, but from working my brain overtime on how to deal with two mad kings at the same time. Father had persistently kept sending attacks to Myrdur, his soldiers roamed Highwall looking for the smallest spot on the wall to slip by and enter Adriata. Urinthia was highly likely aiding my father. The sceptre pieces were like fog in wind—for each step closer, we took three back. The Fogling were surfacing and doubling like frogspawns. And Kilian…he'd made me prisoner again. I wanted out of his cage. I wanted out of feeling like my brain wanted to split in half, like my heart was being ripped out of my chest. I hated that I was not afraid of him but still feared who he was. And I was right back at the square where I was running from him. This time, however, I was just spinning in circles inside bars made of shadows. How could I get out of this one cage when we were both hunters?

The gurgling sound of drowning made me come back to reality.

My boot was on the back of someone's neck, holding their face inside a bucket of water while they thrashed for air. The room had been too dim to recognise who, but I'd make the count later. I watched with a crooked smile on my face as he squirmed and wiggled till the glorious moment his body went slack as a dead fish. So little fight. So little life. So disappointing.

A soldier pushed the door slightly open, casting some light into the empty space. "Someone is here to see you."

See me? Even Cai or Alaric refused to interrupt me when I was down here. Nia usually could stomach it, but I'd forbid her from coming down here. I knew what went through her mind. She would want to talk to the bastard who had sired her. "Tell them my visiting hours are closed."

"Snow?" A light voice called for me and my attention perked up.

My, my, right at the mouth of the wolf and I wasn't even that hungry.

Kicking the body away, I tried to straighten my leathers, tucked loose hair behind my ears to tidy the locks that I had not combed in days and gave the soldier a smile. "Good?"

He blinked all of me in. "Maybe don't smile." When my grin fell, he winced. "Or do. Moderately."

The corridor light assaulted my vision, and I rested a hand on the wall to keep me from swaying. It felt like blood shot right down my legs all at once and I almost toppled to the ground had my soldier not steadied me.

Driada stood before me, gaping and eyes wide. "Snowlin," she whispered my name almost with anguish, her russet stare she shared with Mal coating with tears. Pity. The damned pity.

My mouth pulled to a smile, but only for a moment because the soldier beside me shook his head. "Who do I owe this pleasure to?"

She shrivelled a small step back. "I wanted to give something to you."

"Sure," I said, lifting a hand to her. "Give it."

She glanced at my extended hand with horror streaking her delicate features. "Perhaps clean up first."

I looked down at my palm thick with blood and then slowly retracted it behind me.

The figure blinking back on the mirror was not hollow like me. What stared back at me had not missed any of the meals I'd fed to it. What stared back at me was a healthy version of what my father had wanted me to become.

My eyelids drooped with sleep and exhaust as I braced myself on the sink counter and exhaled slowly in an attempt to control the tremble over my body. "Mirror, mirror on the fucking wall. Who's the maddest of them all?"

I snorted, my laughter bouncing around the empty space.

I'd really lost it, hadn't I?

I must have truly lost it because what stared back at me, those black shadows quivered and neared, whispering, *You.*

Snow, my Snow, wake up, my mother's voice brushed past my ear, and I shook my head, attempting to ward off the dizziness before pulling away and draping on some dress Pen had left for me on the bed.

Driada had patiently waited for me in the great chambers overlooking river Taren that flowed on the valley between the two sister mountains where the castle was located.

She smiled and shifted on her seat a little when I approached, her eyes glowing at the teal dress I wore. "That was your mother's favourite colour."

"I'd rather you don't mention her," I said, taking a seat on the settee opposite hers.

Her smile faltered a little, but it didn't drop. It never had dropped in my presence, always so radiant. As if she was greeting an old memory. "I see Nia is not with you, not that lovely boy either."

"Both busy. As I was." I hadn't seen them in days. Cai never left Myrdur, not even for a moment. Nia had sent a letter yesterday that she was going to stay longer in Eldmoor to follow around a few Isjordian soldiers travelling down to Heca. Visha was attempting every locator craft in her cookbook and had locked herself in her cave. Pen was too scared to utter more than a sentence after she'd seen me drag a councillor's body to the terrace and feed it to the crows piece by piece. Tristin was dealing with the Fogling attacks. And I'd been avoiding Alaric. Perhaps he'd been avoiding me. But I had not been lonely. Not one bit. Not when that gravelly voice in my head had been answering all of my conversation and even entertained my jokes.

"Have you eaten at all?"

I tilted my head back. What was this, torture by small talk? "Plenty."

When she'd dried all motherly questions, she brought something from behind her. A stack of stained and worn out pearl-coloured envelopes wrapped in a little violet bow. "This—I've wanted to give you this back when you were marrying Kilian."

What trick was this?

When I didn't make a move to get them from her, she lowered them to her lap. "I couldn't think for the life of me where I'd stored them." She touched a shaky hand to her head, and I noted her nails that had turned a shade of violet. "But I was searching for a pair of my pearls and found them in one of my jewellery boxes. They are my exchange with…her." She brushed a thumb over them. "We were young then and we said nothing smart, but they are a piece of her."

A piece of her. I didn't want a piece of her. This is how hunger began. And I knew this one hunger could never be satiated. My mother was dead.

She pushed up from her seat and sat next to me, leaving the envelopes in my hand.

Reaching the stack, I decided to pull one out. The black ink had faded and murked in places, but I could recognise that handwriting better than I remembered her features. The prettiest handwriting I'd ever seen. I retracted my fingers from the paper, afraid my touch could sully her words. Afraid I'd dirty this memory with hands that had trampled all over it—sullied her memory by doing all that she'd been against, sullied it by touching with softness the man that had killed her.

My dear Driada,

The weather has been kind to our lands, the sun, too. Anemones have bloomed on every brick they could find, and they remind me so much of you, of your violet silks and laces that your father trades. They make me long for your presence in Olympia. My brothers treat me well, but they would rather spend their free time with ale on one hand and a woman on their lap.

The kingdom is vast, too, but I find myself looking out at sea, trying to make out your father's boats, fishermen who get to taste the salt and sun on their skin and lungs. I wish I could be like the sea—

My eyes drew shut.

I couldn't.

I couldn't.

My mother had wishes and dreams and friendships and a family. She'd had them all. And I'd never gotten to know them. There was nothing I knew of her. I didn't want to know this person. I was too afraid to know her. This isn't the mother I knew. This was Serene Skygard, not my mother.

"Did your son tell you to do this?" I asked, handing her the envelopes.

She frowned. "Why would he ask me to do this?"

All that I felt a moment ago vanished, pure hatred settled coldly on my veins. "I don't know, Driada. Why would you come into my lair right just as I was trying to figure out ways to play with him? My sympathy is divided between injured pets and a wasted death. You would have had a better chance at gaining sympathy if you'd gone down on all fours or died before I could use you against your son." I tapped a finger on the envelopes. "Not that."

"I thought they would have made you happy. It is the only reason why I came."

That made me laugh a little. "Or you thought this would soak my black heart to tears."

"At least keep them," she said, putting the envelopes on the space between us. "You remind me of her so much. I think you would see yourself in there."

My mother was nothing like me. And I was nothing like her. "My mother was weak. Are you calling me weak?"

"Then you do not know your mother at all."

"No, I don't. Your son killed her when I was barely eleven years of age. And now his mother is trying to tell me what my mother is or was. Ridiculous is not even a word to describe it."

"I shouldn't have come."

"No, but we can make the best out of a situation. Stay for dinner," I said when she was about to stand.

She stood a little hesitant. "My sons must be waiting for me to join them."

That was before you chose to come here. "Stay."

"Are you asking or threatening?"

My smile was easy. "Why would I threaten you, Driada?"

"Yes, Ada," Alaric said, coming inside the room and almost jogging to her side, shooting me a look of disbelief. "Stay for dinner."

The old man had kept staring at me all throughout the meal and had given me that 'I know what you are trying to do' look one to many eye rolling times.

"So," I said, lowering my fork over the most unappetizing meal I'd ever eaten. "Do you have any other family in Adriata?"

Alaric grumbled, "Kid."

Driada rested a gentle hand on his arm. "It is fine, Ric. There is no harm in knowing. No," she said to me. "My mother passed away shortly after I lost my second child. Father said it was grief and then grief for my mother took him too. I was an only child, and my parents were both orphans."

"You had another babe after little Mal?" Alaric asked.

Her smile was sad, but still so warm and gentle. "Stillborn."

My guardian sighed. "Bet your husband gave you grief for that."

She laughed a little, a small glaze coating her eyes. "No, he was relieved. It was a daughter. He wanted no daughters. Kilian was the most upset. Mal was too young to even understand. I don't think anyone even remembers her anymore."

Kilian would, some part of me wanted to say.

"That would be it," she said shyly, continuing to eat. "He is his father's son, if there is something he knows best is loss. Kilian keeps his circle small, and he is prepared to lose it all if he must. Besides you, it seems." Her smile was forlorn. "When they told him you were dead I realised he would never be ready to lose you."

I lowered my spoon down and spat the food on a napkin—all that honeyed shit was giving me nausea. "He really sent you here to write me all this poetry, didn't he?"

Alaric shut his eyes. "Kid."

I lifted a brow at him. "I'm curious to know the Night King's strategy, Alaric. Aren't you? How do you think he will deal with the enemy who has sworn to level his lands to a graveyard? And I know first hand that he fancies playing dirty. First playing me and then sending his sick mother to do this dirty work. So utterly fascinating."

Her brows bunched with so much pain. "He loves you, Snowlin."

I pointed a finger at her. "You're funny. Mal takes after you."

"Kid, enough."

"Enjoy the rest of your meal," I said, standing and straightening my dress. "It appears my taste is for another sort of food. Less talkative. And a little more bloodied."

But there was someone else waiting for me at the doors.

Tall, angry, smelling of fire and blood.

Cai's hooded stare was wearing all sorts of shadows. I recognised eyes that had seen death not moments ago. "You're not going down there again."

"I can't let them rot on their own. It would be rude of me."

"You're coming to the training courts with me."

"I'm dressed pretty. No."

"Let's go dress ugly," he said, grabbing my arm and dragging me to my bedroom.

"Alaric called you, didn't he?"

"No, someone else did. I knew I shouldn't have left you alone."

I groaned, dropping my head back. "I'm going to kill the little carrot."

He shook his head. "This attempt of yours to redefine the word sadistic needs to end now."

"Attempt?" His offences were never quite this personal and this one hurt.

He shot me a dark look over his shoulder that prompted me to seal my lips.

Each new breath I took burned. Had my lungs tightened?

"You've become weak," Cai hissed, his arm tight around my neck.

"I didn't stretch," I panted.

He let go of me and I stumbled a few steps back. "You've lost muscle and you're not eating."

"You're not sleeping. Your turn."

"Once before," he said, blocking my hit with his elbow and swirling in place to twist my arm. "I've seen you like this. Ten years ago."

I shook my head. "No."

"You saved Nia yet you felt as if you'd betrayed every foundation you believed on. You tortured yourself endless. You were torn. You didn't eat. You didn't sleep. Tell me this is not exactly the same?"

"It's not the same."

"How is it not?"

I shook my head. It was not. It wasn't. Nia was just a child. A suffering child. A sweet girl who became my sister. I still hated myself for distancing away from her when I learned who she was. Back then the wound had been fresh, still oozing blood, and I'd reacted the best way I knew how to react at something that had wounded me once. But it was not the same.

"How is it any different?" he demanded, shoving me across the court. "You care about that bastard."

I shook my head. No. I didn't.

"Is that why you keep drowning yourself with blood and screams down there?"

"No." And they did more than bleed and scream. He was on a roll with his offences against me today.

"Yes." He hooked a leg under mine, and I collapsed to the hard floor of the court.

"He killed my mother."

"And if he hadn't?"

"But he has."

He breathed realisation, chest expanding. "You don't hate him."

Not nearly enough. Not nearly as much as I should. "I…I think I'm losing it, Cai."

"Is it like before?"

"No. Worse." I swallowed. "I'm going insane."

"You're allowed to, Snow. What he did to you was beyond messed up. You can feel insane. Just come back. As long as you come back." He reached a hand to help me stand and the sleeve of his shirt pulled up a little to reveal a massive violet bruise on his arm.

"Cai?" I asked, taking his hand and pushing the sleeve back to reveal a massive bruise stretching from his elbow to the wrist. "What happened?"

"Some Verglaser almost tore his arm off," Lazarus said, coming to lean against the court fence.

"Not how I remember it, Lazarus," he said, pulling the sleeve back down. "If I remember correctly, I saved your feathers from becoming some type of ice sculpture."

"You think so highly of yourself," he grumbled with disdain.

Cai threw him an amused look. "Shouldn't you be kissing my arse like you used to do when you wanted her attention? Or are you trying some type of new trick now to get on her bed for the entirety of two minutes?"

The winged male snarled, his stance changing to stand taller, his feathers ruffling all threat and too much male energy.

"Go on," I said, leaning back on my elbows on the ground. "This is very entertaining."

My friend looked irked. "I don't entertain zoo animals."

Lazarus ignored Cai and turned to me. "Might I have a word."

"Have your word."

Cai sat on the ground beside me, leaning as I did. "Should have grabbed a snack for this."

"Privately," Lazarus growled.

"This will be as private as it will get," I said. "I have an audience with someone in the dungeons later. Would you wish for that to be our private moment? I've always wanted to paint those feathers red."

I could have sworn the Volantian man flinched a little. Lazarus had a special creep when it came to my dungeons. He'd never even stepped foot down there after I'd defeathered and skinned a Volantian after the man had a hard time accepting the word *no* from a woman and took what was not given to him willingly. Oh, and then I had him boiled in a cauldron in the middle of Taren. But I still think it was the defeathering part that bothered Lazarus—the man had such a complicated relationship with his wings.

He glanced at Cai shortly before clearing his throat. "Meet with me before nightfall."

"I hold court meetings during the daytime, Lazarus."

He stepped forward. "Snowlin, I am not buying this married woman act anymore."

"Oh, her annoyed woman act is pretty obvious," Cai said, grinning. "Your man-whore act, too."

"Stay out of this," Lazarus growled at him.

My friend guffawed. "Seems like Snow wants to stay out of this, too."

"What does my wife want to stay out of?" Kilian's voice boomed against the glen where the training grounds stretched. And like a dark command, everything seemed to halt at its might.

Warm shivers crept up my spine and I spun, looking at him and then at the skies. Night-time.

Kilian's glacial look was bordering murderous for some reason. It softened when he raked it over me. And then turned something of fear when it landed on the winged male behind me.

One look. One. Look. That's all it took for my breathing to pick up for me not to hear anything but my heartbeat pulsing in my ear.

"Go wash," Cai said, standing. "I'll entertain your...*husband*. Perhaps Lazarus can show him a trick or two." My friend turned to the Volantian man who was glaring unrestrained at Kilian. "Lay an egg or something for us, Lazarus."

Kilian grabbed my arm when I slid past him, my whole body seizing. When he raised a hand to my face, I flinched back. Slowly, watching my reaction as he did so, he brought his fingers to my mouth. Why did I have to fight and resist to lean on that touch? "Your lip is bleeding."

I pulled my arm free and spat blood at his feet before bolting to my bedroom balcony.

Pen had dug her comb in my hair, carefully pulling and tugging on my locks till they were free from all knots, while throwing careful glances at me as I had yet to call on her little snitch. She was practically sweating and panting but looked well pleased with her job.

She jumped upright and grinned wide when she spotted someone else in the mirror reflection. Six feet four inches clad in black and kingly might, leaning on the door frame, watching me—every corner and curve of me that was poorly hidden under my short nightgown. "Kilian!" Her eyes went wide and then drifted to me and my glare. "I meant...you're here, you very horrible...bad, bad...king."

He looked a snap away from laughing. "Hello, Penelope. How have you been?"

She tried to contain her smile and fiddled with her braid like some schoolgirl. "I'm training to become a Crafter. Apparently, I have a cousin. Apparently, the Grand Maiden is my aunt." She frowned. "Apparently, my grandmother is a bitch. At least so says Snow."

Kilian raised an amused brow. "All exciting findings for you." His silvery gaze swivelled to me. "Hello, my missus."

The way he called me tickled my belly with nerves. "What are you doing here?"

He slid his hands in his pockets. "I've come to take you myself. My gardens have had enough, and I just changed the grass today."

I stood and reached close to him. "My nightmares are reserved for night-time only. They don't start at sunset. Don't disturb my peace this early again."

His eyes flashed and then slowly travelled down my body. "Noted. Penelope," he called, still looking at me. "Could you bring something else for her to wear? It's...cold in Adriata."

And when I shivered under his scrutiny, his jaw clenched tight and that stupid dimple made an apperance.

"Pen, try and take a step out of this room."

The little carrot halted with a foot over the door threshold.

His stare steeled with challenge. "She will do nothing, go."

"Try me," I said, tilting my head to her and flashing the redhead a grin.

She shuddered and retreated back inside the room.

He unbuttoned his jacket and threw it over my bed-end stool. "Fine by me, love. We are staying in Olympia tonight. Penelope, since you're still here, bring her something to eat. I thought it was thundering for a moment."

The redhead sprinted out before I could draw one word out.

Slowly, he took off his shirt and laid on top of the bed covers, sprawling over my silver satin sheets like he belonged there. No man besides Cai had ever sat on my bed.

He caught my glance and amusement flashed through his stern features. "Your father had sent soldiers through the old inner tunnels today. Larg caught them as they were coming out. Albius made us aware of the new path they were taking around the mountains and through the Sea of the Dark. It seems he wants to find our sceptre piece next."

I nodded.

"We've started searching our temples today," he continued.

Again, I nodded.

There was a long beat of ringing silence.

His voice was glazed with ice when he asked, "Will you not speak to me at all?"

"Not if I can help it," I said, sitting before the mirror and running the comb through my hair again.

Silver irises traced the length of my hair before travelling to hold my stare hostage in the mirror. "Heard my stepmother was here today."

"Oh?"

That made him smile somehow. He sat up, looking around the room before pulling a bedside drawer open and picking up a book—one of my books. Something on the cover made his brow jerk up and I realised too late what it was because he was already flipping through it when I shot up from my seat.

There was a clean smirk on his face as he went through each page I'd made notes on.

"Give it," I said, reaching for the book but he extended his arm back, holding it away from me.

"Why? I'd like to know why you found...Sybil being eaten out by her lover so fascinating that you've done unspeakable and underlined with ink every line on the page."

I reached for it again and he extended it further back and away from me.

Climbing on the bed and over him, I tried to reach for it again.

"You look pretty up there," he said, smiling, and I noted I was straddling his waist.

My hand shot to wrap around his throat and his mouth pulled up to a massive grin. "Harder, love."

Hells. Bloodied hells.

I let go of him and crawled back. Standing and heading for the bathroom to wash my hands. If I felt his scent on me, the lingering feel of his skin on mine—I was going to go mad. I scrubbed and scrubbed till my skin was red and raw and I was panting. Dread climbed up my throat and I watched as my reflection on the mirror trembled like fire touching snow.

He laid beside me all night, staring in wonder at my glistening ceiling. Not a word. His reaction to my red skin and whatever he'd seen on my face had been more than enough.

After he left at dawn, I rolled to the side he had slept on, smoothing my fingers over the sheets still lingering with his warmth and I couldn't help but sink my face in his pillow and inhale the scent of lemon flower he'd left behind. A hole pierced through my heart and a sob wracked through my body.

Sick.

I was sick.

So sick.

My mind crawled with venomous thoughts, and I stood, reaching for my dagger and stabbing the sharp blade onto the mattress and pillow, over and over, till I'd exhausted all my strength. Till my chest pumped fast with air. Till I grew too light headed to think of anything at all.

The soft feathers were flying everywhere, and they stuck to my wet face and bloodied palms as I pushed up and headed out of my room.

Alaric didn't stop me when he saw me—not this time. Neither did Cai. Nor anyone that passed me as I made my way down to the dungeons.

Snow, please, my mother's voice echoed around when my hand rested on the dungeon door handle.

A silent gasp left my mouth when a cold phantom hand rested on top of mine. *Please.*

"Just close your eyes, ma," I whispered, pushing the door open and all traces of her presence around me disappeared.

He didn't come the next night. Nor the other next. Nor the rest of the week. To my luck, he'd been kept plenty busy by his court and only spent a few hours in his bedroom each night. Whether I had many to rely on and trust to help in my rule, he didn't. He checked on everything—severe or not, it had his attention. I'd heard him argue many times with his captains and generals regarding orders they had issued themselves without seeking his permission first though it had been nothing a king should worry himself with. He counted signatures, noted whatever document he signed, kept thick journals with copies of each document. The Night King was a paranoid psychopath.

Right after cleaning up, I bolted to Amaris, electricity skittering around me even after just to make sure I'd scorch his precious gardens. The man was obsessed with his flowers.

Soldiers littered the grounds everywhere, they clustered the entrances, murmuring to one another while wearing spite in their faces as they traced each of my movements. Uneasiness had turned to annoyance pretty soon after I'd started coming to Adriata.

Someone muttered under their breath in Darsan something resembling my mother's name and I stopped, turning to them. "What did you say?" I rarely paid attention to their offences, but I was bored—I wanted to play.

He clenched his jaw tightly, steeling a look ahead and refusing to answer me. Courage was a funny little warm. It came out of butt cheeks to scream and once it felt the outside cold, it slid right back in with all the shitty audacity.

Stepping right before him, I trailed a finger over his sweaty brow. "Why are you sweating, dear?" Slowly, my hand slipped right over his heart, thin ice gliding over my nails to form claws. "When you can just bleed." The tiny organ was warm in my hand and the owner was piled like a dump on the ground.

Weapons were unsheathed, bows were stringed with arrows in my direction, and I barked out a laugh when the soldier nearby raised a black steel sword to my neck.

They wanted to play as well? I dropped the heart and stepped closer till the black metal was cool against my skin. I fought the tremble. Fought it till my jaw was hurting from how hard I'd clenched my teeth. "I had planned to torture some other soul tonight, but yours will do just fine."

Everything went utterly quiet out of the sudden and the soldier lowered his weapon and stared wide eyed somewhere behind me.

He stood there, his shirt and britches dirty with specks of soil, hair dishevelled and falling over his silver eyes that had veiled completely black. "Kneel," Kilian ordered, his voice a lethal frost that made the warm air shiver, and every soldier went down on a shaking knee and knelt before me. "Now bow, face down, no one dare even look at her." The soldiers did as told and Kilian cocked his head back, surveying all his men. "Good. And that is how you respect your queen." Pulling each finger out of his gardening gloves he asked, "Why was it hard to comprehend the first time I taught you that, hm?"

I could feel it—the way fear shivered in the air and how the current suddenly charged with too many loud heartbeats to count.

The soldier before me sputtered blood from his mouth and collapsed to the ground, his body turning ashen like charcoal before blasting into little specks of black dust.

I shuddered, my shoulders bunching and that stomach turning fear crept up my throat. Though they couldn't be seen, I felt the crawling shadow monsters from my nightmares circling me.

He turned to the rest of the soldiers, regarding them as he calmly said, "Everyone who raised a weapon in my wife's direction will come tomorrow morning to my court chambers with your own two feet. Leave goodbyes behind to your loved ones. That is all the grace that I'll offer and perhaps the last."

What was he doing?

They all bowed their heads again and shouted in unison, "Yes, my king."

The air was chilled against my skin. I could taste their fear on my tongue. And I could taste his magic, too. Thick with spice of dark terror and death.

Why—why was he doing this?

As if nothing had happened, he turned to me and gave me one of his smiles. "Hungry?"

Willing my feet to move, I backed away and walked toward the castle, trying my best to breathe out all the fear of feeling his magic brush so closely past me and the flash of forget when he looked at me. Why did I keep forgetting who he was and what he'd done to me?

A massive arm wrapped around my waist, and he pulled me against his body. "I asked you a question. Are you hungry?"

Again, I didn't answer. If I opened my mouth, I'd scream. I wanted to scream. But if he knew I was losing my mind he might think he had already won over me. This is what it was, wasn't it? This was what he'd intended to do to me.

He leaned in my ear, hot breath raising gooseflesh all over me. "Cheese. Bread. Grapes."

"What?"

"Trying to rouse this little beast," he said, smoothing his other hand over my stomach and my body surrendered to his touch. "Pie. Mushroom pie. Mushrooms on toast. Fried mushroom and cheddar. Chestnut mushroom. King oyster." My stomach growled as if on command and he chuckled in my ear, my knees weakening. "There it is."

Electricity zapped my body and he hissed, letting me go. "Your foreplay is a bit advanced," he said, blowing a breath on his hand. "But I like it."

Slowly, I took steps away from him till I stood in his bedroom.

Rage surged to the surface. I wanted to hurt him. I wanted him to hurt me as if only to invoke the monster who'd been haunting him since I was eleven. As if to only invoke every deadly thought I'd had about this man before I could put a face on him—before I put this face on him.

But he was not scared of me. He was not scared for anyone either.

Except—

He lowered a tray of food on the bed. "Love?"

When he got closer and closer to me, I picked up a glass from the table and threw it with all I had to the wall, shattering it to tiny pieces. "Don't come near me."

Now I had to fight with my own head. I had to fight my own thoughts. In the midst of all the battles raging around me, I had to fight my own self.

Snow, breathe, my snowflake, my mother's voice breezed by as I wheezed for air.

"I can't, ma," I whispered back, fighting through light-headedness and grasping the table corners to steady myself. "I can't breathe."

His expression splintered and he stepped back and faded away, leaving me alone only to return with Cai moments later.

After letting my friend inside the room, he stepped outside and shut the door.

He didn't come back inside that night. But his slow heartbeat pulsed from behind the bedroom doors where he remained till I left at dawn.

CHAPTER SEVEN

Monstra

Kilian

For a week, Snow had come at nightfall and left right at the first second of dawn. A full week. She had barely said a word to me, to anyone. She'd laid in the far corner of our bed, eyes wide open, with no rest whatsoever.

And it had done more punishment to me than to her. Perhaps that is what she had wanted.

I expected her to fight me on the decision, use the opportunity to torture me only the way she knew how. And perhaps she was. Seeing the purple shadows under her tired eyes that had lost the flame to gilded frost, the slight sway of her feet from exhaust, her thinning frame, had made me reconsider this bargain over and over again. Perhaps it is what she wanted.

I wanted to let her go. After that night, I was ready to let her go only so she didn't have to ever panic the way she did. But I couldn't.

I was not a good man.

And I wanted her. I was greedy for her.

Selfishly, I was going to hold on to her.

Dawn was yet to grace us, but she pushed her body up and got out of bed, making her way to the balcony doors to stare at the skies ahead that dared refuse to obey her silent order to raise day.

"Glaring at it won't make it come any sooner."

"You never know."

I stood, taking a blanket and throwing it over her shoulders. She didn't push it off, but she did take the smallest step forward and away from me. "While you've become the master of night, my love, I'm afraid day can never be as infatuated with you as I am."

She cast me a glance over her shoulder. "Is that what we are calling it now? Infatuation?"

Sliding my fingers through her hair, I pulled her attention to me, and she flinched just a little. There was panic in her eyes, but not one resembling fear so I didn't let go. "You usually don't like when I use the 'l' word." I tapped a finger to my shoulder and lower to my stomach. "I have an important meeting later, would rather go without any holes in me."

"You can use the word lie just fine, darling."

My grip on her tightened as I backed her to the glassy doors. "Lie? Do you think I'd lie about this?" Did she really believe that?

"No. I'm sure there is much worse you can do." She moved the small dagger she had aimed over my heart upward till it rested right under my chin. "In all honesty, I did expect you to be all kinds of wicked, just not this. I survived you. Twice. And do you know what that makes me?" Learning in, she whispered, "Your victim." She dropped her head back on the glass, a smile playing on her lips as she lifted the little blade over my chin to rest it on my lip. "And they call me twisted." Her blade grazed me, and a droplet of blood beaded on my bottom lip. She went to her toes and licked the path of blood to my mouth before leaning in my ear and whispering, "I'll show you twisted. Survive me. I want to play with you, Adriatian."

Fuck.

Sliding under my arm, she clicked the balcony doors open and backed away towards its edge. Her eyes never left mine as she brought the dagger to her tongue and licked my blood away from the blade. After throwing me a wink, she bolted out of sight.

I had to rest a hand on the glass to steady myself. Hells. All damned hells. This woman was making me crave punishment like a man starved for pain.

The weather in Sitara was at the warmest it had been in months. Snow had held to her bargain and pulled her hand of work over Adriata. No more eudemons had stepped in my lands for days, no sightings of unblessed ships sailing by my ports either. No more lilies of the valley growing all over cities.

Triad took my side as we walked across the villages that had been ruined during the eudemon attacks. "You haven't brought her to meetings yet. Court should start getting used to her sitting beside you."

"It is not time yet." Was all I said. Not until I made sure she didn't fear being around more Adriatians that she didn't know.

"The people are saying that we have righted our wrong from thirteen years ago. Some are saying that the queen has brought blessings along with her."

"Perhaps they are not entirely wrong." In a very small fiendish sense. "Though what we allowed to happen thirteen years ago can never be righted, Triad."

He heaved a long sigh. "Her blood is Krigborn and that is for sure. Her wit is testament to that. But the Krigborn are cold and merciless—she is not cold. She is frost, cruel. She does not aim to kill. She aims to punish. The Krigborn get what they want quick and fast. They don't torture their prey, they hunt to eat. Your wife enjoys the hunt more than the feed."

"It is how she was taught. Take the world, bend it, twist its bones and dry its blood—it is how you can make it yours. It was how Silas raised his three children. I've seen a small part of his cruelty on her, it was enough to convince me that I didn't want to imagine the rest. And no, Krigborns don't torture their prey, they torture their own children to become a sharp blade for which they use to torture others."

"Do you think she can be fixed?"

Fixed? The word made me bristle though I knew Triad had not meant it as such. "There is nothing wrong with her. Nothing. Not one bit. She just needs to learn that there are other things a human can be besides what Silas has taught her to be."

"And you'll teach her?"

"No, I'll be there to see that she does learn." It's why I made this bargain with her in the first place. See that she doesn't lose to her own self amid all that was going on.

The old city lay on a cliff overlooking the Sea of the Dark. While the coast was clear, blue and sun kissed, the further away from land you looked, the more you could see and feel the lingering presence of Golgotha's creatures that herded in the depths.

"It was said that the Octa Virga resided in Nephthys," I said, staring ahead and over the black smog and thunder that marked the land of the eudemons. Though many had attempted to, no one had crossed the dark waters. How had the king of Seraphim sailed through them to the gods' forsaken island clouded in Golgotha's magic and Crafter veils?

Triad followed my line of sight. "The Octa Virga. Never had I thought I would have heard that spoken aloud. My grandfather used to recite me tales of the Ithicean guardian whose feathered wings lit with white fire would come alive. This was not how I imagined fairy tales coming to life—not as

Silas's leverage over the realm." He sighed and faced me again. "We know nothing of it. The queen will know soon enough that your bargain was barely a hoax to steal time."

"I plan on finding it, Triad. My bargain was a true bargain."

"And then what? Hand it to her?"

"You have very little faith in my wife. And if your reasoning is that she is Silas's daughter, I suggest you rethink it. We have a common enemy. And he is more hers than he is mine."

"Answer me only this, Kilian," Triad said. "Once time comes for her to claim her revenge, will you fight her? Will you protect Adriata?"

A soldier ran toward us, red and sweating. "It's the queen. She's left a...a body in Amaris, one of the old councillors."

Hells this woman. "Make sure that it is removed."

The soldier blinked a bit confused. "My king, he...he is in...small pieces." He cringed a bit and swallowed like he was ready to gag. "The animals are already...picking them up."

Triad chuckled and ran a hand over his face. "I think I like her." When I pointed a look on him, the ancient Aura shrugged. "She wants to send a message and she well sent it." He patted my shoulder. "Your wife has prepared herself well to face her fear. It is time Adriata faces theirs."

My corridors were unusually littered with guards. The place I kept clean of weapons and violence. The place which I called a home and where my family could roam without feeling suffocated. It was unusual for soldiers to disobey me. Though there was something else more unusual—grown men and women that I'd trained myself, shaking and sweating from fear.

Distress of all sorts clouded the air. Angry, scared, agonised and expectant distress.

It was past sunset and almost time for Snow to retreat to Adriata. But the fear was not worn with expectation, but with caution.

Mal exited his room, looking battered up and tired. Attempting to button his shirt and failing from the shakiness of his fingers. "She came an hour ago. Made a few you call soldiers shit their flowery knickers and went to your room," he said, patting my shoulder and walking past the corridor, whistling some sort of a wrong pitched tune.

A running water sound came from my chambers. There were blood spatters on the door handle and bloodied boot prints all over my bedroom floor trailing to a pile of grey leathers, the ones that Snow and her soldiers wore.

Had she been injured?

My attention snapped to water sliding and spreading all over my tiles, escaping from under the bathroom door.

Immediately, I rushed towards her. The whole bathroom floor had flooded all over with water that poured from the overflowing bath. She laid back on the tub, her head hung over the edge, eyes tightly shut, her long hair matted and shining a murky ruby. Water rose to her neck and was overflowing all over. It was murky and stained a dull crimson—blood.

She looked peaceful yet the most disturbed. Was she asleep?

I felt the hum of her heartbeat drum all over the place till it suddenly snapped to a steady beat. She almost startled me when her hands broke from the water to clutch the side of the bath.

"Husband," she croaked, sighing and dipping further in the water. "How did you leave Sitara?"

Shadows slithered away, afraid, and this time not from me, but from her. She was unusually chirpy—different from how she'd behaved the whole week. "Got your gift, if that is what you are asking."

"Hm." She tilted her head back to reveal a crooked smile. "Your street dogs looked famished. Aren't I generous?"

"Very," I said, moving to the other side of the bathroom to shut the tap that had poured enough water to rise to my ankles.

She raised her gilded gaze to look up at me, staring through that hooded expression like she once before had—back in Isjord. Like I was her plaything. "You look afraid."

"You look like you've been bad."

She bit her lower lip. "I'll play a game with you," she crooned, trailing a finger over the water surface. "One of hide and seek." When she rolled her eyes up at me again, a wicked smirk lifted on the corners, and I knew then that she'd done something beyond fearful.

"No games, Snow, it was what we bargained on," I said, freeing myself from the jacket I wore. She'd made me feel like I had chains and cage bars all over me with one sentence alone. I'd seen how she played her games. How to cheat them, too.

"I am only playing along," she said, leaning back and dipping her hair in the water, working her ruby stained hands through her blood matted locks.

"It wasn't I who started the game." She hummed to herself. "Though I might have suggested it. Loosely."

"Snow," I warned. "What have you done?"

She flashed me a grin. "Hide. And. Seek."

Fuck. I was in deep fucking trouble.

A fist banged on our door, loud and panicked.

"Come in!" I shouted, moving toward it. My brain was scrambling and working to figure out whatever she had done without breaking the bargain.

Larg breathed hard and heavy, face stained with terror. "Merle's children," he wheezed out. "My partner's children. My stepchildren. They are gone. She couldn't find them all day."

My eyes drew shut. Fuck.

"Hello, Larg dearest," Snow shouted from the bathroom and then cackled loudly. "Better run, my darling. Seems like trouble will keep you away all night long. What a shame." The silence after those words was filled by the chilling tune she hummed.

Larg shook his head. "It can't be...she couldn't have done this," he muttered, staring wide eyed toward the half open bathroom door. He took a step forward and then two back, disbelief like no other filling him. "She took Merle's children?"

I went back to her. "Where are they? If you want me gone, I will go. I'll leave you alone for the night."

She slowly shook her head. "Not good enough. I want to play."

"Snowlin."

She leaned on the tub side, batting her lashes at me. "Yes?"

There was only one way to win her games. "You want to play?" I asked, bending down to her face.

She nodded.

"Let's play."

"Very good." She leaned close, her nose slightly nudging mine, her eyes dropping to my mouth. "Hint. Where can a running child be when at night they cannot see? Where can a running child be when at home they should really be?" She lifted a hand to my jacket lapel, pulling me close till our lips almost met. "You have till dawn." Leaning over my ear, she whispered, "Run."

◆○◆

And so we ran. We had searched almost every corner of Adriata. Almost every forest and lake and rock and city and sea. The Snow I knew would never hurt those children. I just knew it. No matter what I had done to her, what all of Adriata had done to her, she would have not hurt those children. I knew it. Because I knew her.

Merle had crouched by the front stairs of her house sobbing till her voice had gone hoarse.

It was almost dawn. I had no choice but to hold back the day. The veil of unnatural night spread over the blanket of violet dawn, holding back the light of Cyra. Interfering with nature was something I could do with ease, but not something I wanted to do at all.

"What if this doesn't work?" Larg asked, surveying the night I'd summoned.

"It will work," I said, running her riddle over and over. Over and...over.

A small light lit on the second floor window. Small enough that no one could have noticed, but I was not just anyone. Not when darkness called my name like a prayer, like I was its god each time light broke it. It called for my command to make the world entirely lightless again.

"Larg," I tried to say calmly, but sleeplessness and anger had laced my voice. "Has anyone checked inside the house?"

Larg swivelled his head round and Merle stood. Her mouth quivered and rounded to the shape of a gasp. "They...they don't come from school till late afternoon. I was at home all day. I...I would have seen them come in."

"My *asteri*, did you check the rooms?" Larg asked his partner, frowning.

Merle shook her head, shivering from dread. "I was at home all day. I would have known. I would have seen them return from school."

"Then who is lighting candles on your second floor?" I asked, pointing to the growing light upstairs. The noise of soldiers and clatter of hooves would have woken them.

Both Larg and Merle ran upstairs and returned sobbing and thanking the heavens while they held the two sleepy children in their arms. The smell of lavender philtre was strong on their clothes. She'd given them a sleeping potion.

Fucking woman.

Larg wiped a large hand over his eyes. "I knew she wouldn't hurt them."

"It wasn't them she wanted to hurt, Larg." It was me.

The old man sighed. "She is angry. That I understand."

I shook my head. "She shouldn't have done this. She shouldn't have done this to you or Merle or the children." She had wanted me gone. And she'd found the best way to have me gone.

"You can pull your magic back."

"No, I don't think I will," I said, cracking my neck. "My wife wants to play." With that, I faded back to my room.

She laid on her back, reading a book and chewing a nail on her free hand. When I clicked the door shut behind me, she flipped to her front and blinked in surprise between me and the window still showing the night sky. "That was...quick?"

"You can say so," I agreed, unbuttoning my jacket. I noted she was wearing one of my shirts. "Didn't you like the clothes I had picked out for you?"

"No. I'm not planning to join a nunnery."

"Are you trying to get me to sign to a priesthood?" I asked, tracing her lines and curves visible through my linen shirt and she raised a brow at me.

"Good one, Adriatian. Bet you gagged a little in your mouth coming up with that."

She had no fucking idea, did she?

"No more dirty little tricks, Snow," I said, slowly walking to pour myself a drink.

"Or what?"

I swung down the liquor and filled another glass. "You honestly don't want to know the answer to that."

The book she held slammed shut and she sat herself up, my shirt slipping down her shoulder. I was too gods damn distracted to even be mad. "Indulge me. You like indulging me, darling, don't you?"

I plopped down on my armchair. Though I was angry, my heart pumped fast because of how she looked on my bed and wearing my clothes—how I'd always imagined it. "The sun comes out when I tell it to come out. Can you recall how I got my name? How the realm regards me as the Night King."

She glanced at the window and then down at the bargain seal on her hand, her breathing picking up. Something else flashed in that entirely too apathetic expression she wore. "You can fool the bargain, but you cannot cheat it."

I raised a brow and pointed my head at the window. "Try and leave. It is yet dawn though time is beyond sunrise, and I did not in fact specify that you might leave at a certain dawn either. The bargain is that you leave at dawn. I, love, am the king of night. Make the connection yourself. Thought we could use this opportunity to discuss what you did."

Her expression was numb as if she'd expected my move. As if it was exactly what she'd wanted me to do. "Then what about Atlas?" There was no look on her face but blankness when her mouth rose to a grin. "You didn't count your ducks, did you?"

Of course. But when you're a man wearing my crown, you have to already make peace with losses. For her…I counted them all. "What about him?"

"I'll do that very bad thing that rhymes with mill, spill and thrill."

"You do that, my love."

She stood, trailing a finger over my furniture. "No, Cai will when I don't return before the sun is up in the skies."

There was something I didn't understand. Though she never let her guards down, or would admit to any sort of defeat, there was expectation in her stare. The way she studied me—as if she was waiting for answers. "You wanted this. You wanted me to do something like this."

She sighed all disappointment, leaning a hip on my desk and picking at her nails, almost bored. "I just wanted to see, really. What could trigger you, how to trigger you. How could I bring the Obscur Asteri out. How could he come out. For whom and when."

The sip of the drink I took tasted less flavorful than water. "Careful, love, your demons might start to like playing with mine."

Her eyes gleamed as she swayed her way to me and braced both hands on the armchair rest, caging me in. Her scent was otherworldly. The way her mind worked was otherworldly, too. She was entirely the most fascinating being I'd come in contact with. "I think your demons quite like taunting mine." She tilted her head to the side, studying me curiously and intently. "Will you really let me kill him?" She hissed, her face scrunching up when the seal flashed in warning—feeling the oath being broken.

I dropped my head back and sipped my drink. "Thinking about it."

Her attention dropped to my neck, and to make the situation torturous she dragged her soft bottom lip between her teeth. "Would you have let me…do that very bad word to Driada or Mal or Larg and his stepchildren?"

"Is it a yes or a no question?"

Her eyes flashed and a little smirk twitched on her mouth. With no warning, blood began gushing out of her nose, spilling down her face and staining my shirt that she was wearing, and I shot to my feet, holding her head down and putting a handkerchief to her face. What in the hells? "Fuck. Look at me, love."

"Do you know," she asked, her words slow and dragged out as she looked up at me. "What poison I've never been able to take?"

The air froze with stillness and grave silence. I noted her paleness, the dilated pupils, the little twitch on her lids and the greyed tips of her fingers.

She pulled down the handkerchief and flashed me a bloodied smile. "The only one I couldn't sip at all because I was deathly allergic to it." She touched her fingers to her nose. "Didn't work as quickly as I thought it would."

Calmness slipped through my fingers and my chest rose like thunder. "Who has the antidote?"

She looked at me in a trance. "So you're sick, too," she whispered to herself.

I grabbed her face. "Answer me!"

Her pupils paced quickly, searching for answers in mine as more blood gushed out. She frowned, the more she looked at me. Confusion marred every part of her features, her body, too, as she backed away from me. "Am I in your cage or are you in mine?" she asked, coughing, blood now dripping from her mouth.

She was not going to do this to me again. She wasn't going to let me lose her again for a game, a plan, for one of her schemes.

I lifted my hand toward the window, tugging on strands of magic tethered to me and the darkness around till it disappeared to reveal the bright, blue day skies and Hemera blazing ahead.

"Go," I said, dropping my hands, surrendering, and stepping back away from her. "Go, please. Take the antidote."

A knock rasped at our door, and Cai came in, looking beyond amused. He threw her a small vial and then turned to me. "The little priest is napping on his bed."

My nerves made the air sizzle with pure death. "You let her do this?"

He surveyed the black flames fluttering around my fists. "*You* made her do this." His grin grew cocky when he faced his friend. "Didn't I tell you? He won't let you be harmed or die. Those murderous wiles really did the trick."

◆○◆

She had left around noon after giving Larg a very...quirky apology. The oddest part was that the man had forgiven her as had Merle. She'd laughed and made my godfather laugh himself to tears and then gone back to her kingdom humming a cheery tune. Like that, she'd come into my world like a hurricane but left like a spring breeze.

The day had passed in a flash between Highwall and the temple search. And before I knew what time it was, she strutted in the room all legs and barely any nightgown. A little more rested than other days and chirpier, too. Had she gotten the reassurance that I wouldn't hurt her? The fact that she had thought I'd hurt her in the first place had weighed me like a ton of iron bricks.

"No more tricks for me?" Though she did play the ultimate one.

"No. You? I'm getting bored as well." Lifting herself on my table, she picked up the apple I'd been eating and took a bite. "How is the temple search going? Must be tiring considering you have one for every lice on a toddler's hair."

I handed her a piece of paper with the list of the temples we had searched so far. "None had a veil or any other rooms besides the main prayer one. Most are used as confessionals or school and activity rooms for children, women and the elderly. Three had more than a basic veil around it and it was only to safeguard a few artefacts of Henah, none worth much magic or price besides spiritual value. What about Olympia?"

"We only have twelve in total. It didn't take long to have them all searched. They are all open spaces with no walls or rooms, no undergrounds or secret entrances. There are similar inscriptions as that in the Isjordian temple everywhere in Olympia, but no sign of the damned sceptre piece."

"What about the one in Myrdur? The dragon temple used to be a fascination for many. And if I remember to have read correctly, it had many rooms and tunnels underneath."

Her eyes snapped to me. "It's completely destroyed. There is nothing but rock left where it once stood."

"Have you searched underneath the ruins?"

"No. But Silas's soldiers are heading toward the Volants. They go over it."

"Have someone search it just in case the magic of the mist and the dead lingering on the ruins are not confusing Melanthe's tracking."

She swallowed hard, gaze drifting to the floor.

"Cai. You don't want to dig up the ruins because of Cai."

She pinned a glare on me. "It's not in the ruins."

My blood turned bitter and envious like it had never before. "I'm jealous how you care for him. Terribly jealous," I said, going over the documents Atlas had found in Sidra. Few mentioned the island of Nephthys and its purpose to guard the hand of the divine though nothing specific about it, but the young priest had been confident that I'd find something, anything if we searched the fine print. Whoever had a hand in concealing the sceptre must have missed at least something.

She huffed, reaching for another apple all across the table, her hair brushing past my fingers, sliding through her locks. Barely a touch, but my eyes drew shut at the feeling I'd missed most—touching her.

"Take a bite," she said, holding the fruit before my mouth. "Gods know you dip these things in poison."

"I was eating them."

"Darling, I bet you drink poison with your toast just for the taste of it."

My eyes drew shut. "Enough, woman."

"Enough what?"

"Torturing me like this. Carve my heart out and be done with it."

Her eyes dropped to where my fingers had tangled through a few strands of her hair before they rose defiant to mine again. "Just take the bite, Your Majesty, before you kill my appetite like you killed my mother."

Perhaps I'd carved my own heart out the day I decided to be her villain.

Holding on her wrist, I pulled the fruit to my mouth and took a bite.

When she leaned back on the table, I noted a thin, red scar stretched on her forearm. "Where did you get that?"

She glanced down at the injury and then at me. "Fogling attacks. The dungeons don't really fight back to my dismay."

Nia had mentioned something about them. I just hadn't realised how much of a problem they were to Snow and Olympia. "How long have you been dealing with these Fogling creatures?"

"Long, for twenty-seven years, but they only recently began turning dangerous. Why, does it make you happy? You can smile if you want."

I grabbed her chin and pulled her face down to me. "I've missed you being sassy with me."

She took a bite from the apple, chewing slowly. A distraction. She was breathing fast, her pulse was all over the place and I could practically read the fear in her eyes. "Tell me you're not scared of me."

She looked offended. "I'm not."

Truth. She was not. "Good girl." But there was something else and I couldn't tell what.

She swallowed. "Are you scared of me?"

"Terribly."

Her pretty mouth curved to a sneer and she pulled my hand away from her face. "Liar."

I couldn't help my smile. "There is something I've wanted to talk to you about?"

"Of course there is."

"It's about your siblings," I explained, and she shot to attention. "Empaths can recognise blood-related individuals, sometimes by magical scent or colour, but that would make our searching field too wide. I want to narrow it down."

"How?"

"With Visha's help. She can trap a small part of their essence collected from someone related to them into a small craft stone and then one of my Aura will use that as a compass or a beacon to fade exactly where it will pick up any connection to it. It will not take you directly to them, but it will close a lot of distance and search space."

She nodded. "I'll tell Visha to come see you."

I pulled a massive Book of Dreams written by an ancient Dark Crafter on top of all my documents. "You can read Borsich, right?"

She raised a brow between the dust-covered book and me. "Yes."

"It's an entry-based grimoire written by Eamon Gorgan Delcour, head of one of the lower covens before he married the second Grand Maiden and father of the third Grand Maiden—he was a keeper of the ship that sailed to Nephthys." I tapped a hand on it. "The man had loads to say apparently. Detailed every toilet break he took and bowel movement amongst all the other goodness he saw during his duties as keeper."

Her nose wrinkled. "Why have you not asked anyone to help you with this?" she asked, pulling the massive book on her lap, frowning down at it as she did so.

"There are only five priests working on this. Only five that I trust as much as I trust Atlas and they are plenty busy already researching. So how about you use that big brain of yours to help me, hm?"

I'd gotten her another chair and she'd sat beside me, making little notes on a blank sheet of paper. Her tongue peeking at the corner of her mouth, eyes pinched on the writing as she tried to decipher the madness of Eamon. She'd wrapped her long locks around her fist and propped her head on it. Prettiest sight I'd seen in a while.

Her eyes rolled up to me, curious at my attention glued on her. She said nothing and I was too overwhelmed by her soft presence to even come up with any words beside the three she hated to hear.

We sat there almost all night long. She'd eaten two more apples and a little past midnight I'd gone and brought little crackers and cheese from the kitchens which she had all eaten as well.

First time that I had not minded her quiet. I'd actually enjoyed it. Studying and watching her in this form. Every sense in my body roared and fought to push my chair closer to her, run my fingers over her face, rest my lips on all corners of her skin and tell her just how much it hurt that I could not speak those three words to her every second of the day.

There was barely an hour left to dawn and she'd not had a sliver of rest, her eyes drooping and adorned with grey shadows. "Why don't you rest a little?"

She yawned. "I can't sleep here."

"I'll light a ton of candles."

She lifted her tired gaze to me. "No matter how bright it is, you always make it dark again. I hate the dark."

My chest hurt—it hurt terribly. "I'll go. I can go."

She swallowed hard, and then pushed to me the paper she'd written on. "There is one mention of a guardian. Presuming it was Aurora. Apparently, she was locked in there with something else."

"Protection?"

"No. Some form of torture. At least Eamon thought so. He has very flowery writing, so he described Aurora's companionship as the highest form of torment." She worried her lower lip between her teeth. "How could a guardian be afraid of anything?"

"They all have weaknesses, not exactly fears. The gods who created guardians perfect their creatures to the point of excellence, sometimes to boast about their skill and sometimes because they adore them as if they were their own children. And right before gods give life to them, they create one single flaw. And that is what distinguishes guardians from gods. A flaw."

"Wouldn't that help us in case father succeeds in rousing her?"

"Possibly." I pulled a pad filled with my notes. "Five hundred years ago, the Elding kings led the resistance against her, and they managed to chain her long enough to break the sceptre apart. Perhaps there could be some more information in Olympia that dates to your ancestors and how they managed to take on a guardian of her power. It could be just that. Her one flaw."

"The grand library was in Myrdur. A lot is lost, but I'll ask Alastair and a few other of the elders in my court. Someone ought to remember perhaps the biggest tragedy in this realm." She sighed. "How can anyone forget about this? About her."

"Magic, fire, fear. A lot was burned, some were made to forget, and others just chose to forget out of fear. You forget that guardians like gods need the power of humans to thrive. If she lays forgotten, her power sleeps, too."

Snow's sleepless features pulled in a snarl. "Let's hope the selfish bitch has tangled in enough cobwebs to think it's a fly."

"Selfish?"

"I said bitch, too."

I was too tired to laugh but I did smile. "Why do you think her selfish?" *Speak to me, just speak anything to me.* Anything to hear her speak a little more.

"Adriatian, what do you call someone who was aware of the damage they were causing but caused it nonetheless without considering the consequences? If she had been unhappy warming Fader's bed, she should have said so. Not go behind his back and cheat on him. With a human at that. Amongst all the godly cock she had available. Fader's ego must have been bruised like an apple."

That made me drop my head back and guffaw. "And if he hadn't let her?"

"You think Fader didn't have enough women and men riding him to let this one go?"

"And if he had been in love with her?"

"He wasn't," she said confidently. "Don't two people in love share one heart? If you hurt, I hurt too? In that sense? Fader is written in holy scriptures and history as everything but a masochist. But he is written to be a man of law. Obey it and you shall thrive. Disobey it and you shall face wrath. How many stories are there in the History of Numen or Ithicea of others he has punished as such?"

"I think sleeplessness makes you quite the little philosopher."

She sneered at my smile. "Trust me, if I had slept a little less before I came to you, I'd have convinced you to join my cult."

"Already convinced. Been a follower for a long time." *A long, long time.* I stood and kissed the crown of her head. "Goddess of my heart, it's sunrise. You're free from me."

Her eyes rolled up at me for a moment before darting lost about the room. She sighed and stood, righting her short gown. "Not yet, Night King, not just yet. I am certain my full first breath in thirteen years will be when I am poking your heart with a skewer."

CHAPTER EIGHT

Tenebris

Snowlin

Alastair, Alaric's father, moved slowly around his small sage coloured kitchen. The man insisted he lived alone at his dying age in a tiny house in the middle of nowhere in Drava. He'd tripped twice after abandoning his crane to move around the cabinets attempting to make me a cup of tea. And I was sentenced to just watch. The grumpy old man took great offence from help. This had started as a daily visit years ago and shortly turned to a weekly one. After his wife had died between Skye warriors during the night of the *Draugr,* he had decided to let his body age rather than live without her. And ageing had taken him fast and with sickness. The old Zephyr had lived over two hundred years and all two human lifetimes had caught up with him rapidly.

A thud shook the ceiling above us and then Penelope shouted, "I am fine. Totally fine. Ouch. Still fine...I think. This room is a mess."

Sigh. I usually brought one of the servants to help with his chores, but the little carrot had begged me to take her by complaining that no one took her anywhere and that I'd imprisoned her inside the castle. She had not wanted any of the freedom I'd given her, and insisted she remained my helping hand despite all my protest.

Alastair chuckled and lowered a teacup before me, spilling half of it in the saucer from the shake of his hands. "You missed sending the new younglings to their climb of Valda."

The blessed tradition. The journey every Olympian took once in their lifetimes—the climb of Valda Acme. The point where skies touched the realm. The place where the old gates to Caelum stood that now had turned to an altar of prayer.

"You missed this month's rituals, too," he continued, taking a sip of tea. "It will be good to show Olympians your face now that you've returned.

Married at that. Ah, that reminds me. We have to get an Olympian priest to give his blessings."

Pouring the spilled tea on the saucer back in the cup, I looked up at him. "I am not married."

"You are married. You signed a certificate before a priest," he said as a matter of fact. "By law that makes you someone else's wife, hen."

"So, I am married. And?"

"Crown the boy."

Tea spittle flew out of my mouth. That made me laugh. Truly. No, it made me guffaw so hard that my ribs hurt. Crown Kilian? As what? The only crown I'd ever crown him with would be a gravestone.

"Hen," the old man said quietly after I'd settled. "This kingdom is yours, meant to be yours and by blood it is yours. But people are what make this kingdom. If they are divided like you've divided Isjord, trouble will ensue. The Volantians will use this opportunity—"

"To dethrone me? I'd like to see them try. I will feed Foglings skewered birds for a whole year." When Alaric had told me about Bayrd and his intentions of solidifying the Volant lands as a separate kingdom, I'd laughed myself to tears. Now, the more I heard it, the more the absurd suggestion annoyed me. Despite bearing the name of higher beings, they still remained my people. And they would all die as such.

"This is not something you can do by force and fear."

"I can do loads by fear alone. No need for force." Bayrd's feathers quivered for a year straight when I got crowned as queen.

He shook his head. "This is not about dethroning you or making them fear you. This is about dividing Olympia. You go against tradition—"

"Tradition sucks."

"Olympia lived because of it and now thrives through it. Your faith, too, is weak."

"I am my own faith," I said, sipping my tea. *My own god.*

"You are a harsh ruler, and your fist is of iron. It is the sign of an Isjordian heart."

"I am Isjordian, old man, don't forget." Why was it so difficult for them to understand that? Or accept it?

"You are the best thing that has happened to this kingdom. Turned rock to unbreakable diamond, your army, leadership and wits could outmatch Silas's. You are everything he is and ten times more. But our lands do not need more war and soldiers and weapons. Our lands need hope. The same hope that is dying by the day while your father tramples over Myrdur, while Fogling tear the young and old, while our skies have not seen light in years."

"I will bring it back. All of that. I made that oath the day I wore the obsidian crown. I made that oath to the dead and the living."

"And you are breaking yourself apart for it." He reached to hold my hand. "Do you think we cannot see? How you are losing yourself, how you no longer eat, speak, laugh. Crown the boy. The throne of Taren will never see such powers as when you two sit side by side. Share your burden. Share it with the most powerful man in this realm."

I stared at him long and hard. Trying to understand what odd lesson he was trying to teach me. Yet there was no lecturing in his features, only truth. "He murdered her, Alastair. Murdered my mother. Your queen. And he murdered me that night."

He sighed. "Had it not been Adriata, it would have been Eldmoor, Solarya, perhaps even the unblessed. Had your uncle sent that letter to the Solaryans, it would have been them. It was a rash decision made by a young king. You must know this because you've made similar mistakes at that age in your rule."

Betrayal tasted the sourest and most foul from those you cared about. "You cannot tell me to forgive him. Even for a dying old man it would be cruel."

"That is for your heart to decide, hen. Decide this with your brains," he said, tapping a shaking finger to my forehead. His eyes went watery, and I knew what was about to come—the sense of guilt all those that cared about me felt. "You've lived through much. Suffered more in eleven years of life than many do in several lifetimes. I put no blame on how you chose to heal what many destroyed and failed to protect. And till the end of my days, I will support you in your claim to mend. But you are queen, besides your heart, there is the heart of millions you have to care for. Crown the boy. Even if for a little while. It will give our people hope and you some rest. Let us taste power after all the trouble we've been through. And you will put Bayrd and the Volantians in their place. Do not forget, Elding child, faith has conquered realms. Give people hope not just your strength, wit and might. Sometimes hope is stronger than all three."

Tristin came into the kitchen, squeezing the large wings tight against her into the small space. "The door was open again, Alastair."

The old man waved a hand, unbothered. "No one will trouble me. My Nia comes by every day to scare the children who knock and hide."

The Skye Commander sighed and turned to me. "There is a little boy here for you."

"Little—" I looked over the window and a nervous Atlas had wrapped himself tightly, throwing careful glances all around him, almost tripping on his feet.

I knocked on the glass and he jumped upright with a hand on his chest. "Come inside," I shouted, waving a hand for him to come in.

Slowly, he made his way inside Alastair's home, staring wide eyed at Tristin's wings. "My...my queen," he bowed and then turned to Alastair and Tristin. "S-Sir. Madam?"

Tristin raised an amused brow at him, and Atlas flinched a little.

"Who is the young one?" Alastair asked, standing to fetch him a cup of tea.

"The priest that married me," I said, tapping the seat next to me for Atlas to sit.

Both Alastair and Tristin stared wide eyed at him. "They come young these days," the tribe leader said, lowering a cup of tea before him. Olympia only had a couple of priests left. The teaching of gods was difficult, it took years and loads of grey hair to be a guide of the divine here in Olympia.

"I-I came top of my class," Atlas boasted, coughing on a hot sip of tea. He cast me a glance and then jerked his attention to a far wall.

"No hard feelings, Atlas, I wasn't going to really kill you."

He blinked rapidly. "H-he had a sword to my throat the entire time."

"Little Atlas, if Cai had any intentions of killing you, he wouldn't have used a weapon to do so. It just probably amused him." Leaning in I whispered, "He likes seeing people writhe and beg for air. And he hates cleaning blood."

Atlas shivered a little, his temples coated with sweat.

Penelope made her way down the stairs, dishevelled and covered in dust, carrying several bags of clothing. "These all had holes, and most were half torn. I'm going to have to throw them away." Her attention caught on Atlas, and she bowed politely, tucking a strand of wild red hair behind her ear. "Hello."

Atlas lifted a shy hand up. "H-Hello."

The way the two blushed made me chuckle. "Why have you come to Olympia, Atlas? Certainly not for our sunshine. You can get a better tan in the hells you come from."

He cleared his throat and brought a small piece of paper from inside his robes. "The king wishes for you to attend a court gathering. It will be your introduction to both courts...as our queen."

I took the paper from him. *Wear red. In case you decide to break our bargain or stab me again. Somehow, I'd prefer it to be the second reason. Yours, Kilian.*

Lighting stuck outside, close to the house, and Atlas jerked up his seat.

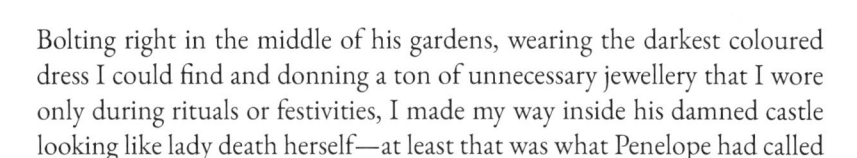

Bolting right in the middle of his gardens, wearing the darkest coloured dress I could find and donning a ton of unnecessary jewellery that I wore only during rituals or festivities, I made my way inside his damned castle looking like lady death herself—at least that was what Penelope had called me before I left.

From the distance, I could see guards taking a step further back though they stood plenty away from me, none daring to look up when I passed them. Their attention concentrated on the very interesting green grass of the gardens.

When guards pushed the beige doors open, there was no meeting room. Only the two Castemont men and loads of food. My stomach growled, a reminder that I had not eaten since yesterday. Did I eat yesterday?

Mal let out a low whistle, raking an amused gaze from the root of my hair to my toes. "Sister-in-law, you look bewitching."

A spoon lifted in the air and hit Mal right in the head. The prince rubbed the spot and said, "That was fair."

"Quit ruining my gardens," Kilian said, his attention to a letter.

I glowered at him. "Quit ruining my happiness."

"That's a big word for you, my love."

"I've got a bigger one for you." Motherfu—

A smirk twitched in his lips. "I'm sure you do."

Straightening my snarl, I cocked my head to the side, studying him. "Why are you wasting my daytime?"

"Sit," he said, pointing to the chair beside him.

All of my body prepared for fight, he triggered me like that. Had this been why he asked for us to be civil? So he could play lackey with me? "I'm not your dog." Politeness melted off me like butter, and then sizzled so hot it was steaming and burning out of me.

He dropped whatever he was reading and turned to me, silver eyes roaming over my body all delight. He looked taken aback for a moment before saying, "Love of my life, light of my eyes, my all, would you please do me the kindness of taking a seat? I'd rather not tire your pretty legs. Not like this, anyway."

Mal snorted, water spurting all over the table.

"Is this why you are wasting my time? Poetry?" I asked, taking a seat next to him and throwing the princeling a handkerchief in his face.

Kilian reached and uncapped a metallic dome from the plate in front of me, setting it aside. "The meeting is in an hour, plenty of time for you to have lunch. But I can read you poetry if that is what you like."

Ice crawled beneath my feet and Kilian shot me a look of warning.

The smell of spice and earth wafted to my nostrils and my stomach elicited a loud groan. I cringed and wordlessly picked up a spoon to stir the dish before me—mushroom stew. Something else caught my attention. The rest of the table had fruit, vegetables, and pies. No meat, no greens. A strange warmth filled me and then I dispersed it as quick as it came by reminding myself just who sat in front of me.

Scooping up some soup, I extended the spoon before his mouth.

Surprised, his brows jerked up.

I lifted it a bit higher, probing for him to try. "Your servants might have a fool's day and cook me poison. I'd hate to sputter blood from my mouth all day long, I've got places to be and people to entertain."

The corner of his mouth quirked. Grabbing onto my wrist, he guided the spoon to his mouth, wrapping those plump lips around the decorated silver. I still remembered how they felt on mine. His taste, too. And from the way his eyes flashed, I could swear he had read my mind.

The air was so thick all of a sudden, choking almost.

"No poison," he said, letting go of me. "It needs salt though."

I nodded and then brought the spoon to my mouth to taste the remnants of the soup and...him. His eyes traced my movement carefully and when I wrapped my lips where his had been only seconds ago, his jaw ticked. Dimple now fully in sight. "No, there is plenty of salt."

After a few spoonfuls of the warm earthy soup, I poked a few baked potato squares with my fork and held them before him again. He ate that and I stuffed a bunch of those down as well. And then the pie. The odd olive bread I'd never had before. Some sort of aubergine dish.

"Woman," he sighed. "Are you trying to kill me?"

"Death by pie would be very fitting to your image, Night King."

He exhaled a long, slow breath and leaned back, looking at me, his tongue pushing on his cheek. "Not calling me Kilian anymore?"

"I'd rather not be on a first name basis with the man who sent his hound dogs to kill me when I was barely eleven." All that salt and spice had bloated my stomach and parched my tongue and that meant I had to drink water. After I filled my cup, I held it before him. "Drink."

"He already tried everything before you came," Mal said, mildly entertained.

My arm dropped and I turned to him. "What?"

His mouth pulled to a wicked smile. "Heard me right, sister-in-law. Everything, from the soup to the condiments to the drinks was tried by him before you came."

Slowly, my head turned to Kilian whose stark face was veiled in some amusement.

"You wouldn't have believed me," he said before I could say anything.

I nodded. No, I wouldn't have. "When is this meeting?"

He cocked his head to the side. "Finish eating."

"Finished," I said, dropping the cutlery. Though my stomach protested that statement.

He shut his eyes and sighed, "Snowlin."

A nerve jumped in my temple from the way he said my damned name.

Mal cleared his throat. "Actually, can we go now? I've got a lady clocking in at the inn with my hard earned money. It hurts me to see it go to waste."

"Get a whore for your brother, too, it ought to lose that stick up his arse a bit," I said, pushing the chair back and exiting the room.

I kept a healthy three feet between him and I, walking besides Mal while he led us to the meeting room.

"He does have a fascinating backside," Mal murmured in my ear, and I elbowed him in the gut with all my strength.

"I'm certain all the ladies will say the same about yours when I put a pike through and through your naked body."

"Ladies will be too busy admiring my front, sister-in-law," the fool said, giving me a wink and trotting ahead.

Kilian pulled the two massive mauve doors and let his brother go in before shutting them right as I was about to enter. He chased my steps till my back met the cold wood and then caged me in. He was so close, too close. Gods, he smelled so good.

He chuckled a little and then looked down at the dagger I held to his gut.

My grip shook from anger—deep red anger that I felt more at myself than him.

He grabbed my wrist and dragged my hand up, resting the blade against his throat. "I'm a very difficult man to kill, love. I'd go for my throat first. It won't kill me instantly, but I'll surely bleed a little and weaken the magic protecting me. And then," he said, bringing the tip of the dagger to his heart. "Then go for my heart."

I tilted my head to the side. "Noted. Any other advice?"

"I'm sure you can figure the rest on your own." He pushed a loose strand of hair from my face, tucking it behind my ear. "There are some very young people in there, I need you to be nice."

I scoffed, sheathing the dagger to my waist. "Darling, I'm the nicest person I know. Do you know what it takes to resist committing genocide on an hourly basis?"

His warm breath fanned over my lips, shivers travelling all the way down to my spine. "I feel for you, love, truly."

Before I could bite out a remark, he pushed the door handle behind me open and I almost back rolled inside the room.

A rectangle half black and half white table took most of the grandiose expanse, the lilac coloured space was bright from the light filtering through the massive windows framing the walls.

Moon and Night court. And I was part of it now.

One by one, the dozen and something councillors, priests and presumably scholars, stood and bowed in holy greeting. Some young, some familiar, some odd, but there was only one face I dreaded seeing sitting on that table. Nesrin.

Kilian ghosted a hand on the small of my back, not touching me, and leaned to my ear to whisper, "I believe you and I have made Nia the same promise."

You will not hurt her. The one I regretted every single day and the same one I knew very well I'd break. Promises were feeble things and there were so many ways around them.

Kilian directed the two of us to the head of the massive table. Once we were seated, the rest followed suit.

Memphis slithered under the table and curled in my lap.

"Gods!" someone jumped up when my morph hissed leisurely at my petting.

"You think a little bite of hers will hurt you when I sit here?" The looks they gave me were hilarious.

Memphis raised her head all offended. *Little bite?* The hiss echoed in my head making me chuckle.

"Is this how it begins? A threat here and a threat there till we wait for you to exterminate us?" Nesrin huffed, crossing her arms. "Have you not had your revenge? Kidnapping the council and all."

"Nesrin," Larg warned, and I raised a hand at the old man, stopping him. "Let her finish, Larg."

Nesrin's face twisted, and I hated how much of Nia was in there too. "Let's say it was fair of you to do what you did, but what have the rest of the innocent Adriatians done to you?"

Funny, weren't they. "I simply operate on an egalitarian basis, dearest. Discrimination is not my sort of thing." I leaned forward and gave her a polite smile. "You pull weed by the roots. Cut it, and dozens more grow. Look at you. Already your father's daughter. How many more *weeds* like you must there be, hm?"

With a sigh, I leaned back and met everyone's stare. By everyone, I meant the only three who were actually looking at me and not at the table or a wall. "Anyone wishes to get anything off their chests? I'm quite enjoying this heart to heart." I waited a minute and then braced myself for pain. "Well, I'll go first to break the ice. One pretty sunny day, I will kill you all. Your mothers, fathers, sisters and brothers, your younglings, your elderly and if I am in the mood, perhaps I'll chase you in the Otherworld, too, to make sure even your souls suffer. I like a bit of irony with my fairy tales. I won't rise from any type of ash, but I will certainly make them. Till the glorious day when I've turned you and your memory to lovely dust, you all will have the honour of being in my presence." The seal of the bargain in my hand burned, my skin felt as if it was being fried over oil when I spoke the words that broke part of the oath I'd given.

Some flinched, some gaped and every gaze in the room went to Kilian. Yet the man remained quiet, leaning back in his chair with a smirk on his face.

"No heart to heart, my queen," Larg said with some humour. "But I do have something of interest in hand." He unwrapped a silk black cloth and placed an emerald quartz stone on the table. Identical to the very same ones Moriko had given me, except there was another circle of much smaller runes around it.

Immediately, I grabbed it and threw it hard to the nearest wall, shattering it to pieces. My breaths were ragged and hard. My hand burned and when I peeled my glove off and there was not an inch of skin uncovered by black tattoos. Melanthe's mint magic scent filtered the air along with something else—something older and more potent. The witch was cunning as hells. "Where did you find that?"

Larg's stare was wide and confused. "Nesrin found it in one of her patrols this morning. Near the gates."

I was dumbfounded at best. "And you just brought it in?"

"It is safe, Your Majesty," a young councillor next to Nesrin said with a mordant expression like I was an idiot. "Whatever the magic was, the Highwall veil would have nullified it. Your Crafter put it back, didn't she?"

A dark chuckle left me when my seal began cracking and tearing. "You dumb little—"

Kilian grabbed my hand to inspect the dark lines. "What is the matter, my love?"

Well, all attention snapped to him at that moment. Bet he'd called me that on purpose. Everything was a little calculated trick of his.

"That was a tracing craft. For the sceptre. Moriko met me back in Arynth and showed me similar ones she'd found. Larg," I said, turning to the general. "How long have you had that stone beyond the wall and the *alaar*?" The whole purpose of the Ianuris agreement was to find a way inside Adriata—to plant trace craft and find their sceptre piece. When Moriko gave me the tracing craft stones that she'd found scattered around Numengarth, I'd suspected that Aryan had planted many around Adriata after breaching through the agreement. But when Visha repaired the Highwall veil back, their magic nullified behind the barrier. It was step one for father and Melanthe. However, if Melanthe was truly getting stronger, who would say that she wouldn't be able to use her craft beyond the veil?"

"An hour or so," he said with worry.

A loud boom shook the ground beneath us, and from the large windows you could see the black fire beyond the Amaris lines.

Everyone shot to their feet, unsheathing weapons and barking orders.

"Sit," Kilian ordered calmly, and everyone quieted down, returning to their seats as if chaos wasn't ensuing outside. "Sound the emergency bells, my people will know to retreat inside their homes. Whoever is hovering about, hold them." He turned to his brother. "Send out the whole Eldritch unit to read for the intruders. We will search the city. Larg, Triad, both of you mark and guard every temple in Amaris. If anyone reaches even a mile close, signal and do not hold back. This is an order of first kill."

The Adriatian council faded out one after the other and Kilian stood, unbuttoning his jacket and folding it neatly on the chair before he offered me a hand. "I'll take you to Taren."

"The hells you are. I'm staying."

He raised a brow and dropped his attention to my dress before nodding. "If that is what you wish."

He faded the two of us right in the middle of a narrow street filled with blazing white painted houses and dressed in all sorts of climbing colourful plants.

Grabbing my hand, he laced our fingers together. "Don't let go of me for any reason."

"Scared your rotten ilk will trip and stab themselves on my dagger?" I asked as he stirred us into the maze-like streets of Amaris.

"You'll get lost, *dahaara*."

We pushed through a panicked crowd of people rushing opposite us and away from a blast. Some sort of fiery orb shot from the sky in our direction and crawling shadows shot out of Kilian, causing the orb to crash against it and splinter in the sky.

From the corner of my eye, I caught a second one aiming for us, and I shot my hands up, forming a layer of ice over all of us, shielding all of the people underneath it.

Everyone stopped in their tracks, looking at me like I was something in a museum. The idiots. "Go, run!"

Hesitantly, all of them backed away and cleared the area of the attack that had charred black on all corners.

Kilian lowered to the ground, picking up some of the soot between his fingers, his brows pinching. "Craft."

There were several other booms scattered around the city and two more just near us. Grand grey mushrooms of smoke soared from behind lines of buildings. This was either a distraction or whoever had organised this attack didn't exactly know what they were searching for.

I bent down and tore the sides of my dress. "Go to the other, I'll go to this one."

"No."

"Yes," I said, backing away.

Very reluctantly, he jogged away from me and toward the blast of black smoke gushing in the separate direction I was going.

Chaos poured from where the blast had occurred, the whole air was grey with soot and smoke while the fire burned a three-floor white building.

Bodies ran in clusters, attempting to escape, and dead soldiers littered the stony grounds. An old woman clutched a small child in her arms, stumbling and falling from the bodies brushing past her. Feet crushed her bony hands while she tried to shield the little girl, and I shot toward her.

Grabbing the little girl from her arms into mine, I held out my hand to her. "Come on."

Pushing the two safely under a stall table hidden in an alleyway, I bent down to them and said, "Don't make a sound."

The older woman nodded, clutching the little child in her arms.

Rushing back to the location of the attack, I searched all the alleys close by till an enormous mauve building rose into sight. There were Darsan inscriptions on the entrance alcove, none I could understand, but from what I could tell, it looked like a city hall or a library.

There were signs of struggle outside, several dead Adriatian soldiers laid over the small steps leading inside of it.

Unsheathing my daggers, I climbed up past them and entered what seemed to be a library. The air was sizzling with something so vile it had the hair on my neck raise from alert. A sort of magic that Crafters usually emitted—it was like the rattle of a snake before they bit you, a warning. Something else was strange, too. The tall shelves ahead were all made of a deep grey almost black metal and all the books were all encased inside fitted boxes of the same metal, and chained to the shelves, all locked. Not only with latches, but with magic as well. I could practically feel the thin layer of craft over them touch my fingertips.

There were no windows and no torches, and it didn't take me long to trip over something and fall to the ground. That something was soft, half warm and wet. A dead body. Lovely. My fingers grazed the wound and I stilled. Several deep dents were on his flesh. Fangs?

Electricity skittered from my hand in an attempt to illuminate my surroundings and I caught a shadow moving to my left between the book space. There was no time for me to chase after it as a three feet tall, massive dog-like creature with sharp canines skidded into sight, growling and barking before launching in the air towards me. A damned Canes. When it reached close to me, I had to blink another take. Its fur had an odd red sheen and the usually black signature eyes all Canes had were red and rabid.

Thankfully, the shelf corridors were wide enough for me to spin in place to avoid the blow, and the thing landed where I previously stood.

It turned to me again, launching in the air, and I ran and slid on my knees under it, embedding a sharp shard of ice in its stomach. The beast landed on the floor, whimpering and writhing till it died. A second one jumped over the tall shelves aiming for me, freezing in the air at my command and landing on the tiled floor with a loud thud.

The floor beneath me had splintered. "That's a waste of pretty tiles."

A shadow caught my peripheral attention again and I ran after it, catching the form right before it took the exit by lifting a tall wall of ice over the doors.

They raised a hand in my direction and my body locked in place. Umbra. Not Isjordian. Panic crawled up my throat.

But to his bad luck, I didn't need to move a single hair to use magic. A cloud of lightning flakes soared around me in a sphere and then blasted, levelling my surroundings to the ground and the Umbra to tiny pieces painted on the wall.

I heaved, breathing hard. Drops of sweat coating my temples from the magic of shadows.

A metal bound book remained where the Umbra had stood, the metal casing was still hot, and I couldn't find where it unlocked. What was this damned book?

The frosted beasts had fragmented into chunks from my earlier blow, but I could still note their strangeness. There was an oddity about the Aitan creatures, and it wasn't the unusual colour of their pelt. Cai would probably say I was overthinking this, but the hounds of Dyurin were calm creatures, triggered only from a sole target that their handler would have needed to command in the old language of gods. For them to act as they did toward me, I had to have been the target, which was impossible considering the Umbra couldn't have known who I was. Not to mention that Canes were not directly trained to kill, they were trained to sniff out magic and nullify it. How would my father have managed to sneak those inside with how guarded the wall was? And this was what they'd come for? A book?

There was someone who could answer me, so I went to seek him.

"Shit," I murmured, remembering, and running back to the alley of the blast. Flinging back the cloth covering the bottom of the tent, I bent down and reached to help the old woman and child stand. I brushed a bit of ash from the little girl's cheek. "You were not scared, were you?"

She shook her head.

"Is your house within walking distance?" I asked.

The old woman nodded, silently.

"Would you like me to walk you there?"

Both nodded this time.

"Where are her parents?" I asked the old woman, hooking an arm under her shoulder to help her limp. Clearly, she needed someone to take care of her, not the opposite.

"Papa left when I was born and my ma has died," the little one said, burying her face in my hair, looking upset.

"Mine too, kid."

She turned to face me. "My ma is a star."

"Mine is a winter sky."

The old woman was staring at me, so I turned to stare back at her. And when I did, she gave me a smile. It left me blinking to myself for a little while. They had no idea who I was, did they?

With one hand, I pulled on one of my diamond necklaces and gave it to the old woman. In Olympia, jewels didn't hold any richness or significant worth, our mines were boasting with them, but they did anywhere else in Numen. "Pay someone to help you with her."

Her sunken face had gone pale and wide staring at the golden jewellery littered with diamonds. "I cannot."

I pushed it to her again. "Yes, you can. It was an order not an offer."

With a shaky hand, she took the necklace and tucked it in one of her skirt pockets.

"Right over there," the old woman said, pointing two alleys down to a small house wedged between two tall buildings. She bowed her head. "Thank you, my queen."

Oh. She knew who I was.

The little girl bowed too, almost losing her balance on her little feet. "Thank you, my queen," she said with a little squeaky voice.

I blinked a little taken aback and bowed, too, before heading toward the city square. Something tugged on my dress and the little girl poked her head to my side when I stopped.

She extended a hand up to me, holding a little half withered yellow flower.

"For me?" I asked, taking the silly thing for some reason.

She nodded and then bolted back into a run toward the house.

"Looks like she chewed you before giving you to me." I laughed a bit as I secured the quaint thing in my corset and then shook my head to reality. I *was* losing my mind.

Amaris was a white and lilac blinding maze. Everything was so linear and similar. Could have sworn that even the cobbled streets were counted in a way that the rocks laid in an identical pattern all over. I might have taken a round trip and not known. By the third alley, I started noting the shops in hopes of finding a way out of the maze.

Just when I thought I might have reached my destination, shadowy forms rose from above and around me, making me halt. Clad in black leathers and armed in the stygian steel, Adriatian soldiers poured out of Amaris alleys, their faces shielded behind a mask and hood as they advanced towards me. Each pulse I counted in the air was furial—not with fear but with anger. As long as that prophecy existed, so did their monster.

"Get her," one called loudly. "Alive or not, I don't care."

The exact words from that night repeating thirteen years later. And flashes of memory chose the wrong time to surface and hold the air in my lungs hostage.

Breathe.

Haziness blurred the figures ahead as I tried to focus, tried not to shiver and crumble back to the helpless eleven year old.

Breathe.

To say that I had not expected this would be a lie. But not the bravery. Thought they would find the easy route and poison me. I did, however, pity our surroundings. The houses were so white and neat to be painted red and dirty.

"Skewered?" I asked, tilting my head to the side. "Or iced?" At my words, clouds of frost spilled from my fingertips, filling the air with white fog and coldness.

Hundreds of ice shards rose from the ground at my command, but the men were quick. Jumping and running in my direction, a black blade on their hand. The look of the steel didn't bother me much anymore. What did, however, was the thought that I might be cut by it again.

They faded rapidly all around me, looking like they were multiplying by the second and attempting to keep up with the movement made me terribly dizzy.

Electricity skittered from my fingers, shooting forward, and many were caught in the blinding bolts. Fading was quick, but lightning was quicker. Immediately, the smell of burned flesh filled the air along with the side dish of screaming.

Shadows around me elongated, slithering over the ground and climbing the house walls till they rose like towering monsters of my many nightmares.

An arrow pierced the electric filled summer air. And distracted by the drown of memory, I almost let it hit me, passing close enough to graze the side of my temple.

Sweat coated my brow. More from frustration than fear. I was power. I was not afraid. Why had my breathing become ragged and my pulse mad?

Mimicking my fury, the air charged heavily and rock, grime and all sorts lifted in the air while the ground crawled with ice.

"Touch her, now!" someone shouted, and a man faded directly in front of me.

Quicker than lightning, I bolted right beside him, my dagger slashing through hard flesh and bone before the man dropped to the floor, burnt to a crisp. I lifted the arm I'd cut off from the man and chucked it to their feet. "With what hand?" I hated how my voice trembled, I hated how I had to trap a sob in my throat.

And before I could let my storm take over, before I could let my rage take flight and protect me, the blue skies suddenly dimmed, slowly coating with crawling darkness, and the men around me froze in place, some screaming and others clawing their throats unable to breathe.

Kilian came into sight, a sword in his hand, his shoulders raising at a scary slow pace that matched his hard breathing. A trail of icy black fire lit with each step he took between the crowd of men. He slashed his sword through a head. And then another and few many others along the way he made to me. The cobbled streets coated crimson, each gap forming a stream of the thick liquid.

He killed for me. He'd killed for me before, to protect his agreement. But this time, he'd done it for *me*. And I hated it.

The closer he came, the more I could see the man that I had not seen in Isjord. A shiver raked through me, and I faltered a step back and then another. And before I knew it, I was walking backwards and away from him.

There was a look in his face, something between torture and pain, something that had made his beautiful face twist with regret. He stopped moving and reached a hand to me in the distance, almost begging. "Love, come to me."

Ice and lightning fluttered around me again, preparing for fight.
Breathe.

For a moment, I was almost afraid...almost. Until I felt his unusual warmth linger in the air and brushing past my skin, until his eyes flashed back to silver and the scent of lemon blossoms lingered in my air.

Night turned back to blue day, peeling my surroundings from grey darkness. And I was awake.

He dropped his sword and slowly, ever so slow, walked to me, watching my every reaction till he stood barely an arm's length away. He towered over me, his hands ghosting over my face. He was covered in soot, blood and sweat and breathed hard. "Hurt anywhere?"

I scowled. "Are you trying to offend me?"

A small smile twitched in his full lips which died shortly when he noticed the graze on my temple. One moment we were in Amaris city streets, the next we were in the meeting room.

While I tried to steady myself, he went to a side table, filling a glass with the amber liquor he usually drank and another with water. He took a sip from the water glass before handing it to me. "Safe to drink."

Dipping two fingers in his drink, he put them atop the graze on my temple. When I pulled away, he gripped my jaw tight. "Stay still, little brat." He took out a handkerchief from his inner pocket and wiped the blood and liquor mess before blowing on the cut.

My knees might have gone a little weak.

After tossing the bloodied cloth away, he drowned back his whole glass of alcohol, which from how it burned my cut was surely only meant to be sipped. Then, he went and filled another before sprawling in his chair like a mad king. There was a halo over him, one that I worried my brain hard to understand how I'd never noticed it before. A halo of might. Dark might. One earned by sheer power not by epics and tales of his doings. The man didn't need to do much, anyway. Not one being in this realm wasn't aware of what he could do.

"Sit, love," he said with a hard edge in his voice.

I drank my water and sat down. "There was no need for interruption. I had it handled." It was under control. My head often played nasty games with me sometimes, but it never failed me, not in the worst of times.

He cocked his head back and unbuttoned a couple neck buttons on his shirt. "I knew you had that handled." What was the mad man trying to do? Have me crawl on his lap? Because it was exactly what I wanted to do right before the sting on my palms grounded me to reality.

"But you see, I've come to realise something," he said, taking a big sip of his drink before continuing, "I've come to realise that I've gained an urge to kill. Anyone that breathes too heavily near you."

"Sharpen your blade, darling," I said, shakily reaching for his drink and taking a sip. Letting the burn of the alcohol soothe me without making my palms bleed any more than they were. "Many breathe heavily near me."

His attention on me turned dark and stern, and when it dropped to my hands, his jaw ticked and that little dip in his chin became visible.

I'm not afraid. I'd not been afraid. Not a day in my life after that night had I been afraid. It wasn't fear. I'm sure of it. It was something worse—a remembrance of when I'd been most afraid.

The meeting room door opened. Larg, Triad and Mal strutted in all deep in deadly concentration. "There was no breach in the Highwall."

"That is because they were already inside Adriata," I said. "Either from when we came for the Ianuris agreement or even before. The trace craft stone was a trick, a distraction. A pretty cute one." Pulling the book from my lap, I dropped it on the table. "An Umbra and two Canes were after this in a library close to one of the blasts. Now tell me, why would my father need to plan that whole charade for a book?"

They all sat around the table, their attention on the metal cased book.

"They were after the Esmeray diaries?" Triad asked.

The what?

Mal held it in his hand, running a finger over the Darsan inscription on the metal. "Ahmes Lore. Why would they want Ahmes Lore? No one is able to read it."

"Who is Esmeray?" I asked.

"A human Henah befriended in her time in Adriata. The woman was even granted permission to Cynth. She travelled back and forth to Numen and Cynth. Transcribed all her travels in intimate detail," Triad answered. "Without Henah knowing."

What? There was such a thing? "Why would my father want that? Could you open it?"

Mal rested a palm over the lock, and it clicked open not a second later. When the metal folds peeled back, it revealed a white leather-bound book with gold inscriptions atop.

Gooseflesh rose over my skin. The air sang somehow and every sense I possessed hummed with warning. For a second my vision dizzied and my breathing grew laboured.

"Love?" Kilian's call echoed from a far distance along with a piercing ring. "Snow!"

When my attention returned, Kilian stood kneeled before me, a palm resting on my forehead. "I'm fine."

"Did anyone touch you?"

I pushed his hand away. "No." When my limbs no longer felt like a gelatinous mass, I picked up the book and flipped through it.

Endless pages were scribbled in black ink in a language I could not recognise. It didn't look like one of Numen, nor that of the old gods. "What language is this?"

Kilian frowned at me and then down at the book. "What do you mean?"

I pointed to a line. "I don't recognise the letters."

It was everyone's turn to stare at me like I'd lost the plot.

"Snow," Mal said, leaning back in his chair. "The pages are empty."

The more I looked at him the more I was starting to think he wasn't joking. But when I flipped the pages open again, they were filled with writing. "Pass me a pen and paper."

All stood and loomed over me as I traced the odd writing onto a sheet of paper. When I'd written a full line, I pulled the paper up and pointed to it. "What does that mean?"

The four men frowned, their expression morphing from confusion to wide panic.

"It is impossible. You can't possibly—" Larg slumped back in his chair with an incredulous look on his face.

"Would someone tell me what you are reading?" I asked.

Kilian took the paper from my hand and tore it to pieces before holding a candle over it and burning them to ash. "They are instructions in old Darsan. How to access the gates to Cynth and ultimately to the rest of the others, too." He sighed, sprawling back in his chair. "Esmeray wrote Ahmes Lore with the blood of a fallen guardian. Only one from the heavens could read them."

"What?" I flipped through the book again. All the scribble and babble made no sense to me at all. "Why is that I can see it?"

"You're part of a prophecy," Triad said, looking at me like I was a puzzle of some sort. "That connects you to the divine in more ways than one. Your ability to read it doesn't surprise me. What does, is your father looking for it. Would this be connected to the white flamed guardian?"

"Possibly," Kilian said, staring at me across the table with a distanced look in his eyes.

"How would one know about their existence?" I asked, ignoring him and the worry in his eyes. "How come my father knows?"

"Adriatians," Mal said, deep in thought. "Someone from the night congregation. A priest or a scholar. Only they would know in detail what any of Esmeray's diaries had in them. Especially Ahmes Lore. It is not a popular knowledge. Kings, queens and courts have made sure it was not popular knowledge to avoid anyone being curious."

Larg sighed. "Won't surprise me if Silas has spies there too."

"Perhaps there is something we have missed," Mal said, tapping a finger repeatedly on the table. "Why would Silas need this, especially if he can't read it?"

"Snow," Kilian said, rubbing a hand over his jaw. "How did they get the book from the chained shelf?"

"The Umbra already had it unchained." The three all shared one of those coded looks and I groaned. "For the love of hells, would you please stop that and tell me too what we are thinking?"

"It was not an Umbra," Kilian said. "It had to have been a Dark Crafter. The shelves are veiled."

I shook my head. "They used shadows."

"Was there anyone else there?"

"No. I would have felt another heartbeat. Especially if it had been a Dark Crafter. My magic and theirs doesn't mesh well." Folding the book back inside the metal case, I clicked the lock shut. "It comes with me to Olympia."

"I have to agree, no one would think to search there," Larg said with a rumbling laughter. His attention bounced to Kilian and the amusement dissipated. "What is bothering you, son?"

The Night King stood like a statue, his attention pointed to my shaking hands. I had not noticed it. When I quickly pulled them back to my lap, he lifted those deadly eyes to Triad. "Which part of the Umbra command was close to south Amaris today?"

"My king," Triad said, leaning on the table. "What you are thinking could lead to an uproar."

Kilian did not look at me as he said, "Could you leave us, love."

"I'm not your dog."

He sighed, his jaw tightening. "This conversation does not end here, Triad. Look at what I asked. I expect a response by tomorrow morning."

I couldn't stand his all-concerned act and I stood to leave. The room suddenly spun, and my feet wobbled. Before I crashed to the ground, strong arms wrapped around me.

I straightened, shaking the dizziness away. "Let go of me."

He lifted me on the table, sheer panic layering his features. How did he do that so well? How could he summon pretend so accurately? "Does it hurt?" His hands moved all over me. "Show me where."

I grabbed both his wrists and pulled them away from me. "Don't touch me."

He nodded and turned to Mal, backing away as he said, "Brother, please have a look at her."

Something inside my chest squeezed. So hard that I felt my heart pop.

Mal rested a hand on my arm. "You were not inflicted. Is it something else?"

"Show me to the room, I'm just tired."

"Kil can take—"

"Show me to the room, Mal."

When Mal left, I let out a long loose breath.

What is wrong with me? I peeled my dress and jewellery off, yet the heavy feel still weighed on me.

I was so tired that my reaction came too late and too meek when Kilian faded behind me and scooped me up in his arms before sitting on the sofa with me on his lap. "What do you think you are doing?"

"Medicine. For dizziness." Uncapping a tiny bottle, he poured a burgundy syrup into a spoon. "Open your mouth, love," he cooed, pushing the spoon between my sealed mouth. After several moments of silent angry stares, he put the spoon down and ran his thumb over my lips. "Come now."

My chest burned like it was being clawed by the inside voice that wanted to shout, to scream. How dare he? How dare he pretend like he'd not been the one to ruin me. "Do you like it this much, seeing me helpless?" I asked, flicking the spoon from his hand and sending the syrup flying everywhere on his pretty tiles.

He sighed. "I am helpless before you all the time. I am helpless before you now. What you are is not helpless." Pouring the syrup in the bottle cap, he lifted it to my mouth again and said, "Resent me all you want. Hate me all you want. Just take this. It's only medicine." He drank a bit himself from the bottle to show me. "Only medicine. Very bitter though, be warned."

"I've had my bitter medicine for today, Your Majesty." Pulling his hand off from me, I pushed away from his lap. "Don't touch me again."

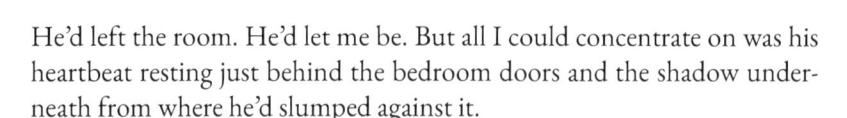

He'd left the room. He'd let me be. But all I could concentrate on was his heartbeat resting just behind the bedroom doors and the shadow underneath from where he'd slumped against it.

A warm bath, dizzying aromatic scents, the soft lull of the fireplace flames and his citrus scented shirt I'd found in his dressing chambers had me drowsy and floating in a soft golden fog.

He'd returned not long after I'd gotten in bed, tucked me nice and tight under the blanket and then disappeared in the bathing chambers.

So silent. So dark though I'd lit dozens of candles around the room. How had I not noticed how dark it got when he was close.

His footsteps and heartbeat were light, I wouldn't have noticed his presence if the bed hadn't dipped behind me when he laid down, close to me but not close enough to touch.

It was only when he shifted to face my back that his heartbeat picked up enough for me to hear. I'd never met someone who could control even his own pulse.

Not long after he'd laid with me and surrounded me with calm, my world twirled into a blanket of dreams that soon turned to my usual hunting nightmares. I was back to running, this time through the streets of Amaris. There was the fire, the screams and the shadows. But this time, he was there too. The face I'd made up to be off red eyes, claws and fangs, leaking inky black tar and growling my name like a chant was replaced with silver halos and warm smiles, no longer chanting my name but singing it like a haunting lullaby that I longed for. When he reached out a hand, I gave him mine. And then he stood there holding me with a touch that began to grow cold, his eyes turning red, fangs extending out of him, my name a hungry call and the hand he held pierced by his claws making me bleed a river onto the white cobbled streets of Amaris.

Snow, a whisper called—his voice. *Wake up.*

With a jolt, I shook awake, taking a deep restricted breath in my burning lungs before coughing. The room was cold—cold enough that my breath misted white. Except that it wasn't cold, I just had made it cold when I'd frozen the side of my bed and half the room.

A massive hand wrapped around my face, pulling my attention to him. No words were said. Nothing. His heartbeat was wild, but so was mine. Perhaps it was only mine. I didn't know. Sense of panic had not quite gone away.

Quietly, he got up from the bed and returned with a wet cloth and bandage. Wiping the blood from my palms before wrapping the angry deep scars with the white gauze. I didn't look at him and he didn't look up at me. I didn't know whether he was angry or mad or sad, but from how hard his features had set when I finally glanced at him, it looked like it was all of that mixed together.

I hated that he pretended to care. Sometimes it almost convinced me that he actually did.

You did this to me, I wanted to scream. But if I did admit how he still haunted me, I'd be made weak.

None of us slept after, we both stood leaning back on the bed poster in total silence till dawn oranges, lilacs and mauves brightened the horizon framed by the tall windows.

"I will never hurt you, Snow."

"I think you've done plenty already." Scarred me in and out.

With the same understanding of silence, I stood and left for Olympia.

Chapter Nine

Brontide

Kilian

Larg sat across from me, enjoying his breakfast. The rest of the table was empty. Mal was nowhere to be found. Atlas, too, was busier than me these days. And Snow had left like lightning at dawn before I could even utter the word *stay*.

"I gather the north temple is burnt to the ground?" I asked, flipping through the identification documents Atlas had found for me, belonging to the men from the attack on Snow. My head hurt when I saw how meticulously that little charade on Snow had been planned. How intricate the web of anti-*Ybris* propaganda was on my land. One priest on my council, twelve more in the same congregation and thirty-two soldiers had been hanged this morning from treason and an attempt against the crown.

For three days, Snow had come at night, laid awake in her corner on the bed and then left at the first crack of dawn. Each time we said less and less, and she looked even more lost inside her head. Looking more wary of me. Almost...scared. And I blamed it on that day—I blamed it on me, for leaving her alone, for assuming I could trust my people, for using my magic when I knew what it did to invoke her fears.

Larg nodded. "Currently looking for more associated with the same clergy. We will get to the bottom of this, son."

I was not one to show my power by fear, but this was the first time I might have actually enjoyed watching the crowd fall silent to my words and threats. "Not the bottom, Larg. I want this thing to have no bottom at all. I'll dig it with my own hands if I must."

Driada entered the dining chambers, chirper than usual these days. Each time Nia brought her back from Olympia her smile had grown bigger. The russet stare that Mal had inherited from her softened and she regarded me like I was an old memory she missed. Clouds of canary coloured happiness gathered around her torso. "Henrik," she said, taking a seat next to me.

She'd never, not once before called me that. "I haven't seen you of late. Where have you been, my dear?" The more she looked at me, the more she withered back to her old self—the old self I remembered her to be when around my father. "Have I done something again?"

She thought I was my father. The man who'd died of heartbreak for another woman.

Larg half stood. "Driada, he is not—"

"Forgive me, Driada," I said. "I'll make sure to visit you more often."

Her smile grew back and she nodded before turning her attention to her breakfast. It hurt my heart to see how she was slowly deteriorating exactly how my father had. First his lungs had bled for the air he breathed without the woman he'd loved and then his head had spun him maddening tales of his past until his heart had grown sick of feeling memory but never touching it. She was suffering like him. Except that she was suffering for a man who had not loved her back.

Something around her neck caught my attention, a thin silvery chain dusted with several small obsidian stones. It emitted something strange, not exactly magic, but a type of magical essence. A sort that when my shadows grazed it, it made them quiver and dissipate.

"What is the necklace you are wearing?" I asked.

She touched a hand to her neck and blinked to herself for a moment before swivelling her head to stare at me with horror. "Kilian, when did you get here?"

"Just now. Where did you get that necklace?"

"Oh, Snowlin gifted it to me. Isn't it lovely?"

The papers in my hand crumbled from the force of my grip. How had Snow managed to step over the bargain again? Had she asked someone else to give it to Driada? "I need you to take it off."

She frowned incredulously. "Why would I do that? And she made me swear to her that I would never take it off."

From an unusually unstirred bottom, anger began crawling up. "Driada."

"If she wants to kill me, so be it," she said, her mouth quivering. "If it makes her happy, so be it. I don't have long in this realm anyway. So do not ask me to take it off, because I won't. And you will not say anything to her."

"Ah, here is my little happy family," Mal said, coming in and kissing his mother's head before taking a seat.

Sigh. He stunk like someone had drenched him in alcohol. "Did you just get home?"

He took a piece of toast and leaned back, munching lazily. "If I say yes, will daddy discipline me?"

Driada's head popped up from her meal. "Henrik? Where has he gone now?"

The piece of bread my brother held crushed in his grip. "Dead, ma. In his plush cosy grave filled with the stink of rot and worms. Right where he needs to be."

My stepmother's face twisted with anguish and pain. "What are you saying, son? Don't speak like that about your father."

"The only father who has raised me has been my brother, not that piece of sh—"

"Mal," I called. "That is enough."

He chucked the rest of the crumbled bread on the table. "I'm sick and tired of you all masquerading the truth. Just tell her when she gets like this. She deserves to not miss the piece of work our father was." With that, he stood and left.

Driada's head hung low, and she wiped stray tears with the corner of her sleeve while quietly eating her meal.

"I will talk to him, do not worry," Larg said, resting a hand on hers.

There was one person he would listen to, and it was either of them. I was sure it was not me either.

A soldier stepped inside the breakfast room, greeting the table and leaning down to me. "There is a woman here. She has been at the gates since last night and demands to see you."

"Demands?"

She nodded. "Very persistently. It has something to do with the queen."

It took me a moment to blink the stagger off. The woman demanding to see me was an older lady, sat by the carriage road and shivering from the cold morning breeze. "You've let her wait at the gates all night?"

The soldier winced a bit. "We didn't think much of it."

"What was she going to do to me? Take me down with her crutches?"

Pushing past the gates, I reached to her, shedding my jacket and throwing it around her shoulder. "Apologies, my soldiers should have known better."

She waved a bony shaking hand in dismissal. "I would not blame them, my king."

"You've demanded you see me. Does it have to do with my wife?"

She nodded and brought something out from her pocket. And as she did so, dozens of swords were unsheathed around me and made her freeze. The poor woman shook from fright.

"Down!" I shouted and they all retreated. Since when have my soldiers turned to agitated killers?

"It is only a necklace," she said, bringing the glittering jewellery out for me to see. One I could recognise. Snow's necklace? "She gave it to me during the commotion in the city. I have a young granddaughter and the queen wanted me to pay for her care. But when I went to the jeweller to exchange it...I just couldn't. He told me the diamonds were the finest and purest he'd ever seen and the gold in the chains," she explained, lifting it for me to see. "It is a fine one, too. It cost too much. You can give it back to her. If she hadn't persisted on it, I would have not taken it, my king."

Something inside of me swelled with pride. "How old is your granddaughter?"

"Just turned five last autumn."

"My wife would be offended if you gave it back." And probably murderous.

"I thought about it as well since she was quite stern in person. This is why I thought to give it to you."

"I'd hate to keep this one a secret. The necklace is yours. Bring your niece over sometimes, my stepmother invites the schoolchildren in the gardens from time to time. It does her well to keep busy," I said, looking over my guards who suddenly became all conscious about their own actions and hung their heads low. "They will know to let you in next time."

She gently patted my arm. "She is a pretty one. Like the night skies—dark hair and starry eyes. Very pretty."

My smile was wide. "She is."

"And she makes you smile."

"She does."

"You love her."

"I do."

There was no movement beyond the Highwall, not a single footstep marked the snowy grounds behind our side of the wall besides the rainstorms that had murked the white floor of Isjord with a mess of brown. The solid mass of stone for the first time seemed like a barrier of protection rather than the usual cage it had been for us. I'd spend many hours of my days in this tower, constantly overlooking the land of Krig. Wondering if everything would have been different if I had not chosen to lie. Every day, I'd looked beyond the city lands laying ahead and wondered if I'd missed her between the crowds of people. And every day, that lie had thickened, hardened and become less a lie and more of a reality. Convincing myself that I'd signed those papers that night to protect my people had become easier to admit, and soon, everyone had accepted it to be the sole truth.

"I-It doesn't make sense," Atlas said, from where he'd sprawled in the corner of the tower room, covered in all sorts of scriptures and ink. "Esmeray lived at the start of times, why would it have anything to do with Aurora or where the sceptre pieces are hidden? N-not to mention that Silas seems to have no trouble locating these pieces anyhow? Why would he go through so much trouble as to steal a book he cannot even read?"

"It is Silas," Larg said, looking out of the tower window where a winged Olympian was pacing back and forth, observing the ground below for intruders. "I would not be surprised if he did have someone to read it."

"What if it was not Silas?" Mal murmured half unconscious. He'd propped his feet on the table and laid back on the chair, sleeping.

Atlas shot to his feet, tripping on his long robes as he rushed to sit near Mal. "W-what would you mean?"

My brother peeled his swollen, blood red eyes open and said, "Don't you think there was too much noise for how Silas usually works? Why would he need to distract us with the fires to get the diary? We would have never expected someone to steal that while he is searching for sceptre pieces. Why would he need something he cannot read? And why did it so conveniently land right in the hands of someone who can read it?"

"You're not wrong," I said, taking a seat.

"Never been before," he boasted with a big yawn before shutting his eyes again.

Atlas put down the book to look at me. "I-If the queen could read it, we could find out if there is something more there."

"Have her read them," Mal said. "Or are you too afraid that she might want to rain down fire on the heavens, too, if she can reach them."

"If Snow wanted to burn the heavens, she would have. Without that book," Nia said, coming inside the tower room.

Unlike other times, her demeanour was colder. No shadows in sight, her hackles raised and ready for strike. I had to ask her about Driada's necklace, but Mal didn't know anything about it yet. And until I figured what it exactly was and how it would harm Driada, I was not going to worry him. Not in the state he was.

"Here to steal my mother away again?" Mal asked boredly.

"We all have our loyalties, Mal. Mine were born and will die with her." She turned to me. "Alaric wants you present at a meeting with the tribe leaders."

I'd met with him a few times, but this was a first. "And Snow?"

"It doesn't matter. Alaric has a big say in her court and not to mention you practically are an uncrowned king of Olympia. Few tribes are acknowledging you as such already. If the majority overruled Snow on the decision, you'd be king of Olympia. Which by marriage rights you are. These are the Olympian rules and even Snow has to work around them sometimes. Emphasis on *sometimes*."

I raised a brow. "Nia, I won't go against her wishes." Snow must be hating this.

"It's a big deal, you know. Olympians only wed once in their lifetimes. Marriage is sacred. To them, whatever is between you is sacred."

"Cursed. It is what Snow would say."

Nia's mouth parted to speak, several times. As if she couldn't find the words. "If you tell her—"

"Nothing will change, if not, all will be worse. Please forget what you have read in my letters."

"How can I?" she harshly whispered, looking at the others as if it was a secret to keep. "What you are doing now is no less wrong than what you did in Isjord."

"I know."

"Then why do it?"

"Because she needs me to be this." She needs a villain and I would gladly be it no matter the cost.

"I don't think I'll ever understand you. The way that you are."

"Does being infatuated spur this extolling side of you?" She blushed. Her shadows did too, and it brought a smile to my face. "So, am I to know who this infatuation is?"

She crossed her arms. "No."

"Keep that up," I said, pointing to her shadows. "And I'll know pretty soon."

She frowned and looked around the room at the rest. "Don't read my shadows."

"Stop making them available for me to read, Helenia Drava." Offering a hand, I said, "Fade us there. Show me that I've taught you well."

With a sigh, Mal shot to his feet. "I'll take this meeting to be dismissed?"

"One moment," I said to Nia and then chased my brother down the tower exit.

I didn't move for a second, standing at the top of the staircase, watching my brother slowly make his way to the stables. Grim shadows of pain, exhaust and distress weighting over his shoulders. He had been hiding them from me after all. And I'd been an even bigger idiot to not have not worried enough to figure out why.

He struggled to untie the reins from the hitching post, and I faded to his side, undoing them for him. "Forgive me, brother."

With a shaking hand he reached and grabbed the reins from me. "I am not your fault, Kil. Only my own."

I clasped his shoulder and turned him to me, his expression was hooded with sleeplessness. "Tell me how to help."

He shook his head and plastered a grin that did not match all the sombre state of his stare that usually was as vibrant as early autumn. "Keep financing that room I use in Meadow Inn and lovely Selia's services on me, and you can still hold that best brother trophy I made you out of father's pens when I was six."

"Sleep at home, Mal."

"I'd rather not," he said, patting my shoulder and mounting his horse.

"Driada needs you."

"Never been needed much before, and she has you."

"You are her son."

"You've been that to her more than I have ever." With that, he rode away.

Nia's steps trickled down the stairs. "Is something the matter?"

"I don't know, Nia. I don't think I know."

Taren was gloomier than usual. Something sinister lingered in the air. Thunder outside almost seemed to touch land. Lightning blared so close it might as well have hit the castle.

I halted when my foot touched a thick splatter of blood on the ground. A trail of the crimson fluid started from one end of the corridor to the other, streaming over the black and white marble floor.

"Is it her?" I asked Nia who seemed equally as stunned as I.

She looked out one of the glassless round windows. "Yes. She's been in a mood for a couple of days now. She won't speak to anyone except Cai when they've gone for a run through Soren Forest."

Since the day of the attack on Amaris, to be exact. She was back to running again. Back to seeing her nightmares come alive.

Nia jerkily glimpsed around the corridors—afraid. Afraid of Snow.

The torches flared and put off, enshrouding the area in some darkness. A scratching sound came in our direction. Like the tip of a blade brushing against the glassy wall of the castle. Time coated in an odd eeriness and cold. Our breaths misting in the air.

"Come now, little mouse," Snow's light voice crooned, coming in our direction.

Lightning hit the ground close to us, the corridor illuminated and her shadowy form fluttered into sight. Splatters of red marred her face, the red thick liquid had coated her arms elbow deep. She dragged the tip of her dagger along the wall making that screeching sound that itched a bad part of my brain. "Mousy mouse, where are you?"

She came to a stop when she noticed us. Her head cocked to the side, studying Nia and I. I almost didn't recognise her. No, I almost didn't recognise that stare. Cold. Dull. Dead. "Have you seen a little rat come this way by any chance?"

When we didn't answer, she moved again, still tracing the tip of her dagger along the wall. This time she hummed something. Something familiar. "Little mouse can't escape me," she sing-songed loudly and it echoed along the corridor. "Little mouse should come out. Little mice should behave. Little mice shouldn't run away."

Nia stepped forward and then retracted back a step again, almost cautiously. "Snow, leave it. I will send a guard to chase whoever you are looking for."

Snow gave her a menacing grin. "I let her out." Her cackle reverberated along the tall corridors when she took in our stunned reactions. "Never played hide and seek before?"

"Enough," I ordered, and Snow stopped.

Slowly, she turned to me, glaring at me through a hooded dull stare. "I haven't had enough." Faster than I could catch it, she shot a hand forward, a bolt of lightning flashed out of her and landed behind me. The packed magic was so controlled and precise it almost stunned me. "There you are."

My aunt stood at the far end of the corridor, covered in blood and grime, limbs shaking with fear and eyes wide, half wild and mad.

"Little mouse is fast," Snow said, moving toward her.

Adriane had frozen on the spot staring at me. I should have felt sympathy. I should, but I didn't. What I did feel was worry for the woman who seemed nothing like herself.

"How long has she spent in the dungeons?" I asked Nia.

She hugged herself tight, refusing to look at Snow. "Too long. From the moment she returns from you till she goes back to you. Cai kept sending her back from the Fogling attacks because she almost lost control of her magic a couple of times and he is not letting her join them again." Her head lowered with some guilt. "I can't go down there with her. So she has been all on her own."

Alone. Snow hated loneliness. And she battled one demon by torturing the other. Why did she always have to fall to their dark pits to do that?

Snow reached my aunt, fisting her hair and dragging her along the corridor. Adriane didn't shout nor scream nor protest. It was beaten out of her. When I pulled my senses open, I winced at the sheer strength of anguish and pain radiating from the woman I shared my blood with. How could one break another like this? I'd never even seen an Empath ruin someone like this—to the point to be begging for death.

"Put her out of her misery, Snow," I said. "There is nothing left of her anymore. Does this even satisfy you?"

Snow cocked her head to the side to study my aunt, the look so predatory it raised my hackles of caution. "No, it doesn't." She looked up at me with a pout, blinking curiously. "Why do they break so easily? It's no fun." She pulled Adriane's head back and slowly dragged the tip of her dagger over her throat, looking at me the whole time.

My aunt's mouth filled with blood, choking as she dropped to the floor. Snow crouched down to her, hugging her knees as she watched Adriane slowly suffocating and bleeding out.

My whole body tensed at the feel of life seeping away.

When all flare of life left Adriane, Snow stood and sighed, wiping the dagger to her sleeve. "Now I'm bored again. Play with me, Adriatian."

I gripped her face and then backed her to the wall. A breath whooshed out of her when her back met the stone hard. "Enough."

She batted her lashes at me, a wild grin spreading on her face. "Enough what?"

I leaned down to her ear. "Playing with me. This little show was not nearly as good as what I've seen of you before." Deranged. Mad. Sick. I was all of those because this woman could set the world on fire and I add more kindling to it to see it grow bigger. This was driving me mad with worry.

She looked down at Adriane's body and cocked a brow at me. "Am I getting rusty?"

"No," I growled in her face. "You're getting too deep inside that head. Remember when I told you that I'd make that my problem, huh?"

Her smile dropped. "You bore me. I ought to see someone who doesn't bore me." My jaw tightened so hard it could snap and so did my grip on her. That made her simper. "You look like you want to gut my throat."

"There are many things I want to do to your throat, but that isn't one of them." *So many things.*

Her eyes dropped to my mouth and when they returned to me, they blazed. The way she stared at me was different, like I was prey for her to catch and a move for her to make. She'd finally made me her quest.

A throat cleared behind us and it wasn't Nia's. An angry Alaric glared at us. No, he was glaring at Snow. "You've dirtied my corridor."

"Whoops," Snow said, giving him a tight-lipped smile.

He pointed a finger at her. "You will clean it."

Snow gaped and made a sound of protest that didn't quite come out as Alaric's finger returned to point at her again, this time in threat before he stalked down the corridor. "I will return to inspect it, Snowlin Skygard."

"Castemont," I called at him, not taking my eyes off my gorgeously angry wife. "Her last name is Castemont."

Alaric halted and turned to us again, chuckling. "Correct," he said, amused, his eyes going back to my wife. "Not a drop on my marble, Snow Castemont."

Snow's face fell, and that signature feral hellcat sneer of hers was in full force when she turned her glare on me. "I'm going to have so much fun gutting you. Pulling your heart out of your chest string by string."

"Clean your corridor first," I said, giving her a wink and following after Nia and Alaric.

Nia chuckled. "You're going to suffer for that."

"Can't wait," I said, holding the door open for her to pass first.

She sighed, shaking her head. "I don't know if you are disgustingly in love or just delusional."

"Both, Helenia."

Every head swivelled to me when I entered the meeting room, most were welcoming, some curious and two particular ones were brewing in frustration and distress.

I'd just taken a seat when someone tapped on my shoulder. "Your Majesty," a young voice called to me. The girl was young, younger than Penelope. Her long brown hair was pulled back and she wore colourful markings on her forehead. "You sit at the top, near the queen."

I looked to where she pointed and was about to tell her that where I sat was fine, but she told me sweetly, "You're in my seat."

"Cori," an older woman criticised. "Forgive her, Your Majesty, she is the youngest amongst us."

A tribe leader? This young? I stood. "It is alright, and please, call me Kilian."

"Well," Alaric said. "We must commence without Snow. She is rather preoccupied with the corridor upkeep."

A few rumbled with laughter and I was fully confused.

The older man sat on my right leaned in and murmured, "He usually makes her bake goods for the villages when she goes on one of her rampages, but this one must have been a mild one."

My eyebrows raised. "And Snow just...accepts it?"

He nodded. "Alaric's word to her is like law. She always abides by his rules even if she can make new ones and overrule any that he could make. Always."

"Why is that?"

He sighed and his shadows dressed in guilt and worry—not for himself. "She knows what happens if she doesn't. It usually ends up with her hurting someone she is not meant to hurt."

My eyes immediately went to Nia who as I expected was sitting in a dark pool of her thoughts.

"She uses my son as the boundary between good and bad because she finds it hard to set it herself," the older man explained.

"Your son?"

"Alastair Drava," he said in holy greeting. "A pleasure to meet you."

Alaric began reading through reports of trading between the tribes. Soon the direction went from the richness of their mines these past few months to the Fogling attacks. I'd never heard of the creatures before and from the distressed sighs and massive number of losses each tribe leader was counting, they were causing massive concern for Olympians. Nimbus Aura were required to maintain dark skies all year round to avoid being attacked by the dark creatures, and that meant produce was not growing, people were often getting sick, and frost was making it harder for the livestock to feed.

"Why don't you allow me to help," I offered. "If these Foglings feed on light then I'm the right person for the job."

The meeting room went silent.

"And you'd do that?" Alaric asked.

"Yes."

Caiden scoffed. "And *why* would you do that?"

I turned to the cocky general. "I think you know why."

He leaned on the table, glaring at me. "And what price will you charge her now? Make her spend every hour of the day in your presence?"

"We made a bargain, Caiden, she asked of me as much as I asked of her."

He snorted. "Sure you did."

"He is only trying to help, Cai," the young tribe leader said.

The general slanted an entertained look on her. "Cori, you wouldn't know a dagger from a pen till it poked your gut with this one."

"That I can assure you as well," Snow said, coming inside the room, fluffing Cori's hair as she went past to her seat. She'd cleaned up, her hair still dripping wet and soaking the black silks she wore. Once she settled, she glanced at me and then threw a glare on Alaric. "Is this your doing?"

The Regent didn't budge, only faced her head on. "He deserves where he sits. After all, you married him, not me."

She huffed a little laugh. "Why am I being persecuted for the hard choices I had to make to save my lands, Alaric?"

"He will sit by you as he is rightfully king of this kingdom," Alastair said.

What?

Snow burst in a loud cackle. "You'll be with one leg on the grave and still crack some good jokes, old man."

The Dravan leader gave her a crooked smile. "It has been voted on."

While my confusion intensified, my wife's amusement died off and she glanced at every face in the room before settling on Caiden. "What?"

The friend rubbed a hand over his eyes. "It was proposed this morning. Majority won."

Thunder cracked outside. Each strike of lightning matched Snow's furious breathing. "You know he is living under a ticking death sentence, right?

You all know he killed my mother, your queen, right? You all are aware I have spent two long years sabotaging his lands and starving his people and I will ultimately make their younglings crackling for eudemons, right?"

"We know," Alastair said. "Till then, he serves as king. Till you two are not bound by sacred marriage he will serve as king."

"You make wise decisions, my queen," Lazarus, the winged male said before standing. "Told you that wasn't a good one."

Caiden and Nia snorted at the same time and the general gave the two a glare before leaving.

The meeting room slowly emptied after everyone had made sure to pass their greetings and introductions to me, leaving only Snow, her friends, Alaric and I present.

It was the Regent that spoke first, "Finish off what you got going on in the dungeons and bury this hatchet."

Snow leaned back in her chair. "Yes, right in their skulls."

"Snow," the older man said. "When I went there last night, there was no human left in them. Only empty, bleeding shells. You've done it, you've gotten to rip their souls out. End them. Now and fast. You've done enough."

I saw something falter in Snow's golden stare. "Perhaps I ought to chain them to the Valley."

What valley?

"No," Nia said this time. "Please."

Cai stood and left without a word. He hadn't even spared her a glance the whole time. Something felt wrong between the two. I knew I had been right when Snow's expression softened to sadness when he left without a single word.

"It's sunset," Alaric said, standing, too. "Fetch your bride away before she dirties my corridors again."

Nia remained behind, nervously fiddling with the ends of her gloves. "Have you killed him yet?" So much distress flitted around her.

Snow looked out of the windows framing a heavy thunderstorm. "Yes."

Nia sucked in a sharp breath and jade relief floated around her along with a string of sadness. "Alright." Before she left, she stopped at the door, turning to Snow one more time, her eyes wet with tears. "Thank you. Thank you for freeing me. Both times. And I am sorry. I am sorry that the man who took part in killing your mother was...my father."

Snow's attention jerked to her. "He was not your father. Never say that again. You're the daughter of Alaric Drava, heiress of Drava. That is who you are and who your father is."

Nia gave her a small nod before leaving.

"That little act with your court was almost perfect," I said. "Who were you trying to convince exactly?" I'd seen real anger in her. Whatever she had shown moments ago was not even remotely close to it. A good facade—one I'd seen her put up with her father several times before.

She blinked slow. "Bayrd, the Volant tribe leader. I can't put you willingly on the throne, not only because I'd rather pluck my own heart out, but because he has intentions of pulling all his tribe away as his own lands and I am sentenced to only bid my people best wishes. Volant is the biggest city after Taren, their kind is one of the rarest in this realm. Volantian soldiers make for a good part of my army, they are skilled Aura and their lands are some of the most fruitful, I cannot afford to let them go, open a civil war with them or to lose their support, not now at least. Alastair and Alaric both helped arrange the meeting this morning where they won sixteen to two in favour of crowning you king. By my order."

"Why would you need me as king?"

She sighed with true anger. "Alastair believes this will help my people. The Fogling and the Isjordians at our borders, they've lowered morale. The land beyond the mist was made a safe haven for them and my people are running away from it because of all that is happening. My people still rely on and love to believe in relic and archaic beliefs. But if it is what keeps them hopeful, then so be it. If they want the Night King by my side, then a Night King I shall give them."

"You have not formally asked me—to be your king."

She took a deep bored breath and rolled her pretty eyes to me. "Darling of my heart, my sweetness, my all, would you do me the kindness and play pretend to be king until I kill you?"

I leaned back on my seat. "I'll think about it."

"Would threatening to slit Driada's throat or Mal's help you think a bit faster?" Her expression pinched with pain and the silk glove she wore burned on her right hand to reveal the band of our bargain flickering bright.

I tsked and stood to get a water jug from the middle of the table to wet my handkerchief and put it over her hand. "Play nice, love."

She pulled her hand away from me, breathing hard. Not from the imaginable pain that breaking part of the bargain had caused, but from anger.

I'd won a round, and from the deadly look on her face, she'd make sure to win ten others from me.

"Was the pain worth it when you gave Driada that necklace?"

She smirked, a wicked tilt to her face and her eyes lit with fire. "Don't like that, do you? Me messing with your little family."

"No, actually, I don't," I said, leaning back in my seat.

That seemed to please her because she was more amused than what I'd seen her be in ages. "Heard of your little outing," she started. "Hanging is not my thing, I prefer bloodier displays, but it was fascinating to see you do it, nonetheless. What will Adriatians think of this cruelty you've committed on your people?"

"That you are mine and no one touches what is mine without deadly consequence."

Her eyes flashed and grew hooded with gilded ire, but she seemed to quickly recover because a feigned smile was plastered back on. "Your paper leashes are unnecessary."

"Love, if I ever leashed you, you'd know."

"How do I say this simply?" Her mouth curved with to a sneer. "Stop putting claims on me."

"I put a ring on you." I looked at her empty fingers. "Though you chose not to wear it. That claim is called marriage. Want me to explain how that works?" I asked, leaning forward on the table.

She mirrored my movement, coming close to my face and tracing a finger over the silver band I wore on my ring finger. "It melted off my finger. Not lightning approved. Are you lightning approved?"

"Are you flirting with me?" She made to pull away, but I wrapped a hand around her wrist and pulled her to me again. "What's wrong?"

Her lids were heavy with exhaustion. It was perhaps why she said, "Everything."

"Let's start with one."

She swallowed. "There was something that caught my eye in one of the Ahmes Lore pages," she lazily said, pulling a folded piece of paper from her pocket and passing it to me. "All the other symbols have a similar shape in construct, clean cut lines and shapes. Mostly made of circles, squares, crosses and rectangles. This one looked nothing like that. Visha could not read it, nor could any of my court or scholars. Olympians were very secluded before and after the attack, the outer world sparked no curiosity for them enough to learn forgotten languages. There was nothing in our libraries when Visha and I checked. I got a feeling that you might know."

And she was right. "The writing is in old Laoghrikrease, the original language the unblessed spoke before they changed the alphabet to match our common tongue. It means: Vas son of Zoltan, born of…Norodoh." What? Picking up the paper, I flipped it sideways and upside down. No, it still said the same. "Love, are you certain these were the letters?"

She nodded and then leaned forward. "Why is the unblessed Isle named in her diary? Who is Vas, son of Zoltan?"

"I don't know. We have very little on any important figure of the unblessed."

She blinked in surprise. "But you can understand their language."

"Only learned it because I was bored, love, it was not in my teachings. Nothing on the unblessed ever was. Now I'm thinking I should have been more bored and learned more. Only to impress a little Winter Princess."

"You're grating."

"And you like it."

She dropped her head back on the rest and stared at me.

I did the same, staring at her.

And we stayed like that till the sun disappeared along with her light.

Olympia was dark at night, darker than Adriata. The blue light torches did nothing to illuminate the room, only vacuumed the place deeper in that enshrouding darkness. And I wondered if she hated that? If it bothered her. If she'd ever been afraid in her own home—all because of the dark I'd shown her.

Her eyes drooped, full of sleep. When her soft sleepy sighs filled the empty silence, I stood and kneeled before her, picking her body in my arms and fading us to Adriata. Once I'd made her comfortable on our bed, I went to take a bath. The cold water soothed all aches of my muscles, and the creeping dark around me soothed parts of my mind. The quieter, the emptier, the more alone I was, the calmer my magic became. If I felt too strongly it became hard to control. A beast that fed from the strength of my emotions. I'd learnt to tame them by feeling less or not at all.

I had only dried off and pulled my trousers on when cries filtered into the bathing chambers. I'd never ran faster before.

Snow had buried her head in the pillows, her body convulsing and shaking, her hands gripping and tearing the sheets as she struggled in her dreams. Her sobs tore me. Her pleas ripped me apart. Her tears—gods, her tears.

The whole air charged with electricity. The more she struggled in her nightmares, the more build-up of magic solidified—till it became skitters of lightning.

I picked her in my lap, swaying the two of us. My skin burned and tore from the touch of her magic, but I held her tight against me. "Hey, I am here. I am here."

"It burns," she whispered through sobs. "It burns so much." She reached a hand to her back, digging her nails hard on the skin, over her many scars. "Please, please stop."

I blew cold air over her back and smoothed a palm over her scars, and soon she calmed in my hold. "It won't burn anymore. I've got you. It won't burn anymore."

Her fingers clung to my shirt tightly, slowly her cries died off and she hiccupped and sniffled as I ran my fingers through her face. "Shh. I'm here." Slowly, her magic quelled and I rested my forehead on hers. She was so near me yet so far. "You're breaking my heart, love of mine."

Was this how it always was for her when she shut her eyes? Was this why she never slept? Why she refused to shut her eyes when she laid next to me?

"I am sorry, I am so sorry," I murmured, hugging her tight to me as I laid us both back down on the bed. "I am so sorry."

She was in my arms again when there was all reason for her not to be.

CHAPTER TEN

Inimicus

Snowlin

The yawn almost tore my jaw. Surprisingly, I felt well rested and relaxed. For a moment I almost rejoiced. Till it clicked that I had fallen asleep and not woken from nightmares all night. What in the hells? In Adriata at that. Right next to my living nightmare.
Sun. Blue skies. Shit. I'd slept through dawn.

The bed next to me was empty and I still wore the dress from yesterday, but all the jewellery was gone and piled on the bed side table. When did I take those off?

Quickly, I shovelled them up and headed for the doors.

"Don't leave," Kilian said. Sat back on his table, he flipped through a pile ton of documents in deep concentration. His hair was wet and the shirt he wore clung to his muscled body. "There is something I need to discuss with you first."

"Discuss it then," I said, facing the windows attempting to clasp my necklaces back on with the help of the faint reflection.

He stood and reached close behind me, taking the clasps from my hands, my fingers brushing his for a moment—only a small and simple moment but my chest swelled painfully from the hard breath I took. Gently, he lifted my hair, piling the stands over my shoulder before fixing the necklace to sit straight on me. I bit on my lip to trap a gasp when he ran his fingers down the nape of my neck, ever so softly. The only man who touched me like he could break me. Perhaps he knew that.

"How did I take them off?"

"I took them off, you fell asleep with them on," he said, trailing a sole finger down my exposed spine and I breathed out a long sigh just to free my chest from the suffocation of what was bubbling inside of me.

I'd missed it. I'd missed that touch. Maybe...maybe if I shut my eyes, I wouldn't feel betrayal against all I believed in. My voice was airy as I asked, "Why did you not wake me?"

I felt him take a step closer to me, his warm breath touched my temple and I shivered. "Why would I wake you? You were sleeping so peacefully." He rested his forehead on the side of my head, trailing a hand up my arm to warm the shivers inching over my skin.

For a second, only for a split second, he was the guard in Isjord. Not the man who had taken everything away from me.

"Open your eyes, Snow."

And when I did, reality crashed over me and I flinched hard.

He moved away from me and my body gradually grew cold again. "Visha came to see me a couple of days ago and she agreed to what I proposed. I've gathered a team to search for your siblings," he said. "They will need to meet up with Visha and decide with you how they will collect your siblings' essence to place the trace craft."

I picked the list he held out for me. Atlas was there but I knew none of the rest. "Where is Mal's name?" Did he think I would trust a single name on that list to search for my siblings?

Kilian rubbed a hand over his eyes, looking tired. "He will not join it."

I crushed the paper on my hand and stalked out of his room. The corridors were almost identical to one another and so were the doors. It took me many tries and turns to find his bedroom.

When I flung the door open, Mal only stirred a little. The idiot had not even made it on the bed because he sat on the floor, his back on the edge of the bed, head hung low with his long, unbound hair covering half of it while he snored fast asleep.

"Wake up," I said, kicking his leg and he jumped to attention.

"Sister-in-law," he mumbled with a loopy grin, stretching his arms, the shirt riding up to reveal a sliver of skin marked with tattoos. "Welcome to my domain."

"Get up."

He cocked his head back and stared at me with those sad eyes he had given me since my return. "I can hear you fine from down here."

I leaned down to his face. "Get up, Malik or I'll give you something else you can see pretty well from down a six-foot grave."

He stood on wobbly legs and headed right to the drink stand, forgoing the glass altogether and chugging the whole bottle.

The moment he lifted the bottle to his lips, it froze. "I need you sober."

He sighed, lowering down the brick of ice I'd turned his drink to. "I'm much fun drunk. The world, too, is much fun when it's spinning."

"Malik," I gritted out.

He cocked a brow up. "Snowlin? Are we going by our ministerial names now?"

"Your brother says he's picked out a team to search for my siblings. I don't want a team. I want *you* to look for them."

He waved a hand, dismissing me. "Nia can surely lead the team."

"Nia is in Eldmoor where she will be for the foreseeable future. She is also, might I remind you, fairly new to her magic. Besides her you're the next I'd think of doing this."

"That you can trust?"

Well...if it took a lie to convince him. "Sure."

"But do you trust me?" I hesitated and he grinned. "You will threaten me with my mother, won't you?"

"Yes." It was better if he already knew my intentions. "Your brother, too." The seal on my hand burned a little and I winced.

"Since I am at such a crossroad I will have to obey, I suppose." With no warning, he pulled the edges of his shirt up and over his head, tossing the thing aside. Like his brother, he was corded in muscles and little scar striations. Different from Kilian, Mal's torso and arms were all covered in black tattoos. They extended everywhere and dipped to the waistband of his britches. He rubbed a hand over his chest and turned around to what looked like a bathing chamber.

I nodded to myself and let out a low whistle at the artwork on his back. "Wow." Shortly startling out of my skin when I turned around to find Kilian leaning on the doorway, arms crossed over his chest and a smug look on his face. He cocked his head back and did that tongue in cheek thing he always did.

"What?" Kicking away a few pillows from Mal's bed, I sat down and leaned back on the poster. His space was not what I'd imagined it to be. It was all soft edges and pale colours, light and sweet. When I tipped my head back, I gaped a little. The ceiling was a mural of bloom. From one end to the other, all sorts of flowers were painted in the most colour I'd ever seen.

"He's done them himself," Kilian said, taking a seat beside me and dropping his head back on the poster to stare at the ceiling. "Mal used to love painting. If he was mad or sad or angry, it was all he did—never lashed out his feelings. Instead, he poured them into paintings. He managed to convince me to convince our father to get him a scaffold to do all that. All the ones in my chambers are done by him, too." A beat of silence followed before he added, "Then it stopped. His hands were no longer stained with paint. His actions were."

I turned my head to look at him. "Why?"

He turned to look at me too. "I think colours dulled for him when he learned what they meant. Human emotion is ugly whether it is in rosy shades of happiness or navy shades of malice. They will always have ugly undertones. Happiness is often shaded with blues of selfishness, and malice sometimes wears pearl shimmering clouds of innocence. It is never simple. And never innocent."

Yet when Mal had spoken of his brother's, they seemed like they were the most vivid he'd ever seen. Pure, too.

"What?" Kilian asked after I remained silent, pushing a strand of hair out of my face. A touch so gentle from such a poisonous hand.

"The way you speak about Mal—you really care about him. Really, really care for him. The type of care that would turn to harrowing pain if he was to be gone."

His fingers stopped on my brow and the look on his face shifted.

That was the most reaction Kilian had ever given to my warnings. It made me simper—my grin was vile. "Yes, Your Majesty, I can and will hurt your brother. And it will taste so sweet. Your pain will be delicious." The seal of the bargain burned at the words, but the pain was rather soothing. "It was my vow to you, *husband*." Slowly, I moved to straddle his lap. "It is your demise I want, not your death," I whispered, running a finger over his pouty lip. This man. This man was the reason for my insanity. Actually, I had to be pretty insane to let him be the reason for my insanity. I wanted him out of my head. For that, I needed him to fight me. Anger me. Provoke me. So I could show him how truly insane he made me. Last night I'd decided I'd get what I wanted from him. But first I had to find out what exactly I wanted from him. Maybe he could be my sickness and my cure.

He sighed, dropping his head back and staring at me with that taunting and haunting silver peer that was the cause of my nightmares and the root of all of my want. *Just once, be afraid of me. Just once let me taste your fear like you tasted mine.*

"You have no idea, do you?" His hands went to my hips and up my waist, leaving shivers behind my traitorous body. The way he stared at me...no man had ever looked at me like that—like he needed me to breathe. "Have your fill, love. I'm feeling pretty damned right now." One of his hands lingered over the thigh slit of my dress, pulling to expose my leg and

I couldn't help but squirm on him, he'd lit me like a match. It was too much. All of it. He had barely touched me, yet I felt him everywhere on my skin—like a cursed mark. "Tell me why you flinch from me," he said, the tip of his fingers brushing my thigh just a little but enough to have me humming with warmth. "Tell me why."

Heat pounded between my legs. My mouth had gone dry, and I was angry—furious at myself. "Because I hate it." *Because I'm terrified I'll enjoy it and want more. Want you more than I already want you.*

A smile painted his face. "My pretty liar." The moment his warm skin met my cold one, my whole body blazed alive in a way only he had ever managed to. Gently, he ran his knuckles on my inner thigh and my limbs suddenly went weak. "The things I want to do to you, Snow. To have you how I want you and to be damned to never be able to. You're my heaven and my hell. Blessed and cursed me. I'm damned. Forever damned."

There was nothing I could do or say, he always found a way to stun me to silence.

He wrapped an arm around my waist, pulling me closer to him so our chests met, and he kissed my cheek before leaning to whisper in my ear, "My divine and my ruin." His soft lips descended down my neck, leaving slow wet kisses on my skin. And I let him. Starved for him—I let him. "Only you could make me beg for ruin." His warm breath rose gooseflesh all the way down my spine and legs, a lick of pleasure trickling between my thighs. "Only you can make me crave ruin," he murmured before running his tongue over my pulse. "Only you."

How did he have so much power over me, dictate my breaths and my heartbeat? My eyes pulled closed tightly. Sick. I was sick for allowing this. He'd made me sick. Purposefully. He still was doing all this with purpose. With purpose to sway me. Perhaps he wanted me to hate myself the way I did for wanting him.

He pulled back and slapped my bottom enough to sting. The smack shook me to my senses, too. Palming and kneading the burn away he said, "Now get off my cock. My brother has enough trauma as it is."

Mal strode in, a towel around his waist as he dried off his hair with another and I pushed from Kilian, sitting back on my spot. My ears felt hot and I was sure my face was probably burning up. Fair mention went to the sweet spot below my belly which still hummed at the memory of his hands on me. If his fingers had grazed just an inch higher, he would have felt and known what his touch did to me.

The younger brother frowned when he saw us on his bed. "Family meeting now, huh? Will this be a common thing? I ought to know when I have company over. Half of the women in Adriata think you've eaten my heart and I'm a puppet of your evil. Imagine when the other half see you in my room."

I scoffed. "I don't eat meat, especially not hearts. And you *are* a puppet of my evil, Mal sweetheart. I'd feed your heart to Memphis though, but she prefers bloodier parts."

"The morph likes livers?" he asked, putting clothes on.

I stood and gave him a pat on the shoulder. "Further down south. She'll even tear it off you, I don't even have to do anything."

He winced and cupped his treasures. "Ouch."

With its own will, my body turned to take one last glance at Kilian, and the idiot winked at me. He winked at me. Winked! "Be good, love."

I grabbed and dragged Mal out of the room, too angry and afraid I might just gut his spleen out and eat it while he watched. "Let's go."

My witch had crossed her arms and stared at Mal like he was a specimen for her to test on. Perhaps he was. But the two knew one another since young, perhaps more than I knew them. His father, the previous king, had been a close supporter of Urinthia's.

From the look on her face, I'd finally found Visha Delcour's bane. Nothing satisfied me more than watching her react.

"You reek of death," my witch said boredly, her dull stare carefully tracing Mal's movement around her chambers.

He sneezed. "You don't smell particularly nice to me either, Visha."

"Don't bring spirits in my alcove, it affects my craft."

Mal mimicked Visha's stance. "Protect your alcove better, witch." He flicked off a bouquet garni hanging overhead, sending it flying across the room. "Death comes with me, it is not something I can control."

Visha's dull gaze turned to me. "I beg of you."

My smile grew wicked. "My pardon?" I asked, cupping a hand over my ear and batting my lashes.

"I don't like working with children," Visha said, pointing to Mal who had quickly moved to explore her herb concoctions by the windows.

"I'm sure children don't like working with you either," I echoed back.

She calmly closed her eyes. "My queen," her voice was monotone, but I knew to recognize when she was annoyed. "Please find another Umbra."

"I'm an Empath," Mal said before accidentally dropping a large vase to the ground. "Shit. Hope that wasn't important." His grin told me perhaps it wasn't accidental.

I picked a garni from her bunch and for some odd reason I sniffed it only to regret it a moment later when the sulphuric smell burned my eyes. "You will work with him, no one else."

She snatched the garni from my hand. "What have I ever done to you?"

Mal chuckled and snatched the garni I held a moment ago from her hand. "Be nice, Visha, we have known one another since before we could walk. This will be fun." He winced at the smell, too, before throwing it out of the window. "That was a disgrace to flowers."

Visha sighed. "It was not flowers. It was sour poison root for the rats." She pointed a look on him. "Seems like it didn't work anyway." Reaching behind the large marble table where she usually performed her craft on me, she grabbed and dropped a red leather grimoire atop. "There are three possible ways for us to go forth with this as I've discussed with Kilian. One: we venture inside your dreams, grab their essence and I place a tracking spell. Most efficient and quickest."

"Two ways then," I said, hoping to sit on the table as she flicked the coffee-coloured paper. Definitely not doing that. A Dark Crafter's duty in this realm was to send off spirits to the otherworld. Celesteel despised denied and ungiven peace after death. The cold god of death was most compassionate in a sense—besides those he deemed unworthy of heavens which he sent right to hells. But those were plenty warm, too, so perhaps he was a gentle soul after all. If my siblings weren't alive, the presence of her magic would banish them off to pass on. And if they were alive, she'd banish my mother.

She parted the grimoire over some strange drawings of a cloak. "The other is to perform a blood craft tracking on them, but if they are under a veil or craft or any other magic, it will not work. Blood scent craft can be nulled under spell."

I shot to my feet and glanced at her grimoire. "But we found Melanthe."

She pointed to a line in Borsich like it was supposed to make all sense to me. "We traced my cousin's magic signature which she and her sister share. You and your siblings all wear a separate magic signature from the mix of your bloodlines. You're an Elding, an already overpowering magic which makes certain essences from you deviate from theirs."

Mal nodded. "Most reasonable one so far is the blood craft if we are lucky enough and Aryan didn't think that far as to use magic to hide them," he said, rubbing a hand over his stubbled jaw. "What about the third option?"

"Manual search," she said, shutting the grimoire. "I will give you a memory potion to access deep parts of subconsciousness, to places and situations you might have forgotten. If they were locked anywhere, it had to be nearby. Otherwise, who would look after their wellbeing? A nearby place you are probably aware of, somewhere Aryan visited, a place where your siblings' magical imprint could be hidden."

I nodded. "Give me the potion."

She reached onto her cabinets and retrieved a flask with lavender coloured liquid inside. "I'd suggest you take it with someone in the room. Though you can direct the memory magic to target a specific thing you are searching, it can sometimes manifest into the spiritual to show you something else. There are some memories our brain locks with the purpose not to ever remember." She gave me a little glance full of doubt before saying, "And I am sure you might have plenty of those."

"Sure," I said, snatching the thing from her hand.

"Before you consume it, think of what you wish to find in your head. I suggest you find a calming environment and someone who centres you. If your thoughts are all over the place it will probably get you lost elsewhere."

"Mhm," I hummed, shaking the glistening bottle to make the lavender pieces at the bottom float around.

It was only a couple of hours before I had to retreat to Adriata, but I supposed it was enough to get this over and done with. Paper, ink, and the potion were set up on my bed. Nia was in Eldmoor, Cai had set up camp in Myrdur, Alaric was in Kvan assisting Cori and Penelope was being trained by Visha in craft so that left me to do this alone.

I sat on the bed, laying the pen and paper before me and then took a sip of the little bottle of lilac liquid that tasted like cat piss and rainbows all in one. There was no time for me to gag because my sight was veiled with flashing blurred sights.

My pulse drummed loud enough to drown the thunder outside and once it calmed, the images sharpened and slowed, allowing me to grasp a clear view.

Isjord. Training courts.

I was on my hands and knees, my fingers smaller and bloodied. I was in my own body, yet I wasn't. No movement I made was my own. I was merely a spectator.

My whole body jerked when a ghostly whip hit my back. Blindly, I reached a hand back to touch my flesh, expecting it to burn, but nothing met my touch besides the old scars. The whip hit again and again. Yet I felt nothing.

"Break, I said," A gravelly voice growled in my ear. *"Break!"*

The man suddenly roared in agony before collapsing before me. I held a rock in my hand. No, not me. Younger me. *"How about I break your toes?"*

Something tugged on my head, and I was no longer just watching—I was one with my thoughts again.

"Hold her back," Renick shouted at the guard behind me as he limped backward with a bleeding foot. *"Hold the goddamn thing back."*

Soldiers surrounded me, but no one dared approach. They'd never come closer than that. Only Renick, uncle and Murdoc could come near me.

"Play with me, Renick," I cooed, and the man shivered with what father had taught me to be a play of fear. Perhaps he was playing with me. No one wanted to play with me.

Suddenly, a hand wrapped around my wrist—a much larger hand, decorated with heavy gold rings that made my body recoil at the memory of the pain they gave me when he hit me. "You're embarrassing, Renick," *Aryan spat before dragging me out of the training courts.* "I'll show you how to break more than toes, Olympian scum."

Father stood on the balcony overlooking the courts, observing everything that went on, and I smiled and waved at him. "Papa."

With one last look of scathing disdain, he turned round and left. And like that, my smile died. I hadn't seen anyone in days. Not my mother, or Alaric. Even Thora and Eren were kept away from me. Father didn't want to see me either. He was getting angrier by the day. I was at the age to bloom my blessing, to become an Aura. I was not giving him what he wanted. Ma, Alaric, Lysander and Eren, all of them had made me swear on the secret and wear the seal that contained the magic I'd bloomed since the day I breathed air into my lungs.

Blood dripped with every step I took, and weariness began setting at the loss of it, but Aryan didn't stop. Not till we reached his side of the castle. I normally never fought against being taken or hurt, it usually never worked and then I just didn't care.

He pushed me into one of his rooms, my feet wobbled, and I landed on the ground with a thud. My palms left bloody prints when I attempted to help myself up and the motion made my back burn, too, the scars chaffing to my shirt.

"You will want to see this," he said, kicking me hard in the stomach. "Stand."

His hit never scared me, but the way my mind commanded me to be still and expect the pain made me afraid that father was perhaps getting what he wanted.

My limbs shook as I attempted to stand again. Barely, I managed to straighten and level a bored look at him and his usually twisted plays. I'd seen enough to get used to them.

He returned with a woman from the conjoined chamber—she had bruised legs, a torn shift and a bag thrown over her face. Had he beaten her too?

Aryan knelt before me, a grin spread wide and vile in his twisted mouth with half chipped teeth. "I've got a little surprise for you and you will love it." *With that ominous promise, he stood and removed the sack from the woman's head.*

Shivers ran through my body and my stomach sank when I saw the face of the beaten woman. She wore the face of my mother. "Ma?"

"Shhh," *Aryan said, putting a finger to his lips.* "Listen to this." *His laugh was odious as he kicked her—as he kicked my mother.* "Speak."

"I...I don't know what to say," *the woman stuttered out.*

She sounded like mother. It was her. I reached forward, clutching her hand in mine, the touch felt unfamiliar but I hadn't seen her in months. Last I saw her, she didn't even want to get anywhere near us—near me because she had held Thora. "Ma, you're supposed to be going with father up north. Why are you with him? Why are you like this? Ma, please, tell me what is wrong?"

Mother's face twisted in confusion before she glanced at Aryan who was red from holding in his laugh. "I am not—"

A hard slap silenced her. Aryan breathed furiously as he grabbed my mother's hair and pulled her head back. "What did I tell you?!"

Mother trembled and cried in his grip and my whole body tensed as I reached for the fire poker beside me and struck Aryan with all my might on his knee.

The impact must have been grave because he dropped down with a cry, clutching his limb.

Quickly, I grabbed mother's hand and pulled us away from the room.

She stopped the two of us, shaking her head and going back to Aryan's side, helping him up. My heart charred and splintered in two. She never chose us. She never chose me. Always someone else. Her kingdom, her secrets, our powers. Why was I never the one to be chosen first before all that? And now...now, him? "Please, ma." *Traitorous tears threatened to leave my eyes, but I'd rather have burned before Celesteel himself than cry before Aryan.*

"Tell her to come here," *he ordered her, pointing to me.*

My mother lowered to her knees and opened her arms. "Come here, child."

Mother wanted to embrace me. She wanted to hold me. I wanted to hold her too. Her embrace was not warm though. It was like the taste of porridge—bland.

I startled when Aryan cuffed a chain to my wrist and pulled me to the wall where he placed the chain against a tall hook. "Make sure to keep those pretty yellow eyes wide open, Snowlin."

He grabbed the fire poker, and before I could grasp what he was about to do, he struck down on my mother.

"No!" *I screamed and thrashed, the chains holding me back. Electricity bubbling beneath my fingertips and it took all of my sheer will to hold it back. To hide it.* "Stop!"

He stopped and turned to me. "Say please."

Never. Never. Never. Mother herself had told us that nothing mattered more to the world than protecting the world. Nothing should matter to me more than not letting father have his victory. To never let him break us, bend us and use us.

He knew that without even me speaking. "I'll still enjoy this regardless." *Again and again he hit her and I crumbled to the ground, sentenced to watch my mother being beaten to her death. He hit and hit her till blood was pooling and separating on the tiles, leaking down under the door and onto the corridor.*

I didn't scream or cry. It was how father had told me—it was how mother had told me, too.

It was dark outside when he had finished. It was dark and I was afraid that it had become darker inside me.

Aryan kneeled before me. "Silas will be proud," *he said, untying me.* "Raised a good soldier. If only you could bloom your damned blessing, you'd serve the goddamn purpose you were born for."

There. That new sense of numbness I'd grown used to settled in me. "Is mother dead?"

He grabbed my face with his bloodied hands, and I shivered. "It was not your mother, you little daft thing. Only an Eldmoorian whore from Ulv Islet prison who used to scam men to their deaths with this little trick of hers."

Shifter elixir. I'd heard of those before. It masked one's appearance to look like another. "Uncle," I said quietly.

His mouth twisted in a sneer. "What?"

"One day—"

"One day I will have your head on a pike and play with the caterpillar that will eat out your brains," I finished the sentence as the memory flared away, and I returned back to my body. It had stopped. The memory had stopped but the bitter taste of it made me reach a hand to my stomach as if the flesh there would be sore as it once had been.

Someone shook me. "Kid?"

Alaric's scarred face sharpened, and he stood in front of me. "What—" A hand went to my throat. It hurt and burned as if I had been screaming.

He ran a hand through my hair and pursed his lips. "Why do you do that to poor old me, kid? Scaring me to death would not be a good idea. It would scare me to *actual* death."

"What are you doing here?" I looked around to make sure I've not sleepwalked to Kvan, only to face him.

He stood there, arms crossed, and his brows pulled in a scowl, staring down at me with those cold eyes that made me shiver. Anger was a strange look on him, the way his face morphed into gelid sternness reminded me who I was looking at. The Obscur Asteri, not Kilian.

"Why is he here?"

Alaric turned to him. "Thank you for getting me, son."

Confused, I rose to my knees. "Get you?"

My guardian took the lilac liquid flask Visha had given me and chucked it into the fireplace, sparks of lilac fluttering in the room. "Whatever you took alerted the bargain you made with him. He tried to wake you but couldn't."

A knock rasped at the door and Penelope peeked her head in before letting Visha through.

She hadn't even properly bowed at me when Kilian said, "I will kill you, Visha Delcour. I will kill you a forever death."

Little specks of shadows materialised in his air to form a shadowy mass around his body, and I jerked a little. When he caught that little movement, his face turned into a mirror of ice and all traces of his magic vanished in a matter of seconds.

Visha didn't even blink at the threat. "The instructions were clear. It is not in my power to dictate how she chose to proceed."

"It is Snow we are talking about," Kilian growled, and the torches blew off leaving the fireplace alone to serve as a source of light. "You should have made sure she was with someone, maybe even stayed there before giving her the elixir."

"I'm not a child, Your Majesty," I protested, standing to my feet.

He pointed a finger in threat and all shadows in the room shivered and disappeared as if they were afraid. "You don't even get to speak anymore, Snowlin."

"Excuse me?"

"Heard me right, you damned brat. Scared Alaric half to death, fully scared me to mine." He pointed that accusatory finger back at Visha. "Let her do something like that again and I swear it to you, Visha, I will deliver you to your mother in pieces."

She winced. My Crafter winced.

Alaric stood, wiped a sleeve to his eyes and patted Kilian's arm. "You seem to be better at this telling off thing than me, son. I'll leave it to you."

Visha bowed and left with Alaric, yet the air felt even heavier—denser.

Kilian crossed his arms and steeled a hard glare on me. "Do you ever think about them? Alaric, Nia, Cai, your kingdom? Do you ever think of anything when you decide to be reckless?" he asked with quiet menace.

"We'd left this caring attitude back in Isjord, darling."

"Answer me."

"I don't think I want to."

He crossed the distance between us in two steps, towering over me with that glacial stare. He breathed furiously, our chests meeting each time, and I backed away. He chased my steps till my back was to the wall, blocking me from escaping the closeness that was beginning to become the reason for my insanity. "Never have I seen a grown man, steeled by war and suffering, a general that legends speak of in high praises of a callous heart that spared none, crying because he couldn't wake his daughter when she was screaming bloody death. Since you do not wish to answer me, I'll answer for you." He rested a hand on the wall and bent down a little to bite the words to my face, "No, you don't seem to care at all."

How dare he? How dare he hold these moral lectures when he was the most immoral one? "Are you quite done?"

He straightened and that gaze turned hooded and scrutinous. "You want to do reckless shit on your own, be on your own," he said, backing away. "I break oath for a night, she might stay in her home." The seal on our hands greyed a little, and then he faded out of sight.

I scoffed at the emptiness I was left in. This was absurd. Did he think this was some sort of punishment for me? Why was everyone acting like I needed any help?

A small noise from the corner of my room pulled my attention and Pen stood there, on the corner. "I don't think anyone quite saw me when I entered."

With a groan, I dropped to my bed.

"He was right, you know," she said quietly, unravelling the curtain ties to block the cold wind of Olympian nights from blowing in.

"Run, carrot, because I'm itching to skin something."

"Skin me all you want, but you were screaming so hard that Taren was almost set on fire from lightning," she huffed before running out of the room.

CHAPTER ELEVEN

Ver

Snowlin

And a punishment it had been. Two nights now that he had let me stay in Olympia. Two nights that I had not shut my eyes not even once—not for a full minute.

The dining room stood empty as I sat there all on my own, without touching my food. My hunger had subdued since my return to Olympia, and everything tasted beyond bland. The memory elixir Visha gave me had done more damage than help. My nightmares were not only of the night of the attack, but they were also of my mother being beaten to her death. Why had the elixir shown me that particular memory out of them all? It made no sense.

Everyone was out running errands and carrying my orders, Malik had chosen to accompany Cai on Myrdur territory after they had sighted a new group of Isjordian soldiers making their way through the ruins. Visha remained hunched over my library in search of a tracing spell to uncover my siblings, blinding herself to the countless words she was reading with no rest whatsoever. I'd sent Memphis with Nia to Eldmoor in another attempt to discreetly infiltrate Red Coven in search of any tell that Urinthia was aiding my father. They were known as lovers of chaos and disturbance—they might be enjoying all that is happening or even recreate my biggest fear and join my father in his march of death across the continent.

I dropped my head to the table, tired from all the disturbing thoughts and hit the cold hard surface several times in frustration. Never had I felt more useless. There were too many loose threads, and my brain was steaming from burnout.

"Usually, it takes you less contemplating and no head banging to eat. What is the matter, love?" The rough, cold voice startled me upright in my seat, the backrest meeting my head with a bang. He'd kept distance from me since two nights ago when he brought Alaric to shake me out of the memory. Like he was mad at me. Like he could even be mad at me in his position.

Rubbing one hand over my red aching forehead and another at the bump forming on the back of my head, I glowered at him.

Kilian stood at the archway, studying me and the untouched food that laid in front of me, his eyes roamed about the large dark dining room and he approached to take the seat next to mine.

"What are you doing here?" I asked, confused at his sudden appearance.

"Why are you not eating?" he questioned sternly, and I narrowed my eyes, annoyed. With a heavy and almost angry sigh, he leaned back. "Did you sleep well last night?"

"Like the dead," I said, shovelling food in my mouth.

"And?" he asked, filling me a cup of water. "Did you reflect on your wrongs?"

My nerves burned, but I kept calm. "I did. I've decided to be good now. My soul is all glued back together, I've taken an open spot up in the mountains with the monks and pray for salvation, taken few more knitting classes to knit scarves for the less fortunate and no more premarital fucking. I've decided to eat my greens, too. It was enlightening, really." I grabbed something on the plate and bit on it only to spit it out after. A carrot. I shuddered.

He smiled and grabbed a slice of the orange vegetable from my plate. "You are married. And greens, huh? That's a good girl."

My tongue bled from how hard I'd bit onto it. Idiot. "Why are you here?"

"Because I know you missed me."

My jaw was locked tight. "To death. Truly."

He smiled and took another one of my carrots. "Visha sent a message for me, something along the lines that I am wanted here. By you."

"What?" Just as I was to argue back to his claims, Visha barged inside the room, half panting, her shimmering red coils still springing back and forth from the force of her run. Visha didn't run. Visha didn't rush. Visha didn't even blink if it wasn't utmost necessary. All alarms of caution rose.

"Your father," she wheezed. "Isjord is in Hanai. They have the sceptre piece. His troops are in Aru, near the sacred land of Ryuu. A vision. I had a vision. I had several visions." That is why she had called Kilian as well.

Both myself and Kilian shot up from our seats and I began shedding my jewellery to the ground along with my dress, heading to my chambers and grabbing the dark grey leathers and my brother's sword.

"The Ryuu you said?" Kilian asked, helping me button up my leathers.

Visha gave him a jerky nod. "The second piece, it has to be there. It makes sense. It is protected and the caves underneath the root of Ryuu could act as hiding space for it."

His face grew dark. "Visha, the Ryuu is sacred ground. Magic doesn't work within the land of the blossom alder."

Pushing my legs into the bottoms, I gave them both a ridiculous look. "So?"

"Why would the sceptre be there?" he asked, kneeling to do the laces on my boots.

After pulling the last button of my britches through, I grabbed and sheathed my sword. "I will find out. Visha, portal me there."

"No," Kilian said, standing. "I am fading the both of us there. Not a chance you are going to risk yourself twice within seventy-two hours. Not on my damned watch." He pulled my hood up and pinned the veil down. "Hold tight, we've done this before, but this is a far journey so we will have to fade a couple of times."

Before we faded, I turned to Visha. "Let the council know."

In a flash, we were in the middle of a white blinding field of snow, buried up to my waist onto a snow pile. Nausea threatened to raise up my throat as I dry heaved for a few moments.

A strong hand rubbed my back gently soothing me. "I'm fine," I blurted defiantly, shaking him off.

"Take a minute," he said, pushing branches of black hair that had stuck to my clammy forehead.

"I said I'm fine."

"And *I* said take a minute," he growled and made no move to fade us again.

"You know I can just bolt there."

"Fine, alert the whole of Dardanes of your existence, let's see how good that will do to you."

"You get a kick proving me wrong, don't you?"

"I think it's you who gets a kick when you defy me."

"Defy you?" I asked, stunned.

He wrapped his huge arms around me, pulling my body flush against his. "You heard me," he bit out and faded again.

Two trips later and we'd breached past the Hanaian lands.

My insides were in knots, but I managed to shake myself to attention. It was eerie quiet, the sway of autumn wind lulled a frightening calm around us and the cascading sunset was not doing it any favours. At least it would conceal us better.

The old forest swayed in colours of mahogany dulled by sunset, it seemed undisturbed. My attention drew to a line of limestone plaques that laid around it for what seemed like miles. There were strange runes engraved atop, some familiar and some not, but then I did doze off on that particular lecture.

"They are here," Kilian said, kneeling and running a hand over the runes.

"Visha's visions are steps ahead. They can't be here yet."

Kilian shook his head. "No, they are here already. The veil of magic is fraying with foreign disturbance." As I made to step past the band, Kilian gripped my arm. "The plaques act as a shield, no magic is allowed beyond their line. Beyond them is the sacred ground of goddess Ryuu."

I jerked from his grip and unsheathed my daggers. "Good thing I rarely rely on it."

We pushed past the limestone plaques and through the maze of the hazel forest. Past the rune plaques it felt like the season had changed. The forest was a shining juniper, and the wind was soft and warm, like spring. My first breath in this part of the land felt different, deeper and unrestricted. For the first time in my life, I didn't feel a cinder block pulling me under. My chest rose and fell faster and faster attempting to salvage what I'd never felt before—normalcy. However, it was odd. Magic still itched at my fingertips. Not as prominent, but I felt it flutter against whatever hovered in the air that suppressed the flow of magic.

Suddenly, my back was pulled onto a hard chest, and a hand over my mouth. Turning over my shoulder, I shot Kilian a glare.

He put a finger to his lips and then pointed beyond a thick section of greenery leading to a colossal elder tree with white blossoms spanning almost all over the roof of the forest—white soft petals shed from its branches giving the wind a sweet scent and a melancholic sway.

Metal clanked loudly, signalling the presence of others. Swiftly, the two of us creeped close to the commotion. Hanaian soldiers held back a group of masked attackers crawling from a passage under the roots of what I figured was Ryuu. The moment I took note of a chest bearing the Hanaian tree of life crest, I pushed past and slid on the fresh soil, my daggers slicing their heels as I spun and manoeuvred the blade back and forth piling lifeless bodies before me. The more blood pooled over the fresh soil, the closer I got to the sceptre piece. Even outnumbered, Kilian and I managed to gain the upper hand over the attackers—the Night King was a titan with and without his magic.

Just as I was about to reach the chest, a blood curdling roar tore through the air and I was toppled to the ground, a massive body shielding my own.

Hells. Every inch of me hurt and felt bruised.

"Kil...Kilian?" I groaned, feeling my ribs constrict every breath I took. Wetness pooled where my palms met his chest and then I felt a wet stream trickle down my neck. Raising a hand to my throat, I touched the warm and thick liquid.

Blood.

I couldn't breathe.

The world began spinning and I tried to lift his limp body from my own. "Kilian?" Panic gave me a strange strength and I pushed till he flopped beside me. Three stripes that looked like a claw mark had torn through his jacket and dug inch deep wounds on his chest. Oh, gods. Oh, gods. "Wake up. Open your eyes, you idiot. Wake up!"

Another roar made me spin in place and I reached for my brother's sword. Glancing behind me at Kilian's limp sight, I held my sword ready. Leaves crunched close to me, and I spun taking note of my surroundings, noting the north flow of wind and the sway of hazel tree branches.

Crunch.

The wind whistled and there was another crunch.

Closing my eyes, I waited and waited till I felt a swift breeze brush my side. My affinity with wind had never been through magic. I was Nubil born. The flow of wind was like the flow of my blood. I'd spent most years of my life trying to understand it and studying it. It spoke to me—in many ways.

I twisted the handle of my sword down and pushed the blade back with the support of my other hand, piercing it on the thing behind me. Hot air and a rotten stench brushed my temple for a second, the steady breaths of whatever I'd stabbed made it seem as if I'd only nicked it with a toothpick.

In a flash, I pulled the blade out and spun, lowering to my knees and pushing it again upright and right on the massive green beast's belly. What...the...hells and heavens?

Viridescent scaly skin dressed every inch of an eight-foot lizard looking wolf. A viscid slaver dripped from its mouth that peeled in a growl to reveal a set of neat sharp fangs.

A shiver crept up my spine. The way its animated dull malachite stare bored onto me—it was almost as if it was actually...*looking* at me. Knowingly. His eyes were remotely and disturbingly human.

Both its claws latched on my blade, breaking skin and drawing black blood from its palms, before pulling my sword out of its wound. Only when it fully left flesh did the thing roar in what looked like pain. The beast faltered back a few steps, swaying on its heavily clawed feet.

Looking around, I noted the dead Hanaians littering the ground, claw marks all over their lifeless bodies. How had this thing killed so quick? Where was the chest? Distracted from my perusal, I'd not noticed the beast disappear from sight.

Kilian stirred, attempting to stand, and I dropped to my knees beside him. "Took you long enough, you idiot."

A pained smile cracked his face and he pointed upward. The green thing pranced from one tree branch to another, heading toward the limestone circle. "Go after it." He gripped my wrist before I stood. "Be careful."

With one last glance at him, I shot to my feet, chasing the fast thing till we stepped outside the ring of limestone. The air around me chilled, my breath fogged white and then ice crept everywhere. The previously russet forest floor turned into frost for a mile at my command. Somewhere inside me tore open like an overflowing dam, my magic hungrier than ever.

The beast suddenly skidded to a stop and turned to me, its gaze flitting between me and the ice crawling and surrounding us to trap it.

"Come on, kitty kitty. Where are you going?" I taunted. Tendrils of ice crawled over the green *thing's* body, trapping it, while tens of shards of ice pierced him all over. The beast didn't even make a single sound of pain as black blood stained the ice.

Movement caught the corner of my eye, Hanaian soldiers riding toward us.

When I reached to grab the sceptre, the thing roared, breaking the ice off his flesh and as if in command to his call, two masked figures faded beside it, the chest between them. Just as quick as they appeared, they disappeared together. Along with the sceptre.

What?

What?

"Shit!" I shouted and the ice cracked and fragmented to dust at my fury. They had the sceptre. My father got his third piece. He was so ahead of me. He had Melanthe, Adriatians, and now this thing. What on Nubil's rocky lands? My brain flitted a thousand directions before drawing up the answer I always doubted. The Ater battles.

"What was that?" Moriko shouted, running to my side, all shades of worried and tired creased her young looking face.

"Does it look like a beast from the Ater battles?" Moriko had fought them for years. If anyone would know, it would be her.

Her eyes widened with absurdity. "No. No, the Ater monsters were somewhat human looking. Whatever that was, it wasn't human." Moriko ran a hand through her hair. "Did they get it? Did they get our sceptre piece?"

Lost of energy, I nodded. "Why was it at a sacred site? The Isjordian piece was at a temple."

She rubbed a palm to her eyes. "They threw us off. We had been circling and guarding every temple in our lands. We might have been looking at this the wrong way."

Something was wrong. My chest contracted with pain and then the bargain band I had with Kilian began burning my skin. Dashing back through the Ryuu, I reached him. The injured idiot stood on shaky legs, holding a palm over the three slashes on his chest still gushing blood.

His skin had turned an ashy white, blood pooled and dripped all around his body and fear curled every fibre of my being as I began unbuttoning his jacket and shirt to inspect the wound.

He looked at me with a goodbye in his stare. Men were so dramatic. "Enough with that." My fingers fumbled with his clothing, trembling like the flutter of a hummingbird.

"This is a bit too public for my taste, but whatever you like," he teased.

I scoffed in disbelief that he could actually joke around with me anymore, especially in the situation we were in. The sight of his gnarly wounds drew a loud gasp from me. I lifted a shaking palm to his upper wound and placed a light coat of hoar frost around the flesh. Barely managing to move my trembling hand down I did the same to the other wounds.

He grabbed my wrist, pulling my gaze to his worried one. "You are shaking, did you use too much of your magic?"

I had barely used a small fraction that I was still able to use from my seal, but I gave him a nod. If I told him the truth—

He wheezed, almost as if out of breath and a sob clawed up my throat at the sight of his wounds. "It is dirty now," I rambled, and he looked at me again. "Salt, I think. It gets blood out of any cloth. I don't know about the cuts...maybe Driada could fix it. Was it a favourite of yours?" From the way the band of black ink was throbbing in pain, I could feel life seeping from him. The frost had sealed his wound and the surrounding skin, but it would only keep him from bleeding out.

A small smile twitched on his lips. "Your nonsense is my guilty pleasure."

Suddenly Moriko was at my side, pushing my frozen state back while she and others surrounded Kilian, putting a mix of leaves and salves over his wound.

"Moriko Uzumi, we finally meet again," Kilian breathed.

The Autumn Queen shook her head. "Save you greetings when you're not bleeding all over my land. Contrary to popular belief, I only feed blood to the soil of my roses."

"Hm," Kilian said, his eyelids fluttering open and shut from blood loss. "Might take that advice into consideration."

The time between Kilian's bleeding sight and now had passed with a blur, barely remembering how I got into the chamomile infused bath that the Hanaian palace servant had drawn from me. The water was more or less icy by the time I forced out of it and paddled onto the wooden floored room I was to spend my night in. Delicate paintings of cherry blossom branches stood against the teal-coloured paper walls and a fragrant sandalwood incense burned at a window corner overlooking a lily pond at the centre of the palace. Hanai was something of a dream. When the painted lanterns lit to create light that the orange-purple infused dusk stole, I decided that perhaps I was in a dream.

A soft rasp against the door drew my attention. A servant girl peaked inside, bowing gently at the waist, she gave me a smile and spoke in Kemeri, "Dinner is ready. Are you to join our queen?"

"Will she have my head if I don't?"

She giggled behind a polite hand. "She is usually reluctant to go for such a difficult limb. Fingers are her favourite."

Cracking a smile, I picked up a robe dress someone had left for me and pulled it on. "This is why me and Mor get along so well."

Stepping inside the room, she reached for my damp hair and untucked them from the inside of the robe, and then grabbed the two ties that kept slipping off between my still trembling hands to tie them behind me. "He is at the dinner table—your husband," she said with a small voice before backing out of the room.

My husband. Still alive.

Lacing my fingers to hide the shake, I headed toward the dining chambers. The palace was a maze on itself—a colourful maze of scents, art and grace.

Light chatter trickled along the corridor. His voice felt like a memory, a making of my mind. But his sight reminded me that I was not being tricked into insanity. Paler than usual but still deadly beautiful, he made my heart race all over again, as it had done so many times back in Isjord. He wore a thin white linen shirt through which I could see all the heavy bandages wrapped all over his front.

I didn't make a sound, yet he spun to me before I'd even entered the room. He watched me all the way to my seat, his eyes never leaving mine. "It is one of many, my love. This is the last we will allow him to have."

I blinked confused. "What?"

He raised a brow. "The sceptre piece."

"Oh." Clearing my throat, I sat on the low table, folding my legs to accommodate my aching bottom on the soft cushion. "Yes, he won't be able to get the rest."

After a reluctant nod, he dove back into conversation with the Autumn Queen and I tried to push some food down my starved body. A touch of a familiar scent pulled my attention to the centre of the dark wooden table. A small tree branch rested in a colourful vase, few white buds sprouting from it.

Lemon flowers.

Immediately, my gaze went in search of him. His brown hair was still wet and fell to his eyes, his perfect mouth moved in conversation, and forcibly, I wrestled my attention away from them only to land on his body. I gulped. The thin shirt he wore was almost sheer, even with most of his hard muscle covered with bandage, his body was something that made my mouth want to adore—teeth and tongue and all.

"A handsome sight, isn't he?" Moriko drew out with snark in her usually composed voice.

She had caught me ogling him. "By all means, you're free to enjoy it, too." Without daring to look up at him, I dug into the delicious meal before me.

"You know my taste is for a different flower."

Lifting the chopsticks to point her in threat, I said, "Call Nia a flower again, and I swear."

Kilian looked confused and dopey, his eyes fluttering open and shut in a weird way.

She chuckled. "She lets me call her that with no issue." Her eyes flinted to Kilian for a moment before they came back to me. "We don't have Medi healers in Hanai, the earth heals our wounds at its pace, but he needs to be seen by one. Whatever that thing that attacked him was, it was a contortion of some sort of dark magic and it could delay his healing. We've given him something for the pain. It should come to effect soon."

Giving her a small nod, I continued languidly chewing.

"Look at me, Snow," he demanded, and my eyes snapped to him. "What is it?"

I couldn't help the way my attention went to his injuries. *I wish you could die without me feeling like I could die, too.* "You're bleeding."

He didn't look down on the patch of red soaking the thin linen, only at me, like nothing mattered. "I've never stopped bleeding, not since last I had you in my arms."

The mouthful of food turned sour mid chew. Light rain pattering on the thin walls was the only sound that filled the deafening silence.

"So have I." The way his silver eyes light almost in hope made my heart ache and all I wanted was to make his ache too. "The sharp sting of scales slithering over my skin, the prickling embrace of a snake, the venomous words of a predator have still left my skin raw and bleeding. I was held by what tore my heart apart. You never warned me of your edges, only made me hold you tighter. As if you wanted me to bleed. Did you want me to bleed?" He hurt me with purpose. I knew he did. He thought me weak, and I hated that he had thought right.

"You weren't meant to."

"Tell me, what was I meant to?"

"Hate me."

"I already hated you."

"Hate me enough to have your fill."

"If anything, you made me a glutton for my purpose."

A soft click on the glass table made the two of us turn to Moriko. "Well, that puts my plan to a screeching halt."

Picking up a spoon, I dug into the next dish. Hunger made me rageful. "What plan?"

"She wants us to make contact with Solarya, to figure out the pattern of the sceptre pieces," Kilian explained.

I scoffed. "Magnus's ego will be too bruised." The Sun King was like the animal he was compared to. Lions and their pride.

"So would mine, if I had one," Moriko said. "Magnus and I are on the same boat. He will find comfort in my failure."

"Then you make contact with him."

She gave me a cold blank look. "The world thinks you dead. How would I explain to the sun rulers all that has happened? How will I justify how Adriata killed you and betrayed Isjord? Sure, they will be pleased to know, but how willing to help him and I would they be? You can act as proof and reassurance of not only what your father has done, but his innocence in this."

"With a method called lies. He can help you," I said, pointing to Kilian. "He knows a thing or two about lying."

Moriko rolled her eyes at me. She rolled her eyes at *me*. The Hanaian queen *rolled* her eyes at *me*. "It would be smart to gain an ally in this, Snowlin. And I am not speaking as a friend, I am speaking as a ruler. If the worst comes to face, we are looking at war."

Well that made me lose my appetite. "Do you think I trust Magnus enough to reveal Olympia to him? With my aunt lurking in all corners of Solarya at that."

"Perhaps you don't have to," she said, looking between Kilian and I. The man still laid back, holding a hand over his wound. "You two are married."

I winced. "Being cryptic is certainly your thing, Mor. Doesn't necessarily mean you are good at it though."

She scowled, pointing her head to Kilian. "You are his queen."

Kilian straightened, a groan of discomfort leaving him. "Not helping your case here, Your Majesty."

She rubbed a frustrated hand over her eyes. "You show as the Adriatian Queen, not the Olympian one. We tell them that the two of you fell in love and Silas intended to use you to get to Adriata and the sceptre, and that Kilian had no intention to kill you. But if you want Magnus and Cora convinced you have to play the part, otherwise he will think you are Silas's spy in Adriata or even Kilian's slave. They have to think you two are genuine. Give them a reason to trust us enough to help."

"By lying?" I asked.

Her eyes narrowed with irritation. "Omitting part of the truth."

"Lies by omission are still lies."

She sucked in a breath and then exhaled slowly before saying, "Point made, Snowlin."

Turning to Kilian, I shot him a questioning look. "What is your say in this?"

"It would be good to forge an alliance, we might be able to figure out how these patterns work. Your father has help—dangerous help. We might need some ourselves, otherwise we are leading in blind. Not to mention that Magnus and Cora are the most knowledgeable amongst us regarding the sceptre. Their experience could even help us."

I nodded. "I'll think about it."

"With both your permission," Kilian said, standing. "I'd like to change the bandage before I bleed all over your table."

I cleared my throat. "Where…where is your bedroom?" Moriko's brows almost joined her hairline, and I shot her a glare. "We have a bargain. I have to spend my nights with him."

"Right next to yours," he said and left.

"A sweet little thing," Moriko said, taking a sip from her drink. "Lemon blossoms."

Standing, I moved to the windows, enjoying the echo of rain. "It's my favourite flower."

"I gathered," she said with a sigh and joined me by the window. The two of us were quiet till she asked, "Do you know the story of my kingdom? How Hanai became two instead of one. Aru and Koy. Spring and Autumn."

"I feel like there isn't much of a choice but to listen. It's either your stories or his presence."

She let out a small laugh. Even that seemed like a wise and calculated move from her behalf. "You can catch him half naked if you leave now, he is probably changing his wound dressing."

Slowly, I turned to her and sneered. "You were to tell me a story."

"Ah, yes. Koy and Aru once were one, the land of eternal spring. As you might know, our goddess Plantae fell in love with Celesteel, the god of the dead. Life and death never touch, and they are bound to circle one another without ever meeting. And if they did, the balance between the two worlds would fall. Wherever Celesteel's feet touched, death touched. And when Plantae's feet touched, the earth came to life. When she walked Caligo, the ashen soil of the Otherworld bloomed with life and the deceased gained part of their living. But what is dead can only come back in such wrong ways, so she was not able to live in the Otherworld as her lover was unable to live in Mankai. After the eight gods descended to Numengarth, their fates continued to precede them in this realm as well. Until Ryuu, Plantae's sister, sacrificed her eternity to feed life into the land Celesteel stepped on, never letting the land he stepped on die. Aru. In Aru both gods could meet and live and love, and they did. For a long time."

I turned to her and said, "That is one of the stupidest things I've heard."

"I do agree."

"You are not making sense, Mor."

"Love is not meant to make sense, Elding queen," Moriko said, turning to face me. "It goes against all sense."

"I take back what I said. *That* is the stupidest thing I've heard."

She was silent for a moment. "The Night King loves you."

"A heart that found it so easy to hurt me cannot love me." He'd only cared for himself.

She sighed. "What is it that you want from all of this?"

I want to want death today a little less than yesterday and a lot more than tomorrow. And I can't do that knowing the harbinger of my pain lives like they've never done me any harm. "My justice."

Moriko didn't say anything. I didn't know if she understood me or not, but she didn't criticise or question my reasons.

"I like her," she said quietly. "More than like her."

"You better. If you show her heart break, Mor, I will hunt you down and show you all the inner parts of yourself you've never seen. You would be surprised to see how tiny your kidneys are."

"The warning. She said you would issue me one." She turned to me. "You reckon we are moving too quickly? Nia says so."

Took me a moment to blink the stagger off. "Are you asking me for advice? On your relationship? With the one I consider closer than a sister?"

"No one would answer me. Servants were too afraid, and my council laughed. Women usually occupied my bed, not my heart. This is an odd place for me to be in."

"Good night, Mor."

Her distressed sighs made me giggle.

The room was dark when I pushed myself inside. I was as blind as a mole-rat in it. "I can't see," I whispered.

Suddenly the room seemed to illuminate, not from light but from lack of darkness. Kilian pushed his battered body up and pointed to the other side of the bed. "Come here."

Shedding the robe, I climbed on my side of the bed, but instead of laying back down, he wrapped a hand around my waist and pulled me onto his embrace.

I froze, my whole body seizing as his hot flesh met my cold one. "What are you doing?"

His face dropped to the crook of my neck and I erupted in shivers at the feel of his hot breath fanning my skin. My heart was drumming against my chest bone so hard it was making me dizzy. "Sleep."

"Let go of me and perhaps I will."

"No."

I spun round fast. "No?"

He winced and groaned from the friction of my body over his wounds. I shot up. "Oh, gods. I'm—" *Sorry.*

His hand went to cover my mouth. "Don't." After a moment, he stretched fully onto his back. "Come here."

Did the Hanaian healers drug him that much? "No."

He cocked a brow up at me and blinked drowsily at me. "No?"

"No, Henrik."

A bright, tired smile crossed his stark face. Gods, I wanted to eat him alive. "Henrik? No one calls me that but a few old bags from the council."

I laid back down. "It's the name you signed my mother's death with." *Henrik Castemont II, King of Adriata.* How many times I played that name in my head over and over, memorising every turn of his pen on the paper.

His face dropped, and he blinked at the ceiling languidly. "Yes. Yes, it is."

"What are you not telling me?" I asked, reaching close to him, my face hovering over his, my hair spilling over his shoulder. The way he looked at me had my mouth go dry.

He entwined a hand through my hair and cupped the back of my neck, drawing circles with his thumb over my skin. I didn't move. I don't know why I didn't move. "That I love you. I love you, Snowlin Castemont."

Seven sweet, hot hells, the way my heart chased to catch its pulse. What was he doing to me? "Skygard. Snowlin Skygard"

"Castemont. That is our surname." He leaned a bit closer and whispered as if someone was listening. "It's in the marriage certificate. I have it on my shelf. Snowlin Castemont."

"It's Sky—" I groaned in frustration. The idiot was drunk in whatever the healers had given him. "Never mind, as if it means anything."

His grip on me tightened just slightly—possessively. "Means you are mine."

A wicked smirk rose on my lips. "We have never consummated our marriage, isn't that fraudulent?"

He wrapped his other hand over my throat and pulled me closer to him. I shuddered. "Try calling it off." He nudged my nose with his, his warm breath kissing my lips. "You have no idea, Snow, how long I've wanted you for. Do you think I'd let you go after going through all that to make you mine?"

His.

"What were you thinking?" I whispered my echoing thoughts. "Letting your council arrange this bargain with my father."

He looked like he was measuring my truth in that question. "That we are desperate."

"What were you thinking when you came to guard me in Isjord?"

"That no one better than I will guard you."

I shook my head. "What were you thinking when you spoke to me?"

His hand moved to cup my face and his stare turned drunk and drowsy with something else. "Gods, I think I've met the she-evil. The prettiest she-evil. So fucking smart, too. And funny—so funny. I wanted to eat her words and her sounds, taste them on my tongue and salvage them however I could."

My pulse stuttered and stumbled trying to catch the steady beat his words had stirred. "When you touched me?"

His tender touch moved to trace the bridge of my nose down to my mouth, and my eyes drew shut. When he spoke, his voice was gravel and silk at the same time, "That by the gods I was fucked. I never wanted to stop doing it—to touch and learn every corner and curve of yours. You were my most selfish act, but the one I regret the least." He dragged my bottom lip down with his thumb. "Perhaps I don't regret it at all."

"I would have killed you that day."

"And I would have let you."

My brows furrowed. I didn't understand. Why did his words feel so true? "Why?"

"Because seeing you happy, seeing you feel free from your past is what I wished from the stars every night."

I hated how genuine those silver eyes were when he spoke. I hated how gentle and soft they became each time he told me he loved me. "Sometimes I could almost believe you. You have that about you."

Pulling me down, he rested my forehead on his. "You believe me, I know it."

I shook my head, struggling to breathe in this closeness—struggling to keep my thoughts straight after...after he'd almost died in my arms. "Why would you pretend in Isjord?"

"Because," he said, his eyes dropping to my lips as he pulled me closer to him. I thought he would leave me with that vague answer as he had done most times, but he added, "I told you that I am a very bad man, my love. The chance was there and I took it. To see and be with the woman I was going to marry."

I rolled my eyes and he chuckled. A chuckle that turned to a throaty groan and then a cough. I hated how worry was my first reaction.

"Lay with me."

"No," I said, pushing back.

With a pained groan, he lifted himself up and caught onto my arm, pulling me to him. He had too much strength for someone so injured. "The thought that I might have died today without getting to hold you one more time made me madder than dying," he breathed in my ear. "So I am going to hold you. And you're going to let me."

I tried to struggle. I did. But I didn't want to. "With a condition," I said, spinning to him. "Tell me what is wrong with Mal."

He frowned. "Why would there be something wrong with him?"

Surely he had noticed. "He looks strangely at me. Like he is...sad." That made me cringe.

He went still, his chest raising quicker. I waited for him to say something. Comment something like Cai would—like it's all in my head. Or at least tell me it's nothing that matters.

I looked up at him. "Will you not tell me why?"

"That day," he started. From the melancholy in his voice I knew which day he meant. "I think I went a bit out of control and he drew my emotion onto him. All of it. I thought he dispersed it back how it is supposed to be. I guess he didn't or couldn't."

"So, he isn't...sad."

Kilian looked at me like he was entertained by what I said. "No, he isn't sad, my love." He opened an arm. "Come cuddle your husband."

Cuddle? This idiot. I kicked his leg with my foot and that made him laugh. "My kingdom," he said, coming down from his high. "My kingdom for a night where I am just a guard and you a princess I never hurt."

"If I...let you hold me, will you shut up?"

He chuckled, his eyes drooping and drawing shut while he nodded. "I want to cuddle you, speak to you, hold you, love you. I want to kiss you," he murmured almost asleep. "I want to do so much. I love you so much. Do you love me so much?"

I'd damn Moriko and whatever she'd given this fool. "No."

"It's alright," he sighed, fully missing most of his vowels. "I love us enough."

Reluctantly, I laid my head on the crook of his shoulder and he wrapped a massive arm around me. Gods...I missed it. How could I feel so safe in his hold when I'd feared his presence alone for years?

"Why did you ask for this? Why did you make me spend my nights with you?"

"Because I don't want to be alone anymore."

I didn't understand.

He let out a sigh, burying his face in my hair and inhaling deeply. "They've made you for me, I could swear on it," he murmured, voice full of sleep.

I think they might have made you for me, too. Just where did they go wrong with it?

For the first time since I've spent my nights with him, he slept. He slept holding me. And for the first time I heard his troubled dreams. With my name on his lips, he panted and sweat in his sleep as if he wasn't holding me. I looked at him—it was all I did for the night. I looked when his face twisted into cries with the same name on his lips—mine. I heard his choked sobs while I contained my own. His heartbeat drummed in the silent air of the night and my own chased after it, troubled as his.

I lifted a hand to his face and wiped away the tears that had slid down his face.

He stirred awake from my touch, my hand frozen on his skin.

"Go back to sleep," I whispered.

He stared at me for a long while. The way he searched my eyes, the way his hand tightened on me as if I were to disappear hurt my heart and I didn't know why.

"I think you might have a temperature. Let me get a wet cloth."

He stopped me from getting up, his grip around me tightening. "It is always how they start. You leaving and never returning. Don't go."

It really hurt. It hurt so much. And I didn't know why. "I will come back." I didn't know why I said it.

"No. Stay."

I rested my head back on his shoulder and shut my eyes tight—tight enough to hold my own tears back. Magic broke the barrier of my fingertips when I rested them on his body. A film of cold permeated the air and chilled his body. He shivered and I carefully wrapped an arm around him, smoothing my hand over the gooseflesh on his arm.

Why is it so hard to watch you hurt? Why does it hurt me to watch you hurt?

PART II
DAY

CHAPTER TWELVE

HESPERUS

KILIAN

She snored softly in my arms as she'd done for nights in a row now. It hurt everywhere and her head was pressing against my wounds, but I didn't dare make a single move to wake her. She was sound asleep and looked so perfect on me.
Morning bright filtered in the room and Snow made a little noise of discomfort. I'd use my magic if only it didn't give her the horror it did. For now, I only raised a hand to make shade over her eyes and she relaxed back, sighing softly.

Her cheek was soft and warm under my touch. My calm storm. Always so close to rage. Always so peacefully violent.

A damned bell rang in the distance along with Kemeri shouts of the new day rising ahead and Snow jerked awake.

Her breathing had gone hard and ragged. "What...what time is it?"
"Sunrise."

Still in half disbelief, she examined the room as if we were in some sort of danger. "Why didn't you wake me?"

I looked down at us, at her body beyond tangled with mine—her arms were tight around my chest, she had hooked a leg around mine and the other between my thighs and hooked that one over my other knee. "You've rounded me like a snake. How could I wake you?"

She quickly untangled her body from mine and pushed away, hauling herself to the end of the bed. There was a look of horror on her face—more like realisation. She ran her hands through her hair, tugging the strands with panic. "I forget," she murmured to herself, pushing up from the bed and backing toward the door. "I forget."

Barely managing to stand, I got myself ready, changing the damp bandages to clean ones. The wounds were gnarly and deep, but not the worst injury I'd sustained. They were, however, odd. Yesterday it had not been so obvious, perhaps from shock, but today I felt a splinter in my magic. Like a chain missing links, attempting to connect and not quite connecting. Like a ghostly arm holding a solid one. Whatever had injured me, it had a similar trace of magic as mine or had been made from the same magic as mine.

Snow and I left our rooms at the same time. She wouldn't even look at me once. And now there was disgust on her face. Her regret hit me hard—almost harder than the pain from the wound.

"The servant said Nia is here. She will take you back to Adriata," Snow said as we made our way to the dining rooms where Moriko waited for us.

"We will return together," I said, and she stopped only to turn and glare at me.

"No."

"Certainly not no. Your knowledge on anything magical is not up to par to mine. Not to mention," I said, tapping a finger on my chest. "This thing that clawed me seems to have a similar magic essence to mine."

Her pretty sun eyes fell to my chest. "What do you mean?"

"It went for my soul, not for my life. In a similar way to how my magic works."

She frowned. "How can it do that?"

"Many ways. One: be created by dark magic. Two: be born out of dark magic. Three: forged by the hand of a divine being. And four: be born out of the divine, that is a guardian, godling or a lower god."

"Moriko said the thing didn't look like it was from the Ater battles."

"She was probably right. Because it cannot be, love of mine, enough worrying your brain with it. Obitus law is the law of the god of gods, it is not something any god and especially us can change. Let's go before the sound of your stomach grows frightening."

"Fine."

"And fine it is."

Both she and I froze on the dining room doorstep. Snow for an entirely different reason from mine as she didn't seem as surprised as I at Moriko pushing her tongue down Nia's throat.

"Moriko is who Nia is seeing?"

Snow sneered. "To my unfortunate eyes, yes."

I cleared my throat and Nia practically jumped three feet back at the interruption. "Kilian…Snow."

"Such an ill-timed interruption," Moriko said regretfully, pulling Nia to a seat.

"How can we be interrupting if we were expected?" Snow asked, angrily sitting on the cushion. If one could sit angrily.

I leaned to her ear. "Why are you killing the mood?"

"Would you not be uncomfortable if you witnessed your little sister being eaten alive by another?"

I nodded. "Thank gods I have a brother."

Snow scoffed. "Trust me, it is no easier seeing Cai do it either."

The spoon stilled midway to my mouth. "Why is that?"

Snow stopped chewing and turned to me with swollen cheeks, assessing my reaction. "Why? You no longer want to set me up with him?"

Moriko cleared her throat, interrupting us. "We have a man from the attack yesterday."

"Perfect," Snow said, beaming.

"Don't hold out hope he will answer," the Autumn Queen said. "My own soldiers tried."

Snow scoffed around a mouthful of grapes. "Your conciliating methods failed you? How odd."

"You're welcome to try."

"No, Mor dearest, you're welcome when I try."

The Autumn Queen remained unphased. "You wear arrogance well."

"It is not arrogance. Getting what I want is what I know best. My skills do not fail me. And speaking about skills," Snow said, turning to Nia. "How did you leave our Urinthia?"

"Melanthe was seen in Heca two days ago. She had visited the lower covens and then left for Isjord."

Moriko said, "My spies sent news that she'd deviated from Asra and Red Coven in her journey. Whatever she did there it was not with Urinthia's permission."

"It seems like she is recruiting Crafters for Silas," I said. "There is no other explanation for visiting the lower covens. He is garnering troops for war."

Snow chewed slowly for the first time since I'd met her. "How is this slipping past Urinthia?"

Nia sighed. "Unless she is allowing it herself. The way she has cut contact with Mor and Kilian, how she has isolated herself and Red Coven from the rest of Eldmoor does not seem normal. Once I get past the veil we will find out."

Not the Urinthia I knew since I was born, but the times had changed and perhaps so had she.

Snow nodded. "Careful."

"Always," Nia promised, sharing a long look with Snow.

It was far too impolite to call the Hanaian prison a prison. Not a holding facility either. The individual rooms were neat and decorated to resemble a normal bedroom. Each prisoner had a view of the coppery forest expanding for miles ahead of Aru from their windows that were not sealed by bars of iron. And each prisoner sat quietly either reading or fiddling with a puzzle while they drank from their steaming teacups. The order in the corridors was immaculate, too. The guards were unarmed, and the prisoners unchained while they moved along them.

Snow scoffed. "Now I know why you have had him for a night in here and he hasn't spoken yet. You are treating him better than my father treats his guests."

Moriko turned over her shoulder. "Sometimes the best solution is the lesser violence."

Snow threw her head back in a laugh and when no one else followed suit, she straightened. "Oh, you were being serious."

The Isjordian soldier stood at the edge of his bed, his entire focus on an empty spot on the ground. He didn't stir, not even when the four of us entered the room.

"Soldier, we wish to speak to you," Mor called. The man didn't even blink, body solid still and attention steeled ahead. "Soldier." He'd already made his decision; his shadows were of acceptance. He was terrified of dying, but he'd made his choice. "Sold—"

Snow was before him, kicking her knee in his face which sent him jerking a foot back in the bed and bleeding. "Want to try that one more time, Mor?" Snow said, before grabbing the man by the hair and dragging him to the ground. She bent down to his face, pinching his jaw tight with one hand. "Do I look familiar?"

The man began shivering when he met her yellow stare. "You're...you're dead. You died."

"Bold statement," she said. "Do *you* want to join me in the Otherworld?"

"I...I won't say anything. I will take death."

"Not that Otherworld, little soldier." She lifted a hand, bolts of electricity skittering and playing around her fingers. "My Otherworld."

"No," he shook his head, breathing ragged and petrified. "No. You're—"

She put the hand on his face and the man screamed, the echo travelling down the empty corridors with a loud boom. Part of his cheek had melted and charred where she had touched him. "I'm, I'm," Snow taunted, waving her hand down to his other cheek. "How did you know where the sceptre piece was?"

Tears poured and mixed with his bloodied flesh, but he didn't answer.

My wife clicked her tongue. "Wrong answer."

The screams were louder this time.

Mor folded her arms tight, a scowl bunched between her brows while her shadows blurred with fascination and a flash of fear. Perhaps she had just realised what Snow was really capable of.

"How?" Snow asked, moving the hand down to his arm, leaving a trail of burned flesh behind.

He shook his head and Snow turned to us all, folding her sleeves back. "You can all leave. This is about to get really up and personal."

None of us moved and she nodded, turning to the man. "An audience. Put on your best performance for me, soldier." Ice glided from her fingers to form claws and she dragged one down his chest, leaving a stream of blood chasing after. Just when I thought the man had grown tired and hoarse of screaming, he shrieked when she dug them in his stomach. "Speak because I promise you, no one will give a damn about your honour, your piety or loyalty where I'm about to take you. Speak because no one will care to invite you in their heavens or hells after my father uses that sceptre to ruin the realm they fought so hard to protect. When you become an extension of his evil. The hand giving him the ability to destroy this realm."

"Our king," he breathed out, "he wants to help the realm. Our lands are rotting because of our faith. This will restore us. Our lands. Our glory. The sceptre will help us."

Snow guffawed, dropping her head back. "Soldier, look at me," she said, gripping his face again. "Do you think he wanted to save the realm with this creature he bred, raised, and trained, huh? The sceptre is the weapon I couldn't become. The monster it will raise will be obedient to a fault. Your lands are rotting because your king has pronounced himself god. He is the god of rot, so he blessed Isjord with taint. The sceptre will help him taint the rest of the realm. By killing millions. Will you bear that fault? Because it will be your fault to bear in the end. In the end it won't matter who made decisions, only those that executed them. Inevitably, this will be on your hands."

Wide eyed and shivering he slowly shook his head, shadows filling with doubt. "No...no, it can't be."

She took his hand and pointed to the golden tattoo band around his ring finger—a sign of a blessed marriage. "Are you ready to take and drag your other half with you there? Will you selfishly punish her because you chose to close your eyes to what your king is doing?"

He faltered with doubt, seeming to consider her words for a moment before shutting his eyes tight. Time ticked through silence. And then—

"I don't know, I don't know how we find them," he blurted out. "The witch and the beast led us to them. We only retrieve them. A couple months back we made respite in General Moregan's camp lines. They sent Umbra inside Aru to place a sort of trace craft all over the land. Some soldiers had seen the witch take blood from the green beast and pour it onto the craft plaques. Some say it was to make the craft stronger and how she is able to find the pieces. They said that the witch drank its blood, too, they said it was why she's become more powerful."

Snow made a gagging sound. "Why would it make her more powerful?"

He shrugged a shaking shoulder. "I wouldn't know."

"The blood of the beast," Moriko hummed with concentration. "It is said in an old codex we found decades ago when we were fighting the Ater battles that Crafters were consuming the blood of Caligo creatures to heighten their magical senses. It helped them summon and portal easier."

"Like mirk root for the Aura," Nia said, her nose wrinkling. "Except more...spiced, I suppose."

Moriko nodded in thought. "There were speculations that the 97th Grand Maiden had used the blood of a Caligo hound. She was a Potioner so many had their doubts as to how one of her likes was able to gather and summon so much magic to create so many beasts."

"Wouldn't that mean the beast is from Caligo?" Snow asked and the room grew grave. She turned to me. "Didn't you tell me that nothing can come out of those gates anymore. You said they turn to ash." You could practically read the panic in her stare.

"What I said remains," I clarified. "The beast cannot be from Caligo, love."

"But—"

I tucked a wild strand of hair behind her ear. "No buts. This thing is something else." I bent down to the soldier. "Have you heard anything about where Silas came across this beast?"

He shook his head. "No one knows. No one goes near it. Soldiers and Aura could barely make it past the first veil, but this thing went and came without a scratch. I've never seen such a thing. I-It certainly might be true that it isn't from this realm at all." He cleared his throat and looked at Snow, "They...they are aiming for Myrdur next—soon. Our ships were barely leaving port before the Solaryans were taking them down. Portalling to Seraphim or the unblessed Isles is near impossible since dark craft weakens the further away from Eldmoor it is cast. Soldiers are saying that the king is in the works of dealing with the unblessed to strike an agreement. They have also agreed to let their ships pick up soldiers from Sayuri Island by filtering them through Hanai. The trip would be dangerous and long, thrice as long, but the king is prepared for the loss of time."

Snow nodded and the man shut his eyes tight, expectant of his final punishment. Yet she stood. "Mor, have a healer brough to him."

The soldier cracked his eyes open. "What...what?"

"You will live to see my words prove right. To see that what you did today helped save this realm. That I didn't lie to you. I won't let you mock me in the Otherworld, I have a reputation to maintain."

"Y-Your Highness," he called as we were about to leave. "When I said soon, I meant very soon. Our troops were ready by Fernfoss yesterday."

"You're too violent," Moriko said as we exited the prison premises.

Snow put a hand on her chest. "I am a pacifist at heart, truly."

"Must be a small heart."

"It is," Snow said with a polite smile, and I feared for Moriko. "But I compensate with cleavage."

Moriko blinked slow for a moment and then breathed out a long sigh. "Safe journey back. When you are ready to see the Ryuu, let me know."

"Thank you for letting me stay," Nia said, clutching Moriko's arm.

Snow kissed her cheek and threw Moriko a glare before retreating to me.

I extended a hand to her which she took reluctantly. "Don't fade us between a brick wall."

"Love, I've never been that injured."

CHAPTER THIRTEEN

INVIDIA

KILIAN

Mal stood on a corner of my room as the Medi healer ran a glowing palm over my injuries that hurt and bled like they were fresh. The pain was not as dire as the fact that I was struggling to fade from one place to the other.
"Don't look so grave, brother. One would think I am weak enough to die from this," I said.

He didn't make a sound or blink at all for that matter besides stare at me, but the Medi healer tending me shook her head. "Wouldn't be so sure, my king. This isn't like any injury you have sustained before. In my eighty years as a healer, it is the first time I've seen something like that. I will send a Magi healer up after I am finished."

"No need."

"Send them," Mal said, all grave and quiet. And oddly sober and clear minded, too.

Someone knocked on my door and I straightened. It was almost night time, but Snow never knocked. And it had not been Snow.

"I heard you were injured," Nesrin said carefully, glancing around the room before stepping forward.

"Council does not need to bring him fruit baskets and good salutes every time he gets hurt, Nes," Mal said, annoyed, sprawling on my sofa. "Who even allowed you to enter this side of the castle?" He chuckled in realisation when her shadows blushed from embarrassment. "Don't tell me you waved some 'I am a councillor' bullshit to the guards."

The councillor's facade twitched a little and shadows she carefully had forced to hide broke to the surface. Disdain and something else—green almost as vivid as envy. "We have grown up together," she said to Mal. "Does it matter what position I hold in court to come see my friend?"

"Yes," Snow's melodic voice filled the room before I could answer. She leaned on our bedroom door, as usual wearing almost close to nothing, her devastating form hidden under a pale grey-white nightgown, obsidian hair loose and piled to one side revealing her slender neck. "When that friend shares his room with his wife, and when that friend's wife is curious to see if you'd bleed more if you were hung upward on a hook or pierced through with a stick like a little skewered chick."

My brows rose. Has she just called herself my wife?

Whatever shadows I'd seen from Nesrin before were gone, all blended between a thicket of fear and hate. "This, us, we have been—"

"Bow," Snow said, taking a step close to her. "When you see me, you will bow."

"W-What?"

My wife stood nose to nose with Nesrin, her stare deadly. "Even at his old age your father knew how to bow. Oh, he even bowed all so well. Has he not taught you?" She took a step closer to her and Nesrin faltered another step back. "Bow. Do it without me putting a boot on your neck, dear, because no one comes up for air once they are under my foot."

The councillor sent me a look of plea before turning to Snow again. She was my queen and hers, too. If Snow wanted her to bow, she would have to bow.

Smartly, she did, and without a second look at the room, she left.

My brother snickered and exaggerated a courtesy. "My Majesty."

She gave him a grin and began moving about my room, trailing a finger over the furniture, the walls, and stopping at a library on the corner before pulling a book out. "I didn't know this room was open to the public."

"It isn't," I reassured, hoping she didn't think people could come so close to her without repercussions.

"That so? Why is your whore running in and out like she pleases? I gathered you spared them some different quarters. The castle is big."

Mal glanced at me and then stood. "I should go."

Snow shut the book and spun to us, resting on the shelf. "Sit, Princeling. Perhaps you can be of assistance to your brother. Help him choose a better one."

"Get out, Mal," I said, standing.

"Stay," Snow said.

My brother looked between the two of us, confused. "The power balance is totally throwing me off right now."

Driada chose that moment to peek her head inside my room. "Son, are you feeling better?" Her smile was wide when she turned to Snow. "Snow, I didn't hear you arrive."

Mal shot to his feet and wrapped an arm around his mother's shoulders. "My mother is in need of me. I'm afraid she wins above both of you."

Driada looked confused as Mal dragged the both of them out. "What need—"

Once they left, I reached close to her, resting a hand over her head on the shelf. I couldn't help it, my attention travelled down her body. "I like it when you're bossy." With a finger, I traced the shape of her jaw. "What I don't like is when you make assumptions without considering facts."

"What facts?"

"That the only woman I'll ever touch is you. The only woman I love is you. And the only woman I want is you. And I'd rather not call you a whore." Leaning in to get washed in her flowery perfume that I'd missed, I said, "Unless you want me to. And still, you wouldn't be any whore, you would be mine."

Her shoulders lifted a bit as if she was cold. "I asked for no explanation, Your Majesty. You may do as you please."

"You were jealous."

Her eyes were amber ice. "No, you like to think that I was jealous."

"Don't worry, my heart, you know I love it. Also," I said, pushing back from her and reaching for a shirt, "it is some petty revenge for all the fucking times I've lost my mind over you. The way men leer at you makes me rethink my boundaries for murder."

"Women leer at you, too."

That made me smile just the slightest and I glanced at her over my shoulder. "Do you leer at me?"

"Why would I leer at you?" Her head tilted to the side and her gaze slid down on me. "Do you leer at me?"

"Why would I leer at you, my missus? You're all for me to stare at. And when I get the chance to look at you, I might as well look good. And hard. Not leer." Something was oddly quiet in her—her quietness worried me. The Snow I know was a tumultuous storm. "How did you leave Myrdur?"

She dropped her head back on the shelf. "The soldier had been right. Isjordians were trying to sneak in a Crafter. We presume it was to study the *zgahna*. Ancient magic is strong, but like all magic there are weak points and leeways."

"How have you kept your kingdom hidden from anyone curious enough to test that?"

She sat on my desk chair, fiddling with a few of my pens. "With an old method rhyming with ill and will. You know—that one bad word."

"All this time?"

"All this time."

"And no one has had a single doubt where everyone is disappearing?"

"Have you heard of the tales about the ruins? How the dead drive you mad and lure you to jump the cliffs?"

"Yes." She smiled and I gaped a little. "They were made up?"

"Nothing a bit of fog, some ugly noises and a few wild boars and crows cannot fabricate. When I was younger, I would call on the mist and go scare a few myself—an old hobby of mine. Olympian spirits are haunted, not the opposite. They loom over Myrdur, but they are quiet, almost serene, and only seek to remain in their home. If anything, the intruders scare them."

"That was smart."

"We are grateful that the mind is a capricious, wrinkly organ, darling." She glanced at the glass I held. "I want a sip."

Why was my hellcat being so polite today? "Have your sip," I said, extending the glass forward.

She blinked for a moment, but then slowly made her way to me, and just when she reached close enough to get it, I lifted it above my head. "A sip," I said, and she frowned at me like ice cold fury, her hand lowering. "I'll give it to you. It's what we agreed on."

Slowly, I lowered down the glass and brought it to her mouth, tipping it up once her pretty lips rested on it.

She winced a little at the taste and I pulled back. "Don't go all crazy drunk on me. It's bedtime for you."

Her eyes drifted down my chest before slowly sliding up to me, and the way her cheeks flushed made me regret that one sip. I didn't want to get those eyes of hers when she was intoxicated—not unless she could look at me like that when wasn't. "Shouldn't have let you drink. You might think I'm a pony as well as that poor lad Simon."

Her mouth ticked just the slightest and she blinked slowly. "That's not how I'd ride you, Your Majesty." Profiting from my distraction, she took the glass and drank the rest of it in one swing.

Sweet hells. "You're wicked cruel."

She made one small, calculated step toward me, her fingers grazing my shirt. "Poor Night King. Are you suffering, my darling?"

I rested my forehead against hers and took a sharp breath, my eyes drawing shut at the scent of lily around her. "Stop it. I beg of you."

"Tell me, I want to know."

"I am."

"Good," she whispered over my lips, lifting her gentle fingers to my face and trailing them over my skin. "So good, husband. Aren't you so good for me?"

Fuck. This torture...I wanted more of it.

With one last wicked smile, she blew me a kiss and then jumped on the bed. Not even a minute after she'd rested her head on the pillow, her soft snores filled the silence.

I went to her side and pulled the blanket over her body. "How can you sleep, my little beast, hm?"

Her response was a deep snore that almost shook the walls.

"Like that, huh?" I stood there chuckling to myself for the next hour till I'd decided that I'd tortured myself enough for the day.

After I'd done a last round check of Highwall, I headed to Taren to get Snow. Later today I had called for a meeting with every priest from every corner of Adriata. Few of them were old—very old. And Atlas had convinced me this morning that the Sidran priests might have been aware of the Octa Virga after he had found some sort of an old scroll with heavenly theories mentioning Aurora as a guardian in their archives. Snow had to be there as my queen. People had to familiarise themselves with her presence or excuse themselves from my court.

Fading was slightly easier now after the Magi healer had mended the flow of my magic that had fragmented from the beast's magic essence lingering in my blood.

The wind howled around me, and the skies of Olympia seemed restless—moodier than usual. It was odd how the emotions of its people were reflected in the skies.

Caiden along with a team of soldiers made their way to the terrace, he rushed orders of all sorts to his men. When he took note of my presence, his face twisted. "Have you come to play king for us again?"

I flicked a bit of dust from my shoulder. "I don't play, Caiden. I am king."

A howl echoed through the mountains and then another. The sound bounced back around the space of the mountain ranges growing closer and closer to us.

"Is that a signal?"

"That is Tratha, a city in the southwest, calling for aid. The tribes echo the sound to us," he explained, peeling off his gloves. Black ink swirled like vines around his hands—Crafter magic. Is that what he'd hid under there all this time?

A blast of lightning hit the skies twice, mimicking the signal howl, and my attention pulled heavenward.

"And that is Snow," he said as she came into view, climbing the stairs to the roof two at a time, pulling her leathers on as she went. She ran across the terrace, and then with no warning, she leaped from its edge into a free fall. Halfway down, her body took the shape of a blinding bolt of electricity and then she was gone from sight in a flash.

A red spark flickered before Caiden and then a wide circle expanded from thin air. A portal. "Handy," he said as his soldiers rushed into the portal one after the other. "When you need to go kill a general's family without being seen." With that, he disappeared inside it.

Casmere. Renick's family.

"Kilian," Nia called, jogging the terrace distance to me. "Are you here for Snow? She just left."

"I saw her leave. I've called for a meeting later on. I'll wait for her to return."

"She could be gone for a while. Fogling attacks are doubling by the day." Her face lit with excitement. "I could show you the city."

"I'd like that."

Taren was fascinating by foot. Houses were made of a dense grey rock, surely to withstand lightning, heavy rain, wind corrosion and constant storms. Not much was made of metal or glass—doors, windows, handles, carriages were all made of wood. The black roofed houses laid in such a way up the mountain face that it resembled stair steps, the corridors between buildings were wide and luscious with life of all sorts.

"There are a lot of bakeries," I noted, counting past several colourfully painted buildings lined with people of all ages.

"Olympians have a sweet tooth. Most of our traditional foods are desserts. People from all over come to Taren for this particular street. And the fact that Snow chooses to invest her own riches into these businesses does not help." She pointed to a small shop just as we turned around the corner of the city. "The owner was in Snow's team when she was training. The girl's family was all killed during a Fogling attack and she became the breadwinner for her two younger sisters. Snow opened a shop for her and hired a cook to teach her to bake. She gives Snow sweets every time she visits the city." She pointed to another bakery where a bald man was laughing along with his customers. "Ewan, the owner, lost his wife with the Skye warriors in the Myrdur attack. He used to sleep in the streets and was poor piss drunk most of the hours of day. His sweet potato pies are Snow's favourite."

She dragged me to the city square that was being set up with white flags bearing the eagle insignia and garlands of white anemones being hung all over. "The monthly rituals are in two days," Nia explained. "People from all over gather to celebrate at the temple under the mountain where river Taren pools. It's the first place Nubil held a gathering with Olympians. People gather and celebrate their blessings for two nights each month. It's also the day younglings are initiated and given permission to make the climb to Valda Acme by Snow. You should come. People would lose their minds if you came."

I chuckled. "Then I probably shouldn't."

We made a stop to an herbal shop where Nia collected and sniffed all sorts of plants. And then to a small hospital located near the barracks where she made note of medicines missing and that needed to be brought from overseas.

We slid further in the city, past the grand library, the temple towers, grandiose rock sculptures from the time of ancient Olympia, through busy streets and quiet corners.

We'd reached the edge of the rock where Taren laid, a balcony overlooking the northeast part of the obsidian castle that stood grand between the crown of mountains when an icy touch of something more than wind brushed the back of my neck.

I turned around, studying my surroundings. Death mixed with something else. Something sinister. Like a stream of death leaking into the flow of spiritual. Had the beast affected my magic this severely?

Between two large boulders of rock, I spotted a small dark passage that entered the mountain. *Angh sragoch. Valley of death* was carved on the stone.

"What is through there?" I asked Nia.

Her attention jerked from the view ahead to where mine had landed and she made a small, startled sound. "I...we aren't going there."

"It wasn't what I asked."

"Kilian, trust me."

Her shadows were turbulent. "Somehow I don't." Passing through the busy streets, I made my way to the tunnel and through. Blue brightness assaulted my eyes when I reached the other side, and I blinked the strange cold air away. My face fell at the narrow valley stretching ahead for long miles. What on the heavens?

Nia latched on my arm, attempting to pull me away. "Kilian, please."

Pushing her off, I walked between the row of half frozen and half alive bodies of people tied and chained to the obsidian walls of the valley. Somewhere beyond life and above death, men and women, old and young lined the space for what looked like miles.

"Who are these people?"

Nia buried her face in her hands for a moment before answering me. "Criminals. Those that got Snow's mercy." She swallowed uncomfortably and reached to touch the rock wall of the valley. The black stone glittered white at her touch. "Taren valley is where Nubil buried his lover, a healing guardian called Meira. They say she gave her own life to heal a human woman and her new-born that the father had beaten and left for dead in this very valley. The immortal became eternal here. Her power lives through the walls, soil and air of this valley. Olympians would come here to heal and pray—they still do."

"I've always had a more creative mind than most," Snow's cold voice boomed through the glen and shivers of fright spiked through all the imprisoned. Leaning by one of the walls, she had crossed her arms across the chest and stared boredly ahead.

"I shouldn't have brought him here," Nia said, stepping forward.

"Nonsense," her friend echoed boredly. "This is the most touristy place in Taren." Pushing from where she stood, she reached close to me. Once she stepped in light, I could see the thick reddish black liquid drenching her grey leathers and the empty stare veiled in purple shadows of restlessness. "A tour, *darling husband?* I keep Adriatians further down. On pikes. They always get the best of my services."

Nia stood between the two of us. "There is a meeting in Adriata."

She yawned and cracked her neck, looking over at me. "Ready when you are."

"You are covered in Fogling blood," Nia remarked, staring at the almost black-grey leathers Snow wore.

"They should be grateful it is not theirs." Snow glanced at her gloved hands and then at Nia. "Actually, it could be theirs, I had a chat with a so-called Leon this morning. Soft like a mushy cherry he was. Popped out of his skin like he was ripe."

Her friend cringed.

When I ran a frustrated hand over the scruff growing on my jaw, Snow beamed. Grinned brightly as though the sun shone again after a storm. "Say it. I know you want to preach me some goodness."

Fading right before her, I pinched her chin between my fingers and lifted her face to me. "I love you like I've loved you since the first day. I am as sick as you and I am sick for you. But this if fucking worrying me."

She blinked slow. "That was a good one."

Not letting go of Snow, I turned to Nia. "Head to Adriata for me and let Mal know that today's meeting has been pushed by an hour."

"You can't order her as you wish," Snow hissed.

"Why not? I am her king, her friend and her friend's husband? Why can't I?"

She batted my hand away. "Because those mean nothing, and you have corrupted her enough to your side as it is."

Nia flinched. "Snow, you know that is not true."

Snow didn't even make a move or sound to deny. "Do as he says. I'm tired."

Nia's shadows glazed with sadness, but she did as told—disappearing.

"Happy?" I asked.

There was no emotion in her face, and it made me all too aware that she'd feigned almost everything in Nia's presence. "Ecstatic."

Hooking an arm around her, I faded the two of us to Taren castle. "Where are the kitchens?"

"What?" she asked, still dizzy from the movement.

Sliding my arms under her knees and her waist, I pulled her up and stalked down the corridors before her senses settled and she fought me like a wildcat. After several wrong turns, I managed to follow the smell of cooking down to the kitchen quarters. Servants rushed from side to side without paying any mind to us as they prepared food of all sorts.

"Snow," a short stubby man bowed. His eyes were so wide they could pop out of their sockets at any moment. "My...my...king."

Snow jumped from my arms and gave him a hard glare. Taking a step between them, I gave the man an apologetic nod. "Kilian is fine. Could you prepare something she likes to eat?"

He took a moment to answer. "Of course."

Grabbing Snow's hand, I pulled us to a corner table. "When have you eaten last?"

"Last time."

"Snowlin."

She dropped her head back. "Leave me alone. Good gods above that is all I ask."

The cook dropped a bowl of soup before her and I put a spoon on her hand. "Eat or I'll feed you."

"When I see your face all appetite vanishes." She smacked both hands on the table and made to leave, but I faded behind her and sat her on my lap.

"We can go at it all day," I said, holding her hips down. "You will find that I am much more persistent than you think. Now, open your pretty mouth for me."

She writhed in my hold. "I'll eat myself."

"You had the choice and refused it." When she wouldn't oblige, I grabbed her jaw and pulled her mouth open, pushing the spoon between her lips. I clicked my tongue. "I could swear you fucking like when I'm an absolute dick to you."

"Good thing you're self-aware, Your Majesty."

"I don't know if I want to kiss, fuck or slap that sassy mouth."

"I want to sow yours shut."

"Be good for me and open your mouth for something other than lies, hm." I pushed the spoon between her lips before she sputtered some remark. "The valley stone," I said, buttering her a slice of bread. She hated eating any sort of soup without one. "It is similar in colour to the necklace stones you have given Driada."

Her glaring attention was on the ceiling, and she didn't answer.

Hooking a finger under her chin, I pulled her face to me. "Thank you."

She bit into the bread almost identical to how Memphis bit into her prey. "Do me a favour then, if you are so grateful."

"What favour?" I asked, wiping a bit of butter from her mouth with my thumb.

"Die."

That made me chuckle. "You'd miss me."

"I'm used to missing. You taught me that."

I placed another buttered slice next to her bowl. "I deserved that." Her stomach rumbled a bit and my brows rose. "Hungry now?"

She went from angry to calculative in a blink. "Hunger," she echoed, still in a trance, looking down at me. Again, identical to how her bonded studied prey. "That's it. I am hungry." Her fingers rested on my chest, moving up to my neck and then grazed my lips.

"Snow," I warned when they slowly descended low down my chest.

A smile bloomed in her face—one painted with intention. "Just a tiny, little taste. You owe it to me. For making me hungry."

"You think that's all it is?"

"I think you know that *that* is all there is."

I pushed loose strands of hair behind her ear, and she leaned in on the touch. "It was more than lust and you know it."

"Right now, I can't remember it being anything else. We both wanted it, perhaps if we'd relented we wouldn't be at these odds."

"You were always more than just a fuck."

"Can't say the same."

"Using all that pretty mouth for lies again?"

"I think you know exactly what will happen if we fuck." She leaned in, her lips almost brushing mine as she whispered, "I've always been a little too obsessed with a particular toy. It would never leave my system till I'd had my fair play with it. Come, play with me, Adriatian, I'm bored." She fisted the front of my jacket, her pretty brows knitted together and something soft touched her icy stare, all roundness and shine. It reminded me of Isjord. Had she pretended then, too?

"Cute, really," I said, bopping her nose. Absolutely adorable.

With a sigh, she let her features smooth back to how they'd been not even a moment ago. At her command, she went from one Snow I knew to the one who she showed to her enemies. "Had to see if my best trick in the bag still worked." She trailed a lazy finger over my jaw. "It used to do wonders on you before. Guess it only worked then because it suited your plan, isn't it so?"

I grabbed her face, bringing it close to mine. "If I fuck you, no one else ever will. If I fuck you, love of mine, you will want to fuck no one else."

"You give yourself too much credit."

"Tell me, have you let any other man touch you since I last touched you?"

"Maybe this might be just the right encouragement."

"Love, you want my cock and you haven't even seen it yet." After kissing that spot on her neck that made her squirm I said, "How about you get off of it now before I am unable to stand from this table."

One short fading distance, we were in Adriata. Snow followed at my side as we made our way to the meeting, still huffing at my rejection. If it made her feel better, my cock was huffing, too.

The room was at a standstill. Two figures stood in front of one another. One fuming in anger and the other drowning in fear—pure opaque fear.

"Nia?" Snow called before pulling Nia behind her protectively. She glared at Nesrin. "You."

Nia suddenly came to consciousness, grabbing onto Snow's hand and pulling her back. "Don't...don't, please. You promised me."

Nesrin began taking small steps back. "I don't know what she had told you, but those are lies. We were children and we played games, nothing more."

Lightning hit overhead and panicked screams broke the air. "Children?" Snow asked, breaking her friend's grip and approaching Nesrin. "Games?"

"Snow, please," Nia called out.

Snow let out a wicked laugh. "You might be right, Nes. Cause I've played some nice games with your father as well. Find the eyeball, loose the wrist, pull the teeth, break the finger. All sorts." She backed my counsellor to the wall. "You like my games, huh? Want to play with me, too?"

"You've killed my father?" Nesrin cried out.

"No. I haven't killed him. He just stopped breathing, unfortunately. There is nothing more fascinating than drowning. Nothing more pathetic than seeing someone struggle and beg and thrash for air. And let me tell you, Nes dear, your father was plenty pathetic." The outside blistered in lightning and Snow's face crawled with black markings.

Nesrin's tears poured while she shook with a deep red hatred and fear.

Snow pushed away from her and turned to face her friend. Something she saw on her face made her take a deep breath and spin to Nesrin again, her forehead hitting the councillor in the face and knocking her back a few steps till she collapsed to the ground. "Looking forward to playing more games with you, dear. Cherish the pathetic breath in your lungs while you can."

The councillor's face was painted crimson as she sunk further down, shrinking from Snow's attention.

I went to Nia, resting a hand on her shoulder and pulling her to me so she couldn't see her sister. "This was entirely my fault, forgive me. I should have known she would be here."

She shook her head. "It is fine. I'm fine."

From the way she had blanched and swayed on her feet, I knew those words were lies without even reading her shadows. "Let me accompany you to our healer."

She shook her head again, "I will return to Olympia."

"Nia, please."

"I swear it, Kilian, I will be fine."

Just as Nia left, Mal chose to show up. His brows rose when he took in the whole room and then grinned when he saw Snow and Nesrin. "Can we do a repeat or a rewind?"

Snow took a seat on the table, and somehow, everyone else followed suit. "I'm in need of a bath, could we speed this thing up?" She eyed the table, frowning the more faces she looked at. "Who are all of you?"

Few stood and introduced themselves, others chose to hang their head low and quiet, not daring to meet her gaze nor letting theirs meet hers—just as I'd ordered it. Each and every one of them had been warned. Perhaps threatened.

I took a seat beside her, putting a hand over her shaking one under the table and she relaxed a little.

"Your Majesty," a small voice called from the side, a young Sidran priestess bearing the waned moon mark on her forehead. She pointed to Snow's forehead, offering her a handkerchief. "Blood...blood is dripping on your forehead."

Snow, to my surprise, took it and wiped the blood away. "Thank you, sweetheart."

The girl flushed red to the tip of her ears and bowed her head.

Atlas nudged my foot under the table and signalled his head to the girl. "You come from the south of Sidra, yes?" I asked and she nodded. "I am told you had something for us."

She nodded again and brought something from underneath the table. "I've found a letter exchange in our library in Sidra. In one of the letters the Octa Virga was mentioned. Very loosely but mentioned. They date from two hundred years ago." She pushed toward us a bunch of scraps reading in Darsan and Borsich. She cleared her throat and nervously fiddled with her sleeve as Snow and I flipped through the faded papers. "It was mentioned in relation to an...*Ybris*."

Our attention rose to her. Snow as usual remained unimpressed.

"Which *Ybris*?" Larg asked, pulling the letters to him.

"None worth noting," she said and then pointed to a specific letter. "It was a study on them. In general. He stated in some of his remaining journals something called an Arx Triad. An old method that Crafters used to protect their covens. Veil, animal, *Ybris*. It is old and cruel," the young priestess said, fiddling with her oversized sleeves and casting a small glance at Snow before continuing. "I believe the elder Crafters who hid the sceptres used the Arx Triad method. Veiled the location, left an animal to guard and tasked an *Ybris* to protect it. He had to have known about the sceptres. Probably very well considering he had information on how they were concealed."

"Oryn," Larg said. "These are Oryn Duncan's letters."

The priestess nodded. "The priest banished to the Danics."

"How would this help us in any form?" Mal asked.

"Not them," the priestess explained. "Him. Oryn Duncan. He is still in the Danics." She brought a compass out of her pocket, old and rusting. "I...I might have borrowed this from the head priest in Sidra. He...he wouldn't allow me to have it." She winced and flipped the cap open to show us. "When Oryn was banished to the Danics, a Crafter spelled him—to keep watch in case he ever trespassed. Apparently, he possessed fearsome magic. He is a prime Empath after all."

We all leaned forward, noticing the arrow pull and twitch west. "I am certain he is alive and can help us," she said confidently.

Snow picked the compass and stood to spin about the room with it. A smile cracked her features and she beamed at the priestess. "Well done."

The young girl bowed. "Thank you, my queen."

Snow sat and then turned to me. "How do we go to him?"

I took the compass, studying it. The Danics. No one went near them let alone enter them. Perhaps once they might have dared to, but Adriatians had not stepped there in centuries. The mountains had been rich with gold and diamonds of all sorts, but the heights had not only been dangerous to climb but a challenge to survive through. Man had killed man for jewels and gold, the earth had turned rotten and a ground that attracted young and old in search for riches only to end up consumed by greed. The bodies soiling the mountain's path had left our goddess heartbroken and her grief had dressed the mountain range with her blanket of night terrors. No one had been able to step more than three feet inside it before running back out. And now, it was the perfect location to sentence someone to solitude or death.

"My love, the Danics are impenetrable. There are several places in Adriata that our goddess sealed for our protection. People were losing their lives mining gold in that region, so Henah sealed the area with her magic. God magic. It is not the same as craft and ten times as dangerous."

She frowned. "Find us a way, Henrik."

I cocked my head to the side. Right now, I wanted to bend her over my lap and smack her backside red and raw. "See what you can find," I said to Atlas.

After dismissing the rest of the meeting, it was only Mal, Snow and I in the room.

I poured a finger of the whiskey Larg had gifted me. Hopefully it would disguise a bit of the discomfort from the wounds across my chest. "Have you considered what Moriko proposed?"

Snow leaned back on her chair with a sigh. "Yes."

"And?"

"We should arrange a meeting with the Vayrs. If this Oryn does not have anything for us, then that leaves us with absolutely nothing." She pushed up and glanced out of the window and over the yellowing sunset painted over the Moor Sea. "Any news on my siblings?"

"I spoke to your witch again," my brother said. "She gave me a trace craft based on some memory she had extracted from Alaric. I'm heading to the North of Hanai tomorrow."

"That is good."

Mal shook his head. "Not entirely helpful. If the essence came from you, it would be better. The emotion you carry, it would—" My brother interrupted himself and took a deep breath. "If you let Visha enter your head, we find out whether they are alive or if we are just chasing a goose hunt."

Snow steeled a look on my brother. "No, I know what happens if she goes in my head. Her presence will banish my mother away."

"I'll enter instead of her," I volunteered. "She can cast the craft from outside and I'll be the one to ground you to our realm and pull you out from the Midworld."

"What makes you think your presence won't do the same?"

"Because my magic has an affinity with death, it scourges the soul. Death is attracted to me, not away from me."

She worried her bottom lip between her teeth and her gloved fingers were clenching and unclenching in fists. "I will have to think about it."

"Of course," Mal said, standing. "With your permission."

"Will you go and get yourself black out drunk again?" Snow asked, leaning back on the wall and giving my brother a berating look.

Mal grinned at her. "Perhaps. Want to join me?"

"I would," she said with a sigh, looking out of the window and lifting her hand to show our bargain seal. "But I'm your brother's prisoner for the night."

"A shame," Mal said.

Snow lifted a hand, stopping him again. "Sober, Princeling. If I catch you drinking—"

"I won't drink, Snow, not when I am looking for them," my brother said, and he had not lied.

Snow bathed and returned wearing a shirt of mine after refusing to put on any Adriatian attire my servants had brought. She'd perched on the edge of our bed, frowning at the Ahmes Lore pages. Scribbling all sorts of madness on a sheet of paper and possibly preparing to ask me to translate them for her even though we'd agreed on the dangers if the copies ending up in the wrong hands.

I was mid-shave when she pranced inside the bathing chambers and jumped to sit on the sink facing me. "Why was Oryn banished?"

"No one knows for sure. Larg said he was quite controversial in his preaching."

"In Adriatian tongue that translates to: went against popular belief."

"Possibly."

"Enough of agreeing with me on everything."

"I do agree with what you just said, not on everything." My hand shook for a moment and then I nicked my cheek with the blade.

Snow sucked in a sharp breath and jumped from the counter to grab the towel which she quickly put over the broken skin pebbling with blood. "Why are your hands shaking?"

"It's nothing."

"Henrik, why are your hands shaking?" she demanded louder, and slowly some realisation set in. "Take off your shirt."

I raised a brow at her. "Love, we ought to start slower."

She rolled her eyes and quickly caught my shirt and undid its buttons. Her stare doubled in size when she took in all the bandage still over my wounds. "Why have you not healed?"

"I have," I said, attempting to close the buttons back again despite the tremble of my hands. "It will take a while apparently. The thing's essence clung to me—to my own magical essence."

She took my hand. "Fade us to Taren, let's go see Visha."

"Snow—"

She pointed a finger at me, her expression turning thunderous. "I'll tie you to that valley with the rest. You will not die from a measly wound, Your Majesty. You will first see real suffering. From my hands."

"I am sure that will go to your plan, love," I assured her. "And I will see Visha but let me finish this."

She hopped on the sink counter and grabbed the blade, running it under water for a bit. "I'll do it." Her legs parted and she gestured her chin for me to reach closer. "Don't be shy now, Henrik. Come here."

I might just like that blessed name now.

Sliding between her parted thighs, I braced on the counter, leaning a bit so she could reach me easily.

"Close your eyes," she said. "You're too close to my face, it's distracting me."

"Distracting you?"

"Yes, you irk me like that. I might just slip and cut an eyeball out."

"Is that so?" I shut my eyes and then felt her gentle hand on my cheek while she slid the blade down my face with the other. Her fingertips scanned my skin, leaving light touches everywhere.

Fuck. She smelled like me. "You used my soap?"

"Mhm."

"Are you wearing my underwear, too?"

"Should I have worn Mal's?"

I rested a hand on her thigh, moving it upward till my fingers grazed the fabric of my briefs.

She gasped a little and I could feel her pulse chase quicker than before. "Any higher and I will cut it."

"Any higher and I would lose my mind."

With a sigh, she continued shaving my face. Her touch was so gentle one would think she could never hurt a fly. She was good at that—pretending.

I couldn't help it. I opened my eyes. She was concentrating so hard, her tongue peeked between her lips and her eyes narrowed on my jaw while she carefully worked the blade.

When my smile couldn't be contained, she became aware I was watching her and blinked ahead at a wall for a moment while a little rosy flush rose to her cheeks.

The fact that I could still make her blush made me mad with happiness. With a finger on her chin, I turned her face to me again. "My blushing bride, eyes on me."

She didn't say anything.

"Why won't you speak to me?"

"I have nothing to say."

"You always have something to say." *Joke with me. Joke with me like you once did.* I wanted my jester back. "I miss your jokes."

Her thumb grazed the little scar from when she accidentally cut me with her dagger. "You were going to kiss me that day. How about that for a joke?"

"It's a good one because I was going to damn all and do more than kiss you that day." Unable to help it, I leaned in and kissed the tip of her nose. Then I brushed the tiny spot I'd kissed with a finger, and she scrunched up her nose all cute and adorable. "Shouldn't have done that when you're holding a weapon."

"Odd that you think I'd need a weapon to kill you."

"It isn't killing you enjoy. It's the hurting. And you can do it better with a weapon."

She ran a finger over my pulse then up my jaw, over my face till it stopped on my forehead. "Where did you get that?" she asked, trailing a gentle touch over the old gash that ran further into my scalp.

I was not sensitive, but that touch made shivers run through my back. "In one of the training courts when I was younger. Back then I wouldn't know better than to injure my head."

She slipped her hands back down to my face, smoothing her fingers over my jaw and neck and my eyes shut at the lightness. Fuck, I was in heaven.

Her touch descended to my collar over another scar. "And that?"

"Dagger."

"It's close to your neck."

"It was aimed there."

"By whom?"

"Some people who wanted to do very bad things to me. Rhyming with shrill and mill."

"Who would do that to you, Night King?"

"Someone who was afraid of what someone like me could become. A Crafter, right after father died. They snuck in my chambers, but I had been awake arranging his funeral. They found me tired but not an idiot. After that no one got close enough to kill me. Except you."

Her golden stare lifted to me, and like a man who'd gotten a taste for excruciating pain, I stared back into it, torturing myself to agony by remembering how it had once shone for me. "I haven't injured you anywhere vital."

Grabbing her hand, I rested it on top of my heart. "Felt pretty vital to me."

Her fingers curled on my chest for a moment and her breathing picked up each time my heart pounded under her touch.

She pulled her hand away and wet a towel, washing the shaving cream away. "I think it's all done." She inspected every inch of my face one last time. The more she looked at me the darker that look got. And when she pulled her bottom lip between her teeth, I almost lost it. "Stop looking at me like that."

"Stop looking like that."

I raised a brow. "Like what?"

With a groan, she pushed me back and hopped off the counter angrily, reaching a hand to me. "Visha, now."

The Delcour heir was less than pleased when she opened her chamber doors to find us disturbing her peace. She stood there staring between the two of us for a long minute before reluctantly letting us through. "Don't touch that, Your Majesty," she scolded Snow, who'd gone to play with a bunch of vials.

My dark head picked a bottle up and then dropped it to the ground. The thing cracked and splintered to pieces. "Whoops. I'll just buy you some new ones."

I pulled her close to me and away from causing more damage. "That was not very nice, my love."

The little mischief put a hand to her chest all offence.

"She is only trying to get me to react. Thinks that I will turn into something resembling a fire wrath if I get angry," Visha said calmly, pointing to a chair for me to take. "How can I be of assistance?"

Snow rushed to my side, kneeling before me and unbuttoning my shirt before I could say anything. "The thing I told you about, from Hanai, it clawed him and he is not healing. Even from Medi healers. Have a look," she said, peeling back one of my bandages.

Visha leaned in and only stared at my wounds, unblinking. For a long time. The Crafter stood and reached a station of herbs and potions that dressed a whole side of the wall. "It looks like nothing I've seen before," she said, returning with a mortar on which she pushed a pestle to grind a collection of herbs. "From the way it has scarred and the veins around the wounds I can tell the irritation is not from any venom." She brushed some type of dry herb mix over one of the slashes, reciting one of her verses, and I could have sworn my skin boiled. "Dark magic as I suspected. You were lucky, Your Majesty."

Snow straightened. "It isn't that bad, is it?"

Visha's look was blank when she answered, "If he wasn't an Obscur, a powerful one at that, he would have died. The thing that has attacked him possesses dark magic. Considering how you described this beast to me, the only possibility a creature of this sort could possess that sort of magic is if it is part of a dark realm."

"No one from any outer realm can step in Numen after the Ater battles," Snow said and turned to me. "Right?"

"There are outer realm creatures in Numen, Snow," I said, and she gaped.

Visha nodded. "Sea of the Dark. Golgotha has always been known to experiment with his creatures."

"But the demon god has been asleep for centuries. And his creatures cannot survive long out of his waters."

"It was only a suggestion," Visha said, slathering a thick brown paste mix all over my wounds and reciting another long verse in Borsich. The pain was already feeling lighter when her magic brushed coolly over my wounds. "The best guess I can make for now."

She handed Snow a new roll of bandage and turned to me. "Come tomorrow as well, I need to extract the magic essence that the beast has left in your flesh and then once it is drained a simple cast from a Medi healer will help."

I nodded. "Thank you, Visha."

Snow kneeled before me and unravelled the long bandage. No one had ever bandaged any of my wounds before. The last I expected to do so was her.

"I hate that you know how to wrap bandages," I said when her fingers started expertly working the gauze around my body.

"It is handy knowledge."

"I hate that you find it handy knowledge."

A little smile. "Bet you don't hate it now."

Hooking a finger under her chin, I lifted her face to me. I needed to see that smile better. "Good thing I don't place bets with losing odds."

Her lips parted a little. "That is my line."

"And you are mine, that makes it my line, too."

Snow frowned, ready to make an angry remark before Visha interrupted her, "The two of you get out. I don't want to hear any more of that."

The chamber doors suddenly swung open and a little, wild-haired blonde girl no more than five, squealed and launched in Snow's direction, knocking her to the ground before smacking kisses all over her face. "Auntie Snow," she screeched all excited.

"Leanna," Snow shouted, "get your beast off of me!"

Quickly, a lithe curly haired blonde ran in the room, a face I'd seen in Snow's council, and lifted the child off from my dramatic wife. The little girl squirmed and giggled in her mother's arms. "Auntie Snow didn't come to see me."

"Auntie Snow?" I asked, helping Snow stand and straightening my shirt that fit like a bed sheet on her.

She huffed. "Don't even start." More than displeased, she turned to them and asked, "Who told you I was here?"

Another woman came into the room. Tall, almost as tall as I, with short white hair and a grand pair of white wings behind her. "We were dining with Alaric when a guard notified us that they had spotted you in the southern chambers. Lila wanted to see you." She crossed her muscular arms across her chest. "I thought you were to spend your nights in Adriata?"

Visha sighed and stepped between us. "Out. Everyone out. Get the child out."

"Pleasure as always to see you, Visha," Leanna said with a deep courtesy before giggling and heading out of the room.

The second we were out in the corridors Visha smacked the doors shut and then bolted it with a thud.

"Your Majesty," the winged woman said, bowing her head to me. "We have not been introduced yet. My name is Tristin, I'm the leader of the Skye warriors and this is my wife, Leanna, leader of Llyn, and our daughter Lila."

"Lila!" the little girl shouted, throwing her hands in the air in a hoorah. "Are you Lila's uncle?" she shyly asked, ducking her head in her mother's hair. "Ma says you and auntie Snow are married."

With a nod, I said, "We are."

She perked up and jumped off her mother's arms, coming to stand before me. "Up. Uncle should hold Lila."

Snow stepped before me and picked the girl up herself. "Uncle is hurt, he can't get you up, you rude ball of fuss."

She giggled and threw her arm around Snow's neck holding her tight. "Lila is sorry."

"Hurt?" Leanna quietly asked, wrapping a hand on her wife's arm.

"The beast in Hanai," Snow explained, cradling the little girl tightly to her and I was suddenly even more enamoured—like she hadn't spelled me enough already.

The tribe leader's eyes sparkled and she jumped in excitement making Snow startle upright. "Llyn has the best weeping bane in the continent. It is the best tea for pain. Nia says so, too. We farm it on our rocks. Let us all go for a hot cup."

"It is late," Tristin said, "perhaps they are tired."

"We are," Snow said at the same time as I said, "That sounds great."

Leanna jumped, clapping her hands together and I could now see where her daughter got her bubbly personality from. She turned to her wife. "Take us, honey."

Like Cai, Tristin had craft inked on her hands and efficiently portaled us before a two-story house right in the middle of a busy alley bustling with vendors of all sorts preparing for the sale of the next morning.

Their house was exactly what one thought their house could be. Leanna's personality was everywhere, from the colourful paintings, the rose walls, the violet dyed furs, red pillows to the delicately painted pearl cups of tea. A little perfect home for what looked like a perfect family.

Almost immediately after we'd entered the house, Lila had dragged Snow upstairs to her room, while the couple served me tea and stared silently while I drank it. Tristin was curious and somewhat distrusting, but her wife emitted colourful clouds of excitement.

"Your daughter is fond of Snow," I said to break the silence. This was odd in every sense to me. I'd never been invited for…tea before. What did one say in this sort of situation?

Leanna nodded. "Snow has been there since I was pregnant, when Lila was born and every day since." My brows rose and she giggled. "Don't be fooled, she likes children." Her eyes went wide and she jumped a little from her seat. "Not to eat, of course. It was a terrible rumour."

"I gather you two are close?"

She shrugged. "Not exactly, but she sort of killed Lila's father and then both my parents and two brothers. She has tied another one to the Valley. We visit him from time to time."

The sip of tea suddenly found the wrong path and I coughed. Leanna shot to her feet, dabbing a handkerchief to my shirt. "Apologies, Your Majesty. It normally doesn't shock anyone anymore."

"Call me Kilian, please," I said, taking the handkerchief from her. "You certainly hold a massive grudge."

Tristin laughed lightly. "Did us all a favour."

"She certainly did," Leanna said, sitting back beside her wife. "Mother and father forced me to marry the tribe's bailiff when I was only a girl. When he would beat me, I went to my brothers who beat me more for daring to object to my husband's beatings and rules." She took a sip of her tea and gave me a smile. "Snow found out through Tristin who'd found me in one of her Fogling patrols in the mountains where my brothers had left me. Snow cut all their heads in front of the whole Olympia, issued a warning and created a safe line of women who could secretly report if something similar happened to them. Right after, I was made the leader of our tribe." She waved a quick hand. "Enough about me. Tell us, how did you fall in love with our Snow?"

It was Tristin's turn to choke on her sip of tea. "Lea."

Leanna frowned. "What? Aren't you curious, too?" She turned to me and leaned in, looking around as if she was to tell me a secret. "A poor soul confessed to her once and after laughing herself to tears she took his sister to bed. Right before him."

That made me laugh harder than anything and Leanna's eyes went wide, blinking rapidly.

Snow found that moment to come downstairs with Lila who rushed to Tristin's lap and curled into a ball. "Lila is tired." She yawned and her eyes slowly drooped while Tristin brushed her wild hair back.

Snow dropped beside me and sighed with obvious distress. Something was weighing down on her. "Llyn is colder than I remember it to be."

"Frost is setting in some of our heights," Tristin said. "The city itself hasn't seen the sun in about three weeks now. Our city is too far up, the Fogling rain down on us in a matter of minutes."

"Tomorrow," I said. "I will come to Llyn and you can order your Nimbus to pull the clouds back. My presence will keep them dispersed enough to let the ground absorb some sunlight. If we can catch one, I'd like to take it back to Adriata for my scholars to take a look."

"No," Snow jumped.

"Love, I can help."

"Not bleeding like a sieve you won't."

"I'm fine."

"No, Henrik, you are not."

"Oh," a little gasp interrupted us, and we turned to Leanna. "Is this some sort of foreplay or?"

Tristin chuckled while Snow glared death at the tribe leader.

I leaned in and whispered in her ear, "Be nice, love."

She huffed. "I'm nice. She is still breathing, isn't she?"

Leanna munched on some biscuits, pointing a finger at us. "You two argue like you've been married for a decade."

"Trying to make it seem as long as it can be," I said, finishing my tea.

Leanna grinned wide and leaned her elbows on her knees, blinking rapidly at the both of us. "More."

Snow shot up and almost launched at her had I not warped an arm around her waist and pulled her to my lap.

Lila giggled and even Tristin smiled.

"Rotten ilk," Snow murmured, leaning back on me. It took her a moment after to notice she'd made herself comfortable on my chest—that it was me she was leaning on. And when she did, she shot upright to her feet. "Time to go." She strutted outside without bidding anyone her usual good night.

I bowed my head. "Thank you for the tea. And the entertainment."

Lila waved a tiny hand. "Goodbye, uncle."

"Goodbye, little one."

Snow huffed and puffed in their dimly lit garden, gathering herself tight from the chilled breeze.

I held out a hand to her. "Let's go."

She crossed her arms. "Not yet. There is a bakery a few feet down the road. Thoughts of murder make me crave something sweet."

The store was small, its walls painted a shade of coral and several rustling wind chimes hung from the ceiling producing a lulling melody every time the northern wind brushed through the parted window panes.

All sorts of colourful desserts were lined on glassy shelves and counters, all which Snow eyed with astonishment. To be a little sugary treat. Had she ever looked at anything else with so much love?

She leaned over the counter a little, looking through the doors leading toward the bakery kitchen. "Samira?"

A young girl popped out of the kitchens, her apron stained with flour and some colourful sort of icing. "Snow, finally. I've just made your usual chestnut cupcakes. Though Nia tried to persuade me and lie that I cannot make it anymore and just sell you carrot cake instead." Her eyes drifted to me and then back at Snow, and then back at me and then back at what Snow was wearing. "Your lover is terribly handsome. If I was your husband, I wouldn't mind if you cheated on me with him."

"I'm her husband."

Samira's eyes doubled and she bowed at the waist, folding herself at ninety degrees. "My king."

Snow rolled her eyes. "Where is your father? Why has he left you all on your own at this hour? Don't you have school in the morning?"

Samira reached to cut a slice of Snow's cake. "I am manning the shop now. My teachers are sending the lessons to my home till I go back. Father has joined the soldiers. They lost about a dozen soldiers in the last Fogling attack. He thought it best that he fights since he is an Aura."

Snow reached a hand to her eyes and breathed out a sigh. "And your brothers?"

"They've joined the Myrdur guard." Her attention went behind us and her golden-brown skin flushed red. "And speaking about the Myrdur guard. Hi, Cai."

The general strutted in looking like death itself and swung an arm around Snow's neck. "Have you come to give him sugar poisoning? Smart. Hi, Samira."

The girl beamed at him. "Did you meet my brothers?"

"Yes, unfortunately," the general sighed, resting a hip on the counter. "I am sending them back."

Samira's eyes widened. "Why? Are they that bad? I swear they train every day."

"Mira, I am done burying fourteen and sixteen-year-olds." The girl flinched a little and Cai reached across the counter to fluff her hair. "I have enough help. You look like you need their help more than I. Go get us our usual."

When the girl left, Snow and her friend turned ten shades of grave. "How many?"

"Twelve."

Snow breathed heavily. "How many of theirs?"

"One hundred fifty."

"Silas is getting persistent," I said. "They've given up from reaching Highwall for the past week. It looks like the Olympian piece is next."

Cai nodded. "How long till they figure out how to breathe inside the mist?"

It was no longer just about Silas finding the sceptre. If Isjord crossed the mist, they would find Olympia.

We sat across one another on a little table on the corner of the shop while Snow ate her fourth piece of cake, utterly enamoured with the colourful sweets.

Caiden's eyes dropped to the bandage peeking out of my shirt and then returned to glare back at me.

I touched a finger to my shoulder. "You have a feather there."

"Fucking, Lazarus," he groaned, fluffing the stuff away. "It's like shedding season."

Snow lifted a spoonful of cake to his mouth. "Careful, he might be wanting to mate with you and ask you to lay his eggs."

He flicked her forehead. "Shut up."

A nerve jumped on my temple when a little swell started turning red on her skin. One day, I was going to round those fingers—

"Cake?" Snow asked, lifting a spoonful to my mouth.

It caught me by surprise, but I ate it and she chuckled. "What?"

She pointed the spoon between Caiden and I. "I made you two kiss."

Her friend shut his eyes and sighed. "Sugar gives her head a rush worse than alcohol. Take her back, she's had enough," he said, taking the plate from her and scooping all the remaining cake in his mouth.

Snow shot up like thunder, ready to attack her friend, but I wrapped an arm around her waist and faded us to Adriata.

CHAPTER FOURTEEN

BESTIA

SNOWLIN

Amaris was one hot humid hell covered in flowers and buzzing insects. I twirled in place as a bee went past me and I almost tripped on the long train of my favourite grey dress. The yellow wee things made me shiver. I hated bees.
"M-My queen," Atlas said, jogging to me, half tripping over the robes that fit him three sizes too big. "I didn't hear you arrive."
"Nia brought me and she went to see Driada. Where is Mal?"
"At the training courts."
"And your king?" I did need his rotten permission after all.
"I-It is his volunteering duties today," he explained. "Children from Amaris orphanage spend four days in the care of the royal court. Mal, Driada, Kilian and I have a day each."
"What does he teach them, rules on genocide?"
Atlas snorted and then covered it with a cough. "He is only a couple corridors down."
Swiftly, I followed after Atlas till we were in front of a square daisy meadow overlooking the sea. Children's laughter bubbled in the air, almost as vibrant as the sunlight above. And he laid there on the juniper ground with his eyes closed and a small smile etched on his lips while children covered him in little daisies. Phantom tendrils of shadows curled here and there in the air, chasing and playing with the children, and each time they squealed when they caught one, he grinned.
Why did it make my chest well with hurt?
"Your Maj—" I slapped a hand over Atlas's mouth and the young priest's eyes almost bulged out of their sockets.
I put a finger to my lips. "Don't tell him I was here." Pulling back, I let go of him. "I'll find Mal myself."

The training courts were a nightmare to find in the castle grounds. I should have listened to Atlas's advice and kept him with me.

This morning, after a quick visit to the dungeons, it had hit me. The memory from the elixir and why I saw that particular one. A place where Aryan could have kept my siblings without anyone knowing. A place that could have neutralised their magic and somewhere far but close enough for him to keep an eye on. Somewhere I prayed long and hard that I was wrong.

My feet picked up a pace when I heard heavy grunts, thuds and clatter of metal. Between feet tall walls of bushes stood a miles long ground of Adriatian soldiers sparing one another. It wasn't hard to spot Mal, his body stood out amongst the many from the ink tattooed on him. He stood back, leaning on a court fence as he directed a group of what looked like teenagers into different fighting stances.

Eldritch Commander. For the first time I could see it. His concentration was deadly, his demeanour dark. For a moment I felt like he might downplay the true him only to disguise this. The chatter, the laughter, the jokes. Perhaps they, too, were only a mask.

He counted and they shifted on his command with heavy grunts of Darsan words.

Many stopped when I pushed through the corridors of the platformed courts, some to stare and others to gape and mumble prayers. Sigh. They never gave up, did they?

When the younger brother spotted me, all of his previous mien vanished—replaced by a mischievous grin. "Sister-in-law," he said, jumping the fence and walking up to me. He gave me a long perusal. "Dressed a bit fancy for a match."

"You wouldn't believe me if I told you how much more gratifying it is beating a man dressed like this. If dirtying silks didn't give me grief, I would have shown you what I mean."

He laughed. "I believe you."

A few men gathered on the platform close to us, leaning on the bannister. "My queen," one said, bowing his head. "We finally get to see you. You are more beautiful than what Mal has painted you to be."

Another nudged his shoulder in a signal to stop. "Kilian will hang you."

Huh, strange. "Die an honourable death and learn to compliment a woman better."

They all laughed to my surprise, and a few others gathered around us, my panic throttling to my neck when I spotted the black leathers and steel.

"My soldiers," Mal introduced. "Part of the Eldritch squadron."

Unease settled in me at the memory of the last Empath I crossed paths with. "Empaths," I said with a sneer I couldn't help. "How joyous."

The men all chuckled, except for Mal. He knew the reason for my reaction.

He threw a sweaty naked arm over my shoulder and pulled me close. "I've known these fatheads since they were learning to shave downwards and nicking their tiny treasures. We are brothers—brothers who know to respect and protect the people I care about. I don't go easy on those that I select under my command."

Somehow, I believed him. With my thumb and finger, I picked Mal's arm and swung it off me. "You stink."

The idiot wrapped it around me again, making sure to rub his sweaty armpit on me. "You're used to my flower-scented brother. This isn't sweat, it's my body's tears from hard work."

I landed a hard punch on his stomach that sent him stumbling a couple steps back and his soldiers blasted in a laughing fit. "Ruined my favourite dress," I said, smoothing a hand over my sleeve.

Mal chuckled and grabbed my wrist, pulling me onto a training court. "Might as well use that situation to our advantage. You taught me some tricks in Isjord, but I never got the chance to show you any."

"Mal, when I kick your arse, I doubt your men will lend you a weeping shoulder."

His soldiers surrounded the court's fences. "Kick it and I'll offer him mine," a blonde one said.

"Not my type, Neo," Mal said, giving him a wink before taking a fighting stance. "Hand to hand, sister-in-law."

I rolled my eyes. "That's a tongue twister for your small brains I bet."

He made a hurt sound and put a hand over his chest. "Don't hurt my poor heart. The deal was to hurt my adorable buttocks."

"They are adorable," Neo said, and the men all laughed.

Mal pointed a finger at him. "Thank you, still not my type. Your sister, however."

The men all made a booing sound and Neo shook his head.

I cracked my neck and took position as did Mal.

He winked at me and gestured his finger for me to approach him. So I did, faking a punch which he caught with his much larger hand. The moment he anchored me to him, I grabbed his wrist and twirled his arm behind his back. The moment we were back to back, I slammed my heel on his knee and he went down. The men cheered and howled. Mal was quick, however, using his free hand to lessen his fall and spin in place to mimic my move, my arm locked behind my back as he slammed his heel on my knee sending me down. "I am a gentleman," he said, holding me tight. "Just not to arse kicking ladies."

"Neither am I," I said, using my free hand to unsheathe the dagger on my thigh and twisting it backward to press it to his back. Gently, I poked his skin.

"Ouch."

"Aw," I pouted, extending a hand to help him up. "Did the mean, arse kicking lady hurt you?"

He scoffed. "Cheater."

With a bright saccharine smile, I admitted, "A proud one." I kicked his leg. "Get up. I need you to do something for me?"

"Homicide?" he asked slyly.

"Not today. Saving that favour for another time."

He raised a brow and stood. "Another thing ending with cide?"

"Why? Do you need permission from your brother dearest?"

He shrugged. "Possibly. He is my king."

"Aren't I your queen?"

"Convenient, isn't it?" he said, ruffling my hair as he went past me to retrieve his discarded shirt. Did he just...ruffle my hair?

He waved a hand at his men. "I better see you sweat those smug smiles off tomorrow."

"Yes, Commander," they said in unison, still chuckling.

"Where are we going?" he asked, taking a long chug from a water bottle.

"There is somewhere I think Aryan could be hiding my siblings."

"Snow, I will take you all around all four corners of this realm," he said. "But you will never know how far and wide these four corners of the realm are. Let Visha perform her craft on you."

"No. I will do everything to find them myself. I can't lose my mother to find my siblings."

He rubbed his eyes, not in frustration it seems as he turned to look at me with the same pair of sad eyes he'd started giving me lately. I hated them. He wanted to say it, I knew. He wanted to tell me what most wanted to tell me. "Are you willing to compromise your living relatives for a dead one?" Except, as always, Mal didn't fear me, and I suspected it had nothing to do with the fact that he thought I was the prettiest woman he'd seen.

I didn't know why I felt like I needed to be sincere at that moment when I told him, "I don't remember her, Mal. I cannot recall a single line of my mother's face. Sometimes I hear her voice in my head, but I cannot match it to a face. Few times when I catch a glimpse of my reflection, I plaster that one on my memories, sometimes a random face I've seen in passing and sometimes I just leave it how my mind sees it—blank, sunken and bloodied. Before that night I hadn't seen her in six months. The words she said to me were perhaps the longest she'd spoken to me in years. Nightmares are all I have of her. It is my only memory. So, yes, I am willing to sacrifice much for my dead mother."

His stare faltered and dropped to the ground. "I...I am sorry, Snow. I shouldn't have said that."

"I don't need you to apologise, Princeling, but I am in need of your services,"

"Is that why you gifted my mother that necklace?" he asked, tying back his hair. "Or why you take her to the healing valley every time she goes to Taren."

I flicked a bit of dust from my dress. "No idea what you are on about, Mal sweetheart."

Mal's attention went somewhere behind me, and I turned.

Kilian leaned on the court fence with Nia at his side. The fool still had little flowers on his head and droopy sleepy eyes that made him look entirely too...adorable.

"Did you get lost?" Nia asked, jumping on the court platform. "That's the wrong brother."

Mal flashed her a grin. "Perhaps the right one."

My friend groaned, dropping her head back. "Do you never get tired?"

"Of being great?" the Night Prince asked. "Sometimes, it's a grand burden to bear."

"Actually." Nia pointed a finger between Mal and I. "You too suit one another perfectly. One massive ego next to another more massive ego."

"The more massive ego was hopefully mine," I said. "I don't do anything unless it is the better, greater version."

Nia shook her head, but Mal laughed.

I could feel his attention on me, like a brand on my skin—one that still burned. I turned to face him. "I'm taking Mal with me."

He cocked his head back and glanced between his brother and I. "Mal will have to eat first, he has been on these courts all morning."

I nodded. "He can eat first."

"Settled then," Kilian said. "We are all having lunch. Nia, you're hungry, too, right?"

"Very," my friend said, jumping from the court platform. "I could hear the rumbling of your stomach to Taren, Snow, come on."

They had me in their trap.

Reaching him, I lifted on my tiptoes and extended a hand to his hair. He was too tall, so he had to bend down a little for me, and I grabbed the little daisy stuck between his thick dark locks. "Lost your flower crown, Princess?"

He chuckled and tapped my chin with his knuckle like it was all normal for us to act like this.

Then I panicked. The type of panic that envelopes you wholly, where you cannot recognise where you are or who anyone is, like the world is suddenly spinning too fast and not at all. Quickly, his reaction dropped, and I knew that I looked as dazed as I felt.

His hand ghosted on my face but did not touch me—he knew not to touch me at that moment. "I didn't mean—"

"I forget," I said, dropping the daisy and leaving after Nia and Cai. I forget who he was and what he'd done. My mind tricked me. He'd tricked me too, made me so comfortable around him, that I could forget just what he'd done. How he'd ruined me.

Lunch was set in one of the patios overlooking the gardens, a large parasol fluttered overhead shading us from the strong sun of the afternoon. The calmness of the spring breeze, the lull of rose scents and the slight buzz of nature life made the moment seem so dreamlike. This was something strange for me, I'd never eaten outside before like this. By the third bee I killed on the table, I knew why.

"Snow," Nia gasped, scooping away another little creature I had my aim on. "Why would you kill them?"

"You've seen me kill stingers bigger than that one."

She slapped my shoulder. "Don't be cruel."

"Oh, killing a bee makes me cruel." I turned to Kilian and extended a piece of some sort of olive filled bread to his mouth for him to take a bite. "Hear that? It wasn't all my kills."

He took a bite and leaned back on his chair. "How much has that list grown now? If I remember correctly, last time it was in the hundreds."

My expression dropped and I turned to look at Nia who was gapping at Kilian. She hadn't been the one to tell him my dirty little secret. The method Alaric had taught me when father was training me to be his weapon—when I had started to kill.

He sighed, rubbing his eyes. "I regretfully have to admit that it was one the only things I could figure out on my own when we were in Isjord, it wasn't Nia."

"Two hundred and five," I said, dipping a spoon on the cold cucumber soup and extending it to him again.

He raised a brow. "You killed more than fifty times that count that day in the battle."

I licked the spoon after him. "You've figured the list wrong. It wasn't all kills that I counted. Only the ones I wasn't meant to kill." Giving him a tight smile, I said, "That other list isn't one I can keep count on. It saves me prayer time for my other sins."

Only ever count those you were never meant to kill, those that were never in your aim, but someone else's and used by someone else. It won't prevent the fall, but it will soften it, Alaric had taught me that. Though guilt had never eaten me after a kill, counting as he had said made me feel a bit more human in some strange sense.

He slanted me an unamused look. "What about the ones in the valley, do you count those?"

"They are alive, aren't they? Those count toward the list of my mercy."

The glass he held stopped midway.

Adriatians and their morals will forever be the paradox that no scholar would ever solve. I leaned on the table, propping my chin on my fists and batting my lashes at him. "Just say it. One's mercy is not for one to give, only for gods to gift."

He took a sip from his drink while looking at me the whole time. "Versed as ever on the Astrum liber, my love. Then why are you gifting mercy?"

"Because, d*arling*," I said, leaning back. "In this realm, I am a god."

Kilian didn't seem too happy at that proclamation. Certainly because of what was said in the saintly books about those with a divine complex. It normally didn't end well. But I wasn't here for a long time, only for a fun one. So that didn't bother me as much as it did him.

"I leave for two minutes and the tensions run high," Mal said, settling on his seat in fresh black leathers and wet unbound hair that seemed to have grown longer. "What did I miss?"

Nia made to say something, but her words caught when her attention drifted toward the castle garden entrance. And I saw my friend crumble back into that little person her fears always made her look like. Nia was mighty and she knew it. She was knowledge and strength and goodness, and she knew it. She was everything this world had fought to rip off her. And I was a foot away from ripping off that fear that made her forget everything she knew of herself.

Nesrin reached our table, her disdain evident as her envious stare bounced between Nia and I.

"Nes," Mal said, slouching back in his chair to squint at the intruder of our peace and my self-control. "What do we owe this unpleasant interruption to? Rather, which soldier shall I dismiss for letting you through to the king's private quarters?"

She cleared her throat and straightened. "I heard my sister was here, I wanted a word."

Lightning struck the sky and the woman jumped back with a flinch. "What did you just call her?" I asked, flinging a butter knife between my fingers that ought to be etched in her eyeball and through her skull.

Nia pointed a hand to the chair before her. "Sit. Have your word."

A smirk tilted in the corner of my mouth at the tone of my friend. That's my Nia.

Nesrin did as told, but seemed reluctant to speak, her gaze going to Kilian more often than I'd prefer. She cleared her throat. "Hel—"

"Nia," my friend said coldly.

Nesrin looked deliciously uncomfortable. "You never liked that nickname when we were younger."

Nia leaned back. "You never liked me much when we were younger, it is beyond me how you would know such a thing as what I liked or didn't."

Nesrin glanced at Kilian again. "We were young...Nia. Very young and our situation was a very difficult one."

"For you. Difficult for you."

"For the both of us." She reached for Nia's hand across the table, and I stabbed the butter knife on the table, quarter of an inch from her finger, stopping her.

I gave her terrified face a smile. "Do that again, please. I very much so would like to hear what sounds you make in pain. How that face will twist when I pull each bone out of your skin and end all our collective woes with a grand symphony of screams. I know how to orchestrate just the perfect piece."

She pulled her hand away and almost imploringly looked at Kilian whose attention was entirely focused on my friend. "You will have to." Nesrin swallowed hard. "You will have to forgive me and help us move forward."

Nia tilted her head to the side, taking her time to answer. She nodded after a while and Nesrin perked in her seat. "No, I don't think I will."

I smiled while Nesrin's face fell. "You are being childish," she bit out with a sneer.

"Nes, Nes," I crooned, waving my knife in the air.

She scoffed and turned to my friend with a threatening stare. It was so patronising it almost made me want to carve each of her muscles out by hand. "What, will you have her kill me like she did with our father?"

The amount of energy I used to hold back gave me a headache. But for Nia's sake I endured.

Nia leaned forward on the table. "No. I am entirely capable of doing so myself. But, *sister*," she said calmly, "be mindful. I don't kill. I poison. I think I like seeing little flowers wilting a thorn."

Nesrin flinched a little—she would have flinched a lot more if she knew Nia the way I did—if she knew what my friend was capable of. "Is that a threat?"

Nia nodded. "It is. I'd prefer that you be aware of what happens the next time you approach me. I well left you in the past, don't cross my present again. Especially going as far as to seek me."

Nesrin pushed out of her seat and made to leave before Kilian called out, "Councillor."

The woman turned with a bright smile on her face like she'd not been part of the previous conversation. "Yes, Kilian."

Kilian? Is that what all members of his court addressed him?

His look was grave, a stoic mask he always wore around others. "Don't interrupt me and my family having lunch or dinner and breakfast at that. It is a precious time. Especially when none of your interruption is a matter of emergency or concerning our kingdom's state of affairs."

Family. The word made me stop chewing and look at him.

She gaped at him, reddening to the tip of her ears. "Apologies, it wasn't my intention."

"I wish it not be your intention for the sake of your future in my court, Councillor," Kilian said, dismissing her.

A small smile pulled on the corner of my mouth when Nesrin retreated with unshed tears in her eyes.

The moment she was out of earshot and sight, Nia turned to Kilian with a small bow of her head. "Thank you."

I linked an arm around her neck and kissed her cheek repeatedly till she was fighting me off. "Nia Drava," I said, "indeed likes to poison."

She scoffed and covered her face with her hands. "Let's not celebrate the fact that I acted as a completely terrible person."

"That you acted as I would have?" I asked, chewing the delicious olive bread. Not offended. I liked how I acted. It was liberating. This bread, gods, it was good.

"With less stab wounds and overall bloodiness of it all," Mal mumbled around a mouthful of food.

She shook her head. "I didn't mean it like that. Perhaps she was right, we were just children."

I turned her chin to me. "I will not let you manipulate yourself into thinking you were in the wrong. I can easily hate something or someone, Nia, if it is only for the way they breathe. For you to hate something or someone certainly takes more than their lung capacity."

"Children or not," Kilian said. "You were hurt from it."

Nia frowned at him. "Don't join the bunch."

"I am not saying you need to kill my Councillor," he said, giving me and his brother what looked like a warning stare. "I'm saying you owe no one forgiveness. Certainly not to those that were not apologetic at all."

That had been why Nia had acted as she did. She'd seen Nesrin's shadows. And that made me even more rageful.

"Sister-in-law," Mal said, taking an apple and extending a hand for me to take. "We have business to attend to. Think very loudly of the place where you want me to take us."

After pulling the hood of my dress up and the gossamer veil over my face, I linked my hand to his across the table and immediately our surroundings changed. The green and warmth of Amaris turned to blistering white snow and dull grey skies. There was a crashing sound and the swirl of waves in the background that suddenly blurred before me. The smell of salt and fish along with the remnants of fading made me retch all I ate out on the murky waters of the Seer Sea.

Mal pulled my hair up and rubbed a hand over my back while I leaned over the small cliff. "That bad, huh?"

I took the handkerchief he offered and wiped my mouth. "What is?"

He gave me a look of apology. "I might have asked Cai and he might have told me. You took mud foam one too many times when we went to sea line cities."

"Don't fret, I wasn't keeping it a secret."

He looked around and then frowned. "Why have you brought us to the middle of nowhere?"

It wasn't exactly the middle of nowhere. I had been here many times before. "Ulv Islet. It's a small island by the shores of Casmere." Only a couple of miles in dimensions, the small rocky land was more barren than the deserts themselves. There was no vegetation and no other life besides the seagulls occasionally taking respite to eat their catch. The Islet was a perfect hidden gem of my father's. One that no one paid attention to either.

I pointed to a wall fort toward the empty north. A towering giant that stuck out like a mushroom in the middle of the small rock. "It used to be a prison. Aryan adored this place."

Mal squinted into the distance. "A prison? An odd thing to adore."

"An undisclosed one. If evil could hold his pets somewhere, he definitely would have held them here," I said. "Aryan could do all the twisted things he liked to the men and women imprisoned here without no one knowing or caring."

Mal tensed, shadows crossing his russet eyes, turning them to black. "How would you know what he did here?"

I got to my feet. "Because he brought me here many times to show me. To prepare me. My kills rot somewhere in here too."

His eyes widened just slightly, enough to see his anger flash through. The Night Prince was different from his brother in more than one sense. But the way they reacted toward me was somehow one of the same—almost protective. It was funny if you thought about it well. The man who sent to kill me and his brother felt protective over me. Out of all the clownery in this realm, this had to be the winning act.

Another waft of sea air carried from the brisk wind, and I winced, attempting to hold down whatever was left in my stomach. "The place showed in my memory from when I took Visha's elixir. Now I think I know why. The prison building had a Dark Crafter buried in its foundations. It fed the place with magic. Magic that disguised a lot of other magical essences. Possibly the ones my siblings have."

Mal and I pushed through the snow-covered rocky paths leading to the stone fort charging with a skin creeping feel of the dead. The kind of dead who spooked evil itself. The prisoners who resided here were the crop of the cut. The horror of all criminals. And it did make killing them somewhat gratifying. I just wish killing was all I did to them.

Mal suddenly pulled me back, staring downward where I almost stepped. "The hells is with this place?"

A stream of black viscous fluid like tar gushed over the blinding snow, gliding in a long path that spilled over a rock and onto the sea. When we reached the tall moss-blanketed dark tower Mal hissed and winced. "Fuck."

The hells. The same creosote liquid dripped from the stone onto the wall gutters that chased down the stream—it came from the tower. It *leaked* from the tower stone.

Just before I reached to touch it, Mal wrapped his hand around my wrist. "Bad idea. It's soul remnants. Very bad souls if I might say so. This place needs to be set on fire and exorcised by a good Crafter. Then set on fire again."

He kicked the main door open, sending the damp wood to splinter in pieces and a chilling crack reverberate through the desolate space.

"What on the bloodied hells died here?" he asked, lifting a hand toward the corridor ahead. The musky scent was replaced with a sharp sweet smell of roses and a blast of a white cloud erupted from Mal's touch. Odd scent for what his magic did.

I lifted an arm to cover my face when the wuthering impact of whatever magic he unleashed sent saw dust, soot and cobwebs blasting in the air.

"Your shadows are white," I said as matter of fact, staring downcast at our two different shadowy figures.

"When I tie strings to the dead, my magic forms a habitat of protection around me by outcasting any darkness from me, including my shadows—anything the dead can cling to. I don't have an affinity with death like Kilian, I only control it through tugs of emotion that linger over the dead and into the spiritual mana. And if I am unprotected, it may attempt to form an affinity with me. By killing me," he said like it made perfect sense.

"How does your brother do it? He was perfectly alive last time I saw him."

"No, but his magic isn't," he explained again, like it's supposed to make perfect sense to me. When he looked over at me, he saw the confusion marking my expression. "You never paid attention to Adriata in any form, did you?"

"How would you guess such a thing?" I could have cared less for anything when I was a child. And after I got crowned I already had too much to worry to bother myself with learning about Adriata. I knew how to kill them and that was plenty.

He gave me a helping hand as we jumped over a fallen pillar. Shouldn't have worn a dress for this, but my leathers felt too saggy after losing weight.

"Never wondered why an Obscur is often called an *Orcus*, why they are called death itself? Soul killers?"

I glanced at the empty prison chambers while we passed through the corridor. "Should I have?"

"Possibly, considering you are now married to one."

"I'm not afraid of him. If that is what you are implying."

"No, you're not afraid of Kilian, but you are afraid of his magic. Still, it isn't what I meant."

I stopped and so did he. "And what did you mean?"

"Kilian taught his magic to read emotion like an Empath, he even went as far as to manipulate his darkness into using shadows instead of darkness itself. I'm not trying to say that Kilian is perhaps the most skilled Obscur since the time of gods, because he is, what I'm saying is that he would rather lose sleep and spend years learning anything else than use his god given magic. Do you want to know the why?"

"Why, Mal?"

"Because an Obscur is also called a cursed Aura—a cursed god blessed." He kicked a rock from our path, leading us further in the corridor. "When a prime Obscur at the time of Henah in Adriata attempted to breach a path to the Otherworld, they were caught by the guardian of death himself. Curiosity might have killed the cat, but it did something worse to the Obscur. The Otherworld guardians are quite the jesters, you know. 'If you wish to see death, be death' was the wording of that curse."

Oh.

"And like that," Mal continued. "The blood of all Obscurs mutated and changed through the curse to what Kilian stands now to be. The very core of death. To be tied with it. Father was an Obscur, it is why my magic, too, is more mutated from other Empath's—why I can control the dead. It is also why Kilian is the only remaining Obscur. Many think that what happened to the dark Aura was fair, mostly those that had seen what an Obscur could do. Gods in this realm of human."

"And to think that I am the one being feared."

Mal scoffed. "Believe me, they fear him alright. But Kilian fears what he can do more than what others fear him. When we take a life, it chips away part of our souls. Fragments, really, but when you are in the position that we are, where we are the face of wars and battles, you really underestimate how quickly your whole soul could shatter."

I didn't know that.

"Is that why he sent others to do his dirty deeds? Because he was afraid of tarnishing his perfect little soul?"

Mal stopped again. For a long while I expected him to say something, but he didn't.

Light filtered through the half-splintered roof of the top floor; the angry winter sky poured a light coat of snow on the sphagnum moss infested floor.

"Perhaps I was wrong," I said, peeking in and out of the chambers Aryan normally used for his activities. There was no sign of any life or any sliver of magic pervading. I would have felt their presence—I always did before, even when we were hiding.

Mal squatted in front of the broken north wall facing the view of the Hollow Sea crashing against rock. "Snow, does this look like a claw mark to you?"

I glanced over his shoulder to a dent near the edge where the wall had broken off. "Looks like it. But—"

"There are no animals on this island and surely no fish crawled from the Hollow to do that." He pointed overhead. "Or that."

Three slashes dented the grey rock.

"They held no animals in here, only Aura and din-Aura, sometimes an unblessed or two. Never an animal." I ran a finger over the dent, comparing the size of my hand to it. "Especially not one of that size." Something clicked in me, and I dropped to my knees, shovelling rock away. "Mal, see if you can find any remnants of fur or scales, anything green really."

The two of us dug and hauled rock and moss and dust like mad.

Mal stopped digging and lifted a rock to my face. A single strand of fibre attached to it. Viridescent green, almost luminescent. "This is getting creepier by the minute."

The thing from Hanai, it had to have been kept here. How and why in the hells?

I dropped to the ground. "How did my father get hold of such a beast?"

"Question is, why would it want to escape if it is under his control?" Mal asked, studying the broken wall. "I'm sure it would know this place has a main entrance."

"Like all of his previous monsters wanted to." I turned to face him. "Why would you assume it is willingly serving my father?" Why would anyone want to serve my father? Why did I feel sorry for it, too?

I got to my feet and searched the rooms one after the other. A thick layer of dust had coated on my tongue by the time I reached the last door, only to find it locked.

My kicks were nothing like Mal's, but I did put almost all of my strength in them. The door, however, didn't even budge.

With a sigh, I turn to Mal. "Leaving a lady to struggle?"

"And miss the entertainment?" He kicked the door, and the wood didn't even shiver.

"Move," I said, pulling him back. I rested my hand on the door and a kick of electricity skittered over it. There was a smell of charred wood, yet nothing was burning.

Some of the dust flaked off from the wood, and at the centre of the door, there were a few odd lines. Some familiar and some not. Tracing a finger over them, I tried to memorise their shape. I cursed my patched memory when nothing would come up when I tried to think of whom or what my uncle kept here back then.

"Snow." Mal pulled me back as something came crawling onto the wood. Several woodlouse, roaches and blackflies began creeping from all over the sides of the door, enshrouding it.

"Dark craft," I murmured. Tinge of mint and dark wood filled the air. "Melanthe."

The two of us jumped back when a thud shook the door from the other side. Then another and another, till the wood quivered on its hinges and the insects went flying in our direction.

"Something is wrong," Mal said, pulling me tightly to his side.

The sound of rock sliding over rock dragged our attention to the broken wall that was no longer a broken wall. When the last square of rock slid into place, the corridor enshrouded in darkness.

My pulse picked up once we were veiled in obscurity. "A trap."

Mal clasped my hand tight. "Fuck," he hissed. "I cannot fade us."

A harrowing roar boomed around the desolate space and Mal pulled me to a run.

"I…I cannot see," I said, spinning my head round in search for just a tiny fragment of light.

"I've got you," Mal said, pulling me closer to him as we hurried away from the beast. "Stairs, Snow. Follow the sound of my steps."

A splitting sound echoed as we reached the ground floor and then the same roar boomed without the constriction of the room.

Hairs rose at the back of my neck when heavy footsteps chased behind us. I felt the wind trickle and shift behind me, and I blindly reached for my dagger—throwing it aimlessly in the direction the thing was chasing us. It had landed on flesh as the blade didn't clatter on the floor or wall.

"Hold on," Mal shouted, rounding me with arms close to his chest. He suddenly skidded to a halt, spinning in place where his body met wood with a thud. The door splintered and I winced when the brightness filtered through. The thrust of the crash sent Mal and I flying onto the snowy ground.

He groaned in pain from bearing all the force of the impact, but still held onto me tightly. "Are you alright?"

I nodded, moving off him and helping him stand.

A pair of viridescent halos glistened from the abyss of the prison tower, its white breath misting in the black air. The way every sense in my body vibrated with scourging terror was one I'd never felt before but at the same time knew very well off. A recognition of sorts, like an old fear or something I was used to.

Mal pulled me behind him like I needed protection and a thick taste of magic wafted in the air. Skeletons broke the snow-covered surface, all surrounding us, and a dusting of shadows began materialising in the air like a shield of protection.

No one moved.

Not us. Not the skeletal forms of the dead protecting us. Not the beast either.

It only stood there. Huffing and puffing white air.

Was it trapped? Why was it not attacking us?

Mal pulled me to him ready to fade us. "No," I said, lifting a hand to stop him. "Wait." Strange, why was its stare so levelled to ours?

Instead of moving towards us, the beast stepped back until it disappeared inside the darkness. Steps of its descent were light and soft, almost too quiet.

Last I remembered, its feet had large claws attached and he stomped enough on the ground to leave massive footprints. The first floor of the prison was littered with rock, wood and mud. Yet there was no sound as it passed through.

"What did it look like, Mal? That thing—what did it look like?" He could see through the veil of darkness.

"Like nothing. It was fog, perhaps from the craft veil around the tower. It could be there to protect it."

"I don't think it was the beast from that day."

He reached closer to the entrance of the tower, frowning the more he stared ahead. "Are you certain?"

"It gave the same sort of alert, but it can't be the same beast. It is too different physically. Father could have created more of them. It has to be more than one. He could be using the one from Hanai to make more. The soldier in Hanai said that he'd seen Melanthe feed on its blood. Perhaps others are, too."

Father was breeding beasts. That meant he was readying for war. If he had succeeded in creating obedient ones without need of chaining and taming, that meant the war was closer than we thought. He was fixing all the mistakes the Seraphim king made when he raised Aurora. There would be no one to challenge the guardian if we were all too occupied protecting our lands from his army of Aura, human and beasts. Father knew he was winning. He was acting arrogantly, carelessly even—it only meant he was certain of his victory.

Then something else struck me. "Mal, I don't think the memory was meant for my siblings. I think it was meant for the beast."

"Do you think you might have come across it before?"

I shook my head. "I would have remembered. I would have felt it like I felt it now. But I didn't even know of its existence before I took the memory elixir." My head hurt from how hard I was pushing memories out of their depths.

He rested a hand on my shoulder, breaking my focus. "Crafter magic works in odd ways. Visions, foretelling and foreboding—in that sense. I wouldn't think about it too hard, Snow."

And I agreed with him. "Henrik better have found a way to that Oryn priest." Right now, he was the only person who could give us an answer.

He raised a brow. "Henrik? Why are you calling him that rotten name?"

"It is his name."

His expression darkened. "It was our father's name."

"Your brother," I said carefully, "he told me about him. And you."

He flashed me a stupid but oddly sad grin. "Bet he recalled it with fondness and deep nostalgia."

"Why do you consider your brother an ally of your father's?"

His amusement fell. "Let's go home," he said, extending a hand to me.

"Taren is my home, Mal, not Adriata. And as your queen I demand you answer my question."

His hand dropped as did his russet stare. "Because no matter what he did to Kil, no matter what hell he made him see, no matter what he did to me or my mother, no matter how he was, my brother never hated him." He huffed a laugh as if he'd just realised what he'd said out loud. "All I wanted was to feel as if I had not imagined all that our father did to me. And him, too. At some point I thought I made it up, like there was no justification for what I felt and that I was wrong. Kil pretended nothing had ever happened. Pretended it was all justified. Believe me, Snow, what he did to me, to him, can never be justified."

"I hate your father, Mal, and I've never even met him." I extended a hand to him. "We're a team of two now."

"Three," he said, grinning only like he knew how to grin. "Cai, too. Though the arsehole is pretending to be all mad and sulky at me right now."

Chapter Fifteen

Supplicum

Kilian

When Snow and Mal had returned last night, they had been beyond disturbed. After they had both fidgeted all night long in my room coming up with all sorts of madness, this morning Snow had rushed to quell her thoughts with violence and my brother with women and liquor. And I could do nothing to stop them both as my duties required my full attention. After a meeting with Albius and Sebastian, a check on the Sidra sealines for any sighting of eudemons, a trip to meet with the young Sidran priestess to discuss my trip into the Danics, Driada's weekly meeting with her healer and ten documents to sign later, I had finally the time to fade to Olympia to meet with Visha.

Taren was quieter than usual, the corridors almost empty and even soldiers were no longer in their assigned positions but looking outside the windows.

"Something interesting outside?" I asked.

They all snapped to attention, returning to their spots and bowing in unison. "Your Majesty."

Somewhere in the distance, over a flat rock on a mountain cliff connected to the castle by one of the bridges, a grand cloud of dust had risen in the air, enshrouding the training courts in a veil of beige.

"It is the queen," one of the men said. "They returned from Kilerth this morning after a Fogling attack." He shot a careful glance to his companion. "Soldiers say she caused a lot of damage near the tribe. Lost control. Alaric is issuing his...punishment."

"Punishment?"

He nodded. "It is usually not this extreme."

Immediately, I rushed to the bridge connecting the castle to the training grounds and faded behind a grand crowd that had clustered around what was happening. When I managed to push through, Snow knelt on the rocky ground of the massive training space, breathing hard and tired while Alaric stood before her, his mouth moving quickly before he shouted, "Up!"

On wobbly legs, Snow got to her feet, her shoulders bunched while she clutched her side. There was no sign of pain on her face. There was nothing there actually. Her look was cold and blank. Empty.

When I went to interrupt whatever was happening, two hands wrapped around my wrists. Caiden and Nia both held me back.

"Not a good idea, shadow boy," Caiden said sternly.

Nia nodded quickly. "Not a good idea at all."

At that moment, there was a blast in the direction of Snow and dust rose in the air from the strength of the wind emitted. The air chilled and ice crawled beneath our feet. She had blocked Alaric's attack with a tall wall of ice. Not how the Snow I knew would deal with an attack. Evade and counterattack—that was always her strategy.

"Come on, kid," Alaric called loudly. "Show me all that attitude you took to Kilerth this morning. You want to go to a fight angry, ey? Show me angry."

Yet she didn't even lift a finger when he blasted another wave of wind enough to have her crashing against the wall of the valley. As if pain was unknown to her, she peeled her body from the rock and stood up again, walking to him.

She uses my son as a boundary between good and bad.

Is this what it was?

"Bet is that she will roll her eyes and he will be angrier than *she* was this morning," Nia murmured to her friend's side.

He scoffed. "Bet is that she won't make a single move to make him angry and the old man will take her to one of them knitting classes."

Nia shook her head, bringing a bunch of wrapped carrot slices from her pocket and handing one to Caiden. "The head of the class is on holiday to see her pregnant daughter. Snow had a servant gift her a massive bag of prunes after she heard that pregnant women get constipated easily."

"Have you two lost your minds?" I asked, stunned at these two while my wife stood there receiving blow after blow without doing anything about it.

Nia offered me a carrot slice. "No, Snow did. Almost wiping out half of Kilerth this morning because she thought a Fogling looked at her strangely."

Snow waddled to us, bloodied and limping. "I swear that thing looked right through my black soul." She swallowed hard at the sight of the carrots, but her nose crinkled in a cringe. "Got anything else?"

Caiden shook his head. "Ate the chestnuts when you were getting your arse beaten."

She shrugged. "Could have been the knitting lady. Thank Nubil I sent her a week early on holiday."

The Zephyr general sighed and handed Nia a few silvery coins.

These two had to be insane.

Alaric strutted to us wearing a deep scowl. "Take your bride away, son. Before she tries to lift another city up from the roots."

Snow frowned at him. "Kicking me away without food?"

"They have plenty of newborn babes to feed you in Adriata, kid."

"Let her eat, Ric," Caiden said. "If she is hungry, her next target might be Amaris and she swore a bloody oath."

The Regent turned to me. "Have dinner with us tonight?" He side-eyed his daughter and said, "We have no serpent flesh and venom to serve you, but her vile mouth will fill your appetite plenty."

"Thank you," I offered, "but I was on the way to meet with Visha. Snow can eat in the meantime."

"You can meet the witch later," Alaric said, waving his hand in dismissal. "Let us sit for a meal as a family. I am sure she has passed to you all the many times I've requested that. And I am sure all the times she's given me your rejection have been justified. Ey?"

Snow scoffed and chucked a bunch of hair behind her shoulder before strutting away irked.

Nia hooked her arm around Alaric's and lifted to plant a kiss on his stubbly cheek. "Don't be angry at her."

"Not angry, little hen. Frustrated."

"Imagine how frustrated she is with all that is happening," Nia said, her gaze following Snow till she disappeared over the bridge heading to the castle. "At least it's been a few days since she's gone down the dungeons. Tristin said all the councillors are gone."

Snow sat beside me, jollily slurping her hot stew, burning her tongue and choking every other spoonful or so from how fast she ate.

I rested a hand on her spoon, waiting for her to chew what she had on her mouth before letting go. "Slower, love, just a bit slower."

Her other hand curled over the table as if she needed the grounding, and she tried to slow her mouthfuls.

Alaric sighed and shook his head to himself. The look he gave Snow told me he knew why she ate the way she did. There was regret in his shadows. "You were out of line today, kid."

"There was no line. Only rock. Very wobbly and curved rock."

He smacked the spoon down. "For Caelum's sake."

She did the same, the silverware almost pierced a hole through the wooden table. The father and daughter shared the same temper. "I told you that there was something wrong with the beast."

Alaric sighed. "There was nothing wrong with the beast. Why would there be something wrong with the beast?"

"Perhaps there could have been," Alastair limped into the dining chambers, setting his crane to a wall and taking a seat. He bowed to me and asked Snow, "What is it that you think you saw?"

"The eyes," she said with a fully stuffed mouth. "They were too...too...human looking. Does no one think of them as strange lately? The way they cluster—Foglings have never clustered before. They never feed on what they kill either, but now they are tearing through human and animal alike. When we pulled clouds back, before they would only hover above our cities and now they break buildings, run through houses. It is almost as if they are aiming to do so."

"They could be evolving," Nia said, returning to the table with a bowl of stew. "Adapting to new conditions. Hi, papa."

Alastair beamed. "You left early. And without breakfast. I made eggs and toast how you like them. Cai finished it all though."

Cai scoffed. "You practically threatened me to eat it all so there was no waste."

Nia scrunched her face apologetically. "Had to leave early for Eldmoor."

"How long?" I asked. "How long have you noted these changes in the Fogling?"

The whole table turned to stare at me. It was Alastair who answered, "About a year or so, but it only got worse last summer. They would not come down on the cities, they'd roam overhead, feed on light and the bustling life below, but never attack. We lived with them for almost twenty-seven years and they'd never been a problem before."

Hells. "Since when have the Isjordians been lingering and dying over Myrdur?"

Every set of eyes on the table doubled, including Snow's.

"But," Nia said, looking over at Cai whose breathing had picked up, "we are burning them and spreading ashes over the Seer Sea."

I shook my head. "Doesn't matter. They are still dying in Myrdur. The magic is potent over Myrdur. The Isjordian soldiers are turning into Fogling."

"He could be right," Visha said, reaching our table and taking a seat. "It is possible. It could also explain why the Fogling are different, more aggressive, too. And why I cannot sense any Isjordian souls lingering in the ruins. If souls have already manifested themselves as these monsters, it would explain that."

Alaric pursed his lips with regret. "And I am afraid there is nothing we could do at the moment besides fight both sides off." He sighed loudly, eyeing his eldest daughter. "Tell me you're not scheming some other manoeuvre of yours, kid."

"I won't tell you, as always," Snow said. "The pre-lecture hurts my morale." She nudged my thigh with hers. "Let's have Visha see you before you wither on me and die."

"Your confessions of love always warm my heart, my missus."

"I must be careful, all the warmth might set it on fire."

"I wouldn't mind the burn, love of mine."

She rolled her pretty eyes. "Shut up."

"What? No sassy remark for me?"

Her fists flowed with electricity and she glanced at every other face that had stopped and gone silent while witnessing our conversation.

She had laid sideways on the bed, half of her body hanging over the edge as she read something she'd scribbled down. Her face had turned red from how long she'd stood like that.

I put the delivery documents down and turned to her. "Love, what are you doing?"

"Thinking."

I stood to fill a quarter of the tumbler. "And can I get you to engage in a less dangerous pastime?"

She pushed up, eyeing me and then the drink I held. "Pour me some."

Kneeling before her, I lifted the glass to her lips. She narrowed her eyes on me for a moment but drank it at my pace. "Tasty?" I asked, swiping my thumb over her wet lips.

She shivered at the burn of the liquor. "Tell me you only drink it to look all kingly and lethal."

"Father used to take me to test the new batches. I suppose I grew a taste for it. Now," I said, drinking the rest of it in a gulp. "What questions do you have for me? The frown tells me there are a couple."

She smoothed her expression and laid back on the bed. "Why could Esmeray travel through to Cynth?"

"She was one of the first Aura in this realm. Henah was very meticulous when she chose to pass her power and she deemed Esmeray one of the finest humans she'd come across in Numen." I took a black leather-bound book from one of my shelves and laid beside her. "Esmeray is also one of the five primes that decoded coloured human emotion for us to understand. Also, one of the five that had visited Cynth with the purpose to learn more about emotion—become it too. They say there was a waterfall in Cynth, that if you washed under the water, it would heighten each specific emotion to the fullest. They stayed there for days till they grasped each and every one to the finest of details a human mind could. One of the five of them was my ancestor, the first Obscur to exist—why I am able to see emotion like an Empath is."

She flipped through the pages of the Anima Book, running a finger over each different coloured section. "This is how you know how to read emotion?"

"Mostly. Some Empaths like Mal and Nia can also feel, taste and smell emotion, so they can interpret it on the basis of how they feel and what they believe it to be."

"But this could be wrong."

I nodded. "Could be, sometimes it is wrong. But the general lines are not. We use Empaths as spies mostly, only they need to learn the very fine lines of emotion because it helps decode a person. The rest, however, only learn to read the general lines between happiness, sadness, anger, contempt, pain, fear, distress, and anxiousness."

"And you? Which did you learn?"

My mouth tilted without much effort. "The very fine lines."

She scoffed and dropped back on the bed. "But of course."

Mal burst into my room like he owned the place and Snow jumped a little. My brother gave me an amused look. "Don't you leave for the Danics tomorrow morning?"

"Are you drunk?" My tone was grating and cold, yet he grinned.

"Not even close. Selia, the usual who is used to my...quirks, was unavailable and the inn was full so they kicked me out. It seems you have confiscated my liquor and apparently all the liquor in the castle and now I can't sleep."

Snow crawled to the edge of the bed, giving me a full view of her backside. "Did you say Danics?" She turned to me over her shoulder. "You found a way?"

I pulled the edge of her tiny nightgown down her delicious back before I gave my brother a reason to never look me in the eye again. "You are looking at it."

She stared around, searching for something in the room.

"My love," I said with a wide grin. "Me, I'm the way."

"Oh. How are you the solution?"

"The same way I am able to do most things on my land—I am an Obscur. Atlas found an old article about an Obscur travelling the mountain range for science, to see if what grew in the mist had any effects on the vegetation—"

"Henrik," she said, interrupting me. "You're babbling and I am a blink away from falling asleep."

Mal chuckled, leaning back on his door frame, watching the two of us with amusement. "I'm going to love watching him make everyone in Adriata call him Henrik. He has always hated using that damned name."

Snow frowned at my brother and then at me.

"Point was," I said, breaking whatever thought was crossing her mind. "I can go inside the Danics magic."

"*We* can go in it," she said, pointing at the two of us.

I laughed. "No." Not taking her anywhere near danger.

"Yes."

"No."

"Yes. What makes you think I trust you not to ruin this."

"Why would I want to ruin this?"

Her face shifted all malice, her eyes sharpening. "Perhaps get the sceptre for yourself and do what my father wants to do."

That made me guffaw. "Love, if I wanted to ruin the realm. I wouldn't need the sceptre to do it." Only a thought and the lands of gods would never see sun or light and life again.

Mal plopped on our bed beside me. "I can second him on that."

Snow glared at him. "How proud you must be to be the brother of death."

Mal took a deep breath and murmured, "Very proud." He fished something out of his jacket. "Adriata is all clear and so is Hanai, including Sayuri island. Visha is preparing for my next trip inside Isjord. I met Albius at Highwall early today and he is going to map out everything for me. He has some doubt they could be in the Islines, beyond the old Krigborn lines. Aryan apparently had a lot of spies inside the court of the barbarian king that kept an eye there for Silas. It is not impossible that they could be there."

She took the paper from him. "You will not go without me inside the Islines. Eren travelled with father once inside the old Krigborn lands and returned half astound. If you lose your mind, who will do all my dirty work?"

"Ah, all this love fills me with such joy." He pushed up, leaning on his elbow to face us. "Brother, how do you do it? It must be so overwhelming."

She read the wrinkled thing with narrowed concentration. "This is why I stab him now and then, so the overwhelm can just pour out of him."

"That so?" I asked, lying down in the little space between the two. "Get out, Mal."

He stretched, yawning and turning to give me his back. "Sleep well."

Sigh. "Malik." My brother had gone to sleep at the click of his eyelids.

Snow stood up a little and blinked at Mal who'd begun full on snoring. "I want to be in the middle."

There was a breeze in my meeting room. A grey leather clad breeze, with deadly green eyes, curly dark brown locks and a scowl. The Zephyr stood tall and unforgiving with his arms tightly crossed over his chest. "I'm coming with you."

Snow stopped fiddling with her grey leathers and gave him a glare. "Why?"

"Not a chance I'm leaving you to go inside this...mist with him alone," he said, pointing to me. "Not with what Nia told me about it."

"Not mist," Mal corrected, lifting a finger.

"Fine," Snow said. "Come if you must."

My brother stood up. "If he is coming, I am coming, too."

"What?" Snow and I asked at the same time.

Mal grinned wide. "He gets to go, I get to go. My muffin and I come as a package."

"Don't play with my nerves, Princeling," Caiden snarled.

My brother frowned. "Why so sour, my kumquat? You used to like when I played with you."

Snow blink between the two, her mouth lifting, and Caiden flicked her forehead. "Not like that."

I touched the little red spot forming on her forehead. "Caiden, do that again and you'll have to learn how to hold a fork with your toes."

Two short fading trips later, the four of us stood at the foot of Danic mountain. Snow made a sound of awe while she trailed the height of the old cluster of rock disappearing between a swirling black vortex that rose to the skies. The taste of magic was thick in the air. Almost thick to the point of suffocating before I weaved a hand inside it and willed whatever was dark and death to make a path for death and dark himself. The old magic parted into a narrow corridor and began crawling away from me, hissing like fire meeting water.

When she took a step inside, her body shuddered. "It's making me tingly."

"Because your magic produces life and this one feeds on it. You are polar opposites."

Memphis unravelled her slithery form from Snow's body and caromed in the air, morphing into a large raven.

"You're riding with me," I said and helped her onto my horse's back before she or Caiden had a chance to object.

I pulled myself up behind her, taking the opportunity to gather her tight against me, till her body almost melted onto mine.

"Is there a reason why you are holding me so tight?"

"Yes," I murmured in her ear, and she shivered a little. "Don't want the mist monsters to grab you from me."

Her body went tight with panic, and she searched the massive black cloud ahead of us. "Mist mon—" Then, her elbow went to my side. She had so much strength for her small form. Gods, a breath whooshed out of me.

"You sure you don't want to hold my hand, my muffin?" Mal asked Caiden with a smirk as our horses trotted anxiously inside the blanket of terror.

The general bristled. "Don't be all cute with me."

"If you're all done flirting, might we go?" Snow said, shivering suddenly. She gasped and then whispered, "I can't see anything."

I rested a hand on her stomach, feeling her pulse beat madly beneath my touch. "I see for the two of us. Nothing can harm you."

Her body relaxed a little. "Why is it not touching us?"

"Because I am not letting it."

"How?"

"I am one with darkness. An Obscur brought prisoners through the mist, abandoning them in it."

"Fancy."

"A perverse punishment to keep saintly hands bloodless."

"Correction," she said. "Very fancy. Blood is a menace."

I leaned forward to kiss her temple. "I meant figuratively, my *dahaara*." She no longer flinched, but her body did that shivering thing that made me think she might as well have flinched. Her being afraid of me was worse than having her hate me.

She cleared her throat. "And what if he is truly dead?

"He was sentenced to solitude, not death," I explained. "Whichever of my ancestors brought him here would have made it possible for him to survive in it. If I didn't know better, I'd say he probably thrived in it rather than survived."

"Why do you say that?"

"Solitude has a way of making you want to prove that you were better off alone in the first place. A poor means of rejecting the feeling of abandonment."

She turned a little over her shoulder. "As crown prince and now a king, I'd think you were the centre of attraction your whole life, at least Eren was. Was it not the case for you?"

"What?"

"You speak as if it is a matter of experience." After a beat of silence, she asked again, "So, did it manage to prove to you that you were better off alone in the first place?"

I smiled. "No."

We'd travelled for about three hours when strange noises began surrounding us. A screech made our head swivel all around though nothing was visible through the thicket of magic.

Caiden shot a hand forward, a blast of wind sending a massive, feather, bat-like creature back into the mist. The wind also disturbed the ashy mist, faint traces of light filtering through. Soon enough we had reached the source. Not a natural one. A beacon of fire was mounted on a tall wooden staff propelling the mist away that had created a dome of protection from the magic of terror. A few metres away stood a bungalow with a wooden fence around it and a few strips of land planted with all sorts of vegetables and fruit.

As I had thought.

We dismounted Memphis who shortly morphed onto her slithery form and wrapped around Snow's neck, hissing protectively around her.

"Magic," Snow said, lifting her palm to the fire.

"Seraphim fire," I explained, pulling her hand down before she burned herself. Unburning fire. "That's how they've kept him alive." Adan's fire fuelled on the spiritual and this dark hole was stuffed with mana of the dark. It would burn till the forever and keep everything in its light's reach alive.

An arrow hit the staff and we all spun in the shooter's direction.

Cai shot his hand forward, a thin shield of air forming over us in protection.

The figure ahead was something between a man and a beast. Peppery grey hair long to his back, with a beard to match, the tall man breathed hard and angry as he mounted another arrow in his bow—ruby eyes bearing aim on Snow. "You are trespassing," he slurred in a gravelly voice, almost as if he had not spoken for a while.

"How can visitors be trespassing?" Snow asked, stepping closer and through the shield protecting us despite the vibration of the string being pulled to her aim. Considering the sharp whistle of his magic breaking the stuffy air, that bow was the last thing Snow had to worry about.

He grunted. "I haven't seen a single soul in two hundred years."

Giving him a beaming grin, she began getting closer and closer to him. This woman. This mad and maddening woman. "Your lucky day then, Oryn."

Oryn's forehead pursed in wrinkles of confusion. His bow lowered an inch and he asked, "Who are you?"

"Snowlin Edlynne Skygard, granddaughter of King Jonah Ren Skygard, heir of skies and thunder, and first Elding Queen of Olympia. Ah," she paused and then pointed a hand in my direction. "And that's Cai, Mal and Henrik."

It was not the time to smile, but I couldn't help it.

He lowered his bow and stared wide eyed at my wife. "Yellow eyes, your magic scent is of pine and hoarfrost—Verglaser magic," he said and then gradually frowned. "Metal and cool rain too. Elding." When realisation set in, his eyes doubled in size. "You're an *Ybris*."

Snow sighed. "Where have the 'how are you?' and the 'fancy to meet you' gone in this day and age?"

Suddenly, he dropped his weapon and reached Snow, taking her hand and shoving her sleeves up. "How? It is impossible."

Mal, Caiden and I all jumped forward pulling her to safety while I grabbed and pushed him off her. "Careful there."

He stared between the four of us. "How do you...control it?"

"Same as you, I suppose," Snow said, righting her sleeves and pointing to his scarred hands coated in black spidery veins. "Is that why they banished you? Because you and I are the same?"

Mal shot me a look of disbelief. What? Oryn was an *Ybris*? No, there was no documentation or proof written about him anywhere. No, this couldn't have been why.

The odd man shook his head. "No, they banished me because I found a way for us to co-exist. It seems the realm has come to terms with us, that I am glad for."

Caiden snorted. "Don't be too glad."

"They have not," Snow told him. "The seal has helped me hide more than help me control my magic."

Oryn frowned and then looked at me. "And why are you here, Your Majesty?"

"You know who I am?"

He gave me a look of disdain. "I can smell a Castemont Obscur even dead. Now, I ask both of Your Majesties. Why are you here?"

Snow reached closer to him. "We need your help."

He grunted in disapproval. "Of course you do. Come in," he said, stomping toward his house. "I have a feeling I might need a cup of tea for this."

"What is your origin, if I might ask?" Snow asked, quickly following him inside.

"My mother was a Lyran Empath and my father a Dark Crafter from Heca," he explained, lowering his bow and arrows at the door, eyeing my brother and Cai still holding a hand on their sword hilts as he did so.

The house was small for such a big man. He had to hunch under the low arches of the doors and ceiling posts. The inside was well lit and warm, with all sorts of dried garni hanging from the walls that had given the space a soft homely scent. There were animal skin rugs scattered all over and a small bubbling fireplace. Everything looked handmade, from the pots and pans to the tables, bed and chairs.

"Fascinating," Snow said, plopping on a wooden bench as Oryn went to fill a pot with water to place over the fading coals of his fireplace.

He huffed, glancing at her with some amusement. "It is one thing to be a spiritual *Ybris* and another to be an elemental. I can channel most of my mana onto the ever flow of the spiritual, but you," he stopped to shake his head, "to bear all the physicality of it even with a seal there has to be a price to it." He stirred the coals with a fire poker, the smell of herbs beginning to fill the cold air of the room. "When I was working to create the seals, I never succeeded in placing one on an elemental."

"You created these seals?" I asked, taking position behind Snow.

He nodded. "Seems like aeons ago now, but I did—I tried. Along with another priest whom the Adriatians chased out of this kingdom. There was an opportunity for us to live—normally. But your kind thought it best that we didn't at all. Fairy tales, sacred books and all dictated that we never would." He brought two metal cups to the table, pouring the bitter-smelling tea and handing it to us before handing two others to my brother and Caiden. "Sit, my king. I won't hurt her."

I slid to the seat next to Snow and Memphis uncurled from her bonded to rest her cold form on my lap.

Oryn glanced at the motion of the morph shortly before turning to ask Snow, "Who crafted your seal?"

"Lysander Delcour."

He was stunned still. "A Delcour? That explains it. He must have used gods markings, that would hold the seal sturdy. But that also might be the oddest thing I've heard today. Odder than a visit from an Elding Queen and a Night King. A Delcour would never agree to such a thing. Their tradition and beloved faith in their god borders between fanaticism and blindness."

Snow sipped her tea, her nose wrinkling a bit at the taste, but she didn't put it down. "Lysander was a bastard born, but one more capable than any of their best Crafters. His belief was more modern than most. When he started working for my grandfather—"

"Jonah, I remember him," Oryn said, nodding. "He always had a fancy for exploring new talent."

"He did," Snow agreed. "It gave Lysander the chance to experiment with this magic."

"Hm," Oryn hummed, taking a seat. His gaze traced the movement of my hand over the morph's head. "Her bonded trusts you."

"My bonded is a clingy little thing," Snow was quick to answer.

Oryn raised a bushy brow. "And if I were to touch her, would she cling to me as well?"

Snow nodded. "Yes, with her fangs. You are still a stranger to her."

He rumbled with laughter. "Would it be so awful to admit that he is your lover?"

Snow coughed on her sip of tea and so did the other two behind us. "He is not a lover."

"Seems like it to me."

My wife ran a sleeve over her mouth. "He killed my mother, almost killed me and my siblings."

Oryn's eyes almost bulged out. Then Snow finished the rest of her story and Oryn listened with fascination. Till fascination turned to horror.

"Your father, a Krigborn king, is assembling the Octa Virga?" he asked, his brows furrowed with more worry than confusion.

She nodded. "He is."

"And you wish to find these pieces for yourself to stop him?"

Snow leaned forward on the table with concentration. "Not all. One, to put under an undetectable craft so he can never find it or somewhere he will never be able to get inside of. Without that one piece he will never be able to construct the whole sceptre. Right now, besides what we are doing to guard our kingdoms from being breached, there is nothing we can do to prevent him from getting to them."

"And you suppose I am able to help?"

Snow nodded again. "We want to find a way to track them. There was a study of yours with our kind and how they were imprisoned to guard the sceptre pieces. You'd mentioned that the elder Crafters who were tasked to hide them created three traps—the Arx Triad. Craft, animal, *Ybris*. We hope that you might know how we can find them."

He sipped his tea. "That was suggested to me, I never got the chance to look far into that."

"Tasked? By whom?" I asked. Did that mean far more people than we thought knew about the Octa Virga?

"A traveller. He'd come across an elder Crafter scroll on his journeys describing precisely that. I found it utmost fascinating at the time. And at the time it was because it was a time of peace. I would have found out more, but shortly after the king banished me here. I think it might have been a sailor or a trader, I am not sure, but he'd stumbled on much more information. It wasn't uncommon for the time to be curious since the burning of Seraphim was only a couple centuries ago. Punishable information, yes, but wildly popular amongst treasure hunters." He rubbed a hand over his overgrown beard and shook his head in thought. "The only way I could have helped would have been if you already had a piece. I could spell one piece to track another. Otherwise, I am afraid you have made this journey for nothing, Your Majesties."

Perhaps it was how Silas was finding the rest of the locations with such ease. But there was something else bothering me. "The Isjordian king did not find his piece first, it was the Solaryan one. How would one start to search for one with the information we have?"

"I told you, my king, there was a grand knowledge among those that seeked it. Perhaps he stumbled upon it. Perhaps someone who has passed the knowledge through generations and kept it a secret sold it to him. It is a kind of treasure if you think about it. One you could buy with coin." He hummed in though. "You said that he has the Solaryan piece and that the sun rulers are aware what the Isjordian king is up to."

We both nodded.

"The Theros library is the mind of Numen," Oryn said, standing to pick up a dishevelled journal to a page filled with all sorts of scribbles and odd language that were most extinct at our age. He pointed a crooked finger to a line art of a tall tower building. "Cyra and Krig were good friends. During their time in Numen, he gifted her all sorts of articles and books and grimoires that the sun rulers preserved fanatically. I wouldn't be surprised if there could be information there. Quite possibly how the Winter King has found out."

Snow jumped a little in her seat and leaned forward on the table. "Talking about books. Father sent his spies to retrieve one of Esmeray's diaries." She snapped her fingers. "Darling, what was the name?"

Again, I couldn't help my smile. "Ahmes Lore."

Oryn's eyes widened a third time. "And did he get it?"

"No, I did before him." She leaned further on the table. "Why would that be a curious thing to my father?"

Oryn seemed disturbed at the thought. "It was said in many tales told by the old that one of the sceptre pieces is guarded at the gates between Numen to one of the heavens. The Ahmes Lore can decode the gates."

The mystery was finally solved. And it was for a far less dangerous reason than I expected. Thank the gods Snow had managed to get it before Silas.

Snow and I exchanged a look. "Which one?" we both asked at once.

"It was only a rumour heard in passing, but if I could presume, I'd think it would be the Seraphim one. The sceptre locations were all concealed by Dark Crafters and Seraphim is the furthest away from Eldmoor from where craft is drawn from. It would be impossible to impose any strong enough veil to conceal such a treasured artefact. One would have thought long and hard how to most efficiently hide the sceptre pieces and leaving a wonky veil to guard one is not in the nature of an elder Crafter."

Snow blinked in thought. "I don't understand. How would he have my father read it?"

The old man seemed surprised at her question rather than what she was questioning, and then startled upright again when she clapped her hands and asked another question, "Why is it that I can read it?"

Oryn, again, didn't seem alarmed at the revelation, but he frowned, looking between Snow and I as if we were meant to already know that answer. "Uh, I am not certain. I am sorry I couldn't be of more help."

He had lied. And by the grave look he gave me, he'd done it for a good reason.

"We have come for another reason as well," I said. "I'd like to revoke your punishment. Return to Adriata. If you wish to still practise, you are welcome to join the priests under my wing. If not, enjoy your freedom anywhere you wish."

Oryn looked taken aback and once the words registered, he slowly shook his head. "I haven't seen one human for two hundred years and I no longer belong amongst them. I never actually did. And to know nothing has changed for us in these past two hundred years, I would rather prefer finishing the rest of my punishment here."

Solitude did have a way to prove that you were better off alone, after all.

"Come to Olympia then," Snow said. "Under my protection and rule."

Oryn stared at Snow with an odd curiosity. "And why would you do that?"

"You're a three hundred and something year old *Ybris*. One with knowledge and I'd like for you to share that. You are also another breathing being who should not be punished for what one cannot control—human fear. I will not apologise for being better, greater. And I refuse to let you do that too." She leaned back on her chair. "Also, I'd like to share my spotlight in Adriata. No fun being terrifying all on my own."

He blinked stunned but his shadows read of fascination. "You're an odd one, my queen."

"Odd?" Snow asked, scowling somewhat offended.

I stood. "Collect anything that bears any importance to you, and we will leave."

Oryn slowly rose from his seat, still indecisive, nervously rubbing his palms to his sides. "This, I suppose," he said, picking up the battered-up journal. "Nothing else."

The five of us lit a torch on the Seraphim fire before we descended the height of the tall Danic. Oryn was beaten from age and the magic fatigue of the Danics, so I had offered him my horse. Memphis had morphed into a mare, carrying Snow while I walked beside her, holding the reins.

The descent was far easier than the climb, especially with the everfire, but Snow kept taking cautious glances around the black cloud we were cloaked in.

"It will do us no harm. Not unless you've come with the desire to mine the mountains for jewels. It is how the magic works," Oryn said to her. He swung the torch inside the inky fog and watched it shriek and fade.

"If you knew your way around it, why did you never try to leave?"

The old man took a minute to think his answer. "The feel of belonging—inside isolation is where I found it."

Snow glanced a little at me and then blinked ahead.

Chapter Sixteen

Marmoris

Snowlin

The sun rulers had responded to our request within the day of contact. Something that had surprised Kilian the most. Adriata and Solarya rooted their grudges on more than the difference of their blessing. It was a foundation built since the time of the gods. The two lovers that were destined to hate one another. Cyra and Henah. Night and day.

Pen and I sat on the edge of Kilian's bed as a servant brought what I was supposed to wear to Solarya in an attempt to convince the two sun royals of our little lie. Most of the Adriatian women I'd seen were soldiers, priestesses or councillors, and they wore an attire almost similar to the men. What laid before us was something I'd never seen anyone wear before.

Pen picked up the black contraption as if it were lit in fire and smelled of rotten egg. "They can't possibly be serious."

"Very serious," Kilian said, strutting inside more handsome than ever, wearing a black ensemble with detailed silver embroidery all over it. He didn't look like a king, he looked like a god. "Where is my missus?" he asked, looking around the room and I sat up a bit. "There she is. Scowling at me." He grinned. "Perfect."

I huffed and turned away from the idiot.

The little carrot helped me get into the tight thing that barely managed to be pulled up my hips. Made of a dark fabric that looked like it sucked all the light in the room, the dress was a beauty of hand stitched golden embroidery that ran along the arms and down the long train that extended almost a foot behind me. I'd lost a bit of weight over the past weeks, but the thing clung to me as second skin, pushing my cleavage so high that it almost reached my chin.

Kilian stopped his conversation with Atlas. His eyes raked me top to bottom and his lip tipped up in a smirk as he said, "You're the death of me."

I was sure my face was burning red from his scrutiny and those words. I've always felt beautiful, but when he said it, I felt a different sort of beautiful.

"Blessed Krig," Pen muttered, grabbing Atlas's hand and fleeing the room like their soles were on fire, letting me deal with him on my own.

"I suppose you look pretty too," I said, walking to him and smoothing a hesitant palm on his chest. Warming up would help. As good as I was puppeteering my manners, it was hard when it came to him. My reaction was to recoil to his touches and his words.

He cocked a dark brow up. "Pretty?"

I nodded and tipped my head back to look at him. "You're the prettiest man I've ever seen." Perhaps the truest truth that had come out of my mouth in weeks.

He smiled, his sad eyes did too. Definitely the prettiest man I knew. "I've never been called pretty before."

"Makes you feel all warm and fuzzy inside, doesn't it?"

He laughed and I was sure my chest constricted because it suddenly became hard to breathe. His smile fell. He must have seen something or felt it, I didn't know how he did it because he never told me how he found out when my thoughts shifted. He traced a light finger over my cheek. "Your eyes. They still do that thing."

Your laugh still undoes me. It was once only mine and I wanted it to be only mine again. Shame washed me all at once and I felt my body grow cold. It was all because of that lie—it wasn't him that I longed for, it was his lie. It was for my favourite lie. He was my favourite lie. "Let's not leave Moriko waiting under the summer sun. The ancient thing might just wither."

He grabbed my arm, turning me to him again. His finger tipped my chin so I could look at him. "I haven't told you today." He leaned in and kissed the tip of my nose and then both my eyes before whispering against my lips, "I love you."

My chest tightened. Those three cursed words. Those three cursed words I'd only ever heard from him. They branded me and they thawed something of mine that was long frozen—the want to be loved. I longed to be loved. If one like him could ever love someone like me. It was all his game. I dreaded how easily he found to play it still. "Too early to start pretending."

He nudged my nose with his, his warm breath fluttering over my skin as he leaned in to bite and drag my bottom lip between his teeth. "I ought to gift you a dictionary," he whispered over my mouth before kissing both corners of my lips and my pulse thundered. He gently raised my chin with a finger so I could look up at him. "Or shall I teach you myself? I am a very patient man. I'll go slow for you. So very slow, my love." His eyes darted to my lips again and he breathed heavy. "I'll teach you all and everything. You'll taste the definition of my every word and love for you on your tongue. And then you'll crave it. Just like I crave you. I want to teach you this hunger. But I will never let you starve—never."

How could one explain this, make sense of it all? Why did I want him to do it again? Why did I want him to whisper those words over my skin again? Maybe...maybe just having him once would satiate me—would make this obsession I had for him go away.

I wasn't sure if I were breathing too hard or breathing at all.

His fingers slipped from my face, and he kneeled before me, sliding the satin black slipper on my foot. Bringing men to their knees had never been something of pleasure, I preferred pushing them to their coffins better. But bringing a king to his knees? I had to reconsider.

"Shall we?" he asked, extending a hand for me to take. "Or you want to take another good look at me?"

"No, I was done."

He chuckled and flipped open the envelope that the sun rulers had sent and recited the old language runes before fading us to the meeting location. The two rulers of Solarya had decided to meet us in Noor Island, a deserted oasis south of Solarya that had been used for political gatherings since the time of gods.

Sun blistered all surfaces, painting the sky azure, the stone a bright beige and the sea surrounding us a shimmering aquamarine. I couldn't make out which was clearer, the water or the skies. The small island was desolate except for a gold painted alcazar standing tall at the height of a hill not far from where we stood. The air was humid and thick with heat, my lungs were not meant for this weather.

Kilian clutched my gloved hand tight as we climbed a set of tall stairs leading to the building we were meant to meet with the rest.

By the third stumble, I decided to gather the train of my dress in my hands. "How do Adriatian women wear this on a daily basis?" I huffed, annoyed.

He shrugged. "They don't."

That made me turn to him with a frown. "What do you mean?"

"Have you seen another court lady wear that?" he said pointing my chin down at me and taking the chance to take another long perusal over my body again.

"Then why am I wearing this?"

"So I can see your backside better," he said and then slapped my bottom. When I began to retort, he lifted a brow. "Utterly in love, remember?"

"Enjoy this as much as you can because I plan to make you regret it."

"I hope you hold to your word. I am looking forward to seeing how you can possibly punish me anymore than you already are." The way his nostrils flared when he stared at me trickled a flutter in my lower belly.

I muttered curses in Calgnan all the way at the top, but all it did was throw him on a laughing fit.

The palace was built like a maze. Colourful cerulean, charcoal and gold paintings of Solarya's history lined the maze-like corridors of the tall ceilingless building. The pearly marble floors reflected daylight right onto the beige walls, making them look gilded.

I came to a stop—something had caught my eye. A painting of two women facing one another. A black-haired tall woman, donned in floating black silks, stood holding a short staff with a crescent moon atop. She faced another woman, with russet long thinly braided hair cascading to her waist, her dark brown skin glistening as if lined with gold specs and in contrast, she wore a short white dress, several golden chains decorating her frame.

"Henah and Cyra," I said, tracing a hand over a Tahuma inscription between them. "The two lovers bound by hate."

"Not hate. Fate," Kilian said. "In her darkness she shone and weakened the black night. In her light she dimmed the blue day. They were fated to dull one another. Even if it didn't destroy them, being together took away who they were. Day and night."

"Anyone," I murmured. "They could have wanted anyone else. Yet they caused one another pain, destroyed one another and then tore apart only to live with the consequences. I guess gods are as stupid as humans are. Perhaps even worse."

"You cannot change who you want."

"There you are," Moriko called, coming from down the corridor, looking like a warrior goddess in the traditional Hanaian clothes. By her side stood Nia, wearing a Hanaian guard attire of a muted green and brass armour. "Lost?"

I sneered and then turned to my friend. "You look atrocious."

Nia smirked while she examined me. "You want to talk about how I look?"

The Autumn Queen wrapped an arm around her waist. "Yes, Night Queen, you want to talk about how she looks?"

"Now, now, ladies" Kilian said with humour, steering me further down the corridor in an attempt to stop me from biting Moriko's head off.

"You're being too hard on her," he murmured in my ear.

"Someone has to keep her on her toes."

"She cares for Nia."

That is what I was afraid of. "Care is overrated. I cared about this little cactus plant once when I was little—perhaps more than cared. I adored it and made it the best of my friends, yet I let it starve and die when all I had to do was water it once in a long time. And do you want to know the lesson it taught me?"

"A cactus is the worst plant to make friends with?"

"That, too, actually, but no. I learned that something that needs my constant care to thrive is tiring. What happens once Moriko realises she has to constantly water this relationship they have for it to exist? Nia wants to feel it, it is how she is. She wants to bask in it. Because she craves it. What happens when Moriko can no longer give Nia what and how she wants it."

A hard lesson I'd learnt from my mother. Except that I'd always been the cactus, and she'd grown tired of watering me though I never asked to be watered much. Her care and the way she cared were like a drug, one she grew tired of giving. I never asked for water altogether, all I wanted was a bit of her sunshine. At least then I would have withered under her rays. But then like every abandonment, I learned to be a weed and feed on my own. And once I did, another's care never mattered much to me—leastways not to crave it.

He suddenly halted and so did everyone. Turning to Moriko and Nia, he said, "Would you give us a moment?"

"Please steer from daggering each other. Let's keep this bloodless, shall we?" Nia warned, following after Moriko.

"This was not about a cactus, was it?" he asked, and I faltered for a moment.

"Twas," I said, folding my arms nonchalantly.

He ran his fingers through my hair. The action was so soothing, my eyes shut, and I accepted the comfort—it was how a woman in love would have acted. "Who would starve this cactus? I would have overwatered you. Made you the best of my friends."

I scoffed. "Me and you would have never been friends under any sort of circumstance."

"How so?"

"I've wanted to fuck you the first time I've laid my eyes on you. And I don't have those sorts of friendships."

The way his temple twitched had me thinking the man was chained and imprisoned—already suffering under my tortures. "Are we pretending?"

"When have we ever stopped?" Liar. Liar. Liar. Sick. I was so sick.

When his mouth began lifting to a smile, I turned on my heels and walked the rest of the corridor distance. At the last turn, a glistening open space lined with chairs came into view. Pillars rose to the open ceiling, and between them, thin layers of gossamer swayed at the touch of the summer breeze serving as walls. In the middle of the pillar circle floor stood a gold painting of the sun and right above the open ceiling rose the heaven of Hemera, parallel to it. The heaven followed the rulers of Solarya, wherever they were, it stood above their heads. A crown in the sky.

King Magnus Vayr sat in a ring of chairs circling the open space that wasn't quite a room. Tall and lean with a rich dark brown skin that became a pool of shimmers under the sun, Cora took side next to her husband. The sun queen was a thing of distinct beauty, something I'd only read of in tales of fairies and nymphs. Magnus on the other hand was a massive man, an inch or so taller than Kilian, long thinly braided hair beaded with gold bands and pearls, his Solaryan attire of a sheer white blouse and a loose white kilt ended above his knees to reveal muscle carved through hard work. The rosy scars contrasting his dark skin highlighted the number of years he'd spent as a warrior in his father's army before he was king. The two were mighty in paeans and panegyrics sung about them, but they were mighty before us, too. The light and the healer. The couple the whole realm spoke highly of.

The couple exchanged a strange look before focusing on me like I was some fascinating creature and I couldn't help the irritation bleeding in my voice, "I am told it's rude to stare."

"You speak Tahuma," Magnus said with some humour, pointing for us to take a seat.

However, on our side, there was only one seat. For Kilian.

"Apologies," Magnus said with absolutely no apology. "We entertained the idea of this meeting without considering you might be telling the truth. You ought to forgive us that we thought it to be but a time wasting sham."

He barked a laugh. "The hunter and the hunted married and in love at that. Who would think of such a carefully spun tale?"

Kilian guided me to take a seat while he leaned on the seat arms, slinging an arm protectively around my shoulders. "Worry not," he said with bite in his words. "We are well accustomed to your quirks. You have been ruling this kingdom for sixty years. It ought to catch up with us."

My eyes snapped to Kilian and his unusual tone.

Magnus's artificial smile twitched just a little. "Henrik was always so soft spoken."

"My father is dead. A fact you are well known with."

I couldn't help but feel strange at the man beside me. The way he spoke was not one I'd witnessed before, not even in his meetings.

The Sun King faltered a little. "As I expressed in the letter we sent, your father was a great loss to this continent. To be taken from sickness at his young age was very unfortunate. We were very sorry for your loss."

"Were you?" Kilian asked with some surprise. "I wouldn't have thought that when you sent eight ships to attack Lyra a week later. The men were quick to speak after some care from our Empaths. The mind is a breakable, dainty thing." He crossed one leg over the other. "Not exactly certain what you were wishing to achieve with that...little gesture."

My mouth parted a little. What? Was this the scale of their animosity?

Magnus laughed—it was one of unease. "A test for the new king."

Kilian looked as stern as ever. "One would think it was a test for a kingdom with a new king. Did I pass this test of yours or fail, Magnus?"

What was he doing? Were we not here to make an alliance?

The Sun King cleared his throat and rested back on his seat. "So, you married the Winter Princess."

"How long does the sun stay up?" I asked, tired of this already. The heat made me irritable.

Cora blinked confused. "Why do you ask?"

I gave them both a saccharine smile. "Since you find time to waste on obvious matters, it might stay up longer than I thought."

Moriko's mouth twitched just a little and Nia nudged her foot a little before saying, "Pardon our enthusiasm, but I am afraid we are in a race against a time we are not even aware of."

The sun ruler eyed us all with suspicion, the umber stare setting on me with some unease. "I find it hard to go into straight conversation considering your *husband* is the first Night King to make contact with us when our kingdoms have disputed since the time gods stepped into Numen." He then pointed to Moriko. "She is the first Autumn ruler to want to join an alliance." He stopped and raised a brow at me. "And you are the daughter of the man who wants the realm in ashes. The same man who created you not long ago to turn this realm to ashes. And now Night Queen. Isn't that so convenient for Silas?"

"Precious concern," I said with boredom. "But twice you have stood by silent when my father was doing more than attempting to raid this realm. And you're just now expressing concern? You are quick to judge us when you took the long route to judge my father. I thought now that he stole from you, you would have grown a pair."

He blanched. Not at my harsh words, but at the mention of stealing. "And what do you know, girl?" he growled all red and malice, enough to make the heat from the sun turn scorching on my skin. Was the summer sun supposed to burn like this?

His tone was grating my nerves and a low rumble of thunder rolled somewhere in the distance drawing everyone's attention to the clear skies.

"Careful, Magnus," Kilian warned.

"Playing knight for your young *wife*?" The Sun King almost mocked, tilting his head to the side to give the two of us one long doubting perusal.

My whole body was already preparing for fight and my magic pushed at the gates, loaded and ready to unleash at the scent of scorching threat lingering in the air. This was a mistake. Negotiations had never been my best trait. Not unless I had whoever I was negotiating with in chains.

Kilian gave my shoulder a squeeze as if knowing what went through my head. "It is not her I am worried about."

The air became too humid and wherever light touched us, it burned. Magnus's jaw ticked. "Was that a threat? In my land and under my sun?"

The spill of magic leaking out of Kilian rose gooseflesh all over me and memory called for me to run—to hide. Suddenly, the day dulled, and onyx crawled over blue, altering the day skies into night. Our surroundings dimmed, too, and we were enshrouded in total darkness.

"Should it be a threat?" Kilian echoed back. He'd done this without lifting a finger. He'd done everything without lifting a finger—only with a thought. It still terrified me the same way it first did.

"Let the sun return," Magnus's voice was low and deadly.

"The sun returns when I tell it to," Kilian said with utter calm. "Now, Magnus, should it be a threat?"

"No, Obscur Asteri, it shouldn't," he gritted out.

The veil of night slowly retracted bit by bit till the heaven of Cyra illuminated overhead again. When the light returned, I noticed the shake of my limbs and one of my hands tightly clutching the one he had rested on my shoulder. With a jerk, I let go. His skin was marked red and scarred from how hard I'd held him.

He leaned to my ear and whispered, "Forgive me, please. Forgive me. I shouldn't have done that. Forgive me."

"Your hand," I whispered back, trying to distract myself from it all—from the way nightmares just flashed before my eyes in broad daylight.

He planted a long kiss on my temple. "It is fine, love. As long as you are." He lifted my chin to him. "Tell me you are."

"I am."

Like that, with two words, his shoulders lifted, his breathing and pulse evened, and his silver eyes settled.

Magnus huffed and leaned back in his chair, studying the two of us intently. "Odd, very odd." He turned to me. "Word spreads fast in a world like ours. I've heard of your reputation."

"All of the good stuff I hope."

"Interesting...stuff."

"I've heard of interesting stuff about you, too, quite recently actually. The little set up you got on the north of Isjord for example," I said, and waited to see Magnus's face morph into discomfort. "Adorable attempt, but father won't certainly let a bunch of criminals get their hands on the sceptre piece before him."

The two rulers perked in their seat, glancing at all of us with some terror. "And what do you know about the sceptre?"

"Plenty that my uncle revealed before he tried to kill me so he could get inside Adriata and get the kingdom along with their sceptre."

"Aryan Krigborn tried to kill you?"

I put a hand to my chest. "A tragedy, really, our family has always been so loving and tight with one another. It came all so unexpectedly."

The king smiled a little. "Still, for your father to sacrifice you—"

"My purpose to him ended the day I possessed no magic."

His brows jerked. "There were rumours from Winter court a few years back that he wanted to make you heir."

"A rumour, as you said."

"We are sorry for your loss, Snowlin," Cora said. "Your brother would have made a great king."

"So am I."

"So, you are aware of the sceptre?" Magnus sighed. "And you are aware that Silas has the Solaryan piece?"

"He also has the Hanaian piece," Moriko said. "And we want to make sure that is the last he gets."

"Damned hells," Cora muttered, turning to her already horrified husband. "He has two already."

"Three," I said. "Considering the Isjordian one."

Magnus blinked away a daze. "Are you certain? Last we know his soldiers still roamed the Isline temple."

"Unless he lied, I presume so."

"This...alliance, how do you suppose we can help?" Magnus asked, still doubting.

"We are here in hopes to stop Silas from making them four," Moriko said. "His Krigborn greed surpasses what many might have thought it to be during their time. It won't be long till he collects them all."

"We want to track and find one piece and place it under craft," I said. "Father can then spend the rest of his immortal life searching for it for all I care. You are the one with the most information out of all of us—you can help us find a piece of the Octa Virga."

Cora said, "I am not quite sure how we can be of help."

"How did you find out where the Isjordian piece was hidden?" Kilian asked.

"We didn't," Magnus said with a resigned sigh. "That witch of your father's has a potent magic stain. When she came to steal our piece, one of our Magi Healers made contact with her magic and managed to contain some of the essence in her. From there we used a Dark Crafter of ours to trace her magic pattern. We tried again not long ago, to ensure the Seraphim piece remains out of their touch, but it seems she has caught a whiff of our tricks. Now not one drop of her magic is felt anywhere."

"But you knew about the sceptre?" Moriko asked. "Before Silas stole it?"

Cora shook her head. "No. Not a thing. In the vault where the sceptre was found there were scriptures in old Tahuma, mostly babbles and riddles, but under where the sceptre was kept, there were engravings in the old language of gods. Mostly runes scattered here and there, nothing easily legible to the normal eye."

I sat a bit straighter. "Then how did you read them?"

"Solarya holds the world's knowledge in its very core," the Sun Queen explained. "We have libraries dating since the time of Cyra still intact. It took us weeks, but we got there. Translated all the inscriptions and then dug for more information with a private group of scholars to keep the rumours from spreading and sending our kingdom on high alert. There was not much, only enough to gather what Silas was planning."

"Anything on where to find the rest?" Moriko asked, hope fleeting from her cold eyes.

Cora shook her head again. "No. The eight Dark Crafters that were tasked with hiding them swore a magic oath to their silence and then...sacrificed themselves. All they knew died with them. The guardian was never meant to be raised again—I am certain of it. This was the only solution to an indestructible problem."

"Where was the Solaryan piece hidden?" Kilian asked. "The one in Hanai was in a sacred land, the one in Isjord is in a temple. The pattern is confusing. Perhaps that could give us some lead."

It was Magnus's time to wince. "Theros, a tomb of a...hybrid Aura. The boy was a prince of one of my ancestors and a whore who turned out to be a Scarlet. He barely reached the age of seven before nurturing his abilities. He took out an entire city up north, the ground there still toxic with his magic, the air burns your skin, and the ground is ash that infects your body with temperature till you boil and die. His remains were dangerous, so he was buried deep underground, layers of layers of protection shielding him and not to mention the Crafter's veil erected after one of the eight Crafters hid the sceptre piece."

How in the hells? "But my father's soldiers got through that?"

Magnus pursed his lips with regret and Cora reached to hold his hand as she answered for him. "There was a beast. Killed two hundred of our men, managed to breach the veil, the Aitan sphinx guarding the vault and the walls of sun magic around the vault itself. Only to come out and kill another three dozen guards before disappearing into the sea."

"This...beast, did anyone see what it looked like?" I asked, my hand going to Kilian's thigh. I felt his body seize under my touch before realising what I had done.

I was about to jerk it away, but Cora followed the motion with intent eyes and now I was locked in place. "A strange beast with green scales like those of a snake, its...drivel still coats the walls of the vault green."

I turned to look at Kilian, my eyes going to his chest where the three slashes were. "The same as the one in Hanai." I then turned to Moriko again. "Are you certain it looked nothing like the ones from the Ater battles? My father could have easily tasked Melanthe Delcour to create them or dig them up from somewhere."

"Certain," said Moriko.

"No," Magnus interrupted, backing Moriko. "It was nothing like the ones in the Ater battles. None of those beasts could come close to inflicting as much damage as this one has."

Kilian rested his hand atop mine and asked the couple, "Can we have a look at your library ourselves, see if there is more we could find, anything that you might have missed?"

Magnus nodded. "Most certainly. We will take you to Theros library tomorrow. Tonight, we dine."

"We will not be staying," I said, looking at Moriko and Kilian to back me up.

"Nonsense," Cora said. "We are talking about an alliance never done before. Tonight, you are our guests. Never in my years have I sent back guests without feeding them first."

Chapter Seventeen

Apricus

Kilian

We'd been shown to our rooms. Snow and I shared one, of course. The Theros castle rested on high rock, facing water. From our balcony, you could see the view of the Hollow Sea stretching far and wide, littered with boats and sailors basking under the sunset, waiting for their catch. There was so much life in Theros despite the serenity of the setting day marking everything it touched with gilt and sparkles.

Snow had disappeared in the bathing chambers for more than an hour now, yet I hadn't heard water run or her even making a single movement.

Flushed red and panting, she peeked from behind the ivory doors. "This. Bloody. Dress."

"You should have just asked me, love," I said, pushing up from the sofa.

She turned around and I swiftly slid the small buttons out of the loops all the way down to her lower back. She took a deep breath as if the thing had been restricting her and I could help but lean and plant a kiss on her spine. And when she didn't flinch away from me, I couldn't help the several kisses I left on her back till her skin puckered with goosebumps.

Her breathing had grown laboured when I turned her around and peeled the dress from her body, leaving her in the shortest, tiniest, silk black slip.

She was exquisite. From start to end, Snowlin Edlynne Castemont was a painting of the divine. Soft curves, sharp edges, made of the most alluring palette of colour and utmost intoxicating scents of flower.

I ran my knuckles from her cheek down her neck and stopped over her pebbled nipple poking through the silk shift. Desire overlooked every decision of mine as I decided to roll the nub between my fingers. They were indeed my weakness. *She* was both my weakness and my strength.

A small, muffled whimper left her and suddenly she trembled. Never had I wanted to read someone's emotions more than now and I cursed whatever didn't allow me to read hers because I had to pull away. My mind began to entertain the idea that she was truly disgusted by my touch.

She took my hand and laid it against her breast, her breathing growing hard, and her eyes drawing shut briefly as if to give her some sense of grounding.

I reached close till our chests touched and slid my hand through her hair, tugging to pull her head to face me. "I am going to need you to use those words. Remember, I can't read you and your heart is beating in a rage of hate against me. I know I can give you pleasure despite what you mean to me and I mean to you, so you have to tell me if you want me to."

She wetted her rosy lips. "So you will fuck me?"

Gods, if my cock didn't just jump to attention. "Pleasure doesn't constitute my cock being inside you." Some of *my* pleasure would.

She slowly lifted a hand close to my face and then flipped me off. "Got a hand right here." She made a sound of surprise and cupped one of her perfectly full breasts with the other, eliciting a groan from me. "There's another."

With that and a big taunting smile, she began retreating toward the bath.

I leaned against a pillar and crossed my arms. "Take a good look, love. I'm sure you want to remember me well for your alone time scenarios."

She stopped and I could swear her cheeks were flushed. "I already had someone in mind. Large and feathery."

My smile dropped and before I reached her, she shut and locked the door in my face. "Open the door, my love."

The water ran and then she let an overly exaggerated 'Oh, Lazarus' moan that made me chuckle. I could fade in there and make her regret that—make her eat her words back as I devoured her. Just the thought made me groan with frustration. A taste of her was all I wanted. I could fade in there and have my fill of her, but I couldn't. Not until she gave me that permission loud, clear and preferably written, too. I hated regret. And fulfilled momentary desire was the recipe for regret.

Instead, I shifted my stiff erection to the side so it didn't strain against the seams of my britches and leaned against the pillar facing the door, waiting till she finished her bath.

It wasn't long till she came back, surprisingly yet not so surprisingly. Her dark wet hair had matted over her face, neck and shoulders. She was breathing hard and frustrated, clutching the top of her towel with a white-knuckle tight grip.

My lips kicked to a smirk. "You didn't finish, did you?"

If looks could kill, I'd be very dead right now. Slowly, I approached her, and she stepped back till the wall stopped her from moving further. "Ask."

She pursed her lips in a tight thin line as a sign of her refusal yet her body ground to mine, searching for my touch.

"Ask, Snow. Say, Kilian, I want you to make me come." I ran my finger over her pretty nose. "Say, Kilian, I want to come on your tongue. Say, Kilian, touch me. Touch my pretty cunt till it's weeping." *Fuck, just ask. I am losing my mind just to have a bite of you.*

When I wrapped a hand over her soft neck she moaned and whimpered at the same time—the sweetest sound anyone has ever made. "Ask me."

Her head jerked in a nod.

"Words. Let me hear them."

She fisted my jacket and rested her forehead on my chest. "Gods damn it, you did this to me."

I'd take fault for that till the end of my lifetimes. "You did it to me, too. Twice, thrice, ten times worse. I am the one that fell in love, remember?"

Her fist hit my chest lightly over and over. She wouldn't relent though I could feel the lust oozing out of her stare, her inhales, those little sounds of frustration she made.

I backed her fully to the wall, my thigh going between her legs and a gasp left her pretty lips. "Say the words."

She gripped my shirt and squirmed, rubbing herself over my leg. All I wanted to do was indulge her, watch her come apart. And tonight, I'd damn all and watch her.

"I—" she panted, and a moan popped off her when I pinched one of her puckered nipples poking through the towel and palmed her soft breast.

Resting an arm on the wall above her, I caged her in. "Take what you want. Make yourself come on me. Use me."

There was uncertainty in her stare, but there was blazing lust in there too. Her hand slipped under my shirt, trailing up and down my torso and my whole body came alive. Every inch of me burned from her touch. "More," she said, moving faster, rubbing herself on my leg. "I want more."

I pushed a little harder on her and she gasped. "My greedy girl wants to come?"

She responded with a whimper, her plump lips parting open and she dropped her head back, baring her neck to me. "Yes," she moaned, biting on her lip to soften those sweet sounds.

I lowered my mouth to suck on her neck, the soft skin gliding between my lips, and I groaned. The sweet scent of her, the feel of her. To gods,

I could swear they'd made her for me. "That's it, ride my thigh, love." Gripping her hip, I guided her movement to a quicker pace.

"Ah...oh, gods." Her breaths grew short and rapid, her hold on me tightening and I knew she was close.

"One day I'm going to have you ride my cock." I trailed small kisses along her jaw and her head dropped back, demanding for more. "That's what you want, isn't it?"

She nodded.

When she didn't give me my answer, I palmed her bottom before giving it a sharp whack. "My words, where are they?"

She shivered in my arms, her fingers flexing and tightening on my chest, her hips rocking against my leg faster. "Yes. Yes, that is what I want. You know that is what I want."

"I like hearing it," I said, pushing my leg against her and watching that mouth part in another gasp. I could help sink my teeth on her. Biting the corner of her jaw softly.

Her eyes lifted to mine and she bit her lower lip to suppress the cry of her climax. She swallowed, breathing hard and ragged, her body still shivering. Fucking pretty.

When her soft body went slack, her head lolled back, resting on the wall and she stared at me through a hooded gaze, her cheeks flushed and her lush mouth a rosy pink. I'd never gazed upon a single thing more bewitching and heart achingly beautiful. This woman. This woman that I loved.

"Were these your favourite trousers?" she asked, wiggling her hips a little.

"They are now," I said, kissing both of her pink cheeks.

I was painfully hard and from how close we were pressed together she could probably feel it, too.

Snow's eyes dropped down and she dragged her lip between her teeth. Her gentle fingers played with the seam of my trousers, poking inside just a little but enough to have me curse all heavens and seven hells. When she looked up, her eyes were all glassy and shy. "Let me touch you?"

Fuck. Fuck. Fuck.

A knock rasped on the door and a small voice called out, "Dinner is being served, Your Majesties."

I plucked away a strand of wet hair matted to her forehead. "Hungry?"

Her eyes dropped to my mouth. "Yes."

I couldn't help but chuckle. When she cracked a little smile, my heart tripled in size. She never smiled for me anymore. Gave them to everyone else, but not me, not anymore. And that had been the worst she'd done to me ever since she'd found out who I was. "For food."

Her hand was still on my torso, trailing gentle touches over my skin. "That too," she said, still breathless.

I kissed her forehead and willed every muscle on my body to pull back. "I'll only be a minute. Get dressed."

She grabbed onto my sleeve like a cat. "But—"

I shook my head and kissed the tip of her nose. "One hunger at a time."

Quickly, I bathed. Thankfully, the cold water numbed my whole body. Resisting the urge to touch her was one thing, resisting the urge to touch myself while thinking of her was quite the difficult other.

Snow was already donning the Solaryan clothes Cora had sent to us. Her long hair had dampened the thin fabric and it had turned almost see through. If that didn't make blood shoot south all over again.

She stood and unravelled something in her hand. "Sit. I'll patch you up."

"I'll do it."

"I'm quicker," she said, pushing me to a stool and coming from behind me to wrap a thin bandage all around my torso and over my shoulder. I could get used to this, being looked after. She did that concentrated face where her tongue poked at the side of her mouth just a little, her brows bunching as she concentrated to get it to wrap around me precisely. "You're healing terribly," she said, tracing a gentle finger down the dent between my muscle and I had to grab her wrist to stop her before I lost it. When she rolled her eyes up at me and noted my expression, her lips pulled up. "Maybe I can ask Cora to have a look at you. She is supposed to be the mother of healers and the best healer in this realm."

"It will heal, my love. No need for that."

"Done," she said, tying a small bow.

Dinner was being served on an open veranda overlooking the blue roofed city. The sun still gleamed on the horizon, though mildly and a burnt orange. It stood behind Magnus's shoulders, giving him a halo that possibly boosted his confidence more than it should because I couldn't look at the man without squinting. And each time I squinted, Snow snorted.

"Your Majesty," Snow called, bringing Cora to attention. "Might I ask for a favour."

The Sun Queen nodded. "Please, call me Cora."

Snow rested a hand on my arm—every move of hers became intentional when she noticed Cora's reaction to them. How much more trusting she became to us. Snow's game of pretend was winning their trust. "We went to aid Hanai when my father got the sceptre piece and the same beast you saw here injured Henr—...my husband. Injured, my husband."

I had to bite down on my smile. The way she said it through gritted teeth almost made me laugh.

The Sun Queen gave her a smile. "You would like for me to heal him?"

Snow nodded.

"I will have a look early tomorrow before I head to our infirmary for my shift."

I leaned on her ear and whispered, "I told you there was no need."

She turned to me with a deep frown. "You are like a sieve. I really don't like sieves."

"You say the most romantic things to me, wife." I kissed the tip of her nose and she sneered.

The table had gone quiet and the two of us were so deep in our food and thoughts we hadn't noticed. When I looked up, Moriko gave me an amused look.

What? I mouthed.

She lightly pointed her fork to Snow's neck, pulling my attention to a little violet mark that I'd left there.

Carefully, I plucked a bunch of my wife's hair to her front to conceal it. Snow didn't pay much mind, entranced by the colourful and flavourful food before her, but the Sun King did.

Magnus looked amused. "So the two of you are really in love, huh?"

"Is it so difficult to believe?" I asked, sliding an arm on the back of Snow's seat, resisting the urge to pull her on my lap and make her come again just so I could hear that sweet fucking sound she made.

Magnus's brows rose almost to his hairline. "You sent to kill her twelve years ago, if I am not mistaken."

Snow froze, her fork halfway to her mouth.

"Didn't you and your wife have a similar background?" I asked and Snow turned to me half astounded. "You killed her family and then imprisoned her before you fell in love and married her. Unwillingly, might I remind you. It wasn't till long ago that she reciprocated your feelings, correct?" Cora's father was a priest with a larger desire than to guide people to their beliefs. He wanted to guide the whole kingdom to his rule. He'd challenged Magnus, had even raised a resistance against the Vayr rule over Solarya with the argument of fading belief and modern practices that was ruining their blessing. Magnus not only had crushed the resistance, opened hundreds of temples and made it a habit to pray every day in mock of what was being said against him, but he'd tortured the priest and kept his family in his dungeons for years. The priest's daughter, Cora, too. Magnus had fallen for more than her beauty and grown a soft heart for her, it was known all over the realm, but Cora had taken years to warm up to him. At least, that is what it was said.

"I see you are well informed," Magnus said, sparing a glance at his now quiet wife and sliding a hand over hers.

My fingers curled around Snow's shoulder. "Informed enough not to make judgements I am not entitled to make."

Magnus scoffed, leaning back on his chair, and pointed a look at Snow. "He has sharp wits despite his young age. I can see the charm."

"I'd return the compliment to Cora, but I'd be lying," Snow said through a mouthful of food.

Cora made a startled sound, but Magnus roared with laughter. Once he came down from his amusement, he cocked his head at my wife again. "I heard you poisoned your half-siblings."

"You have heard right."

"Heard you became a Captain in your father's court, fought for the position yourself."

She had stuffed her mouth so tight with food her cheeks had swollen. "Your hearing is still intact, Your Majesty."

Magnus laughed again. "It surprises me, that's it."

Snow dropped her fork and leaned back in her seat, seizing Magnus like he was seizing her. "Do not tell me that is because I am a woman?"

He shook his head. "Because you are your father's daughter. Trickery is in your blood. I'd never think you would pass up the opportunity to fight an unfair fight. It entertains you Krigborns."

Snow levelled a bored look on him. "Heard your father beat your mother. Are you your father's daughter, too?"

Magnus laughed again and pointed a finger at us. "You come prepared."

Snow only shrugged. "It's in my Krigborn blood as you said."

"You remind me a bit of Jonah," Magnus said with a sigh. "He was a clever man. Unforgiving, like you. But the kindest and most gentle ruler I've met in my time as king. During the time of the Misae drought that plagued our island, when my people were starving and dying, he offered help. We refused it, of course. It was unheard of for us to accept pity, so he bought all of our catch that was going to rot away and then all of our spices. He paid more for that spoiled batch than I would have ever, and I bet he never fed it to his people. But he saved us. He was a great man."

"He was," Snow said quietly. "And I am nothing like him, Your Majesty. I would have let you starve off and die."

Magnus's brows rose and he turned to me. "Do you think so, too?"

"No," I said. "She would have picked a fight with you, thrown you here and there till you'd bleed and ruined a few of your furniture, and then she would have dumped stacks of coins before you as pretext to make up for the damages she caused."

The sun ruler slowly smiled and nodded. "You know her well."

"You have no idea," Snow murmured to herself.

"So," Magnus said, "An alliance."

The Solaryan morning sun was blinding, but it didn't seem to bother Snow. She snored softly on the bed, cocooned in the middle of the enormous thing and drowned by the sage coloured cottons and pillows. Her sleep had been sound for the most part and when I'd felt her distress, I'd gathered her in my arms till she calmed.

"You two match one another well," Cora said, ghosting a palm up and down my wounds, a beam of light emitting from her fingers. The Sun Queen had been more than punctual, arriving at dawn in an attempt to heal my wounds.

My gaze never left her sleeping form. "She'd say otherwise."

"How come you went against the odds?"

Sighing, I leaned back on my seat. "Most people pray for rain, I prayed for thunder."

Cora spared me a smile. "I've met her once before, you know, at her aunt's wedding to my son. I doubted she remembered me, and she didn't remember me. She was the rudest little girl I've ever met."

A smile ghosted on my lips when Snow made a deep snoring sound. "I've met her before as well. Before everything and the agreement with her father." I didn't know why I admitted it to Cora.

"Before the attack, you mean?"

I nodded. "At Urinthia Delcour's coronation, when we were children. And few times after."

Cora's hand stopped hovering and she looked over at my sleeping wife. "Something tells me she doesn't remember this either."

"No, she doesn't."

A bell rang from outside somewhere in the distance, surely to notify morning hours and it seemed to startle Snow awake with a jolt.

She stared ahead, wide eyed, her cheeks red with wild hair plastered to them. She was panting for air. "What...what time is it?"

I flicked through the pages of the book a servant had brought me this morning about the Abendrot tomb in Theros. The burial of the royal *Ybris* and the location of the sceptre piece. "Sunrise."

She looked around the room and then at the bed where she laid. "Where did you sleep last night?"

I flicked to a tunnel map that ran sideways. "I didn't."

"The bed is big. I could have taken the other side."

"I can't sleep unless it is in total darkness. They keep the torches outside lit at night too. It was too bright." I shut the book and went to her, sitting on the edge of the bed. "It wasn't because of you." Dropping a kiss to her forehead, I stood. "A servant brought you something to wear. I'll wait for you outside."

The same servant girl who I'd asked to bring me the book stood outside of our bedroom. I flicked the book open to the page of the map and turned it to her, pointing to the entrance of it. "The entrance noted here is right in the middle of Theros, but your king mentioned that someone left through the sea not through here."

She nodded and then pointed to a spot in the Theros sealine. "The inner caves have a few exits here. Children play there all year long, you can catch some colourful fish there, too."

"And would other maps have these exits noted?"

She thought for a little while and then shook her head. "I wouldn't think so. They start big but go on very small." She lowered her hand down to her knees. "They only come to about here and you have to crawl through them diagonally. Some are even smaller."

"Who else would know about these?"

"All other children in Theros. Everyone has been there at least once. Some sneak to see the Abendrot tomb, though they shouldn't really."

Magnus had a rat. Someone on the inside had given him the information an Isjordian surely ought to not be aware of. Was it his own son? But the Brogmere lord that Snow had killed had no clue about the sceptre whatsoever. If he'd been the only means of contact between Silas and Otis, the Sun Prince, that theory would prove wrong. It had to be someone else.

Snow came out of the room, her brows pulled in a frown. She had a hand over her chest and another clutching her dress to the side. "Who got me this?"

The servant girl gave her a smile. "Queen Cora selected it herself. It suits you well."

"Give her our thanks," I said, and the girl bowed her goodbyes.

"I can't go anywhere."

I turned to her. She looked mighty fine to me. "Remove your hands."

She shook her head.

I took her hand covering her chest down and Snow cringed as the fabric parted into a deep V that dropped all the way down to her belly button. Fuck. I then took her other one down and the white gossamer parted to reveal all of her thigh all the way up her hip.

"It doesn't cover my seal either," she said, turning round to reveal the deep plunge of the back that ended barely above her hip.

Fuck. "Fuck."

"I know. How the hell do I hide that?"

"You look deadly, Snow."

"I need you not to be a man for a moment."

"I think it would be hard to be a woman at this moment, too." I shed my jacket and threw it over her shoulders. She promptly pushed her arms through, and I buttoned the jacket only till midway.

Hooking a finger under her chin, I raised her face to mine. "What?"

"Hm?"

"Don't *hm* at me. What is it?"

"Nothing."

"Good try." I pinched her chin and lifted her face to me again. Her eyes darted all over, the usual feistiness in them blurred with regret. Though I couldn't see the colour of the emotion, I tasted the bitterness in my tongue. "Last night. It's about last night."

Her jaw clenched and she put a bit of distance between us. "I better sleep in a bonfire these days. To get a real sense of what waits for me in hells."

"You could be put in one of the frozen ones. The god of death probably knows all about your skin troubles and would want to punish you."

She smacked my hand away and glared murder at me.

I offered her a hand which she took—reluctantly. "No gloves?"

"I couldn't find where I left them last night. Perhaps a servant took them. As long as I keep them covered," she said, showing me her scarred palm that had fresh scars too.

There were not enough shades of colour to show how much it hurt me to see Snow still soothe by hurting herself.

Theros library stood massive between the city buildings, the beige rock was painted in gold and cobalt, figures of gods and guardians adorning its walls. Guards loitered the grounds in every corner of the city, encircling mostly in the library's distance.

"Precaution," Magnus said as we climbed the stairs to the entrance. "Silas knows we hold valuable information here. If he was brave enough to rob a tomb in the broad daylight of our goddess, I wouldn't hold it past him to rob this one as well."

Magnus had been right. The library was a colossal giant of knowledge. Shelves ran several floors tall with feet long ladders attached to them, all over filled with books and scripts of all sorts.

Nia sneezed and waved a hand in front of her face. The dust and humid musk was heavy in the air. "The library is safe. Silas's soldiers will collapse from allergies before taking a second step in."

Snow pointed to a gilded copy of the Astrum liber perched on a plinth. "Look, your favourite book. Maybe this edition has a bonus chapter you can indulge yourself with. You know, all that godly goodness."

Magnus laughed, shaking his head as he directed us further inside the library corridors until we reached a golden metal door guarded by two sentries. *For the king's eyes only,* the engraving on it read in Tahuma.

"My personal collection and some very precious pieces," he said, ushering us inside.

The room had no windows or other exits beside the door. Hundreds of small holes in the ceiling illuminated the much smaller area, pouring like beams of liquid gold onto the floor that was painted in geometrical motifs of all colours.

Snow lifted a palm and looked up to the ceiling, the beams showering her in a divine glow. If one could paint the heavenly, it would look somewhat like what I was seeing now.

From the corner of my eye, I caught Moriko staring at Snow's hands with a deepening frown. The dozens of little half-moon scars had made shadows of curiosity and worry mottle the Autumn Queen.

I slid my hand over my wife's and laced my fingers with hers, to cover attention that she probably did not want. Snow blinked in surprise for a moment but didn't object, only took close place by my side.

Magnus retrieved a stack of books bound in black leather and placed them on the round table in the middle of the room. "It might look like a lot, but most are vague tales and praises of the prime gods, few guardians and very little on the white flame guardian. You will need someone with knowledge of the old language of gods." He patted the books and sighed. "Anything else that catches your eye, do let me know."

The four of us took a seat round a library table when Magnus returned with a massive dust-covered edition of Numen History and Ithicea History, interwoven in a chronological conjecture with one another.

Moriko and Nia scrolled past the thick pages in search of any mention of Aurora while Snow and I searched the records of all guardians of Ithicea.

"This shouldn't be difficult, right?" Snow asked, tracing a finger over words. "If she was Fader's lover, her name would be painted all over these."

"Except that it isn't," Magnus said. "It looks like they really wanted her gone from all mention in history."

History. Wiped from all history.

"We could be searching the wrong volumes," I said, standing to reach the shelves. When Adan and Seraphim flashed in sight, I stopped and pulled their sacred liber out along with any tales and folk whispers. "If anyone would forget to wipe out something it would be there," I said, pouring the books full of lush fairy tales and lore on the table. "In history books it is said that a fire guardian ruined Seraphim, and I believe history has not lied or tried to conceal her identity. Aurora was guardian of the white flame and if I remember correctly," I said, tapping my finger on the sacred liber of Seraphim, *Phlegethos*. "Fire has both a spiritual and elemental aspect that is why Adan was in charge of making guardians for Ithicea. He moulded all the guardians he created from different fires."

Flipping through the book, past the praises of gods and sacred hymns, I stopped at the mention of Adan's guardians. "Abiz, the silver flamed guardian of order, servant of Ithicea, child of Empyrea. Agni, the golden flamed guardian of riches, servant of Ithicea, child of Empyrea." Flipping past the pages, and countless guardians, I stopped. "Aurora, the white flamed guardian of peace, she who guarded the balance of realms, servant of Ithicea, child of Empyrea."

Magnus was at my side staring wide eyed at the book pages. The paragraph was short. Stating how she was shaped by him and descriptions of the immense magic she possessed. Her power was of the purest form of fire and perhaps the finest of its sort. The touch of her white fire could burn air itself and her words scorched all untruths.

The king traced a hand over the page. "We presumed Fader would have never taken a lover created by the gods. We presumed she was Ithicean born or a child of the lower gods."

Snow lifted a Seraphim folk whispers book, pointing to a faded drawing of white-haired woman with two broken white wings while laying over another body—a male's body. Aurora's lover. "The white flamed guardian that fell for the human man from—" Her eyes went wide. "The human was Vrammetheni. It doesn't make sense. You cannot tell me that the real reason why the western continent remained primitive was because Fader lost one of his lovers?"

"Fader is not petty," Magnus said. "He is might itself, but he is kindness by nature. To find wrong and right it has always been his purpose. He wouldn't have never abandoned a whole civilisation because of this. There were far greater reasons written in holy scriptures detailing why the gods did not take part to bless that side of Numen."

"No, love," I said, agreeing with Magnus. "Guardians did not descend from Numen till after the blessing, till after the unblessed were deemed of rotten hearts. If she fell for the man, it had to have been after."

"What happened to the unblessed man?" Nia asked, flipping through the pages of folk whispers.

"Presumably died, if not by the hand of gods, by that of humans or by humanity itself," Moriko said with a shrug. "The unblessed never live longer than their forties, anyhow. They are infected with disease and famine. Gods would probably have let him rot with the rest of his people. The most ironic end considering his lover would continue to live on forever."

"Hells," Snow murmured, frowning at a page of the thin colourful folk whispers book. "I thought there would be nothing on the name. Vas son of Zoltan. Born of Norodoh, the human man excelled the skill of any blessed soldier. Slayer of the Vilewrath, the beast of Moor, that haunted many of their travellers. The unblessed man became more than man. In the eyes of his people, he became what the unblessed believed him to be a...god slayer." Her wide stare lifted to me. "Why is that name in the Ahmes Lore in a folk whisper? Why is the name of Aurora's lover on the Ahmes Lore?"

I turned to Magnus. "Have you ever heard of this beast, the Vilewrath?" Solaryans were sailors, schooled, fed and beaten by the sea. They lived to tell tales and stories of their journeys.

He nodded. "As a child, years ago. It is an old sailor's tale. Many still speak it when they travel west of the Moor, but it was never told who slayed it."

"Perhaps concealed," I said.

Moriko picked up the book and then frowned. "Does this aid us in any form?"

"This name is in the diary codes to the heavens, the same one Silas attempted to steal from Adriata. It has to make sense somehow," I said, moving to peruse the children's tales, folk whispers and tellings shelves all over again.

Snow stood at my side. "Are we searching the Vilewrath?"

"Yes, my smart girl," I said, fluffing her hair. "Anything you can find on it."

The shelves were heavy with knowledge of all sorts, in most languages spoken in Numen—even those lost to the times.

"Will we not speak of it?" Snow asked quietly as she browsed through book after book.

"*It?*"

"Would you prefer I give it a name?"

That made me chuckle. "So, what is there to say about it?"

"It will not happen again—"

"It is all up to you, my love. If you want me or not, if you need me or not."

She snapped a book shut so violently, dust clouded overhead and made her cough. "Let me finish."

"I *did* let you finish. Didn't I?"

She hit me. Went to her tip toes and squared me with a book on my head with all she had. I did deserve that. "It will not happen again if you are not part of it. It was an exchange, nothing more. I won't owe you anything."

"Owe?" That made me pause and turn to her. "I was part of it perhaps more than you were." I backed her to the shelf, caging her in. The way she looked up at me reminded me again just how much I'd enjoyed it. Leaning to her ear, I whispered, "Never heard of a sweeter sound than the sound you make when you come. One day, love of mine, when you give me the honour of touching you again, you will be screaming my name, too. That'll make it a whole lot sweeter."

"I don't scream."

"I beg to differ. But then again you do like me begging," I said, trailing kisses down her neck, and her hands shot to my chest, clutching my jacket tight. Her mind was torn because one moment she pushed me away, and the next she couldn't get me close enough to her. "Ask. Just ask and I'll be at your feet. Or do you want to hear me beg for a taste of you? Do you want me to beg for you to come on my tongue? I could bet you taste as sweet as heavens, my sweet villain."

She whimpered when I sunk my teeth on her neck and then kissed the sting away. So dizzying. Her scent, her shape, her mind. It was all cast for me, and it spun my mind with violent want. "Ask and I'll do it." I held her face to me while I rested my forehead to hers. "Ask because I am losing my mind."

Just when her lips parted for her to speak, a throat cleared to our side. Moriko stood with her arms crossed tight across her chest and a stern face judged the position she'd caught us in. "I hate you. Oh, I hate you, too," she mocked with a bored tone. "I will kill you. Oh, I will kill you, too."

Snow slid away from me and brushed some dust from her shoulders. "I, for one, said more than that. Second, have you ever had a good, angry, hateful fuck?" she asked, tapping her shoulder and marching away.

The Hanaian queen gave me an assessing look. "Think I liked her better with your mouth on her. Kept her quiet enough."

Straightening my jacket I said, "I quite like her loose tongue, Your Majesty. Sometimes more than when it is in my mouth."

With a heavy sigh, she shut her eyes and turned to leave.

Snow and the others were already flipping through the books, searching for any mention of Vas attached to the sea monster he'd slain.

There was mention of the Vilewrath all throughout Numen mythos and tellings, but very little on its disappearance. However, the children's books were thick with information.

Vas was born in the sea, son of a tradesman and a highborn Norodoh woman. Many paragraphs told of his accomplishments, from the eradication of sea beasts to pirates and illegal trade made on the Moor. He was a hero in the unblessed west, but he was a hero to the blessed too.

Nia shot up from her seat. "I've got it," she said, waving a book before us. "Aurora met him in Adriata. Look. 'Sight first cast under Henah's starry sky, a breath first shared in Henah's land. Worth and unworth met, yet the two shone like the stars they were under that night. Enamoured with her beauty and her kind, the unblessed man believed for the first time that there was a divine. Enamoured by his tenancy, his crystal eyes and his tender smile, the white flame guardian believed for the first time that the gods had been unjust to omit help in Vrammethen. They tasted the beauty of night and the perks of the dark to enjoy one another—to fall for one another. But when the sun shone the next morning, Aurora's betrayal was clear to the heavens. She'd betrayed Fader. His trust, his care and his love. Mostly, she had defied his power, his word and his ruling. To mingle with humans was ill-advised. To mingle with those with hearts darker than the tar pits of Golgotha's heaven was forbidden. A violation. The two unfated lovers were not divinely punished. For the divine refused to stoop to the gall they'd committed." Nia blinked at the pages, running a finger along the inner spine. "It was torn. The next page was torn."

"Vas was made to live out his human years and she was chained to the realm," Moriko said with a sigh, pulling Nia to her lap, and leaving a kiss on her shoulder. "Predictable, my *ahana*."

Nia trailed a finger under the next page. "The next part starts with Aurora being trapped. 'The silver gilded guardian was trapped in the silver gilded sceptre. A gift, a curse. The realm now possessed the power to turn Fader's mercy into either. As the magic remained unstable, so did the Numen folk. Carefully handed to those that feared neither magic nor death, Red Coven kept the divine object where no one could step—Nephthys Isle. Protected not only by the magic tether of all Eldmoor witches, but by the hand of the mighty Golgotha and his creatures laying lair in the Sea of the dark.'"

"Visha mentioned that," Snow said and grabbed the book from Nia to read the title. "The insults to the divine. A prose poem mythos written by—" She frowned at the cover page. "E.V."

"Esmeray Vassenas," I said. "First a scholar then an author before becoming Henah's confidant. Safe to assume all this occurred during the time she lived."

Nia stood and rushed to the shelves again. Everything had narrowed down. We now had a time frame to match and line everything up.

Snow dropped back in her seat. "Also safe to assume that they have wiped out this in any history book of that time too. We are now back where we started."

Her friend dropped about a dozen or so more books on the table. "All written during that period of time. Mostly Eldmoorian. One ought to speak of the sceptre."

Moriko picked up one of the thin, colourful editions. "Doubt that they were teaching children where they hid the sceptre pieces, *ahana*."

Snow pointed a finger at the Autumn Queen. "First time you called her your flower I pretended my senses had dulled from the dust. You say it a third time and I—"

"Be nice now, love," I said, pulling her threatening finger down.

Nia snickered, bringing a packet of almonds for Snow to munch on them. "Yes, be nice now."

Sneering like a little feral cat, she pulled the treats and dove inside the book pages. "This was why I hated these stories when I was a child," she scoffed, flipping through them with disdain. "So much colour and pretty words for the gruesome truths they were based on. Sam told me Alaric didn't speak for a whole year after the Ater battles because of the horrors they'd seen. Yet 'Seven Red Tales of Numen' paints the soldiers with a smile on their faces and a puny sword."

"They are for children, Snow," Nia said quietly.

As if in realisation, my wife's hand stilled on the page. "For children, yes."

We looked through the library, each to one corner. We'd spent hours doing so, and before we knew it, that titian glow of sunset filtered through the ceiling windows.

Snow was behind me, raking her attention over the stacks of books when she let out a gasp. She carried a book in her hand, shaking it in amazement. "Marianne Hawthorne," she whisper-shouted at me. "The unpublished copy of Blood Bound, the recollection of tales: The two lovers of Saratuza." She fluttered the pages open full of unadulterated marvel, so rare to see. "Do you think he will let me have it?"

I lifted a brow at her and her excitement.

The book was snatched from her hand by Moriko whose stare turned wild when she read the title. "You don't read that sort of rubbish, do you?"

Irked, Snow snatched it back. "Let's not shame readers for what they like to read, shall we?"

Nia must have heard the commotion because she poked her head from behind a shelf and came to us. "Marianne Hawthorne. Oh, it's the unpublished—" Her enthusiasm diminished when she looked up at me and Moriko. "What? She is a woman of refined literature."

"What literature?" Moriko asked, crossing her arms and giving Nia an amused look.

"Uhm." Nia's gaze flinted to Snow for help, but she was too entranced by whatever she was reading on the pages of the odd book. "Women's literature?"

Attracted by the commotion, Magnus joined our group. He frowned at the title Snow held. "Is it something worth your interest?"

"Yes," Snow and Nia said at the same time.

"You may have it," he offered and the two beamed. "Anything else?"

I pointed to a couple dictionaries I'd set aside. "Besides those, I don't reckon there is anything else of much help."

He nodded. "You're welcome to peruse anytime you wish, son."

"Actually," I said, "would it be a possibility for me to return sometime to view the Abendrot site? I'd like to see how the beast has managed to get past the Arx Triad."

"Of course."

CHAPTER EIGHTEEN

Praeteritus

Snowlin

I'd been knocked around the training platform like a ragdoll. A ragdoll with ragged thoughts. A ragdoll who was going to make a few others very mad with a decision I'd made after we'd returned from Solarya a couple days ago.
When I lost my balance, Cai hooked a hand on my elbow and pulled me back to my feet. "Concentrate or go."

"My bones are a bit rusty, no need to be nasty."

"Yeah, all that time down the humid dungeons really rusted you well."

"I haven't been down there in—"

"Two weeks, I know."

I was going to say a while. But it seemed like he'd counted. Had it really been two weeks?

He grabbed my jaw tight, angling my head to the side where his dagger had grazed me. "I'm not explaining to your *husband* how you got that."

"Scared of him?" I taunted, pushing his hand away.

He scoffed. "Did you see how he looks at anyone who raises a decibel of their tone with you? Nia told me what he did in Solarya. If he called night over the land of day without a second thought, right before Magnus Vayr, I'd be an idiot not to be afraid."

I lifted my daggers up and took my stance. "It's an act, Cai. He thinks I'll find it in my black heart to spare him."

He pushed my blade down with a finger. "Do you really believe that?"

"What is there to believe? Do you really think that man could care for me?" I asked, nudging his weapon. "I need this. Either fight me or get someone else up here."

He shook his head. "You're not angry, you're confused. Confused doesn't do well when we are both holding weapons."

I dropped both daggers. "I am not confused. Hand to hand then."

And like that, Cai had me on the ground in two swift moves, a knee pressing on my spine. "Snow!"

"Fine," I sighed, surrendering.

There was a flurry of thunder brewing in me, yet I couldn't make it rain so I sought the closest thing to relief. Murder.

Murdoc sat tied to a chair before me, his viscous brown eyes boring into me as if they still had power to tear me. He stared blankly across to where I sat before him, and despite the cold darkness of the dungeons I could still make out his features pursed in an ever-angry scowl.

"You were always so angry. Still are," my voice broke the echo of water droplets that had restlessly pooled on the ground behind him.

Murdoc didn't answer, only stared. He was never lost for words, and if they were ever robbed out of him he always relied on his ability to hurt physically.

"At some point I thought you were going to kill me. At some point I wanted you to kill me. It would have been easier than having to do it myself," I confessed, my chest feeling lighter somehow at the confession. "It would have been easier on my mother, too—she wouldn't have blamed herself. Eren and Thora wouldn't have been as sad either. Like me, they would have held onto you like an anchor. Your death would have given them purpose and then relief." A bitter laugh left me at the memory, and I dropped my head back on the rest, tired. "It was such a pretty little plan. I spent nights thinking it through. To my rotten luck something worse happened. You proved to be just an abusive coward and I became addicted."

My hands subconsciously curled to fists. "Pain became my addiction and you became the dealer. Eren thought I took Thora's place to protect her." Tears were suddenly rolling down my eyes, not from the ghostly touch of pain I sometimes felt when I recalled the memory but remembering how I volunteered for Murdoc's punishments instead of my sister for my own twisted reasons. I'd beg him to take me instead of her, and he would. I needed the pain and he had plenty to offer. "I came because I wanted to hurt, and she knew. Thora knew." I was sure she did. The look in her small face still sent shudders through my body. My little sister knew everything. She sensed everything.

Pushing to stand, I reached Murdoc. "That's enough heart to heart, I suppose." Fisting a bunch of his hair, I pulled his limp lifeless body to the ground and crushed the wooden chair he'd sat on with my heel—spreading the wood as kindling over his body. I'd pushed too far and too hard, the valley stone couldn't have helped to keep him alive at the point I'd beaten him to. He was dead after a few of my administrations. Perhaps it was for the best. Coming down here had only twisted my rage, not soothed it.

"Tristin," I shouted.

The Skye warrior's shadowy form stood tall at the door. "Yes, my queen."

"Bring me a torch."

The blue flame illuminated the dark room and made visible all I'd done to Murdoc. One might say I'd take it a bit far. One wouldn't know how much further I could have taken this before his weak-willed heart ruined it. His body lit almost immediately after I threw the torch over him. The cooked rat stench was livid, but I wanted to watch him turn to ash.

Tristin cracked open a small silver tin lined with neatly rolled cigarettes and handed it to me.

"Thought you quit," I said, taking one.

"Only in front of Lila. Leanna and I have a sneaky one once in a while."

I snorted and held the cigarette head to the fire before inhaling a puff of the clove scented tobacco. We both watched the priest burn to the bone. Burned. Because that is how I wanted him out of my memory—gone like dust. "I thought about burning him alive, but all the screaming ruins it for me sometimes. You know, like when you see the food actually cook before it is served to you. It ruins the eating experience. Doesn't that bother you as well?"

She slanted me a bewildered look. "I've known you for years, yet I question your sanity every day."

What was sanity, really? Have I ever been sane? "Much easier to just accept that I am insane. It doesn't offend me as much as questioning it does," I said, pulling my feet out of the wet boots I wore and warming them up on the fire. The wet prune skin sensation ticked a nerve the wrong way and it was a waste of a fire if no one used it.

"Snow," Sebastian called, jogging inside the dungeon room. He winced at the pungent scent and my bloodied sight, but quickly recovered.

"A bonfire," I exclaimed, ushering him in. "Do you have any snacks with you?"

"No, unfortunately I come unprepared." Taking a clove cigarette from Tristin, he lit it on the fire "Who are we burning?"

"Murdoc."

He nodded. "Explains the stench."

"But he burns rather nicely." I turned to him. "Any news for me?"

He took one long puff and then flicked the rest of the cigarette in the fire. "It is confirmed, your father's men have successfully infiltrated Adriata through Kirkwall with hopes to retrieve your uncle. I let them through like you asked me to. What do you want us to do next?"

"They will definitely retrieve someone," I said. "Have a soldier of ours direct them onto the Adriatian isles out in the Moor Sea and get Mal for me."

Tristin held an arm out, blocking me from leaving. "I'll have to report to Alaric that you are thinking of doing something about this."

Did she just use the 'I'll tell your father' threat on me? "I'm shivering, Tristin. Truly," I said, throwing the cigarette butt on the fire and giving her a wink before heading to wash the stench off of me.

Midway to my room, Alaric caught me. His features pinched in a cringe when he smelled what was on me. "You're smiling. Where have you been?"

"The dungeons. They are lovely this time of the year. You should visit."

His face twisted a little when he reached close to me. "I gather you've burned someone?"

"Getting sharper by the year at your young age."

The moment he took note of my red eyes, his expression fell. He knew immediately who I had burned. "Kid, look at me." He rested a hand on my arm, the most comfort he knew how to give, and the smile I'd put on faded. "Don't expect it to be all fixed now. You carry all that he has done to you, not him. Now that he is gone, it won't mean all that it will be gone with him. It is not what will heal you."

"It felt good, Alaric. You've known that truth of mine for years. You know I don't do it because I have to do it or because I think it will make me feel better. It feels good to hurt. Liberating. The more he screamed, the harder I wanted him to scream next."

"You are not cruel, kid. What you are is not cruel. What *he* has made you is cruel."

"I only know how to be cruel. Nothing else makes sense to me anymore." If I behaved humanly, how he had tried so hard to teach me, I felt like a tear in the reality—like I didn't belong. Like my purpose was wrong.

His hands fell to his sides. "You can't let them win. You can't let them ruin you like this, kid."

"Already ruined," I said, passing him and heading to my room.

Pen was already there, tidying the sheets like I hadn't spent every single night for the past two months in Adriata. She hurried to the bathing chambers the moment she saw me and the noise of water running filled the emptiness of sound. The grey of my room that I loved, the silver satin sheets, the silver bedstead, furniture, the glittering grey stones decorating my ceiling that I pretended were the starry night sky when I squinted—they all seemed so dull all of a sudden. And so did the quiet stormy sky framed by my balcony. The world was numb. Or perhaps it was just me.

Pen didn't say anything. Not when she peeled my bloodied clothes off. Not when she scrubbed the dried blood from my hands. Not when she ran the sponge over my scars and I flinched. Not when she helped me dry off and sat me down to brush my wet hair. Not when I stared at that dark reflection of mine shape shift into a giant of terror. Not when tears rolled down my eyes.

She didn't say anything, but she cried along with me without a single word.

She wept harder than me.

I really didn't understand. I understood none of it. Why I felt like I did. Why did nothing feel like I'd imagined it to be? Why the scars on my back still felt fresh every time I took a deep breath. Why I felt so little again. Why even dead, Murdoc had so much power over me.

I'd never cried then. Why was I crying now?

I'd gotten my final word—my final punch. I'd given him a piece of my own cruelty, yet it didn't satisfy me as I thought it would.

Pen wiped away the heavy tears streaming down her face. "Should I," she hiccupped, still crying. "Should I get you a peach? It makes me happy when I eat them."

That made me smile. "I'd like that."

She rushed out and returned shortly, out of breath, cradling a bunch of the fuzzy fruit.

They were sweet, I'm sure they were, but I tasted nothing but ash. "What time is it, Pen?"

"It is sunset," she murmured through sobs.

I stood, reached my balcony and bolted to Adriata.

Sunset in Amaris was almost as warm as a lover's hand on your back. For a couple of moments, I stood in his balcony marvelling at the twisting of colours that were beginning to paint dusk. As I saw the skies shift, a wave of peace brushed me. Or perhaps it was the cool summer wind of this cursed kingdom. Whatever it was, I wanted it again. It made me feel something—something warm.

The glass doors behind me slammed open. "Snow, what is the matter, my love?" Kilian's voice had taken a deep, worried edge. When he spun me to face him, his gaze widened and cracked. "Please tell me you're not hurt." His hands touched every inch of my body in urgency, searching for wounds. He'd never find them. All the wounds hid under healed scars. They'd even managed to trick me.

Why doesn't it feel enough? Will it feel the same when I kill you? I wanted to ask him that. But I was too afraid of the answer. Too afraid to even think about what I was meant to do to him. "I want you to enter my head, find my siblings."

He stopped, searched for something in my stare then said, "Alright." His thumb brushed underneath my eye. "Alright."

I lifted the peach I held. "Want a bite?"

He leaned in and instead of aiming for the peach, he lowered his mouth to my neck and dug his teeth on my skin. Hard but not hard enough to hurt. Just enough to have all sensation return to my body and light it all alive with heat. He kissed the sting away and when I moaned a little, I felt his mouth stretch to a smile over my skin. "Sweeter than sweet," he whispered in my ear. With a last kiss on my cheek, he pulled away and I almost bellowed. "You could have stayed in Taren tonight. I will have to go to Lyra for a while. One of my scholars wants to try something about the Foglings and needs my help." He traced a finger over my jaw. "Mal is in his room if you wish to stay here. I can ask him to sleep on the sofa if you want."

"I don't want to go to Taren. My knight in shining armour can stay in his room though. He snores worse than a hog."

His thumbs brushed my eyes that were still wet with tears. "What happened?"

I took a bite from the peach. "I don't think I like peaches."

"Snow."

"I think it's the fuzz. It makes my brain think I'm chewing on a ball of hair." With that, I handed him the peach, pushed past him and did a little run before jumping on the fluffy bed and diving inside the covers.

The bed dipped and my heart shivered with anticipation. *Don't ask. Don't ask.*

"Can I ask?"

Sigh. "No."

He slid a hand under the blanket and held mine. I didn't hold him, but he held me sturdy enough for the both of us. "Is the problem murderable?"

That made me smile. "Too late for that."

"You killed them good?"

"I never kill bad."

"Was it Murdoc?"

How did he know? How did he always know? "You said you wouldn't ask."

"I didn't specify what."

My finger brushed a little raised flesh on the side of his wrist and his skin pimpled with goosebumps. "How did you get that?"

"My hand got stuck on a human bone."

"How?"

"We'd been stuck on an island down in Eldmoor. Most of the Celesteel's blessed lands are a death trap for those that rely too much on magic. I had no weapon besides my hands. My younger self didn't aim as tactically as I do now, back then I just aimed to kill what wanted to kill me."

He let out a tortured sigh when my hand slipped further up his arm, stopping when I felt another scar. "And that?"

"My armour broke, and the metal dug into my skin. Someone hit me with a mace and my quickest thought was to block it with my very breakable arm."

When my fingers brushed another one, he answered without me even asking. "Sparring with Mal. We were both piss drunk and it was raining. I slipped before I got the first punch in. There is also another one on my back from the same day."

He told me about each and every scar on that arm till my eyes hooded with sleep.

The room was overly crowded. Cai, Nia, Alaric and Mal had leaned on a wall in the far back of Visha's chambers. All concentrating on the craft halo which Visha had spent the last hour drawing on the floor.

"What if he fails to pull her out?" Cai asked.

"I won't," Kilian responded calmly.

"But what if you do fail?"

Mal pushed from where he stood and squatted before the halo, studying the patterns. "Then I jump in."

"It won't be necessary," Kilian said, now starting to lose his patience.

"And what if you fail?" Cai asked Mal.

The Night Prince raised a brow at my friend. "What's with you?"

Cai's gaze darkened. "Simply finding it hard how the two of you could possibly care to bring her back."

Kilian's head swivelled to Cai and stood, reaching my friend face to face. "How many times do I have to tell you?"

Cai straightened too, reaching closer to Kilian. "I simply cannot comprehend how you can care for her after everything you've done."

"She felt safe enough to ask this of me, Caiden. If you find it hard to believe me then believe your friend."

"If you wish to argue, please do it out of my chambers, you are bothering the dead," Visha said quietly as she lit the candles around the room. Red flame spurted from the wicks, fluttering crimson light and darkening shadows. She handed me a piece of obsidian with a little white rune engraving on the top and pointed for me to sit inside the circle. "To trap their essence."

Kilian sat as I did, facing me.

"Hold hands," Visha said, settling just outside the circle. "Don't let go during the trip back and forth, he is your grounding to this realm."

I peeled off my gloves, throwing them out of the circle and held Kilian's hands. They were warm—always so warm.

He rubbed his thumbs over my scars and his jaw tightened with tension, that little chin dimple flashing.

It was tormenting. My tongue darted to wet my lips and he looked up at me. The corner of his mouth lifted up when I couldn't help but look down at his chin again.

"Don't gloat," I sneered.

"Can't help it, you're leering at me. I like it when you leer at me. Keep leering."

Visha began chanting in Borsich, the candles in the room fluttering like mad and a strange wind picked up and swirled around the craft circle.

My eyelids drooped, heavy with sleep, and suddenly I fell into a downward abyss. Spinning and spinning till the ground felt solid beneath my feet.

I jerked upright, breathless, reality settling around me again and I swayed on my feet.

Kilian stood beside me, studying our surroundings, a sturdy arm around my waist to hold me upright.

The room was familiar but dressed in the old beige colouring of my childhood. Isjord, but not quite the Isjord I remembered. Something was odd, the way time felt old and yellow stained like a memory but not quite.

The door opened and a soldier stepped in, passing right through me. He had long, red hair pulled half up in a tail, tall and strong features and donned the white uniform Isjordian soldiers wore on the solstice. We were in my memories of that night. The Solstice from thirteen years ago.

"Lin," he called, searching the room. "Come out. Your father is asking for you."

"Lysander," I whispered, part overwhelmed and part guilty for ever forgetting how he used to look like.

He searched the room all over, under the bed and tables, the bathing chambers before he returned frustrated to leave. I knew what he was looking for. I knew what he had not been able to find that moment.

"The curtains," my voice shook when I spoke. "You didn't check the curtains."

Moments after he left, a small form came from behind the large emerald curtains. The white dress that fell too low and hung a size too big still looked too big and long for my petite frame. No one really cared about me then. If I dressed or not, if I looked my part as princess or not. No one cared. Not that I had ever wanted them to care.

I'd recognise that little girl anywhere. Not from the dark hair we shared and the yellow stare that we both despised, but from the way she wiped her bloodied palms on the corner of the curtain and put a fresh pair of gloves on as if she was born without pain.

Suddenly, I remembered that now I had to share this memory with someone elsc and I turned to glance at Kilian. He stood lost in a world of his own. Staring at my young form in a strange trance. As if he too was visiting an old memory.

A smaller Memphis slithered past little Snow's shoulders to turn into a small cub. She kneeled beside her and whispered, "Find my brother."

Go find him yourself. I wanted to shout those words when Memphis prattled away on her small legs. The first mistake I'd made that night. I'd hid.

The surroundings suddenly shifted in a murky mist and we were no longer in my bedroom. My younger self ran along the corridors, and we followed swiftly behind as she navigated between heavy bodies of soldiers and terrified Isjordians. Screams, cries of help, the taste of smoke were now in the air. The moment the Adriatians had opened their attack against Tenebrose.

I trembled at the sight of my brother approaching, his white attire littered in blood and soot while he slashed his sword over Adriatian men. How had I forgotten? How had I forgotten how my brother looked?

"Eren," little me called my brother's name like a battle cry, drawing a small dagger and weaving through bodies toward him.

My brother gathered my smaller form in his shaking arms. "Find mother," he panted. "Find mother, she went to the gardens to search for you. They are looking for the three of us. Don't let the Adriatians see you. They want us. Don't let anyone see you. Do you hear me?"

Younger me shook her head. "No, we will find ma together."

He ran a bloodied hand through my hair. "I have to get to Thora first. I have to get our little sister out of the fire. I will meet you there."

"Eren," little Snow cried out. "Please."

He stood to leave toward the engulfing fire. "I will be right behind you, I promise. I promise you, Lin. I am right behind you."

"Liar," I whispered, and then shouted at the figure disappearing between the ash, "Liar!"

Time warped again, floating images flew by and past us. My cries begging Cerelia vortexed around us. Flame. More death. Blood. The hounds chasing and sniffing around for us. Memory of me catching Moreen guiding Adriatian soldiers toward the winter gardens as she hid. Till all of a sudden, the air cleared, and our surroundings sharpened.

A black-haired woman searched the winter maze frantically, her white dress stained and wet from the snow carpeting the floor of the gardens. My mother. It was my mother. "Snow!" Her hands shook as she cupped them over her mouth. "Come out, my snowflake. Please!"

"Ma!" Little Snow flew in sight and my mother sobbed with relief.

"You look like her," Kilian said quietly.

"I couldn't remember her," I whispered. I'd forgotten what she looked like. In my dreams she has my face and other times a contorted mess of blood. My beautiful mother.

My heart cried, it wept so fiercely, but my eyes refused to blur the only chance I had to see her again how she was.

And even that got cut short when Adriatian soldiers flooded the gardens, doubling in number by the second while Moreen hid herself behind the garden walls, grinning herself to tears.

Protectively, my mother pushed me behind her. Lifting her hands heavenward, a wall of wind raising between the two sides shielding them. Magic that she hadn't used since her kingdom had been destroyed. Magic she'd refused to use because it reminded her so much of her pain. But she'd used it then—for me, to protect me.

"Run," she said to me, her body quivering from magic which had not cursed through her for twenty-seven years. "Run, Snow. As quick as lightning, as quick as Nubil, do not turn, do not stop, and do not fear. Run till all you hear is nothing, till all you see is nothing, till you are so alone, your thoughts echo in your ears. Promise me, Snow, you will run and you will live, promise me."

"No," my smaller self cried with conviction, flickers of lightning gathering around her small wrists. "Not until you promise you will run with me."

My mother smiled brightly down at me. Perhaps one of the first times she'd done so in a while. Maybe it was why I believed the next words she said, "I will be right behind you, I promise."

A bitter laugh cracked from me. I laughed and laughed hysterically till I couldn't breathe. Promises and promises. "Watch," I said to the man beside me. "You don't want to miss the best part."

As soon as I'd taken off, my mother had given up, shadows slithered from all corners, like tentacles they latched onto her limbs. Quicker than a flash of lightning, black steel jutted out of her chest, life vanishing from her eyes within moments.

Our location shifted till we stood beside little Snow. She'd crouched to the ground, a look of horror painting her face as she saw from a distance her mother bleeding out on the cold ground.

"Get up," Kilian murmured beside me, and my attention jerked to him.

Little Snow didn't cry, nor scream, nor mourn at that moment. She looked given up, staring between where mother's body laid lifeless and the burning castle.

There was little I remembered from that night, but I remembered the thoughts crossing me at that moment—wanting to go after them, to die with them.

A screech came from the sky and Memphis landed beside my smaller self. A second later, Lysander portaled close by. He'd used the morph to find me.

"Go!" he shouted at me. Swirls of red magic twisting around his fists. "The city gates are open, run toward Sabble Abyss and hide."

When she would move, Memphis dug her teeth in my dress and began pulling both away. They didn't get a chance to go far before Lysander was overwhelmed with men attacking him from all sides. All too quickly, Memphis was twisted around a few Adriatians, and I was running toward the gates when a man reached to grab my long hair in his fist.

I flinched, my hand going to my hair on command at the ghostly touch of that memory and Kilian jerked forward, as if he could stop what was happening.

The man pinned my smaller body under him, but I had stopped thrashing. I didn't remember this part. The part where I'd given up.

Have you heard about the death of a thousand cuts? The words brushed in a whisper past my ears.

He took a dagger out and dug it onto my cheek. "Have you heard about the death of a thousand cuts?"

My fingers went to my scar as I watched the Adriatian carve it on my younger self. I don't remember it hurting.

A brush of warm wind tickled my cheek. Not wind. A gust of magic. Kilian looked like he was not breathing and breathing too fast at the same time.

I flinched a little when a tear rolled down his cheek as he watched what happened ahead. And when his mouth slightly quivered, I tore my eyes away from him.

Little Snow didn't scream when he dragged the tip of the black steel from my cheek down my neck and shoulder. Little Snow didn't cry. She didn't fear. This was the moment I'd realised my only reason to live, the flash of wanting to take.

"Sorry, mother," little me whispered, before resting her palms on the man. There was a sharp zap of light and then black dust flew where his form was supposed to be.

Bloodied and dizzy, she shot up and then took in the men surrounding Lysander before approaching them. Her fingers moved slowly by her sides and the sky cracked in blinding light at her conduct. I looked a fearsome thing, not because of the crimson staining my skin and white dress, but because I was something to fear then. Without lifting a finger, bolts of white electricity crawled over the snowy ground. The second it touched the men, only black dust from their remains was left behind. This was the moment I lost faith in promises and oaths. I could have saved my mother had I used my cursed magic. I could have saved Eren and Thora, too. But I swore. Sworn an oath and promise. That promise made me lose them.

Lysander was panting when he kneeled before younger me. "No magic, Lin. Remember what you three and your mother worked so hard and sacrificed so much for. You swore, you all swore, never to let your father win. Now go!"

"At what cost, Lysander?" I murmured and flinched a step back when his eyes met mine over little Snow's shoulder. Could he see me?

"At the cost of never living through what he was going to put you through." He smiled. "Say hi to my daughter for me."

The surroundings warped again. It grew darker and colder. I'd recognise the trees surrounding us with my eyes closed. How many times had I traced their forms and made shapes out of their branches to keep myself from falling asleep.

I searched the white ground for what I'd partly forgotten. A half dead younger me with a half dead younger Memphis in my hold, keeping me warm. We stayed like that for three days. For three days we had not moved and hid under layers of forest and snow. A dying heart next to another dying heart. We'd not yet bonded at that time, but the animal had stuck to me like we had been closer than what any bond or blood could have made us be. Memphis's heart had slowed almost with mine, willing to die with me.

Kilian reached close to them, running a ghostly hand over my smaller form's face. In that same moment, little Snow shifted and cracked her eyes open to stare at the grey skies pouring soft flakes over the forest floor. Memphis perked too and nudged her for a pat which I'd never denied. "Remember, M?" my smaller self asked, running a small blood-crusted hand over the matted and wet fur of the morph. "Mother said that if she ever left us for the heavens, she'd become a winter sky, full of snowy storms." She nuzzled the morph's neck. "Will we make pretty winter skies, too?"

Kilian dropped to the ground and covered his face. His shoulders rose furiously and suddenly his body shook with a sob. "Forgive me," he muttered between shaky breaths and cries. "Forgive me. Forgive me."

I backed into a stump and slumped to the ground as stray tears left my burning eyes.

Like that, I watched Kilian mourn his doing. I wish I hadn't—not like this. He should have mourned it with my blade cutting him piece by piece. With him suffering as I had. With him losing everything before losing his life. Why did it look like he was suffering just the same—perhaps worse? Why was he suffering?

Why?

"You were such a disobedient child, but that day you listened." The words were so airy for a moment I thought I'd imagined them.

I stood and spun round at the realness of that voice. Like an older reflection of me, she stood in white, her long black hair waving at the touch of wind. I had forgotten the green of her eyes. How they resembled the vibrance of a forest after rain.

Her fingers lightly grazed my face, they were cold, so cold. "My beautiful girl." Turning her gaze to Kilian, she bowed her head just slightly. "Kaliantha's boy, you have grown into quite a handsome man." The smile she gave her killer was sickly sweet.

I took a step forward and then another till I was within a hand's reach from her. This couldn't be. I reached to touch a creation of my troubled mind, yet I met soft flesh. "Mother?"

"Don't frown, my snowflake," she said, reaching her hands toward me and pulling me into her embrace. "You look entirely too much like my brother when he was about to give me a scolding."

"How?" I asked, tightening my hold on her, afraid she'd leave me again. "How?" I shook. I shook so hard I couldn't form a thought. She was holding me. My mother was holding me. "How?"

"There is not much time, my Snow, you cannot stay long in this realm. You've already spent too much time here." She pulled back and reached to hold my hand. "Find Eren and Thora." Something warm appeared between our hands. The obsidian Visha had given me glowed white for a moment. "Their essence. All of my memories I have of them. All of my love for you and for them, my snowflake. You have it there, it is now yours. Use it to find them."

"What?"

A tear slid down her cheek. "My last sacrifice. One I will gladly make to have you join them once again."

Sacrifice? "What are you talking about?"

Her gaze went to the little form on the cold ground covered by snow. "I thought I would lose you. For three days I saw my child get one breath closer to death, since then I bound myself to you. I could not find the strength in me to leave you." She turned to me, her warm hand caressing my cheek. "You were always so strong. I need you to be strong again." She turned her gaze to Kilian and a chill spread through my spine. "I need you to thank Visha for me."

I broke away from her touch, shaking my head.

Her smile quivered. "I visited her a while ago, asking to bring you and Kilian to me."

"Why would you do that?"

"I need you to be happy, my snowflake. For that to happen you have to let me go." She turned to Kilian again. "And he can help me make you happy."

"No. He cannot help you. He will not help you." I shook my head. "He took you from me once, he will not do it again." I turned to him. "You will do nothing. You hear me? You will do nothing!"

"You will help me won't you, son?" my mother asked, pleadingly. "Please. There is nothing left for me to wish in this realm for anymore besides this. Let me join my family in the skies. Let my daughter be rid of old memories."

"Are you certain he asked?"

No. No. No.

Heavy tears slid down her eyes. "More than ever."

My magic erupted, leaving the boundary of the seal, but nothing happened. I knew gales of it were seeping out of me, but nothing was happening. "You won't. You won't. Please, please," I begged Kilian. I hated the weakness in my voice, the way my words softened. "Please."

His silver gaze dropped to the ground, away from mine, before meeting my mother's and a sob ripped out of my throat. He was going to ruin me again. He was going to take her from me again. "Please."

Suddenly a crafter's halo formed below my feet, runes began surrounding it one by one. *Seal. Trap. Hold. Forbid.* Visha. I was going to kill her. "Visha!" My knuckles bled where they met the shield, the thin layer of air staining with blood. "Visha!"

My mother cried, her eyes never leaving mine. "This is the right thing to do, my snowflake."

No. No. No.

The craft had frozen me in place, my whole body weighing the size of a boulder. "Do this and I swear it to you, I will make all you love hurt and bleed!" I shouted, panting for air, drumming against the invisible shield holding me back.

But he didn't hear me. No one heard me.

One last time she turned to me, her beautiful face filled with love and bliss. Was she that happy to leave me? Was she that happy to be rid of me? "Be...happy."

When she touched Kilian's hand, a vortex of black wind swirled around her and suddenly all that was left of her were specks of golden dust that floated toward the skies.

I screamed. I screamed so hard the world blackened. I screamed so hard I felt the guards of my seal open and then...then I fell and fell in what looked like a pit of nihility.

It was so dark, and I was blind in it, but my body was no longer falling and solid ground dug onto my knees. Sobs tore through my lungs, but I couldn't hear them. I knew I was crying when I felt the sting of a burn in my throat and wetness pool down my cheeks. I knew I was shaking because the earth below me constantly slipped from my palms and my grip had weakened.

Come back to me. Come back to me. The words repeated over and over till it echoed in the hollow of my head. They repeated till bright cracked across my sight and my fingers finally dug in stone. One by one, the blurred figures took shape, concern marring their features, particularly his. The male sat affront me had death painted on his pale face, as if he had seen it and been afraid of it. His palms rested on the ground besides mine, fingers intertwined with mine, but not touching me.

"Snow?" He tried to touch me, but I crawled back.

"I hate you." The coarse sounds came out as harsh as they sounded, they burned my chest more than my throat. "I hate you. I hate you!" The scream bounced back in an echo.

Yet he didn't waver. No, he was solid stone and ice.

More tears spilled from me. I realised something I'd refused to accept before. That I was finally grieving. These cries hurt. I had not grieved my mother. I'd shed tears of anger and burning revenge, not that of sorrow. It made me cry harder, the selfishness in me. The inhuman in me that had not grieved her own mother. It would not stop—pain of loss poured like a stream out of me. And my sobs turned to raspy screams. I'd forever lost her now. He'd now taken her away from me forever.

"Snow," he called again with worry, reaching for me.

"Don't!" I bellowed and then my vision blurred red. Not figuratively. I felt the thicker liquid pour over my cheeks and wet my palms and the ground crimson. My lungs seized breathing and I panted. My mind overflowed with emotion I had never felt before.

Another kneeled beside me, hands resting on my shoulders. I leaned onto the touch, recognising the comfort of my friend. Suddenly I could breathe, but it was not me—it was him. Then he did something he had never done before, he wrapped me in his arms and let me in a little piece of him that he gave no one—proximity. "Remember when you first came to me," Cai said calmly, in a way he only knew how to be calm. "Alaric promised me a good chunk of gold if I could bring you out of your room." He laughed at the memory. "I tried for weeks. You wouldn't even speak to me let alone follow me outside. And one day, I took a long trip to the baker's before coming to you because I knew it would be just another useless attempt and being late would not be an issue. Whether it was night or day, you refused to speak or come out. The first time you even acknowledged me was that day. No, actually, you acknowledged the cake."

"Is that chocolate cake?" Cai's mouth fell open, bits of the sweet falling out and I wrinkled my nose. "That was disgusting."

"It is cake," he said, slowly, as if he was treading on glass. "We can go get some if you want. They have all kinds."

"It was worth it," I whispered in his chest. "The best chocolate cake to this date."

"The first time you went out and I figured my trap. Take you to the baker's every goddamn day."

"Can't believe I still have my teeth after how many sweets we ate that summer."

"Let us go to the baker's again, Cakes."

I slinked onto him, tired. "I am not hungry."

"Please," he whispered, holding me tight against him.

"Alright." I felt my eyelids droop and the world blank.

The fresh breeze and the sound of rain pattering on the walls woke me gently, like the whisper parents woke their young child to—like Leanna woke Lila. My head hurt but my body felt as if it was made of feathers—relaxed. When I felt the brisk wind that smelled of rain and electricity, I stopped mid-stretch and cracked my eyes open. Sleep. I slept.

Without dreaming.

Without seeing her.

Slowly, I lifted my body up, the greys of the room coming to focus. I was in my room in Olympia. And there he was, sitting at the foot of my bed, his head bent down, attention over the bargain runes on his hand.

"I am going to kill you," I said, before launching toward him.

Quicker than me, he grabbed me mid-air and flipped me to my back. Pinning my arms over my chest like he'd once done before. He was panting with fury. Not often had I seen this side of him, even before he had been accusatory and curious—this was angry. "I will not apologise for what I did because I'd do it again. I might not be here for long so I'm going to use all my time and all my might to leave you as whole as I can. I'm going to take care of what holds you back. I'm going to take away every toxic thing you hold dear and you're going to hate me so much, Snow, and I will not give a damn. Till I leave this world I'm going to make you so angry that you are going to wish you had not taken that deal with me!"

I squirmed and thrashed under him. "I hate you! I hate you!"

"Hate me then. Hate *me*!" His jaw was set tight. "Me, Snow. Hate me. Why...why do you hate you?"

I stilled. "Why are you doing this to me?"

"You know why! You know why," he repeated softly, voice filled with such anguish that it made me shiver. "Tell me you know that I've never pretended for a moment. Tell me that you know that. Do I love that terribly? Do I not know how to love? Have you not felt it at all?" There was true doubt in his eyes. True fear.

I have. I have and I hate it. How can you love me? You of all people.

"You're right," I said, my body going slack. "My father loved my mother once. She was broken, hurt, depressed. She hated the world and herself, she hated us, too, at times. You're right, I think you do love me because it feels exactly like that. Like you're taking everything from me just to make yourself happy."

He leaned close to my face and his mouth pulled in a snarl. "If you think you will guilt me into letting go of the most precious thing this world holds, you're wrong. I broke you, Snow." His voice shivered as he repeated, "I broke you. And mark my promise, I will piece you back again. Every broken fragment I shattered, I will find it and I will make you as whole as I can again."

I shook my head. "No, this isn't love. It's an obsession. You're obsessed with the idea of me. The idea of the girl you almost killed. Is this your redemption, gaining my likes so you can secure your spot in Cynth?" I raised a brow. "I assure you, that would only kick the cinder of the fire you'll be burning on in Caligo."

He pushed close till our lips grazed, my breath catching when the electric feel of that touch heated every inch of me. "I'd be doing you a kindness, remember. Not to leave you there all alone."

And that was it, I thrashed violently. "Don't you dare! Don't you dare use words I said to him."

He froze. "Him?" There was some hurt in his face. "You said them to me, Snow. Me!"

I shook my head. "For all I know, he died that night. And you're just the man who tried to kill me thirteen years ago."

"Don't deny me," he said, anguish in his stone-cold voice. "Don't deny me the small piece of you that I had. It is my treasure. I found it. It belongs to me."

"It was a lie."

"It was mine, nonetheless. Mine, Snow."

This was madness. This was utter madness. "Get off me."

"Push me away," he growled. "I know you can. Push me away."

"The bargain—"

"Fuck the bargain, we both know you can hurt me without killing me. You can hurt me all you want. You've already hurt me a plenty, so push me. Come on," he goaded, breathing hard. "Come on, Snow."

I couldn't.

And he knew it.

We both knew it.

He rested his forehead on mine and whispered, "Come on, love. Push me so I know to hold back with you. Push me so I know to stay away from you. Maybe…maybe I can really try this time."

"I want to," I breathed out, shaking my head. "I swear I want to. I swear I want to hurt you, push you, kill you. I swear. And I swear one day I will. There is no escaping it. I will kill you." When he let go of me, I didn't push him off nor did I wrestle him to the ground. Instead, I fisted his shirt and said, words burning my mouth, "But…I need you. And I hate it…hate it so much. I hate you so much. Hate that I want you. You did this to me. And I hate it. I hate you." Frustration, so much of it, it wrapped around me like a second skin and I couldn't tear it off. He'd confused every part of mine. Mostly my head. I needed him out of my head.

"You hate me," he breathed, caging me in under him again.

"I do."

His silver eyes blazed. "And you want me."

"I want you."

"Say that you want me again."

I slid my hands down his chest till the seam of his shirt touched my fingertips and then pushed it up till it went over his head. Leaning forward,

I left a kiss on his biceps and his eyes drew shut. "I want you." From the tortured way he breathed, he was not going to give in. "Make a deal with me?"

"Stealing my lines now?"

"Wouldn't they be mine too?"

He dragged that soft bottom lip between his teeth to hold back a smile. "What is your deal, my queen?"

"We pretend. We continue our lie."

"Your lie."

"Will you argue with me on this again?"

"Yes."

"Fine. My lie."

"There are conditions. You can pretend I am the Kilian you remember, but don't pretend to be Snow from back then. Don't feign care. Don't smile at me if you don't want to smile at me. Don't touch me unless you want to. Take what you want from me. Use me how you want to. You don't have to pretend at all."

"Don't you want it to feel fair?"

"Nothing about this is fair," he said, leaving kisses all over my face. "Not when I love you harder than I need to breathe."

My chest constricted, blood rushing to make my heart pump harder. "If that is what you want."

"Where do I sign? There?" He kissed my brow, both my eyes, my nose, my cheeks. "Or there?" he asked, tipping my chin up, his tongue darting to lick the seam of my lips before he bit my bottom lip. How I loved that. "Tell me," he murmured over my flesh, trailing wet kisses down my neck. "Tell me what I should do to you. Tell me what you like."

You. Anything of you.

His hands travelled over the sides of my body till they met the end of my night dress. "Tell me how you like to be touched." He reached under and began rolling the fabric up my body and over my head. The open chill of Olympia pebbled my skin, but the scrutiny of that hungry dark stare set in on fire. "Licked," he continued, chasing a trail with his tongue between my breasts, stopping on my neck again and sucking on my flesh. "Sucked." He grazed my jaw with his lips as he moved to whisper in my ear, "Fucked."

A gasp drew out of me when his hand went between my legs to cup me. His fingers pulled on the seam of my underwear before dipping inside, the pad of his fingers grazed that sensitive bundle of nerves and I moaned in response without being able to help it. Knowing it was him—his touch—made it even more thrilling.

"Like that?" he asked, leaving torturous kisses on my neck.

"Yes." I gripped his wrist as his fingers started tracing circles over the apex of my thighs. The sensation of his mouth on my skin and his fingers on me was almost blinding.

When his fingers moved further down, gliding over my wet centre, he hissed in my ear. "Fuck, so wet." His eyes held mine as he slowly slid a finger inside me, thrusting in and out of me severely slow, and my breaths grew to chanting puffs. "Is your pretty little cunt soaked for me?"

"Please," I breathed, fisting his shirt tightly. *More. More.*

"Answer me," he ordered, pulling out and slapping me between my legs.

I jerked a little from the sting and squirmed, searching for his touch again, my body growing hot. "You know the answer," I whispered back, afraid of what uttering those syllables aloud could do to me.

"Good." He lowered his mouth over a nipple, and I plunged my fingers through his thick hair to keep him there as he tortured me with lips, tongue and teeth while his finger torturously circled my core.

"I want to taste you. I want to see if you taste as good as you do in my mind," he whispered, kissing his way up to my jaw. Bringing a finger to my mouth, he pushed it in between my lips. "Taste that?" he asked, tongue darting to lick my lips coated with my taste. "That's what's mine tastes like."

Sweet hells.

His lips left a hot trail as he kissed his way down my body. A trickle of gooseflesh rose where his warm breath fanned over my skin.

I cried out, clutching the sheets in my fists when his mouth lowered to my core, making every inch of my body pound with warmth. His tongue flicked over me once and my thighs quivered at the sensation, at the sight of him between my legs, the soft touches he left on my thighs, his finger disappearing inside of me. It was all too much—so much.

My body arched off the bed and my hand shot to his hair, half wanting to push him and half holding him there while I rolled my hips to meet his movement.

His eyes rose up at me and something he saw in my face made his mouth pull in a stupid smile. He groaned over my flesh, sucked and nibbled till I became a puddle of need and sweat, till release hummed and throbbed over my body. A second finger entered me and picked up a pace, thrusting in and out.

My breaths grew quicker to match what was rising inside of me.

More—I wanted more.

His tongue darted over my entrance. "The taste of you," he breathed, ravishing me. "I'll never get enough of it." When his tongue plunged inside of me, all of me, my mind and body, went tight as a bow and my sight dizzied for a moment as release rippled like a tidal wave. He didn't stop, holding my thighs apart while licking and kissing my release till I'd grown light-headed and delirious.

My teeth scraped my bottom lip hard enough to draw blood to drown out my moans.

Just when I'd stopped shaking...he did it again.

And when he decided to stop torturing me, he sat up on his haunches, his mouth still glistening with the remnants of my release as he perused every bit of me sprawled before him with burning relish. He studied every curve and corner, every little scar and dip as if he was trying to remember it all. Our eyes locked for a moment and he swiped his tongue over his lips. "I think I've got a poor imagination." He leaned down, trailing kisses up my stomach and my body shivered. "You are fucking delectable." With one last innocent kiss on my cheek, he dropped beside me before gathering my naked body in his arms.

I shuddered from every little innocent touch he gave me after. Every nerve ending in my body still twitched from the saturated remnants of my pleasure.

My thigh brushed his hardened bulge and I looked up at him, running my hand down his chest and sneaking it between the button space of his shirt to touch his skin. The need to feel him was overwhelming everything. "Let me touch you." I trailed my fingers down the dent of his hard muscle and felt him twitch under my touch.

"No, love."

"Why? I want to hear you come, too. I want to taste what is mine, too."

He shut his eyes tight and groaned as if he was in pain. "Not how I want you to."

Was he really not going to let me?

He tugged on my cheek. "Don't look at me like that. It's breaking my heart."

With a sigh, I rolled to my side of the bed, and threw the covers over me. "I thank you for your services," I said with a yawn and heard him chuckle.

He wrapped an arm around me and buried his face in my hair. "And I thank you for the meal."

I writhed in his hold. "I don't like being held." Liar. I was angry. I wanted to have a taste of him, too. To know what he sounded like when he came. I wanted to see him as he saw me. I wanted him to be at my mercy, too. Just the thoughts poured pure rage in me.

He threw a heavy muscled leg over my own, completely trapping me. "You will like being held by me. Now stop squirming. If your arse touches my cock one more time, I will tie you to the post, have you ride my face and not let you come. Even if you beg."

Sigh. This was going to be one long, tortuous night. The back of my hand brushed an indent in his arm before I decided to trace my fingers over it. As always, his skin pimpled with gooseflesh and his chest caved with uneven breaths. And it made me smile with victory—I could render the Night King breathless with one touch. "How did you get that one?"

He told me about it. He told me all about the other dozen or so I asked. Detail after detail, little important bits that I'd never think to pay attention to in my surroundings. All of his scars taught me a lot about him. How good his memory was, how many he had, how much attention he paid to everyone and everything, how he never blamed anyone else for them but himself. He told me about them till I fell asleep in his hold. Till I was sated with warmth, comfort and peace.

Chapter Nineteen

Bimaris

Kilian

I stirred awake. The bed beside me was empty and a clattering noise was doing my head in.

Pen paced back and forth between the chamber rooms in a hurry. She skidded to a stop and stared wide eyed at me. "You're awake." Immediately, shadows of anxiousness and fear burst from her.

"Was that not your intention with that god awful noise?"

"Ah," she said, raising a duster in the air for me to see. "Didn't realise I was being that loud." She bowed at the waist. "Apologies, Your Majesty."

Pushing from the bed, I picked up my discarded shirt from the bed-end stool. "She is not here, Penelope. Your head remains safe if you keep calling me Kilian. And by the way, where is she?"

Her eyes dropped to the ground, and she made to leave the room.

I faded in front of her. "Penelope, where is my wife?"

She covered her face with her hands and muttered something unintelligible that made me grow more anxious by the second.

"Penelope," I growled.

She lifted her stare at me and said, "Isjord. She went back to Isjord."

I let out a little laugh. Last night must have made me extremely dizzy. "Repeat that again for me."

She took a few small steps back. "Mal helped her too. It wasn't just me and Visha."

That was it, today I would kill my brother.

Four confused individuals stood before Visha, a sleepy Mal and a very guilty looking Penelope, in the meeting room of Taren.

"One of you speak," Cai growled, hitting a fist on the table. "Now."

Visha blinked boredly. "This morning she got Sebastian to take her back to Isjord in pretence of being your captive," she said, pointing to me.

Tipping my head to my brother, I asked, "How are you involved in this?"

He yawned. "She wanted me to take her to our prisons on the Moor Isles and let the Isjordian soldiers pass through to her easily."

He would be dead by the end of this meeting.

"Silas will buy none of that," Alaric said, shaking his head as shadows of worry and anxiousness clouded him.

Visha placed a small flask containing a clear liquid on the table. "Liquid cuts. She took it. And she looked pretty believable to me."

Liquid cuts. Liquid cuts? She was going to be the end of my patience.

"Visha," I said calmly, taking the flask and crushing it in my fist. "Are you telling me you gave my wife a torture elixir so she could look—what did you say again—believable?"

Nia put a hand on my shoulder. "Kilian, calm down," she said, pointing her chin around us. The place was crackling with bursts of dark, crawling and extending out of me.

Memphis flew in from the open balcony and shifted onto a large cat, striding to me and resting her face in my lap, huffing and letting broken strangled yowls.

Yeah, I know, Memphis. She made a fool out of us both.

The Zephyr general glared at my brother. "I expected it from you. But from you," he said, pointing to Visha. "Explain this to me again, witch. You not only let Snow go with her crazy plan, but you helped, too?"

My brother put a hand on his chest. "Oh, pet, be gentle with my feelings."

Caiden gritted his teeth and tilted his head in warning.

The Crafter didn't even blink as she answered, "She built a convincing case. If we are to further this anywhere, it has to be done this way."

"Please," Nia said, standing. "Can we not pretend that any of us would have been able to stop her?"

"She will never find where Silas has hidden the pieces," Alaric said, shadows darkening with fear.

"What I'm afraid of is that she will," I added.

"She wants answers. Not to find the pieces," Visha said. She pushed five envelopes on the table. "She has left tasks for the five of you in the meanwhile."

Each of us opened our letters and collectively sighed at her very sparingly used words.

Find them. This damned woman.

"She wants me to return to Eldmoor and not come back until I've made contact with Urinthia," Nia said.

Mal flipped the letter back and forth confused. "What did she mean by 'behave'?"

Cai crumpled the paper and threw it to the floor before standing and stalking out of the room.

His friend leaned down to pick it up and smoothed the letter. "Protect our home."

Alaric ran two hands over his long hair. "If Silas catches her."

"She won't be caught," I said, half lying to myself. "She hid herself well. I never even doubted she had magic." I turned to the Crafter. "How are we to communicate in case anything happens?"

"I've inked craft on her. She will be able to call you through your bargain." She pushed a second envelope for me. "She wants you to free her from the bargain till her return. She has signed a temporary blood oath—you need to sign next to her."

The paper half crinkled from my tight hold. She's put me on a crossroad. Not only would I ruin her plan if I didn't sign, but I would also expose her to Silas, too.

I dropped back on the chair, running a hand over my frustrated face. Had it been my fault? For last night?

"What am I supposed to do with 'behave'?" Mal asked, still confused.

Visha sighed. "She's left something else for you. Follow me." The two left, bickering all the way down the corridors.

Soon Alaric and Nia did the same. But I stayed there for a long while, doing what Snow did with utter perfection—overthinking.

Had it truly been because of last night? Had she regretted it?

When I reached the terrace, Caiden stood there. Waiting, it seemed, because he had pinned a glare on me and crossed his arms tight over his chest.

"You do a poor job at hiding how you feel, and I'm not talking about shadows," I said.

"Sort of was the point."

"I take it that I have an answer for what is bothering you?"

"Why does the morph trust you? The beast doesn't even let Alaric breathe near her."

"Are you able to lie to her if I tell you?"

He scowled. "Why would I need to lie to her?"

"Because you wouldn't want her to know this."

He took a moment. "Tell me."

And I did tell him. From the start of it all. How and why Memphis trusted me. How she had trusted me long before becoming Snow's bonded. How she had obeyed my order and remained beside Snow, protecting her.

And he stood there. Taking it all in silence. Though the man had an expression of stone, his shadows were all over the place.

Commotion sounded in the clouded air above us and not long after, a pack of the winged men landed on the terrace floor. The general, Lazarus, among them. And when he spotted me, his expression turned sour and his mouth twisted to a snarl. "Seems like she chose to go back to her father's lair than be here where she has to see your face every second of the blessed day and cursed night."

"Shut up, Lazarus," Caiden said, annoyed.

The man growled. "Easy for you to speak. He is not forcing your woman to do gods know what."

That made me bristle. And there was no jealousy I felt. It was rageful jealousy. "How is she your woman?"

"She and I have history."

"And that entitled you to her? History?"

"Listen," he growled, coming chest to chest with me.

"Listening," I said calmly, reaching closer to him. "It seems like you've lost that ability, however. You are more man than you are bird, yet you seem to share the same brains with your counterpart. Do you know who you speak to? The things I can do to you without even lifting a finger or batting a lash? There is one thing you owe me if respect for your king is not something you can comprehend, you owe me fear. Don't provoke me with unnecessary courage. You will not only find it a futile effort, but a very costly one."

"This is not a debate I need to have with you." He pushed away from me and made to leave, stopped by my extended hand.

"She bears my last name, swore the same oath as I. She is mine in more ways that you can ever imagine. Now, any man might not have an issue with you staking claim on their wives, but I do take great offence. And believe me, Lazarus, you don't wish for me to take said great concern."

The rest of his men left first, and he followed suit, throwing a glance or two behind his shoulder at me.

Caiden cocked his head to the side in amusement. "Snow would have had a laugh with all that alpha arsehole energy."

I cracked my neck back and forth in an attempt to free some tension. "Don't worry, I will certainly give her something to laugh about once she is back."

"I think I understand now," he said, tilting his head back to fully examine me. "Why you seem to charm everyone. I think I'm charmed."

"Flattered. Hope you haven't formed this new opinion because of the kiss we shared."

He laughed, he threw his head back and fully laughed. "You're not that charming, Night King."

"It's alright, General," I said, brushing off white fluff Lazarus had left on my uniform, "not all of us have taste."

Nia jogged to us and took position between Cai and I, looking panicked and then stunned. "Oh."

I raised a brow. "*Oh* what?"

"Thought you two would be strangling one another."

Cai blinked at his friend before looking up at me. "I suppose she knows all of it."

"She does."

The Zephyr general nodded, planted a kiss on Nia's cheek and disappeared inside a portal.

Nia's eyes were all hazel and round and happy. "You told him."

I nodded. "Take us both to Moriko."

The same happy eyes shot wide almost to horror. "Why?" She cleared her throat and softly repeated, "Why?"

The Autumn Queen perked from her seat at the sight of Nia and quickly dismissed the members of her court from the room. "My *ahana*," she greeted before rounding an arm around her waist and pulling her for a kiss. "Who do I have to thank for this?"

Nia hooked a finger in my direction.

Moriko gave me a bored look. "Kilian, is there something the matter?"

"Snow has gone to Isjord."

Her expression didn't change. "Did she?"

Sigh. "You helped her with this, didn't you?"

She nodded. "A couple of the soldiers that Silas had sent for the rescue team were from Brisk. Ibe notified me first before I passed the news to Albius and Sebastian."

"You didn't tell me," Nia said, moving a bit away from Moriko.

The queen quickly closed the distance and pinched Nia's chin. "*Ahana*, the woman had a—"

Nia quickly waved a hand. "Never mind. I am sure she did something she should have not done. I just didn't know Snow had been planning this for a while without anyone knowing."

Moriko nodded. "Snow has a smart head on her shoulders, a reckless one, but extremely smart. It is why I decided to let her threaten me. I know she will make something out of this. She has to, otherwise Silas has already won this war." She smiled down at Nia. "Are you staying?"

I cleared my throat and the queen's smile died back to that hooded sternness she possessed. "Yes, Kilian."

"The Ryuu. I'd like to visit the underground where the sceptre was kept."

She sighed with disappointment and nodded. "Sure. And then Nia stays."

"Actually," Nia said. "Nia goes. Goes to Eldmoor. To finish important tasks like Snow is in Isjord."

Like this was all my fault, Moriko turned a scathing look on me. "This is your wife's fault."

"You helped her."

"A misjudgement on my behalf it seems." She straightened her clothing and said, "The Ryuu then."

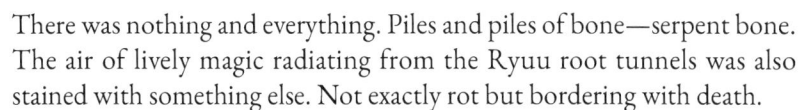

There was nothing and everything. Piles and piles of bone—serpent bone. The air of lively magic radiating from the Ryuu root tunnels was also stained with something else. Not exactly rot but bordering with death.

"Three headed hydras," Moriko explained as we descended the root tunnels. "A creature Dyurin created by imitating Cerberus, the three headed guardian of the hells of rot. The god of animals often compared that particular place to our realm." She shone the torch over a piled of long thin bones and dried scaly skin. "You have to kill this three times, but we only found one injury on most of them."

I bent down to touch one of the greyed carcasses and the pain in my chest turned sharp, shooting right to my head and making me sway from light-headedness. My magic screeched in the air, gusts of scorching darkness bursting, making the humid air hiss with death and mist.

"It appears I was right," I said, straightening, taking a deep breath that sent more pain through my wounds that seemed to tear as though fresh. "This thing is an *anima accissor*."

The queen frowned. "Soul killer? Impossible."

I tapped a finger to my chest. "It still is going after my soul through the remnants of its magic. The hydras have three lives but one soul. It is how that thing has killed them with little effort."

"Only the god of death can gift such magic. Besides the Obscur Aura and the weapons we forge with all the elements of the eight gods, nothing or anyone can be an *anima accissor*."

"That we know of." There was very little we knew about some dark magic. Mostly because there was not a lot to learn from. And then because there was no need for it to be used.

"It is worse than we thought," Moriko said, frowning at the pile of serpents. "The beast still possessed magic within the veil of Ryuu, killed the serpents and—"

"*Ybris*, the last of the Arx Triad."

She sighed. "Are you certain you wish to see this?"

"Though I did faint before you, Moriko of Hanai, I am not faint of heart."

She nodded and led me through further underground until we reached a grand cave about the size of my castle. The ceiling was hanging with roots and bright with a lime-coloured stone that shone like the starry night. In the middle of the room stood a body dispensed in the air, burning unburnt inside a crisp blue fire. The boy was young. Too young. His body slashed all over and mutilated in such a form that his features were completely gone.

"The everflow of his magic will keep his body young forever. He will burn as such till the end of Numen. We can't even bury him. But Ryuu will keep the outside safe from his magic by absorbing it."

"Anything on whose son it might be? It could point us to the elder Crafters."

"We looked in the archives after finding him here. It didn't take us long since there are not many *Ybrises* born in our time. His mother had sold him to a Dark Crafter right before he'd bloomed his blessing, no name was noted."

Sold. A mother had sold him. My eyes drew shut when I noticed the little makeshift bed at the far corner of the cave and the many wooden toys scattered here and there. Five hundred years. This little boy had been here for five hundred years. Alone. Scared. In the dark.

Moriko rested a hand on my shoulder. "Calm, Kilian."

I let the dark unravel from me and envelop the boy's body, death flying inside the hearth of life and around an unending well of magic. The fire began dousing and his body dropped from the height, powerless—entirely lifeless. The gift of my magic. It could take life from anything and anyone.

"Don't," Moriko warned right before I faded to catch him.

He was light. So light. Barely bones and no flesh.

I laid him on the ground while I knelt and dug out the soft soil with my dagger. I dug and dug till I'd made enough space for his body. Wrapping him with my jacket, I put him on his resting place and spread the soil over his body. There were no remnants of a soul inside him that I could send to the skies. Nothing. He couldn't be happy in the heavens either.

Moriko kneeled beside me, resting her palm over the scattered soil. A bed of gypsophila blooming in the purest white.

The world had failed him. His mother had failed him. Everyone had failed him.

PART III
TWILIGHT

CHAPTER TWENTY

Anguis

Snowlin

Dressed in Adriatian rags, hair dishevelled to a mess, fresh scars across my whole body—I looked like the perfect victim as Sebastian carried me in his arms down the corridors of Tenebrose castle.

The doors opened as Sebastian brought me inside the meeting chambers. Gasps and loud murmurs floated between those in the room.

A strange large rough hand rested on my face. Barely holding myself from flinching away and cringing, I cracked an eye slightly open enough to make out the stern features of my enemy. Father stood there, observing me with both doubt and a strange frown on his face.

"How was she found, where?" he questioned Sebastian who lowered his head, closing his eyes with distraught—like I had taught him.

"Tortured and imprisoned by the Adriatian king's prison quarters when we were looking for His Highness, prince Aryan. We lost twenty men trying to bring her out, but she is alive. Our Adriatian prisoners said she had disappeared the night before her wedding," he answered, just as I had instructed him to.

A lie twisted with another lie to deceive the liar of the whole lie himself.

My father would hardly fall for this, but I only needed him to doubt himself long enough to keep me here till I had my answers.

He said nothing and out of the sudden took me in his arms, bringing me to his chambers, shouting orders to his guards to call for a healer and not letting anyone disturb or hurt me.

Different from before, there was a thick light barrier and a metallic tinge of dark craft surrounding him. Protection? Was father that afraid? Oh, my.

The moment after he left, I opened my eyes to the real prison I had brought myself to, the chambers that once had really been my cage.

The healers came not long after father had called for them, they tended to my injuries which the liquid cuts elixir had done a marvellous job in carving. To my good luck, for the past few months I had lost weight enough to hollow my cheeks, so I did look the tortured and imprisoned part. Servants had come to tend to me, but I had kicked them all out, half shouting like a madwoman till they had been so afraid they had almost run out of the room. I bathed calmly and dressed in my mother's floaty grey dress brought by the servants at my request. I wanted to show my poor condition to my father who was the most distrusting of all.

I sat by the bed in silence, staring at the blessed frost storm raging outside. It was the end of February and spring had a foot out, yet winter didn't seem to have fainted at all in Isjord.

The doors of the room opened, my heart beating the sound of the drums of death as I slowly turned to face him.

"Good to see you again, my child," father said quietly but with such venom.

Half unplanned, I jumped from the bed, charging towards him, hitting and kicking him violently till my lungs were left gasping for air. He stood there taking it all without moving. "Good?" I frowned at him. "Good that you sold me off to them despite my protest, good that I was about to die in their hands, good that you were made a fool?" I asked in my best hurt voice. Nia would be proud of me—all the theatre she had dragged me to watch finally served me some purpose.

He closed the doors behind him and turned to me once again. "We did not know of their intentions." Of course he didn't, but he knew of his own, to kill and attack Adriata as well as myself in the process. It was hard to hold back a laugh. He was fooled, just not the way he was finding out he was.

"But you knew of them, father, you said it yourself that they had asked for me. Did this not make you doubt them the slightest?" I began with playing his own game. "And that attack had probably been by them so they could have brought their wretched guards in pretext to guard me to spy on Isjord, but your judgement was clouded by your dreaded spite. One that had me almost killed and my friends dead," I shouted.

His eyes went wide as he shifted uncomfortably around the room. The attack had been his, but I wanted him convinced of my ignorance—ignorance that had been enlightened by my dear dead uncle.

"Why did you disappear after the wedding?"

Painting distress on my features, I ran a shaking hand through my hair. "Someone...something was waiting for me. I don't remember much. There was a tower and masked men. Shortly after, Adriatian soldiers burst through the tower and I was thrown into the Adriatian dungeons."

"These men," he carefully pried, "who were they?"

Yours, you wily bastard. I shook my head. "Rebels or soldiers I presumed, anyone with the *Ybris* grudge against me. There wasn't time to question anything. Everything happened so quickly and I passed out most of the time."

He went silent, his yellow eyes rounding and sharpening in an attempt to see past my answers.

"They did not even bother to make him a prisoner, you know," I pushed on an already salted wound—the perfect distraction. "They killed him right in front of me, like they had done with the rest. Piece by piece they dissected him till you couldn't even puzzle together to think it was a human." With that, I waited and watched.

His breathing grew laboured and there was a light tremble on his clenched hands. Exquisite. The portrait of hurt. Poor father.

I turned away from him, covering my face with my hands, unable to hold my laughter any more at his hurt reaction. Tears flooded my face from how hard I'd suppressed it.

He approached me from behind, putting a hand on my shoulder and pulling me in a hug.

The seven hells?

I froze, my body convulsing with anger. To keep my hands from wrapping around his neck, I gathered them into fists, digging into my palms and thinking of my grounding over and over till my breath grew normal and he let go of me. I had to let him comfort me. Only the weak needed comforting. Signs of weakness brought underestimation. This is why even wolves often wore the mantle of sheep to trap the shepherd. Father needed to underestimate me.

"Why did they keep you alive?"

Was that what he wanted to know the most? "They tried to work if I was hiding magic, they thought me the weapon you wanted. Their disappointment was grander than yours," I responded, wiping my face from tears. "Probably to use me against Isjord, too."

He cocked his head to the side. "I had an army sent there after you disappeared, not a small one at that, how did they fend them off?"

The taste of doubt in his words pushed a little anxiousness in me, it was too soon for him to pace my game. "I don't know, father, they took me the night before, but from what I have seen they are just as powerful as Isjord if not more. They have lied, whatever they have told you, you have been lied to, father. They have deceived everyone. Everyone." I wanted him to fear

Adriata and not think of any other funny thoughts. I wanted him far away from what soon was to become my kingdom as well, away from Kilian's lands, far from hurting him.

He seemed to believe my words for a moment before backing away, looking slightly dubious again. "I sent for Alaric, too, we found your house in Fernfoss empty. Why was that child?"

I blinked, utterly confused. "Alaric? Why would you send for him?" I questioned, pretending to gradually realise what was happening before lifting my gaze to his again. "I told you that the antidote was not anyone you knew. He has probably gone to look for me after learning what's happened. Funny isn't it, how it all circles back to your actions?"

He rubbed his forehead at my words. "You are right, it was wrong of me to doubt your words. Forgive me, Snowlin," he offered, and my eyes widened at his apology, one that I had ever heard before from him.

Sunset was pale on the clouded skies of Isjord when I sat by the window. "Mister and Miss Graben in Fernfoss village, our neighbours. They looked after me for a few summers while Alaric was working in lumber, they are the antidote." Well, lie, lie and then another lie. There was no mister and miss Graben, they were both Olympian guards in Fernfoss who overlooked the approach of Isjordians, and they certainly had not looked after me any summer which I had all spent in New Olympia and most certainly they were not the antidote. Visha had left two vials of Alaric's blood with them before I decided to return to my father whom I knew would ask for it. Whom I knew from uncle Aryan that had sent for Alaric. You have to have a perfect lie for the perfect deceiver. You cannot juggle a ball without throwing the other first—a truth for a lie. As much as it saddened me to awaken the washed-out gnomes, the antidote was my truth to gain his impenetrable trust.

"Thank you, my rose," he offered with a nod.

"I want my quarters back. To stay till you find another merchant to bargain me off to. No one would want a useless princess around for nothing, right?" I asked spitefully.

He gathered his hands in fists and his jaw tensed yet he did not say anything but nod in agreement as I walked past him, half limping towards the corridors to my old bedroom.

The servants had readied my chambers in no time. Father had not bothered me for three days, but he'd left written messages with my breakfast. Empty words and wishes for my quick recovery.

And for three dreaded days I had to remain bedridden while my feet were itching to explore.

Today he had sent word for breakfast, so I readied myself onto a velvet sapphire long sleeved gown and gathered my hair with a tie behind my back. I had not let servants in my quarters, nor help me. For some odd reason they were all new faces, including the guards patrolling the castle.

I halted. A bell trickled in the distance, the same as it had for the past couple of days. Thrice a day, the sound ran for a whole three minutes. A curfew? Was it because of the Adriatian fear?

A servant came down the corridor opposite me, her speed picking up and her head lowered when she saw me. Grabbing onto her arm, I stopped her and she startled out of her bones, her pulse drumming so loud it was giving me a headache. "What is the bell ringing thrice a day?"

She swallowed hard. "I...I—"

"Wrong answer," I said, jerking her close enough so she could feel the dagger I held to her gut. "Try again."

"We haven't been allowed outside the castle walls," she said, fully shaking. "His Majesty had all new staff brought to the castle not long after you arrived. My father was indebted to the royal treasure and he gave me as payment. I am not allowed anywhere without my handler. I swear it, Princess, I know of nothing beyond the walls. Only as much as you. The bells have rung thrice a day, every day since I've been brought here."

"Who is your father?" I asked, letting her go and sheathing back my dagger.

She blinked confused. "My...father? A...a clam merchant south of Brogmere, Your Highness. Why do you ask?"

"Do you have any other siblings?"

She looked even more confused now. "A brother."

"Younger?"

"A year older."

"And what does he do?"

"Not much. Father will pass him the business, so I suppose that."

"And what did you want to do?"

"I don't understand," she said, hugging herself tight.

"Before you were given like a sheep to my father, what did you want to do?"

She thought about it for a moment. "I was good at school. Mother had taught me to read and write well and I'd worked down the print shop a few times when they needed a pair of hands. That—I wanted to do that."

I nodded. "That and much more you will get. I'll trade it with you. Freedom, choice and good coin to get you far from here."

"What?"

"In exchange, I want you to do something for me. Tonight, come to my room, and bring the earrings I somehow lost today at breakfast." Tapping a finger on the diamond in my ear, I gave her a wink and headed to breakfast.

A test. To see if loyalty had swayed in these difficult times for Isjord. And confirmation to see if my father had rehired help to keep me ignorant and spy on me.

Father sat alone at the head of the table, his eyes slightly perked up when he spotted me, and I almost felt a flash of pity for the tyrant. All old and alone.

Bowing, I took my usual seat by his side. The second I sat, my stomach roared, but I was not hungry. Something hit my senses and I shot to my feet, clicking a red glass window open before retching my stomach out.

I stood there for a while till weakness hit my knees and the tip of my nose turned red, till I felt my father's hands on my back and his jacket over my shoulders. Shutting the window and shedding the jacket, I sat back down. I could not stand his stench of darkness and death—I missed my tangerines and lemon flowers.

The perpetrator that twisted my stomach stared me right in the eye, a large mackerel at the centre of the table. I hated fish more than I hated meat, their scent alone made me dizzy. Eating it was another story.

Taking a tangerine from the fruit basket, I brought it to my nose, drinking in its scent till I forgot the one coming from the fish.

"I have sent for the antidote, your brother and sister will join us soon enough," he said, munching all pleasure on the white fleshed creature.

Laughter overtook me at the use of those words they had never deserved, the words that almost felt dirty when he used them for Fren and Reuben. Father only looked at me with disappointment in my reaction. "And the crone? How is mother dearest?" I taunted playfully and waited till his features dropped to downturned lines. Father wearing his tar dripping heart on his sleeve? Oh, my.

"How did you get those documents?" he questioned without answering me.

I leaned back, sipping in my goblet while taking in the tension in his face and body at the mention of Moreen. The old fox had been one of his most trusted spies in his court. Ah, the betrayal he must have felt. "Under your very nose as everything else has been these past few months. It's not her fault, you know—that she hated and tortured my mother." He turned wide eyed at my words as if he did not know. "Yes, tortured, you heard me well. But the point was the lack of her fault considering it was yours to begin with. Now tell me, what did you do with her? I left it in your hands hoping you would punish her well, but seeing your reaction it appears I might make the matters my own after all."

He leaned back, studying me as I was studying him, as if we were two of the same kind. Perhaps we were. One fed by greed and another by hate. "Don't doubt yourself, my child, you know me well. She has received the punishment she deserved for it."

I didn't doubt his word, he was very little forgiving when it came to such a thing as treason, especially from someone under the wing of his most trusted. I was twisted, but father was forge bent in his ways, so I was very pleased with his response.

A wicked smile crept on my face, stretching ear to ear, and I threw my goblet up in a toast. "Father, don't make me like you. It is more dangerous than having me hate you."

He let out a rumble of laughter and clicked his goblet to mine.

The world was so loud in its silence. Sat on a furry rug, I stirred the crackling embers of the fireplace over and over till my arm was sore and the poker suddenly felt too heavy.

The knock at my door made me jump upright. Nissa, the young servant who'd pledged to my side, peeked just her head in. "His Majesty would like you to attend dinner with him." She bowed, dropping a folded piece of paper inside before leaving.

Two days from now, when the shift changes after lunchtime, there will be no guards guarding the northern exit into Tenebrose.

Perfect.

My hair fell loosely in waves down my back, a rosy silken short sleeve dress clung tight around all my body, draping to the floor—no black rose anymore. Today I was a plain pink dandelion. It suited me, made me look severely innocent. A complete lie, but I was here to fool anyway.

The second the dining chamber doors flew open, my eyes and smile grew wide with excitement and amusement at the sight of the two yellow radish sprouts in front of me. Fren and Rueben sat on my father's right, their pale beige faces almost blank until they opened their blue eyes. Startling really, if they caught you by surprise you could lay an egg from shock. They both had hollowed and thinned ghastly.

I sat across from them, but their gaze remained down to their food—they were scared but I could read anger there as well, their grips had tightened as if spoons and goblets could grow tiny legs and sprint away.

"My, my. Did you not miss your little sister?" I asked, clicking my tongue and my father let out a sigh knowing what was to come. "Venomous behaviour really, disrespect that is."

Reuben choked and coughed his water, and I threw him a handkerchief from across the table. "Worry not, it doesn't really poison my spirit."

The eldest half breed finally managed to muster some courage and lifted his gaze to meet mine. "I see even the Adriatian king couldn't break your rabid character, there must be no hope really," he sneered.

My smile grew wilder at his comment, finally the boredom was leaving my body. "And a bit of poison managed to lubricate your arse to bring out that little worm of courage, there must be some hope really."

Flaring in anger, he threw his goblet towards me and before I could move away to dodge it, father lifted his palm and released a wall of ice preventing it from hitting me.

Reuben and Fren stared in shock towards their father who was panting like cold fury, which surprisingly didn't seem to be directed at me.

He turned to Reuben. "Is this how your mother has raised you? If you cannot win an argument, and with a woman at that, hit them?" Well, well, since when did my father grow a backbone of rightness? Father's eyebrows gathered in a frown as he crossed his arms. "Dealing with council, deals, trades and much more is a war itself, a war of words and banter. Do you plan on hitting them with your goblet as well if you cannot overtake them? How is your sister more versed and prepared to face them than you are?" he criticised.

I knew how. I was a queen, and he was a stuffed solstice turkey.

Reuben and his sister froze at his words and their eyes began to grow slightly wide, probably taking my father's words as a hindrance to the bastard's position.

Father wiped his mouth and stood to leave.

"Could I see you for a moment, later?" I asked and he accepted with a nod, leaving me to my entertainment.

Fren did not hesitate, she dropped her cutlery loudly to the table. "What did you do to my mother, you wretched bitch?" I liked the new fire, but it didn't suit her pitchy voice that sounded like a violin played by a horse.

"You need to ask father of that, not me, dear. This time I truly did nothing, it was all sweet, old, withered crone."

I waited by the winter gardens, emptily staring around the dreaded snow coated bushes and conifers. How ridiculous. My name was Snow, yet I had a deep dislike for it.

Father came down the corridor with two others and separated by the gates of the garden, heading in my direction.

"We should make this our official meeting spot, you always ask me to come here," I said with irritation. My eyes had rolled to the point of headache when his courtier had let me know where he wanted to meet.

He approached, putting a hand on my shoulder and I stared down at the unusual affection that was growing common between us lately—bloody disgusting. "It is your mother's garden. We used to sit here almost all the time. She used to insist we eat here during the summer months when the snow was not as severe. She even came up with your name while we were sitting here one night. I thought you remembered that and liked it here, was I wrong?"

My mind started boiling in anger at how lightly he mentioned her, as if he truly cared for her. "Yes, I hate snow," I answered, flicking away the white frosted mess atop a bush.

My father laughed, like thorns dragged through silk, and it gritted on my nerves. "Serene hated it as well, she kept repeating that for months when she first came. When she decided on your name I questioned her choice, but she explained that she wanted to name you after it so maybe she could learn to love it just like she loved you."

My eyes shut tight from grief at her memory—I missed her so much. "She never told me," I said, straightening, not wanting to seem affected by his words. She never had the chance to, because of him. He was the cause of all my trouble. "I want to return to your court, make me Captain again. If I spend one moment in my chambers and in this garden, I will begin stabbing everyone purely for entertainment." He had to otherwise my return here would have been for nothing. I would have thrown down the drain precious time that I could have spent finding another way of procuring a sceptre piece. I could have even planned a raid of his castle to look for his own sceptre pieces, all those days of endless wall staring could have been spent another million ways.

He narrowed his eyes at my determined expression but nodded in the end. "Very well, but I will put a few conditions, some you might not like."

"Get me out of the castle and I might even let you chain me to a watcher," I said eagerly. This was my opportunity. His plans were now in the open to his council, whoever or whatever was helping him would be there and it would not matter what conditions he put.

His dark low laugh rumbled about the empty winter garden. "That won't be necessary. See you at the meeting this evening," he said, patting my shoulder before leaving.

And I might or might have not danced a cheery jig across the garden returning to my chambers.

Time had not ticked or went slower than it had the moments before the evening. I quickly made my way towards the meeting chambers. The corridors were cold and empty. More than usual. There was not a single servant I recognised, not a soldier either. Father had wiped the castle clean of anyone from before.

Something made me halt right in the middle of the corridor. A wind of a familiar chilling sensation brushed past me, one that made me bristle and had me reach for the dagger under my dress.

I searched the dim space, but it was entirely empty. A far window creaked behind me, the pane had blown open and brought heavy snow inside.

Maybe I was being paranoid.

The meeting had gathered when I arrived, all the spots on the table were filled with lords, generals, captains and all sorts. A few priests, too. What under Nubil's skies?

I spotted the Lord of Arynth, Sebastian, and Celdric, who I'd left in charge of Brogmere, all my allies and a new face. She was young. Pretty and blonde. Prim and proper, buttoned and ironed like she was all ready for the first class in preparation school. Gara. The new Grasmere lady. And my loose oar.

The rest of the room turned to me, bowing their heads—except her. "I see Malena has raised her bitch well," I hissed in her ear when I went past her, and she jerked a little.

Amongst them the trained pet Reuben sat anew, stuffed and pampered in a soldier's uniform, sticking out like a sore thumb. The first time I had seen him present in a meeting. Strange considering the only blade he'd lifted was a butter knife.

"My, my, Reuben, did you finally squeeze a pair or did father strap them on?" I said, making my way to a seat.

There was another new face amongst the bunch. Dressed in a general's uniform, three circlets above his breast pocket, olive skin, a scar across his dark eyebrow and over his dull green eye, his hair slightly curled at the crown as it came shorter on the sides. Extremely handsome by my previous standards had they not been overtaken by the silver eyed snake. He was probably Reuben's age—too young to hold his position as general in Isjord's court of the usually wrinkled sandbags, and his presence radiated strongly of a different type of serpent from their breed. And something told me that my father had recruited him because of that.

He surveyed all of my movement with a smirk. And when I sat near my father's chair which was next to him, his eyes were still following me. "You must be his daughter," he said in a chilling deep voice.

I turned to study him. "And you must be his lover."

He threw his head back, laughing, and the whole room took turns staring at us both. His amusement dropped from laughter to a wide smile. "Are my assumptions wrong?" His eyebrows cocked up as his eyes perused me some more—shamelessly.

"No, just very presumptive. I am myself before being his daughter. Snowlin, Princess, Your Highness. Though I would have preferred something along the lines of 'you must be the most beautiful woman I have seen'," I teased, batting my eyelashes.

He studied my features, his eyes fell to my lips before he answered, "You are one of them."

I cocked an eyebrow up. In complete honesty I was half offended. "Why, is there another?"

My father came in as he was about to answer, we stood and bowed and when we sat back, he murmured close to my ear, "Yes."

"Your mother?"

He howled with laughter once again and father turned to us with a scowl, an assessing look pinching in his face while he glanced at the two of us.

Schooling my features to the penance of grace, I bowed to him once again.

He cleared his throat and turned to the young general. "I see you have met my daughter, Demir."

Demir leaned forward. "Yes, Your Majesty, the most beautiful woman I have ever seen," he answered, and I turned to him wide eyed and surprised at his lack of fear or critique from my father. He winked at me and relaxed back in his chair while my father remained unusually quiet and passive.

The Winter court began discussing and reporting their usual sleep-inducing digits and issues, Celdric and Sebastian did the same—unusually well. I had chosen right with them. Hours passed and they had managed to almost lull me to sleep more times than I had done myself upon my return to Isjord. Maybe one of them should do that in my chambers at night.

"You will be under General Demir's watch," father said to me, and I shook awake. "He will dictate your position. I'm sure it will be valuable to all of us to have such a skilled soldier in his team."

"Why are you allowing this, father? You have a thousand better trained soldiers to allow that one in your army. Again," Rueben said spitefully, dragging everyone's attention. Green was a good colour on him.

I leaned in on the table, crossing my arms over the table. "That is one venomed remark, dear. Why such a poisoned attitude? I was never the bane in my father's way," I teased, and the room chuckled under their breath. Except one. Gara glared at me from the corner of my eye, giving me a perfect confirmation of my vantage against her.

Very oddly my father remained quiet, shuffling at his papers, not answering to Reuben neither silencing nor attempting to reprimand me for my behaviour like he usually did. Something was not entirely right—I could feel it. His unusual show of affection and liberty he had given me felt forced and wrong. He was up to something or he did not really trust me, not the slightest. Was Demir his new obedient puppet, had that been the reason he assigned me under him, to keep me under control? He had truly chained me to a watcher after all.

Demir leaned in near my ear. "I think we will get along just fine."

Flinging my hair to one side, I said, "I'm sure we will."

"You have no idea how confused I am right now Snowlin," Elias said, coming from the opposite end of the servant dining chambers. "Should I be going on one knee, or do you not expect formalities undercover?" he asked quietly, taking a seat across from me.

"My subjects don't bow, they kiss my toes."

He shook his head and laughed. "Didn't expect Silas to let you inside the court so soon after your return."

"My charm still does wonders."

He lifted a brow. "So I've seen. You and Demir have become a topic of discussion."

Of course we had. But it hadn't been my intention. The man was a loaded chamber of secrets locked twice. "Why had no one told me about him?"

Elias shrugged. "He didn't have much of a position in court before. Your father used him like a mop. Sending him here and there to do most of his dirty work."

"Father seems to trust him. He trusts no one. And speaking on trust. I heard he pulled your marriage to Fren at the beginning of Summer."

"He and my father have been picking up each other's short sticks lately," he grumbled, picking up one of my cookies and dunking it in my milk. "Would not be surprised if he is planning to have my old man killed so I can take his position. And with that, he has the full sealine as his."

That made me laugh a little. "You mean mine?"

He looked around the empty chambers that I knew no one frequented at this time of day. "You're forgetting Grasmere. Venzor, Casmere and Brogmere are all fishing ports, Snow. He sat me down a while back, sometime after Fren and I had been promised, and asked what I thought about joining Grasmere as a naval base. It was not long till I heard from the Isline Captains that he'd levelled down two forests up there and hired hundreds of Senchi Aura from Hanai to forge new ships. This is growing concerning, Snow. As if he is keeping measure in case the...sceptre fails."

Whether it was one caused by the divine or one by the one pretending to be the divine, war drummed ahead of us. "I need you to tell me everything about the new Grasmere Lady. Everything, Elias."

Chapter Twenty-One

Animus

Kilian

Even though Adriata and Olympia had kept me plenty busy, each day that had passed since Snow's return to Isjord was longer than the previous. Not only did I miss her fiercely, but I feared. Truly, she'd taught me fear.

After I passed the news of her return to our Solaryan allies, Magnus had invited me to study the sceptre piece location deep under the city of Theros.

Along with two of his soldiers, he guided us through the Abendrot caves that connected to the tomb carrying the *Ybris* who served as vessel for the sceptre.

"She is either brave," he said, holding a glowing palm up as we manoeuvred through the tight tunnels, "or insane to try and deceive Silas by returning right in between his claws."

"She is not afraid of her father as much as she is worried about his intentions."

"Someone might call that noble."

"Snow's world is small, but if anyone dares to threaten it, she will open war."

After tunnels and tunnels of salty rock, a sea cave flashed in sight ahead. A dim giant space that spread for miles.

Magnus sent several spheres of light floating over the clear blue water under us and towards the stalactite covered ceiling. The cave expanded wider and wider, the further the light spheres went the more I could make out a small rocky patch island standing in the middle of the hollow cave.

A rowing boat waited on the shore of our side to carry us through.

"The water is acidic," Magnus warned. "In case you thought to freshen yourself up."

The land in the middle of the water was small, but big enough to hold a broken crypt. The boat halted and Magnus extended his hand forward to lift a glistening barrier. "The only thing protecting the tomb is my shields of magic, the veil was broken by Silas's witch," Magnus explained as we stepped on the small patch of land. He sighed and pointed forward. "Don't ask me how because I can't tell you. No one can tell you how a young witch like her is able to break elder craft."

"An Isjordian soldier had caught sight of her feeding on the beast's blood. Our Crafter thinks it belongs to Golgotha's herd. Probably explains how Melanthe Delcour's skills have all of a sudden seem on par with her aunt's."

He shook his head. "Never had I thought a Delcour witch would stoop so low as to serve Silas let alone dirty her blood with a beast's."

Two soldiers pushed the broken stone of the crypt away to reveal a set of steep stairs descending downwards. The smell was of rotten flesh and salt. Something told me it didn't belong to the *Ybris* buried down there. The corridors inside the crypt were wider than I'd thought and lush in stories drawn along the walls. Solaryans were storytellers and visual people. Impeccably talented at that. From what I gathered, the story told of the *Ybris* buried here. And it wasn't a pretty one.

A green glowing speck splattered over one of the drawings caught my attention and I came to a halt. There was a dip in the stone of the wall under it, like a claw mark.

"I wouldn't touch it if I were you," Magnus warned. "The fluid of that beast is corrosive. It will eat your flesh off."

I unsheathed a dagger from my baldric and dipped the tip in it. "Are you saying this came from that beast?" The dark metal didn't budge when I collected the liquid in its blade. Adriatian steel was a gift in a sense.

"Yes." He pointed a hand further in the corridor. "There is more you need to see."

Sheathing the dagger in its scabbard to preserve the liquid, I followed him. My feet halted when I noticed what laid ahead. Bones atop bones piled along the corridors, all above a puddle of viscous green. Human bones.

We reached the end of a corridor and Magnus placed his palm on the wall—it lit in golden streaks that spread all over the corridor walls in a maze-like pattern. Once the whole space was lit bright, the wall shifted to the side to reveal the actual Abendrot tomb. Six pillars rose to the high rocky ceiling, a bright cast of glittering dust floated in their middle carrying a small body dispersed in the air.

The form was almost as if it was alive, still preserved perfectly.

"Magi healers channelled his own magic to create a barrier around him that will protect the outer environment. Since all hybrid Aura magic is ever flowing, the shield around him feeds from it and will preserve all danger he presents, for eternity," Magnus explained. He pointed behind the pillars, to a pile of large bones and teeth. "The Aitan sphynx, guardian of the tomb."

The word around them built you to expect a grandiose ancient creature of power, but what had remained of it was no less than horrifying.

An Aitan sphynx burned unburnt. A gift Aidan, god of fire, had given to his long-time friend, Dyrin, the god of animals, who had moulded the creature from the earth of his own realm. These animals were rare. They carried the very essence of Dyurin's heaven. They were dubbed the rulers of all animals. Not only because they were strong, but because they carried nine lives and nine souls. One gifted from each prime heaven in honour of them and their greatness.

I kneeled by the pile of remains and picked a heavy piece of what seemed like a fang. "How did it get past this?" For it to die, it had to have been killed nine times, one after the other.

"Nine times," Magnus said, echoing my thoughts. "When we found it, it had nine wounds. All fatal."

"And the heart? Where is its heart?" The heart of an Aitan Sphinx had no price. Not all of the gold of my kingdom could buy one. Its properties were endless. Some said it could feed immortality even to an unblessed. The magic of the nine heavens the sphynx carried stemmed from its heart. Even dead, the remnants of the raw magic were strong.

"Gone," Magnus said. "It was expected. Silas would never miss such an occasion."

Fuck. Another thing that in the hands of the Winter King that could turn into a fatal weapon.

Snow had been right to panic.

This wasn't right. Something wasn't right. No, it felt terribly wrong. So wrong that the flow of mana shivered in the air.

I stood, almost dizzy. A sharp pain struck my chest and a palm went to my wounds.

"You are bleeding, son," Magnus said, coming to my side and throwing my arm over his shoulder to balance me.

My lungs begged for air. "Show me the exit. Show me where the thing made its exit."

Magnus shook his head. "You are too unwell. We can come back down after my Cora has a look at you."

"My wife is in Isjord putting herself at great risk for this cause. The sooner I solve this, the sooner I have her back in my arms." I shook my head attempting to ward off the dizziness. "Which way?"

Hesitantly, Magnus directed the two of us to further into the cave. Streaks of light filtered through coin sized holes in the cave walls. They intensified the further in we moved till they got big enough to fit a human body through.

I let go of Magnus and studied the trickles of the green viscous mucus in the ground that seemed to stop right before the adits leading to the open sea.

"From memory," I asked. "How tall do you remember this thing to be?"

Magnus rubbed a hand over his greying beard. "I'd say about seven to eight feet."

I stood up and reached the exit openings, attempting to fit myself through. Failing as the holes narrowed the further in you got and were only big enough to barely accommodate my body. "Now tell me, Magnus, how did that thing fit through there when someone of my size barely can?"

The Sun King gaped for a moment and attempted to fit himself through one of the exits and then another, only to fail each time. Realisation crossed his features. "It transforms. It was human."

I nodded. "Someone of a shorter and smaller stature than us."

"Seems like the work of Silas's witch."

"From what our Crafter has said it is highly doubtful that Silas's witch is capable of forging such a beast. But we might finally be able to find out what it exactly is," I said, pointing to the dagger I'd dipped in the green mucous. "I will have our Crafter take a look at this."

He nodded, rubbing a frustrated hand through his beard. "We were so occupied dealing with our dead and our losses that we didn't pay attention to many things."

I clasped his shoulder, the movement making me wince from the shooting pain it sent through my ribs. "No one would have been prepared for that, Magnus. There is no one to blame but Silas."

Reluctantly, he nodded, though his shadows read of troubling concern. "I will have someone go down the adits, see if they can find anything down there."

Almost everyone had gathered in Visha's quarters, and that annoyed the young witch beyond measure. But then, Visha was easily annoyed. Even as a child she'd liked quietude not only because it focused her magic and kept chaos intact, but because she'd been the centre of attention before even being born. Not for being the next Grand Maiden, but for being the future bride of the prince of death.

Caiden impatiently tapped his foot as Visha poured a bubbling red liquid over the dagger coated with the green mucous. "Come on, witchling," the general pushed through gritted teeth.

Alaric clasped his shoulder. "Patience, kid."

The Zephyr dropped his head back with an annoyed groan. "I'm going to chain her when she returns. Chain her, Ric. She went out there knowing this thing is lurking god knows anywhere near her." He'd reacted the worst at the news of what I'd found out in Solarya. What I'd observed in Isjord came back to me. Caiden was not afraid for Snow. He knew the best out of all how capable she was. The fact that she was out of his reach and out of his protection had roused a massive cloud of trouble around him.

Nia stood from her seat and faced her disturbed friend. "I could go to her."

Caiden pointed a finger in warning. "If I have to worry about you, too, I will lose my mind. I swear, Nia, think of stepping in Silas's land after we found so many traps and I will personally chain you. Open a book or make some...tea for yourself, you're not going anywhere."

Nia lifted her hands in surrender. "Alright, okay."

"Could you argue outside of my quarters?" Visha spoke quietly, still concentrating over whatever she was concocting. "You're upsetting the spiritual."

"You're upsetting my spiritual, witch," Caiden said, settling back in his chair beside me. I felt him turn to me. "How are you so calm?"

"I am not."

"He is badly injured," Visha said calmly, still in her bubble, not even looking at us. "The spiritual is screaming with his pain."

"If it is bothering you," I said, standing. I hadn't considered that.

She lifted her head, finally looking at me. "It will upset her. I did after all make an oath to heal you." Her eyes dropped to my chest and she calmly—almost boredly—added, "You are bleeding."

Nia gasped when she looked over at me. "Kilian, you need a healer."

"I am fine."

Caiden stood, a frown etched in his brows as he looked at the blood coating my shirt. "I will go fetch a healer. I have no intention of dealing with Snow if shadow boy here dies before she kills him."

Just as he left, a soft knock rasped on the door and all of us rose in surprise when Elias Venzor himself walked into the Crafter's chamber. He let out a low whisper of awe as he studied Visha's space. "Snow did tell me you had switched one den for the other."

The Crafter shut her eyes slowly and let out a sigh. "Why are you here, Elias?"

"You know one another?" Nia asked.

Elias walked to Visha and threw an arm over her shoulder. "Best pals since the age of two. My grandmother, may she rest in heavens, was Eldmoorian and a friend of Urinthia's. Visha and I used to bathe in the same basin."

Wasn't this world small?

The Crafter pushed him off and gently righted herself. "Not by choice. Explain why you're here or I'll turn you into a little blonde mouse."

"I called him," Alaric said, pointing to a chair. "Come have a seat. Quickly, I don't wish to chase a rodent down my corridors again."

He took a seat and threw a glance at the collection of bones laying on Visha's marble table. "That your lover, V?"

The witch didn't even spare him a glance. "Yes."

He nodded to himself. "Could tell. You've sucked the soul out of the poor guy."

Alaric chuckled at Visha's stunned expression more than at Elias's joke. "I gather the two of you know one another well enough."

"Yes," Elias said. "Pretty well I'd say. Until she decided to vanish from the face of the realm and not let anyone know why. Not even her friend. If I even dare call myself so."

Visha lifted her indignant stare at him. "Missed me, didn't you?"

He smiled at her. "You probably have missed me more, V."

Calm and collected, she asked, "How is Snow doing? I presume you haven't made all that journey here to waste my time."

The Venzor heir nodded. "Good, considering the General she was put under."

"What General?" I asked.

"Demir. He returned shortly after you left for Adriata. We hadn't seen him since Silas had tasked him to Seraphim about a year or so ago. Weren't expecting him to return either since Isjordian troops are still in Heyes, presumably to retract their sceptre piece."

Nia stood, suddenly anxious, but then so was everyone. "Why wouldn't she be doing well under his command?"

"Demir is a sick son of a bastard. He chews his prey then plays with it then chews it again." He cocked both hands on his hips. "Snow, however, seems to be doing great with him."

"Stop playing around, rich boy," Caiden said, nudging him hard with his shoulder as he came in with a healer. "What did that mean?"

Elias casted a small glance at me before saying, "The two seem...close."

Close?

That made Caiden chuckle somehow. "Snow is probably spinning the poor guy in circles to get him to speak. She probably thinks he has some sort of information. I pity whoever gets her attention."

Elias shook his head. "Demir shouldn't be messed with. He is not—" He looked at all of us. "He is not me. I was...enamoured with Snow, he is obsessed. Like he got a new toy to play with."

A glass shattered on the marble floor, and we all turned to Visha. The Crafter stood frozen, her eyes veiled red and her body convulsing.

Elias ran to her side. "V?"

"Don't touch her," I ordered, and he stopped right before her.

The ground beneath our feet shook, furniture clattered banging on one another and flasks blasted in the air, shattering to pieces.

Cai lifted a shield of air, enshrouding us away from the chaos. "Someone shake the witch awake before she turns Taren to dust."

The tremors stopped all of the sudden. Visha gasped awake, breathing hard and dizzy. "As I'd predicted," she said too calmly for what she'd just been through. "The beast is not created by my aunt. Nor by the god of demons. The beast is of Caligo. It is made of death. Its soul smells rotten like it has been dead a long while—a really long while." She went behind the marble table and pulled a red grimoire. "But there is no beast of Caligo who carries the rotten smell, they are all made of pure death and unable to die." Her eyes glowed red and the grimoire flipped open, the pages rapidly fluttering till it stopped with a snap, parting on the pages illustrating some type of beasts. "It makes no sense."

"If it turns human as Magnus and Kilian presume," Caiden said, "the beast could be made of Caligo blood, like the Ater battle monsters."

Visha tensed, her grip on the grimoire turning her knuckles white. She glanced shortly at Alaric who'd blanched at the mention of the wars and then shook her head. "It is impossible. No beast can cross the threshold of the heavenly gates."

And she was right. It was impossible. Obitus law—the law of realms. All that were born and existed in one realm can only stay and exist in one realm until death. It was not just any law that prevented it. It was a godly law—the law of existence itself. Not Silas, not the gods themselves could they turn it around unless Fader himself ordered it.

Nia chewed on the tip of her glove. "Melanthe could have dragged something out with her from there."

"Still," Visha said, letting her shadows for the first time visible in sight—panic. "Impossible. No matter her skills, it is something that defies nature itself."

"Then how do we make sense of any of this?" Caiden asked, standing and running a hand through his hair. "The temple in Isjord, I remember I barely made it past the half the veil all the nine times that I entered. Ryuu. Abendrot tomb. This thing is able to go through them all. This thing is what's collecting his sceptres."

The room grew grim.

If we made one step forward, Silas had found a way to push us ten steps back.

CHAPTER TWENTY-TWO

Superus

Snowlin

Since the meeting, I've been watched like a hawk. Guards seemed to all keep an eye on me, where I went and who I met. Priests were oddly now circulating the castle corridors, all wearing a look of surveillance each time I passed by. The beast was nowhere to be seen, nor was the witch. I should be looking for both, but there was something else bothering me at the moment.

Three times a day, a bell rang outside the wall of the castle every day on cue. Curiosity had eaten me for days before I decided to venture into Tenebrose to see what all the commotion was about. Like Nissa had promised, the northern gates were empty when we passed through.

The two guards accompanying me murmured to one another, surely uncertain on how to get in my way. They kept close pace behind me, but from the corner of my eye I'd caught several more trailing in disguise just behind us.

The second bell of the day rang just in time as every day and I sat in a bakery's storefront eating a lemon glazed muffin, expectant.

"Sit," I said indignantly to the two hunks of ice beside me. "You're blocking my view."

"The king doesn't wish for you to be out in Tenebrose at this hour, or at all," one of the stiffs of ice said. "It is a dangerous time, and you are far too recognizable."

I levelled a glare on the soldier. "And what are you and the rest of the bunch behind the bakery with me for, to feed me gossip and check my lipstick? Don't make me repeat myself. Sit. Down."

The two exchanged another annoying glance and then signalled the men behind us to pull back.

Three muffins and several bell rings later, a throng of Isjordians and their dead ancestors' pants gathered in Tenebrose city square. Such a crowd and for what?

A young priest took centre stage on the square's platform usually used for hangings. After a bow to the thick crowd, he took something out from between his robes—Eirlys book. "*Ner Krig't khôlda, zel Hodr khôlin.*" *With Krig's blessing, to Hodr heavens*, he greeted loudly in old Ysolt, holding holy sign.

"*Ner Krig't khôlda, druval ât wâlkya da,*" *With Krig's blessing, might they welcome us*, the crowd echoed back, and I stopped chewing.

What the—

They all kneeled before the platform, bowing their heads as the priest began reciting tenets and exalts to Krig and Hodr.

Holy hells.

My two guards murmured among one another, again, and I turned to them. "Did the Night King hit me hard on the head or are these stiff praying?"

The two tensed, shooting more careful glances to one another. "They are praying, Your Highness."

"Huh." Taking a big bite of my last muffin, I stood and dusted crumbs off my pretty dress. "So, all the bell rings are prayer times?"

The other nodded. "Yes."

"And Tenebrose gathers like this at all times?"

Another nod.

"Willingly?" I asked again.

This time the response was delayed and interrupted by another glance to his comrade.

I patted his chest. "Got it." Father was forcing these prayer sessions. Question was why? The man never did anything without purpose.

The priest shut the book and a soldier handed him a thick bunch of what looked like leaflets. On his command, the Isjordians stood, and he flicked the papers in the air for them to catch. "Today's lessons," he said, before bowing and descending away into the corridors of Tenebrose.

A hand wrapped around my wrist when I caught a leaflet. One of my guards held me tightly while he pried the paper from my hand. "It is time to return to the castle, Princess."

He stilled, his whole body raking with a tremble. "My paper," I said, holding a hand up at him while the other held the dagger etched just a little inch on his gut. Once the crumpled leaflet was tucked in nicely between my breasts, I pulled the blade back and wiped it on his sleeve. "Touch me again. I haven't gutted an ice block in ages. Dying to see your heart melt in my hand."

Sure, father would be made aware of every single detail of my adventures and my findings, but there was very little I cared about and very little he could do, really.

In the privacy of my chambers, I smoothed the crinkled paper and sat by the fireplace while I took in every word of madness inked in it.

It took me a moment to process that I'd really read what I did. The grave talks about not believing and losing faith. The punishment and the odd nonsensical detail of being a non-believer. The use of kingdom funds to enrich Isjord with temples. Nothing made sense. Why was father looking to force and make his people into believers?

I'd chewed half of my fingernails off before deciding to throw my cloak on and make way to a side of the castle that had probably fermented under dust. There was something I needed to confirm.

Another set of guards waiting for me outside my room and the first thing that struck me was how idiotic father must think me to be. The two were not even remotely Isjordian.

"Umbra?" I asked with a raised brow, and the two tensed. "No, let me guess. Empaths." When I clapped my hands together, one flinched. Adriatians and that was certain.

"Not sure what you are talking about, Your Highness."

"Sure you don't," I said, strutting down the corridors and onto the piercing chill of the winter night.

Whispers began itching my ears as the two guards argued with one another when they noticed where I was heading.

"You are not meant to leave the main castle quarters of the castle at this hour," one said.

"As you see, I am. And what will you do?" By this point, I don't think I cared.

None made a move to stop me when I reached my destination. Just as I'd expected, there were lit torches and snowless paths instead of cobwebs and dead prayers in the old forgotten gates of the castle temple. The altar path was squeaky clean, all statues of guardians were freed of their cobweb scarves and mossy coats. Now you could vividly see the deception, not only feel it lingering in the dirty air filled with prayers of the wicked.

A hooded figure stood kneeled before a gilded stone dais where a tall figure of Krig sat. When I was young, I'd come here and paint moustaches on him with charcoal and a faint grey line above his upper lip was still visible. Should have given him nose hair instead, he still looked handsome with facial hair.

The smell of mint and trickery hit me first before the thick taste of dark magic. "Changed faith so soon, Mel dear?" I asked, kneeling beside her. Two fingers to my brow and two to my heart, I murmured the holy greeting to Krig. I might have added a vulgar word at the end since Alaric had taught me to personalise my prayers to feel closer to our faith. If there was one god I held the most grudge against, it had to be him. The one who claimed to see all yet let my father call all cruelty alive in his name.

She pushed the hood back. "What brings *you* to faith again?"

Fishing the flyer from my corset, I gave it to her. "Father. Isn't he just inspiring?"

Her temple twitched just the slightest. "He is. To restore faith in a forgotten land is a great act on his part. A rewardable one."

A town of clowns this place was. "It is. A grand one, actually. But who would have thought? My father, a believer?"

"Say what you want to say, Snowlin."

I plucked the flyer back from her. "Your hair is terrible and clothes in that colour wash you out entirely. You have to stop letting a five-year-old dress you in the morning and your gardener shear your locks, sweet lamb." Gesturing the holy greeting again to Krig, I stood. "If father wants the attention of the divine, he ought to stop playing god in the first place. They don't bode well with human competition." Fader had been robbed of a lover he could have easily replaced and stomped around like a child, throwing tantrums that have cost the realm millions. Imagine if they were stolen respect.

"He doesn't want their attention. He doesn't need divine attention. Not when he commands it the same as them."

That made me stop. My eyes drifted to the flyer. How had I not noticed? The priest. The preaching. Aurora. Ruining Numengarth. There was no mention of Krig, no mention of Hodr. They were not the pieces of greed—they were the ladder to his position amongst gods. Claim Numengarth as his realm. He did want to become god. By proxy. He was making Krig his proxy.

He'd lost his damn mind.

I turned to her. "You and your aunt were inseparable from one another. Why did you choose to stay in Isjord after your mother died when you could have become the Grand Maiden's second?"

"I'd already made one choice. To stay and serve your father."

My attention perked. "But you soon betrayed him, and he hung you. For betrayal. Because you betrayed him. See where I'm going with this?"

Her stare turned cold, the old foxy mask slipping on. Or perhaps off. You never knew with this one. "A slip from my behalf. I deserve the punishment I got."

That made me snort and then blast with laughter. "Oh, hen, you're insane. Truly."

"You'll never understand."

"No, I'll never understand. We were both groomed to be his pets, dearest. You wear your leash with pride and I wore mine with shame."

The second I arrived at my chambers, I rushed to the closest mirror, peeling back my sleeve and resting a hand on the reflective surface. "*Glaoigh kail.*" *Show my husband.*

The surface twisted almost immediately and three figures took shape before me.

"Fuck," Kilian said, coming close to the mirror. "Fuck, Snow."

Blood rushed and warmed at his sight. He'd left stubble growing on his face. His hair, too, was slightly longer and I decided I liked it. "Good to see you too, husband."

He tensed, angling his head in warning. "Don't be all sweet with me. Not when you left like that."

Nia jumped from behind his shoulder trying to take a peek. "You look pale."

A hand went to my cheek. "It's the damned weather. My pores are the size of a hell's crater. I'm desperate for one of those green, herby masks you make."

"Love," Kilian said, rubbing a hand over his eyes in frustration. "Your pores are fine. It has been more than a week since we got any news from you. Sebastian and Albius had only seen you in passing once days ago, Elias is gods know where and you only just now contacted us. I thought...I thought something had happened."

"Father has isolated the castle, the servants, the guards and every other staff is completely new. He also hasn't called a meeting last week at all. He went up north himself a couple days ago. I presume to check on the war camps."

Visha peeked from Kilian's side. "There is something wrong, isn't it?"

I nodded and Kilian looked like a lion ready to prance. "Father is completely odd. Kegan, the Seraphim king, was he a believer?"

"He wasn't. Why do you ask?" Kilian said, folding his arms across his chest, wincing a bit as he did, and all thought flew out of my head.

It took me a moment to concentrate on his words. "He...uh, father, he has mandated prayer, reopened temples and even built new ones." Pulling the flyer from my corset, I pressed it to the surface of the mirror. "This can't be normal. It has to do something with the sceptre, I am sure of it."

"None of the Lords have mentioned anything of this sort," Nia added.

"I don't think they have paid mind. Not unless they've actually read these or sat through one of the preaching sessions. Call Bash or Celdric for a meeting and question how long this has been going on. Isjordians think my father is trying to bring faith back because the land has turned to complete frost. You can barely go outside these days without getting swept in a snowstorm." Turning to Visha, I asked, "Does this have to do with the sceptre?"

She took a moment. "I believe so."

"Aryan said that Kegan lost control of Aurora and the guardian ended up destroying Seraphim. Could he have lost control because of his belief? We all know gods and guardians fuel on our prayers, wishes, and need to believe. Could it be why father is trying to convert his people, so history doesn't repeat itself?"

"Possibly," Visha said quietly. "It was said that those impure and distanced from belief could not touch the sceptre, yet alone command it to their will. This was Kegan's mistake—he underestimated the laws of gods all while wanting to use their divinity for his benefit."

I shook my head. If father's wicked hands lost control of the sceptre it would be worse than him using it. "This would be a disaster. If father forms that damned sceptre—"

"He won't be able to," Kilian said confidently, and my own confidence suddenly mirrored his. "Not with all of us and him alone. Remember what took Aurora down in the first place. Just as the realm did back then we will take your father down."

"What of Eldmoor, Nia?" I asked.

My friend worried her lip between her teeth. "Urinthia is in this in some way for that I am certain. Visha sent me to a brothel near Red Coven, the one the Crafter guards frequent. The women there say an Isjordian soldier or two had rested there this last week alone. But Red Coven is up on high alert, their veils stronger than ever. Looks more like Urinthia is hiding from your father, not aiding him. But she knows more than anyone of us does. This is what makes me doubt her intentions more than anything."

"Witch," I said. "Why did my father hang Melanthe? What was she and your mother doing?"

The witch paled a little. "It is not for me to say."

"Visha, I'll pluck that tongue and make it speak myself if I have to." I smacked a hand on the mirror, making it shake. "What was so grave that my father hung the daughter of a Grand Maiden?"

The red witch took a long glance over my friend and Kilian. "She was consorting with a Lord at the time. She came to my mother to seek his protection."

"Protection from what?"

"From your father."

"Why would my father—" My eyes drew shut and an angry laugh shook my body. "Melanthe was my father's lover?" She'd betrayed her oath to Red Coven because she was my father's lover?

"She was your father's property."

"Speaking about your father's property," Nia said. "We have news on the beast. Kilian obtained some of the beast's spittle from the Solaryan caves and Visha tested it. The thing is a product of Caligo."

Confusion rushed to my head all at once making me dizzy. "What?" But Kilian had reassured me. And he was rarely wrong.

"Further reason for you to return to me now," Kilian said.

"Further reason for me to stay longer," I said, reaching the mirror close enough that I almost bumped my head to it. "Seraphim—the gates to Empyrea, this is how my father would have reached it. This thing is made of magic from heavens." I turned to Kilian. "You said—"

"And I still stand by it, love. I don't know how your father unearthed this thing, but it is not of heavens and that I am sure of. I also believe it transforms. It turns into a human. The Abendrot exits leading to sea from where it had escaped after retrieving the sceptre piece in Solarya were too small to fit its size. Unless it turned."

Human? It was human?

"Keep your eyes open, Snow," Nia said. "It could be anyone around you. Perhaps even a servant."

"You'd be suggesting I'd even closed them in the first place." The way Kilian's brows pulled together after I said it made me regret saying it.

The Bruma halls went starkly quiet when I strutted inside. Soldiers halted their sparring and bowed while I made my way through.

Renick stood between the courts, observing and shouting orders to his Aura.

"Nick dearest," I said, creeping behind him and I could swear he flinched a little. "Where is your whip? You liked using that more than your voice."

He bowed his head. "Your Highness."

Verglaser Aura were doubled in mass from the last time I'd been in Isjord, they blasted their magic from all corners ahead, yet none as powerful as I'd expected them to be. None as powerful as the ones I'd fought in the ruins last year. "Your recruiting has expanded. Is father lowering his standards?"

"We've lowered the age of acceptance."

Children. My father was using children in his battles and cleverly thought that forcing people to pray would help him garner godly approval of his good heart. Bet Krig was enjoying this more than anything. "Have you stopped giving your soldiers mirk root?"

"Yes, a couple weeks ago now."

I clicked my tongue. "Need you to start giving it to them again." See, I never claimed to be the nobler monster—if there was ever a competition for the better sort.

"What?" he stuttered out. "I cannot do that. Symptoms are showing quicker now. The Bruma command lost one hundred Aura last week alone. It won't be longer before Silas catches on to it."

"Renick dearest, I do not care. Give mirk root to them. It is a command," I said, pointing to his wrist where our band of bargain was hidden. "Besides, it would be a shame to slit Fiona's throat before your eyes and let wolves pick her organs apart before I let your soul be consumed by the bargain." If we faced war, I needed father to lose as many of his Aura as possible even if it meant we had to double our troops in Myrdur to handle their attempts of breaching through the *zgahna*.

He breathed furiously and distressed, running his hands over his greyed hair over and over.

"There is not much of a choice. Don't act like this is a struggle because it's not. You are scared of dying, Nick dearest. So is your daughter considering how much she begs me to spare her," I said, a wicked smile on my face. How much fun this was. Reaching close, I brushed the pad of his shoulder with the back of my hand. "Renick. Your life hangs by a little thread that I am pulling. Ah, did you know I also hold a massive pair of scissors over that thread, too?"

He nodded. "I will give them mirk root."

"That's it, good pet," I said, patting his chest. "Break apart, just like that."

He shook a little, his jaw tightening with anger. "You are the same as your father, worst even."

My grin was vile. "You worked hard, Nick dearest. Time to reap what you sowed." That same sensation blew in the air rousing my magic to alert, and I turned to look around. The beast was hiding around the castle, I was sure of it. "Tell me," I asked, still looking around. "Where does father keep his little green pet?"

Renick's stare jerked about the court space. "You...you know?"

"Not my answer," I crooned.

He swallowed. "No one knows. Besides the witch and Silas no one does. I've seen it once in passing in Moregan's camps. Heard the rest from my Aura."

"Why did I see it in Ulv Islet a few weeks ago?"

He shortly glanced at me and then our surroundings. "The Highwall Canes," he explained. "Till the witch worked her way around them some time ago. The veil over the prison disguised the beast's scent."

Of course.

"Snowlin," Demir called, jogging to me. "There you are."

Damn it.

I shot Renick a look and he greeted Demir before backing away into the courts.

The odd general gave me a curious look. "Are you and Renick close?"

Pointing my chin at the training courts I said, "He used to make me bleed all over those floors."

He cringed. "A grudge then?"

"I don't worry myself with grudges, Demir." Were they even grudges if I'd made him weep and bleed and sworn off his life to me?

He waved a hand for me to follow him. "Come meet the team."

A pack of buff men stood in a separate hall, laughing and joking with one another. There was a strangeness to them, and I didn't know how to explain it. Their heartbeats were too quiet for that of a human.

They all turned in unison when Demir and I approached, their noses wrinkling and expressions souring. Was this Melanthe's experimental batch? Had they all fed in the beast's blood?

The closer I got the more my senses roused. My skin prickled at the whiff of their magic staining the cold air with a smell of a rotten corpse. It was enough to confirm my every doubt.

"Snowlin was Captain before, she will join and maintain her title as such in our team." He clasped my shoulder, his thumbs drawing circles. "I finally get to work with you, Princess."

Chapter Twenty-Three

Galanthus

Snowlin

Demir was an exhausting man. For three days straight he had dragged me all along Tenebrose without the attempt to even step near the gates let alone leave its walls. I knew that was not his normal route because half of the time he had no idea where in Tenebrose we were and even got lost several times during our city guard duties which a captain and no less a general normally ever had.

Father was doing it to test me, so I obliged to every rotten demand Demir gave me. Get a cat down from a tree, which I did. Separate a bunch of wailing children who poked their eyes playing snowballs, which I again did, but with deep reluctance because tearful screaming children amused me. How their faces twisted and how loud they wailed from the light prickle of pain, it was entertaining. But Demir didn't think so.

Today was the first day he had called a meeting with his captains, and I allowed myself to get half excited. The meeting chamber was filled with dozens of familiar and unfamiliar faces. Captains, Renick, the northern lords and a particularly unfamiliar one I'd never seen but heard of before, were in attendance.

The woman wore the three circlets on her breast pocket, her emerald attention stone cold on a document she was reading. There was a deep, old rosy scar that started from the middle of her shaved head and down to her forehead—a scar I'd seen before. Ulv Islet. Father's little loyal toy was from his personal dungeons. The person single handedly dealing with all matters of the sceptre was a criminal who my father had tortured before?

As if noticing my attention on her, she cocked her head to the side and gave me a leary look before bowing her head in greeting.

Moregan. Ulv Islet. The war camps. The beast. This was starting to feel too easy. Morgan was the beast? Well, there was a way to find out. Ask her. And where better to do so than surrounded by my father's court.

I leaned in on the table and batted my lashes innocently. "Have we met before?"

The odd general glanced at the room, aware of the attention before meeting my gaze again. "No, I would not think so, Your Highness." Her voice was gravel and ice. Probably from all the screaming time I remember she did back on Ulv Islet.

Narrowing my eyes, I said, "You look oddly familiar."

Her brow quirked up a little. "I am very recognisable, Princess, someone must have described me in passing."

"No, I'm sure I've seen you before. Somewhere resembling a very dingy, dark dungeon far at sea."

Her breathing picked up a little, signalling me that she was uncomfortable with any of the information coming out in front of those in attendance.

Concentrating on her rising chest, I counted all heartbeats in the room. The ratio was minus one. No heartbeat came from her.

The other captains shifted uncomfortably, and chatter began growing as did Moregan's discomfort. My, my. Was she really father's dirty little green secret? How did this one manage to turn to that green thing? Her Verglaser stink was potent, but not potent enough to emulate the beast's scent—not in any way triggering my senses either.

Demir strutted in the meeting chambers all energy and sat atop the table, ruining my little moment. Shortly, he took note of my presence and threw me a wink. And as he did so, I marked another day down till I'd pluck that eye out.

"I've selected a team I want to take up north, to deal with the vandal attacks," he began. "They've doubled in size and have reached all the way up to the face of Islines where some of our people reside."

North? What vandals? I'd told Magnus that father had gotten his sceptre, so why would there be any—

Hells. Had father not gotten his sceptre piece yet?

I almost perked up in my seat when he called my name, "Snowlin, you are to come with. I already have your father's permission."

"Of course," I offered politely, but my insides were churning with excitement.

"We leave tomorrow at dawn. I suggest you all head for rest." He turned to me. "You too, Princess."

And I suggest you rip your own spine out. "Will do."

"Ah, Snowlin," Demir called just as I was about to leave. "Your father expects you for dinner."

This filial daughter act was going to be the death of me. I hadn't acted obedient a day in my life and now I knew why.

My mood picked up when I saw who had joined the radishes and father for dinner. Melanthe stood there in all her crimson might and sat right in my bloody seat.

"Princess," she purred, lifting herself a little from the seat to bow at me.

"Mel dear, you're in my seat," I said, pulling the chair beside her and sitting down. "But stay, I bet your leash doesn't extend to here."

Her face fell and she glared at me. Look at her feeling all offended again.

"My rose," father sighed and pinched the bridge of his nose, tired. "How was your day?"

I plucked a grape from the fruit platter. "All the better now. One can only once see the dead, snow spirits and a king in one table together. Trying to get a good look before it ends."

"Glad you are entertained," Melanthe drew out, stabbing her fork hard on her food, making the metal screech against the porcelain.

Leaning forward, I cocked my head at her. "So, dear, where have you been sneaking to lately?"

She stopped mid-chew and turned to me slightly. "Concerned, are you?"

"You've got to be cautious, Mel sweetness. No one knows what lurks in the shadows. What hungers for you."

Her mouth pulled to a sneer. "I am not afraid, Snowlin. You forget, I have already died once."

"What a fond memory." I lifted the cup to a toast. "Here's to second chances."

Her eyes widened a little and she brought a hand to her stomach. Something bad stirred in mine from the way her fingers curled protectively over her clothing. Then I heard it. A slow hum. Not entirely a strong heartbeat, but strong enough to send webs of panic shooting through me. Melanthe was with child.

Father rested a hand on her shoulder. "You shouldn't strain yourself."

I almost knocked myself over when she rested her scarred hand atop my father's and said, "It will be fine. She is fine."

She? Oh gods. *You'll never understand*, she had told me. Hadn't she been right? The servitude that one could explain with insanity was because of this? Howling laughter blasted out of me till I almost choked on my own air. "You two know?" I asked the two quiet radishes. When they remained bitterly silent and glaring holes onto the table, I laughed, again.

"Father," I called, still hiccupping with laughter and pointing at the two half breeds. "Two wrongs don't make a right, but my congratulations, honestly. To all of us. From a circus to a carnival." Turning to him, I lifted my cup to another toast. "I hope you get your desired outcome from this. The one that me and my siblings failed to give you." I hated how betrayal filled my stomach so sourly. Had he even loved my mother when she had loved him so? Wasn't that what people in love did, held onto one another even if only their memory lived?

"There is always a lesson in failure, my rose."

"My, how wise you must be by now."

He smirked—his face lit with amusement. Not his usual reaction to my insults. "Wise," was all he said. I was convinced this man is evil himself. I pitied the child she held, the future that babe would have if she even lived long enough to have one.

"If there are no more surprise children for me to figure out, I ask for permission to leave. As you know, Demir's team leaves early at dawn," I said, coming to stand.

Father nodded. "Have a good rest."

Before I left, I bent down to Melanthe's stomach and said, "Be safe, little sister. You need all the luck there is because your ma is a wicked witch and a little bit of a nasty bitch."

Melanthe tried her best to hide that snarl but failed and ended up looking like a constipated chick.

First thing I did when I reached my room was head to the mirror. Peeling my gloves off, I rested a hand on the reflective surface. "*Glaoigh kail.*" *Show my husband.*

Visha had warned me the magic could take a while, but this was taking too long. Each second that went past, my heart drummed loudly against my rib bone. Why did I have to tell him? I could just keep it to myself, it was nothing, really. "Come on. Come on."

The mirror surface finally twisted and there he was. Half-naked, the gnarly scars in sight and ruffled hair almost as if he had been asleep. If it was evening here, it would be before sunset in Adriata. Kilian, asleep? At this time of day?

He rubbed a tired hand over his eyes and approached closer. "My love?"

Hackles of panic rose. "Why were you sleeping?"

"Couldn't sleep the night before," he said, shaking his head. "What is the matter? Is there something wrong? Do I come to you?"

"No, nothing like that." Did he just lie to me?

His face hardened. "You are worrying me."

I was worrying myself, too. Actually, he was worrying me more. "He...father and Melanthe, they...they are having a child. The witch is pregnant...with my father's child. Why were you not feeling well?" I asked, stepping closer to the mirror.

He shook his head. "Nothing to fret over." His fingers moved lower on the surface as if he was touching me. "Did it upset you—finding out about Melanthe and now this?"

"I don't know what it did, but I'm not upset. This isn't upset."

"You're worried."

"Why would I worry?"

"Because you know what it feels to be Silas's *Ybris*."

"But I do not care."

A little absurd smile pulled on the corner of his mouth. "You care more than you think. Think about it, love. Are you thinking of the future or the past?"

"Both."

"Then you are worried."

"Maybe I am. But not for the babe. Worried that she is somehow incorporated in my father's plan. This doesn't feel like my father. He's had the chance to have more heirs and thankfully never did, but he has had the chance."

"You're overthinking again."

"No. There is just a lot of thinking going at once. Not overthinking." I should be writing this down and making up a dictionary of my own. Why was I trying to justify it?

"I can't stay this far from you any longer. Come back."

"Not yet. Tomorrow I head to the Islines with my father's General."

His jaw ticked. "Demir."

"How did you know?"

"Elias," he said with the same disdain in his voice. "You didn't even say goodbye. Was that night that terrible?"

I gulped. "It wasn't terrible, and you were so peacefully asleep." I'd never found a man adorable, let alone when they sleep, snore and drool. But I'd caught myself twice smiling down at his little sleeping face—my stomach had done that somersaulting thing and my toes had curled like an infatuated idiot.

He did that insanely annoying thing with his tongue pushing on his cheek and I couldn't help but feel frustrated and giddy. "Not terrible, huh?"

"Mhm." I cleared my throat. "I suppose we should bid goodnight."

"Are you tired?"

"Not really."

"Then talk to me."

"But you're tired."

He gave me a little smile. "Not anymore."

My eyes went to that little dimple in his chin.

"Love?"

"Yes?"

That somehow made him smile again which then ended up making me feel faint because my heart galloped at the sight. "You answered."

I shook my head. "What?"

"To love."

"Oh, my mistake."

That made him throw his head back with laughter.

"You make me dizzy," I said.

"Concerning," he said, cocking his head to the side with humour. "But I like it."

"I don't."

He sighed and placed his hand on the mirror again. There was this look on his face, something between enamour and sadness. "Love, my love," he whispered.

"Henrik." A yawn suddenly made me all teary. He had that effect on me. I'd never felt safe sleeping next to someone. No one had ever made me feel safe enough to fall asleep near them.

"Go rest now."

I nodded. "Good night."

"Good night," he said, backing away from the mirror. "I love you, Snow."

The image faded, reflecting my sight back and it made me flinch.

The most beautiful dark he'd once called me. What I saw was neither beautiful nor the most beautiful. Nor someone you can love. How can anyone possibly love what I was? Would father love his new daughter?

We are born to simply be tolerated, Eren had once told me when I had asked why other children got hugs, sweet words, colourful toys, pretty pink bows and sweets without giving anything in exchange. I'd often wondered why they were adored and not beaten like we were. I was born to simply be tolerated. Another lie Eren had told me.

We were born to be hated.

I tilted my head to the side, the dark figure on the mirror mimicking my movement. "I don't think I like that one lie…Kilian. I hate it."

I'd readied myself before dawn and waited by the stables for Demir to show up. The man walked side by side with Melanthe, the two were deep in conversation as they reached the stables. The ease between the two made me extremely curious and equally confused. They behaved like old friends around one another.

When the witch took sight of me, her mood turned sour and she put a hand over her stomach, almost protectively.

"Calm, Mel dearest, I don't really like the taste of them when they are that small," I said, pointing my chin to her stomach. "All soft bones and no flesh."

Demir chuckled and the witch threw him a deadly glare.

She stepped on something and stopped, lifting her foot to inspect the little flower she had crushed in the snow. Something shifted in her stare as she reached to pluck it and hold it before her like it was a blade dipped in poison not an innocent little flower. "Galanthus," she said quietly. Her eyes flitted to me and then below my feet where I'd crushed some of them. "Snowflower."

My blinks were slow and confused. "Do you want an applause or something for guessing it right?" I asked, saddling my horse and joining the rest riding away. Did pregnancy make you daft?

Demir rode beside me as we left the Tenebrose walls. "They are a sign of spring," he explained quietly. "Do you see any spring?"

"It is just a flower, Demir." I'd tricked an entire kingdom with just a flower. Made a fool out of them all with a tale.

"Like you're just a Princess?"

I turned to him more bored than annoyed. Of course he doubted something, everyone did. "No. Because I am not just a Princess, like you aren't just a General. You want to open that discussion?"

He threw his head back and chuckled. "I like you, you know. You're nothing like the rest of Isjord. There is an air about you."

An air about me? "Why do you compliment like you're born before the ascension of gods?"

"Calling me outdated?"

"Severely unaware of his outdatedness," I said. "Almost as if he *is* outdated."

When we reached the foot of the Islines, the villages came into sight. The tone had turned gravely. Not like last time. Now, the place stank of ruin and death. And an oddly nice parsley smell that made my stomach gurgle.

The only few houses still standing were guarded by Isjordian sentries and had bars and had several deadbolt strike plates on their entrances. The place had turned to a graveyard.

We reached a tavern, the same one I had stayed at the last time I was here. Once Demir gave us our assigned rooms, he turned to me. "You will remain here. The rest of my team will continue to travel up north to the furthest village by the old Krigborn lines."

My eyes bulged out. He wasn't really going to take all the way here to just leave me to guard the village. Or maybe this was his plan to begin with. Distract me while he goes and gets the damned sceptre piece. "Why aren't I coming with?"

"You were Captain previously, that means your rank is the highest in the team after me. You will maintain guard here."

I stepped before him, stopping him from leaving. "You could stay the night, why are you rushing there?"

He gave me an amused look. It would have looked entirely too slimy if not for his good looks. "I like the eagerness, but those were your father's orders. It's too dangerous for you to be with me." He leaned to my ear and whispered, "When I return, maybe you can help me compliment you better."

My smile was uneasy, but he clearly couldn't tell because he flashed me that grin again before sidestepping and leaving the tavern.

Muffled sounds came from the end of the corridor just before I reached my room, and I went to press my ear to the chatty door. "I don't understand why we had to remain down here," someone said with indignation.

"The mountain entrances to the temple are many. He won't be able to enter them all in a day."

Hells.

"Moregan's team said they had information that the Solaryans had found entrance up there," another said. "You know Demir, he will be done in an hour if they have found the easy entrance. The beast is with us. I heard it travelled with Moregan."

"He should have just let the princess back in Tenebrose."

"He was given an order by the king. It would have been suspicious for her not to be the only soldier in our team not to join. And you know all the rampages she went on during her time as Captain when her father denied her something." He clicked his tongue. "Spoiled royals."

Steps approached the door and I dashed to the other side quickly, flinging my door open and dropping on the bed.

The beast was with Moregan. Or Moregan. And they finally had found how to get the sceptre piece.

It was set. Tomorrow I would enter the temple again.

CHAPTER TWENTY-FOUR

Serta

Kilian

I awoke in a puddle of sweat and a dull burn on my arm. The seal of bargain between Snow and I had ebbed and almost faded. Something was wrong. Quickly, I got dressed and faded to where the seal directed me to.

The cold hit me first, and then the snow began coating my hair and clothing before I gathered a sense of my surroundings. I groaned when I saw where I was. This damned woman.

Few feet away from me stood the temple in the Islines.

Without thinking it further, I stepped inside the veiled temple. The space was completely enshrouded in darkness, but my senses were brighter in it. If not, I saw even better.

Between the statues lining the second entry of the temple, I made out her figure navigating between a large round archway under the god of gods, Fader.

"This relationship between you and peril ends now," I said approaching her.

"Gods!" She startled, dropping her torch to the floor.

"Close, but you can keep calling me Kilian."

She breathed hard, a hand over her chest and the other gripping the hilt of her sword. "It's not him," she whispered to herself.

"It is me Snow." Grabbing her hand, I pulled her to my chest, letting her feel me as I felt her after weeks of not being able to touch her. I breathed her in and kissed every corner of her face. Sweet gods and blessed heavens, I'd missed her. "We have not entered the Crafter's enchanted veil yet."

She swallowed. "How do you know about that?"

"I entered it about a hundred times when I lost you that day in it. I recognise the way around it by heart."

She backed a step away from me. "You shouldn't be here."

I lifted my hand, showing her the inked bargain that had begun fading under the foreign veil of magic. "You are tethered to me."

"I'm getting the sceptre."

"Not until we figure out how to cross the veil."

She shook her head. "Father is determined to get it this time, I know it. He has sent a team to the Islines to enter the old Krigborn lands and find other entrances. It is a matter of time before we lose this one too."

"Then *we* are getting the sceptre."

Her jaw tightened. "No."

"Yes."

"You're a living sieve, you idiot."

"But living, nonetheless. Either we go together, or no one goes at all." I reached chest to chest with her. "Go on, say no."

She dropped her head back and groaned before turning on her heels and continuing down the temple.

The room was just as I had remembered, a small flicker of light circled around the room illuminating the drawings and the numerous statues about the walls and ceiling. We both looked down as red liquid filled us to our ankles.

Snow squeezed my hand tight, her eyes jumping about the room. From the way those golden irises had thinned, I knew we'd entered the veil and she was seeing and hearing things that could drive a sane person to insanity.

A bulbous light jumped about the ceiling, illuminating the dark charcoal drawings. At the centre stood a white winged woman with her hands bound together, eyes painted in a pale starlight and her hair a blinding ivory.

At her side was a long thin sceptre, wrapped in engravings in the old language of gods.

Aurora and the sceptre.

When blood had reached Snow's shoulders, I lifted her up and she wrapped her legs around my waist, holding tightly onto me.

"What is that?" she whispered, seeming almost out of breath.

I looked up to where she pointed. At Aurora's side stood another drawing, the figure of a heavily chained man kneeling at the centre of a circle made of moon phases.

Her lover?

Snow whimpered in my arms, burying her head in my neck and clawing my body. The crimson thick fluid had reached my waist as I guided the two of us towards the other side of the room.

"Stop, please," she called in almost a cry and I pulled her tightly to me. She let out a soul tearing sob and writhed in my hold. "Kilian."

I stilled at the whisper of my name. "I'm right here," I said, softly pressing my lips to her forehead and lifting her body higher. "I've got you."

The veil had only affected her. They called it the veil of fear, one of the many tricks Dark Crafters had under their sleeve. It brought to life what you feared most by tricking every sense in the body. Sometimes almost too vividly. My biggest fears had gone a long time ago and I had made peace with most of them anyway. Fear was also taught out of me, with steel and fire that had marked me inside and out—it had made me a master of it. Until I met her. Then I had to re-learn it all over again. Re-learn to fight it all over again.

"What do you see, my love?" I asked as moving became difficult. "Tell me, we have to fight it away otherwise this will drown us."

She pushed from me, her eyes completely veiled black. "Let me go, I have to get to them."

"It is not real, Snow," I said, tightening my grip around her at the same time she began thrashing with a force no woman of her stature and height can possibly possess. "They are not real. Not inside here."

"Let me go!" she bellowed. "No! He's killing them! Gods, please. Please!" Her cries shattered me—entirely shattered me. "Please!"

"Almost there, my love. We are almost there."

She kicked and punched and scratched me with all force of her body as I pushed to reach the end of the room. "Let me go! Let me go!"

Sobs wracked her body and mine along. It was painful to hear them.

Holding her tightly, I kicked the wooden door repeatedly with my foot, the density of the blood straining my every movement and with Snow wrestling me, it took me several long moments to push it open. Wood cracked, sending the door to split and push open just as the blood reached my neck.

When we stepped on the other side, all evidence of the blood soaking us had disappeared. The remnants of the veil, however, still lingered within Snow who hiccuped and shivered on my arms. I held her so tight, but it felt as if I couldn't get her close enough. "It's over. It's all over."

"One...moment. Allow me one embarrassing moment," she murmured, still clinging onto me.

"It will be our secret."

"Our secret," she breathed and rested her face on the crook of my neck. After she'd gathered herself, she looked up at me. "Why didn't it affect you?"

I wiped the tears under her eyes away. "I have only ever had one fear. And it came true."

"You can put me down now."

"I don't want to."

A screech made us both turn to attention.

A gust of wind suddenly blew in our direction, almost toppling us and before we knew the cause, a large, winged animal was aiming its talons at us.

Snow jumped from my arms and we both unsheathed our swords just as it came in close reach. With a few manoeuvrings between Snow and I, the beast was cut to pieces, and we were both bone tired as if we'd been wrestling a dozen of them already.

"What in the hells?" Snow said, turning to inspect our surroundings.

Like a curse, screech after screech filled the empty space.

I pulled her behind me. "Seems like we have to share that secret with all of them."

We were inside what looked like a massive stony cave. Sharp stalactites of salt and earth hung from its ceiling and its walls were made up of hundreds of hive-like dents where more beasts nestled.

The cave was bright so there was a source of light coming from somewhere. "There," I said, pointing behind a large bulldozer of rock erected in the middle of the hollow space. Small rays of light peeked from behind it. "Our exit."

I linked my hand with hers and began slowly walking toward our escape. Every white pair of eyes tracked our movements with intensive attention.

"Come beasty, beasty," Snow cooed nervously. "We taste terrible."

"I beg to differ." She tasted what one thought heavens tasted like.

She stumbled a little and turned to glare at me.

Just as we were about to reach the exit, a large feathery body dropped before us. Not long after, one by one, the beast descended from their caves and rounded us from all sides.

Claws and teeth the size of an arm and covered in ashy grey feathers—nothing I could recognise. The second protection of the Arx Triad.

"We are still inside the veil, right?"

I nodded, lifting my sword up. "Can't feel any magic."

Snow swung her sword, bolts of electricity circling around it. "Why can I?" Two black lines creeped from under her clothing towards her neck and then to her forehead.

"Snow," I warned, panicking, seeing as her seal was quickly opening.

"If I am quick about it, we can get out of here in time before it cracks open."

I began to object, but she suddenly let go of me, sheathing her sword and raising her palms in ahead toward our exit. Thick strands of lighting exploded from her, the room filling with blinding light and shrieks of what seemed like pain. One after the other, the feathery bodies dropped to the ground, scorched. The rest of the creatures rose higher in the air to avoid Snow's lightning and the path ahead of us cleared—long enough for us to run through to the bright exit.

We crossed the threshold, meeting a blinding light. It was as bright as it had been in Solarya, perhaps even more so. Pollen and the smell of wood circled around us as we turned to see a thick willow forest grow in front of us. It was not a Crafter's veil. I touched the leaves and the ground, everything looked as real as real could get. Trees whooshed at the light warm breeze, and the air was filled with the sound of woodpeckers and songbirds. Too tired to question our surroundings, we dropped to the ground for rest. First the veil and the monsters, my whole body ached. Couldn't imagine how it was for her.

"Pretty amazing, aren't I? For a monster, I mean," she teased, panting, the black tattoos doubling and tripling across her skin. "Why...why could I use magic?"

"Your guess is as good as mine."

"And what is your guess?"

"That the veil probably couldn't suppress all of your magic and that is why your seal was opening quicker."

"Ah."

"Ah?"

She shrugged. "Was hoping for something more mystical somehow."

I lifted a hand in the air and a phantom tendril of shadows twirled from my palm. I could use magic now, too. "It is feeding from my mana." And there was the cost.

She stared at my creation. "Why?"

"I can't feel the flow of the spiritual ever since we crossed the cave, but in here I can feel my magic."

"You are my first ever visitors," a light voice called from behind as both Snow and I shot up, our weapons at ready.

"For the love of bloody heavens," Snow groaned. "What is that?"

A little girl giggled from where she sat on top of a rock, swinging her bare feet playfully from under her light rose coloured gossamer gown while the breeze lifted her beige straight long hair around. This is where normal ended. She had a branch jutting out of her forehead like a horn. My senses rose to alarm somehow despite her fragile appearance.

Instinctively, I moved to cover Snow and the girl let out a light laugh. "From what I saw, she does not need your protection," she said, pointing behind us as the cave exit we once came through warped into the air and disappeared. "Monsters of our sort never need it anyway. It is you who might need the protection."

The *Ybris*. Only a girl—a child.

Snow stepped to my side. "What is this place?"

The girl hopped from the rock. "A purgatory of sorts, you're partly in Caligo and partly in Numengarth. Crossing neither yet stepping neither. A between land." Trees groaned with each step she took, almost drawn to her. "I guard the sceptre as you might have already guessed. It gets pretty lonely here but now I am saved." She stopped a few feet from Snow, eyeing my wife with a curiosity I didn't like. "How are you so grown? Has he brought you down here to trap you with me?"

Snow frowned at her. "Trap?"

The girl blinked with confusion but nodded. "Did master Blackwell bring you here?"

"Who is Blackwell?" I asked.

"The Dark Crafter who chained me here."

Blackwell was dead and she was a forever prisoner of wherever this was.

"Has there been anyone before us?" Snow asked. "To come here and look for the sceptre."

The girl sighed. "A few, but not many manage to pass through the veil to begin with." She perked as if in remembrance. "There have been many trying to come play with me these past few months, few that have managed to even pass the feathery beasts in the cave. But they all die so quickly. And they rot even quicker," she said, sounding almost upset.

Snow's face tightened at her words, and she extended a hand to the girl. "We need the sceptre piece, young lady, where is it?"

The girl blinked rapidly and moved back as if scared from Snow. "Master has promised to free me if I protect it well and I want to play before I kill you."

"The sceptre piece and I'll send you to play in the Otherworld," Snow demanded again.

I winced a little bit at her harsh words, considering the way the innocent looking child's eyes widened and teared up in horror. "That wasn't very nice, my love."

Snow gave a look. "Would you rather I let her kill us, or worse, free the jolly bird onto our realm?"

Good point. Bad priorities.

The little girl's face shifted with a wild scowl, soon her hands tightened in fists and her hair floated furiously as if under a vortex of wind and her body gradually turned to complete blue ice. The shift caught us by surprise, and we gawked at the creature she became. Ice crept all around her, freezing the forest as it aimed for us. Backing away from her reach, our backs met a large tree trunk stopping us from going further. Suddenly, branches curved around our bodies trapping us under them. Verglaser and Senchi. Ice and Vegetation.

I swung my Adriatian steel upward, cutting through the branches and freeing myself and Snow.

Snow let out a bolt of lightning, the magic not even reaching close to the girl as she blocked it with hundreds of thick branches. Blow after blow from Snow, she blocked and attacked twice as hard. For each burst of ice Snow summoned, the girl doubled it. Black tattoo markings had doubled on Snow's face from the amount of magic she'd called from the seal. When her hands began to shake, I knew she had pushed beyond her limit.

"Enough," I said, pulling her hands down. "If this is an in-between world, the flow of your magic through the seal to Caligo is cut."

She breathed hard. "You suggest we die?"

"I suggest *you* don't die."

The hybrid girl was not only strong, but she was extremely smart, trying to tire us out without sending the last landing blow. "She is playing with us, like she said," I told Snow, while I furiously cut through the tentacles of branches coming in our direction.

"Play with me!" The girl screeched and the earth almost shook as if in command. Trees twisted their trunks and then furiously shook till they pushed from the ground as if alive, walking on their roots toward us.

"We are getting beaten by a ten-year-old," Snow panted, grasping her daggers with shaky hands.

I gathered her in my arms. "Shut your eyes."

"Why?"

"Because I can't have you see what I will do."

Her dark brows pulled in a frown. "What happens if your magic exhausts your mana? You're not an elemental."

"You doubt me too much, my love. Shut your pretty eyes."

Snow slowly closed her eyes, and I pulled her face to my chest before magic emanated from me. Darkness splintered and fed on light, withering and spreading all its horrors. And soon, the sky turned dark, the air thickly cold and a piercing scream rang in time as tendrils of my magic filled every nook of the forest. Just when I felt the last flutter of life leave the forest, I pulled back all of my magic. Night turned to day. But what was once dark could no longer bear light.

My vision had dizzied from the use of magic, my limbs quivered as if I'd gone months without food or water. I dropped a kiss to her forehead and gathered her tighter against me. "I don't want you to open them."

"I am not afraid." Snow's markings had reduced, her tremors too. She spun round and a light gasp slipped past her gaping lips when she faced the remnants of my magic.

"Liar," I murmured, swaying on my feet, my vision already dusting with black specks.

She didn't deny it, only stepped toward the mess of death.

The ground and trees had turned to charcoal still figures and grey ash floated around us, frosting the ground silver. Even the blue sky had dulled to a grey. There was no more life of any sort. The air, too, was polluted with the ghostly touch of lifelessness.

We both stared at the girl's lifeless body as it slowly dispersed to dust leaving behind a short metal bar carved around in silver vines and flowers—the sceptre piece.

Snow reached forward but pulled away right before grabbing it. "You take it. Visha said no one unworthy of gods should leave a trace on it. The sceptre apparently manifests in the energy around the ones that hold it."

I turned to her with mild amusement and confusion at the same time. "And I am worthy? Interesting judgement coming from you at that."

She rolled her eyes. "Just grab the damn thing—" Her words were cut in half when the silver rod began humming. Three runes in the old language of gods flickered alive in the metal and glowed white.

"*Hur ma'hazur kahaz,*" Snow recited the language of gods in a trance, her eyes flashing white. The sceptre piece glowed and warmed up till it burned my hand.

Kneel to the power, the wind whispered, gyrating around us furiously, lifting rock and ash in the air. *Hur ma'hazur kahaz.*

Electricity began skittering in the air, gathering around Snow, encircling her body like a vortex and her face twisted with pain. She dropped to the ground, heaving and wincing from pain. "Stay back! I don't know what is happening." She reached a hand over her shoulder, digging her nails on her back and let another soul shattering scream as bolts of electricity gathered atop, forming what looked like a pair of wings.

I kneeled before her, my heart stammering out of my chest from fear. "Open your eyes, my love. Look at me."

Slowly she peeled her eyes open and looked up at me. "I don't know what is happening."

"Concentrate, Snow. Feel where it pours out. Point it to me."

She lifted a trembling hand and put it on her chest. "Here."

"Good." I inched a bit closer to her and she panicked, crawling backward. "You won't hurt me."

She shook her head.

"Feel it, my heart, concentrate solely where it pours from." I inched closer again and this time she didn't back away. "Concentrate."

She shut her eyes and attempted to control her breath.

"Open your eyes. You can't concentrate on the nothingness, it is too vast. Concentrate on something around you."

She opened her eyes and fixed them on me. She concentrated on me as she breathed in and out. Though her look was distant, she was still looking at me. Slowly, afraid that I'd send her panicking again, I unravelled a tendon of shadows and let it crawl over her skin. She gasped, the more touches of my magic slithered around her, the more her breathing evened. It took her a few minutes to quiet the stormy rage of her magic, but she did it. Her body went slack, and before she dropped to the ground, I gathered her tired form in my arms.

Unable to help it, I embrace her tight, nuzzling my face in her neck, breathing her in.

"How...how did you do that?" she murmured.

It was beating. It was still beating.

"It has never happened before. Not like that," she said, taking a deep breath. "You're squeezing me." Her gentle hand tapped my back. "Kilian?"

Kilian. I breathed out a deep sigh, still not letting her go.

Her hand settled on my back, and she held me too. She held me for the first time since that last night in Isjord. Before I ruined everything. "This is how I die, huh? Squeezed by a giant piece of Adriatian flesh. And he is my sworn enemy at that. Not a bad way to go, you smell like heaven."

"Did you hurt a lot?" I asked, running my fingers through her hair, unable to keep my hands off her. "Did it hurt you hurt a lot, my love?"

Her mouth parted, but no words came out. She only stared at me before shaking her head. "Not a lot."

I stood, helping her up and then grabbed the sceptre piece. The silver piece of rod did not feel unusual, despite the ominous looking engravings, it felt just like a hunk of metal. The runes were gone along with the strange vibrating light. Perhaps Snow's magic had triggered it and the guardian's magic had triggered Snow's.

A spark flared before us and a portal cracked open, showing a coniferous forest glazed with a thick mass of snow. Isjord.

The second we were at the other side of it, stepping on Isjordian soil, the portal shut, carrying all memory of what had happened there.

"You're bleeding," she said, looking at her palms and then at my chest. Her eyes cast down at her own chest coated with my blood and she trembled. "I think you're bleeding, Kilian."

CHAPTER TWENTY-FIVE

URO

SNOWLIN

Despite all the time we had spent in the temple, no more than moments had passed on the outside. Luckily, we had returned before Demir's team had. I still had unfinished business in Isjord. The beast, the diary. I still had to figure out how my father found out and retrieved his sceptre pieces. If I was quick about it, I could even make time to try and find where he had hidden the Solaryan and Hanaian pieces.

The tavern below the inn was filled with the soldiers returning from Demir's little expedition. All had a sullen look on their faces, eating their food without a single word amongst one another.

There was so much to take in. To hear among their whispers. Yet I couldn't concentrate.

Did you hurt a lot? I'd never wanted to tell someone more than him how much I hurt. Why did he always ask?

"Tired already?" Demir asked, approaching my table. He examined me in his usual flirty ways and my skin had learned to unconsciously creep at him. But it wasn't just his behaviour that did it, his whole being radiated a burning strangeness. Something lifeless and sinister.

"Just bored, dear, what's next? You want me to knit with the ladies tomorrow?" I asked, taking a sip from my drink.

He laughed. "No, I would not make you do that. You are better with a sword than a knitting pin. We are to return to Tenebrose tomorrow either way."

"My, the snow monsters in the mountains not liking your advances either?" I teased, faking a pout.

"At least you are," he said, and I halted my goblet midway before putting it down.

"Am I?" I raised my eyebrows, crossing my arms and leaning back. "Are you?"

His features dropped for a moment and he studied me slowly, different from usual. "If you are patient enough you might hear that answer."

Ugh. No, thank you, but why not now? I pulled my face in a teasing grin hoping to push on some hidden wounds. "Patient? Are you married? Is your wife sick? Waiting for her to die? Such a decent man, who would have thought." Taking my tray loaded with enough food for the hunk of Adriatian muscle waiting upstairs, I stood.

His face stilled as if my words really had poked at the centre of the target and he reached to grab my arm, stopping me. "We are leaving early tomorrow. Be down at the stables at dawn."

I leaned close to him. "You're burning, Demir." He pulled his hand away from me with a jerk. "Odd. Didn't you just come from outside?" I asked, flicking some snow from his shoulder. "Goodness, you're sizzling." *Must be all that delicious blood you're feeding on.*

"Good night, Snowlin," was all he said, before exiting the inn's diner like a slighted beast.

Pushing the door with my hip, I managed to enter the room without scalding myself with hot soup. Kilian was not there, the bed was still made, and few candles flickered about the room, creating massive shadows. The floor creaked from the bathing chambers and a half naked chunk of Adriatian flesh made its way towards me. I almost let out a low whistle at the sight in front of me. His shoulders were wide and stretched in hard muscle, six hills rose over his lean stomach that were now marred by three slashes and two deep lines traced down his hips pointing to a very delicate area that I almost traced before averting my gaze to put the food down to a table. The man had fainted on me and I refused to let him fade back to Adriata. In his condition, I wouldn't be surprised if he faded and lodged himself between a tree trunk.

I cleared my throat and turned to him. "Brought you food."

He eyed the tray and nodded in thanks before sitting on the edge of the bed, attempting to apply salve to his wounds.

"Eat before it gets cold." With that, I left to take a bath.

He had eaten his food when I returned and was rounding bandages across his wounds. In a sloppy, most male-like attempt at it.

Grabbing the salve, I kneeled in front of him, applying it gently to the wound on his skin. "You have not applied enough salve, the bandage will stick to your wounds, you idiot. Apply generously. Look, it's written on the bottle." I'd exchanged a gold circlet for it, this princess held no coin. This princess was actually poor if you thought about it.

"Stand, I don't like you kneeling in front of me," he ordered quietly.

I looked up at him. "I am sure that is up for discussion if I was doing something else." Leaning forward, I blew his wound to help the salve dry. That got me a pained groan from him. And the way his muscles twitched almost made me gloat with victory.

His hand slid to my neck before slipping through my hair and pulling my head back so I could look at him. And it was all it took for my thoughts to turn all shades of filthy.

"Don't fucking smile at me like that."

"How should I smile at you?"

"Not like you want to suck me off."

Batting my lashes and putting on an innocent smile I asked, "Better?"

I was too focused on my job at hand and startled when he hooked his hands under my shoulders and lifted me to his lap like I was a feather. "I give up," he rasped, pushing a strand away from my face and kissing my cheek. The way that silver stare bore on mine with glazing hunger made my heart pulse madly against my ribs.

"What?"

He rested his forehead on mine and let out a long sigh. "I give up. I will be just that. I will be just a fuck. I'll be your dirty secret."

Had I hit my head that hard? "You will? Why did you change your mind?"

His hands slipped to my waist, thumbs working in circles over my skin and my breath hitched. "Because I am desperate for you. Any piece of you." I was not sure if it was the caress or the words that spread electric heat over my spine. Whatever it was, it licked my body with shivers. "And I don't think I want to die before having you. I don't want to die without hearing you call my name while I come inside of you."

My toes might have curled a little from the image he painted in my head. I reached to rest my palms on his shoulders, my fingers skimming his muscles, unrestrained. "Do we add this to our deal?"

He chuckled, grazing my chin with his lips. "My wife is a rigorous businesswoman."

"Where do I sign?" I asked, leaning forward and planting a peck on the corner of his jaw then a few more down his neck.

He drew me closer, the move shifting me right over his hardened erection and my body floated with waves of delicious heat. "The things you do to me, Snow."

I swallowed hard and tried not to squirm on him. My core had caught fire and I missed his touch.

He weaved his fingers through my hair and just held me for a moment despite the way his body was fighting the urge to grind against mine. "Do you need me?"

I thought it was obvious. But he wanted reassurance. "I need you."

His hands moved further down on my body, over my arms, my waist and down my thighs where he tortured me with light touches until I began taking in short and sharp breaths. On the way back up, his fingers caught on my nightgown, pulling it up my body till it was over my head and on the ground. His eyes were on me when he leaned forward and took my nipple on his mouth and groaned around it. The vibration travelled all down my belly and straight between my legs where wetness began gliding.

He kissed his way up to my face while his strong hands kneaded and palmed my breasts, fingers playing with their swollen centres. He stilled for a moment, his lips resting not a hair away from mine. A silent question.

"You can kiss anywhere but my mouth," I said.

"Was our first kiss that terrible?"

The way his breath touched my lips shot more want in me than any kiss would have ever. "No one would want a repeat of that."

He grinned wide and cupped my face to kiss the bridge of my nose. "This is my spot anyway."

Every sensation in my body was erratic. No one...no one and nothing had made me feel this much with a touch alone, with how they looked at me, spoke to me, breathed near me.

"You will really fuck me?" This felt unreal.

He clamped my nipple between his thumb and forefinger, tugging and rolling the swollen nub before leaning in to suck on my neck. "No, not tonight at least. Tonight I will make sweet love to you." I gave him a hard smack on the shoulder and he chuckled, his fingers circled my breast, tracing its shape and I shuddered, arching onto the touch and seeking for more.

"Oh gods," I moaned when he bit down on it. Heat pooled on my lower stomach and I rolled my hips, searching for some relief for that ache below. The towel around his hips was the only barrier between us and it was torturous. "Kilian, please, I want you inside of me. Please, please." I was so ready for him.

He chuckled against my neck. "So polite," he drew out, his fingers softly descending down my back and over my bottom before they brushed between my legs, against the wetness gathering there. "Fuck, you're soaked, love." He brought his fingers to his mouth, licking all of them clean, one by one, and giving me a massive grin. "I missed your taste on my tongue." He pinched my jaw and probed my lips open with his thumb before sliding his tongue in my mouth.

Sweet hells.

I closed my lips around his tongue and tasted myself and him. "Please," I breathed. I was losing my mind.

He wrapped an arm around my waist and flipped us over on the bed so I laid on my back. He knelt between my legs, nudging my knees apart so I was sprawled before him and his eyes flashed, trailing slow over my naked body. I could tell all restraint was snapping from the way he breathed.

"I want to see your cock."

He chuckled. "I'm sure you do," he said, lowering his mouth at the apex of my thighs, kissing and sucking on that bundle of nerves till I was a puddle of sweat and moans and withering and whimpering—melting like liquid iron onto the sheets. His tongue licked a trail over my slit and hummed before thrusting it inside of me. He devoured me, his licks and kisses were not savouring like it had been that time, the man was hungry—mad with hunger.

My hips jerked, thrusting forward when he sunk two fingers inside of me, pumping in and out so torturously slow that I whined, almost to the brink of tears. "You idiot."

He left wet kisses on my inner thigh. "I have to get you ready for me, love, I don't want to hurt you. You're fucking tight."

My back arched against the bed when his teeth grazed the swollen nub that throbbed with nearing release. His fingers curled inside of me and picked a pace, blinding light flashed through my sight, and I put a hand over my mouth to drown the scream as climax rippled through and seized my body with shakes of fluttering pleasure.

His fingers pulled out and he smeared my come over my sex as he climbed over my body.

I opened my legs so he could sit between them, and my hands reached to touch his chest, muscles twitching under my touch and my gaze dropped between us, over the only thing keeping him clothed. He'd never let me touch him. I knew he was big since we'd slept close in Modr, but never felt him with my touch. How would he feel inside me?

My gaze jerked to his, the silver rings were drowned in shadows, they looked black. I slid my palm further down the ridges of his muscled stomach till it grazed the towel seam. Paying with the edge till he dropped his head down with a groan. "Snow," his chest caved with stuttering breaths. He grabbed my hand and pushed it further down, till my palm glided over the hard length of him.

I might have gasped a little as I tried to fist the base of his cock, fingers barely wrapping around him. He was silky smooth in my hand and so hard. And long. And thick. Would he fit inside of me?

He drew in a sharp breath, eyes dropping between us to watch as I rubbed him and smeared a bead of come leaking over his tip before he wrapped a hand around my wrist to stop me.

"I just want to feel you."

His chest moved fast. "You will feel me aplenty when I am inside of you."

A shiver trailed down my spine.

My whole body seized when he lowered his hips over mine, his cock pressing on my sex, and I rolled my hips searching for some friction. And he watched me, almost utterly fascinated as I panted, my body arching off the bed searching for his.

He trailed his fingers so delicately over the dip of my collarbone, the swells of my breast, the flat of my stomach and back up as if he was studying the stars—so intently and transfixed. "Say it again. Say my name again," he said, moving his hand over my hip and thigh to guide my leg over his back.

"Kilian."

The man groaned as if he was in pain. "Do you know how long I've waited for it—to hear you call me that again? Do you know how you've ruined me?" he asked, reaching between us. I sucked in a sharp breath when his cock nudged my opening. "Answer me."

"Yes." I knew.

He rubbed the tip along my slit, coating himself with my wetness and my mouth parted with a moan. "Look at you still ruining me."

"Please."

"I'm going to go slow."

"No. Hard."

He kissed my nose. "Thought you were going to scream and run from me when I showed you my cock. I am going to take that as a compliment and that you've never taken someone as big as me." There was no time for me to blush because he slid a small inch in, his hand tight on my thigh as if he was trying really hard to hold back. "So." A kiss on my cheek. "Very." Another on my brow. "Slow." He kissed the tip of my nose and whispered over my mouth, "Relax, my love. I'm barely in." Slowly, his cock buried a few more inches inside me. The fullness stretching me with a delicious sting, the pleasure beyond overwhelming. Because it was him. It was him. Just the knowledge that it was him inside of me sent a tremble all over my body.

"Fuck," he hissed, lowering to drop kissed on my cheek as my muscle twitched around him. "You feel so good, love."

He moved a little, and I bit my lip, trying to suppress a moan that would have been heard three floors down from the thin walls. My body grew warmer than it had ever been, lit inside like a match as he slowly thrust inside of me, burying a little bit deeper every time he entered me. "So do you. Ah, that feels so good," I murmured. His palms slid over my hip, the curve of my thigh, holding tight as he picked up a pace, sliding in and out of me tortuously slow until the sting turned to that curling sensation. "Gods, Kilian," I moaned, looking between us where he disappeared inside of me.

"You want to watch?"

I nodded.

He sat back on his knees, looking down on me spread out before him, his cock glistening as it slid in and out me. And then he fucked me. His hands held my hips sturdy as he pounded hard inside of me—relentlessly.

My head dropped back, and I'd clutched the sheets so tight that my nails were ripping through them. His hips thundered against mine, the sounds of our bodies meeting one another grew louder and harsher, my skin heating and turning red where we joined.

Kilian Castemont was not gentle. Kilian Castemont didn't do gentle. No. The man fucked.

His grip on my hips was bruising as he plunged in and out of me with such force the bed shook on its hinges. Too late to worry about my moans.

He bent down at me, slowing a little as he trailed a hand from my hip to my breasts, playing with their hardened centre, kneading and squeezing before trailing that hand to wrap around my neck. The pressure, the pleasure, the warmth in my belly made my eyes roll back and I moaned. "Kilian, shit."

"I knew you could take me," he whispered over my mouth. "I knew you would take me so well." His free hand slid down my belly to my core and I jerked a little when he rubbed the pad of his finger over the sensitive flesh. The pleasure was blinding. Every part of my body curled from the fluttering sensation. I didn't know if I was breathing or whimpering or moaning because whatever was leaving my mouth was drowned by the sounds of his body meeting mine, the hinges shaking and the bed frame rocking against the wooden floor. "Come for me, love. Soak my cock. Come all over my cock."

I grabbed onto his back, anything to hold, nails raking down his muscular spine as his thrusts grew punishing, faster, harder. And I couldn't think or see or breathe, nearly delirious as my climax crashed hard like an angry sea against rock.

"Fuck, I love that sound." He didn't stop. Gripping on the head board above me, he held on tight as he rammed his cock inside of me, prolonging my release and chasing another.

His brows bunch a little, making the little space between them wrinkle and his mouth parted just slightly. His eyes bore into mine and he let out a small, pained groan before I felt him spill inside of me.

His thrust turned gentle and unhurried as he left soft pecks all over my face. "That's my girl," he murmured, kissing both my cheeks, sinking his teeth gently on my skin and tugging playfully. "Pretty and blushing."

I could swear my vision had gone blurry for a few seconds as he held me against him to gather my breath.

What had we done?

I knew the signs of addiction. The rush to have more. The feeling of always wanting more. To crave it every moment of the day.

Kilian Henrik Castemont had just become my new addiction.

He breathed hard and so did I. We stood there, forehead to forehead for a long while.

He pulled out of me and rose to his haunches, staring down at me, his muscled chest still rising and falling rapidly. And there it was. That little smile that had me look away like a shy schoolgirl. "I want you every day like this. On my bed." His fingers circled my swollen sex and I flinched. "Fucked red and raw and stuffed with my come."

Chills ran through me.

With one last look at me, he stood and headed to the bathroom, and I got a full peep of his backside.

Gloriously naked and carved like a god, he came back holding a damp cloth. Sitting on my side, he propped my legs apart. I winced a little at the friction of the cloth against my skin and he stilled. "Sore?"

"A little."

He petted my thigh and left a kiss on my knee. "I'm sorry, love."

"I'm not."

He dug his teeth on his bottom lip as if to hold back a smile and continued to wipe the mess he'd made.

The mess. Oh gods. "Do you take the potion?"

He bent down and kissed my belly. "Yes. I'd like for the mother of my children not to hate me first before I have them. And besides, unless you want us to hurry, I'd like to have you for myself for a bit."

I kicked his shoulder with a foot. "Not funny."

He chuckled, grabbing onto my foot and kissing my ankle, tongue swirling over my flesh, and my core heated again. "It was a little."

After dressing me and wrapping us with a blanket, we laid silently on the bed, my cheek pressed to his warm shoulder rising and falling with still rapid breaths. Did we just do that? I would have done a little dance of victory if I wasn't laying on him.

"You said that you'd make sweet love to me," I croaked in the ear-piercing silence.

His hand worked through my hair, pulling it aside from my face. "That I did."

My head jerked up. He looked confused, his brow slowly raising in question. "What?"

I swallowed hard imagining his definition of fucking if this was sweet love. "Nothing." My fingers brushed a slash on his ribs. "How did you get this one?"

Again, another morning I woke up with another thing to hate. There was so much of it lately, but the blissfulness of waking pressed to his warm body was one I shouldn't need to try so hard to hate. Because I should already hate it.

I wished the dull throb between my legs, the violet marks all over me and the soreness of my thighs were the only remnants of last night, but I felt him everywhere. Mostly where I didn't need him to be—in my head.

Pushing my upper body up, I leaned on my forearms and stared at his sleeping face. That permanent starkness etched even in this form. Finding the beautiful in things was something I always struggled with, yet I found him the most beautiful.

He cracked his eyes open and shifted slightly under me. "Morning, love."

"I didn't hurt you last night." I'd laid on him all night long, slept without any nightmares, not waking once and without hurting him.

He ran a lazy hand over my naked spine. "You didn't. Did I?"

"It's a pain that I like."

He stilled with panic. "Love."

"Not like that, Kilian. It feels like you're still inside of me." Resting my chin on his chest, I looked up at him. Just looked. And he too looked back at me. While I studied him in this new form of bliss and calm, he only looked at me still in what I could gather to be disbelief.

Slowly, a little smile tugged on his lips. Lips that had kissed every inch of me. "If you keep staring at me like that I will have to damn your mission and take you back with me," he said, voice gravelly with sleep. It's vibrations sending a shiver trickling on my skin.

I huffed. "You think too highly of yourself, Adriatian."

A yelp left my mouth when he flipped me under him. Lowering to kiss my neck, he whispered over my skin, "Tired of me yet?" He ran his knuckles over the side of my body, leaving a trail of gentle fire that scorched my skin deliciously. My breath caught when his fingers circled over my hip and then between my legs. His lips pulled in a smile over my ear, while he traced a single finger over my sex and found me as he had expected—wet and wanting to be touched again. "I guess not."

I jumped a little when he slapped between my legs, and then drowned a whine when he pushed away from me. Panting half from frustration and half from annoyance, I wrapped the bedsheet around me and stood after him. "Where are you going?"

He glanced back at me as he began dressing. "It's dawn, they must be at the stables by now. Unless you've changed your mind and are coming with me."

I imagined all the manners of how I could suffocate him. Hands around his neck would be too arousing for me so I decided that I'd have to hide his pretty face behind a pillow.

Suddenly, he laughed, and when he turned to fully face me, a massive grin stretched over his deadly handsome face. Cupping my face, he placed a kiss on my forehead. "Plenty of time when we are not running out of it."

"You did this on purpose."

He frowned all so innocently. "What exactly?"

"Fucked me so I would want to come with you."

He kissed the tip of my nose. "Made love to you. And, did it work?"

With disrelish, I started dressing. "A fair try." Unfair really.

"Fair try, huh?" With that, he walked to the bathroom and left me to simmer on my own nerves.

We were silently washing our faces side by side when he turned to me and said, "Ah, let that general touch you again and I will cut his wrists to damn your whole damned plan."

"You're in no place to make such demands, Kilian."

He gripped my chin, bringing his face close to mine. "Are you sure about that?"

I gulped. "Yes."

He nodded. "Glad to see you're feeling well enough to lie again."

Heavy footsteps and chatter trickled from outside signalling my squadron was ready to leave. Kilian helped me put my jacket on, buttoning it, tidying my sleeves, smoothing the sides. And lastly, adjusting my remaining circlet to stand straight. "Why are you all red for?" he asked, kneeling to help my legs through my britches and then push my feet through socks and then boots.

"Why are you dressing me?"

After lacing my boots neatly, he stood to his full height, towering over me. "Because I didn't want to leave just yet."

"Go, Kilian."

"Anything else? Hair clips or pins you need me to tie your hair with?"

I rolled my eyes. "Leave."

He cupped the side of my head and lowered to press a kiss to my cheek. A very long one. "Goodbye, my love," he murmured to my ear before fading away.

"Goodbye."

Demir narrowed his angry viridescent gaze on me, his nostrils flaring as if he was sniffing the air. "You have another scent on you."

I scoffed. "Good morning to you, too, General."

"Why do you have a male's scent on you?"

Trying to hide the panic that question rang in me, I donned a grin. "What are you, a dog? And I do have another *male's* scent on me. Who I bring to my bed is none of your concern."

He mounted his flaring brown and black spotted horse with a look of disdain on his usually ever pleased face. He was slowly slipping. "It is a concern. You are my Princess and I serve your father."

"It is certainly vital for him to know who his daughter brings to her bed, you must rush ahead, Demir, tell him how I was fucked just like all your little expeditions up north," I retorted, mounting my horse and nudging to trot ahead of the squadron.

Half way to Tenebrose, a soldier rode towards us as Demir's team and mine made a halt.

"Messenger," he yelled.

All of the squadron turned to curiously eye one another at the halt. Why was a messenger sent to us? Did father want Demir back on the mountains? Had they noticed something after Kilian and I had gotten the sceptre?

The soldier brought out a piece of paper from his satchel, pointing it to me. "A letter for Her Highness from Captain Elias Venzor," he said, handing it to me.

What was the fool thinking, making our exchange so public? What could have not waited that he had to send a messenger and in front of Demir at that?

The young general was staring at me with an arrogant smirk. "Seeking more consolation or is it strictly business with the soon to be brother-in-law?" he asked, angrily. His reaction somewhat pleased me, my old flirting skills were not all so rusty after all, he seemed to have truly taken a liking to me. However, father would be aware of my communications with Elias, who was soon to be very hardly punched on his perfect jaw.

I opened the letter. One short sentence was written across and signed by Elias Venzor.

Meet me at the Bear tavern in the north of Tenebrose city, at once.

I studied the piece of paper back and forth as if more writing was to suddenly show up. Pearl paper. Neat writing. Elias. At once?

I handed the piece of ridiculous paper to Demir, who read it before narrowing his eyes at me. "Permission not granted."

"I outrank you, General. Remember that this pretty face is a Princess." Bowing my head, I greeted farewell and charged forward to meet the eager fool who had sent the letter.

The city was unusually quiet and so was the tavern who had always boomed with noise and music.

"Hello?" I called as I entered a completely quiet, empty and dark tavern. There was not a soul inside. Sigh. I had just entered a very poorly thought through trap. An amateur had me in his grip, my condolences were soon in order to the poor soul. A presence behind me tickled my senses and I stilled as a cloth covered my mouth and a sack fell over my head.

How many times could one princess be kidnapped?

―――――◆◇◆―――――

My head had dropped to the side, I cringed at the pain across my sore neck. I had been tied to a chair so tight that droplets of blood dripped from my wrists, every movement and friction sent a shooting pain up my arms. Barley, wheat and old pine wood had scented the dusty room that was coating my airways, it smelled of a storage room. Before I could let my imagination take course, the sack was pulled back from my head exposing my sore eyes to the bright room. A storage room as I had concluded, empty as blitzes of sunlight flinted onto the large hollow room. The wood floor cracked as a tall lanky figure stepped from behind me into view.

Reuben took a seat in a chair afront me, crossing his arms and legs satisfied at his achievement. Grinning ear to ear, his blue eyes burned with a sickening flame of vileness, eager to take what he wanted from me. Retribution.

This idiot was going to ruin my plan.

I let out a short laugh and his smile finally dropped. "Step one: demand of the kidnaped. I can tell you are new to this, but own to your actions. As painful as the torture of being stared at by you is, it is not entirely deadly."

He jolted up and smacked me fiercely across my face, his ring scrapped and drew blood from my lip. The metallic taste of blood felt electric, I could fry this radish in a fraction of a second. However, he had just given me a brilliant idea. A better plan.

He sat back, my blood coating his fingers. "Till the end a feral mare, just like your mother,"

My jaw locked. "Oh, Reuben, you are stepping on very pungent shit right now."

"Let me not remind you of the remaining dead breed of yours. Don't worry, you will join them when I have had the rest of my fun with you." He stood to retrieve a clear bottle of a red potion. "Where has he sent my mother?" he demanded.

"To her rat hole?" He struck me again. This one I had to give to him, it really stung. I spat blood at his feet. But I needed it to sting more. "Mommy left you without a tit to suck on? Aw, who's powdering your arse now?"

"You will answer me," he threatened, striking me again.

"Or what?" I pushed, grinning. *Come one, hit me harder.* "Will you run to daddy dearest or hit me again, hm?" A terrible satisfied laugh left my throat—he was so very dead.

His nose flared, an angry red cringe twitched and patched in his horrendous yellow face as he twisted the cap of the bottle open, pouring half the liquid to my arm. The moment the red potion touched the skin of my arm, screams of pain erupted from my throat. The liquid stuck to my skin, crawling all over and under my clothes, scorching my flesh with a branding burn.

I trembled, beads of sweat covered my body and my skin shivered from the pain that dug almost bone deep. I calmed my stuttering breaths, releasing a thin layer of chill above my skin, but it didn't subdue the pain—not the slightest. The potion was magic. Crafter magic.

Reuben laughed as he took a seat again. "Liquid fire. Dark Crafters really know their evil," he boasted, shaking the bottle with the rest of the red fluid. "This is how they burnt, right? Siblings should share everything, even pain. Feel how your rotted breed burnt, taste the feel of it before you taste the bite of my steel, you whore."

"Reuben, Reuben," I muttered breathless, shaking my head, "You are in for a treat, dear. Better clutch that crown tight, who knows I might bring Eren back just for the sake of it, and I am not speaking from the dead."

His face fell just a little, but enough to recognise that fear. The fear of knowledge. The half breed knew. "Your brother is dead. Has the pain reached that far up your head?"

"Is he though?"

He faltered. "What game are you playing?"

"My favourite game of taunt or truth. It seems you're hiding something."

Another wave of anger flared in him as he stood, unbottling the cap of the liquid fire.

I rolled my eyes up at him, a wicked smile spreading wide as electricity floated about the room and he took a startled step back.

The door of the storage room burst open. Quickly, I shifted my magic shut as Demir and Elias broke inside the room, wide eyed and gasping for air. They assessed the room, the blood on my face and the burn marks on my hand and arm, their expression growing livid before they unsheathed both their swords towards Reuben who in Reuben fashion charged in a run before being plunged down by a very inhumanly agile Demir.

Elias quickly came to my aid, untying me. "What did he do to you, Snow, why did you let this happen?" he murmured, examining the burns.

Soldiers broke about in the room, seizing Rueben as the young general kneeled in front of me wiping the bloodied mess away, tucking my sweat matted hair behind my ear.

Reuben stood, shaking and furiously pulling between the two soldiers that were holding him. His face had reddened, veins had made their ways to the surface as he shook like a rabid animal. "I will have your blood one day, Snowlin!"

I let out a loud wicked laugh and strode up to him. Knocking my forehead right in his face and enjoying the sight of blood splattering his face. "Say that again, Reuben, it sounded real profound."

His rage broke him free and he charged towards me again, but Demir moved quickly, nailing a punch in his fragile face that had probably never even felt the pain of a slap before. Reuben landed with a thud on the wooden floor.

Ouch.

"No honour among the wicked, ey?" I teased, as the young general turned wearing a pinched frustrated expression towards me.

"No, not when he has painted your beautiful face like that."

Elias's brows hiked to his hairline at that statement. He nailed his piercing gaze on me and whispered only for me to hear, "I thought you were smarter than to fall for this, was I wrong?"

No, he was not wrong, but he was very right at the same time. Great ideas are born amidst very compromising situations, and I was going to enjoy the unravelling of this plentifully. "Did I?" I asked, leaning back in the chair. "Fall for this?"

He scoffed, shaking his head. "Thought so."

"You found me quicker than I had thought, how did you do it?"

It was Demir who answered, returning back inside the storage room, "I met Elias by the gates, he had not sent for you. Didn't even recognise the writing on the paper you left me. Your scent was everywhere around the tavern and all the way here."

"My, my. You *are* a dog,"

"Call it a gift—a blessing," he said as he poured water over my arm.

I rode with Elias who had been quietly observing the whole scene without commenting. Breaking my line of overly thinking the last twenty-four hours, he spoke silently behind me, "You are good, Snow."

"Which part exactly? If you are to stroke my ego, do it properly."

"All of it. It appears he is not immune to your charm either," he said, pointing his head in Demir's direction. "Though Kilian shan't be happy that another man called you beautiful so openly. Let alone when he finds out you didn't roll your eyes at him."

I threw my elbow back at the teasing mongrel. "Kilian? Since when are the two of you on a first name basis?" Since when had the Adriatian bastard managed to charm another on my side of the game?

"I respect him."

Respect?

When we arrived at the castle, father had been waiting for us. He'd gone completely red, not from the cold but from the tight anger flaring in waves around him. The moment Reuben's feet touched the ground, father struck him hard, making him leap back and onto the floor from the force.

Inclining my head down, I hid my giggles. This felt amazing. How I had craved his punishment for all that he had done to me and my siblings. And who better would hand them to him than his father dearest?

"Are you hurt, my child?" he asked, turning to me, in a tone full of worry that I had never heard before. I wanted to ignore the minute note of sincerity but somehow I couldn't. Some deep part of me—very deep part of me—wanted to acknowledge it.

He brought my hands up to examine the burns and huffed a heavy sigh.

A tear slicked down my cheek, then two. I hated this, with the strength of my life. The care that I had missed for twenty-two years of my life, only to receive it in the end when it no longer mattered. To receive it when I had his trust, when I had to prove who everyone and myself were to him—for me to be hurt by his indirect touch. But I had to endure it. For the sake of what I was about to do.

"He has hurt you," he said, reaching to wipe away my tears, before gathering me in an embrace. For a second, like I had never done before, I allowed myself to soak in his warmth—my father's skin creeping warmth. I allowed myself to feel what I should have felt for my father all the years of torment I have received because of him. I took a deep breath, my body tightened in a flaming rage that had made me want to freeze his heart and crush it to a thousand shards. Two layers of barriers kept me from committing to my thoughts, but once they were down, he was not going to have my mercy. I would not freeze his heart—I would carve it out and feed it to him. The ultimate evil—he stood over me, his filth and stench spread all over the continent.

He let go of me. "He will be punished for what he has done, worry not," he said, watching Reuben fighting and writhing between the hold of soldiers.

The half breed's eyes had gone wide with wild hate and anger. Somehow, he managed to break free from the soldiers and came toward us. "No, you cannot trust her, father. I did it for us. Look what she has done since she has returned. Our family was fine till she came back. Till her rotten kind came here again, like her mother, whores of Olympian blood!" he spat.

Oooh, good one, Reub.

My father's features smoothed to a terrifying calm and Reuben began choking and coughing. This time it was not my doing, father had grasped him till he dropped to the ground, his hands running over his throat as he struggled to breathe.

I placed a hand on my father's arm, pulling his attention to me. "Let him go, father, he is harmless and his words pitiful if not worthless. He was begging for his mother, maybe you ought to send him her way," I said, and turned to head towards my chambers before I changed my mind and enjoyed watching my father choke the radish to his death. For now, I needed him alive.

My feet dragged painfully over the snow-soaked ground, my skin had set on fire and the cold around me did nothing to soothe it.

Demir came to my side. "Let me carry you to your chambers," he offered. The only one that was ever allowed to do that from the day he had carried me from the winter gardens would be Kilian—he would have also known what to say to soothe me out of my cluttered thoughts, he always had the right words to calm me out of them.

"I want to walk."

"You left that letter with me purposefully, you knew it had been a trap," he continued after some long silence.

"Yes," I admitted. "Elias would never write to me, let alone one of the finest quality of paper that only my father uses. Did you think that stitched writing belonged to a man who was raised as a soldier since a child? Only an idiot would underestimate me and begin a plan like that. The execution of it was just as short-sold. It was either Reuben or one with balls looser than that wimp."

He halted, turning to me. "But he got to hurt you."

I let out a tired giggle. "Small price to pay for the satisfaction it gave me."

Demir lifted his hand, turning my face to examine the cut on my lip. "Be careful, Princess, when you sift this much snow you make mounds behind. What will you do once you want to return and they are on your way?"

I pulled my head away from his strange touch. He always pretended he had everything on me, as if he could read me. There was none with that skill but the silver eyed snake. "Climb, melt, pierce through, part in half, fly over. I have lived a life that has forced me to dig holes and pile rocks with my every decision. Once you are accustomed to the suffering, you master the pain, Demir."

"Why do you put yourself through it still, if you are so versed in it?"

I moved down the corridor and he followed closely behind me. "Force of habit, I suppose."

He laughed. "Vengeance is not a habit. And is it truly vengeance if you hurt yourself in the process?"

This time I halted, turning to face him. "Did you truly get hurt if you have achieved it in the end? Everything you do, even breathing, requires effort."

His mouth pulled to a strange smirk. "We are more alike than you think, Snowlin."

My eyebrows rose at his words. "And who are you to avenge?"

He leaned close to me, his green eyes unnaturally bright all of a sudden. "The gods," he said, pointing above us.

I let out a sardonic laugh. "How have they wronged you more than they have wronged the rest of us?"

"In many more ways you know. I don't hand secrets that easily, your pretty Highness." He threw me a wink before turning around to leave. He was something I could not quite understand. Strangely skilled but not an Aura, my father's general and his trusted dog—a dog that was neither respectful nor scared of him which confused me further.

CHAPTER TWENTY-SIX

Lux

Kilian

It had been four days since I'd had Snow in my arms. Four days since the night I couldn't get out of my head. And four days too long for me to start thinking I'd imagined it all.

Visha had almost dragged me to her quarters to tend to my wounds which had now almost fully healed on the outside with the help of Cora Vayr. She'd insisted on a daily visit to Theros because Snow had sent word to her privately before she'd left—with a polite threat attached to it. Thankfully, the Sun Queen understood Snow's mechanisms and found humour in her violence.

"This is entirely unnecessary, I'm feeling much better," I insisted, unbuttoning my shirt.

Visha silently handed me a letter, not even bothering to say anything. It was how she had always been since she was young. I don't think she even realised how much she resembled her mother down to every mannerism.

Make sure he sees you every day, my spies are noting all of our moves. Fail me and I will knit myself a scarf with those red locks of yours. –Sincerely, your beloved queen.

"She is delightful as poison, isn't she?" Visha said, folding the letter back between her grimoire.

"It just happens that poison is my favourite taste."

"You both make me sick, and I intend to keep my hair," she said, completely stern, making me chuckle. "Don't laugh, Your Majesty, I know her better than you. She has done worse to others. At least she didn't threaten to turn my skin to leather stools like that poor unfortunate soul a few years back. Now lay back."

Oryn rumbled with laughter from where he had sat in a small corner, perusing and studying all sorts of vials laid before him. He was adjusting well in Olympia. After he'd gained some weight, lost the beard, the overgrown hair, and dressed properly, he looked like the man of his worth.

The cold marble bit on my skin as I laid to face the ceiling. "What are those marks?" I asked, pointing upward. Burnt lines marked the obsidian stone ceiling that had broken in places.

Visha glanced up. "Snow's attempts to be freed from the seal. When it opens even just the slightest, I have to close it, but it resists. Her magic is like its own form. Its own creature."

"How often has it broken?"

Oryn's attention rose to us again and he listened intently.

"Last time was after the Isjordian battle. But not enough to do any damage. There hasn't been any instance when she has lost true control of it, if that is what you are thinking."

It wasn't what I was thinking. Did it hurt her, when it broke? Did it hurt her like that day when we fought the *Ybris*?

"It hurts her," Oryn said, probably having read me. "There is nothing without pain. Nothing without cost. And I think you better than anyone know that, my king."

The adept Crafter swirled a bunch of burning incense that smelled rottenly sour over my wound. "Your magic has trapped some of the beast's essence. I've extracted most of it," she said, bringing a small flask and bottling some of the white smoke. "I might be able to put a trace craft on this thing and chase it."

"Can we keep this between us?" I asked, standing to put my clothes back on. "If Snow thinks she can hunt it, she will hunt it."

The Crafter seemed to not understand my point because she blinked blankly. "That was the point of the trace craft."

"Visha, I'm starting to think you have something against my wife by aiding her get in the most dangerous situations."

"Don't underestimate her. Her capabilities are beyond any of our understanding."

"Is that why you left your mother? To help Snow find and push these capabilities of hers?"

Oryn lifted his head up from his small workstation and then ducked it back down not a moment later. He knew something. But I wasn't sure if *we* were meant to know. I'd learnt in my years studying the Celesteel blessed to never question their silence and never poke it—it was a beast better not roused.

Visha went to the cabinets, placing the white smoke flask beside a few others. "You know very well why I left Eldmoor."

I did. To outrun her fate. The fate that was sealed and pursued her since the beginning of her ancestors. The fate of the 103rd Grand Maiden, the one promised to the 7th Prince of hells, Son of Celesteel and Plantae. The bargain that the 3rd Grand Maiden had struck with hells so she could bring her own daughter back. Among seven sacrifices she'd given to each gate of hell, this had been the last one. A bride.

Still, it didn't justify why it was Snow who she had picked to hide behind. Any king or queen would have taken her as their Crafter in a breath. "Funny how you ended up right on Snow's side. Funny how you crossed a whole deadly mist to be beside Snow where you could have gone anywhere."

"There was no craft involved in my crossing, the *zgahna* let me."

"Why would the *zgahna* let you through?"

"It called to me on one of my visions. The same vision I saw a white flaming woman with grand gold-streaked wings and Snow facing it. It asked me to guide the Elding Queen to her destiny."

I stopped fiddling with the sleeve buttons and looked up at her. "A vague reason for such a strong Crafter like yourself. You know your visions are implausible and most of the time a game of your own magic. A test."

She shook her head lightly. "Not to the future Grand Maiden. My visions have never failed me. I saw you get injured in Hanai, I also saw your trip to Oryn Duncan, the man my uncle modelled the seals after. I do not tell what I foresee for I am cursed to change the course of fate if I do. Tampering with fate means tampering with gods and what they have planned. Though many brace for the consequences, I have to admit, I am not brave enough."

"That I can attest to," Oryn mumbled.

"Visha, are you saying the guardian will be woken?"

"No, for that I am not sure, that part of the future must still be in the writing. I only know that Snow will have to face her one way or another." She reached onto a shelf and pulled a tray of colourful stones. "The trace spell for the Skygard siblings is finished." Picking a ruby one out of the bunch, she handed it to me. "Hand this to Nia since she is heading to Eldmoor this afternoon, I will have another one ready when you return to use in Adriata."

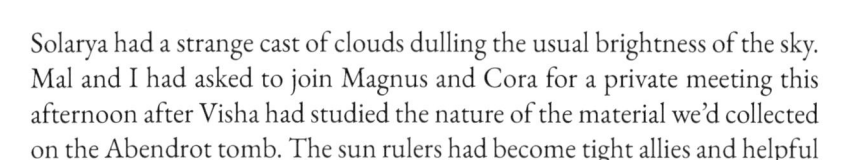

Solarya had a strange cast of clouds dulling the usual brightness of the sky. Mal and I had asked to join Magnus and Cora for a private meeting this afternoon after Visha had studied the nature of the material we'd collected on the Abendrot tomb. The sun rulers had become tight allies and helpful ones, too. They deserved to be kept up to date with everything.

"What is the cause of this bliss of yours? It's giving me allergies," Mal said, flinging a hand in the air as if to push my shadows aside.

"What is the cause of any of my bliss?"

"I'd like to say that it is I, your most loving brother, but then there is a certain dark head that comes to mind."

My mouth pulled to a smile. "There is."

"Don't be creepy."

"How am I creepy?"

"Smiling to yourself and all."

"I thought you said I look happy."

"Now you're just being creepy."

Small footsteps interrupted our conversation and we turned to the sound. A petite blond woman came to view, with eyes of yellow brown and a pale skin tinted red by the sun. She didn't wear the attire of Solarya but rather one I'd grown accustomed to seeing in Isjord. Bright colours, tight laces and puffy skirts.

"Heard Magnus had made foreign friendships," she said boredly. There was curiosity in her shadows different from the blankness in her features. "To think that it was the Night King was never anyone's guess. How is my niece?"

Eleonor Krigborn. The youngest Krigborn royal. "I'm not sure. You would know better. Your brother knows the way in my lands rather well."

She raised a hand to cover her laugh. "No hard feelings, I suppose. And in all fairness you were done a favour. She would have drained the soul out of you."

"I like to think of it as that, too," I easily lied.

Her attention perked a little and then travelled all over me. "You should join my husband and I for dinner one night."

"I think that would be an excellent idea."

Her brows rose in surprise as if she hadn't just offered it herself. "Yes, well, let us know when."

"Tonight," I said, and Mal turned to stare at me. "Since my time is limited and I am already here for the day."

Eleonor blinked wildly. "Tonight? Oh, tonight. Of course. I will have a servant sent here to direct you to our home in White Bridge."

"Excellent."

She left more confused than when she came.

"What on the hell's hot coals were you thinking?" Mal asked.

I dug onto my pocket to reach for the source of my madness and fished out the warm rock that had not stopped buzzing in the presence of Eleonor Krigborn.

The red ruby glowed bright and still vibrated on my hand, though less and less till it came to a stop. "It's the tracing craft Visha placed on Snow's siblings. I was meant to hand it to Nia before we came, but she'd left for Eldmoor already."

Mal took the ruby in his hand and raised it in the air, waving it around a couple of times. "Are you telling me this thing detected something?"

"Yes, when Eleonor came."

"White Bridge," Mal said in realisation. "They are in White bridge. It only makes sense for Aryan Krigborn to bring them there. She mans the island, and her husband has probably served as Silas's spy countless times. It all makes sense."

"Possibly. There is one way to find out. Tonight."

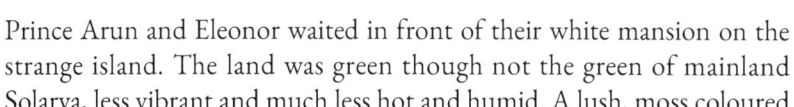

Prince Arun and Eleonor waited in front of their white mansion on the strange island. The land was green though not the green of mainland Solarya, less vibrant and much less hot and humid. A lush, moss coloured roof of trees was what the eye caught mostly on all sides of the horizon that weren't water. The white mansion of the Vayr residency was the only discrepancy in the scenery.

Tension and discomfort bled between the two hosts as they greeted and welcomed us inside.

The stone buzzed in my pocket and the heat radiating from it almost tore a hole through my clothing. We were close. But how close?

"It is much cooler in White Bridge compared to mainland Solarya," Mal commented as we sat down on a veranda overlooking the Hollow Sea. Dinner was laid out for us with all sorts of delicacies. Eleonor had dished out the best she could find considering the only thing not gilded was the actual food.

"We are closer to the Winter kingdom," Arun said, glancing at his wife. "Also, this part of Solarya was not entirely blessed by Cyra and her warmth. Most occupants are also pagan. They pray to some of their own beliefs of Cyra, not to the holy script." He waved a fork in the air. "You know how that goes down with the gods and heavens."

I leaned onto the seat. "And who do they exactly bow to?"

Arun's fork stopped midway to his mouth. "Father, of course."

I turn to glance at the sentries surrounding his property. "Yet no Solaryan guards." The stink of Verglaser magic was more than obvious. An odd choice of guard. But then, was it really?

Arun's features sharpened and he cut his food a little harder than necessary. "I like to keep a personal guard around my house."

"Of course," I said.

"Your grounds are lovely," Mal commented awkwardly, giving Eleonor a wide charming grin. "I presume the lady of the house is to congratulate on the decor."

Eleonor smiled at my brother. "I enjoy looking after the grounds, it gives me something to do."

"No children?" I asked.

The two wore their emotions in the open, not even a sliver of need for me to read their shadows.

"No," Arun said. "No children. We are unable to have any."

The only thing I couldn't grasp was the severity of their reaction. "I'm sure there are many children out there that need a family, love and care—if you wish to have any," I said.

Eleonor's mouth curled up a bit in distaste. "I will not raise what is not mine. Children are not stray dogs to house and bathe and…pet."

Good. I'd wish it upon no child to have a mother like such.

"Indeed," Mal said, stepping hard on my foot. "They are not."

Apparently I was glaring at the woman.

"How did you come to do business with my father?" Arun asked and laughed. "Almost slipped my mind, it was the first thing I wanted to know."

"Common interests," I said, folding my cutlery on the plate. "After the Isjordian attack it was clear Silas had no intention of submitting to the agreement, so I needed to make another."

Arun blinked with surprise. "All the way through to Solarya?"

"You're suggesting I rather make a silk and spice trade with the eudemons instead since we share territory?"

The Vayr couple laughed uncomfortably. It was obvious the two didn't have many social interactions between these walls because they wore their emotions like a fresh haircut—nice and trim. "Of course not," Arun said, waving a hand. "Solarya has gained a strong ally in these challenging times, we are thankful."

"The sunset falls lovely on the pond," Mal commented again.

"It does," Eleonor agreed. "It looks even more captivating when it falls over the lake behind our premises."

"I'd love to see such a sight," Mal said with a grin and throwing my wife's aunt a wink.

A bloody wink. Gods. And the woman blushed ten shades brighter than the salmon before us.

I glanced at Arun, hoping he missed the odd interaction, but he was entirely too entranced by his green beans.

Eleonor cleared her throat and turned to her inattentive husband. "Sweetness, shall we give our guests a tour of the premises. It would be a shame if they leave without seeing the archway you built near the lake not long ago."

The Sun Prince nodded. "Whenever you wish."

"Thank you for the food," Mal offered, standing. "Ready now, before the sun disappears."

Arun was still chewing when he looked up, confused at my brother's eagerness. He swallowed and stood, too, wiping his hands on a table towel. "Let us then."

The golden sun was perfectly cut in the centre as it sank down the Hollow Sea. There was a mild chill breeze and a faint trickle of locusts still chirring in the distance as we followed the walkway through the lightly beige tinted grass. Since we'd left the veranda, the obsidian in my pocket had almost burned a hole through my wools.

Now, if I could get Arun and Eleonor not to pay attention for a small minute so I could spell the ground of White Bridge to direct us to them.

As if reading my mind, Mal swung an arm over Arun's neck, startling him. "Architecture, huh? I fancy myself as a bit of an architecture fanatic." My brother turned around to me, forcing Arun to do the same as he was still holding him on a tight head lock. "Kilian on the other hand has a fancy for flowers." He patted Arun's shoulder. "You've got some stunning gardens, too, Your Highness. Go peruse, brother, I am afraid he and I have a lot to discuss. About all this architecture."

Eleonor stepped to speak, but my brother swung his other free hand over her shoulder, pulling the couple tightly to him and steering them further in the thicket of sun burnt shrubbery. He kept jabbering about arches and angles the whole way until they disappeared from sight.

Backing myself into the direction of a forest mass just across a pond bridge, I fished out the obsidian that was vibrating and pulsing with heat.

Movement still sounded close to me, and I opened a fraction of magic, sending faint tendrils of darkness travelling through the forest onto a target, invading their mind with emptiness.

The ground sang when I placed the obsidian down. "*Moonus.*" *Show.* Once the rock began to glow at the call of magic, I smashed the heel of my foot down on it, sending it to splinter to shards. A vortex of red swirled around the spot and grass scorched underneath, forming the shape of a rune. The cross symbol with the arrowhead meaning *here.* The magic had been absorbed by the earth and would act as a compass to direct us to find them with some of Visha's other tricks.

Thora and Eren Skygard were alive. They were alive and on Whitebridge Island.

Snow…I had to tell Snow.

"Brother," Mal shouted as he chittered and laughed with the two Solaryan royals. "Have you lost your path?"

Fishing out a dagger from my baldric, I dug it into the ground, ruining the rune mark.

"Here," I said, slowly approaching them. Arun looked confused and annoyed, but Eleonor was trickling with shades of suspicion. "Didn't wish to offend you by relieving myself into your roses. If you've quenched your fancy of architecture, brother, shall we head for return?"

Mal sighed with feigned disappointment. "I'm afraid so. But this was the loveliest time I've spent in a while."

"Do visit again," Arun said as he and Eleonor walked us to the boat docked at the private bay facing the house. "If this alliance persists, we are to see one another more often. Perhaps, share more than our fancy of architecture. A trade or two?"

"Definitely," Mal said, tapping his shoulder again and bowing to Eleonor shortly before leaving toward the boat.

I bowed my head to the two of them. "I thank you for your invitation and hospitality."

My brother paced back and forth on the deck, stopping in his tracks when he saw me. "Tell me all."

"Let's go get my wife."

CHAPTER TWENTY-SEVEN

Opacus

Snowlin

Ever since we'd departed the Islines, the air had shifted. A zap of pinching electricity hovered thickly in the air constantly raising my hackles. There was something wrong with the way Demir regarded me, the way his movements felt more calculated and guarded, the spurious tight smiles he gave me from time to time and the last calculating look he greeted me goodbye with. It almost had me convinced that he knew of what happened and that I had the sceptre piece. If Cai were here, he'd tell me I was overthinking it, but he was not and there was a fat chance I wasn't bordering on paranoia.

A couple of days had passed since father had sent Reuben gods knew where. But that had been the same number of days since I'd last left the castle grounds. Not once had I felt the beast's presence, not anywhere I'd looked. Nissa had told me that Moregan's troops had travelled back north, and I was starting to believe the general might be closely related to the beast—perhaps was the beast itself. I'd met Melanthe here and there in passing, no words had been spoken but she regarded me rather curiously now.

An hour ago, Nissa had dropped off my dress for father's eightieth anniversary ball that was to take place tonight. Eighty years of a plagued realm.

"The unblessed arrived last night, Your Highness. The three island Princes and an emissary from Comnhall," Nissa murmured while she secured my corset. "The servants say your father met the Princes privately right after they'd settled. Alone. With no other court members in presence."

"It is odd, the unblessed have never been invited to such gatherings before. My father would have rather chewed his foot."

"Many were surprised, too," she said quietly, helping me fit myself into the murky sapphire dress that was made for the body of a fourteen-year-old and washed my complexion. This was my role now, the devoted daughter and Winter Princess. Couldn't say it was my best played act, but I was managing.

Nissa combed my hair, pinning a few dazzling diamonds here and there to match the colour of the fabric. I squared my shoulders even though the corset dug into my ribs each time I did so and huffed out a sigh. Demir—he was my primary target tonight. I had to get him to speak.

"Any news on where they have taken the half breed?"

She leaned in a little. "Kitchen staff were saying that the fishermen had seen him being loaded up on a ship going toward the unblessed Isles. It is thought that the king has sent the consort back to her ex-husband's family. Perhaps he has sent your half-brother there, too."

That made me smile. "Perhaps. Perhaps unfortunate weather will find his way and his ship won't make it there at all." I stood, facing Nissa. "Perhaps it will be a tragedy."

She blinked, seemingly confused.

Quickly, I scribbled a note and placed it inside an envelope before giving it to her. "Make sure to hand this to the Lord of Kirkwall or Lord of Brogmere. They will know what to do. They will also help you leave Isjord."

The servant nodded, looking afraid. "Thank you for everything, Your Highness. I wish you well."

"Goodbye, Nissa," I said. "I hope you find luck with the future you are chasing."

Two guards trailed behind me as usual as I made my way to the ballroom. The string music floating down the corridors was pinning me with a headache already. Maybe I should have just returned with him.

"Unusually tense, are we today?" Demir's sleek voice came right over my shoulder, and I froze. How had I not felt him get that close to me?

Plastering a calm face, I turned to him. "Let's switch attires, it ought to loosen me up a bit," I said, trailing a finger over his jacket embroidery. Somehow the Isjordian garments never seemed to be fitting to him, they rather fit him as costumes. "Besides, Isjordian attire never fitted you. They must wear less imperious clothing wherever you truly come from."

His eyes twitched just the slightest, yet it was enough of a reaction.

My fingers stopped over his chest. Utter silence. No echo. No noise. No movement. No...beat.

He grabbed my wrist hard at first and then loosening as though he had caught himself a moment too late. "A village boy that never had much to eat, less to wear will never find these wools comfortable."

"Village boy, you say?" I raised a brow and stepped closer to him, his cloudy green eyes narrowing down on me. "Tell me, Demir, from what village do boys without a heartbeat come from? I only know one and Celesteel would feel rather offended if I regarded the Otherworld as a village."

Challenge rose in his features, his jaw ticking and he, too, took a step closer, our chests now touching and his face hovering over mine. "Tell me, Snowlin, what girl can escape the Night King?"

"Can't tell you," I whispered. "I'm a woman." My grin grew at his visible anger—the first time he'd shown me such a side. "Calm down, village boy, your pedestrian lies don't bother me. Letting a witch play with your lifeline is only your concern, not mine."

Pulling the domino mask over my face, I turned on my heels toward the buzzing room that boosted with chatting mouths from all corners of Isjord. Few greetings and congratulations later, I managed to part from the crowd and take a seat next to my father.

"You look beautiful, Snowlin," father said, sweeping his gaze all over me. He looked too pleased with himself, almost as if he had scored a victory. "You've always made my dais shine brighter than the gold."

I froze at the compliment and shuddered when he gave me what looked like a warm fatherly smile. The rattle and the snake. All felt so wrong. "Thank you for the dress." Offering him a smile that probably resembled at best a cringe, I took my seat. "I see we are missing Melanthe."

He surveyed the guests filling the ballroom to the brim. "It would do her no good to be part of the celebration. Her pregnancy is a difficult one."

Funny this one, wasn't he? Had he worried like this for my mother too? "Father?"

He turned to me. "What is it, my rose?"

"Truthfully," I said, holding his repulsive stare. "When did you and Melanthe begin your relationship?"

There was tension in his face. "It doesn't matter."

"I suppose it doesn't anymore." There was a dull ache in my chest for my mother. She'd once loved this creature I called a father. The worst part was that she had loved him till her last moments. And that enraged me. "But father." He turned to me again. "I am curious to see its end."

He regarded me for a moment as if he was taking my warning with caution—different from how he always did. Strange.

Lords, scholars and all sorts of fawners lined before us to kiss compliments up my father's arse. It wasn't long before I was half dozing and drooling on my fist.

"Snowlin," father's voice boomed too close to my ear drums. "Snowlin, the Breshall Prince is asking for a dance."

I shook thoughts back into my head, noting the young unblessed prince standing with his hand reaching out to me, a stunned look on his eerily pale face. In Fernfoss, the unblessed had prospered, thrived even, and lived longer, too. The one before me, however, looked like he'd been brought from the graves, puffed in lace and dipped in white powder and rouge—looking like he was held upright by strings.

"Of course." My mouth curved with a sneer when his leery brown eyes roamed over my scar for a long while.

He pulled us between a parting mass of bodies and rested a hand on my back. "I'm told there is great beauty under that mask," he said with a too primed common tongue accent, eyes drifting to my scar again and that thin moustache twisted a little like he was displeased at his observations.

"And I'm told correct about you."

"And what is that?"

"There is a great lack of brains up there," I said, pointing my chin to his head.

He tried to disguise his snarl with a creepy smile. "Impolite as every other of your sort."

"Superiority does that to you. Inferiority hasn't treated you nicely, but it sure did get you a ticket to my father's ball. The more uselessness under his foot, the greater he feels."

"He wishes to make an alliance with us," he gritted out near my ear. "Tell me where is the inferiority in that?"

Pride was a fickle thing, and I knew how to play it like a fiddle. "To be on the receiving end of pity is nothing to boast about. What can you possibly have that he wishes to have? Disease and famine?"

He bristled. "Access and knowledge, Princess. Far more valuable."

"And you're telling me father needs *you* for access and knowledge?"

"Primal knowledge. The same one your kind seems to have buried underneath their mistakes."

With a saccharine smile I said, "My, you're trying too hard here to impress this princess. Pray tell, how could you come up with that lie?"

"It is not a lie."

"If you say so."

It seemed like I'd struck his last nerve because he asked a little too tense, "*Anima accissor*—you know what that is?"

Soul killer? What was he on about? "Should I know your fibs?"

"It is what your sort calls a weapon, an object or a person. One that produces a type of magic that scourges the soul. Your petty gods gifted you all sorts of blessings, but you still rely on our goods to create anything of the sort. *Anima accissor* is made out of metal untainted with magic."

"And you possess it?"

His creepy blue stare glowed. "Most certainly. Our mountains are rich with it. And for the right price it will be your father's."

What in the hells did my father need unblessed metal to make *anima accissor* for? The old weapons were used during the times when the gates of heavens were open and when all sorts of creatures would sneak their way into our realm. All that was divine could not be killed by humanly weapon or force so *anima accissor* were forged. And that is exactly where my lesson ended on the subject because nowadays they bore no significance whatsoever.

The music stopped and I pulled back, bowing my head gently at him. "Thank you for your cooperation."

His face fell while he watched me dive inside the crowd.

What was happening? What was truly, truly happening? Father needed the Esmeray diaries to get the Seraphim sceptre piece. But why did he need the *anima accissor* for? Was it another part of the same puzzle?

I stopped between a throng of bodies, struck by my own thoughts. Did father need the weapon to fight whatever heavenly guardian that was guarding the sceptre? It had to be the only explanation. Was he planning to kill a guardian of the heavens?

A hand wrapped around my arm. A bloody hot one at that and I spun around to face the intruder of my thoughts. "You wouldn't leave without giving me a dance, would you?" Demir asked, giving me a smug look. He took my hand and rested the other on the small of my back.

For a split second, his attention went to the Breshall prince, and it made him tense a little.

The more I looked at him, the more it seemed to click. "Demir. That is a Seraphim name, isn't it?"

His mouth twitched a little. "It is."

"Which village in Seraphim are you from?"

His fingers tightened a little around mine. "You wouldn't know."

"Humour me. I'm bored, you're bored. We're all bored."

"Maskan. I'm from the north of Maskan."

My brows raised. "Maskan?" I let loose a giggle. "I was terrible at geography. Wouldn't know for the life of me where that is. For the heavens, keep this conversation going and just tell me where it exactly is. Or shall we sit in uncomfortable silence while you have your little sway between the rich?"

His grin was wide, and his eyes flitted to the Breshall prince again. "Just outside Heyes."

"You learn something new every day. How lucky for you to have been recruited by my father. How did that happen?"

He stilled, stopping the two of us from swaying till bodies began bumping against us. "Lucky, as you said."

"You must have possessed a great pair of skills."

"I do."

"Are you a Scarlet?"

"Not an Aura."

"But you possess some sort of blessing?"

"Yes."

"Melanthe's blessing?"

His attention returned from the unblessed prince to me. "Of a sort."

"How is that working for you? I mean, in regard to getting the sceptre pieces. Being green and ugly certainly must do you some favours to find them." If I had to give up a layer of my own lies to unmask his so be it.

His feet stopped again, and with him so did I. There it was. Tight mouth, glaring eyes and sharp breaths. Like a fox caught on a snare.

I put a hand over my mouth and gave him an innocent smile. "Oh, you never mentioned the sceptre, did you?"

He bowed his head. "Thank you for the dance."

"Most welcome," I said, bowing back. "Ah, Maskan is lovely this time of the year, is it not? The Azar unburnt Isles flourish in March. Had mangoes on the Maskan temple terrace about fourteen years ago at this time. You should definitely visit, Demir. Though I'd suggest you take a guide. Maskan is certainly not just outside Heyes." This idiot was not from Seraphim.

Those dull green eyes twitched, and he'd grit his jaw so tight I could almost hear his teeth crush on one another. He cocked his head to the side, dull eyes suddenly shining with menace. "That wasn't smart, Princess."

"Why?" I asked, batting my lashes. "Will you tell my father? Oh, do tell him, I beg of you. I'd like him to answer a few of my burning questions about the secret that *you* revealed to me during a night of passion we had in the Islines. Everyone must have heard me that night at the inn. Me and you, I mean. After all, you act all so enamoured with me, how could you have kept such a secret." I put a hand on my chest, pulling my features to imitate pure distraught. "Oh, father, how could you keep this from me? Demir told me all about it. He told me everything. How could you?" When his face wore a layer of panic, I dropped my hand and gave him a smile. "And this can't be all that much of a secret matter. Perhaps everyone knows even." I raised a hand to stop a dancing individual who I had not the slightest clue who it was. "My excuses, fair sir. Do you happen to know about Aurora's scep—"

"Enough," Demir said, grabbing my wrist and glancing around for anyone who might have heard.

My smile was polite when I turned to him. "See, Demir dearest, one mouth of secrets can become a crowd's gossip leaflets. And how jolly, everyone from every corner of this realm is gathered here in this very crowd for many days of celebration."

"That wasn't smart either."

"Not an intelligence competition, dear. But I am still outrunning you. A secret for a secret?"

"This isn't a child's game."

"No, but it is mine. Tell me, how can a beast's blood make a witch stronger?"

He let out a furious sigh and cast another careful glance around us. "How would I know?"

I waved him off. "Never mind that. How does one find where the sceptre pieces are?"

The look on his face was ferocious. "Again, asking the wrong person."

"I think not. But do point me to someone who might be willing to tell me."

His mouth pursed tight, and he tugged tighter at my arm, bringing me closer to him. "Princess."

"It's Moregan isn't it?"

He faltered a little. "Not sure what you are asking."

"Huh." A sliver of that familiar wind brushed my neck and I glanced around from the corner of my eyes. The same sensation I'd felt in Hanai began intensifying around me and my pulse raced. Morgan was up north. Why did I feel it here? "Let go of me, Demir. You're bruising this precious Princess."

He let go, looking around stunned as if he had just lost control without knowing.

Hells.

Flaming hells.

There were slashes in both his palms. One right across the bottom of his fingers and the other over his thumb. Identical in both hands.

Then it struck me.

In Hanai, the beast had grabbed my sword.

A lithe, bony hand rested on his shoulder and we both turned toward the interruption. "May I have a word," Melanthe said, looking more dishevelled than normal. "Privately."

Just like the sensation came, it faltered. And it confirmed my realisation. The beast from Hanai wasn't Moregan. It was Demir.

Ulv Islet—it had been him in his human form. Not Moregan. Not any other beast. Him.

He bowed his head to me. "Excuse us, Princess."

"You're excused. Demir."

He halted and turned a little over his shoulder, those dull green eyes glistening a bit more vibrantly than usual.

Perhaps turning my back to him was not a smart idea, not when I'd just found out he was my father's beast. But I was dizzy, so dizzy from knowledge of all sorts assaulting my thoughts from all sides.

I had to get out of here. If that thing had scented me…if Demir had scented me back in Hanai—

There was something wrong. That I knew from the moment of my return. Had he known all this time? Did my father know, too? The way he'd reacted to me, to my words and actions.

Father stood up from his dais, making his way down to me and I froze midway to him. He extended a hand to me. "Dance with your father?"

Four walls were caging me in, nearing and nearing. A game—I'd entered my father's game when I returned. He'd played me all this time.

Before I could answer, a hand slid over the small of my back. A gasp trapped in my mouth at the possessive touch curling over my waist and the way his thumb circled over the fabric covering my skin. "Your Majesty," the cold voice that had whispered sweet nothings and promises over my flesh not long ago greeted my father. "Could I steal this turn? I am afraid my party will soon retreat. I'd hate to miss this opportunity."

My father seemed taken aback for a while before giving him a nod.

Sweat trickled down my temples and I couldn't make my body move at the tension coursing me. What was this idiot doing here?

"Just a moment," father called as we began retreating to the dance floor. My fists bunched half in anxiousness and half in anger at this foolish divulge that would risk all my work here in Isjord. Not when I was so close to cracking what my father was up to. "You're the Comnhall emissary, aren't you?"

Kilian turned round and gave him a nod. "Yes, our king sends his best regards."

What emissary?

"Stay a while after," father said, retreating. "I didn't get to greet you when your side of the party arrived last night."

"We were held up at sea, our ships only touched land this morning. I will see you afterward, Your Majesty," he replied, politely. And it seemed good enough for my father because he sat back in his blood dais all too pleased.

Kilian's hand remained on the small of my back while he stirred us to a corner with bodies pressed together swaying in a slow waltz. Six feet four clad in white and a silver barocco mask concealing his beautiful face, he stood out amongst the crowd like a sore thumb. Or perhaps he stood out to me.

A shiver permeated me when he pulled our bodies close, his palms resting gently on me. The memory of those hands on me was still all too fresh and my body reacted on command the more I thought about them.

"You idiot," I hissed.

"Missed you, too, my *dahaara*. Smile pretty for me, your father is watching us."

Curling my lips in the fake smile I'd mastered all these years, I looked up at him. Like an anchor at sea, my body had loosened from tension in his arms. "What are you doing here?"

"Taking you back."

I let out a chuckle. This one was pretty real and angry. "No. And what did you do to the real emissary?"

"He is still sleeping on the ship. Nia made a blue argain mix to put him in a nice week long rest."

"You idiot."

"Already said that."

"Go back."

He leaned to whisper in my ear, "This is not how you greet your husband, missus." The hand he rested on my back slid lower and lower till it grazed my hips. "Did you not miss me at all?"

"Would you prefer I keep our lie or tell you the truth?"

"Either will do, I never fail to distinguish a true lie from your mouth. Actually," he purred, "lie to me. I like it when you put in a little effort in our marriage."

"You have to go," I said, clearing my throat and ignoring how shivers had spread all over my flesh. "I'm not finished with Isjord."

"Call it finished right now because I have found them."

My feet stopped and I looked up at him. He was not lying to me. "Are you certain?"

A nod. "We need to get out of here, now. Visha is waiting by the north wall to tear Melanthe's veil so I can fade the two of us out. He is still watching. Pretend to agree with something I said and take my arm."

I did as told without turning to look at father as Kilian led us out toward the corridors he probably knew by heart. Once we bypassed the main corridors and reached the far north corner that led to the back gardens near the wall, Kilian pulled me to his arms, backing me towards a wall till he was pressed tight against me.

"What are you doing?"

"Waiting for Visha to signal us." He lifted my mask off and smoothed a thumb over my lips. "And enjoying the sight of my wife. Who knew I was insatiable?"

I reached for his mask, pulling it away so I could see him, too. My mouth went dry when his full rosy mouth curled into a smirk. Unlike him, I'd always been insatiable for him. "My father could have recognised you, you idiot."

Taking his mask, he placed it over my face. "He couldn't."

My words came out muffled. "I did." By touch alone.

I swear he could hear my thoughts because he flashed me a grin so unlike him. "I'd recognise you, too, my love." He rested his forehead on mine, the thin mask separating us. This layer, sometimes invisible and sometimes not, was always there. We wore it each time we were with one another. A truce to hide the truth. We were pretending—that is all it was. Another lie.

"What are you thinking?" Kilian said, dragging me out of my thoughts. His hand had spanned over my neck, his thumb smoothing over my pulse. "It's too loud for how quiet you are."

"You wouldn't enjoy hearing these thoughts."

"Don't say regret because I will believe just anything, Snow, but not that."

"I wish it was regret that I felt. Perhaps I wouldn't want to hate what we did this much."

"Why don't you hate it?"

"Because I am twisted like that. And because I know once this is over, I will enjoy the look of hurt on you more than your death."

His grip around me tightened and I ground on him, feeling every inch of his body touch mine. "Gods, I love it when you speak murder to me."

A scream tore through the air, both of our attention snapping toward the end of the corridor.

"That is the signal."

"Oh."

I must be wearing how I felt because once again he read me all clear and gloated with a grin. He lowered to kiss a trail from my jaw to my ear where he whispered, "I would rather fuck you against the wall of our bedroom, love. Nice and slow, you know I like to take my time with you."

One moment we were in the castle corridors and the next out in the blistering cold night and surrounded by towering frost-gilded pines. I never remembered winter as harsh as it had been this year. Though the season was year-long and unending, it did soften during the warmer months. By this time of the year the ground would have seen at least an hour of sun a day—it is how I always remembered it to be. Yet Hemera had not kissed the land not once since my return.

Even in the dark, I could make out Visha's luminescent green eyes as she approached us, a hood casting shadow over her grim face. "That veil was crafted almost too perfectly." Today was a day of many firsts. First time I'd seen Visha look concerned. "I don't understand. Her skills have always been subpar to mine. Melanthe has gotten stronger."

"Or your skills are ageing rather less perfect than hers," I said, my teeth clattering.

Kilian shed his jacket, throwing it over my shoulders. "Remember, she is taking that beast's blood."

"The beast," I said, pushing my hands through his jacket. "I know who it is. Demir, the young general."

"Fuck, Snow," Kilian hissed, running a hand over his eyes. "You've been near that thing all this time?"

"Let us hurry," Visha urged. "There is something in the air tonight. And I don't like it."

"Where is it that we are going?" I asked, following them through the thicket of the forest.

Kilian said, "Malik waits for us in Brogmere."

"Why there?"

He linked his fingers with mine and walked us toward the edge of the forest. "Because I don't trust the Solaryan rulers to ask for permission to fade within their shields." Before I got any more confused, he explained, "They are in White Bridge, in your aunt's and her husband's lands of rule."

A wave of excitement and shock went through me all at once to make sense of how I really felt. "Eleonor always favoured Aryan, for them to be working together isn't surprising."

"It is not all, Snow. I doubt Magnus and Cora were unaware of this. For them to be under their nose for this many years seems folly to me," he said regretfully. I knew he'd gotten close to Magnus and got along well with him—Kilian was disappointed.

I shook my head. "They both have the seal. They could easily pass for humans. But true, I wouldn't want to risk them."

"And exposing them, you and inevitably Olympia to the Solaryans in the process," Visha said absently, hooking her bag to the horses waiting for us. "We will figure out the analytics in Brogmere. Might we go before you are less of a Crafter? My bones have never known a cold like this."

I faced Kilian. "Why are you not fading us there?"

He lifted me onto his horse before following suit behind me. "Apparently Melanthe has put a trace on magic all over the land. Elias warned us that Canes were littering the port, city and castle grounds when the guests were coming through to the celebration. My magic is potent—she has probably realised my presence in Isjord by now. If she figures where I've faded next, she will get the animals to sniff us out."

Three hours of a ride through the Sable Abyss Forest, away from the main roads which would have cut it to one, we reached Brogmere. My limbs had frosted over despite the warmth from Kilian's body and his jacket.

Celdric, the Olympian I'd left in charge here, awaited us at the gates. After several dark alley turns to conceal us from any potential spy of my father's, we reached a small lone house just nearing the south wall of the city.

I had barely even got down from the horse when the door banged open, startling everyone. A beaming girl ran towards us till I was engulfed in her smaller embrace. "You came!" Lara whispered, hugging me tightly.

"You have grown a head taller," I said, fluffing her yellow hair. "Have you grown a head smarter, too? Last I heard from Celdric, you were caught sleeping in class."

That made her pull away and sulked. "Soldiers don't need to learn how to hold a feather, they need to learn how to wave a sword."

"Right back at school you need to go," Kilian said, kneeling before her. "A sword is yielded not waved."

The both of us rolled our eyes at his words, but she flew in his embrace shortly. Reluctantly, she pulled away and glanced wordlessly yet full of questions at the both of us.

"You are allowed to like him, Lara. He is my enemy not yours. Though I wouldn't get attached to him. My enemies don't remain enemies for long."

She clutched Kilian tightly as if I were to take him away from her. "Why is that?"

"Because I will kill him."

"Glad to hear that I still have a chance," Mal said. He leaned on the door frame, arms crossed over his chest and a knowing teasy look on his face that jumped between me and his brother. "Come on, sister-in-law, we both know it's me you really want."

"Don't you have better things to do than flirt with my wife?" Kilian asked, throwing a heavy bag to his brother.

Mal caught the thing as if it were weighted feathers and threw me a wink. "Ready for tomorrow?"

I nodded. "You?"

He threw a look behind where Kilian was directing the horses to a stable. "Are you sure you don't want him to come with us?"

"The first thing my siblings will see after I free them won't be their mother's killer."

Mal's features tensed, a tick hammered in his strong jaw. Whatever he wanted to say got interrupted as Kilian's hand slid over my back to wrap around the nape of my neck.

Oh, gods.

I was more than certain I was flush red, even my ears were burning. This felt way more intimate now. His hold and touch felt like a claim. Why had I allowed him to have that?

Even through the torment of thoughts, I leaned on him.

Whatever silent conversation went between the two brothers had Mal clear his throat and plaster his usual smug expression back on. "Lara's grandmother has made a mad dinner. I bet you both are hungry."

Dinner went mostly silently. Except for Lara's fight chatter and hand gymnastics on how to yield a sword, the rest were quiet and focused. Mal had concentrated on an empty spot on the wall like it held all secrets to this realm. Visha on her grimoire and Kilian on driving me to the brink of madness. He paid attention to Lara and her grandmother yet his hand on my thigh was his focus. Back and forth, he massaged and petted my flesh with the hand he had slipped under my skirts. Going far enough to tease me and have me panting with need.

When I had enough of squirming in my seat, I grabbed his hand and spoke in his ear, "What are you doing?"

He took a bite from an apple and turned to me. "Whatever do you mean, love?"

"You idiot."

He kissed my temple and leaned in to murmur, "Yours. Only ever yours."

When I went back to my soup, everyone had gone quiet, staring between Kilian and I.

Mal leaned back on his seat, narrowing his eyes all amused on the two of us. "So, Henrik."

"Don't call me that."

Mal pointed his chin at me. "Why can she call you that?"

"Because one day she will give me Henrik III and the only thing you will ever give me is a headache."

I gaped. Visha's fork slipped out of her hand. Mal grinned like a wolf. Lara's eyes were huge while her grandmother blinked stunned between the two of us, unsure.

Kilian on the other hand? Unhinged. Eating his apple.

"If you won't choke on your own words," I said, standing. "I hope you choke on that apple."

His laughter trickled all the way outside. I'd barely stepped on the snowy porch when strong arms and warmth wrapped around me. My eyes drew shut and I listened. I felt.

"Do you imagine it is not me?"

I slowly turned to him, frowning. "No." If anything…it was always him.

"Why do you always close your eyes?"

I like to feel it all. Without distraction. Fully. "I don't know."

His thumb brushed my pulse. "What is it?"

For some reason, I decided to tell him. "What if they don't want to come with me?"

"Why wouldn't they want to come with you?"

"What if they hate me?"

"Why would they hate you?"

"What if they—"

"I want to kiss that mouth if only to shut you up."

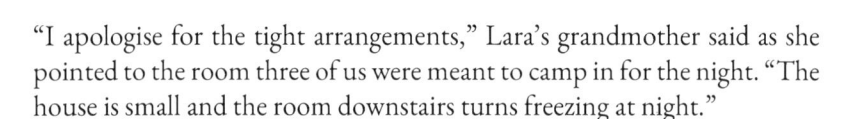

"I apologise for the tight arrangements," Lara's grandmother said as she pointed to the room three of us were meant to camp in for the night. "The house is small and the room downstairs turns freezing at night."

"That is alright," Kilian offered.

Mal scoffed and shook his head, pushing inside the room. "Easy for you to say."

He, Kilian and I were to share the room, and Visha with Lara and her grandmother. It was the only arrangement that made sense.

While Mal attended to create a soft spot on the ground for him to rest on, I demanded to check on Kilian's wounds.

"See," he said, running a hand down the still angry, rosy flesh of the wounds. "Will live a while longer."

"He almost lost a leg once," Mal said, laying down on his makeshift mattress. "The bastard will be just fine."

Kneeling before him, I uncapped the salve Moriko usually had made for him and applied it to his scars. "Love," he said, hooking an arm around my waist and hoisting me up. "The ground is cold."

Before I stood, some ridiculous part of my brain made me lean forward and plant a kiss on his stomach. "Done."

He leaned back a little, his eyes fluttering with sparkles. "Kissing my pain away?"

"For the love of the crescent heaven," Mal grumbled. "Please go back to daggering one another."

"Talking about daggers," I said, weaving my fingers through his hair and pulling his head to me. "The Breshall Prince told me something about *anima accissor*. Father was buying metal from them. But why would father need to create weapons when he is breeding beasts and assembling Aurora?"

Kilian didn't seem alarmed by the news. "Did he say specifically that the metal was used to create weapons?"

"No. But why else would father need it?"

"*Anima accissor* is often used as a token to strengthen the walls like we've done with Highwall, and that would make the veil stronger—unblessed metal is potent and the main ingredient in creating it. This could be the sign he is suiting up for war, preparing for any response. Silas knows Solarya is aware of the Octa Virga. He probably expects resistance from other kingdoms once he starts to attack. The same resistance he will not have the time to deal with while Aurora tries to turn the realm to ash." He rested a hand on my hip, gently pulling me closer to him. "What are you thinking?"

"If I tell you, I will get the Kilian lecture."

"So bad things that will have bad consequences and bad outcomes."

"Ha ha."

He smiled a little, pulling me closer and closer to him. "If you're going to laugh, do it fully so I can hear it."

Mal sat back up from his makeshift bed. "Sacred Cynth, is he always like this? How did he get you in bed speaking like a flower girl?"

"With his huge c—"

Kilian quickly wrapped a hand around my mouth and Mal howled with laughter. "Well done, brother."

The man narrowed his eyes on me. "Glad the size is to your satisfaction."

"I'm glad, too," I said, jumping in the bed and ducking inside the covers. Very glad.

He followed suit, pulling me flush against him.

I cocooned in his chest, the feel of being held was enough to lull sleep into me.

The younger Castemont still twisted and turned, making the floorboard creak. The only thing keeping me awake.

"I feel bad for Mal," I whispered. "Shall I tell him to come up here, there is plenty of space."

"I really don't want to kill my brother," he murmured from where he had buried his face in my hair.

Slowly, I spun to face him and wrapped my arms around his body, hiding my face in his chest.

"Better?" he asked, kissing the crown of my head.

"Mhm."

"For the love of all gods, don't do anything in my presence," Mal sighed.

"Ah, Kilian, right there, ah," I moaned loudly and the man holding me shook with laughter.

"Very funny," Mal said, turning his back to us.

"Kilian?" I asked, tucking my hands under his shirt.

He pulled us closer. "Hm?"

"Good night."

"Good night, my love."

CHAPTER TWENTY-EIGHT

Sudus

Snowlin

We boarded an illegal ship to Whitebridge early this morning in a northern Brogmere wharf while Visha and Kilian took another to travel further west. Once they were outside of Melanthe's veil they would be able to fade to Olympia without being traced.

Even though we were almost reaching land, the thought that I would get to see my siblings soon had not settled with me. The fact that they were still alive had settled with me to begin with. It felt like all this time I'd chased spirits to sedate my grief and it had helped, but now, it was coming true. What would they be like? Would they remember me? Would they hate me for running? Would they even want to come with me?

Malik stood solemnly still and quiet beside me, silently observing our surroundings, ready to jump at the sound of danger.

Men, women and children had taken shelter under deck, travelling hidden towards the warmer lands. It should have surprised me, but it didn't. Isjord was said to be the capital of Numengarth, but it wasn't kind to many in the ways it should be. Work was hard and life was a standstill of frost, short days, long nights and the four walls of your house. It paid well to keep you prisoner of your own lifestyle.

My face was hidden under a hood and a scarf, but few were not sparingly glancing at me, they were fully staring at me.

"Golden eyes," a little girl spoke from her mother's lap. "Ma says not many have gold eyes."

Horrified, the mother slapped a hand over her daughter's mouth. "She is tired, miss, forgive her."

The girl bit her mother's hand and spoke a little too loudly, "But you said only the prime Verglasers have yellow eyes, ma. To see the sun in their eyes even when they feel the coldest. To be reminded—"

The mother shut her daughter up with both hands.

"That heat lives within us and the cold without. To not allow our hearts to grow cold," I finished. My bloodline was the hearth of blistering ice. Eons ago, Krig's Aura had grown so powerful that they'd become something of fear. Afraid that magic would overtake their humanity, Krig had gifted one last thing to his strongest Aura—the eyes that I loathed.

"A pretty tale," I said, reaching into my pocket and handing a piece of chocolate Lara had given me before the trip to the little girl. "For the gruesome truth that Krig blessed needed reminders to behave humanly." Pulling the scarf down to reveal my face, I put a finger over my lips.

Both the mother and daughter gasped and then quickly nodded before curling in silence.

The ship successfully reached shore and we soon moulded with the tight moving crowd toward the large port. The stench of fish, guts and salt was heavy in the fishing city, but the mud foam I took when we boarded ship had numbed my stomach from reacting.

"Why did you show your face to them?" Mal asked as we parted the heavy line of buyers and sellers.

I ran a hand over my forehead that puckered with sweat beads from the heavy sun. "They needed a reason to not be afraid and I gave it to them."

He flicked the roof of my hood. "Thought you liked being feared."

"I do, but I like controlling fear better."

The sea line town was one united cluster of bodies hurrying from one side to another. Mal had grabbed my arm after almost losing me in the crowd twice. A bazaar stretched in the frontlines of the city, filled with all sorts of vendors bargaining their trade with everybody passing their stalls.

"We need a compass," Mal said, dragging me over a line of stalls.

My gaze caught on something while he perused for the compass. Tens of white sunstones of all shapes and sizes were laid on a jade velvet stand.

"It is a good choice," an elderly lady sat behind the stall said as she fanned a large azure parasol to her face. "Sunstone symbolises new beginnings. A new day ahead and a bright future. If you wear it out in the sunrise—"

"It glistens," I said as a dull ache throbbed in my chest like an old wound reopening. Had he been here? Had Sam stepped here? My eyes drew shut, hoping to feel his presence at least one more time. But he was gone. Like my mother was gone.

The woman stood and pointed to a sun-coloured stone. "Might I suggest this. Amber would match your eyes."

"I am not here to buy."

"Two," Mal said from behind me, handing the woman two silver Dar and plucking two amber necklaces from the table.

I didn't even get to object before he was clasping the necklace on me.

"The other," he said, lifting the second necklace. "For the smaller Skygard. When we find her."

"I can't wear this, Mal."

"Sure you will. Consider it a wedding gift." He threw an arm over my shoulder and steered us into the crowd again. "Pass it to my niece."

With a groan, I elbowed him in the stomach and he turned red more from laughter than pain.

Once we reached the edge of the town, I removed my heavy clothing and wore the thin cloak Mal had purchased in White Bridge east port, hoping to blend in and not become a subject of curiosity to Solaryan soldiers.

Once we reached a thicket of forest, we dismounted. It was presumably deep enough in its centre considering we'd travelled for the past two hours without rest. Mal pulled a map out of his bag and the compass he bought. Apparently, the map was Visha's creation. The white parchment paper was dusted lightly in shimmering fine black specks, crafted to guide us through to them.

"Your hand," Mal said, pulling a dagger from his side. He dug the tip on my finger and let the flood drip onto the white map. "It will take us to those of your blood."

For a few tormenting long moments nothing seemed to happen. I sighed and sagged with relief when trails of red began a path along the map. A short path, meaning we were close.

A new sort of panic settled in me and breathing became difficult. I couldn't...I couldn't breathe.

"Snow?"

I turned to face Mal whose face was shaped with concern. "This is not a dream, is it? Actually, it feels a lot like the beginning of most of my nightmares." Me chasing after my siblings. Finding them, but not being able to reach and save them.

He reached close and cupped my face. "It isn't a dream. Look, I'm touching you and Kilian hasn't magically burnt me to ashes with the power of his mind."

That earned him a grin.

He removed his hands, lifting them in the air and absently looking around. "I wouldn't put it past him, however." Pulling the hood back over my head he said, "Let's go find them."

We followed the map till it brought us to a small village where we left our horses. The closer to the end of the trail we got, the more my pulse made it hard to hear anything besides. Only Mal's reassuring concentration brought me back to my senses now and again.

He stopped abruptly. "It separated."

I looked over the map he held and saw the trail divided into two. "They must have separated."

"Wouldn't that mean that they are roaming freely?"

"I don't know, Mal." That feeling of bitter sense of wrong crawled at the back of my head like a painful rush of blood. Perhaps they chose to live far from me, far from everything? Perhaps they were happy. Perhaps they wanted to be left alone.

We decided to follow one of the trails together. If this was a trap it would be easier to get out of it together rather than separate. The thicket of the sunburnt forest grew clustered the further in we got.

Suddenly, Mal grabbed my elbow and hauled me back, resulting in both of us rolling over on the ground from the force.

"A shield," he said, rubbing where a sharp branch had dug on his thigh. "Look up."

At a small space where the green forest ceiling was scarce, light hit the air in front of us and a reflection bounced back from thin air. Picking up a rock, I threw it toward the shield. The thin layer of magic bounced in a rainbow-like wave, but the rock landed safely on the other side.

Mal squatted before it. "Looks like a well thought trap."

"Or a prison."

An agonising while passed while we searched the perimeter which the shield was over. It wasn't just over a chunk of land—it went on for miles. The analytics of the shield were not adding up and at this point it did feel like a trap. Was it to keep out or in?

"It's too close to the village," Mal said as we met halfway. "A hunter or even children could pass through here and notice this. This isn't the work of a Glare. Their magic is solid and physical like that of a Verglaser, like every magic of an elemental is."

I shook my head. "I would have recognised the scent of dark craft."

"Perhaps," he said, pushing a hand through the shield, "not dark craft. Could be the work of a Magi healer. Those white witches aren't much better. If Kilian was here he would have made some sense of this." He turned to me. "I say we go in."

I grabbed his wrist, pulling it out of the shield. "*I will go through*, the last thing I need—"

Before I began to disagree, he grabbed my hand and pulled the two of us across the thin shield. "You were saying?" he asked, flashing me a smug grin.

"Malik Castemont, you damned idiot."

"You're welcome. Now let's go. The sun is almost down and we both know you're practically blind in the dark."

This idiot.

"Shit," he hissed, shaking the map and compass. "Shit."

I grabbed the map and noted the now dried patch of blood. Opening a part of my magic, I called electricity. The moment the flush of magic skittered between my fingers, relief filled me. "I can use magic."

"Just not dark magic. Definitely the work of a Magi healer."

"We were close, it can't be far from here."

We dove further and further in the forest before we decided on a break. The heat was too much and too soon after I'd spent weeks freezing over in Isjord. My lungs were on fire and my skin felt like sandpaper over my bones.

"What's that?" Mal asked, reaching a woven basket and a bow that laid resting on a bole nearby.

Before he even reached close to it, a hooded figure jumped from the tree crown above, a dagger in their hand that was aimed at him.

Mal faded away in time before it even grazed him.

Quickly, the hooded figure spun on their heel, twisting the dagger between their fingers aiming toward Mal again.

The hand on my sword froze. My head repeated that dagger motion over and over. The familiarity of it struck me with memories.

It goes over and then under. The trick is in the wrist, twist too much and it will move quicker and then lose balance, Eren's voice boomed in my ears as if it was as fresh as that day.

Mal faded right before them, grabbing onto their wrist and spinning them round to have an arm wrapped over their neck before pulling their hood down.

Angry emerald eyes hit me first, and then the rest of memory flushed through in an aching throb in my pulse. The same soft features, the same round stare, the same pouty mouth and the same long dark hair that we shared. She resembled nothing of the little quiet girl I remembered her to be. The one who liked her hair neatly plaited, who made bows out of dress scraps dyed pink with rotten cherries that Ken saved us. The girl—the woman—standing before me resembled nothing I once remembered her to be. She was beautiful. Grown.

She thrashed in Mal's grip, strands of wild hair falling over her face. "Let me go!"

When she turned to glare at him over her shoulder, a smile crept over his face. "Well, hello, little bird."

It was real. She was real.

"Thora?" I asked, taking a small step forward. If I moved too suddenly, would it all disappear—would she disappear again?

She stopped writhing, her gaze snapping to me. Stillness. It was as if the whole world had halted its rotation. It felt as if anything else didn't matter when my sister's gaze found mine.

I pulled the hood down and her expression shattered, breaking into fragments of pain and confusion.

"Thora?" My knees weakened and I crumbled to the ground, tears streaming down my face and blurring the figure of my sister ahead. "Rora?" It was not a dream. It was not. I could not breathe. My sight had fogged as I called for her again, "Rora?" Would she heed my call or would she disappear like smoke?

She took me in for a long moment. Noting every detail of my face, from my scar to my hair to my eyes. "S-Snow?" She shook her head and squeezed her eyes tight. "Can't be. Can't be." Tears stained her cheeks and she sobbed, dragging her fingers through her hair. "She is dead. She is dead," she repeated, covering her ears, and then sobbed louder when she opened them to find me standing before her again. "Snow."

"Rora," I whispered between tears.

She ran and threw herself in my open arms, pressing her face onto my hair, holding me tight as if I'd disappear. She shook, her hands were firmly pressed to me as if I might just slip away. Her cries tore my heart and mended it altogether at the same time. "Where have you been? Where have you been, Snow?"

I held her. I was holding my sister again. "I am here now. I am here."

Her cries grew louder, turning hoarser. "You were dead." She pulled back, lacing her fingers through my hair, searching me like I might still be a fiction of her imagination. "He said you were dead, Snow. He said the Adriatians killed you and mother. Is she alive, too?"

There was hope in her stare and I was going to break it. My throat was clogged, and my words came out choked, "No. She died that night. The same night I thought you died."

I expected her to falter at the revelation, but she only nodded like she'd made peace with her death. With mine, too. "Did Aryan tell you where we were?"

I tensed, anger roiling in gales through my heated blood. "No, I killed him before he could."

Her mouth parted in surprise. "You killed...Aryan?"

"Freed his big head from his ridiculously small shoulders."

She winced a little and then laughed. It was still the same. The exact same bubbly laughter. And it hurt my heart—terribly and so fiercely. "Did you play ball with it like you used to tell him?"

"Heavens," Mal murmured to himself, settling next to the chestnut basket.

"I did," I said, and we both giggled. "Hung it on a pike, too, but it festered with flies, not caterpillars."

She ran a sleeve over her watery forest eyes. "Eren did tell you butterflies don't grow like that."

"He did," I said, reaching to smooth my fingers over her face. She was real. All of it was real. "He did."

Leaves rustled from our periphery. "Thora, what—" The deep edged voice stopped when I stood and turned round to face him. Tall, much taller than I remembered him, my brother stood there, mere feet from me, staring at us. Hazel eyes, black short hair like he always kept it, that little scar over the bridge of his nose and the other across his upper lip when I made him trip in the kitchens—all were still there. My brother was truly here. His gaze jumped from me to Thora. "Tell me gods aren't playing cruelly with me now."

A sob crawled over my throat at hearing his voice again. "Gods wouldn't know any other way," I said, my voice shaking.

He let out a teary, choked laugh and I ran, jumping in his arms. I felt ten again, when he would haul me round and spin until I saw stars flash in my vision. He still smelled the same. Like pine and snow. My brother still smelled like my brother.

"How?" he asked, breathless. "How?"

"I ran," I whispered, my eyes welling and pouring hot tears. "I ran away."

His hand cupped the back of my head. "You did well. You did so well."

That broke me. Broke me entirely. My heart wept again. "You promised," I accused, squeezing him tight. "You promised me."

He held me tighter. "I am sorry. I am so sorry."

Tears flooded my eyes. "When did you get so tall?" I asked, refusing to let go of him.

"Why haven't you grown at all?"

I smacked his shoulder and he put me down. Sadness dripped from the corners of his expression as he ran his finger over the scar on my cheek. "I am so sorry, Lin." He cupped my face, still staring in awe. "My little sister."

"Why are you eating my chestnuts?"

I turned around at the indignant sound of my sister. Mal had sat cross legged on the forest floor picking on chestnut skin. "Why, were you going to eat them all yourself?" he asked, giving Thora a long, slow perusal.

"Who is he?" Eren asked, protectively standing at my side.

Mal shot up and extended a hand to him. "Malik Castemont, at your service."

Eren shook his hand, fully confused. "Castemont? You're Kilian's brother? Little Mal?"

Both Mal and I stared wide eyed at my brother. "Do you know of him?" Mal asked, glancing at me apologetically.

Instead of answering, Eren looked puzzled as he asked, "Why are you with my sister?"

"Complicated to say the least, but long story short, she is married to my brother," Mal spouted out before I could stop him.

Both my sister and brother gave me stunned looks and I might have winced.

My brother blinked confused. "You married Kilian?"

"Stop addressing him by his name," I said, a bit too angrily.

Eren raised a brow. "Do you not call your *husband* by his name?"

I winced again.

Eren's eyes turned hard. "Did father have something to do with this?"

"You will want to take a seat for this one," I said, dropping to the ground.

After telling the both of them the whole story, the two sat in silence while processing all I'd told them while Mal and I ate some chestnuts.

"Scary," Mal murmured beside me, and I turned to him. "How much you two look alike and how much you actually don't."

I followed his line of sight that ended at my sister. "We looked almost identical when we were young." It was why my uncle loved to hurt her.

I swallowed a hard lump of hurt down at the memory of all she'd been through because of me.

He passed me a peeled chestnut. "Do you think they've thought about it enough or shall we return another day?"

I kicked his leg and he laughed.

"The Octa Virga," Eren called absently, staring at the ground. "Is it stronger than...us?"

I nodded. "She is a guardian of heavens—guardian of the white flame to be precise. Father has hit his stroke of luck."

"But you have a piece."

"Yes."

"And Kilian is helping you with all of this?"

This time I frowned. "What part of 'I was planning to burn Adriata to the blessed grounds before father got in my way' did you not understand? We have a bargain, one soon ending when I kill him for what he has done." The word *kill* trembled and shattered on my lips.

My brother's dark brows knitted together. "You can't possibly blame him."

That made me frown. "You can't tell me otherwise. Not when I was left picking pieces that he broke."

"Lin, Kilian was barely king. If anything—"

The skies rumbled from the fury swirling inside my chest. "Enough. Enough saying his name as if he isn't the reason why you and Thora grew up to be some people I don't know."

Eren glanced at the skies before saying, "You know Aryan did all of this."

"Our uncle only lit the flame, but Kilian blew the rest."

"Lin."

"Don't try to reason this with me. Not when you do not know half of it."

He rested a hand on my face. "What matters is that we survived."

Disbelief. "Wait till you find out how."

His hand fell and he stared at me as if he didn't know me—as if I was a stranger. Perhaps I was.

"Can we not fight already?" Thora asked, gathering herself tight. "It looks scarier now that you're all grown."

Commotion drew all of our attention. Heavy footsteps seemed to be approaching us from all directions, the lowering sun extended shadows to cloak them from sight.

"Soldiers?" Mal asked, pulling shadows from sight to reveal any hidden assaulters.

Eren unsheathed a dagger and so did Thora. "No, these are not just any soldiers, Lin. They are Magi healers. The shield must have alerted them when you stepped in it. You both need to go. Now."

Stunned, my attention snapped to him. "I'm not going anywhere without the two of you."

He shook his head and pulled his sleeves to reveal two strips of white ink around his wrists. "We are both bound by magic to this land. A coven of white witches sealed us right after the Solstice attack. Old magic, Lin, threaded to their goddesses' realm through portals. We are chained to the shield. Go, both of you, now. We will think of this later." He cupped my face and kissed the top of my head. "All that matters is that we have you back."

No. No. No. I wouldn't leave them, not again.

"The shield," Mal called as hundreds of bodies surrounded us. "Snow, all magic is physical." When confusion drew in all of our faces, he groaned and grabbed my brother's wrists, pointing to a white rune and then to the shield. "Physical, Snow. And you have loads of that to match."

"No," Eren ordered strongly, suddenly resembling our father all too much. "This is old magic. We have tried. We have tried for years. This would open your seal."

Thora nodded, tears pouring down her face again. "Go."

I turned to Mal. "The moment that shield cracks, I need you to fade them out of here." He made to object, but I shook my head. "Promise me that you will take them when I say so."

He grabbed my arm. "Then I will come back for you."

"No, I will bolt to you. For any reason, don't fade back. Promise me, Mal." When he wouldn't budge, I yelled, "I won't owe your brother any more than I already do. Not your life—I won't. Promise me!"

The second he nodded, I drew all that held my magic back out of the way. Pure euphoria settled in my chest. A sense of being full yet plenty empty drew my pulse louder than normal. A roaring dam gate with too little bank to fill. I felt the static lifting me in the air. Aiming at the shield, I let all the magic pour out of me. A thick bolt of lightning hit the sheer surface of sun magic, the forest loud and bright from it. The ancient magic resisted the attack, feeding from the tether of mana attached to Hemera. But not for long. The humid air trembled, packed with electricity and the sun magic shivered in the air, splintering and fragmenting.

Once I saw the ceiling crack, I peered down at Mal and gave him a nod.

My sister screamed, launching toward me, but Mal was quicker, hauling her onto his arms and grabbing Eren to fade. One moment they were there, and the next they were gone.

Soldiers surrounded me the second I lowered to the ground. Some were frightened and most stunned at what I had done.

Ice blistered the forest ground and then sped to all directions, trapping the men to the spot. I felt dozens of heartbeats hum in the air, my senses separating each and every one of them by the flow of their current. *Thirty-nine. Fifty-four. Seventy-eight. Ninety-one. One hundred and ten. Two hundred. Three hundred and two heartbeats.*

My limbs trembled, each movement of my hands conducting magic no longer out of my own control. *More and less*, the two sides of me screamed as black veins marred my hands, showing just how far till I lost all control I was. Red and white stained the dimed auburn of the forest. Three hundred and two more lives that I didn't mean to claim were taken today.

Once the last heartbeat hummed in the air, I shut my eyes tight. Not seeing didn't make what I did better, but the beast within fed from violence, and the beast without lost humanity within with each act of wrath.

All three hundred and two heartbeats were silent, and so were the many animals I felt litter by from before, but the gates would not close no matter how much I tried to will them shut.

Feel it where it pours out, concentrate and will it shut. I tried to do what he'd taught me. Over and over again. But my magic was too far opened. The tips of my fingers were beginning to change into a glowing silver, and soon...all my limbs, too.

CHAPTER TWENTY-NINE

Nix

Kilian

Oryn and I stood side by side on the highest tower in Taren castle, expectant. It was just past sunset and there was still no news of Snow and Mal.

"Your queen will be fine," the old priest said. Yet it offered no comfort to my distress.

The sun had peeled all the light from behind the grey sky of Olympia when we spotted three figures fading by the terrace.

A dark headed girl screamed bloody death in my brother's arms—not my dark headed girl. She was shorter than Snow, her ink black hair longer, cascading almost beyond her back and her stare was of a rainforest emerald. "Take us back!" The castle floor blistered with ice, growing and spreading all over and downwards.

"Rora, calm down," the tall black haired male next to my brother said, but the girl had slid too far down her panic. The air was misting with frost and the Olympian sky suddenly poured soft flakes of snow.

Linking an arm around her waist, my brother pulled her against his chest and put a hand on her face. "Calm down!" he shouted and then softly added, "She will come back, I know she will. She always does. From the dead, from the living. She will always come back."

Pray to gods he wasn't talking about my Snow. Pray to gods all he said was true if he was talking about my Snow.

He had not used any of his magic, but as if he had, the dark haired girl suddenly went lax in his grip and the ice halted from spreading. She looked around, her breathing growing to panting when she realised what she had done. "Why...why are we so high up?"

I didn't give him a chance to reply because I fisted my brother's shirt, almost shaking from fear. "Where is she?"

He shook his head, running a trembling hand through his eyes. "She will come."

No. No. He'd promised me to never let her out of his sight, to keep her safe. I gripped him tighter. "Mal, where is my wife?"

The sky gurgled with flashing thunder. It was her. It had to be her.

One strike of lightning hit the distance and part of my soul began cracking. By the second one I was losing grip of reality and the world began swaying as it had only once done before.

"I can't lose her again, please take me back," the girl cried, clinging to my brother's side. "Please."

"I promised her," was all he said.

Her jaw tightened and the air chilled with frost. "Promises mean nothing to her!"

The sky above us swirled into a vortex and lightning crashed on the terrace. A body swayed between the burning and frozen mist. Blessed be all heavens that decided she would return to me.

But she hadn't returned to me, something else had. Something with a bright pair of electric wings spreading wide behind. When the white mist cleared, her glittering figure became clearer. Long dark hair floated around her and every inch of her body sparkled with bright white glowing veins—her eyes, too, no longer gold but a glowing white.

I reached a hand forward. "Snow?"

She tilted her head to the side, like a hunter studying prey. The skies behind her framed a horrifying thunder that cracked heavy over the mountain ranges around us.

I didn't stop. Not until I was barely inches away from her. She didn't hurt me. And though she was glittering with lightning, the air around her was colder than winter itself.

Slowly, I let night unravel from me, letting it slither in the air and all over the ground till it girded her. When her magic came in contact with my darkness, it doused and faltered—hissing like ice meeting fire. Like all other things did. But she had enough life in her to battle my death.

The essence of her magic smouldered, and her eyes unveiled from the unnatural glow to reveal my suns. Her body went slack and my shadows held her up till I gathered her exhausted form in my arms. Black lines were still spreading over her neck and face, the seal was opening or it had opened.

The journey from the terrace to Visha's quarters was a blur. Words were muddled and touches were ghostly as I rushed to find the Crafter.

"Put her down," Visha ordered the second I showed at her doors, pointing to the massive stone table in the middle of the room. She shut everyone out, bolting the doors closed despite the calls and screams from outside. She rolled Snow onto her stomach and tied her ankles and wrists to the table posts.

"What are you doing?" I asked, grabbing her hand away from Snow.

"She gets unpredictable when I close her seal. I suggest you leave as well. Now let me go."

Oryn rested a hand on my arm and slowly pried my hand away from Visha. "It will be fine, my king. You may go."

Backing a few steps I said, "No. No, I'm not going anywhere."

"Snow will skin me for letting you see this," Visha said, tearing through Snow's shirt with a dagger. She gasped at the sight of the seal. "She's never let it open so far." Black tentacles of ink spread from the circle of the seal, crawling and pulsing as they expanded and thickened to cover every inch of her skin.

"She can do it," Oryn said, folding his sleeves back and reaching to hold Snow's head. Flutters of a bright magenta smoke wavered from his body till it enveloped him completely.

"Move back," Visha ordered. The witch's form began glowing red till the halo surrounding her flickered and shivered like a crimson fire, mimicking Oryn's magic. The air sang from the dark magic—a hymn of the dead. My own senses shivered, feeling the spiritual crack open and form a tear in space between Numen and Caligo like a gate—an invisible portal.

"*Tāha ār I dāraiokt ōn āet tāhōs.*" *I call upon all gates of his magic*, Visha recited followed by Oryn, and Snow's body enveloped with phantom flames.

And as it did so, she let a soul tearing scream and her hands violently pulled on the chains. The more magic Visha drew from her, the more she struggled.

Lightning skittered all over the room and the outside howled with thunder. Dark deep rumbles rolled over the mountains of Taren and echoed all over the valley till the castle shook on its foundations. The black ink on Snow's back shivered and began shrinking the more Visha chanted her craft.

My wife thrashed, her shoulders arching while she tugged on the chains holding her. Blood dripped from under her gloves, soaking the white sleeves of her blouse.

I couldn't watch this. Damned be the realm. Damned be all for all I cared.

Visha extended a hand to the side, stopping me. Her eyes had veiled a glowing red when she turned to me. "Don't. This is what she wants."

What Snow wants.

Helpless as ever, I stood there—watching.

Numbness had set in by the time Snow had stopped fighting and the seal had closed and magic had faded away into whatever hole they'd opened between this realm and the Otherworld. Tugging her bounds off, I picked her up in my arms, and she snuggled her face in my neck. A small sigh came out of her as I pressed her closer to me.

Her lips moved to form a word over my skin.

"What is it, my love? What is it, my heart?"

"Spring." The words were airy and soft.

I held her tightly against me, pressing my lips to her cheeks. "Do I still smell like it?"

She nodded.

I rested my forehead against hers and whispered, "You scared me."

A light smile ghosted her lips. "I'm a scary person."

Oryn stood before us, lowering his folded sleeves and glancing between Snow and I. "You need to teach her to control her magic without relying so much on the seal. Like you control your own magic."

"It is not the same," I said.

He pursed his lips and shook his head. "It is in a sense. Elding Aura lay on a scale between elemental and spiritual magic. But that is not her issue." He kneeled before us. "Her issue is that she leaves rein to emotion. She is angry and thunder blasts. She is frustrated and ice blisters. She is happy and the sky is shining. Teach her to disconnect her emotions from her magic. You, my king, have already mastered that control as your magic is highly relying on emotion." He pointed at her. "Teach her your ways."

"What ways?" Snow asked.

"I believe your husband has to take the time to explain them to you," Oryn said, standing. "War will come even if not led by the divine. Battles are short, but war can last for years to no end. You need to learn to use your power, not let it learn to use you."

A knock rasped on the door and Snow tensed in my arms. "Don't let them see me like this."

I turned to Visha and said, "Tell them that the bargain demands I take her to Amaris for the night and that I'll return her at dawn."

As soon as Visha nodded in confirmation, I faded the two of us to my bedroom.

The sun had just kissed the sky with lovely hues of burnt orange and red, barely the start of sunset in Adriata. There was a fresh set of white roses on my table and a note from Atlas.

For Snowlin. Tell her I am happy she reunited with her family.

I set her down and threw my jacket over her exposed shoulders that had puckered with gooseflesh.

"He is a cute kid," Snow said, taking a rose out of the vase.

"He will forever hold a grudge if he hears you called him a kid and cute."

"Our secret then."

I kissed the tip of her nose. "Our secret."

She yawned and made a pained sound when she attempted to stretch. Immediately, panic filled me and I searched her body for injuries that I might have missed. And even though I'd found none, no part of me relaxed.

"Bathe me," she said, and I did as told. Pulling her with me and filling the tub with hot water and tons of those smelling salts and herbs that she liked.

Once she was out of the torn clothes, she helped me get out of mine and I lifted her in my arms, dipping the two of us in the water. She sighed when the heat enveloped her body, leaning back to rest on my chest. "What method, Kilian?"

"It is a practice Obscurs are taught before our blessing blooms. We meditate to facilitate emotion, control it to our desire and maybe even get rid of it completely."

She looked over her shoulder at me. "Rid?"

"Yes," I said, lathering her arms with soap. "Strong emotion can sometimes accentuate our magic, so we train to douse or raise them, but emotions such as greed, jealousy, envy, those are completely useless to us and only hinder and disbalance our emotional state and therefore our connection with the spiritual. So we train...to get rid of them."

"And you want me to do that?"

"No, I think Oryn didn't mean it like that. I think he meant to teach you self-soothing—to draw power instead of letting your emotions do it for you."

"Like when we met the *Ybris* at the temple."

"Yes, sort of like that."

"And that would work?"

"I believe it would help you control just how much you draw out from the seal and even store outside of it like most elementals do so you don't have to ask for magic that pours out of you."

"Alright then," she said, spinning round a little to lay on her side before resting her cheek on my chest. As always, her fingers began skimming my skin till they landed on a scar near my shoulder. One she already knew how I'd gotten it.

"You made me afraid today," I murmured, dropping a kiss to her hair.

"I think I always make you afraid, Adriatian," she mumbled half asleep.

"I had thought I'd got rid of it, Snow. First thing I learned to get rid of. Never felt it for myself or anyone. Only for you."

Her breathing had slowed, expression went lax with drowsiness, but she managed to whisper, "You make me afraid, too."

She'd rested for a while. Sleeping soundly in my hold. When the water started turning cold, I very hesitantly brought the both of us out of the water and wrapped a massive towel around her. Once I'd bundled her up in my arms, I pushed the bedding out of the way and laid her down. When I cradled her to my chest, she sighed and said, "At least you're not six foot four for nothing."

"From the beginning of my existence till the end of it, I am all for you and all yours."

She sighed and snuggled closer to me. "Sprouting poetry again, husband?"

I nudged her nose with mine. "Don't act like you don't like my verses." Throwing a leg over hers and tucking her tight to me, I said, "Sleep."

As usual, she tucked her hands under my shirt, laying her palms flat against my stomach and melting in my hold. And sleep swept her away in seconds.

She was awake before I was. I could feel her staring at me and couldn't help the smile tugging on my lips. The way she always did this made a part of me glow with warmth.

"You're awake."

"The force of your thoughts woke me," I said, cracking my eyes open. It was still fairly dark outside, the sun just breaking the surface in a dim purple light. My attention glued on her and how divine she looked beside me, her long hair pooling all over us. The other day I found a bunch on my table. They were everywhere actually, and I liked it. It meant that she was really here and that I'd not grown a concerning level of daydreaming.

I ran a finger down the bridge of her nose and she wiggled it as if it tickled. "You're a painting."

"I know I am," she said, raising on her elbow and giving me a sultry look. "Should I have a portrait done for you?"

I wrapped my arms around her and hoisted her atop of me. "Why, when I have the real thing." This realm's moon hung on the skies, mine laid beside me, smiling and radiant. And for a moment, a split moment, it was full again. My moon had the sun in her eyes, too. So when she was happy, not only did she glow but she shone, too.

She kissed one of the scars on my chest and then the other. She kissed all three of them and then my chin. Her touches, her lips, her caress were gentle—always so gentle. Fuck, I must have died and gone to heaven.

"You smell like lemons," she said, nuzzling my neck.

Lemons? "I use a citrus soap."

"It's from a soap?" She frowned, abruptly standing and leaving the bed, heading toward the bathing chambers. Only to return with a bunch of my soaps in her hand, sniffing them one after the other, dropping whatever she didn't like. "None. You smell like none of them."

"I use the last one you dropped."

She picked it up again and sniffed it one more time before dropping it again. "No, that smells bitter. You smell sweet. Like lemon flowers."

"I smell like flowers?"

"Lemon flowers, be precise." She climbed over me again, laying her head on my chest. "Laundry detergent," she said to no one and pushed her head up. "Take me to the servant chambers, now."

That made me chuckle. "They use unscented detergent because scents irritate Driada's lungs."

"Oh."

"Maybe I've picked it up from the gardens."

"No, you smelled like that in Isjord too."

"A mystery. Come," I said, getting the two of us up. "Let's not make them wait any longer. I'm sure they are anxious to see you."

It didn't take long to find them. Already in the dining room and anxiously waiting for Snow.

Her sister jumped from her seat and ran almost knocking Snow on the ground. The two were like two water droplets from afar, but immensely distinguishable up close. It looked utterly unreal to me that she was joined with her loved ones—how unreal it must seem to her. "You should have stayed yesterday."

"That is entirely my fault," I explained.

Thora uncurled from her sister and turned to me. There was the same sort of steel in her emerald eyes resembling Snow's. "Twelve years might have passed, but I know the way her brain functions." She bowed her head. "You must be—"

"Kilian," Eren called, interrupting the younger sister. My old friend greeted me with a tight embrace. Almost fourteen years and he'd not changed not one bit. He was alive—he'd been alive for all these years.

"Hello, old friend." If I was finding it unbelievable that Eren was here, how unbelievable was all of this for Snow?

"Hello, crazy bastard." We both chuckled and when he pulled back, his stare flitted between his sister and I. "You did it. You married her."

The whole room went quiet.

"What are you talking about?" Snow asked, gradually frowning.

This was not how I'd planned for her to find out.

Eren looked surprised. "He hasn't told you?"

I could see Snow's gears spinning and cracking furiously attempting to work out what was happening. "Tell me what?"

"He was going to ask father for your hand," Eren loosely explained before I could, and Snow's brows dipped lower. "After you met at Urinthia's coronation."

Snow's look shifted wide with bewilderment. "Urinthia's coronation? I haven't met—" She froze. Her expression falling. And falling some more. I saw the crash before I felt it—the realisation that I'd been lying to her.

"You're the grey eyed boy?" Thora asked, a bright smile stretching wide on her lips. "She never stopped talking about you for months."

She'd remembered me. The thought shouldn't have made me smile because Snow looked like she wanted to tear my head off.

"I never stopped thinking of her either," I said, planting a kiss on Snow's temple. "I will go now. All of you must have so much to catch up with."

I made it halfway down the corridor when a gloved hand wrapped around my wrist. She breathed unevenly—her gilded stare searching me as if it was trying to remember and make sense. "Were you ever going to tell me?"

"Would it have made any difference?"

She stared at me as though it was the first time she'd seen me. "You pretended you didn't know me. I remember you hating me to death when we met and now…now I hear this. It's ridiculous. I don't understand. It's ridiculous, Kilian. Tell me."

"Pretend, my love. It was all pretend."

"It was too convincing."

"I had many to convince, not just you. The whole council, the whole of Adriata. Myself, too."

Her chest rose furiously. I'd never seen her more at war with herself. "Why?"

One truth—I would tell her this one truth. "Would you like to hear how I killed my father?"

She frowned and took the smallest step closer to me. My chest tightened when she didn't back away from me as she always did. "How?"

So I told her what no one else knew. The one secret I'd carried alone. "When I was a boy, I told him that I liked someone. Perhaps more than just liked. We'd spoken once and only had stolen faraway glances at her, but I told him that I could see a future with her, grow old and never be bored. Old, yes, because the girl was human. At least so I thought then. I would have given up my eternity for her. And I would have not regretted it. Father cried that day. The first time I'd seen him cry. First time he'd been happy for me. He fell sick the next day and died a week later. Heartbreak—I reminded him of his own heartbreak because I wanted to be with that girl. If I had not said anything—" I shook my head and she stepped closer, her other hand holding onto my jacket as if she needed to steady herself. "If I had not wanted you so madly, this would have never happened. That night would have never happened. You would have been happy." I rested my forehead on hers and finally breathed the words out, "I am sorry. I am so sorry, Snow."

She was struggling to breathe. "This can't be real. It cannot be. It cannot. Tell me it wasn't you. Tell me it is not real. Tell me that fate isn't truly that twisted."

"I don't wish to lie about this."

She stared at me. She stared at my eyes for a long time. "How did I forget? I always hated the stormy skies, and the dull grey of winter. But then somehow they became my favourite thing. How could one like the colour grey? It is such an odd colour to like."

This was madness. Utter madness. "You are making me entirely too happy right now."

Stunned—she was beyond stunned. Something else lingered behind those twin suns—something grave. "Were you really going to marry me?"

I nodded. "Father already knew and approved of it. He had already sent word to Silas and were going to meet to discuss the possibility of a union. He died shortly after."

"And the agreement with my father? Did it have to do something with this?"

"No, I was going to come to you at your pace. I was going to find you someday because I'd sworn it to you whether you wanted to marry me or kill me, it didn't matter. The agreement just sped up that process."

She shook her head. "Why keep this from me?"

I ran my knuckles over her cheek. "I didn't. I wrote it all to you. After Nia told me you chose to throw the letters away I figured it was a truth better left untold. And you'd long forgotten me."

She raised a hand to my face, tracing a delicate finger over my eye and her expression cracked. It would never change our fates. Nothing would. I knew her so well. I knew her mind better than I knew her heart. And I meant one thing in her grand scheme of things—a means of retaliation. She needed it. And I would give it to her.

"Are we still stealing time?"

"Always, my love," I said, kissing both her eyes and she breathed out a sigh. "But I am a better thief now. If I am stealing, I better do it well." My attention went behind me, where Thora was standing at the door, waiting for her sister whom she hadn't seen in thirteen years. "Stay in Taren tonight. With your sister."

She nodded. "Alright."

Chapter Thirty

Caelifer

Snowlin

Eren still had an indecipherable look on his face after Kilian left. Thora too. Both looked confused.
But I was more confused. Them being here. What Kilian had told me. This felt a lot like one of those messes my brain made up when I wanted the world to disappear and reinvented it myself.

My head hurt—it hurt terribly as I tried to recall that memory that Kilian had kept for fifteen years. How had I forgotten?

"Someone say something," Thora whispered carefully, looking between Eren and I.

It was Eren who leaned forward. "So, Kilian—"

I rolled my eyes and my brother howled with laughter, gales of laughter. Till he ran a hand over his eyes, mouth quivering as he said, "Thought I'd never see you roll your eyes at me again."

Thora frowned at him. "Something happier."

Alaric ran into the meeting room at that moment, breathless and panting. Tears streaked his red cheeks as he took in Thora and Eren. "Gods, blessed gods." He opened his arms wide and Thora flew onto his embrace. The same as she'd done when she'd been little.

He pulled back to cup her face, his eyes spilling with tears. "You're all grown."

"You look old now."

He chuckled. "Yeah, nice to see you too, Thora."

She cocked her head to the side to study him. "It must be that dreaded beard."

Alaric pinched her nose making her yelp. "You never change, do you? Rottenly sincere."

My sister shrugged. "You told me to never lie."

He laughed. "I did, didn't I?" Alaric's attention softened and melted again when he looked at my brother. "Son."

Eren and him shared a long embrace. The two had been the closest to one another. Eren was the son Alaric always wanted and Alaric was the father Eren never had.

"Forgive me," Alaric said through sobs. "Forgive me for not being there that night. For letting your mother die, for losing you, for making Snow hurt the way no child should ever hurt."

"Nothing to forgive you for," my brother said. "I bear the guilt for making all the wrong decisions that night."

The food I was chewing began turning bitter. "If we are all quite done pointing fingers and bearing guilt, might we please sit down. You're giving me indigestion."

Eren cocked a brow at me. "Some things never change."

Alaric laughed and clasped his shoulder, "Trust me, not for one moment."

Thora tilted her head to me. "Men in this family are too emotional."

I smiled at her and she smiled back at me. Had we ever smiled at one another before?

It was her who looked away first, lowering her tear glazed eyes to the table and swallowing hard.

The air was awkward. We'd all gone silent. I never ate in silence. I wanted to know it all. How they had lived and how they had grown. If they had suffered, if they had been in pain. But somehow I couldn't. Somehow, I didn't know how to form those questions. So I only stared at them, glancing between my brother and sister and holding back tears.

It was real.

If I extended my hand to touch her she would not vanish between my fingers.

The dining room began filling with people arriving for breakfast. The more greetings, tears, hugs and blessings I heard the more the ache in my chest soothed. It was real. They were real.

Sebastian came into the dining room, bowing to all of us. He stood taken aback, staring between my sister and I. "You do look alike."

"Eren," Alaric said, "You remember my nephew, Sebastian."

My brother offered him a polite smile. "Of course."

My spy bowed again at him before regarding me with a troubled look. "Silas has gone mad over Isjord looking for you."

From the corner of my eye, I saw Thora and Eren tense. "A little bit more madness won't hurt him, Bash."

"My queen," he called, sternly. "He is turning over every rock in Isjord. The Night King was masquerading as the unblessed emissary and now Silas thinks or likes to think the unblessed have something to do with this. He is practically holding them all hostage in Tenebrose. You have just given him a pretext to attack the unblessed and raid their lands for the sceptre and the metal. The unblessed Isles will do nothing to aid the Vrammethen mainland. Not when there is reason. Comnhall will be the next Adriata and he will get his metal with no trade at all."

"You said the unblessed are still in Isjord?"

He nodded.

"Keep an eye on them for now and let me know when they will set sail. As for Silas, I will have Kilian send out news to father and the whole of Isjord, it ought to keep my father from using this golden opportunity."

"Their ships are anchored in Grasmere, Snow. Gara controls all their itinerary and the Isjordian fleet that will escort them out at sea. I'm afraid we are blind there still."

"Did you receive my letter from the servant?"

His mouth tipped up. "Yes. I did. And the package is secured."

Stabbing my fork on a carrot, I forced it into my mouth, hoping the vile taste of the vegetable could tone down my amusement. And it did. "Well done, Bash."

Alaric was frowning at me. "What package?"

"Do you really want to know?" I asked, sipping on some water. "It won't do your heart any good."

"This is so strange," Thora noted, munching on a piece of bread. "You really are queen."

"Wait till they bend down and kiss my toes."

Her eyes went wide and she giggled.

Lazarus came next, frowning as usual. "Saw your husband on the way out," he growled, taking a seat and tearing through an apple.

My sister studied him head to toe. First impressions had always been very important to her. It took only one look for her to lose all interest in someone. "Must have truly been a humbling experience for you." And there was her judgement.

He frowned. "Who are you?"

"Thora Isa Krigborn."

Skygard—I wanted to correct. But this was foreign land to her while I'd spent the past decade engraving myself as a Skygard. What if she hated it here?

Lazarus shot up from his seat, glancing between my siblings and I. "You've found them."

"Actually," Thora drew out with a polite smile. "Her husband did."

He cleared his throat and turned to me. "I've left soldiers holding Fogling guard. I'm leaving for Myrdur tonight. There have been sightings of squadrons with Crafters travelling through Tenebrose."

"Make sure no one makes it past the ruins and get Visha with you to plant hexes around the Volants."

The winged general nodded. "I think we should hold forts in our mountains. I've got a feeling we are nearing the time where we won't be able to hide anymore."

Something crawled up my stomach—something resembling fear. And I hated it.

"What happens if they make it past the ruins?" Thora asked. "Won't the old mist hold them back?"

"Crafters are feeding on a beast's blood, their powers have gotten stronger. Snow believes they could find a way through it," Alaric explained. "And Silas will find out about Olympia."

Eren and I crossed the obsidian bridge connecting the castle to the city. I had brought him with me to see the kingdom—his kingdom. He was not only the crown prince of Isjord, but Olympia's as well, which meant he was the true king and I held his position. Eren deserved my seat more than anyone in this realm. This was my kingdom, it would still be mine—always. Nothing would change even if Eren came into power, perhaps all would be better.

The city was at its busiest, the whole mountain face bustled and roamed with carriages, merchants, children and those busy tending to their business. My chest expanded with pride at how far we'd come.

"I would have never imagined this," Eren said, taking in the expanding city. "Mother told me stories, but the greatness exceeds anything she has ever described."

"It is so much more than this. More than you can ever imagine. The kingdom expands for uncountable miles, all hidden right before your very eyes. Not only surviving but thriving."

He gave me a smile and wrapped an unsure arm around my shoulders. "I have heard more about you from your people than I had thought I knew about my little sister. I could not believe this wild child had become the queen they had described. Mother would have been so proud just as I am right now."

I'd forgotten how his words felt. How warm and comforting they were. "I want the best the heavens can offer for our kingdom and now I think the best this kingdom can have stands before me." I halted and turned to face him. "You were the crown prince, the throne I am holding now feels as if it doesn't belong to me. I will pass the crown to you. You are the true king of Olympia."

He frowned. "There is no such thing as a true king or queen, that throne is yours. I am no king, never had any desire to become one either despite how I was raised." He rested a warm palm on my cheek. "Can we please speak of something else."

We spent the whole afternoon just chatting and walking the grounds of Taren. He'd changed a lot. But so had I. Yet nothing felt odd about it. And all worry melted off my shoulders before it was noon.

As much as Eren had made it my decision, I was smart enough to know that it wasn't mine alone to make. So I gathered a meeting with the tribe leaders.

Cai arrived first. His grey leathers rugged and worn. When he dropped to the chair next to mine, he let out a long, tired sigh. I had not seen him in weeks.

"You look...tired?"

He slowly turned to me. "Your compliments always flatter me. Apologies even more."

"Cai—"

"How many times do we have to go through this, Cakes? How many times do I have to go through this?"

"Not for long. Bear with me till then. I will try and stay alive until then."

He frowned at me. "And after. Will you try and stay alive after?"

"Depends. Will I be getting my salted caramel candy?"

He reached into his pocket and threw me one. How in the hells did he have them at ready? "Say stupid things like that again and I'll make sure to grow a pepper bed over your grave."

"That is terrifying."

He threw me another candy. "Shut up."

Oh, damned hells. I almost forgot. "Cai," I said, munching on the sweet. "Don't flirt with my brother."

My friend cocked up an amused brow. "Why would I flirt—" His words got cut in the middle when Eren strutted in the meeting room and sat across from him.

I rolled my eyes when Cai's smile grew serpentine. "The brother, I presume."

"Eren," I said. "This is Cai, my best friend, my general and someone I've had the honour of calling my brother for the past thirteen years."

Eren bowed his head. "Pleasure, Cai."

My friend's grin was wide. "Pleasure is all mine."

Oh gods.

The meeting had fallen silent after my words. They looked mad at what I had proposed.

"With all respect to you, my queen, and His Highness," Gilmor, the Lanner tribe leader, spoke first. "But we chose you not because you were heir, not because of the bloodline you carried or the power that you channel—we chose you because of the sacrifice, tears and blood you poured onto this kingdom since you were no more than a child. You wore the obsidian crown and took the reins of trouble without being asked, without doubting, without faltering. Not once."

Grunts and nods of approval followed. It left me a bit astounded.

Had it been what they had thought then? When I wore that crown, all I remember seeing was fear. A Krigborn queen on an Olympian throne. An *Ybris* with powers she could not comprehend herself.

"We saw it in you the day you lost your team in the mountains. You wore no grief, no pain, only the pride and the hard work of the soldiers you had lost. You stood the day we buried them—that very difficult day for only a sixteen-year-old girl who had faced and battled the guardian of death—solemn, like a queen," Darron, the eldest of us and leader of Alder, said. "Then we heard your pain and grief in the troubled skies, echoed in your cries at night as you counted name by name every soldier you had lost every night in your nightmares for months. When you make the trip to their graves every year though you knew them for barely days. We knew then what we had in front of us. A warrior strong enough to battle the storm, compassionate to soothe the wind, with knowledge that paved rocks and the confidence of a lightning strike. All qualities of an Olympian ruler. The same we saw in your uncle, your grandfather and your every ancestor before. We saw it then and we have kept seeing it every day since. You are queen. Have you ever questioned why we crowned a child to take the throne?"

"The Olympian throne was empty."

"The Olympian throne needed a leader," he said. "It needed you. Your Krigborn wits and your Skygard heart."

I looked over at Alaric and saw pride in his smile. "We are people of the skies, kid, we all see despite what you know how to hide well."

Eren nodded at their words and turned to me. "It appears we all agree. What do we say, little sister, shall we put this to rest?"

I nodded.

Bayrd leaned onto the table and Cai dropped his head back with a sigh, anticipating whatever the Volant leader had to say. "There is another matter at hand that needs to be discussed as we are dealing with matters of the throne."

"You never lose a feather, do you?" Cai said and I caught my brother's smile at my general's words.

Ignoring him, Bayrd turned to me. "We have all three grandchildren of Jonah here and we have no need for a foreign king. It feels like a matter of time before you truly crown him before our people, your mother's killer, as that. Is that what you want?"

I knew he was attempting to goad me. But what I didn't know was why it was working. It was true. The bargain was ending—should have already ended. And the lifeline Kilian was attached to with it. The way that thought filled my stomach with discomfort made me angry. Why did what I'd been waiting for years made me uncomfortable?

"What I want, Bayrd, is to have reassurance of support when my father opens war toward the continent."

"It doesn't feel like it."

"And do tell, what does it feel like?" Cai pushed through clenched teeth.

"Like a lie," Bayrd said fearlessly. "And for the sake of your people, I suggest you take action to put such rumours at peace."

"Whose rumours?" my brother asked, tilting his head to study Bayrd. "Presumably yours?"

The man bristled. "With all due respect—"

"Don't start a sentence speaking about respect when you have no intention of being respectful," my brother said. "I might have only arrived yesterday, but I helped my mother raise this kingdom from its foundations. I have known you since the day she made you leader of the Volants. People speak. It is not so difficult, Bayrd. To know."

I tapped a finger on the table. "Let's cut it short, shall we? What is it that you want, Bayrd?"

"Resume your engagement to my son. Two true Olympians on the throne, ruling by one another as gods have dictated from the start of our times. Better than anyone, my queen, you know the consequence of marrying another kind. We Olympians adore the spiritual, live by it and for it. We haven't had a single king or queen who has had an unblessed marriage. Yet you wear no band of blessing, nor will you ever be able to get it from the gods if you marry him. Not to think of heirs which you could never have with him." He glanced at a few other tribe leaders who he surely had discussed this with and had obviously disagreed with him from the scathing look he gave them. "Though a piece of paper can suffice many, we Volantians will not put our sacred laws behind."

I turned my attention to Lazarus who had remained silent all the way through his father's words. "Is that what you want?" Men and their selfishness never ceased to disappoint me. I needed to know who was pushing this. Who did I have to kill, son or father?

Cai cursed under his breath and Eren scrutinised me with uncertainty.

"You were all I ever wanted," Lazarus said. "And I do think my father is right."

I nodded. "We will continue this meeting another time." Perhaps a beheading could clear up my mind.

As the room began to empty, Bayrd turned to me one last time. "Consider it well, Your Majesty."

Two beheadings? I leaned forward. "You'd be rather surprised, Bayrd, but I've considered everything rather well. Have you?"

"It will not be my fault if my people wish to distance themselves from Olympia."

The air chilled. "It will not be my fault either when I pull the *zgahna* over the Volants and let the rest of you become skewered meat for Isjordians and Fogling. This is my land, not because you or the land fear me, but because I am the land and I am fear. Think well, Bayrd. Are you willing to be the face of disaster?"

"I'll be whatever is best for my people."

"Mine," I bit out. "My people."

Bayrd said nothing.

The meeting chamber's doors had barely shut when Cai said, "You better be considering this well, Cakes."

"I am."

"Lazarus is a prick," he snarled. "His father is worse."

"Good thing I am not making Bayrd king then."

He growled. "If you do this just to spite Kilian and to shut up Bayrd, perhaps your brother should have taken that offer when he had the chance."

"Don't throw me as bait," Eren said.

Cai cocked his head to the side, giving my brother one prolonged perusal. "You're too handsome for bait. Perhaps…an offering?"

My brother smiled. "Still bait with a bow."

"You'd look good with a bow."

"Assumptions," Eren hummed. "Do I assume you are presumptuous by character or good with your imagination?"

Cai's mouth twitched at my brother's words. "A bit of both?"

I slammed a hand on the table and then pointed between the two. "If you must be like that, do it when I am not present. I'm feeling that slice of lemon cake I ate back in my mouth."

Cai pointed back at me. "Don't do it to spite Kilian."

That made me frown. Had he been recruited in Kilian's little fan group? "You two friends now all of a sudden?"

My friend gave me a coy look. "You and Lazarus more than a short ride before dawn now? Emphasis on short."

Eren's eyes doubled in size. "You and that general—"

I raised a hand. "Don't finish, please. And no, not anymore."

My brother nodded and leaned back. "Does Kilian know?"

My temples throbbed. "I will pretend you didn't just ask me that."

"Kilian knows," Cai said and turned to give me a wide grin. "Had the unfortunate opportunity to hear first-hand how Lazarus has handled you. Kilian would have grilled him. Almost grilled him. But the birdbrain was smart enough to back away first."

Oh gods.

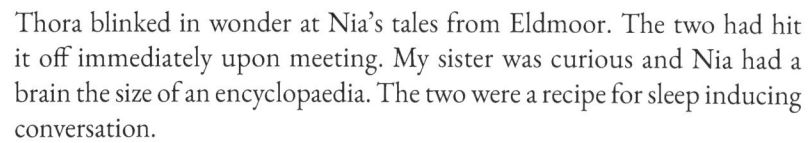

Thora blinked in wonder at Nia's tales from Eldmoor. The two had hit it off immediately upon meeting. My sister was curious and Nia had a brain the size of an encyclopaedia. The two were a recipe for sleep inducing conversation.

"So," my little sister said, arranging her cross-legged position on my bed. "You planted a poison in their borders? To nullify the veil around Red Coven?"

My friend who sat facing her nodded. "It will take a while to grow, but yes, essentially. Blue gyre is the opposite to mirk root when used carefully." She pointed a finger over a tiny blue three leafed flower on her book. "It has to be planted with silver otherwise it will bear no effect. Before I dropped the seeds, I had them dipped in powdered silver. It will eventually weaken the veil enough for me to go through."

Thora blinked half amazed and confused, flipping through Nia's book. "There are material things that can nullify magic?"

"So many."

My sister gaped a little. "How do you know all of this?"

"I wanted to be a healer once."

"Once? You don't want to be one anymore?"

Nia shook her head. "I was asked to heal a criminal during my apprenticeship, and I refused to help someone who deserved to rot for what he'd done. Apparently, a healer has no choice in whom they heal, the duty is to just heal. You cannot be selective, but I couldn't help but be selective."

My sister nodded vehemently. "I'd have to agree with you."

I'd not said a word. Only listening to the two go back and forth about things as simple as life itself. And I listened. Stared. Until they'd both had fallen asleep after exhausting their voice cords with all sorts of conversation. Now wedged between Nia and Thora, I laid back on the massive bed with no desire to sleep while the two snored softly.

If I closed my eyes, would it all disappear?

Could one be afraid to be happy?

The little clear sparkling stone decorating my ceiling glistened and it was all it took for me to think his words. How had I forgotten him?

A shadow flickered on my balcony, and I immediately rose from the bed in its direction. Carefully stepping around Nia so I wouldn't wake her. Flutters crawled my body with anticipation as I tiptoed outside.

"Can't sleep?" he asked, leaning on the ledge of the balcony.

My eyes raked over his half naked frame and I swear my mouth watered. Walking to him, I traced the thin faded scars he had gotten in Hanai and his muscles twitched in reaction to my touch. "No. You?"

"Not when you aren't." Lifting me at the waist, he put me on the balcony ledge, separating my knees so he could fit himself between. Softly, he petted my hair then my face before both his palms began kneading my thighs. "How are you so beautiful?"

Putting my legs around his hips, I linked my ankles together and pulled him flush against me. "Heavens owed it to me. It was the least they could do after everything."

He chuckled, running his knuckles over my cheek. "And I owe them a thank you. It helps that you're pleasant to my eye. Compensation for the hardship on my ears."

"Ah, a real charmer you are, husband. Thank the gods for that bargain with my father or you would have lived a life of solitude."

His gaze went dark. "I would have."

"Kilian?"

"Hm?" With a finger he tipped my chin up to look at him. The moment he saw through my distress, a deep frown pulled between his dark brows.

Touching the silver band on his ring finger, I said, "I need you to end it. Our...marriage. It is only a piece of paper. It won't mean anything more or less, you know."

The Olympian night darkened as did his expression. "Tell me why."

"Now that Eren and Thora are here, my people will feel safer. The council might ask that I resume my arrangement with Lazarus. A true Olympian union. One that would be blessed." I'd never marry anyone. Never again. I don't think I could. But it was time he and I broke the ties stringing us together little by little before they tangled even more along the lie we'd enshrouded ourselves in.

His hands left me. "No."

"I was not asking."

"If he thinks I will hand him what's mine on a platter, he is wrong. Severely so." He backed away and then he was gone, fading out of sight.

I dropped my face in my hands. Hells, why was this so hard for?

"Come back," I whispered into the emptiness.

Like a prayer, he faded back and strode to me, lifting me up again and I immediately locked my arms around his neck and my legs around his waist.

"Forgive me," he whispered as he nuzzled his face on my neck. "I shouldn't have left angry. Forgive me for getting angry."

"Will you do as I said?"

"I didn't say that."

That made me laugh and me laughing seemed to make him laugh too.

Why did I enjoy these small moments of domesticity between us? The simple embrace, the soft laughs, the small touches. With him I felt starved. I craved them more. And he seemed to always know what I yearned for because he gave them to me regardless.

How had I not remembered him?

"Love?" He eyed my gloved hands. "Why are you wearing them to bed?"

Immediately, my fingers curled to fists. "I don't want them to see."

"They deserve to know of your pains and aches, my heart, enough hiding from those that care."

"They will worry."

He peeled a glove off and kissed my fingertips. "As they should. They will figure it out one day as I did. Believe me, the part where you have to guess and doubt and fear is worse than being told the truth."

"Spouting all sorts of philosophies now, Adriatian?" But he was right.

"That seems cosy." I startled upward at the interruption. Nia leaned on the balcony door, arms crossed and severely amused.

"It is," I said, wiggling my locked feet. "Want to try? He is big enough for two."

Kilian made a choking sound and nuzzled my neck to hide his chuckles. "You do realise how bad that sounded."

"What is—" a sleepy Thora said with a yawn, coming from behind Nia. Her brows almost met her hairline. "Oh."

Oh gods.

"We have been caught," Kilian whispered and then kissed my neck before letting go of me to face them. "I apologise, ladies."

"You don't look sorry," Thora said, and Nia laughed.

"I am not, actually," Kilian offered with a cocky grin.

Thora assessed everything with her usual scrutiny. "Alaric is taking us to Drava tomorrow, to celebrate our return. You should come with us," she offered.

"I don't think—"

"Come," I said quietly.

He turned to me a little surprised. "I will then."

"Can you," my sister started, a little nervous, "can you get down from there, Snow?"

I jumped from the balcony ledge and my sister flinched back in the room. Immediate worry cursed through me, but I didn't get a chance to look further into it as she went back inside.

"What was that about?"

Nia looked behind her and then at me. "She hasn't been near a window or the stairs at all. Looks like the height of the castle scares her. I faded us to Taren because she couldn't walk the bridge during our walk."

Heights? "She has never been scared of heights before."

"I'll find out," Nia offered. "I know how to be gentle with other people's secrets without scaring them." She pointed a finger to me. "Don't try. Your approach to other people's feelings is too aggressive." With that, she left Kilian and I alone again.

"The gears are spinning," he said in my ear, his warm breath making me shiver.

"They are."

He turned me to him and gave me a long kiss on my forehead. "Good night, my love."

What? I gripped the hem of his trousers "They know you are here, why would you go?"

Slowly, his brows went up. "You want me to stay?"

"Stay," I said, pushing him back till the balcony ledge stopped him. "Entertain me, Adriatian, I'm bored." I was tired—really tired, and sleep kept pestering me for a while now. But if I shut my eyes, I saw what I'd been seeing every night in Isjord. Nightmares. However, this time I was not running from monsters of night, I was running from myself. Because every time I stopped, he was in my arms bleeding, life seeping away and fading. And I held the dagger to his heart.

He ran the back of his finger down my cheek. "How about I tell you a story?"

"Sure," I said, leaning to rest my head on his chest. "Tell me a story." Anything to distract me from what I was going to do sooner than later.

CHAPTER THIRTY-ONE

Oscen

Thora

Olympia was my ultimate nightmare. Wherever I looked and whenever I turned there was a tall fall. Thankfully, the training courts were between a long glen stretching along the two highest peaks of Taren. Bodies moved chasing one another, sparring and duelling yet all I could see were blurred figures. My mind had already drifted to another place not long after we'd gotten here. To a world that was mine and mine alone. One small—so small that only I could fit in it. An empty one, but one where there was no one to hurt or hurt me.

Someone threw an arm over my shoulders and I jerked upright. "Where did I lose you to?"

It took me a moment to jump from my safe haven to reality, and when I did, Eren stared at me with a frown like always. "Just thinking."

"Of what?"

"Things."

He turned tense as always. "Rora."

"Please, can we not? I swear it is not like before."

"What is not like before?" Snow asked, coming to kneel before me. She reached to rest a hand on my knee but pulled away.

"You're going to hog them for yourself all day?" Cai, her friend, called, crossing the training court distance to us. His eyes slipped to my brother for a small moment before they focused on Snow. "You could have taken them to see the north, the south. And you brought them here."

That had been because of me. Everywhere we'd seen today had been flat land.

Snow stood. "Why are you dirty?"

He slung a hand over her neck. "Someone has to do your dirty work in Myrdur."

My sister tensed and I could feel the alarm from the way her eyes settled. "This early?"

"They had made camp in Fernfoss last night. All were young, probably excited to do their part."

"How young?" Eren asked, he was tense too, but a different tense from Snow. He worried.

Cai's look was downcast. "Young."

"What is with all the grimness?" Another voice came from behind the two. Malik. Kilian's brother. He winked at Cai and slapped his bottom. "Looking all cute, my muffin. The ruggedness really works for me."

My brother's brows were a bit higher than usual. "You two—"

"No," Caiden said quickly. "He is just an arsehole."

Malik frowned. "Cai, my sweet, careful, some people might think we are friends." He sat next to me as the others began chatting about Myrdur, sprawling on the bench, and I glided a bit further away. The movement was small, but his attention snapped to me, gaze travelling from the tip of my boots to my hair. "Little bird."

"Thora."

He eyed the bow on my hair. "Wasn't that what I said?"

I frowned. "Is it a hearing or a comprehension issue?"

His mouth pulled up in a slow smile. "I've got something for you?"

"For me?"

He brought out a little yellow stone pendant and put it on my hand. "Apologies for the colour choice, but I made the assumption that your eyes were the same as your sister's."

No one had given me jewellery before. Quickly, I undid the clasps and put it around my neck. "Thank you, yellow is one of my favourite colours. It's Snow's eyes."

Suddenly, someone sat between us, forcing us to part. "Quit bothering her," Nia said, and I laughed.

His eyes slid to me again, but only for a moment. "Did you put Moriko to sleep with one of your spicy contraptions? How is it that you are not in her bed at this hour in the afternoon?"

The two began bickering and snarling at one another, and I felt overwhelm coat my attention to a glazing white and fill my hearing with a swarm of bees.

So many people. So many people loved Snow. Snow was so loved. She'd not been alone. For that I was grateful.

She already had a family. A beautiful family.

Would we ever fit in that?

My presence felt ugly, malign. Unwanted.

A winged woman dropped from the skies and I jerked a little. She was clad in all grey, leather armour and an expression as hard as her armour. "My queen, might I have a moment. Sebastian is here with news regarding Grasmere."

My sister nodded and then threw me an apologetic look. "Tonight. I will see you tonight."

Snow was queen. She had duties and responsibilities, and she was fighting off our father. Again. And again. As if it hadn't been enough back then when she fought him for the three of us, tooth and nail, head-to-head.

"Tonight," I said, and she backed away, disappearing with lightning.

"So," Malik said, looking between Eren and I. "Who's the dragon and who's the dire wolf?"

Penelope, who I found to be uncle Lys's daughter, had found me a pretty, long sleeved, blush dress that had belonged to my mother. The satin was cool over my skin and when I spun on my toes, the fabric floated wide around me. I'd always wanted to try doing that. She'd brought me one of my mother's diamonds as well, but I kept the amber stone that rested delicately over the square neckline of the dress.

A gift.

For me.

It is meant to be a good night for us. To gather and celebrate our reunion. The one I'd prayed so hard for. Yet I was dreading it because I couldn't even cast a minute glance out of the castle windows without feeling like I couldn't breathe.

"Hey," Nia said, holding my hand tight. "I will fade us there. You won't have to see a single height."

Despite being extremely grateful, that made me flush with embarrassment. But Nia was warm and kind like no other, she had not pried more even though she knew of my vice. Snow on the other hand wanted to, only held back by Nia considering what I heard on the balcony last night. I wasn't sure if I would be able to lie to her if she asked me. I always lied terribly. The only secret I'd ever kept in my entire life had been the one about our magic. And more often than I liked to remember...I'd almost failed to keep even that.

"Do you have something that could help me, like a potion? For height sickness?"

Nia pursed in thought for a moment. "There is something, but is it the height that bothers you or something else?"

Nice try. "The height," I said confidently, and it seemed like she believed me. I didn't want to lie to her, it felt wrong.

She nodded. "I'll get you something."

Snow strutted in the room dressed head to toe in red and a little 'wow' formed on my mouth. The gown she wore was something I'd never seen on anyone before—flimsy silk and delicate gold chains with little bright rubies decorating it. Mother's silks were beautiful but far too modest compared to what Snow was wearing. Mother's frame was modest, too, Snow was much taller and fuller than her. My sister was beautiful.

"They grew," I said, and the two friends blinked confused before I pointed to Snow's cleavage.

Snow grabbed her breasts and stared down at them. "They did. Why didn't yours?"

The comb I held flew in her direction without warning, hitting her straight on the head.

She chuckled. "We'll look for them, do not worry."

Just seeing her smile like that and joke so lightly made me fly to my feet and wrap myself around her again for the one hundredth time today. The Snow I remembered had never been like this. Had never smiled at me like this.

She held me tight. "Do you hate it here?"

"No," I said truthfully. "I don't hate it at all. It's just so high up."

Her fingers brushed the rose-coloured silk band on my hair. "You could have stayed down in Fernfoss, but there are too many Isjordian soldiers roaming around."

As always, even thirteen years later, she was my blanket and my shield. She'd always protected me with all she had, even if all she had were bones and flesh—she'd used her own body to save me from harm. Did she resent me for it? For being the burden she didn't want to bear when she was fighting all sorts of her own demons and father. Had my sister hated me? "I will be alright, Snow. I think I've never been better."

Her brows gathered for a moment, and when she glanced at Nia she straightened her expression and gave me a smile. "Let's go."

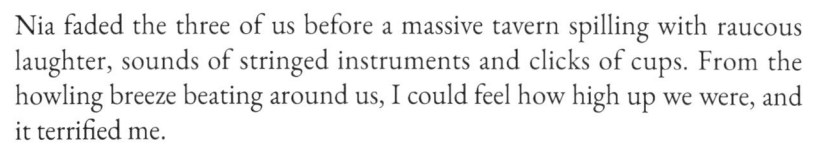

Nia faded the three of us before a massive tavern spilling with raucous laughter, sounds of stringed instruments and clicks of cups. From the howling breeze beating around us, I could feel how high up we were, and it terrified me.

We'd not been restricted in White Bridge, but I had not seen much despite the little freedom we'd been given. Places like taverns were not what most deemed lady-like so I'd avoided them even there. This would be my first time. Would they think me too much of a prude if they knew that?

Bodies jumped in the air in a strange unison, not the same as that in ballrooms. The music, too, was not soft and coordinated, but bouncy and almost cheerful. A faint smell of alcohol and fresh bread circled the air and made my stomach growl with hunger. Olympian food was suiting my taste buds well.

Alaric had sat along with a few court members I'd met yesterday and a woman I could not recognise. She had a sweet smile and honey eyes, it seemed like her and Alaric went along well. All the men along with a severely stoic woman were already seated at a far end table by the corner of the tavern, all deep in conversation.

First thing I noticed was Kilian's reaction to my sister. His normal expression was so grave and cold that it was the most noticeable, like someone lit a candle in a very dim room. And when she took a seat beside him, his hand slid under the table to hold hers. And my sister did not push it off.

I didn't not understand this little agreement between them no matter how much Snow had explained it to me.

Nia exchanged kisses with the woman who now I knew was Moriko, the queen of Hanai and her lover. The stern queen whispered something in Nia's ear and she suddenly looked unaware of the world surrounding us as she blew in a bubbly laughter, her cheeks flushing red and eyes twinkling. The two stood and disappeared between the dancing bodies.

Everyone looked…happy. And it made me all too aware of my own self. My skin felt uncomfortable, the seat under me was too hard, the world too noisy.

Our table was suddenly surrounded by a bunch of ladies, all flushed red from liquor and dancing. They pried my brother first, then Caiden and Malik, luring them to the dance floor. Kilian politely waved them off one after the other, clutching to Snow for dear life so no one would take him to dance. The two were whispering and glaring at one another, their expressions going from liquid warm to cold as ice and then soft like clouds. So difficult to understand.

Once the three of us were left alone, he lifted Snow to his lap, making me choke on a sip of my drink.

Snow immediately went mother wolf as she'd always been, extending a tissue across the table. "Are you well?"

I waved her off. "Wrong pipe."

She nodded and leaned onto Kilian, the move so minute no one would have taken much note of it. But I did. Because I knew my sister leaned on no one. She never let anyone feel like they were needed. Snow had tried to teach that to me, too—how to exist in a world where we couldn't rely on anyone, not even our own mother.

A hand grabbed Snow and snatched her from Kilian's lap—the younger brother, Malik. He steered Snow on the dance floor, swirling her round and about, jumping and laughing with one another. And Kilian was still looking at her the same.

"I think I like that," I said out loud before I even realised the sound was my own voice.

The king raised a dark brow, it made him look entirely too handsome and slightly less terrifying. "What is that?"

"How you look at my sister."

He glanced at Snow, his eyes doing that thing where they softened to molten silver. "How do I look at her?"

Just like that. Like she makes your world shine. "Like she is the sun and you've only ever seen night."

His mouth parted a little. "That is correct."

"She can be rain sometimes, though."

"I like that, too."

"With big, angry, grey clouds and loud thunderstorms."

He chuckled and I realised then, when he took another peek at her, that the Night King was in love with my sister. "My favourite sort."

The Night King was in love with my sister.

Kilian was in love with Snow.

He leaned back on his seat, levelling an examining look on me and it suddenly felt too clustered around me, like I was in a box. Was he trying to read my shadows like Empaths did? "What worries you, Thora?"

"Much," I said, sipping on my drink. The ale was sweet here, it smelled of honey.

He cocked his head to the side. "You're good at that."

"At what?"

"Giving people the answer they want. Shrinking. Getting rid of their attention on you."

"That is a horrible trait to have," I said. "Reading people."

"You do it as well."

"Except that I don't point it out. I do it for my own benefit. In the privacy of my own thoughts."

"Because you struggle to comprehend another's actions, thoughts and feelings."

"You're doing it again."

He smiled. "My apologies."

"You never look sorry."

"That is because I rarely am."

"Go dance with her," I said, pointing at Snow. I wanted to see that look again.

He glanced at my sister again who was being passed back and forth between Eren, Cai and Malik. She was laughing like I'd never seen her laugh before. "She is pretending the trouble doesn't exist. I'd only remind her of it."

At that moment, Snow looked over at us, at him rather than us. Her grin fell to a soft smile and she extended a hand to him in the distance. The two held a quiet moment, like the world had gone all silent and still around them, like they were the only ones standing in the room, and his breathing picked up. Of all I'd ever seen...I struggled to understand this.

"I don't think you were right, Kilian."

He bowed his head gently to me and headed to join my sister. The music shifted to a slower jig, and he pulled her close to his body, holding her so carefully as if she was made of glass. His hands trailed gently and ever so softly over her back and she relaxed in his hold. When she tipped her head back to look at him, he dropped a small peck to the tip of her nose and gave her a smile I'd only ever seen him give her. Such an innocent little gesture yet my cheeks were hurting from smiling like a mad woman.

She stared at him as if she saw wonder and she wanted to keep looking at it.

A body landed close to my seat with a thud and I jerked upright from surprise.

"Why the tears?" Malik said, swiping a thumb under my eyes before tipping my chin up to look at him. He frowned the more he looked at me.

"They were of happiness."

"No such thing as tears of happiness, little bird. If it made you tear up it had to hurt first."

Pulling the corner of my sleeve, I wiped my eyes. "I think you are looking at this too much like an Empath and too little like a human."

His touch dropped and I pushed a bit further back from him on the stool.

"You're right," he admitted quietly, leaning back and taking a long chug of his drink.

"Maybe not," I said, taking a sip of my own drink. "What would *I* know about being human, right?" My giggles were nervous and he seemed to catch onto them—it made me panic. "Please don't read my emotions."

"I am not." Yet he was looking at me oddly.

"Oh. Why?"

He glanced down at my necklace. "The only privacy I like to violate is that of my brother and my enemies."

I nodded. "I am thankful then."

"Would it be that terrible, to have someone understand what you yourself can't understand sometimes?"

"I'd rather be confused than emotionally naked. Actually," I said after a long swirl of my drink, "I'd rather be naked altogether in front of a whole crowd than be emotionally naked."

"Huh." He threw his arm back on the stool rest and stared at me like I'd said something curious.

"What?"

"Your sister would probably say the same."

I laughed. "Then you know nothing of Snow. She'd rather you knew just how burning red her anger is. Or how...dark her hate is. It would terrify a person or two. It was terrifying to most back then."

"Hate is not dark."

"What is it then?"

"Love."

"Odd."

"It is dark for a reason," he said, picking the end of a long hair strand that had blanketed the stool rest. I tensed, my whole body going taunt while phantom memories tugged me back to moments I wished to forget. "Love is never just one emotion. It is lust, jealousy, anger, care, happiness and when you blend so much colour on a palette, what do you get?"

My attention is entirely too focused on his finger twirling my hair and barely managed to murmur, "Something dark."

He nodded, looking up from my hair to my eyes. "Quite right, little bird. Something dark."

Noting his distraction, I yanked my hair out of his touch. "Don't call me that."

He cast a side glance at me. "It suits you."

I'm neither little nor a bird. But what would I know, I hadn't had a single decent friendship or relationship with another human being in forever—or maybe never? The bare thought of someone breathing near me made breathing difficult.

"Where did you fly off to?" Malik asked.

My attention caught on my sister and Kilian again. He had his forehead rested on hers as they swayed slowly in a circle.

Malik startled me again when he rested a single finger between my brows. "Why the frown?" He followed my line of sight. "Ah. They'd make a monk frown, too."

"Malik." His name shivered in my lips and the man turned so close to my face, I could tell apart each of his lashes, the split of umber and russet in his irises, how he smelled like misty mornings and roses.

His brows bunched together and he regarded my face with curiosity. "You're redder than a tomato."

"You're too close." I pushed away from him only to almost slip from the edge of the stool.

Malik hooked an arm around my waist, pulling me back on the seat before pushing himself to the other end of it. "Why did you frown?" he asked, pointing to my sister and his brother.

It felt comfortable to confess because I told him the truth, "I've seen much of my sister. Never that. I always trailed after her like a tail she never wanted. She faked smiles and laughter, sometimes care, too. And love. Not because she didn't care or love us, but because she didn't know how." I feel a tear slide down my cheek again. "I'm thankful and regretful at the same time." But I was angry, too. Angry at the world for denying me my peace. At my father. At my uncle who died before I could kill him. My mother who I couldn't even remember. I was angry. So angry at the world that had moved on when mine had stopped.

Pushing from the table, I stood and hurried outside before I'd blister the place with ice. The tavern was inconveniently overlooking a large cliff falling miles downwards and my insides churned while my head spun with panic. Immediately, I turned my back to the height, facing the tall mountainside that rose so high up it disappeared among clouds. And he stood there. Hands on his pockets, blinking slowly.

I waited to read the judgement. Waited to see him mock me. Yet he didn't do anything, just watched me as I watched him.

"You don't like heights, do you?" he said, closing the distance between us while I stepped back. He appeared in front of me in a blink and clasped my shoulders, anchoring me in place. "Why do you do that?"

"I don't know," I answered honestly. "Can we please move away from the cliff? Please?"

One moment we stood before the tavern, the next between a cluster of grey stone buildings. Drava was melancholic at night. If you shut your eyes, you could hear the distant waves crash against rock. Streets were empty besides elderly men playing chess in the candle-lit night. Their laughter and cheer warmed my heart and hearing them speak the language I'd long forgotten broke it altogether. We reached a fountain twirling for feet upward, sputtering water around in the shape of a rose. The breeze carried a sense of blue too. And just like that, my sight blurred and tears burned trails over my cold cheeks.

Malik rested a hand on my back in comfort, but the moment it touched my hair, my breathing seized.

I froze. Panic crawling like hot coals over me.

"Thora?" Malik asked carefully.

I pushed back from him, wiping my eyes with the corner of my sleeve. "Shall we go back?"

"Will you not tell me?"

"Tell you what?"

"What just happened."

"Nothing happened."

He tensed, his strong jaw ticking. "Thora."

"Malik," I said, righting my skirts. "Take us back."

He stepped toward me, coming close—too close. I had to tip my head back to stare at him. He wrapped an arm around me and pulled me tight against him. Hodr. I meant...Caelum. My whole body curled with flutters and warmth. "If I touch your back," he said, running his other hand over my spine and then lifting a brow as if he expected something to happen. Something was happening, just not what he thought. "No? Hm, maybe if I touch you here." His hand slipped on my arm before slowly gliding up my shoulder.

I swallow hard. "Malik."

His fingers made their way through my hair and my whole body seized. "There. That."

My eyes clenched shut and the air chilled and howled around me, bits of frost grazing my skin. "Please, please, please."

"Woah, little bird," he said, resting a hand on my cheek and everything felt lighter somehow, so I opened my eyes.

It was like a snap. Like someone ordered it to stop. "Do you use magic on me?"

He blinked a moment. "Yes. Yes, I did."

"Oh, it works well."

His mouth quirked up a little. "So I've heard." He pulled back a little. "Will you not tell me?"

"No."

"How about this? Let's be friends, you and me. Friends tell one another everything, a silent oath of secrets. We both confess and we both never tell."

"I've never had a friend before, how would I know that is how it works?"

"Let's learn together."

"What if you tell me a silly one?"

"I'll make sure to tell you a good one, Thora."

I swallowed. "You first."

He sat down at the edge of the fountain, and I followed suit. Was he really going to trust me with a secret? Did he have to know my own so badly that he was willing to give up his own truth? What if I couldn't keep it?

"When I was younger," he started, "just after I'd bloomed my blessing, father found out I was more capable than most Empaths. In my sleep, I'd been able to call on the dead and we'd woken to an army of them waiting right outside my window. He'd never been prouder of me. He'd never been proud of me at all. I was the second son that his court had forced him to have, something he'd never even wanted. But he'd wanted me that day. And I knew shortly after why Kilian never liked the attention he'd given him. To be able to utilise those capabilities, I had to make friends with death. Know everything about it. Know it well. Know it before and after. So he locked me in a room with seven sick men, women, and children. For seven days. I had no medicine to give them, no bandages to wrap their bleeding wounds, he only gave enough water and food for me. I had no milk for the babes. For seven days, I watched and felt them die, one by one. I learned so much those seven days. That is how I became Eldritch Commander."

I wasn't breathing. I couldn't breathe at all.

"Your turn," he said, brushing it off with one of his grins.

"Back then." I swallowed hard before continuing, "A priest called Murdoc would lock us up in a tower and…and—" My hands shook and I locked them together on my lap. Not even Eren knew this. "He would do things to us, like beat or flog us, and that was on a good day. He liked to use Crafter magic on us too. Liquid fire and elixirs of the same. I…I was much younger than Snow and Eren. It was thrice as easy for me to bruise and thrice as hard to heal. Snow would take my place. In the beginning it only was a couple of times, but then I stopped going all together—she had permanently taken my spot. One day, Snow didn't return after Murdoc had come down from the tower, so Eren and I went up to look for her."

"When we entered the tower," I went on, hiding my shaking hands under my thighs, "Snow had climbed up on the balcony and was swaying back and forth on the ledge. Blood, so much blood. There was so much of it everywhere. She was bleeding everywhere. Her neck was marked, her face, her arms. There wasn't a place in her body without a wound. She wouldn't come down from there, no matter how much we called for her to. I think she didn't want to come down. There was no more of my sister left that day, she was so given up. I begged and yelled for her to come down. But then she did turn. With a bright grin on her face when she said my name and came down to hug me, as if nothing had happened. I know if we had come any later, she would have…jumped. The thought of any height makes me sick." Thick tears rolled down my face and I wiped them with the back of my hand. "It's pretty stupid, isn't it?"

When I turned to face him, I found his eyes already on me, they were completely black. There was something cold in them. Icy cold, like death. His chest rose at a terrifying pace, all too controlled as if he was preparing to hunt prey.

"Malik?"

"And the hair?"

"We said one secret."

"Thora?" Snow's voice echoed softly, and I turned to my sister. Kilian stood behind her, glancing between his brother and I with a cold calculating look in his face. Sometimes he made me afraid—he made me afraid all the time, actually. "Why did you two leave?"

"I needed some air. There were too many cliffs around so he brought me here."

"Do you want to go back to the castle?"

"Why don't you let her stay in Adriata till she gets used to the heights?" Mal said and I froze. "No one knows who she is. Kilian and I will be around her all the time, she will be safe."

Silence howled between the four of us.

Snow looked hurt, but she nodded. "If she wants that."

"Only for a little while," I said and hated myself when Snow gave me a smile and nodded

CHAPTER THIRTY-TWO

Intempestus

Kilian

Snow stood before me, legs crossed, her eyes shut, breathing in and out while an orb of lightning enshrouded her in—her body levitating with it. The taste of her power was overwhelming the cool air of Adriata. "Breathe in," I said, and when she inhaled the orb grew bigger. "Good girl. Now out." And when she exhaled it shrunk back. Her attention was more focused than before after hours of practice we had done for a week now. She'd worked on all her emotional triggers and how they affected her magic, bit by bit, and she was getting progressively better. Until—

"Open your eyes." And when she did, the magic surrounding her shivered a little and began patching in places and escaping in others. The burning shadow standing beside me resembled a wolf, nothing that could make even a child fear, but to Snow this was her one fear. The same happened even if the wolf had been a butterfly or a songbird.

"Love," I called, bringing her attention to me. "Stop trying to convince yourself you are not afraid."

"You're not making sense." She took a deep breath, but her magic began growing and growing till I had to lift a wall of darkness around her to quell it.

Snow collapsed back, breathing hard. "It is much easier when I just blast things around." She turned her glare on me. "You're a terrible teacher."

I was going to bend her over and sm—

"Why is it easier for me?" Thora asked. Unlike her sister, she'd been able to find the hang of it in no time. But with Thora, concentration was something she commanded with ease. She slipped in and out of consciousness as if it was oiled.

"How do you do it in battle?" Eren asked. He'd leaned on the court, observing and studying his little sisters, but had refused to join our practice. From what Thora had thrown here and there during dinners and odd conversation, Eren had a strained relationship with his magic. He also seemed to struggle watching his sisters use magic.

Snow shrugged. "I call as much as I can from it. Like taking a big swing for a punch."

"That is why your seal keeps opening," I said. "Again."

She made a face. "Adriatian."

"Love, sit up, close your pretty eyes and do that again for me."

And so she did. Again, and again. Until the afternoon heat began glazing us all with sweat. She was still struggling to trust my magic, but that was not the biggest issue. It only meant Snow had not grasped control over her emotions. My wife's struggle was that her Elding side overwhelmed the balance that Thora had. Ice and wind were both elemental. The Elding drew partly from the spiritual and until she could manage to use her emotions to her advantage, to quell and rouse them appropriately, they would always cause her trouble.

"We're done, love." She didn't answer. "Snow, my heart, open your eyes."

"I think she is asleep," Thora whispered and pinched Snow's cheek. "See. Asleep."

I was an idiot. A damned idiot. I'd tired her to the point that she'd fallen asleep upright.

Gathering my wife's body in my arms, I stood. It was not nearly sunset, but she probably needed the rest. "Help me get her ready for bed?"

She nodded and followed beside me to our room.

"How are you getting around the castle grounds?"

"It's nice in here," she said while pulling Snow's jewellery off of her. "Warm. The food is good, better than what Eren used to cook for us. Nia also brought me some Olympian snacks to keep in my room."

"Snow struggled in the beginning," I explained. "Knowing who she was surrounded with."

Her fingers halted on Snow's hair piece. "I...I didn't see much that night, not as much as she might have. The hall was set on fire before I saw any Adriatian soldier. And then Aryan showed up. I guess my evil is not everyone's evil. Your people don't bother me." After we tucked Snow in bed, she sat on the ground, watching her sister sleep. "She never slept like this. So peaceful."

"She is tired, having to deal with so much in Olympia with Silas and the Fogling all over the cities and here, too." We'd been called four nights in a row at Highwall, and we'd spent the rest of those nights waiting and ensuring whatever disturbing scent the Canes had picked up were not Silas's beasts. Silas was lurking nearby, and Snow swore she could hear his…rattle nearby. And I never doubted her.

"And I think," Thora said, fully sitting on the floor and running a hand through her sister's hair. "That she feels safe. I've seen her tired plenty of times, exhaust kept her even more awake."

Safe. Had Snow truly ever felt safe in her nights here?

She stood and blew off a candle and then another before I stopped her. "She doesn't like the dark, Thora."

The little sister blinked at me, brows pulling to a frown of realisation. "Will you always love her like this?" she whispered, blinking the glaze of her eyes back. "Even when it is time for her to come after you?"

"Always."

Snow had woken a couple hours later and had sat along with Atlas, Thora and I in my private library, studying Eamon's Book of Dreams. She had reached the last quarter of it and was struggling to keep her nerves grounded and not cross the Otherworld to chase the man and squeeze the life out of him over and over again.

"Love," I said, putting a hand over the page she was reading. "Leave it. We don't need to find out about Aurora anymore."

She took my hand and put it on her thigh, lacing my fingers with hers. "I want to know what her flaw was. What stayed with her in that tower. What we found in Olympia was useless. How could my ancestors have defeated her, a guardian, without knowing how to fight her? There has to be something."

Her curiosity was a beast that fed on her anxiousness. The more she knew, the more uneasy it made her.

Thora raised her head from one of the colourful pages of a Demon Grimoire illustrated with all of the beasts of Golgotha that an ancient Adriatian scholar had observed in his studies on the Dissiri creatures. I was convinced Silas's beast was not of Caligo and the only way to prove it was by cancelling out other dark creatures. And the young Skygard had a brain that worked at the speed of light. She'd compared half of it already to the sketches Magnus and Moriko had provided for us. "You said the piece reacted to you when you touched it."

"No," I said, cutting whatever the young one was suggesting.

"Finish, Rora," Snow said, smacking Eamon's diary shut.

The younger sister glanced between her and I. "Perhaps not."

"Wise girl," I said, going back to my research on the Ater beasts that the 97th Grand Maiden had created using humans and Caligo beast blood. Any attempt to find any loophole on Obitus Law had failed so now I was back to studying any form of mutation in Numen that could have mimicked the beasts with a little bit of craft manipulation. Though the 97th Grand Maiden had been a psychopath, she'd created a revolution within the community of Potioners. More dared experiment with dangerous and unknown substances. But Melanthe was a Summoner so that complicated my research. "What are the chances that Melanthe's sister might have created a potion to create her sister a beast?"

"Slim," Visha said, strutting in along with Oryn. "Aradia can fix you a nice little potion for your headache, but that's it. And besides, I've been keeping an eye on her for years after Melanthe died."

Oryn glanced over the journal I was reading. "If a Potioner had made the beast, its essence would be of dark magic not made from dark magic. No Crafter is that good, my king."

"Visha," Snow said, trailing a finger over the table. "Could we establish a tether between the sceptre and I?"

"Love," I warned, and the woman turned, blinking her lashes all innocence. "Not only is it too dangerous, but we could trigger the guardian."

"Actually," Visha said, and I sent a scathing look to her. "Never mind."

From the look on Snow's face, she was not going to let this go.

"This...thing," Thora said carefully, running her fingers over the sketch. "There is something strange with it."

Snow leaned over to steal a glance. "It's the eyes, isn't it?" Of course she had doubted something. Nothing missed her sharp eye. Nothing. The more details something had, the better she remembered.

Thora nodded and pulled a much smaller book from under the Book of Demons and pointed to a few creatures we often had seen in history books from the Ater battles. "The Ater battle monsters' eyes, the Caligo beasts drawn from the Crafters, Eudemons and even few of Dyurin's creations, they all had unusual eyes. Uncle Lys used to often say that our eyes were what made us most recognisable from other creatures, they were a gate—a gate to the human soul, and much could be read from eyes alone. Gods made sure no human could be able to conceal such a gate, so no magic, earthly, divine or dark could change them. But Demir's eyes in his beast form are human, too human even."

"Would defeat all of our theories that he belongs from Caligo or Dissiri," Oryn said. "Well thought, Princess."

"At least then we had some sort of answer," Snow said, slouching in her chair and narrowing her eyes on a wall. "Don't you all think that this beast and the sceptre are fitting a little two perfectly with one another, like a key to lock. Melanthe is using his blood on the trace crafts, she's drinking his blood, too, Demir is also on its own collecting these pieces like he knows how. In Hanai, it was clear it was the first attempt at retrieving it as it was in Solarya. It took two of us, an Elding and an Obscur, to go through it. We were lucky I could call my magic inside the veils and that Kilian can turn air to ash."

"Is that what you were looking for in Eamon's diary, mention of the beast?" I asked.

Thora leaned forward, glancing between all of us. "But that would mean this thing has been living amongst us for hundreds of years."

"Not impossible," Visha said, scribbling in her journal.

Snow chewed on her lip. "But Demir is not an Aura. And even so, it would mean he is a five hundred plus years old Aura." Her head tipped back. "Perhaps it was Moregan not Demir. That woman is odd as well. It could be that Demir is not the original beast, he could have fed from her." She glanced at her sister. "Do you remember the bald woman with a scar on the middle of her forehead from Ulv Islet?"

Thora shivered and gagged a little. "Yes. But her name was not Moregan. Uncle would poke open her wound all the time and he called her something else." The younger sister clicked her fingers and groaned from frustration. "Skadi. Yes, that's it. An unusual name. Who would name their child after the mother of Krig?"

Oryn frowned. "Skadi? You don't mean Skadi Krigborn?"

All of us spun to the old Crafter.

"You know her?"

He nodded. "The banished old Krigborn queen for the Islines. I spent some time in the Islines when I was a seminarian in the old temples there. Her younger sister dethroned her and kicked her out of their lands afterwards. If you are thinking her to be this beast, I am afraid you are wrong. Skadi was born around the same time as—" He cleared his throat. "As my son."

"Your son?" Visha asked.

The old priest blinked rapidly, lowering his glazing gaze down. "Uh, he...he died. The seal did not work on him."

Snow frowned.

"I am sorry, Oryn," Thora offered.

The old man pursed his lips and went to his book. "It was a long time ago, Princess. But no, the old Krigborn queen is not our beast. Not unless what the young one said is true. Though she could have easily fed from it and turned into one herself. She was a powerful Verglaser. It could actually be that none of them were the beast. It could be that both of them have fed from it."

Snow nibbled on her lip. "No, Oryn. I know what I felt. Demir introduced me to a few soldiers who had possibly fed on the beast's blood. Their essence, the way their magical presence felt against mine was completely different. The original beast is either Demir or Moregan."

"Children," Driada said, sauntering in with a frown. "You didn't join me for dinner."

At the mention of food, Snow's stomach howled.

My stepmother put a hand to her face to hide her smile. "I'll have the servants bring something down here for all of you. Have you seen Mal anywhere?"

As if roused by his mother's worry, Mal faded inside the library and swung an arm around her shoulders. Dishevelled head to toe, marked all over his skin with what looked like...lipstick. "Is this where you are all herding now? Searched every room in the damn castle to find you in this rat hole."

Driada smacked him over and over till he was chuckling, attempting to hide his head. "At least have the decency to bathe after returning from that hells house."

He kissed his mother's cheek. "Missed you too much, woman. Was there a mention of food? I'm starving."

He sat beside Thora as servants filled out tables with foot, but the younger Skygard had been concentrating on her research rather than eating. And this seemed to bother my brother somehow.

Mal pushed the side of crackers, pies, fruit and cheese to her. "Eat, little bird. You need to become a big one."

She didn't answer, only kept scribbling on her paper.

He tapped the table and she still paid him no mind.

After heaving a long sigh, he grabbed her jaw and turned her face to him. "Eat, Thora."

"Appetite writhed," she said calmly, pulling his hand away from her face.

He glanced down at the Demon Book before her. "Queasy stomach from that?"

"No, from the sickening cheap perfume wafting my nostrils."

My brother frowned, looking somewhat confused at her. "Apologies, princess—"

"Apology accepted," she said, turning her attention back on her book and wiping a hand over her cheeks.

He cocked a smug brow up. "I'll ask Selia to be less generous with her perfume."

"Don't inconvenience your whore for me, Malik," Thora said, giving him a polite smile and standing. "I can just sit further away." After finding a spot near where Visha was sitting, she continued her research.

Odd. These two had been inseparable since Thora had come to live just two doors away from our rooms.

Snow chewed slowly, looking between her sibling and then my own. She turned to me a little. "He doesn't smell that bad, does he?"

"I think they are fighting." Had my brother done something again?

Snow blinked. "Why? They have been getting along just fine."

"They are just bickering, love. Let them be."

"Last I remember us bickering like this," she said, putting a slice of apple on my mouth, "you almost kissed me."

The recall to memory made me smile a little and I slid my hand over hers. "It is not like that with them if that is what you're trying to get me to say."

She chewed on a piece of cheese. "My manipulation is no longer working, huh?"

"Working just fine, but I like calling you out on it just to see you accept it." Leaning in, I kissed her shoulder and then her neck. "One of the many things I like about you."

"So," she started, glancing at her sister and then at Mal who'd kicked his feet on the table and was napping. "The two—"

"They are friends."

Caiden came inside the library all grave and curious, eyeing the shelves, the walls, the stained-glass ceiling and then the rest of us. "Research? This is how you all research?" he asked, kicking my brother's chair leg that sent him flying backwards to the floor. "Glad to see you're eating, Cakes."

She threw him an apple and he caught it mid-air. "Where is Nia and why were you forced to come all the way here?"

He took a bite from the apple and pointed at her. "Your brother kicked me out from the Myrdur camps and told me to go rest in Taren where trouble came to find me straight away. I'd barely stepped one foot in the castle. Get up, it's news from Bash."

Snow shot up from her seat, dusted her dress and headed to leave. Well, almost headed to leave, because I pulled her in my lap and rounded my arms around her. "I love you," I said in her ear. "Be safe."

She shivered a little and nodded. "I will."

"No goodbye kiss, my muffin?" Mal said, straightening on his chair.

Cai threw him a middle finger and my brother laughed.

Sebastian? Why was he calling for Snow?

Chapter Thirty-Three

Martius

Snowlin

Larg dragged me along as we squeezed past the narrow and hidden corridors of the Highwall. The same that Esbern Kirkwall had used for his illegal trades.

The old troll had huffed sigh after sigh ever since I'd asked him to bring me through the wall without telling Kilian. There was a risk of fading or portaling in Isjord. With Melanthe's nostrils being on high alert, I wouldn't be surprised if she could sniff us out all the way to Olympia and through the *zgahna*. This had been our only choice.

Cai followed quietly behind me, a hand on my elbow to keep me from tripping in the dark tunnels.

I knew we'd reached the exit when my skin puckered from the Isjordian chill that had all of a sudden turned burning. Sebastian was already there, waiting along with a few soldiers. All surveying the surroundings with high alert.

"You stay here," I said to Larg.

The tall man frowned. "Over my dead body, my queen. Wherever you go on this rotten soil, I will follow. And I will protect. I've given an oath. With my life. And I won't break oath no matter how mighty powerful you are."

"You're massive," I explained. "Not a good trait when you want to hide." The man stuck to me like a barnacle everywhere I'd stepped in Adriata. He growled at anyone who dared give anything more than a polite smile. The day I returned from Isjord, he even shed a tear for me. A tear. Was it age? Did age make men sensitive?

The troll's shoulders dropped a little, as if he was trying to make himself smaller, and he flushed. "Then I will stay back. I will never endanger you or your mission."

"Take what she says with a bucket load of salt." Cai patted his arm and followed after Sebastian through the thin strap of forest separating the city and Highwall.

It was barely past sunset in Amaris though night had already blanketed the winter city. But it was rather quiet. Too quiet. Even the howl of wolves was so faint I thought I could have imagined it.

"Curfew," Sebastian said as if reading my doubt. "A week ago, Silas set a curfew for all of Isjord. The guards do ground checks on the city all night after it."

Hells, my father was losing his plot.

We reached a bungalow right outside the city line, hidden away by the forest, snow and the shadow of Highwall.

"She is inside," Sebastian said, opening the door for Cai and I to enter.

The air was grave and frosted inside the small space lit by the fireplace and odd candles. The energy was all so severe and dramatic.

"Hello, Gara," I said, going round the table and taking a seat before her.

Her hair was still neatly pulled back, her clothing ironed and prim, not a thread in sight, and it somehow annoyed me. "You will come to regret this, Olympian bitch," she snarled.

My, my. "Oh, will I?"

She banged a tight fist on the table. "Using another Lord to call me here with lies and threats was your first mistake."

"What was my second?"

She bared her neat teeth at me. "Messing with me."

I looked past her and signalled Cai to let my leverage step in. All dirtied and beaten, Reuben stood with his head hung low by my friend's side.

The Grasmere Lady shot up from her seat attempting to reach her bound lover when Cai lifted a sword to her neck. "Down," he said, motioning his sword to the seat and she sat. "That's it. Good dog. I'd make you apologise, but she likes apologies with screams and Isjordian bitches bark a little too loud."

Gara bristled and Cai's grin turned vile.

Not a beat after, she turned to me. "You will let him go. He is the heir of Isjord. You better pray your father does not find out."

All the delusionality was starting to wear on me. Did they truly think my father cared? "Father had sent him back to Comnhall. To his mother. He had no intention of bringing him back. Especially not when father is expecting a child and presuming many more once he resumes his plague over the realm. He is no heir. Never was. Though father liked to entertain the idea just to keep the spoiled batch looking like a real happy family. You know how important image is to you Isjordians." I lifted my attention to Reuben. "I am only taking care of discarded rabble. But it seems that one's trash is another's treasure. Am I right, Gara?"

The Grasmere Lady remained silent. "If you think I will betray your father and Isjord under any circumstance, you are wrong. If you hurt us or kill us, much worse will come your way. He is the heir, and I am to be his wife! You cannot kill us so spare me my time."

Twas my first choice, but then the endless cycle of choosing a Lord or a Lady was too time consuming. I needed Grasmere now. And by now, I meant today.

I stood, fisted Reuben's blond locks and dragged the little worm all across the room while he squirmed away with tears and boogers hanging off of him. The whole time I watched Gara's reactions crack to surface and her sweet little face morph to terror.

I sat back in my chair, the half breed kneeling before me. "Have you ever been struck by lightning?" I asked and the two held their breath. "No?" Leaning forward, I stuffed Reuben's mouth with a piece of cloth and let electricity skitter around my fingers. "There is always a first time." When I rested my hand on the half breed, the Grasmere Lady shot up from her seat and screamed my eardrum out.

The little rat started smelling of burnt hair and flesh and cried like a babe. Probably shat himself like one, too.

The woman shook, eyes wide on me. "You're...you're—"

I stood and reached her. "Your worst nightmare. And do you know what nightmares do best? They don't kill, dear, they haunt."

Her frightened bright blue eyes drifted to Reuben. "What do you want?"

She flinched when I trailed a finger around her face. "What do you think I want? It isn't all so difficult to guess what I could want from a stuffed doll with a title. I want to play."

Her soul almost flinched out of her body when lightning struck very close outside.

"Don't touch her," the half breed called hoarsely, trying to sit himself up. "She is with child. You will hurt the child."

Ugh. I pulled away. Was it contagious? Why was everyone left and right pregnant these days?

Tilting my head between the two, I asked, "What will it be?"

Reuben shared a look with his lover and lowered his head. "Pledge...pledge to her. Do what she asks."

Gara shook her head, breathing steam out of her flared nostrils and backing away from me. "You might be heir," she said to her betrothed, "but your father is my king. Never. I'll never pledge to you." She spat at my feet and made to turn around had I not fisted her hair and dragged her back to me.

She struggled in my hold as I backed her to the wall, pushing her face to the cold surface. "You misunderstand me," I hissed in her ear. "Bringing you here was kindness. Resisting the urge to rip out his heart, the heart of the creature you carry and then yours is truly, truly tempting, my dear. It was my original plan. But I am out of time. So, I will rip his heart first and then my friend by the door will portal right at your sister's doorstep in Grasmere, your family house is lovely by the way, and he'll rip her heart too and her children's. And if that doesn't convince you," I said, tugging on her hair and bumping her head hard against the wall. "I will send a letter to my father detailing how your father has been trading with Solarya even after the ban and that his ships send and retrieve Magnus's spies back and forth for dirty coin."

Her eyes grew wide with horror. "That is not true. That is not true!"

How funny, wasn't it? They still feared my father more than I despite what I could do. They still feared more for their pride. I supposed it worked in my favour that shame for an Isjordian was worse than death. "I could have easily ended you, Gara, I just chose not to." I pulled back and let her go, heading to Reuben. "Brother, I'll send Eren your regards." Ice crawled over my fingers and I plunged my hand in his flesh.

"Wait!" Gara screamed, clutching on my arm right before breaking the flesh of her betrothed. "Wait...wait."

And that is what I called diplomacy.

She swallowed. "Don't tell the king. Don't tell your father."

"I expect we have a bargain?" I asked, extending a hand to her.

And like that, a twelfth band of bargain wrapped around my arm, marking me with pain, a black mark, a promise to tear my soul and another victory.

The cold air was assaulting when I stepped outside. But it had stopped snowing and there was a clear night sky above us. So very odd.

"It's strange, isn't it?" Sebastian said, looking heavenward. "The first day of spring yet it is cold as if it is the first day of winter."

"First day of spring?" I asked, spinning to him.

He nodded. "It's the twenty-first of March."

Kilian was still sat on his desk when I arrived in Amaris. His head hung low over a massive binder as he flipped and made notes all through it. We were gearing up for war and we didn't only have numbers to count, but also losses. He was making sure the second remained low.

"Hello, love," he said, without removing his attention from the numbers and letters. "How was your day?"

"Boring." Untying my robe and setting it on the sofa, I walked to him and sat myself on his lap. I lifted a violet anemone up to his face. "For you."

He took the little flower, confused.

"Happy birthday," I said, leaning in to kiss his cheek.

He gave me that smile he had only ever given me and rested his forehead on mine. "This is the best gift I've ever received."

"The flower?" Even I had received better.

"You, the flower. Mostly you. Though I do love the flower."

I leaned in and left a small kiss on his neck and then another until I heard those little breathy moans and whimpers of his.

His hand on my thigh began moving higher up till it grazed the lacy edges of my nightgown. "Do you need me?" he asked, eyes dark with want, staring at me as if he was starved.

We'd not had a single moment to ourselves since that night in the Islines. I didn't need him—I was desperate for him. "I need you."

He lifted me onto his table and reached to pull the thin red underwear off of me. When he took note of the colour, his lip tilted up. "Did you wear them for me?"

"No, I like red." Liar.

He pulled a little cupboard open, stashing the delicate lacy things on it and going on his knees before me. The sight had me smiling like a fool. "Like that, huh?"

Yes. Yes. Yes. "I thought your knee hurt."

"There is this one prayer," he said, kissing his way up my thigh. "That I'd like to leave at this altar."

Hooking his hands under my hips, he dragged me to the edge of the table and flicked his tongue over me. The sensation of his mouth had me panting, my knuckles turning white from the force of my grip that could almost crush the wood in splinters. He played with my body, knew every inch of it like his playground. His fingers curled in me, hitting that one spot while his mouth and teeth grazed my core.

I felt something warm wrap around my limbs. Phantom shadow hands swirled around me, pulling my legs avert till I was splayed out to him completely. They brushed past my nipples and neck till they summoned hot attention on every inch of me.

His tongue slid inside of me, fingers still circling me until he had me calling all sorts of prayers and curses. "Fuck, Kilian."

His lips and tongue and—

And that.

His fingers and shadows thrust in me while he kissed my thighs, and I felt his magic slither down my stomach and—

My body arched on the table at the toe-curling sensation brushing the apex of my thighs, substituting his fingers. They teased that thrumming sensitive nub, flicking and circling while Kilian's fingers picked up a pace thrusting inside of me. "Yes, right there." The hum of pleasure built up and up till my vision spotted and I was crying out my climax with his name on my lips.

His hands held my thighs apart as his tongue flicked over me till he'd lapped up every bit of my release, till he'd licked every shudder and shiver off of my skin.

When he stood, my fingers fumbled with the buttons of his britches, rushing to free him. He chuckled at my eagerness, leaning in to leave a gentle kiss on my mouth. It wasn't until I almost melted into it that I realised what we were doing.

I froze. So did he.

He'd kissed me.

The first time since that day.

One moment we stood there, forehead to forehead, utterly quiet. The remnants of that kiss still wet on our lips.

His heart was loud but so was mine.

If all it took was one kiss.

"Forgive me," he breathed out, cupping my face and kissing every inch of it. "I didn't—"

"Where did you leave off?" I asked, kissing both his palms and then guiding them down my body again.

The way he watched as I pushed his hands down my breasts, down my stomach and between my legs, had my body come to life once again. One look. That was all it took.

One look.

He wrapped an arm around my waist and turned me around so my back was to his chest. A hand slowly descended down my stomach to tear my nightgown off while his mouth left torturous kisses on my neck. "If you want me to stop, I will stop."

Quickly, I wiggled out of the nightgown scraps. "I hope to gods you are trying to be funny with me."

He chuckled in my ear, his warm breath making me shudder. "I'm being serious, my little beast. My hunger is a bit severe, and I'm done being patient."

"Then you must know how I've felt."

His grin was massive as he slid a hand over my jaw to turn my face to him so he could lean in and bite my lip, drawing a bit of blood and sucking on my flesh till I'd grown twenty shades of frustrated and wet. "I'm fucking delirious at your taste."

The same warm sensation wrapped around my ankles, pulling them apart, and slowly, he pushed my torso down so I laid flat on the table, the same shadows wrapping around my wrists too. "Look at you," he said, trailing his fingers over my spine. A gasp trapped on my throat when he smacked my bottom. "So ready for me." There was not a moment for me to gather myself because he crowned me and fully pushed in, filling me and seizing both my air and my voice.

"Fuck." He stilled just a little, waiting for me to adjust before he began thrusting in me hard and then fast, then harder and faster till our bodies were rocking as one, his hips smacking into mine. "You were made for me, woman," he growled, thrusting a bit deeper and my nails dug on the table from the curling sensation.

Yes—

"My god, Kilian." His name on my lips was prayer and plea, one which had obliged every time his cock thrust deep inside my body.

His hand went below my belly, pulling my upper body up while he pumped in and out of me hard enough that my vision had dizzied a bit. And when his fingers travelled to circle my core torturously, I shuddered and my knees weakened, the only thing holding me upright was his shadows.

"Your god?" The grip of the hand he had on my hip turned bruising as he kept me anchored while he pumped in me.

"Mine," I said, pushing my hips back to meet his thrusts.

"That I am. Yours." His mouth latched on my neck and his paces slowed a little despite how hard he breathed. "Always yours," he murmured, running his tongue over my ear. His other hand slipped to my breasts, kneading and squeezing, pinching and rubbing their hardened centre, eliciting a string of moans from me. "My weakness," he whispered in my ear, slapping one of them and then palming the sting away. "So fucking pretty with my hand print on them. They'd be even prettier with my come over them." Whispers of affection, praises, wet kisses, warm shadows and the sound of our joining balanced me right at the tipping edge of release.

He wrapped a hand around my neck and plunged harder into me, it was fierce and hungry, teeth and nails. Each thrust of his hips cut off a breath and made the next one even harder to take. He fucked me to oblivion, till patches of stars flashed in my sight and his name was no longer a call but an order—till the only word I could remember was his name. "Kilian."

He buried his face in my hair, inhaling me and surrendering control to his body, as his own climax chased mine. His soft groans matched my gasps as I felt him spill inside of me—fill me only how he could.

His shadows slithered away, softly petting my sensitive flesh as they retracted back to their owner

Every inch of my body had gone slack, my knees trembling and weak when he pulled out of me and spun me round to face him. Our chests synced, our breathing matching. The first thing he did was lift my gaze to him, searching for something there.

I opened my mouth to speak and then closed it and then opened it one last time before giving up to the astonishment. He'd fucked me speechless.

And it seemed he had found what he was looking for because he smirked like only Kilian Castemont could before picking me up in his arms and heading to the bathing chambers.

"So, what prayer did you make?" I asked, wiggling my feet as he carried me to the bath. I'd never felt fuller. My appetite was satiated and if I craved any more, I only needed to take a bite.

He chuckled and nuzzled my neck, feeding more warmth into my chest. "That's between me and my faith."

After setting me down on the sink top, he went to fill the tub, sprinkling ten times the normal amount of salts and soap.

"Are you trying to cook me?" He cast me a confused glance over his shoulder, and I pointed my chin to the bath. "Spicing me up nicely."

"Thought you liked the crap."

"A handful, Kilian, not the whole container."

"You've never said anything before."

"Twas funny."

He bit his stupid lip and sauntered to me, lifting me up and soaking the two of us in the warm water filled with a foot of bubbles.

I leaned my head back on his shoulder and rested a hand on his knee, feeling the thick scar over it with my fingers. It was jagged and rough, and I could feel the bone under the new tissue. It somehow made me tilt my head up to look at him. And he was already looking at me. "Why do I know so much about you from scars?"

His hand went around my jaw, rubbing his thumb over my cheek and he dropped a kiss to my forehead. "What do you want to know, love of mine?"

"Your magic, how did you become so good at it?" I was curious. After Mal had told me how his father had forced him into accepting who he was, I always wondered if it had been the same for Kilian.

"I thought you didn't want to learn me through my scars."

Shifting to my side, I looked up at him. It made me afraid to ask. To know his pain. "Which scar?"

He took my hand and put it on his head. "There."

"Tell me."

He kissed my palm before setting it down on his chest, over his beating heart—the same heart I had in my fist each time I closed my eyes and dared to sleep. "It is not that interesting."

"I want to know."

He rested his forehead on mine and let out a sigh. "I always liked the sun. My favourite colour was yellow. I liked the warmth of the day, the blue of the skies, meadows with daisies. The night sky was a wonder, but one that I didn't adore with fascination only with respect. Being born as an Obscur I'd offended Henah plenty, I am sure of it. But I'd made my father disappointed. The same disappointment he took out on Driada and Mal. So I forced myself to be good at it."

Always the sacrifice. The way he put others first made me admire and loathe him at the same time. "How?"

"I stayed in it. I stayed in the dark. All sorts of dark. Rooms. My own head. Dungeons. Alone. Alone with death, the dying, the dead."

"When you say death, the dying, the dead—"

"Exactly what you're thinking."

"Why?"

"You cannot learn from books what you can experience yourself, the range of dying can teach you just how many shades of death there are. There is no spectrum big enough to fit that."

"How long did you do that for?"

"For days. Weeks. At some point for months. And when I came out of the dark, the dark was all I knew. I'd mastered it. Pulled it by strings. I found peace in it too, it became comforting. It grew like a symbiote, no longer something I could pull out of the spiritual—it was already in me. I learned to become it, create it, use it, force it into submission. Mould it to the shape that I wanted it to be used. I studied all those before me and I fixed all their mistakes. Eventually there was no mistake to correct. And I became the man who summons night in the middle of day."

When my eyes dropped from his, he hooked a finger under my chin and demanded my attention back at him. "Did I bore you?"

"You can never bore me, Adriatian."

He bit his smile back. "Because I play with you?"

"Because you're the game I can never seem to stop playing."

He nudged my nose with his. "It looks like I fuck all the compliments out of you."

I wanted to kiss that smirk away. I wanted to kiss his scars and pain away, too. I wanted to kiss him.

From the way he returned my gaze, it looked like he wanted to do the same.

Shifting around, I spun to cradle his lap, rocking my hips against his length till he hardened under me. I kissed a path up his neck, tasting every inch of his flower-scented skin, and he hummed, trailing gentle touches up my spine that turned to a burning lick of pleasure.

I lifted my hips and reached between us to palm his length before slowly lowering myself down on him, taking as much of him as I could. Sweet hells.

He leaned back on the bath, his head cocked back and arms sprawled wide as he watched me ride him with a stupid smirk on his face. I slowly rose up and down his length, my body shuddering when my hips grinded against his to reach that spot inside of me that sent every sensation in my body pounding with warmth.

"You're killing me, woman," he groaned, his head dropping back, eyes shut as took him ever so slowly—gently. Only so I could see that tortured look on his face. Lips, tongue, teeth and fingers, I teased and marked each inch of his body while I took him.

And just when the man started groaning, whimpering and struggling to breathe like I was holding him prisoner, I rested my palms on his chest and rode him harder, the pleasure making my sighs turn to loud moans that grew and echoed louder in the massive bathroom.

His hands slipped down my hips and his own pushed forward. I gasped when his cock sunk deeper into me. "Tie your legs on my waist."

I did as told.

He faded us out of the bath, lowering me to the sink as he started pounding in me like a starved man. "You make me crave torture," he rasped in my ear, his hand weaving through my hair, tugging back so he could lower his mouth to my neck. "Sweet, flowery torture." His teeth dug into my flesh, pleasure melded with a bite of pain and pleasure rolled through me, my thighs quivering. "Look at you coming all over my cock. So fucking pretty."

He didn't stop, nor slow. He thrust harder. And harder. The sounds of our bodies meeting one another grew erratic. Prolonging my release till it joined his.

We both heaved, holding one another till long after. This was madness. Absolute madness. I liked madness. And I think we were both a little mad ourselves.

He pushed a few wet trends away from my face and grabbed my jaw, smiling down at me and breathing hard. "Are we okay?"

Light-headed and breathless, I nodded and looked between us where we were still joined.

He pulled out, and his come dripped out, too. "If you could only look at my face with that much fascination."

There was not enough energy for me to bite out a snarky reply. "Funny, aren't you?" I tried to slide down from the sink, underestimating the shake on my legs as I almost ended up collapsing had he not hoisted me in his arms and back in the bath.

"Stubborn woman," he said, pulling me onto his chest and kissing the top of my head. "Who I love."

Kilian's hand was still wrapped around mine as we and Mal made our way down to the dining chambers in Taren and I didn't want to pull away. Not after he'd called me his more than fifty times and made me call him mine about one hundred more. Would it matter if we played pretend outside of the bedroom?

We must have missed lunch with everyone because the only ones we found there were Lazarus and Thora in a heated stare down.

"Why is that pigeon sitting with your sister?" Mal asked, somewhat defensive, before pushing past us and taking a seat by her side.

Thora jerked a little at the intrusion, she always had a thing about attention. Always blurring out anything that was not in her focus. It was something that had worried Eren countless times, especially when she would blank out in the middle of danger.

"Why is Nia not with you?" he asked my sister.

"I am not in need of a babysitter, and she was busy."

Kilian and I took a seat by one another, and Lazarus stared his disdain and almost vocalised it before Mal asked, "What ruffled your feathers today, birdman?"

My general threw his spoon on the table and pointed a finger at me. "You missed the meeting this morning, then breakfast with your family. Did he bargain you to abandon those too?"

"That is none of your business," Kilian said calmly as he buttered a slice of warm sourdough for me. The man had the patience of saints.

Lazarus's chest rumbled with a growl. "Damn right it is. Just because you force her to share a bed with you doesn't give you rights to her."

"I let him fuck me on the same bed, too, Lazarus," I said, chewing the warm sage scented crust. And the room went quiet.

I didn't need to look up to feel Lazarus's betrayed puppy eyes. He was a big boy and one who knew I had no intention of reciprocating his feelings.

He stood and pushed the chair back, sending it flying across the room before stalking all upset and heartbroken out of the dining chambers. Splintered prides were easier to repair than cut-up genitals. If he spoke to me or Kilian like that again, I'd feed it to him.

"If I remember correctly," Kilian said, placing another buttered slice next to my bowl and leaning in to whisper the rest, "I didn't actually fuck you on the bed."

I raised a brow. "Want me to call him back?"

He gripped my jaw with a hand and licked the corner of my lip. "Perhaps I ought to just fuck you on the bed then."

"Really?" Mal called indignantly. "In front of the young one?"

Thora coughed on a sip of tea and turned to Mal with a dumbfounded look on her face. "I'm not a child, Malik. And you're only four years older than I am."

The younger Castemont shut his eyes tight. "Just cooperate, will you?"

"Cooperate? What are you sullying my sister with?" Eren asked as he came into the dining chambers. He kissed the top of my head and then Thora's before taking a seat.

"Sully?" Cai asked, plopping down in a chair beside me. When did he come? "It is Mal we are talking about. Thora is probably past saving now."

Mal chucked a butter knife at my friend who caught it mid-air and began cutting his food with it. "Thank you, princeling."

Pen and Visha came in together, chatting and murmuring to one another. The second my Crafter noted Cai and Mal, she bowed her head to me and left the room.

Pen had a massive frown on her face, her gaze narrowed on Kilian. She sat down, crossed her arms and stared at him up and down. "Are you a rabid dog?"

Kilian stopped chewing and slowly glanced at me before turning to Pen, confused.

The little redhead pointed a finger at me, particularly on my neck. "Why do you bite her?"

Surely red had crept all over my face and ears.

"Because she likes it," Kilian answered calmly, buttering me another slice of bread.

I smacked him hard on the back and he chuckled before grabbing my face with a hand, his fingers squeezing my cheeks, as he bent down to kiss my nose. He threw me a wink, too.

I took the buttered bread and ate it, meeting every curious and amused gaze on the table with a narrowed glare.

Alaric's whistles grew closer to us and he strutted in with a bright crooked smile on his face, taking a seat at the head of the table. "Morning, children." He pointed a fork to Thora. "Your hair is lovely, kid. It suits you."

My sister touched her sloppily braided hair. "Driada did it for me."

He made to say something to me, but shyly retracted back, a red flush creeping on his face. What in the heavens?

Cai shovelled food quickly down his throat before he rose to leave. It had been barely a minute since he'd sat.

"Cai," I said, grabbing his arm. "Eat properly."

He shook his head, still chewing. "Myrdur is infested with Isjordian rats of all sorts."

I grabbed a piece of bread and stood with him. "Let's go then."

One by one, the whole table rose, and Cai dropped his head back with a groan. "No, you all will finish first."

"How about we all eat," Eren said, looking at Cai. "And then we all go, hm? Sit, General."

I stopped chewing. General?

My friend's mouth twitched just a little and he sat back in his chair, resuming his meal. By the end of lunch, the muscles in my eye had gone sore looking between him and my brother. The more they glanced at one another the more I was convinced that—

"Why have you called Vidarr, kid?" Alaric asked, calling me to attention. "Last I know you'd sent him to Seraphim to check on your father's camp."

"Putting your nose in the business you never like to smell, old man. My spy's business is stinky stuff." Vidarr did the heavy lift work over the west of Numen.

He gave me an assessing look. Ohhh, he knew something. "Does it have to do anything with the fact that Grasmere is in your hold?"

Every cutlery on the table went quiet.

He pointed a finger to my shoulder. "Saw you leave last night for Adriata with a new bargain on your arm. Considering you'd sent Sebastian after your banished half-brother to hold him prisoner, and that his pregnant betrothed is Gara Grasmere, the chain fell right in the correct links."

Sigh. You could not keep one secret in this kingdom.

Kilian slowly turned to me and peeled the dress off my shoulder with a finger to reveal the bargain band. "How did I not notice?"

"Remember how distracted you were making all sorts of prayers?"

The look on his face was utterly blank. Was he stunned?

"By half-brother," Eren said slowly. "You mean Reuben? You are holding Reuben Krigborn prisoner?"

"No."

"Lin," he warned, trepidation pulsing through his summer forest eyes.

"He is a guest in my dungeons."

He sighed with disappointment, but I saw fear flash through my sister when she asked, "Reuben is here?"

"No," I said. "Reuben is in the dungeons."

Myrdur had been restless. Not only from the spirits that had not passed on or the constant attacks from Isjord. The *zgahna* was no longer whispering, it was now rumbling like thunder. And I didn't understand why. I already had a sceptre piece and that meant he wouldn't be able to form the Octa Virga. Was war that near us?

We all sat on the ruin rock wiping blood out of our hands and weapons that was still hot on our clothes and metal. For each attack, father had doubled the number and I was sure that sooner than later his curiosity would get the best of him and he'd send the beasts.

Eren frowned over the ruins' distance, hazel eyes murking with shallow pain—one I'd seen before when mother used to take an evening off from grief and tell us about the night of *Draugr*. "They were barely teenagers. We killed children."

"Silas is eliminating the lower links first," Cai said, plopping beside me, stealing my drink and taking a big gulp. "But those lower links can still walk themselves toward the *zgahna*. And considering the witch has gotten particularly witty and wily these days, I wouldn't find it odd if they could breathe through it."

"How long have you been casting guard over Myrdur?" Eren asked, turning to us.

Cai leaned forward, resting his elbows on his knees. "For the first decade you couldn't step in Myrdur even if you wanted to. The floor was tar, it burned and ate your flesh and soul. Souls clung to the land with all their might. I was around sixteen, living in Kilerth and training with Alaric when we first heard of the scavengers lurking in the ruins for gold, diamonds, artefacts. Then came the Crafters stealing and digging graves and bones to strengthen their craft." My friend breathed hard and his eyes dropped stolid on the ground. "Wearing my people around their necks and wrists like jewellery and belts. The unblessed grew curious, they too came and ventured, trampled the ground and took a stone from a ruin or two as a memory of their visit over the graves of my family. Solaryans wanted to see if they could shine life inside the ruins again—they left before even trying. Hanaians planted Soren and left after their roses withered in this soil. Isjordians came last. About two years ago. Curious at first. We thought they wanted to make sure someone was not rebuilding Olympia and now we find out about the sceptre. I've been guarding this land for almost half of my life."

Eren kneeled before him, resting a hand on his knee. "It won't be for the rest of it, Cai. We will deal with my father, one way or another. And you will get to walk these streets again. Not to guard them. To live."

My friend leaned forward, inches away from Eren's face. "Such a king like promise, Your Highness."

I blinked between them, eating the cashews Cai had given me. Did they even see I was sitting with them?

My brother's eyes dropped to Cai's mouth. "You seem to like them regardless."

Standing, I unsheathed my sword. "I'm sure someone just called for me. Oh yes," I said, cupping a hand over my ear. "Second hand embarrassment, I'm coming."

"No," Eren said, grinning. "What is embarrassing is that my little sister has kissed the man I want to kiss."

Nubil. "You told him?"

Cai shrugged. "Transparency." He smirked and looked down at my brother still kneeling before him. "You want to kiss me?"

And that was my cue.

By the time I bolted to Adriata, all my limbs were sore.

Mal sat with Thora and Driada on the garden patio, they were all chatting amongst one another, laughing and smiling. Deciding not to disturb their peace with the scent of battle and trouble, I headed upstairs to Kilian.

He too sat among the snake fire of battle and trouble, but his scent was of spring flowers. "Hello, love."

Too tired, I took off my leathers and climbed into bed. "Good night."

I tried to sleep. Tried really hard. But my mind was still fighting and planning and buzzing. So I stood, wrapping the sheet tightly against me and crawling in Kilian's lap. He rounded his arms around me, that sweet scent of his working like a lullaby hushing all other noise.

Safe. So safe. Like a net. But I was fish out of water, and I was struggling to breathe somewhere I didn't know how to breathe in. And he was teaching me. Little by little. To get out of the waters I'd known all my life and learn to live on this land.

His fingers kneaded my sore muscle, his lips leaving kisses on the crown of my head and that land felt warm, my lungs stronger. "Should I come to bed with you?"

I shook my head. "Just speak to me, anything."

"Do you want me to tell you about my day?"

"Yes. Tell me."

The second I rested my head on his shoulder, and his voice formed long verses of the most random sentences, sleep took over—dreamless, spring scented sleep.

CHAPTER THIRTY-FOUR

Dius

Snowlin

The moment I bolted back to Olympia, I knew something was wrong. Soldiers were frantically running all over the corridors, several Volantians were dropping from the terrace rushing south.

"Myrdur is under attack," Cai shouted running toward me. "Kvan and Amur, too. Head north to Amur, Tristin and the Skye are heading to Kvan to help Cori."

Why was my father so persistent in crossing the mist, had he not realised he'd lost the sceptre? I shook my head. "Send someone else north, Cori needs more help."

He clasped my shoulder. "North, Snow. Volantians are down in Myrdur. You can get there the fastest."

Reluctantly, I obeyed. Bolting at the outskirts of the village so my lightning didn't attract the Foglings to the city. The whistle of Nimbus hiding up in the mountains ran once and then twice before the Amur skies slowly began crawling with dark, angry clouds and the city disappeared under a thick layer of fog.

My Aura were quick, but not quick enough because the dark creatures poured out like ants from behind the closing curtains of clouds.

Electricity gathered around me, and I sent a bolt upward to the skies. Like moths to flame, the dark creatures screeched and changed direction, gathering in a vortex above me.

"Damned hells," I muttered to myself when I saw the number of Foglings circling above and downpour on me like autumn rain.

My soldiers began running toward me, but I lifted a hand, stopping them. "Get the city under clouds. Go!"

"But—"

"If any of them get to the city, I will kill you all myself."

Reluctantly, they all pulled away and as did Memphis who hovered the skies, attempting to stay away from the lingering beasts overhead.

The rock I stood on blistered with ice that crawled all around me and pierced upward onto a Fogling body. Ice was easier to control, my aim more precise but from the way the creatures had surrounded me, it was no task of precision. They were crowded around and above me in such a way that I couldn't see at all. It was almost becoming as dark as night.

Finally, I decided to drag every inch of electricity I could control and blast it around us. Over and Over. Yet the more I killed, the more showed up, attracted by the bright lightning.

The mountain blistered with my magic that clung to every rock and atom of air. The height rumbled and heat scorched anything that was alive where I stepped. With each breath I took, the sputtering lightning dressing my libs expanded. And then I felt the gates of mana ram open. I stopped and drew my sword. If my seal opened I was more dangerous to Amur than the Fogling. It had to be done the good old way.

The skies cried heavily as I swung my brother's sword back and forth, impaling one Fogling after another. When I killed one, two more showed up. They were multiplying by the moment, and I was running out of energy to keep myself upright. But bolting was all it would take for my seal to break. And I wasn't sure if I'd make it to Visha on time.

The rain soaking my leathers was heavy and held up my punches. Or perhaps it was the tremble of exhaust that did it.

One by one, they dropped to the ground, clawing the stone in my direction, their mouths hungry and their swirling dark stare mad. Once, these creatures were an Olympian—at least the dark part of the soul remaining from them.

I looked up at the pouring skies, breathing quicker than what my lungs allowed. "You really don't want me up there. I swear, you don't want me in either heaven or hells." My throat burned and my pulse was erratic as I pushed my sword through body after body. "You really don't want me up there."

My grip gave up, loosening from the shake permeating me and the sword dropped to the hard rock with a clatter. I frowned looking down at my dishevelled state. My spirit would be mocked and dragged to bits by fellow spirits.

Sigh.

What a fucking terrible way to die.

The surrounding air grew heavy with magic and all of a sudden, tentacles of dark rose from the ground, enveloping the surroundings and rising to the sky, turning day to night. The creatures screeched in anguish and I felt a trickle of blood dripping from my ears.

Before I crashed to the ground, a strong pair of arms hoisted me up. If I was tired enough to not recognise that touch, I could never be tired enough to recognise that sweet scent of his.

"I've got you."

When I cracked my eyes open, he stood there, looking down at me. The inky black air that touched me was warm, but the moment the creatures enveloped in it they turned to ash.

Soon, it got so dark I could see nothing.

So dark that I had to clutch Kilian hard to feel like I wasn't slipping in it. Perhaps he didn't want me to see. But he didn't know...that I was no longer afraid of the dark.

"You're safe, my love." He rested his forehead on mine and I got to breathe him in.

"I've always wanted to be saved," I murmured, my tongue loose from fatigue or perhaps from how safe it felt to say it. "At least once, I prayed to be saved. Have you come to save me?" I sighed again onto him, my body melting to his as though every fibre of mine wanted to feel his. "How is it so much easier to say things in the dark?"

"Because they stay in it. Whatever happens in the dark stays in the dark."

I lifted my head up, presuming I was looking at him because I couldn't see anything.

"You're staring at my nose," he said with some amusement.

"I wanted to stare at your mouth." I reached a hand to cup his face, slowly guiding my fingers to find his lips. "Whatever happens in the dark stays in the dark, right?"

My heartbeat was solid against his, both competing which would give up first from the force drumming against our chests.

He didn't answer...because his mouth was on mine. So warm. His touch, his breath, his caress, his lips and tongue. I longed to feel warm. He was soft and tasted a bit like the liquor he always drank, and his kisses were just as strong. Demanding, devouring. Intoxicating.

"You taste heavenly, my sweet sin," he whispered over my mouth before crushing his lips to mine again. Kissing Kilian Castemont was like walking through fire on a rainy day. Kissing Kilian Castemont was agony—kissing him was the sweetest agony. It made me want to suffer.

He held me so close, tightly pressed to him and it wasn't nearly close enough.

It took us a few moments to gather our breath. To gather sense about something that made absolutely no sense at all. How...how could just one kiss...one kiss...colour so much negative space on a canvas that had been blank for so long—so vehemently.

How?

When darkness began dispersing, I let go of him and he let go of me. His mouth was rosy and swollen, the remnants of what we did painted on his stare, too, glazed with dark want.

Fogling laid on the ground the colour of ash, frozen with their mouths and eyes wide open as if they'd seen their end before even dying. Perhaps they had. The Obscur Asteri was the dark and the dark was death.

"Let's go see the city, make sure none of them strayed from the flock." He extended a hand for me to take and in a flash, we were at the centre of Amur.

The stony streets were empty, houses locked and dark. I could feel the fear of my people in the air. I felt the horror they went through. And my heart bled.

A few curious looks peeked from behind curtains and then people began pouring out of their homes and onto the city square, surrounding us and rejoicing.

"Thank you," an elderly man offered, rushing to us despite his limp and the crane. He bowed to us, offering Kilian a string of dragon larch beads that many used to count their steps to Valda. "My queen, my king. We thank you."

My king.

Kilian took the small gift, eyeing the engraved wooden spheres with curiosity. "I'll cherish it well. Thank you."

"For your own walk to Valda," the man said. "Hopefully one day you will convince your wife to accompany you, too. She can make her fist climb as well."

Kilian's stare grew with curiosity, and after the man backed away he asked. "You've not made the climb?"

How did he even know about it? "No. Surely Alaric ratted me out plenty on my bad Olympian behaviour."

"It was mostly Alastair," he said and pocketed the small gift.

A little boy rushed to us, a few colourful sweets in his hands. "For you. To thank you."

Kilian kneeled before the young boy, fluffing his hair and taking the candy from him. "How did you know they were my favourite?"

The boy's eyes doubled in size as did his smile. "My mama sells them in the city, she makes the best corn candy in the whole of Olympia."

Kilian popped some in his mouth. "I will make sure to visit here more often then." He stood and offered me some.

Corn sweets? His favourite sweets were sugar rolled in balls?

I picked an orange-coloured bead and popped it in my mouth. The strong artificial sweeteners made me wince, but I gave the boy a smile. "Thank you." Once the little boy was out of earshot, I turned to Kilian and made a gagging sound. "You can't possibly be serious. These are sickly sweet."

He raised a brow at me. "They are. Because they are corn *sweets*."

I looked around and made to spit the candy out, but he grabbed my jaw, stopping me before I did so. "Don't you dare," he said, and then probed my mouth open with his thumb. He took the half-eaten candy from my tongue and put it in his, licking his fingers as he did so. "Persimmon flavour is one of my favourites."

I made another gagging sound. "There was a flavour besides sugar in that?"

He gave me a small, amused smile and nodded.

Maybe I was willing to try another if he liked them that much. I looked down at his palm cradling the small candy. "Which is your favourite?"

Without hesitating he said, "You."

Idiot. "Your taste is questionable," I said, smacking my tongue to the roof of my mouth in an attempt to wash away the sugary taste. Better no more candy for me.

He kissed my cheek. "My taste is exquisite."

If I could blush, I would, it's just I was freezing and that would have required an insane amount of heat. My insides, however, were twirling like little spirits under moonlight. What the frozen hells was the matter with me?

After throwing the rest of the candy in his mouth, he reached into his pocket and brought out a small stygian cube about the size of a chestnut. "I finally worked it out. How to keep the Foglings away from the cities. One of my scholars dissected the beast and found their trigger. A tumour grew welded to their hearts, a black mass that fed on light. He took the essence and tested it on many counter elements. Darkness worked best."

My mouth parted in awe, and I stared at the small thing he held. "That?"

He nodded. "Oryn helped me make these. Adriatian steel carrying the essence of two Obscurs. The king that died in the mountain and mine—to reinforce it. The creatures don't need darkness to stay away from it, like the clouds the Nimbus are creating. The essence alone will keep them away."

He looked around and went to a round well positioned in the city square, dropping the cube in it. "I will have one made for each tribe. Order your Nimbus to pull away the clouds."

"I don't think that is the best idea."

"Snow, tell your Nimbus to pull away the clouds. If anything happens—which is highly unlikely—I am here."

The Nimbus stood guard atop the rocks surrounding the city. Cupping my hands around my mouth, I whistled the signal twice to alert them to pull away the clouds. The fast palpitations of anticipation had my hackles raised. I reached for my sword only to find the sheath empty so daggers it was. Many other sentries around the city followed suit, and we waited as clouds pulled to reveal the clear blue sky of midday.

We waited and we waited, weapons and magic at ready, but nothing happened. Then we waited some more, and minutes turned to an hour. And nothing happened.

Nothing was happening.

Claps and cheers made my reality snap in place. People circled the streets rejoicing with one another, muttering and crying prayers as they stared at the sun and sky with blissfulness and hope in their tearful eyes.

Hope.

He'd given them back their hope.

I turned to Kilian who was smiling at the blue skies of Olympia. "I—"

"It is my duty," was all he said.

I nodded. "Could you take us to Kvan? The Skye warriors and Cai are there, but I just want to check if everything is alright."

Kvan seemed darker now that I'd basked under the sun. I couldn't wait to break the news to the others on what Kilian had found.

"I'll pay a visit to the western cities first," he said, backing away from me and I nodded.

"Wait," I said, grabbing onto his arm. "My brother's sword. I think I dropped it in Amur."

"I'll get it."

When I didn't let go of him, he raised a brow. "Yes, love?"

I didn't want him to leave. Not when I still felt him all over me. I wanted him to bring night and kiss me again. "Nothing," I said, turning and diving into the narrow streets of Kvan.

The further in the city and past Fogling bodies I went, the more I realised the sun wasn't the cause of the lowering and the calamity over the city. One by the other, ravens took spots on the building roofs. Their cawing grew, reverberating in the quiet of the valley of Kvan and I spotted Memphis on the high tower of the city library, eyes shut and her head ducked down—then her pain slithered down our bond to fill my chest with a swarm of augur.

A throng of people stood in the middle of the city square, circling around something. Faces were pulled in mourning and something began emptying inside me. All of the sudden...I began to feel dull again.

Cai showed up before me, his face hard with shadows and specks of black blood. The man who'd seen distraught and never faltered had it now painted all across his face. And if I'd felt dull before, the pain of my friend became my own and I felt anything but dull.

"Move, Cai."

His head dropped and he pulled his fist tight together before moving aside and letting me pass.

The crowd parted for me, and Cori's small frame laid on the ground covered with a blanket. Her tribal marking had faded in places and her long brown hair streaked with white paint fanned on the dirty ground. Some elderly said children were of the heavens, they were pure and kind, and could smile the sun back to the skies. I believed in little, but I believed in that because of Cori.

Why had they laid her on the dirty ground?

I dropped beside her and waited for my senses to pick up the thrum of her vibrant heartbeat, the same one that fluttered so loudly and alive as always. Perhaps I was tired from the fight before. I had to be tired because I couldn't hear anything. She had to be freezing laid there. "Cori?" She didn't answer.

Reaching over her, I put a palm on her chest. The hollow in my chest suddenly filled with something—something harrowing. "Where is it? Why can't I hear it?"

A hand rested on my shoulder. "Snow." It was Nia. Why was Nia crying? "She is gone."

Gone?

What...gone?

I ran my trembling hands over my head, clutching my hair tight, pulling and waiting for the pain to snap me back to reality. "What will I say to your mother, Cori? What will I tell her? She made me promise. She made me make a promise. A real one. It was her dying promise. It was her dying wish for me to keep you out of harm's way."

"No one saw her," Nia said, kneeling beside me. "She joined the soldiers without being seen."

I dug my fingers on my scalp, the burn no longer soothing, only reminding me how much the threshold of my pain had changed this very moment. No. Not Cori.

Someone reached to move the blanket over her face and I jumped, grabbing their wrist. "Don't touch her."

"Let go, Snow," Tristin said. "Don't do this to her, too. She deserves to rest."

Her, too? Slowly, I peeled my fingers from Tristin's hand, and I watched Cori's young pale face disappear behind the cloth.

Nia held me tight. But not tight enough. I stood, anger holding me up because my legs had given up. I met every stare around me while rage filled me to the brim. It tipped with need for carnage, to punish whoever had made me break my promise. "Who was responsible for watching her? Who was watching her when she went to die?"

Someone stepped forward, an elderly woman I knew well. Cori's governess. The woman who had stayed behind when Cori's mother and father, the previous leaders of Kvan, had died during a Fogling attack. Cori had been but a wee thing when the governess had taken over to raise her. She'd raised her as though her own. "Whatever your punishment is, I will welcome it, my queen. My Cori is gone. My babe is gone."

Quiet had fallen over the city. They knew how I punished. They knew no one survived my punishment. Maybe for the first time ever, I reconsidered. For Cori. For the little girl who had only ever known this woman as her parent. So I said, "Let her death be punishment enough for you."

The elderly woman's eyes splintered with tears. She sobbed silently, limping toward Cori's lifeless body. From her cries, I realised I'd given her a worse punishment than death.

Bells went off around Kvan, one after the other they echoed around the southern mountain range and then like dominoes, a signal from the Volants rang off in the distance, the echo carrying it closer and closer to us.

A winged Volantian broke through the clouds, landing right before us. Part of his wings were torn and he had three gushing wounds on his stomach. "Isjordians are crossing the mist," he wheezed, before dripping to the ground with a thud.

My feet began backing me off, carrying me with a mind of their own—itching to run. When I couldn't feel my sword on its scabbard, I pulled one laying on the ground from a dead soldier and backed away.

"Snow," Cai bellowed. "No!"

I took off in a run and just when I was far enough from hurting anyone, I bolted.

The *zgahna* screeched in my ears when I landed in front of the thick mist. Pulling my hood up and my veil down, I descended the mountain face toward Myrdur, where I could make a dozen or so bodies making their way to me.

The mist whispered in my ears as I moved through it. It swirled around me, dressing my limbs till I was only a grey shadow—it became one with me. The essence of my elders. The essence of all the Elding before me.

"*Raghair*," I whispered retreat and the ancient magic echoed the sound around the ruins for my soldiers to leave before they were caught in what I was about to do.

Electricity skittered below my feet and the ground charred with my every step as I descended the ruins of Myrdur, breathing fury.

When the Isjordian soldiers spotted my form, weapons were drawn and heartbeats shifted.

The mist slithered around my arms and then extended into tentacles in the direction of the men. The moment it touched their swords, they were sent flying back onto the air. Electricity zapping in their metals.

The soldiers didn't hesitate, unfolding their magic, sending sharp blisters of ice flying in my direction. The mist vortexed in front of me, swallowing their pathetic attacks and I gave them a touch of my less pathetic one, sending bolts of lightning piercing right through their guts. It didn't take me long to have all dozens of them turned to charred flesh.

Right as I was about to step back into the mist, a blood curdling roar filled the air. One I knew well.

The green thing dropped from the sky right in front of me, sending the rocky ground to splinter in half. Its nostrils flared, sniffing the air and then carefully, it took one step after the other toward me.

The mist twirled around me and turned to skitters of electricity before darting to the beast's direction.

The thing didn't even flinch from the hit. Not from the many others. It was merely feet from me when it jumped in the air and above me. Thankfully, the mist reacted quicker than I did, solidifying above me like a shield. The thud from the beast landing above me reverberated through the ruins of Myrdur and the mountains groaned.

"*I command you,*" I whispered to the mist, my voice transcending through it. And it obeyed me, to my command.

The white fog roared as it rolled down the Volants towards us. Arms made of white mist grew from within it—hundreds of them. Moving from under the mist shield, I backed further and saw the elder Elding magic take action. White phantom hands grabbed onto the beast and tied around it while the thing struggled and roared.

Once the beast was tied to the ground, I unsheathed the whitestone sword I'd grabbed from the Kvan soldier. The weapon felt heavier than the one I used, but it would do.

The beast lay trapped right before my feet, its heated breath vaporising my leather boots. In one swift swing, I impaled one of its arms and then the other.

The *zgahna* trembled when the thing roared so loud the ground shook. My skin pebbled and every sensation in my body prepared for a fight. Something felt unnaturally wrong. Not like the sense Foglings gave you. Not like the sense of darkness. Something far worse. Far more sinister. A call of a magic I could not recognise but still felt familiar with.

I stumbled a step back, aghast at what was happening before my eyes. Flesh materialised and crawled from where I cut his arms to grow into a new pair. The green beast breathed hard as the flesh regenerated, its green eyes lifting to meet mine.

I stumbled another step back when its mouth twisted almost to a smile. "Should have gone for my head. That grows slower," the thing growled.

Blessed seven sweet hells of Celesteel. The thing spoke. The thing was conscious in this form? But—

Bracing itself in its new hands, the beast rose itself up, tugging the tentacles of mist hard enough they snapped and dispersed in the wind. One after the other, the beast was free from their hold and standing eight feet tall before me. Those malachite eyes went to my sword and its fang filled mouth twitched more.

I looked down on the borrowed sword I held. Then it hit me, my attention going from the three visible scars on the pale green abdomen to the arms to the non-existent ones where I'd cut its arms. In Hanai, I'd struck it with my brother's sword, and it had worked.

For each step forward the beast took, I took another back.

"Scared now?" the thing growled, still chasing my steps.

My steps wobbled, a sense of fear marring my features and I trembled with each step I took back. The way the beast's expression grew into what one can only call amusement made me realise how entirely too human it appeared to be.

The thing hadn't made a move to attack me, only chasing my steps back and revelling in my fear—almost enjoying it. "I spy with my green eye," the beast crooned in its gravelly breathy voice. "A little fearful—" The beast didn't finish. He was rather preoccupied with choking and gasping for air.

I stopped and lifted a brow, a smile stretching wide below my face covering. "Welcome inside the *zgahna*." *Demir*.

The thing cocked its head to the side and frowned, still heaving for air.

I took another step back. "Welcome inside the hell with no air," carried by the wind, my words echoed around the mist. "I command you to kill." Like the hiss of a snake, senseless words and buzzing carried through the air and the fog thickened around us till it became so dense that breathing was impossible.

Choked sounds and then a hard thud signalled the effect. The mist parted for me while I stepped toward the unconscious beast.

"Ugh," I gagged, wrapping my hand around its slithery wrist. It took me a full hour to pull the thing's body from the mist. I would have left it there like I'd left many others, but now I knew it could regenerate. How long could the thing breathe without air? That is if it even needed air to breathe. How long till a new pair of lungs grew and it could die and regenerate itself all the way across the *zgahna*? The more I thought about it, the more worrying scenarios formed inside my head. Perhaps father had figured the way inside the ancient magic.

When I reached Myrdur ruins, I slashed the sword through its neck and bolted along with it and its head right in the middle of the Hollow Sea. The waters were icy, within seconds hypothermia was going to set in.

"Hope something in here finds you tasty, Demir." I pushed from it as it began sinking underwater and then bolted back to Taren.

My breath misted and I left water puddles all along the blue lit corridors of the castle. I saw him first amongst the others. Shedding his jacket as he rushed toward me.

I sighed when the lemon flower scented warmth surrounded me. He breathed furiously, holding me tight, running his hands to my sides to warm me up. "To gods," he swore. "To gods you do that again."

"It speaks," I breathed out. "It speaks and it's conscious in that form and it grows limbs. It can grow back its head, too."

He pulled back, staring at me like I had gone half wild.

Eren showed up to our side and he ran his hands over my head and through my hair. "Did you hit your head somewhere?"

I took a moment to stop the chatter of my teeth. "The beast from Hanai. I am sure it was Demir—it had the scars I gave it back then. He was in Myrdur, crossing through *zgahna*."

Nia came into sight. "That thing was in Myrdur?"

Visha peeked from behind Nia.

"Yes. I cut his head and tossed both onto the Hollow Sea."

They all stared like I was now fully mad, except one. The red headed witch stared blankly downwards, the emerald pupils jerking fast up and down.

"What is it Visha?" I asked.

She raised her wide stare to us and I immediately saw what I rarely saw from her—panic. "It's not made, Snow. It's born from the magic of heavens, if nothing kills it and it regrows limbs. This thing is of heavens."

"Maybe our whitestone swords do not work on these creatures because Eren's sword injured it, it still had the marks of the wounds from where I stabbed it."

"Your sword is something called an *anima accissor*," Kilian said. "Soul killer."

I frowned, turning to my brother. "The smith said it bore no magic."

"The smith was right. It bore no magic because it is magic itself. The metal was of Olympian soil, forged with Seraphim fire, under Cyra's light, beaten with the black steel of Aldric, quenched in Crafter blood and Isjordian snow, and the emerald stone is the heart of an Aitan sphinx. It was made for an Elding. It was made for you, Snow. Everyone just assumed I was the Elding since I was the eldest."

"You tell me this now?"

"It was not meant to bear any meaning to us. We swore to never use our magic."

"*You* swore," I said through clenched teeth. "You."

My brother's face fell and I immediately regretted my words.

I looked around for the one who usually mocked my thoughts. I waited for him to laugh at my conclusions to make me calm about my panic, but I couldn't find him. "Cai. Where is Cai?" Where was he?

I pushed through all that had gathered around me and ran toward his quarters only to find them empty. Reaching his balcony, I bolted to Taren, searching the usual taverns he frequented only to find them void of his presence. Kvan. Lyn. Amur. Kilerth. Drava. Volant. I searched every tribe only to find him nowhere. Where was he?

Light rain began pattering on me and it was slowly turning dark. Panic settled again. The same panic only he could soothe.

Panic. He'd panicked, too.

I bolted to Fernfoss, searching the village by foot and when I found no trace of him, I ran through Soren.

He'd leaned back on a billowing alder, eyes shut, his mother's pendant in his hand.

I'd stopped running for a while now, but he never had—my friend was still running.

Slowly, I sank down next to him. "She is with her parents now."

He turned to me a little. "You believe none of that crap."

"I'd like to believe it just this once," I said, gathering myself tight. "Believe it with me, Cai. It's an order. From your queen."

"And if I disobey?"

"I will have you banned from every bakery shop, Drava to Fernfoss."

His expression turned cold. "You wouldn't dare."

"I'll even have someone paint you a portrait and hang it around each shop with a reward if they ever catch you buying any sweets. Then, I will write a decree that by my order no cook, professional or not, can ever bake you anything. Ever. You will live a life of savoury foods until you beg for me to end you. And then—"

He chuckled a little and wrapped an arm around my neck, rubbing a fist on the crown of my head till it burned. "Alright, alright."

"It was not your fault," I whispered. "Tell me that you know that. Tell me, Cai."

His head dropped back on the tree. "It isn't. But if I could blame someone, it would be me."

River Taren flowed languidly along its distended bank, unbothered by the crowd of people gathered beside it or the light drizzle that made its surface ripple like velvet. Cori's funeral was packed with all sorts of faces I'd never seen before. Family, they all said. They were her family, yet when her parents died, it was the mother of another that raised her.

I loathed funerals. Loathed them more when *I* had to bury someone I cared about. A child I cared about. Just a child. Little Cori was a child.

How many like her had I bid goodbye in this very same river?

How many more did I have to bury?

Tears were dry, the dull of white garments was comforting and most were chatting about their own memories of Cori—they were all lively and innocent memories that caused the small crowds to lighten with laughter. And I was grateful.

There was only one body hunched over the small wooden casket. The only one who was never afraid of mourning. He'd done it thousands of times. Become a slave of it by now. Alaric wiped tear after tear, a hand resting on top of where Cori laid below. He'd bid goodbye to her mother and father not long ago—buried under the same white painted wood.

Alastair had taken to reading the rituals after I refused to utter a single babel of gods. The elder tribe leader stood tall and strong despite his broken age—the luxury he'd given up right after his human wife had died. He'd given up his eternity...for another.

Immediately, I sought him in the crowd, only to find him already staring at me.

Come here, I mouthed.

Shortly, after pushing through the crowd, he stood by me. It wasn't till he wrapped an arm around my shoulders that I realised I'd been falling and falling. His sturdy touch had just caught me.

"Mourn her," he said only for me to hear. "There is no one to avenge, Snow. Just mourn her."

I don't think I know how. I only seeked that—retribution. This time, however, there was no one for me to demand retribution from. Silas? The gods?

What Tristin had told me still haunted me. *Her too*, she had said. I was holding Cori hostage, too. I had to let her go. She deserved to be among her family.

A few young girls broke from the crowd, they rested colourful rose bouquets on the small coffin, marking the dull grey of weather and mourning with a vibrance of the prettiest flower I'd seen.

A snort left my mouth, and I couldn't help the laugh that followed suit. I paid no mind to the attention on me and I laughed hard and even harder. "Cori," I said, pressing a shaky hand to my mouth that couldn't hold back the remnants of bitter amusement and something else that made my body quiver. "She...she—" The damned laughter would not let me speak. "Cori was deathly allergic to flowers."

I'd not realised the tears wetting my cheeks until Kilian pulled me into his chest, hiding me from the world. When he made to pull away, I clutched his jacket tight and hid my face between the flaps. "Don't let them see me like this. Don't let them see me weak." *Hide me. Hide me like you hide the truth of our end.*

I stayed like that, breathing in spring in a world of cruel winter, through the last calls of her life, through the sung praises of her infectious youth, through the torch lighting her small wooden coffin and till they pushed her away onto the Taren River that would soon flow onto the lakes hidden under mountain caves. It was said a guardian of Caelum resided under there and would fly your soul himself toward the gates.

Today I made another wish. I wished that all tales of heavens and gods were true. For Cori, I wanted them to be true. For her to meet her mother and her father and be happy.

"She will go now," Kilian murmured in my hair. "Look at her one last time."

And I did as he said—I watched the small boat carrying her flame down the river and disappear between the tall valley.

CHAPTER THIRTY-FIVE

IMBER

SNOWLIN

The meeting room was grave and silent. Where Cori had once sat, a wrath of white chrysanthemums stood. No one dared to remove them even after days of her passing. It was like all weather had paled since she'd stopped from sitting in my court. If I let them take away the flowers, it would be winter again.

It was Moriko who spoke first, "Silas is not stopping at all. He is fully readying for war. He's lost his guardian, but he has not lost his army, nor his monsters. My spies have caught sight of his soldiers still in Eldmoor, Seraphim and even down to the unblessed. I am not sure if he has realised that he is missing a sceptre piece or not, but even so, I believe he is trying to gather an alliance." She pushed two scrolls to Kilian and I. "Those were counted two nights ago."

Kilian unrolled the papers and sighed at their content before passing it to me. "He is planning to do this the plain old way, isn't he?"

The numbers—they were endless. Humans. Aura. Dark Crafters. And possibly more monsters wherever he'd hidden them.

Albius leaned forward. "It is time, Snow. Claim Winter court."

Eren tensed as I knew he would. But salvaging with peace was not something I could do. Nor had I any intention of trying to do so. Not with my father at least.

"She can't, not peacefully at least," Alaric explained. "Not when Silas has distanced every Lord and Lady out of his plans. Not when he has full control of his Aura and soldiers, these new beasts he has created or the foreign Aura he has gathered from all sides of the realm. How long before he dismisses his court and reigns despotic rule over Isjord? The man is a self-proclaimed autocrat. How much more do we need to see him do without his court's approval? How much do your personal armies have? Five thousand? Ten thousand?" My Regent scoffed. "Isjord has over four million soldiers, two million Aura and a set of probably thousands of beasts."

"Eight million soldiers," Albius said with a grave tone. "And four and a half million Aura."

Sebastian added, "And probably thousands more in recruiting as we speak. Word has it that there have been boys and girls seen leaving homes at night toward the war camps up north. Another fair mention goes to the new deal they might be striking with the unblessed. We have no numbers on the unblessed, but I would think they have plenty of human lives to spare in their search for the glory Silas is offering them."

"Not to mention that geographically they'd attack Adriata first," Cai said. "Then Silas has the continent in his clutches—surrounded."

"I'm afraid I might have to add a bit more fuel to this fire," Nia said, coming into the meeting room along with Mal. The two were worn out and bloodied and fear shot up to the root of my hair. "Eldmoor is aiding Silas."

Mal plopped to a chair, tired. "Every witch from Asra to Heca has gathered in the capital and are being picked up from soldiers at the borders between Aru and Brisk. Elias just sent Memphis back with word that the witches are being housed north of Tenebrose and servants say the Crafter chambers of the castle have been reopened."

"Oh gods," Alaric grumbled, and it wasn't on the news. He was staring at me. "What now, kid?"

"Do we have any news on the unblessed princes?" I asked Sebastian.

He nodded. "They are planning to leave in three days' time."

Leaning back on my chair, I said, "Numbers versus numbers. It is how my father has made the whole realm be at his fear. I'll give him numbers."

"The unblessed are pledging to your father," Albius said. "There is no way to persuade them otherwise. I've seen the three princes, Snow. They are blinded by what your father has offered them. They will not sway."

"No one said anything about persuasion, Albius. I'm not good with words as I am with actions. Father will lose their support and metal."

"You're too sure," Moriko said.

"I'm never too much of anything, Mor dear."

"We must make the Vayrs aware of it all," Alaric said. "They deserve to be aware of who they are siding with."

"If you are thinking of an alliance, you are thinking of war," Moriko pointed.

"This doesn't seem like it can be avoided," Nia said, taking a seat beside her, linking a hand with her and I could swear that the Autumn Queen's shoulders relaxed a little.

She seemed shaken by the thought. "Are you ready to plan one? Are you ready to plan a war?"

Kilian rested a hand over mine under the table. "If we have to, we will. Question is, will we have allegiance?"

Mor sighed and nodded. "Hanai would be honoured to fight beside both of you."

Both of us.

When did the wheel turn?

When did we become allies in all of this?

Thora pushed from the balcony pillars where she'd leaned all through the meeting and set down one of the war gaming figurines on the middle of the map splayed on the table.

"You have discussed everything," she said, picking up the king figurine. "Except for killing our father."

"Rora," I said, my smile wide. "It was the first thing I've considered, but the bastard cannot be killed."

She frowned. "How so?"

Sebastian leaned in. "He has a craft veil around him and a Magi healer has also tethered lifelines to him, feeding mana onto him. Other people—countless people. You won't know how many times you have to kill him to actually kill him. Not to mention he is protected all around all the time. And I am not talking about Isjordian soldiers."

She set both hands down on the table. "Snow killed the beast. We kill the Magi healer. And we kill the witch."

Visha flinched a little, throwing her pleading gaze at me which soon went downcast—my witch knew I'd done worse.

"The witch is pregnant," I revealed. "With our father's child."

Thora faltered a little step back, the figurine she held slipped and fell to the ground with a clatter. It took her a moment to righten herself, a cold armour rising over her emerald eyes. "Does that make her unkillable?"

"Thora!" Eren called.

The look on my sister was one I recognised well—it mirrored my own. "Why, brother? We've been made to kill worse. Remember? I do. Because we didn't get to shut our eyes like you, Eren. I watched and so did Snow. This would have never happened if—" Her jaw tightened. "If you had let Snow kill him that night."

Every eye in the room came on me, including Kilian's.

"One of my many good moments of being comfortable with violence. He'd taken away this very adorable plush toy I liked," I said, giving everyone a tight smile and a few loosened up but Eren's expression floundered, his head lowering.

"She was nine, Rora," he said. "Nine."

"Then you should have killed him," my sister said.

Mal stood and grabbed her arm before I could say something. "Come on, little bird, let's have a chat." He took her over the balcony, his mouth moving slowly while she stood before him with her arms crossed and a vacant look in her face—it was empty, like she wasn't even inside her own body anymore. And Mal noticed, grabbing her jaw with a hand and shaking her head a little. To add more to the oddness, she snapped like that, her attention became warm and she nodded and talked back to him, normally.

"Did your brother use magic on my sister?" I murmured to Kilian.

He looked over at them, silver irises narrowing before he shook his head. "No. He doesn't use his magic like that. Not even with Driada."

⋅⊰◈⊱⋅

Mal waved a hand in the air across the gardens and ran to me, struggling and fighting the sleeves of his shirt as he attempted to slide it down on his sweaty muscular body. "That is nice of you to visit me."

"Where is he?"

His smile dropped. "Could have just pretended that you missed me, sister-in-law. The fool is fixing his gardens."

Atlas had a pair of large shears in his hands and was sweating a bucket attempting to catch a bunch of branches overgrown atop a tall bush. Kilian, however, was nowhere in sight. Had he left poor Atlas to do his work?

"The two are joined to the hip," I said, noting the young boy struggling from the heat and labour.

"Kil found him."

"What do you mean *found*?"

"On a trip to Sidra. After we rested in a tavern for food before returning to Amaris, we heard a small child cry behind a rubbish bin. He was barely five, wearing a large nappy and covered in dirt, eating a half-eaten loaf that had more mud in it than bread. My brother refused to leave him. He refused to let anyone take care of him, too. Atlas slept in a room near his till not long ago. Ate with him and followed him everywhere, meeting, trials at Highwall and even patrols out at sea." Mal laughed. "He even called Kil *papa* for a while. Funniest part was that Kil let him."

How little did I know of him.

Atlas chose that moment to turn and wave a bony hand to us, and I suddenly found another human being...adorable?

Mal strode to the young priest and slung an arm over his shoulders, the boy's posture drowned by the fool's much bigger and taller one. "How is young Atlas? And where is your father?"

I smiled a bit, but Atlas went beet red. "Don't start again."

Mal pinched his cheek. "Why? I think it's adorable."

"It's embarrassing," Atlas said, trying to escape Mal's hold.

"If Kil is your father, would that make me your mother?" I asked, taking a seat on a bench, facing the honey scented white rose bushes.

Atlas went crimson to the tip of his hair.

"Enough, you bullies," Kilian said, coming from behind a maze wall, holding a large sack of soil on his shoulder before dropping it to the ground. He was messy, dirty, sweaty, ruffled, and gods help me, he was a treat I wanted to devour. He fluffed Atlas's hair. "Are you alright, son?"

Mal and I laughed till our bellies hurt, and Kilian, too, showed us that perfect grin.

Annoyed and embarrassed, Atlas picked up his shears and trotted away further in the garden.

"This is how we will be now?" Kilian asked, taking off his gardening gloves. "Bullying children."

"I am not a child," Atlas bellowed from a distance.

Kilian nodded at him with a little smile on his face. "My pardon, I meant grown boys." When he turned to us, he regarded me for a long moment. A lick of pleasure shot up my spine from the way he raked his gaze all delight over my body. "That is nice. Is it for me to take off?"

Suddenly, it was really warm. Too warm. Especially between my legs. I'd spent too many nights away from him trying to deal with the Isjordians in Myrdur. "By the buttons this time, preferably. It is one of my good dresses."

Mal clapped his hands and gave us both an annoyed look. "Signal for me to evaporate from this realm." And he was gone in a blink.

Kilian came to kneel before me, resting his hands on either side of me before leaning in and dropping a kiss right on my chest, between my breasts. "I'll have a thousand made for you."

"The last time I let you dress me I almost suffered a stroke. No, thank you."

He chuckled and the sound was so soothing somehow. A tendril of thick black fog materialised from thin air, crawling over his body and then over mine. The lick of magic over my skin was warm, almost as warm as his hands when it brushed over my cheek to tuck a stray strand of hair behind my ear. It still triggered my unconsciousness, but I was getting better and not fearing it. I knew why he often let small parts of it linger around us—to make me comfortable around it, teach me not to fear it. It was working. "What do I owe the pleasure of seeing you in broad daylight?"

I kicked back the hem of my dress and pushed off my slipper, trailing my foot over his thick muscular leg before pushing it under his shirt. "Several reasons."

His brow rose and he sucked in a sharp breath when I lowered my foot over his crotch. "Dangerous reasons, considering you need to distract me to convince me to help you."

"Did it work?"

He leaned in, leaving small kisses down my leg and then my foot. "I've been at your mercy ever since that day when you grabbed that sword off of me."

My face was solemn but there were inner parts of me smiling. "Hm, is that so?"

"Enough chatter." He put my foot down before gathering me up and slinging me over his shoulder like a sack of soil.

"You've dirtied me, you moronic piece of Adriatian flesh," I shouted, wiggling like mad.

He smacked my bottom, hard. "Reason for you to bathe with me."

"Sister!" Thora shouted from somewhere in the distance and Kilian paused while I lifted my head to grasp where she was coming from. "Oh, why is she up your shoulder?"

Kilian put me down. "Long story, young one."

My sister frowned and blinked slow. "Why am I either young or little to you two brothers?"

"My missus here," he said, pointing his chin to me. "Is little, too."

"Fair," my sister said and uncrossed her arms. "Did you tell him about where we are going tomorrow?"

Kilian turned to me with a raised brow. "We? And where are *we* going tomorrow?"

"Nowhere," I said. "Right in the middle of nowhere. Well, right in the middle of the Hollow Sea where fifteen ships of unblessed folk are travelling back to Comnhall."

"Are we to deliver them a sweet farewell on this trip of ours?" Kilian asked, crossing his arms.

"Yes, to their Otherworld." I frowned. "Do they have their own Otherworld?"

"They rot in the ground of their birth, according to their tales," Thora said, nodding with confidence. "Technically they will not rot because the Hollow Sea is festered with scavenging creatures who will not let flesh waste. There is also the matter of the salt levels and water pressure. Ultimately, their skeletons will pile at the bottom of the sea. There will be no rotting process."

"What she said," I offered to Kilian who was now slightly gaping and looking all stunned at the two of us.

"Keep explaining, ladies, you're not helping your case just yet."

"Oh," I said. "Yes, as I was saying. The new Lady of Grasmere has provided me with a detailed route of their trip. Father planned to escort them out of the Hollow channel himself to see that they cross without being noticed by Solarya and safely onto Moor. So my Aura will make sure Isjordian sails drift far away from the unblessed and we will make a trap for their ships. Once I've made sure not a single piece of wood swims back to the unblessed, I will send news to their king through a spy of mine explaining to them how they were ambushed by Isjordians on their way back and my father's intentions of invading their lands. Not only will whatever agreement of metal trade they have with my father end, but I highly doubt there will be peace between the two kingdoms."

"Is that why you are dragging Thora into this?" he asked. "To make it more believable that it was Isjordians who did it?"

"Actually," Thora said, raising her hand. "I volunteered. I've never been on a ship before."

"Was hoping you would get her convinced that she was not needed," I said.

Thora sat up taller. "I am coming, and I will see the ship. Meet you both tomorrow morning. Mal has promised to take me down to Lyra to see the prophecy. I keep debating with him that I am not the dragon but the dire wolf. My wind magic is not nearly as strong as the ice part."

"What about dinner?" Kilian asked. "Do I ask the cook to make you the potato bake?"

"No, I'm having dinner with Larg and his family." With that, she turned on her heels and left toward the gardens, hopping along to a melody she hummed.

"She is getting along well here," I remarked.

Kilian pinched my chin. "She is slowly getting used to Olympia, too, my love, it will be fine." He huffed a long, long sigh and then threw me over his shoulder again. "The bath and then you got some convincing to do."

"Are you suggesting I use my body to sway you to help us?"

He smacked my bottom. "I was talking about your mouth, little beast."

"Ah."

"Ah?"

"Will you finally let me?"

He laughed, hard. "Words, woman. I meant words."

The cliffs of Llyn were what I as a child thought heavens looked like. The breeze brushing my cheek was not cold yet not warm, just a subtle perfect in between that made the glistening sapphire view ahead even more magical. Sound of waves crashing against the tall rock sung a lullaby along with the chorus of seagulls rushing overhead. The scent of sea was salty yet not fishy and it made Llyn perhaps the only seaside that didn't make me sick.

"I wish you hadn't picked my territory to go get yourself in a mess," Leanna said, nudging my shoulder with hers. "Alaric will serve my lungs on a platter to my child if anything happens to you. At least take my Tristin with you."

"Her feathers get in the way."

She chuckled. "Will this work?"

"When has anything I've done not worked?"

With a sigh she turned to face me. "Well—"

"Fuck off, Leanna."

At that moment Kilian, Alaric, Thora and Tristin all walked up to us.

"Be nice, love," Kilian said, coming to stand by me.

Leanna chuckled again and now the whole kingdom was about to find out the Night King had just scolded me.

"Volantians are already hovering above them after they sent off the Isjordian ships inside the northern storm," Tristin said, pointing her chin at the expanding distance of the Hollow Sea. "If you find trouble, signal and the Skye warriors will portal to you."

"Won't be necessary," I said, reaching my sister to pull her hood up and her veil down. The leathers fitted her perfectly. A little too perfect. I never wished to see her in them. Every time I've worn them, I have either taken a life or lost a life. "Ready?"

She nodded and we both grabbed hold of Kilian's extended hands. The fading was rapid. Vast sea surrounds us and from the deck of the ship Kilian had just faded us to, you could see the Isjordian Islets in the distance behind.

Thora rushed to the edge, looking down at the waves crashing on wood. "Nice."

"Hey," a man below deck shouted in Laoghrikrease. "Who are you? How did you get on the ship?" More men gathered below us, all aiming some sort of weapon in our direction.

The hair on the back of my neck rose when magic littered the sea air. Shadow tentacles crawled over the wooden floor till they reached the men. The moment they mingled with their shadows, the men dropped their weapons and stood frozen aghast. "Find the prince. Check the great cabin first."

We manoeuvred around the still bodies and rushed to search around. And there he was, snoring on his two-seater while his ship had barely left Isjordian waters. They were idiots, truly.

Thora kicked his leg and he jolted upright before startling further back in the seat when he saw us. "Come on now," my sister urged, flinging her dagger up at him. "Get up, sir."

"What on the crown's rubies are you?"

Thora caught his ankle and pulled him from the seat, dragging him all over the floor as we walked back to the main deck.

Kilian raised an amused brow at me and I only shrugged.

With one swiping motion, I parted the Breshall prince's hand lined with dozens of glittering and colourful diamond rings.

The man screeched like an alarmed cockatoo who'd forgotten to coo at dawn.

"Shhh, sir," Thora said, looking around the other ships, at the sailors gathering to see what was happening. "Men are so sensitive."

Kilian chuckled at my sister and grabbed the rest of the prince, fading back to Olympia.

"Ready?" I asked, extending a hand forward to Thora.

She nodded, crouching down to the ground and resting her palms on the wooden floor. "Ready."

At both our command, the water surrounding the ships froze. Magic poured in gales from us. Massive, sharp stalactite shards of ice surged from water and pierced each ship, destroying men and wood.

The wind howled and turned frosted—soon, snow began pouring from the skies.

By the time Thora and I had channelled not a scratch of our magic, a graveyard of frost floated in the lost middle of the northern waters. Sails creaked from the wind of the Hollow Sea, the only sound around us. Even the life below us had disappeared.

Kilian faded back with someone—someone who had worked for me for years long now and a good friend of Alaric's. An unblessed spy of mine that had kept a good eye on the Vrammetheni continent for years.

"Vidarr," I said, throwing him the prince's hand. "You know what to do."

His teeth lined with gold gleamed. "Yes, my queen."

Kilian's attention had focused behind me on the wreckage we'd caused and the lives we'd taken. Even if he couldn't see the bodies buried under frost, I was sure he could feel them. Every muscle on his body tensed. "There is something travelling with them," he said, pulling all of us close.

Something bumped hard below deck and the wreckage shook, causing water to break and the ship to quickly turn to the side. Kilian grabbed Vidarr, my sister, and then me before fading us on top of another close-by ship.

Something tore from the rubble. Something green and large. Something resembling the beast from Hanai, but not quite so. It looked too human, its figure was of a man, his face was of...nothing I could describe properly—if a cobra and a wolf had a child and made it green and scaly and breathing out a strange green mist.

The thing went on its fours, his chest rumbling like two marbles hitting each other each time he breathed.

"Father had offered them beasts," I said, coming to realisation and unsheathing my sword. "Hells. He was going to trade beasts for the metal."

The creature's head snapped to me. In one swift move, it leaped in the air and over to us, a deep rattle vibrating in the air and piercing our eardrums.

Kilian grabbed and faded us on top of another wreckage. We'd barely settled on our footing when the thing appeared before us again, running on its fours quicker than any animal I'd ever seen.

Thora's hands shot forward, sharp stalactites raising dozens from underneath, piercing the creature over and over. But the thing broke its body out of the ice, digging its teeth on its own limbs and tearing them apart till he was free again. Bloodied and half torn, the creature heaved green froth and mist as all lost limbs began growing back.

Seven hells. This thing, too?

Kilian's darkness began pooling around us and shooting toward it. "No," I said, grabbing his arm and his magic doused, disappearing in thin air. "Not turning it to charcoal. I want to see something. Pierce it with your steel. Go for its head."

My sister's eyes bulged as she tried to manoeuvre her magic to keep the thing from nearing us. "What, why?"

Kilian already knew what I wanted to see and faded beside it, his metal cutting though the beast's head. Like I'd predicted—green flesh began crawling like worms and slowly mended itself till its head formed again.

Kilian faded back to my side. "This isn't good."

"My turn." I bolted right beside it, impaling its arm. A moment. Two. And the thing roared, clutching its arm that gushed blood like a stream. Spinning my steel around, I dug the blade through its heart and the green thing dropped to the wooden ground—dead. Its flesh began turning ashen and flaking. And soon, the creature's body was gone like dust in the wind.

We'd all struck still.

It couldn't be.

No. No. No.

All creatures killed by *anima accissor* were of...outer realms? "The blood they have fed on made them unkillable," I said, leaning back on a sail. "If these things cannot be killed without an *anima accissor* that would mean—" Horror rained on me. We had nothing to kill them with. And father had broken laws set by gods—he'd found a way to defy nature.

Kilian bent down, touching a bit of the dust left by the beast. "I don't understand. The Ater battle monsters could be killed with a crane even. They were fed Caligo beast blood, too, but besides the terrifying exterior, agility and strength they possessed no other similarities to the beast they were fed on and mimicked. These—" He shook his head. "Something is not right. It makes no sense how they are breaking the Obitus Law. It makes no sense at all."

"We have nothing to kill them with," Thora said, dropping to the broken deck. "And if father is selling these beasts wouldn't it mean he has plenty to spare?"

"What kills a heavenly beast?" I asked and their attention snapped to me.

Kilian shook his head. "Love, the process is far too complicated and we do not even have what is required to create them. That is not mentioning the smith. There are barely any elder smiths who have passed the tradition of creating *anima accissor*."

"No, but we are left with no other option. We have to try, and it just happens that we have found one of the ingredients." I turned to my spy who was studying the wreckage from the beast. "Vidarr, there is a change of plans."

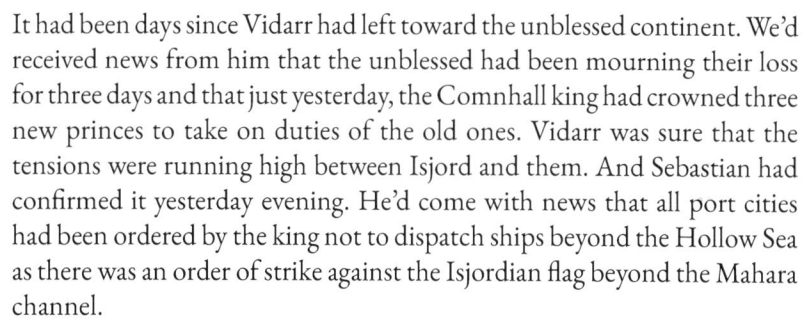

It had been days since Vidarr had left toward the unblessed continent. We'd received news from him that the unblessed had been mourning their loss for three days and that just yesterday, the Comnhall king had crowned three new princes to take on duties of the old ones. Vidarr was sure that the tensions were running high between Isjord and them. And Sebastian had confirmed it yesterday evening. He'd come with news that all port cities had been ordered by the king not to dispatch ships beyond the Hollow Sea as there was an order of strike against the Isjordian flag beyond the Mahara channel.

"We've never made deals with the unblessed," a young councillor in Kilian's court said. "Never in our history. We cross their waters and they know not to cross ours, and that is the closest to a deal we have made with them."

"That means we've made history," I said, glancing at the moon clock on the wall that had ticked endlessly since Kilian had gone down to Vrammethen to propose an agreement to the Comnhall king.

"And if they deny it?" he asked.

I slanted a look at him. "The unblessed happen to fear Adriata more than any other kingdom. Their king's ego will be boosted beyond rejection knowing a blessed king, the Night King himself, is proposing a trade and an agreement to them out of all. And, dear, have you seen your king being a king? If anything, I am afraid they might hog him there tonight with how long they are taking."

Larg raised a brow at me. "He's been gone for an hour."

An hour? Surely it had been more than that.

"Why is it that you've gathered only us?" a priest asked, looking around at the lack of the Moon court in presence.

"There are very few who I want to know about this," I said. "Father has someone inside the Adriatian court and that I am sure of. It just happens that I know all about you and your families—so go on, dare be that person."

A few laughed and others nodded in agreement.

"And then?" a young councillor asked. "After we've gotten the metal, what will we do?"

"First we deny Silas what he wants badly enough that he was forced to tie an agreement with Vrammethen. I am still thinking through the rest."

"There is nothing I've enjoyed more than seeing you outsmart your father," Triad said.

"There is no outsmarting him, Triad. He is well gifted by his cruel god, but what I can do is disarm him. You can never make my father prey. You can try. But I would not suggest it. With him, you have to strike quick and fast."

A young captain cleared his throat. "My queen, Kilian had planned a trip to Sitara this afternoon to check on the new railings we have put on the cliffs to keep away any eudemons. We need someone to approve them so the metalsmiths can continue dressing the rest of the bay."

"I will go," Mal said, yawning and dropping his feet from the table.

"I will come with." He gave me a strange look. "Mooncakes. I want some." Cai and Eren were in Myrdur, Thora had gone to Hanai with Nia, and Alaric had led a group of younglings to Valda Acme and would spend the night there. I didn't want to go back to an empty bedroom.

The seaside was terror and beauty at the same time. Half of the waters were pitch black and the other half a clear bright azure. The line separating Golgotha's territory was grim and lifeless, not a single wave or ripple on its surface.

After we'd checked the railings, Mal had taken me to a little shop with an old woman sat beside a coal stove frying mooncakes.

The woman glanced at me now and then. For each flip back and forth of the dessert on the stove her gaze rose to me. While her curiosity was at its peak, I never felt or saw a flash of fear or disgust.

My stomach growled and she howled with laughter, startling me. Quickly, she wrapped the mooncake in a tissue and put it in my hands. "Eat—eat loads, but stop thundering in my shop, ey?" she said, tapping my belly.

Mal grabbed my arm and dragged me outside before I had a chance to show the old woman what real thunder looked like.

Distracted by my anger, Mal lowered his mouth to my mooncake and took one massive bite. "Testing for poison," he said, chewing. "No poison."

My mooncake remained a crescent moon. "I will kill you."

"Sure," he said, throwing an arm over my shoulder. "Let me know when, I'll wash my hair first."

I took a bite of my crescent cake. "Fear me, Mal."

He fashioned a bow. "Yes, Your Majesty."

People ushered in the streets, peeking their heads from all over to take a glance at me. I waited for the panic to strike, for my vision to blur with shadows, but neither came. I breathed out a long exhale, looking around the little glassy shops filled with all sorts of colourful tokens and trinkets. Moons, stars—so many of them.

Torches lit all around, casting the light that sunset was robbing. It gave the city a haze that made it look entirely too dream-like.

"They never light the torches."

My attention swivelled to him.

He pointed his head to the elderly climbing ladders to the tall torches. "They are lighting them for you, so you can see."

For me?

Stopping before a little shop painted violet and white, Mal waved to a short, stubbly old man who sauntered to us. "Prince Malik." He eyed me and then bowed. "My queen. How are you finding our little city?"

Were Adriatians trying to make small talk with me? "Not little by any means." My feet were aching. The fool hadn't warned me how steep the streets were. I rarely walked anywhere.

"I suppose when you never leave it, it does become little."

My eyes fell to the little artisanal hair clips made of sparkling little yellow gems and copper metal that were laid all over the shop and his working space.

He lifted a thin clip dangling with copper chains that had little crescent moons and yellow stones at the bottom. "Women and a few men who have taste wear them on the summer equinox, the day our moon is the brightest and closest to our realm—Dolunay. Our goddess removed her own clip and gifted it to a little girl during the first Dolunay. My ancestors have been making these ever since for people to exchange them with their loved ones."

My smile died a little. Summer equinox. Would we still be at these odds till then? Would Adriata be my ally till then? Or would my revenge have resumed by that time?

"A gift for you, for your first Dolunay in Adriata, to exchange it with your loved one. It is nothing of much worth but please accept it," he said, reaching for my hand and handing me the clip.

I took off one of my earrings. "I keep no coin with me."

The man looked offended. "It was a gift, my queen."

"Thank you, Pietro," Mal said, taking the clip and sticking it in my hair. "This is my mother's favourite shop. You'll give her a bad face with the merchant."

"Why don't they hate me, Mal?" The question was out before I could stop it. "They either hide it well or are terrified of me. But his heartbeat was calm and he didn't have that look on his face. The same one...the same one from back then."

He stopped fiddling with the clip. "The issue with my people is that the minority spewed hate but the majority never attempted to squash it. Their biggest fault and guilt they bear is that they never did anything. Not hating you, Snow."

"Pietro, I am taking three others. Put them on my brother's tab," Mal called to the shop owner, picking three more clips. He lifted the delicate things before my face. "Would little Skygard, Nia and mother like these?"

After finishing the rest of my dessert, we walked the shores of Sidra, my feet meeting sand for the first time and it amazed me. So warm, so friable, so satisfying. Why were people buried in rocks and soil when this existed?

Mal put his massive naked foot on mine, stopping me from digging my toes in sand again. "You can only do it enough hundreds of times and it will still feel the same." He looked ahead at the fading sunset and stars glazing the russet sky all over. "We should have brought Thora, it rained when we went to Lyra."

"She trusts you," I said, squinting toward the apricot sunset.

"I trust her."

I blinked. "Why?"

"I don't know why or how or when it became so but it is so. I told her my darkest secret and she told me about hers. After that it became addicting, and I told her all of them. Thora Isa Skygard owns every and each of my darkest secrets. If someone can bring me down, it would be her."

My little sister had dark secrets—ones that she kept from me. "She can't keep secrets well, you know."

He smiled a little to himself. "She's kept mine."

I sighed. There were things I couldn't understand, and this was one of them. Perhaps I didn't have to understand this at all. Friendships did bloom from most inconvenient situations—I was testament to that.

I dug my toenails on top of his foot till he hissed from pain. "Go get me another mooncake."

CHAPTER THIRTY-SIX

Opto

Snowlin

Not even a second after I'd entered his room, I was thrown over his broad shoulder and dropped on the bed. He'd come this morning from Comnhall with good news, but I'd been too busy managing court in Taren to come and see him earlier no matter what duty I tried to ditch. For two very long days, he'd made friends with the unblessed king, secured the metal shipments and a guarantee that Silas would not get a fraction of it. Just as I knew he would.

He crawled over me, pushing my knees open to settle between them, caging me in till we were chest to chest. His silver eyes turned molten the more he looked at me. I was sure my own resembled his at that moment. Our breaths were synced, and he was so warm against my cold skin. So perfect.

"Hi," he said, a grin stretching wide in his handsome face. It warmed something in me—something long cold and forgotten.

"Hi."

He kissed the tip of my nose. "How is my gorgeous girl?"

Happy. Afraid. So afraid. "Hungry."

"Food is on its way." There was a knock at the door. "Right on time," he said, standing to take a tray of food brought by the servants and laying it on the bed. All sorts of aromatic scents wafted from the silver domes covering the plates and my stomach rumbled.

"Come here," he said, pulling me to sit on his lap. "I need you close to me."

Once I got comfortable on him, he pulled the silver domes to reveal the food and it took me not a second to dive in it—had he not stopped me. He grabbed my wrist and guided the spoonful of stew to his mouth. But as soon as he'd tried everything, I dug in—eating so fast my jaw was hurting.

Resting his hand gently on my arm, he pulled the next spoonful of food I held back on the plate. "Chew that first, my heart."

And I did as told, but there was a shake now on my fingers and a feel of wrong crawling on my skin. Like when you dream of being chased but you cannot run, stuck in place.

As if he had sensed it, he kissed my cheek and murmured in my ear, "We cannot outrun the past, but we can set the pace in the present. Nothing can harm you, my love. You are strong, smart and your husband is not to be messed with."

I tilted my head back to look at him. "Still playing guard?"

"With what is mine to protect? Always."

His words didn't stop the uneasiness or the overwhelming trepidation, but it was comforting. And I realised it was all I'd ever needed. I didn't want to ask how he knew my truths. But his words were like a prayer I needed to fulfil.

Like that, I ate, sometimes at my own pace and at others guided by him. By the end of my meal, I'd established a good in-between and even surprised myself.

He took the tray away and I rolled on my back, sprawling on the bed with a groan. I'd eaten too much. "That damned olive bread."

He stood up to fill himself a glass of the amber liquor he always drank, drowning a glass all at once before filling it again.

I pushed up, resting on my elbow. "I want a sip."

His dark brows jerked with amusement. Stepping before me, he grabbed my jaw with a hand and probed my mouth open with his thumb. He took a sip and brought his lips over mine, barely touching, as he spilled the amber liquid from his mouth to mine.

Hells. Seven hells.

I gulped, the burn of the liquor made me wince a little and the man chuckled. Burning hells and heavens.

From the way his silver eyes glazed black, he'd read it in my stare—the desire pouring out of me. And his own mirrored mine. "Do you need me?"

"I want you, Kilian."

Candles blew off in the room, pulling a dimness over us. And soon, walls of black rose around us, enshrouding us in absolute, pitch-black darkness. Then...his mouth was on mine rendering me senseless, dizzy and utterly mad. His lips and tongue were wet and warm with the taste of liquor, and I drank him in—devoured him. We were both breathless, yet none of us made to pull back for a breath of air. As if drowning was euphoric. Perhaps this one was. My hands were everywhere on him, while his slowly descended down my body, lighting my flesh with warmth, my mind with spring scented torture and my belly with jitters.

He pulled a little, only so he could murmur, "The shaking, is it fear?"

"No."

And he kissed me again, hungrily, till his kisses grew bruising and my body hummed with need to be touched—to have him close to me, feel his skin over my own, each and every muscle of his melt to mine.

He pinched a nipple and I gasped. "You know how long I waited just to hear that?" he asked, gathering my breast in his palm and lowering his mouth to suck on the swollen nub over the fabric of the silky nightgown. He dropped his hips flush against mine, grounding forward and I moaned at the taste of what was to come. "And that one." His other hand slipped to my neck, tightening just slightly and my eyes rolled back. "Perfect, just perfect," he murmured, pressing his lips to mine, plunging his tongue in my mouth so I could get a full taste of him.

I bit his lower lip, and he groaned. Hells, that spot between my legs liked that too much. "Kilian," I moaned, lowering my hands to his hard muscle to unbutton his shirt. "Do you know what you sound like?"

I could feel the lines of his smile as he left kisses on my cheek. "Tell me."

After peeling off his shirt, I wrapped my legs around his torso and flipped both of us over so I stood on top of him. I could see nothing, but for some reason I was certain he had a stupid massive grin on his face. "You sound like mine," I said, leaving kisses down his throat and the man let out a tortured whimper when I sunk my teeth on that spot between his neck and shoulder. My body seemed to like that because flutters hummed below my belly and my core tightened.

"Fuck," he hissed when I slipped a hand on his britches and palmed the hard length of him.

He had me out of my slip and underwear in one tear before wrapping an arm around my waist and pulling me down to him so he could kiss me dizzy again.

He tugged his britches off, and I squirmed on him, my centre rubbing over his length for any friction, and I moaned in his mouth when the contact sprung rapture over me.

"That's it, rub your pretty, little cunt on me." Slipping a hand between us, he circled my core till I was breathing hard and moving faster over his length. "Get my cock wet, love."

My fingers dug on his skin as I rubbed myself on him "Kilian, please, I want you inside of me."

"Ride me, little beast," he said, slapping my bottom hard and kneading my stinging flesh.

"Yes, sir." Another sharp whack. "Ouch."

That made him chuckle. "Up," he ordered, slapping my bottom again and I lifted my hips for him to enter me.

He easily slid inside of me, the fullness made me gasp and him groan, my nails digging a little on his stomach at the feel of him slipping deeper and—

Oh gods, too much.

"All the way down, love," he said, guiding my hips till his entire length was buried in me and I trembled a little. "That's it, you can take it. You can take it all." This was so much deeper. "Open your pretty eyes."

I forgot he could see me.

"Don't blush now," he said, wrapping an arm round my waist and pulling me closer so he could take my nipple on his mouth and thrust his hips up a little.

Slowly, ever so slow, I moved, rocking my hips and riding him. Leisuring in his delicate touches, his soft sighs and breathy little moans—his kisses. I revelled in them. I didn't know I'd longed for affection till he'd given it to me.

He let out a pained groan, his fingers digging in my thighs as I began riding him hard and then harder, taking him like I knew he liked it.

"That's it," he cooed, wrapping an arm around my waist and pulling me down to him again. "That's it, love. You're doing so well. Fuck, look at you."

He held me tightly to him, his mouth never leaving mine as he lifted his hips and thrust up. My body surrendered when he plunged inside of me relentlessly.

Pleasure teased every inch of my body. I was close—so close. "Kilian, harder, I want it harder," I breathed, my nails digging in his hard biceps. "Please."

He flipped us over and guided my legs to wrap around his hips. "Hold tight, love."

He pressed his lips to mine, swallowing my moans and whimpers while he almost fucked me dizzy. Soon, my pants grew shallow and so did his and before I grew out of breath, release cascaded through me, rippling with warmth over every inch of me—seizing every sense.

His thrusts grew punishing, his little breathy moans made me tingly all over again. This man could only breathe, and my body would be ready for him. It was my time to swallow his grunts as he came inside of me. His lips were so gentle against mine, our tongues slowly twisting around one another, unhurriedly, while his body steadily slowed over mine.

We stood there, holding each other and trying to catch our breaths—with him still inside of me. "Kilian, you will have to do that all over again if you stay inside me a second longer."

He kissed me again—hard. "It doesn't sound like a complaint on your behalf."

"Twas a warning," I said, nibbling on his lips.

He chuckled, rolling us to the side and gathering me to his chest.

"I want to see you," I said, and at his command, darkness dispersed back to reveal a soft navy hued night filtering through the room.

When I looked up at him, he'd closed his eyes and had a little smile playing on his mouth. "Let's have a bath and we can do that again."

He bit that plump lip of his and said, "Let me relish it, woman. I want to remember every detail of that—of you." He kissed my brow and sighed. "You haunt me, woman. You always will—you've been haunting me for fifteen years and I am still consumed just by the thought of you." His fingers played with my hair, and I sighed from the overwhelm of senses—the overwhelm of his words, the closeness, the caress. "I'll take that you've missed me as well."

"How would one come to such a conclusion?" I asked, sliding my palms down his body, muscles twitching under my touch.

"Keep doing that and we won't make it to the bath."

"That sounded like a proper threat."

He rolled me onto my back and caged me under him again, reaching a hand between us and over my entrance, spreading his release all over my sex before sliding inside me again. He took me again, almost hungrier than the first time. And just before we'd agreed to head for the bath, he took me a third time—slower, our bodies moulded to one another, his eyes never once leaving mine, soft touches, savouring kisses and low sighs.

The muscle ache was combined with a strange bliss, and the sweet scented, steaming bath water had turned me into a complete puddle of bones and flesh as Kilian held me between his parted knees, my head resting on his chest.

The two of us were silent for a long moment before he said, "What?"

"Nothing." I wished. I wished his father hadn't died and that my own would have agreed to the marriage proposal. I wished to have seen him, stolen glances at him when he would come to Tenebrose to meet my father. I wished that he, too, would have stolen glances of me. I wished I had remembered why grey was my favourite colour. I wished he'd known that I loved that colour because of him. I wished that once I'd been old enough, I would have married him. I wished.

Then all of the sudden those feigned memories I'd never lived dulled and dimmed when I remembered what he did not know of the girl he'd met at Urinthia's coronation or saw in passing in Arynth. How I was behind doors and before mirrors. How there was no life in me. How much he would have hated that girl.

"I've lost you again," he said, running a finger down the bridge of my nose.

"I don't think I've ever been found, Kilian."

"Then let me find you."

Only so I could be lost again? Silence rang for a moment. "Why do you like me?"

"Like?" he asked, lifting my chin with a finger. "I liked you once when I was a boy and I like many things about you, loads—so many. But I love you. What I feel for you has surpassed like a long while ago now."

He loved me.

Right after he made me scream all shades of pleasure, he'd gotten dressed to attend a meeting. Leaving me alone and bored in his room with a promise for more when he returned.

A glint of silver caught my eye on his table and utter boredom made me shoot to my feet and pick up the heavy king chess piece. Except it was not a chess piece. The bottom had his royal seal. A crescent moon with vines and a dagger going through it. I knew it too well. I'd seen this mark plastered on ten different documents retrieved from the Adriatian men after the attack in Tenebrose. It struck me hard—the memory and my actions. My mother, my siblings, that night—him. And then came the convincing that it was all but pretend. It was all it was—pretend. For a little while we were playing a game of forgetting. Only a little while longer.

Just a little while...I wanted to have him just a little longer.

As I set the seal down, my attention caught on the last document Kilian had used the seal on. Not on the words. On the signature. *Kilian Castemont.*

With a finger, I pushed the paper back to reveal the other under it. Another signed document with an identical signature. My heartbeat grew erratic as I flipped through all the papers on his table one after the other.

Kilian Castemont. Kilian Castemont. Kilian Castemont.

My world swayed for a moment before I rested a hand on the shelf to balance myself. No, I was making this up. My head had to be making it up.

I stopped, picked a document up and traced a trembling finger over the curves of his name. Over and over and over till the pad of my finger was sore and the paper felt too coarse against my skin.

He hates that name. He never uses that name, Mal's words floated around the room.

Then came his words, *Only a few old bags from the previous council called me that.*

I rushed out to his balcony and bolted to Taren. The second my feet touched the roof of my castle, I almost ran to find Nia.

She perked from the dining chair where she'd been hunched over whatever poison she was grinding on the mortar and raked her gaze over my half naked form. "You really need to stop taking fashion advice from that courtesan."

"I need his letters."

She frowned. "Whose?"

"Nia, I know you still have his letters. I know you didn't throw them away when I asked you to."

Her features pulled in an apology. "Will you throw them away if I give them to you? I really don't want you to throw them away. Not those words. You can't throw them away."

All my limbs shook, but I managed to say, "No...no, of course not. Get me the letters, please."

It took her seconds to fade back and forth to her chambers with the letters. But too many seconds too long for my brain to lose all sense of comprehension from incredulous thoughts. One moment then two and ten, I sat on the cold marble ground just holding them. My fingers shook over the lilac paper, over the broken black seal. And finally, slowly, I pulled a letter from its envelope. I waited, calming my nerves, my eyes shut tightly while I breathed in and out. And when I opened them, I saw what I didn't want to see. Yours...*Kilian Castemont.*

It read the same on the next one I opened. Also on the next ten. *Yours, Kilian Castemont.* The curve of them, the slightly slanted angle he wrote, the delicate end tails, the sharp dots on all the 'i-s'. They resembled nothing of the clean-cut signature of the attack orders. Henrik Castemont II. He'd written *Henrik Castemont II*.

"It wasn't him. It wasn't him, Nia," I repeated, my fists bunching to give me some grounding that kept slipping away from me. He had lied to me. All this time, he'd lied to me. It had not been him. When she remained silent, my eyes shut again. "You knew."

She said quietly, "I did."

A bitter laugh left me and my whole body burned with ire. "Who was it? Who signed off on the attack?"

She bit on the skin of her cheek. "He won't say. The only thing he has told me is that he'd fallen very ill on the day of the attack, and he'd awoken to the chaos. Driada told me he'd not spoken a word till the day that they had found you alive. She said he blamed himself for everything and that is why he took responsibility for it."

I threw the letters on the ground and stalked to the closest balcony, bolting back to Adriata.

He was there. Expectant. Staring over the mess I made on his table. From the downcast of his gaze, I knew he was aware I had found out more of his lies.

"Who are you trying to protect?" I asked calmly, my hands curling to fists.

He bent down to pick a discarded letter. "No one."

"Liar!" I shouted. "You damned liar and your damned lies. Who are you trying to protect? Why are you letting the real person behind that attack escape my judgement? Who is it that you are protecting?"

"No one," he repeated, and I turned into fury.

The outside blistered with thunder, a deep dark rumble reiterated over Amaris, and I could feel control slipping through my fingers. A cloud formed over my vision and the bargain seal on my hand pierced with an intense burn already sensing what I was about to do. He too knew what I was about to do because he turned to me, worry etched in his features and a flutter of his usually calm pulse was caught by my senses. "I will rip every heart in this kingdom, one by one if I have to. And you'll watch mine bleed if you must."

I rushed for the balcony and bolted right in the middle of Amaris. Screams tore the electric air and flutters of fleeing bodies passed across my blurred vision.

I grabbed onto the first body that had the misfortune of bumping into me. Before my hand dove onto their chest, a large hand spanned over my wrist to stop me. He spun me round, my back to his chest, his arms embracing me. "Don't, please."

The air chilled at my command and spread from under my feet to blister the whole of my surroundings—trapping people in it. "I like you begging. Beg some more perhaps I'll consider."

"If you do this—"

"What?" I asked, cocking my head to the side to look him in the eye. "Will you fight me? Will you kill me? You can stop me if you want. One name. Give me one name."

"It was me."

"Liar." I pulled out of his touch and bolted again. This time landing in the outskirts of Amaris, a quaint little white housed village. The tip of my fingers itched for carnage so I obeyed. Magic ushered out of me, skittering around my body and climbing onto the forest greenery till flames erupted around me. The burn from the seal had long dulled now.

Someone faded behind me. It was not Kilian, but the presence was familiar. "I did it, Snow. I signed the document that night."

Magic froze around me. Frost climbed trees, grass and rock, dousing the fire. Slowly, I turned to face the reason for my demise. The true evil of my nightmares. Only to find him. The person who'd been nothing other than a light hearted dream one had when they slept out in a meadow on those warm summer day sunsets.

Kilian faded between the two of us before I even managed to say something. He raised a hand to his brother and shouted, "Go!"

Mal shook his head and took another step forward. "She deserves to know, and I should have said something sooner."

Kilian tensed and fisted his brother's jacket. "You gave me your fucking word. I said *go*."

He'd taken his brother's place. Kilian had taken Mal's place.

Oh gods.

What he'd once said to me—how he had to convince many that he hated me. Had he convinced everyone that it was him who had signed off the attack? How old must have Mal been then? Why was I thinking this? It didn't matter. I had been a child then, too.

Hesitantly, Mal faded away leaving Kilian and I alone amidst the frost. "He lied," was the first thing he said, running a shaking hand through his hair. "He lied."

Till the end—was he going to do this till our end? Was he going to let me kill him without telling me the truth?

"I don't think he did."

Kilian took a step back. "It was my fault. It was my fault, Snow. If I hadn't fallen sick that day, it would have been me who signed it."

He wouldn't have signed it. The Kilian my brother spoke of, the one Driada and Mal knew, the one I'd grown to know, would have not done it.

"It is all my fault," he said, dropping to the ground. "He was only a child. The council had threatened him with Driada. A child would know no better. I made him swear on his life and Driada's that he would never tell."

"Why did you take his blame?"

Kilian's stare turned cold and distant. "He was the first person I've ever cared for and loved. I would have never known how to care for another being had it not been for him. No one had taught me—I had to learn it myself. I learned it through Mal. If I lose my brother." He shook his head. "I can't lose my brother. Don't make me choose, please. I love you both."

My whole world had turned on its hinges and now I stood on a ground I'd never stepped on before. The ground of uncertainty. Why was I uncertain?

"All you've ever done to me is lie. You made me feel disgusted for letting my mother's killer touch me, for wanting you to touch me. You made me convince myself that I was sick beyond repair. Do you know how many times I've drowned in self-loathing because of this lie?" I shouted. "Did you not care? Did you not care at all? Was it all lies? Were any of your words true?"

He stood and just when he reached me, I stepped back, his hand froze mid-air to me.

"You selfish bastard."

He took another step toward me, and I took another back. I watched as his face fell and wrinkled with despair. "It's still all my fault."

"That was for me to judge."

He tried to reach for me again, his hand shook. "I'll tell you all. Everything you want to know. From the start of it all. Come to me, please."

"I don't think I want to."

He made one last attempt to reach me and when I backed away, his expression cracked. "Please."

"You want to take his place, Your Majesty," I said, making my face the surface of ice blistering from within me. "Then have his place back."

I bolted with no aim. Landing in the middle of Soren Forest in Fernfoss. The greenery groaned and shifted at the feel of my presence. But strangely, the forest habitants didn't jolt to run from me. Instead, flower folk, wind and forest spirits approached me, cautiously. Another first.

A glittering little thing landed on my lap resting a small palm on my much bigger one. Another followed, leaning on my leg. And then another landed on my shoulder.

Soft white flakes of snow touched the green floor of the forest, gently creating a pelt of frost. The grey sky was the loveliest it had ever been. Looking up, I whispered, "What do I do?"

But my mother was gone now. And I didn't have any answer. For the first time my mind was empty—without a single thought.

Something I didn't understand was happening. Something I'd never felt.

My eyes blurred and before I knew, a single tear slid down my cheek. The wind spirit fluttered her sparkly wings and flew close to my face, reaching her tiny hand to catch my tear. I watched the drop turn to glittering dust that got carried in the wind. "You're melting."

"It is called crying."

She shook her tiny head and lowered to press her palm to my chest. "Here."

"I don't want it to melt," I whispered. I steeled it to ice myself with the purpose of never melting.

"You were never the Queen of Ice, you're the Queen of Skies." She flew close to my face again, resting her palm on my forehead. "They are rainy and stormy, blue and black and violet and orange, they thunder and cluster in soft white clouds. They pour out snow, but they never freeze."

"You're awfully opinionated for such a wee thing."

"You are big, yet stupid."

I sneered at her and she giggled.

The spirits gasped and then fluttered nervously around me.

"It's concerning," Mal said, coming from behind me. "Befriending forest folk at your old age." He came and sat cross legged before me. A black rose in his hand.

Mal had signed off the attack.

Mal.

Not Kilian.

He'd done it to protect his brother. His young brother.

Mal had been a child.

But so had I. Since when did I have a moral compass? All I wanted was my justice. I'd fought so hard for it. I'd lost nights of sleep and days with my loved ones to plan my revenge. This was not how it was meant to go.

"Is that for me?" I asked, extending a hand to him.

"They were created for you," he said, handing me the flower and suddenly the delicate thing weighed the size of a brick. "He had a Hanai Aura create a seed with what he remembered of you—with what your brother had told him of you, what he'd studied, what he'd heard. All that he could gather. Kilian created the scent of the flower from what you reminded him of. The sun, the moon, the stars. Mostly everything that shone. And then made the colour black because it was what makes shine—the night inside you that made it all glow. My mother told me that a few weeks ago when she was in one of her...moments—I never knew. Perhaps if I did, I wouldn't have found it so odd how much he admired them. If I'd known how much he lost that day, I would have never kept it from you."

I stared at the flower, frozen at his words. It couldn't be possible for one to feel like that for another. Not for me at least. Not for what I was. Yet...he'd felt all of that and still lied to me. He was going to let me kill him. He would have let me kill him to protect his brother.

"I don't think I would have killed you, Mal," I confessed. "But I would have found a way to hurt you. Perhaps I already have."

"I did it, Snow."

"Your brother did."

His face morphed. "Snow," he called with quiet terror. "Please."

"I know no mercy, Princeling. And I will take what I am owed. From your brother. And eventually all of your people."

Nothing had registered today. Nothing I'd done or said—I don't know if I'd even done or said anything at all. All that had tried to talk to me had backed away eventually and left me alone with my tremulous thoughts. Thoughts that had always been sturdy. Thoughts that I'd carried for thirteen years and filled me with hope—hope that I'd get my justice one day.

It hadn't been him.

And in a perfect world where I was not forged with fire and violence, I would have gotten my happiness. In that perfect little world where he'd never been the man I'd sworn to kill, I would have perhaps loved him as he loved me. But my story never began with 'there was a happy, little princess'. The princess was a villain. And as all villains do, I, too, would meet my villainous end. And I'd make sure that it was glorious. For the sake of the girl who'd been kept alive for thirteen years with the promise of retaliation.

There was one last thing that tethered the two of us together. Perhaps the last thing. And perhaps for the last time, I walked the Amaris castle corridors to his room—our room. Only to find it empty.

The candlelight on his desk was dying and flickering on the last bit of wax, a patch of ink had dried on a document he had been signing and his jacket hung on his desk chair neatly as he always left it.

He had left in a hurry. And my only prayer was that he was alright.

I kneeled before the jacket, running a finger over the dark velvet before I gathered the fabric and brought it to my face. It smelled like him still.

If he was gone, would I ever see spring again?

I laid on my side of the bed and waited till dawn began to crack the skies, blowing shades of mauve inside the room. He'd returned only an hour ago from wherever he'd been, looking like death and smelling of soot. His breaths were heavy and tired when he laid beside me and I ached to turn to him, to check if he'd not been injured and bury myself in his hold. Comfort him like he'd comforted me many times. Just hold him.

My palms throbbed from how hard I'd dug my nails on skin, yet it had done nothing to soothe the pain on my chest. When a trickle of blood rolled over my wrist to soak the linens, he seemed to hold his breath. Besides my pulse, the room went dead quiet for a few moments.

He jolted from the bed and in a blink stood before me. Eyes wide in terror when he saw the blood coating my arms. "Fuck."

When he reached out to touch me, I scooted back on the bed. "Don't touch me."

He grabbed my ankle and literally dragged me to him before throwing me over his shoulder. He plopped me on the bathroom sink, taking my hands under the running water. Fury was painted on his face while he washed the blood from my palms. "You're going to stop doing that."

That made me laugh. "Sure."

"No," he gritted out, holding my jaw with a hand. "You're going to listen to this. You. Will. Not. Do. That. Again!"

"Don't shout at me!" I yelled back.

"Then don't do this anymore!"

"I will do what I want!"

"The fuck you will!" He weaved a hand through my hair, holding my face close to his. "Hurt me, love. Hurt the world. Hurt someone that hurt you. Speak your anger and pain, shout it, scream it, whisper it, pray it to the gods, to hells, tell it to those you love, tell it to those you hate. Lash it out if it is so hard to hold in. Break a window, someone's bones, someone's heart. Cry it out. Laugh it out. Share it. Give it all to me if you want. I swear, love, I will carry it for you. I'll drain every bit of it out of you and hold it in me till forever. You only need to ask. Ask, please. Ask me to take it away. Ask me to take all your suffering. Enough…enough with this."

Why did he have to care so much? Why did he have to care for me? I was fine with no one caring. It was fine when they all left me alone. He ruined my peace. He had ruined it all for me.

There was nothing else I could say or do, so I hopped down the sink, and rushed toward the balcony. I'd not even reached the door when he wrapped an arm around my waist and lifted me up. "I wasn't fucking finished, Snowlin."

"I was!"

He lowered me on the bed and pinned me down, crossing my arms over my chest. "I need you to promise me."

That made me throw my head back with laughter. "You're crazy. To gods, you're madder than me."

"No, love, I'm insane," he bit out to my face. "Deranged. Sick. When it comes to you I'm a fucking lunatic. Now, you're going to promise me. You're going to give me a big, fat promise that you will not do that again."

He made a small sound of pain and dropped his forehead to mine. Blood dripped down my hand and soaked my white shift. And for the first time, I shivered when the thick crimson liquid touched my skin. "There. Have my anger and my pain," I murmured, pulling my dagger out of him and stabbing him again, and then another third time. He just stood there and took it. This would have been so easy for us. The guilt, the anger, and the strain I'd gone through all because of what he had hidden. Why did he have to make everything so complicated?

"Why…why do I keep missing your heart?"

He lifted his head to look at me. "The day you want it, I'll direct you to it."

For the first time, tears welled my eyes and I allowed them to pour. Unafraid of being weak. He'd made me unafraid of everything. Night was just a sky, darkness was just the dark, my shadows were just shadows. He'd taken all fear from me—all besides being happy. He'd made me terrified of being happy. The warm wet drops slid down my face and he leaned down kissing each of them away. At this moment, I realised that I'd never felt more loved in my existence. Not by anyone. Not ever.

"You will do what you must do." His fingers were gentle on my cheeks, he trailed his touch all over as if he wanted to remember. "Because you deserve the world, love of mine. The piece of world that I own is yours, have it all."

"I am going to ruin you," I whispered.

"Ruin me."

"Will you fight me back?"

His thumb drew circles on my temple. "I'll fight you."

"With all you have."

He nodded lightly. "With all I have."

"Alright."

He kissed my cheek repeatedly till I was squirming and almost giggling, and it somehow made tears flow heavier. "Let me hold you one last time."

I nodded and he wrapped his arms around me, pulling me close to him. We stood like that for a while. Body to body, sharing a breath and a pulse, our hands tangled on the other. At least till he spoke.

"I, Kilian Henrik Castemont, free you from the vow made of blood, flesh and bone, ash, and soil. No longer bind you to our bargain."

More warm hot tears poured out of me. "I, Snowlin Edlynne," I whispered through trembling lips, "Castemont, free you from the vow made of blood, flesh and bone, ash, and soil. No longer bind you to our bargain." The seal burned on my hand painfully, but there was another ache much fiercer in my chest.

"Give me my promise," he whispered in my ear.

Right now, I would have given him everything and regretted nothing. "I promise you."

"The paper is in the second drawer. Tear it, burn it. It's yours." He kissed my temple and pulled back. There was no last glance or a last goodbye before he left the room.

I pushed up and ran after him. "Kilian."

He turned and opened his arms. And in a breath, I leaped in his hold. The boy who was going to marry me. The man who married me. My destiny. My ruin. "Goodbye."

He shook his head, burying his face in the crook of my neck.

"Say it back," I urged. "Say it back. Tell me goodbye."

"Goodbye, love of mine." He pulled back a little. "You know that I love you, right?"

"I do."

His smile was watery as he let me go and backed away from me. "Good. Very good."

When he turned his back to me, tears poured hot and burning.
I will do what I must do.
He didn't turn back.
I will do what I must do.
Not even once.
I will do what I must do.

PART IV
DUSK

Chapter Thirty-Seven

Fulmen

Snowlin

The air was grave in my chambers, just as it had been for the past four days since Kilian and I had broken our bargain. Pen hadn't said a single word and neither had Thora who'd crouched to a far corner inside my room that did not face the balcony. She'd glued her attention to my arm, likely over the missing band of bargain that no longer inked my skin.

My little redheaded servant peeled my jewellery off one by one, a routine that Kilian had done for the past few months. "At least you don't look like a rabid wolf tackled you," she huffed. "Marking a royal woman like that is so indecent." Everyone around me had grown to adore Kilian. It wasn't only I that had lost him. And from the way she secretly wiped a stray tear or two away, she'd lost him, too.

I ran a finger over a little faded mark on my collarbone and my eyes drew shut at the memory of his lips on my skin.

"Are we at war with Adriata now?" she asked quietly.

"Not yet, carrot. Not yet."

But soon.

Mal faded on my balcony, striding inside my room with an unusual grimness in his face. He bowed his head to me and scanned the room for my sister. "Come, little bird, mother and the rest are setting down for dinner. I've asked for your favourite potato pie to be made."

My sister hugged her knees tightly, not looking at Mal. "I won't come to Adriata anymore, Malik. I thank you for all that you have done."

The princeling frowned and shot me a look. "We agreed she could stay a while longer."

"We did," I said, looking over my shoulder at Thora. "You might go to Adriata."

She stood. "I'd rather not." And then dashed out of my room.

Immediately, Mal ran after her and returned dragging her behind him. "I don't want to go." She writhed, trying to pull away from him, but he was much, much stronger than her.

He grabbed her jaw with a hand and turned her face to me. "Say bye bye."

"Bye bye," she mumbled between squished cheeks before the two faded away.

I'd just laid down on my cold bed when Nia came into my unusually dark room. She tossed her jacket and boots and then threw herself beside me.

Shuffling to my side to face her, I rounded an arm around her waist and rested my cheek on her chest. I'd missed her. I'd missed her so much.

"Do you want me to light a candle?"

"No."

"Snow—"

"I am tired, Nia."

She sniffled a little and swallowed. "I know."

"Why does it feel like I am losing though I am not?"

Her voice quivered as she whispered, "There are no winners, Snow. You were both bound to lose in the end. He's lost too."

"Nia."

"Hm?"

Tears rolled down my cheeks at the warm comfort of my friend. "I am sorry that I cannot be better. I want to, but I can't."

Visha paced round and round the oval meeting table, making me dizzy. "It is impossible," she muttered more to herself than anyone. "It is impossible."

"Visha, take another step and I'll feed you to my morph." We'd all been on alert since yesterday. Father had returned his attacks all of the sudden, they'd even doubled and tripled. And last night, Visha had felt something tamper with the veil she'd lifted over the sceptre piece.

Her footing halted mid-air and she turned to me. "Melanthe has managed to trace the sceptre piece through twelve of my veils. All night last night, I've crafted veil after veil and my aunt has broken them all. She is hunting that sceptre piece like a hound."

"Could it be the child she is carrying, why her magic has surpassed yours?" I'd heard what motherhood did to witches. It was the stage of life where their power stood at their strongest.

The whole room turned to stare at me. It was Alaric who spoke first, "You can't possibly think of doing what I'm thinking."

Tilting my head to the side, I gave him a bored look. I'd done worse. "A small price to pay." Hooking my thumb in Mal's way, I said, "And besides, how long till they get to her anyway."

The Night Prince lifted his hands in surrender. He'd remained our only contact with Adriata. "In all fairness, she is right."

For the tenth time today, the Myrdur call echoed through Taren. Tens of Volantians flew past the meeting room windows rushing toward the attacks. Father had been persistent these past few days to the point of concern. It was certain that the Olympian sceptre piece was the next he wanted to get. Had he not realised that he'd lost one?

Cai burst through the doors, breathing hard and stained with blood. Blood that looked like his.

Both Mal and I shot to our feet immediately, rushing to him.

"The fuck, Cai," Mal said, hooking an arm around his waist to support his weight.

My hand shook when I pushed his long brown hair back to expose a deep gash on his forehead. "Who did this?"

He grabbed my wrist. "Whatever they are sending, whoever those Aura were, they weren't just taking mirk root, Snow, they were amped up in something else. Something worse. And the beasts," he heaved. "They can breathe in the mist."

That was all it took before I was rushing toward the balcony and bolting in the middle of Myrdur. Mal faded beside me not a second later.

The air was grave and packed with an insane amount of magic. The heavy stench had every sense of mine raised in caution. For the first time, the smell of death in Myrdur was overshadowed. By more death.

It was not only hundreds of Isjordian soldiers advancing forward, but there were also massive green forms half resembling the beast from Hanai and half human. It wasn't an army, but it was plenty.

"We have Canes at the Highwall and none picked up any scent of beasts. This can't be good," Mal said with some panic, before dropping to his knees and sinking his hands on the muddy ground. And before I could ask, skeletons broke the barrier of mud and rose in dozens. He whispered something in Darsan and the dead launched forward, tackling soldier after soldier.

"I think Melanthe has found a way to trick them."

"Then we are fucked, Snow."

"Die," I warned, pulling out my daggers. "And I'll drag you back from Caligo from your balls."

He grinned, unsheathing his sword and hopping forward while I raised my hands toward the misty Volants.

"I command you," I ordered and the white *zgahna* rolled down the face of the mountain, spreading over the Myrdur ruins and surrounding me. The second the fog veiled me, every inch of my body fuelled with electricity, white bolts skittering around and spreading over the floor of the ruins.

The dead rose from one side, taking down and slaying soldier after soldier while the rest fell from the touch of my magic.

The green creatures roared enough to shake the rubble stone of the ruins and launched in the air towards Mal. Immediately, the tentacles of my mist shot to block them mid-air, shielding Mal enough for him to fade elsewhere.

He reappeared beside me and more skeletons rose from underneath the ruins to tackle the soldiers.

Our surroundings chilled and then shards of sharp ice flew towards us. Quickly, Mal rose a layer of shadows blocking the attack. "We can keep pushing them back, but we can't kill the beasts, not without getting close to them. What do we do?"

I took a moment, calculating our odds—theirs, too. How much we would risk if we let them cross the Volants. If it would be possible to not lose them inside our mountain ranges—some which even Olympians had never stepped on.

Unless.

A smile grew on my lips. Dispersing the mist around me, I looked up toward the ever-clouded roof of Myrdur. The skies were mine to control, it was in my blood, but I'd never done it before. Not willingly at least.

I raised both palms heavenward and called to it. *Come on. Come on.*

"Any time now," Mal crooned nervously, flinging his hands back and forth to orchestrate his killer shadows.

From the sliver of skin between my gloves and sleeve, I could see the black tattoos of the seal spread and thicken. The skies shifted and groaned with thunder and the movement of clouds changed, swirling and spreading rapidly. There. Sun light cracked between the dark grey clouds, hitting the ruins for the first time in decades. The skies parted at my command, revealing the bluest of blue. Grabbing Mal's hand, I pulled the two of us back. "Three. Two."

A screech broke the air and then several more followed until Fogling rained down in hundreds down Myrdur. Their piercing screeches made gravel and ruins quiver, and all Isjordian attention rose heavenward.

Hungry as ever, the black creatures batted their membranous wings creating vortexes of wind which sent soldier and beast alike shooting up in the air. It had been more than weeks since Kilian had banished their presence in Olympia, I bet they were starving.

"Grab a soldier," I said to Mal. "And fade back to Taren. I'll be right behind."

He faded between the battle of monster fighting monster and disappeared with a petrified Isjordian in his hold.

Backing toward the Volants and into the *zgahna*, I watched the ruins splatter with Isjordian blood and bones, making sure no one managed to escape the creatures.

The ground cracked a few feet before me, and a massive Fogling body stood there, looking at me. Those baleful red eyes slowly peeled back to reveal soft green irises that were so human I almost startled. The beast gently bowed its head to me, dropping to a bony knee. My magic hummed, the mist behind me did so, too—it sang and drummed, and my chest tore. A lullaby I'd heard hundreds of times before. A song of woe. One sung in rituals and mourning. One that made elderly shed tears and taught our youth grief. The same one Alaric had hummed to me before sleep every time he could. It spoke of that day's loss—the cursed night of *Draugr*. Lyrics of the Olympian bravery, the Skye sacrifice, the Isjordian cold and the Elding brothers who'd lit themselves as lightning to hold back troops as Myrdur folk hid in the Volant caves till their bodies had turned to ash and whisper. My chest sang, too, it rattled with heavy sounds of pain.

There was no way to explain how my senses feted, rejoicing in recognition of another like me. Elding blood meeting Elding soul. Like called to like, and I faltered a step back, filled with an emotion I didn't know I could even feel before. "Grandfather?"

The beast lifted its head again, its stare glazed and watery. Something rumbled from its chest, an ugly noise that usually made my skin creep suddenly made my heart hurt. A call—one of pain. Though I couldn't tell how, I knew it was that—I felt it. The moment was gone, my magic quelled, the buzzing of the mist returning, and its eyes veiled back to red before it launched into air and toward the throng of battle.

That moment I made a promise. It wasn't one of retaliation.

With a weeping heart and raging fury, I bolted to Taren.

I'd make my father a sacrifice to my lands. I'd part his flesh layer by layer of muscle and spread him all over my land, for worms and crows to feed. I'd let him rot right in the lands he murdered. I'd let his soul tarnish and dust while he watches my lands thrive.

The meeting room was empty besides a few. Tristin and Mal stood above the terrified Isjordian soldier knelt on the ground.

"They will never confess," Cai said, dabbing a cloth to the gush on his head. There was hopelessness in those emerald eyes that had never faltered with nothing but hope. And it made me rage more.

Mal extended an arm, stopping me before I got to the soldier. "I will get him to speak."

I knew both Castemont brothers well, if there was one thing they hated, was tampering with life through their magic. It taxed them. It taxed their souls. It was the bargain that came with their power. "No, Mal. I can get pretty convincing myself." Nothing really taxed my soul as much as it taxed my annoyance threshold.

The soldier writhed, pushing himself back till the wall stopped him. "Don't hurt me, p-please, please."

Bending down to his face, I said, "Fairly easy. Tell me where were you headed?"

He shook his head and sealed his lips tight.

"No?" Resting a palm on his chest, I let a trickle of electricity curse out and he spasmed, dropping to the floor. Fisting his hair, I dragged his bleeding body along the corridors of the castle, all the way down to my dungeons. I had no patience to be civil today.

Mal chased after me, looking around my dungeons astounded. "I like the decor. It has personality. What paint is that? It's given the wall a nice texture."

"Blood."

"Cynth," he murmured, closely taking my side.

Stopping before one of my favourite cages, I gripped the soldier's face and showed him a piece of my work. The thin form hung upright by two chains, the portrait of suffering. A man who'd been so terrified of pain he'd cut a little girl's hands. The man I'd had the pleasure of showing that same pain he thought he bargained my friend's hands for—I'd done that for almost ten long years, and it still didn't feel enough.

"See that?" I taunted, shoving his face between two metallic bars. "I show him death once a week and then I bring him back to life the next. And then I do it again and again and again. He is getting old, would you like to be my next toy?"

The Isjordian shivered and when the half dead man made the chains rattle, he shot upright, startled. "Alright," he cried. "Alright."

That was easy. "Let me ask again. Where were you headed?"

He shook and his words were muddled. "The sacred gates, Valda...Valda Acme. The ancient gates to Caelum. The one that is said to be up in the Volants. The one from the sacred books."

Mal gave me a thumbs up, but I was left blinking to myself for a couple of moments. That had never happened before. Were Isjordians losing their blessing? "In Valda? You're telling me what you're looking for is in Valda?"

He nodded. "We were told the guardian of the gates was tasked with its protection. The one living in between worlds."

Well that was just silly. "That can't—" Then it clicked. The Esmeray diaries to the heavens. It wasn't the Seraphim gates—it was the Olympian ones. The sceptre had been right under our nose all this time. Damn it. "Not only did you think you could open the gates, but challenge a heavenly guardian for the sceptre, too?"

He blinked rapidly, avoiding my stare. "We have the artillery."

I snorted. "You mean the beast?"

He nodded.

Leaning down to his face I said, "Has mirk root fried your brains that bad? I killed the thing."

He gaped, eyes shooting wide open. "How...how do you know about that?"

"I've got the artillery. Actually, I own the artillery. Now answer me."

"It is not dead—the beast is not dead. It is not capable of dying...so I've heard."

Hells. I should have known. "And what is it capable of?"

"It killed an Aitan sphinx, broke through the Ryuu caves filled with serpents, and almost got through the veil in Isjord. Almost."

I lifted a brow. "Almost?"

He shivered and suddenly gaped as if he'd caught himself saying too much.

I tipped my head back and smiled. "The thing fears something. Something grave I gather. I thank you, soldier." At the snap of my finger, a shard of ice pierced his chest. I stood, levelling a stare on my favourite prisoner. "It will bring you a few tailed friends to keep you company."

Mal had pointed a scowl at an empty spot on the ground. "Why did they want the Esmeray diaries if this thing is of heavens?"

"I don't know, but nothing surprises me anymore."

"So Demir is still alive."

"Not sure, Mal. The green beasts do look alike." I pointed my chin to the dead Isjordian. "Could have easily mistaken it for one of the others."

He swung an arm around my shoulders. "We're a good team."

I scoffed. "I thank you for the moral support."

He bowed his head a little. "My pleasure, sister-in—"

"I'm still married to him, Mal."

"I thought—"

"The paper is still in my drawer. In one piece."

He didn't say anything. But I think he knew. He knew why I hadn't torn that paper yet.

We walked back to the meeting room. A Medi healer was already tending to Cai's wound while Alaric kneeled beside him, and from the way his mouth moved rapidly, I'd imagine he was nagging at him for getting injured.

"Someone hand me a map of Valda," I said, taking a seat.

Cai perked up, pushing the Medi healer away to frown at me. "Valda? Why Valda?"

"According to the soldier, the Olympian sceptre piece is there," Mal explained, plopping beside me.

"I'm getting it," I said, and everyone suddenly shot up and crowded me. "If they cannot feel a trace of it then they will stop trampling over my lands."

Alaric shook his head. Different from the rest, there was a strange worry on his face. "You cannot go to Valda Acme."

Odd. Valda Acme was part of our most ancient traditions. To make the climb to the highest point in Olympia and pay respect to Nubil and his greatness at the gates was a ritual not a single Olympian, old or young, had ever abandoned. Cai had made the climb twice. Nia, too. As queen, I should have made that journey the moment I wore the obsidian crown. Before today, I'd rather die with a potato sack on and let the Midworld have their laugh than bow before gods.

"Eventually, I would have made that trip, Alaric. It is our tradition. Remember? The same ones you love respecting so much."

The thrum of his heartbeat picked up and the air around me stirred. "You don't understand, Snow."

That made me frown. "Either make me understand or enough with the nagging."

Thora shot up from her seat. "Kilian could come with you." She blinked in everyone's reaction and slowly sank in her chair. "Or not."

Alaric nodded nervously. "Yes. Take the boy with you."

"Visha," I said, ignoring them all. "Do you have my map?"

"What map?" Eren asked, coming inside the meeting room. When he took note of Cai, he rushed to his side and kneeled before him, a hand on his cheek. "What happened to you?"

"Do I still look handsome?"

My brother blinked at him. "Yes."

"Then nothing happened." My friend pointed his head at me. "She is making the climb to Valda."

Eren stood and nodded. "I'll come with."

"I'm going up there with no purpose to pay respect to any god, Eren. You will remain in Taren. If anything happens to me, you are heir second to me."

The climb was steep, it usually took my people a whole day to reach the top. But conveniently, I'd bolted halfway up where the veil of heavenly magic stopped me from bolting any higher up.

Valda Acme. The gates of Caelum. The entrance to the heavens of Nubil which eons ago were open to his blessed. Now a prayer altar of his greatness.

It was a tradition for an Olympian to make this climb at least once in their human life. It was a tradition to honour the greatness Nubil had left behind. To conclude all, a whole bunch of sh—

Lightning hit overhead, crashing on rock that sent flying stones overhead. Well, that wasn't me.

I knew I was out of form by the third break I'd taken not even halfway through the climb. Valda was a rough mountain of dry rock, dusty air and parched shrubs turned the colour of sand. There was not much life close to the *zgahna*, and those that attempted to create life here were shortly forced to move because of what the long exposure to the strange magic of the mist did to one's mind.

After tossing the empty water bottle to free some weight from my shoulders, I continued toward the stark climb. How did children do this? How did the elderly do this?

It always amazed me how my people took this climb to the gates. It was one of the traditions everyone without exception held—to touch the land closest to the gods. More than an act of affirmation, it was one of adoration. My people were thankful to their god, they were blessed with one who had often listened. But like all gods, he too had forgotten about this land. And without blame. Who would want to watch over phoney faith coerced from fear of hells?

A thicket of cloud immersed me all of a sudden and then I saw the glint of metal far ahead. The plaque of Valda Acme stood only feet from me now.

Ahn ghuh go blasaidh. Here stood The God.

A familiar yet strange warmth kissed my insides, like a caress. The air was sweet and electric, it danced around with my magic as one. If the skies had a limit, this would be it. The cliff was deserted besides two metallic pillars rising several feet tall till they disappeared in the cottony clouds.

The sky shook with a deep rumble like no thunder could cause. "Have I come on a bad day?" I muttered to myself, unravelling the letter containing the cypher to the gates.

Wind picked up till it turned to a vortex that carried dust and gravel swirling furiously in the air, and clouds parted, letting the brightest streak of light peak through and drop right at the two erect silver metallic pillars that stood in the middle of the rocky terrace of Valda. The sole heartbeat of mine suddenly doubled, not because my liver started pumping from anticipation, but because something came from between the two pillars. Not...something. Because what stood before me looked neither human, nor animal, nor a demon. The woman was tall, her dark brown skin adorned with silvery bands, chains and diamonds all over, her curly white hair was cut to her chin and streaked with bands and beads of silver. Her irises matched, a grey so white it could almost startle you if you turned round too suddenly. It wasn't the hair, the unearthly beauty, the eyes or the strange muslin dress floating in the air and doing absolutely nothing to hide her breasts and lady bits that surprised me. It was the glowing white band around her neck and a massive pair of wings that did. Her wings were thrice the size of the Volantians and streaked with silver flakes, the feathers on the ends glowed, too.

The guardian of the Caelum gates, I would suppose. But I had not called upon her. Not when I didn't even utter a single letter of the cyphers.

She bowed her head.

I turned and looked around. Oh, she bowed to me.

"Welcome, Snowlin Edlynne Skygard Castemont, granddaughter of Jonah, last guardian of lightning, to the gates of Caelum. I'm Calandra of Caelum, guardian of the gates."

Maybe all the gild and the glow had hurt my hearing besides my eyes. "What did you just call me?"

Her mouth tipped up. "I was told you wouldn't be impressed."

I blinked to myself for a moment. "Pray tell, by whom?"

"Nubil himself," she said proudly. "He said nothing heavenly or godly would ever strike you as curious."

A deep frown gathered on my brows. "And he knows that from that one time we braided each other's hair or when," I paused for dramatic effect. "Oh yes, when he didn't give a damn about my realm and left it to burn to hells."

Her eyes flashed with warning. I could bet my good cheek she wasn't used to hearing such things about her beloved god. "He sees."

"Through his arse cheeks?" I asked. "Because that is one dimmed and shit covered sight he got there. Now, what did you call me?"

"Last guardian of lightning."

"Aura. I'm the last Elding Aura."

"Guardian. Guardian of lightning," she tried to say politely, but the tick on her temple was clear even from where I stood.

"Aura that guards the power of lightning."

She closed her eyes and huffed a sigh. "No. I meant guardian. Guardian like me."

"Do I look anything like you, lady?" I looked around. Was this some sort of test for the sceptre piece?

"We come in many shapes and forms. Sometimes we are made of the purest elements, some are born into this life either by being a child of a guardian or a lower god, and some simply carry the bloodline of a distant ancestor. And that last one would be you."

I was starting to think this wasn't a joke. "What distant ancestor?" Some form of panic began curling in my chest. I was an Aura—a hybrid Aura. No one had told me anything about any ancestors.

"Zephyr. You might know him as the first king of Olympia, but heavens referred to him as the great guardian of lightning, second to Nubil. He descended to Numen centuries ago when gods still walked the realm. He fell in love with a human woman. Because of what happened with Aurora, Nubil was forced by Fader into giving Zephyr an ultimatum. Either leave the woman, return to Caelum and never see her again, or lose his wings and live here to die his human death. Because he was the last to carry the power of lighting in Caelum, the decision had to be met with much more sacrifices. To not lose the heritage, his bloodline would continue carrying the Elding bloodline. To live as Aura amongst the other magic folk, but not quite as such. The Elding were never gifted their magic, they were born out of magic. It is why the Skygards were the only to possess the magic of lightning. This bloodline would carry other guardians of lightning to preserve the ancient magic. And return to Caelum to retain their seat as Nubil's second, if they ever desired to do so—if you ever desire to do so."

My knees weakened a little and I stumbled a step back. No, I would have known. Someone would have known. I was not...I am not a guardian. I am an *Ybris*. Someone would have known. It would mean that my uncles, my grandfather, all my ancestors were of heavenly blood. But they had been Aura. Our holy script said so, too. The Elding were Aura. "What did you mean to live as Aura, but not quite as such?"

"You're not part Aura, Snowlin. You're fully Aura, as you are fully a guardian. Your blood is of heavens."

"I'm an *Ybris*," I said as if I was trying to convince myself that everything I knew was a lie.

"Correct. The ultimate one. Aura and guardian."

"Meant to destroy the realm, lady. The prophecy says so."

She frowned and it suddenly seemed like the skies frowned too because they dimmed with grey clouds. "The prophecy does in no manner indicate so. It sings to the power you and your siblings carry. It sings of your might. It was a signal of your birth, of your existence. One that has not occurred ever before. Guardian and Aura, a blessing. A miracle either heaven expected and no other realm has seen."

"Miracle?" I asked, my nerves pinching tight. "Did my father know this?"

"Which father?"

A shaky bitter laugh left me. "Alaric knows?" She nodded and the solid ground beneath my feet turned to mud. Is that why he didn't want me to make the climb? "And Silas?"

"No, not fully to comprehend the true amount of power you possess or that you are a creature of heavens. But he was aware of the power of your bloodline when he sired you three, if that is what you are asking."

"Creature of heavens?" I asked, irate. "I'm cursed to carry some old bloodline, cursed to bear the reality of a monster only to find out I am a divine one." The skies thundered mimicking my fury and she flinched a little.

"It is beyond us to control human nature and their reasoning for fear."

"It is in your divine preaching!" I shouted, thunder crackling.

Her white eyes lifted heavenward for a moment before she answered me. "All written by men and heard by human ears. We do not interfere in their way of belief, only judge the way they adhere to it. Faith is personal. Something you share with yourself and the gods alone. If they chose to fear you because of shared belief, they have lost that bond. What you are is far from monstrous. Your existence is not blessed, it is the blessing itself."

"I'm no blessing that I can assure you."

Her stare drooped with what resembled pity and it made me sneer. "Unfortunately, fates and gods have a way of testing the goodness out of us. To make sure you carry their expectations with the best of intentions and prosper under the weight power bears on one's shoulders. Your fate writes you to be great. A hero to your realm. But as all heroes—"

Laughter bubbled out of me and her words were cut in half. A hero? All heroes were saintly martyrs. When I died, it would be with a stomach full of vengeance and blood. The gods expected me to be rained on pain and walk myself to sunshine? I had to suffer so I could thrive? They made me something of fear and carried no responsibility for it. "I need the sceptre piece. It is attracting unwanted attention to my kingdom."

She blinked astound for a moment before lifting a hand toward the skies and a silver rod materialised from thin air in her grip.

I extended a hand to her. "Throw it." Not planning to go anywhere near her.

Her white brows rose. "You want me to throw the sceptre piece?"

"Heard me right."

Surprised, but she did as told. The moment the metal touched my hand it flashed and the three same runes glowed bright on it. It triggered my magic in a way of warning. And the same excruciating pain throbbed in my veins that cursed with electricity.

"You have affinity with it. Like calls to like. Make good use of what you are able, guardian," she said, inclining her head in a bow.

Guardian. Ybris. Human. What in the hells was I? Perhaps I was a bit of all—the worst bits of all three. "You underestimate how human I am," I said, taking a step back and then another. Calandra's eyes bore an understanding of my thoughts even before I spoke them. She read it in my smirk, felt it in my raging gaze. I pointed an end of the sceptre to her and her great wings shuddered just a little. "*You* underestimate just how unforgiving and immoral humans are. You underestimate a part of me, a small part, truly. But that is not the worst of me, believe it or not. You don't know how rotten the divine is—your sort." I chuckled. "I mean, our sort. Selfish. Greedy. Those are the tip of it. Your—our kind—is what brought this reign of terror in this realm in the first place. To ask of me to fix your mistakes just doesn't seem fair. Now watch the flame you lit feed on kindling you forgot under it."

"Snowlin," she warned, stepping from the gate podium to me and the barren stone sprouted with life. White anemones grew under each step she took.

Guardian. She said I was one. Why had my steps only ever left charr behind?

I lifted a palm and she stopped as if my word was command. "In this realm it's Your Majesty. And I was not finished. As I was saying, I am part unforgiving, petty, feeble, breakable and part rotten, selfish, greedy. All that and with a great shiny crown. Do you know what that means for this realm?"

Her features turned cold and tense.

"Exactly. It means nothing," I said. "Nothing good."

"What are your intentions?"

I smirked at her and waved the sceptre piece. "To make acquaintance with a long lost of my sort. You must know her, too. I'll pass Aurora your greetings."

Her face contorted with wilderness before I walked backwards to the cliff of Valda Acme and pushed myself off the tall height.

Falling was euphoric. The wait for the crash, for the world to turn silent and dark, the build of adrenaline and anticipation of death that I would cheat right before it got to me.

Before my body crashed against rock, I bolted to the top of Taren castle.

The air was too thick and it barely reached my lungs. It felt as if the mountains drummed when I descended down the castle corridors. Perhaps they did. The thunder I'd set the sky alight with had turned to a lightning storm that blasted like percussion. I could feel electricity licking around my body passing through the wide corridors. A chill spread in the air, cooling and misting my breath white. Rage—I felt like rage.

For twenty-three years I lived loathing my existence, hiding and being fearful of who I was. Ashamed even. For twenty-three years I'd been lied to by the person I trusted the most in this realm. For twenty-three years he had let me think I was the pure abomination of evil desires and greed. For twenty-three years he'd not once had helped me soothe the self-gnawing feeling of wanting to perish. Of feeling less. Of feeling dirty. Of feeling tarnished and chipped. And now? The gods had plans for me? Is that what Alaric wanted to become of me? A vessel for gods' good deeds? A puppet? The very same thing my father wanted to make of me? Take me from one wicked master to the other?

I came to a halt.

Kilian stood in the middle of the corridor in all his calm. Clad in all black, looking his part as the Night King—cold and distant. It had been days since I last saw him and right now there was nothing I wanted more than to run in his arms and let him tell me it was all alright. Though there was no such thing as alright, for a moment he would have made it seem so. "You will regret everything if you don't calm down for just a few moments."

So he'd been told. What had he thought of me? To know someone like me could be what they called the purest form of the divine. "I am calm, darling," I said, my voice smoother than ever. "What makes you think I am not calm, huh? Perhaps finding out that I am the same sort of rot I've loathed, scorned and despised all of my existence? Perhaps that it took one sentence to turn me from an earthly monster to a heavenly one?"

He tensed. Must have sensed me too, because shadows flickered around the corridor and a lick of warmth touched my exposed skin—his phantom darkness had surrounded me. To calm or contain me, I didn't know. But it wasn't working. "Alaric would never do anything to harm you. He must have thought it best this way."

"Too much thinking for how little it was required of him."

"It is Alaric, Snow," he said, as if that was an argument for reasoning with me.

"Yes. How simple, isn't it? Simply Alaric. Simply the man I trusted most, intricately lying to me."

"He told me everything."

"And he told me nothing."

His hand rose just slightly before it went back to his sides. He wanted to touch me. I wanted him to touch me too. "If you had known, would it have changed anything?"

I wanted him to understand. How could he not understand when he knew me better than I knew myself? "You once asked why I hated me," I said. "I didn't answer you that day, but you were right, I do hate myself. It isn't you, or your people, or gods and their heavens, not my father either—it was me. I hate me more than anything. I hate myself so fiercely that I like to hurt myself in any way that I feel helpless—in any way to make the monster helpless. I hate myself to the point I want to punish myself because that is what you do to those you hate. I hate me, Kilian. And there are only so many ways to hurt oneself, but I found them all."

He faltered. That stoic shield cracked and twisted and iced with pain. He looked like he was injured and bleeding. When he stepped close to me, I didn't back away. Not when he hooked a finger under my chin and grazed my lips with his. Not when my eyes drew shut from the ache clutching my chest—the ache that pounded my heart for just a look at him. The same ache that begged, pleaded and cried for me to forget it all—to let it all go. "Snow, my Snow. If only you knew your own heart like the rest of us do. If you only knew how the rest of us love you. My light."

"I am not yours," I whispered back.

"You will always be mine."

His. In such a way that no one should belong to another. I was his. And it was ripping me apart.

But I was a woman who fed on pain. The fiercer it was, the more it fed me relief. I took a step back from him. This wasn't what I need now. No. What I needed right now was not to unload my anger and soothe. What I needed was to salvage it. I threw the sceptre piece to him. "Give it to Visha."

I bolted where I knew he would be. Where part of my consciousness spent most of his afternoons.

Myrdur was eerier at sunset. Not because the dark came with it, but because it somehow looked like less of a graveyard and more like a city that was once filled with life.

Cai sat atop an arched ruin, staring ahead further into the ruined city. "My grandmother used to say that she could taste sunset in these streets." He pointed to a broken house just as I settled beside him. "Apparently, above that terrace you could taste it best. Like fresh sweet dough and rosemary with a touch of apple. I can't smell it," he said, regretfully. "Never could, no matter how much I tried. To me it only smells like...death. Alaric found me sitting here a few years after you came and I told him that. He laughed and said that it was because the building beside had been a bakery, the smell had come from there." He laughed and my chest constricted at the pain he no longer hid from me. "All this time I've lived with the illusions they have put in my head, the one my grandmother used to tell me and then Alaric, you, Taren, travellers and every single one who could spare me just the smallest detail of the life here. The life I missed and lost. The life I was supposed to have."

"Why do you keep coming here?"

"For a few hours I'd like to live in it. What is and was of me is in here. I don't know what I am in the world outside because I was never meant to survive. I was just...lucky."

That hurt my heart. Knowing that he had thought so made me hate myself. I should have been there for him like he was always there for me. "You're my brother. An Olympian general. Son of a fallen hero. You are Cai. You are the boy who saved me." I reached to rest my hand on his. "You are all those in my world and much more in many others."

He laced his fingers with mine and held my hand tight in his. "So," he said, his mouth twitching into a smirk. "The Adriatian fool was right, you are a heavenly being."

I pulled my hand away and smacked him on the head.

"You will want to take that back," he said, rubbing his head before pulling a bunch of salted caramel candy from his pocket.

I went to my knees and bowed deeply to him. "Forgive me."

He chuckled and threw a piece of candy at me.

"I can read it in your eyes," he said, staring at the fading sunset while we ate the delicacy. "You want to rain down hells."

"And if I truly want to?"

He considered me for a moment. "I will be right beside you. Just as I promised that first day."

I sucked in a harsh breath. "It will not be pretty."

"It is an ugly world, some flames ought to decorate it."

"There is something I need to do first."

He nodded. "Don't skewer the old man. He is harmless."

I backed away and bolted to the second highest peak in the Volants. Right between two cliffs that framed Volant, the city that touches skies. There were many reasons why I adored this part of my kingdom. The old Olympian architecture from centuries ago was still holding up, all white carved arches and columns, the old path laid with grey granite tiles and the massive stone hands covered in moss that helped the heavy waterfall pour over the city edge and fall over miles down below. Once, gods themselves had walked over this very path.

Everyone stopped in their tracks as I passed through, few children gathered behind me, following me around as I made my way to Bayrd's home.

Tristin landed before me right about as I was reaching Bayrd's mansion gates. "I cannot stop you—"

"No, you can't," I said. "Did you know?"

Her expression remained cold as always as she nodded. "Most of your family history was burned during the night of Draugr and a lot was kept a secret by the Skygards themselves, but father keeps memoires in his study. And there have always been whispers. People talking. Rumours of your magic." She rubbed her eyes. "For heavens' sake, you've grown wings and call skies as if they are yours. If you weren't of guardian blood, I'd still think you of heavens."

"And Bayrd knew."

"I am not here to protect my father, Snow. I am here to protect my queen," she said, glancing behind me, over the crowd of children spying behind us. "So don't do this. You've never killed for power or to take power. Don't make your people fear you the same as they fear Silas."

The words were unsaid, but I heard them. *Don't become your father.*

The old mansion's doors creaked open and Bayrd pushed through. From the way his expression fell and how his head hung low, he was expectant of death. "My queen. What calls you to my home?"

"I want you to resign your position," I said, stepping forward. "Hand your duties to Tristin as Lazarus is already my General and part of my court."

He glanced between his daughter and I, tension bleeding through his greyed features. "Are you asking?"

"I am ordering." At my word, the sky greyed without effort at all, mimicking the thunder in my voice. "This land is mine no matter your beliefs and differences. The air is mine. The sky is mine. The gravel beneath your feet is mine. These people are also mine. And you've always known that, Bayrd. That I will always be more related to them, hold more importance to them than any man could. Not only because I am queen. And you took a chance from my ignorance. Attempted to profit from my ignorance. Desired to claim my city and my people as your own. You speak of divine laws when I turn to be, as you know, divinity itself. You broke not only my laws as queen, but those older than time. This kingdom is made of thirteen, but its heart is one and will remain one. To suggest otherwise calls for death. You've done much for my Olympia, you helped people of my own tribe hide in these mountains, for that I owe you gratitude and respect. But it doesn't mean I owe you subjugation. Tell me, Bayrd, can they ever bow to you how they can bow to me? Can you protect them how I can?"

Uncertainty and challenge crossed his face, but he inclined his head in a bow. "Tristin will be prepared to represent Volant in court."

Turning round, I raised a brow at the little, curious spawns who'd probably spied every word that had come out of my mouth. "Who wants to play ball?"

"Me!" they all screeched in unison, and I chased them around and between the ancient buildings of the city till my thighs burned and my lungs had expanded to the size of a cushion.

CHAPTER THIRTY-EIGHT

Copetum

Kilian

War was at my doorstep and there were a thousand things I had to arrange and think about yet there was nothing occupying my mind beside her. Wherever I turned there was a piece of her. I felt her everywhere. She was forever a part of me. Knowing her, she had reached a tipping point when she'd learned of what she was—who she really was. And worry had exhausted my ability to exhale fully.

A gentle knock rasped on my door and then Thora popped her head inside. The only thing that shone a bit of light these days had been her—she'd shone it on my brother and Driada, too. I was glad she was able to stay a bit longer. "Would you mind taking me to Taren. I can't find Mal. Some of the servants say he has already left for Taren early this morning."

Mal? Why would he be in Taren? I stood and threw my jacket back on. "I'll take you."

She took my hand and a second later we stood at the roof of Taren. Bright daylight stretched over the endless skies, and the city ahead seemed to glow in it. Even the mountain faces had received a virid glow.

The younger sister tugged my sleeve. "Help me get down the stairs, you know I hate the height."

"Thought you were getting better."

After practically dragging me along, she gave me a coy smile over her shoulder. "I am."

"Thora," I warned.

"Perhaps you can see Snow. It has been days and she won't come out of Visha's lair—she's even slept there. Her poor hair has gotten all tangled. I know you must at least feel sorry for that, your hands are always in her hair."

"Don't get me in trouble now."

"You're right on time," Alaric said, coming from the other end of the corridor. The man looked like he'd lost fifty years out of his lifetime. Was Snow still not speaking to him? "Join the court meeting."

"I don't think that is right, Alaric, and you know it," I said, bowing. "With your permission."

"Join," Snow's cold voice echoed from the end of the corridor and my chest sighed with some relief. There were deep shadows under her eyes that had gone a dull amber. Damned hells, this woman. Making my heart bleed without even breathing near her dagger. "I think you might want to sit this one in."

Alaric's expression pursed with apology, and he tried to reach a hand to Snow, but she pulled away from him wearing violence in her face.

Not like this. I didn't want to leave her like this. Fragmenting to pieces again. Not when I'd had her so whole in my arms not long ago.

The air was cold. Snow's court had filled the meeting room, my brother and her siblings joining too. What was Mal doing here?

Bayrd, the Volant leader, was replaced by his daughter, Tristin, and I was sure Snow had a hand in his retirement. The discussion had switched from the Fogling disappearances to the shipments from Drava they were expediting to the unblessed isles, to the new sceptre piece in our hold, but I paid attention to nothing.

My attention was on her. Her expression was not only void of emotion but filled with something darker. Detachment.

Several times I'd attempted to catch her attention yet nothing.

Just once.

Just one more time.

Look at me one more time.

Just look at me, love.

I needed to see those eyes. I needed to see what they were saying. I needed to see her troubles. Only this one last time.

A knock rasped at the door and Snow finally lifted her gaze and met mine. Gods spare us all. The look she wore chilled every fibre in my body.

Visha entered the room, bowed at the table and turned to Snow. "We have found the location for the Adriatian sceptre piece."

The court went wide-eyed at Visha's words. Quiet terror reigned among her court. Looks were exchanged between many. Few aimed at me.

We have found the Adriatian sceptre piece.

Snow wanted to search for the Adriatian piece.

Her expression finally cracked, not in the way I thought it would. A smirk tilted upward in her lips. "Brilliant work, witchling. Prepare what I need."

Alaric stood and raised a hand for Visha not to leave. His shadows mottled with distress. "What is going on now? We are not in the need of any other sceptre piece and Adriata is well guarded now. Silas will find it difficult to raise the guardian."

"That is correct," Snow said, leaning back and directing a scathing look toward Alaric. "Silas will not awaken the guardian. I will."

Silence echoed in the room, stunned at her revelation. And so was I.

Alaric looked around the meeting room, pleading for someone to object, but the tribe leaders ducked their heads in agreement with Snow. No one was opposing Snow's words. Not even his father.

Alaric shook his head. "I will not allow you to play god, Snow. I will not sit around and watch you become Silas."

Snow cocked a brow up at him. "You can stay standing up if you wish and it appears that I *am* god, Alaric."

"I am Regent—"

"You're no longer Regent, I've demoted you from that position."

"Snow, my love," I interfered.

"Cai is now acting as my Regent," she said without missing a beat. "Seeing you have been incapable of providing your queen with the correct intel. I need a hand of support not a backstabbing one. There is plenty out there already."

"Son," Alaric turned to Cai. "You cannot agree to this."

"I already have," Cai said blankly.

Eren leaned forward, resting a hand over Snow's. "May we discuss this a bit more, Lin."

The older brother winced a little when she turned her cold stare at him. "There has to be a discussion to discuss."

He shook his head. "What do you intend to do once you awaken Aurora?"

She pulled her hand from his. "Finish what I started years ago. Wipe Adriata and Isjord out of the map. If I am feeling up to it, perhaps some more."

Thora jumped from her seat, her mouth gaping in disappointment. "Snow, you can't...you can't be serious."

"Though the thought that I will get to see them set on fire makes me amused, this is not a joke," she said, cocking her head back to give her sister an indifferent stare. "You will find that I can be serious at times, little sister."

Thora's assessing gaze bore on her sister as if trying to work out what was going on inside her head. "Why would you want destruction when we fought so hard against it, when we endured what we did? Why are you giving up now?"

"*You* fought so hard against it. I only followed sloppy instructions," she said. "The same instructions that had me watch our mother bleed a bloody death because I had to hide what I was. Which by the way happens to be divine. Can you just believe that?"

Her sister recoiled, hurt and speechless. Her voice was meek when she asked, "It won't bring her back, Snow. You know that. What will dipping your hands in more blood bring you or this kingdom?"

Snow blinked boredly. "When I do it, I'll let you know what it will bring me, Thora. It certainly will be something."

It was Nia's turn to object, "You have everyone here. Everyone you fought to have beside you."

Snow measured her friend's words. "Yet I am unsatisfied." She turned her gaze to me. "Our bargain broke. We owe one another nothing. Consider this the warning for what is to come."

I shook my head. "I'll keep my end of the deal till you find the Adriatian piece. I know my land better than any. I'll help you get that and then you'll be rid of me."

"No. What makes you think I trust you to help her now?" Cai almost accused.

Lazarus shot to his feet, feathers ruffling. "Yes, what makes you think you can do that now that she is free of you?"

"I will go with them," Thora said and then turned to Lazarus with a cold bored gaze. "And you might sit down, feathered man, no one asked for you to defend anyone. Certainly not your queen from your king—her husband might I remind you."

Mal chuckled. "You tell him, little bird."

Lazarus blinked stunned a moment before he sat back down, embarrassed.

Snow's jaw tightened. "You will do no such thing."

Thora met her stare dead on. "Why, will you stop me? Will you chain me like father and uncle did? Will you hurt me and hold me and beat me too till I obey you?"

Snow faltered a little, speechless.

"I will come as well," Mal added.

"No," both Snow and I said.

He cocked an amused brow at the two of us. "Why, will you stop me? Will you chain me—"

Thora gave him a smack on the shoulder, and he chuckled some more.

And like that it was decided. The four of us would go to retrieve the Adriatian sceptre piece tomorrow.

The meeting room dispersed, leaving only the four of us and Visha to prepare for tomorrow's travel.

Lake Astrid was not a sacred ground like the other Octa Virga locations. The shadowed lake was a reminder of human nature. Asterin was a graveyard of those that put greed before their life. Once the waters had been rich with life, a home to creatures of water and land, half human and half fish. We called them nereids or lake nymphs. Fascinating creatures that the god of waters, Roto, had gifted Adriata in passing when he'd visited my kingdom. The creatures had lived peacefully, thriving in their waters until humans had made contact. Nereids were not social beings, their language was poison to human ears and their singing was deadly, it lured one onto the waters till they drowned—magic that was meant to protect them from harm. But it had lured one too many to their shores, dragged onto the depths of the waters till they had drowned. News had spread fast in my lands and curiosity had grown along with lies to attract attention. Some had said the nereids opened gates to the heavens of Roto and had voluntarily entered their waters in search of them. Others said the nereid songs cleared your soul to guarantee you heavens and had listened to their singing only to end up in the Otherworld.

So many lives were lost in pursuit of those lies that Henah had been left with no choice but to seal the land with magic like she'd sealed the Danic's. Just like the veil in the Danic's, this too was a dark one—one that only the goddess of darkness could cast. The magic was a warning to those that disobeyed. And those that disobeyed found a darker end in the mist than what they would have found in the lake.

Visha had kept staring at me the whole time Mal explained the condition of the location we were to visit. There was an odd look on the young

Crafter's face. Almost resembling worry. "I think you shouldn't go tomorrow."

Her words made everyone go silent and turn to attention, staring between her and I.

"It will be fine," I assured. "Continue, Mal."

"So, are the nereids still in the water?" Thora asked, looking disturbed by the thought.

"They are," Mal said. "Scared?"

She shook her head, steeling on an expression of fierceness. "No. Curious how we will avoid dying by a song. It would be a terrible way to die."

"No one will be dying, Rora," Snow said boredly. "At least not tomorrow."

Moriko chose that moment to enter the meeting room chambers. She dropped a red flower on the meeting table. A red spider lily. "Why do you grow that on castle grounds?"

Snow scoffed. "Do I look like I do the gardening in my castle? And have you not noticed nothing can grow on obsidian rock?"

Moriko pointed to the flower with persistence. "I plucked that from the wall outside."

Snow looked at the flower and then Moriko with an annoyed stare. "Too much fuss for a flower, Your Majesty."

"That is the omen of death, Snow," the Autumn Queen gritted out without her usual calm.

"It's just a flower," Snow said.

Moriko pointed to the window. "Look outside."

Mal and Thora went to the balcony and froze. Slowly, Snow and I rose, too, and what we saw made us both take a step back. Red spider lilies had sprung all over the face of the obsidian castle, covering the black rock in crimson. An ominous blanket swaying at the touch of wind that dusted the air with sweet pollen and soft notes of warning.

"Why has the bride of death visited your door?" Moriko asked.

"She is your goddess, Mor, figure it out yourself," Snow said, heading inside the room again.

I caught Visha still looking at me. An indecipherable look on her face.

"Why are you here?" Snow asked, taking a seat.

The Autumn Queen sat across Snow. "I am told about the changes to your plan."

"Nia is quick."

"I am quicker," Mor said, coldly. "If you chose to pursue those goals, I will pull all of my support given you. I cannot in good heart watch you do what your father was about to do."

"By all means," Snow said. "Do as you find fit."

Moriko turned to me. "You are going to let your wife do this?"

"She is free to do as she wishes, and she is not my wife." It hurt to utter those words aloud.

The Autumn Queen shook her head and rose to leave, reaching onto her pocket for some type of white root. "Nia told me you would be needing this. It will help you breathe underwater. Consider this the last thing I will do for you." She left, without bidding goodbye.

I stood too.

Snow did not spare me a single glance. I'd lost her—I'd lost her again.

"Wait," someone called, chasing behind me. Thora was panting as she reached me. "Wait."

"Mal will return with you. I will see you at dinner."

She caught my arm. "You can stop this, Kilian. I know you can. You can convince her. I know how she looks at you. I know there is something there. I just know it. Please, please. I know...I know you can stop her."

"Thora, I don't want to stop her."

She frowned and her stare shivered with confusion and hopelessness. "What...why?"

"I gave her my promise."

Chapter Thirty-Nine

Illunis

Snowlin

Dawn was finally bright in Olympia. The lands had not seen the skies change colour for the past two years. And this was all thanks to him. He'd made it possible for my people to live under the clear colourful skies of our god. It almost felt unreal.

I was beyond tired from lack of sleep, and exhaust was settling heavy over my bones from spending days chasing the Adriatian sceptre piece with Visha and Mal. My body had given up on this long ago, but there was no convincing my thoughts. I worked for this half of my life. Days and night and more days and nights, I'd spent calculating every move of mine. I'd played the realm as I played chess. By my own damned rules. And I was winning. I was so close to winning. But now I was playing a game I didn't even want to play anymore. And I was still winning.

Someone stood beside me. "You probably don't want to see me right now, kid," Alaric said. "But you have to give this old man a chance to say something before you leave on this journey. In this life, I don't regret anything more than words unsaid. I lost someone I deeply loved because I was too afraid to say what I wanted to say. Even though I will make sure to be with him in heavens and explain that to him, you've tempted the hells too much for comfort."

That made me chuckle.

He took a deep breath and continued, "The day you were born was the hottest day of the realm, yet the skies thundered like heavens were about to crack open for all of us to see. Your mother knew Eren was not an Elding though you all have the blood of Zephyr. She knew *you* were the moment she felt you squirm in her belly. And she was terrified of the burden you would hold on your little shoulders. So terrified, she couldn't bear to look at you. Serene couldn't spare herself a glance without guilt. Your mother planned a great deal of things. She took much responsibility upon her—"

"Except for raising her children. I wanted her guilt, Alaric. I wanted crumbs from her If I could get them."

"You have to understand."

"I'm done understanding. There was nothing to understand. You were there. Mended my wounds, helped me to sleep, fed me, brushed my hair—you were my mother and my father. And I appreciate you so much for it, but I needed her, too. What she and you owed me was the truth, to the three of us. It was one thing to be raised as Silas Krigborn's monster and another to convince yourself that I was the monster that many spoke of, that he wanted to create. To hate myself." Shakily, I peeled my gloves back and showed him my palms. "To hate and hurt that monster because it was the only way to control it."

Gently, he took my hands in his and tears flooded his eyes, his mouth trembling. He studied each and every scar, his expression shattering with each look. This was why I'd never done this. "Forgive me, kid. Forgive me." He shook his head. "How have I not known this?"

"Because not long ago, even I thought nothing of it. Till him."

Alaric looked up at me with red teary eyes, brows knitted together. "Till him?"

I nodded. "He made me promise," I said, putting my gloves back on. "That I would stop. So I have."

"You have?"

"It is difficult, but I am trying." My voice shook a little when I said, "He never breaks his promises, and I will not break mine." Reaching inside my leathers, to the little pocket I'd made especially for it, I took out Sam's necklace. "I don't think being alive will ever feel right or that hate will not forever corrupt my heart. I cannot be fixed, Alaric. I don't think I can watch it glisten on a spring sunrise." Taking his hand, I placed the sunstone necklace on his palm. "But you can. Help me honour Sam's wish. Let it see the sunrise it deserves."

"Kid," Alaric said, putting the necklace back in my hand. "That day will come."

I shook my head. "No. I chose it so." Pushing the necklace back in his hand, I stepped back. "Pick a pretty one. Pick a pretty sunrise."

He tucked the necklace close to his chest. "Every day since the moment you three were born, all I've ever seen are pretty sunrises, kid."

Slowly, I reached close and wrapped my arms around him, sinking my head in the comfort of his chest. He smelled of cloves and autumn breezes—he smelled like home.

His sighs were heavy and pained. "Why out of all the things this realm has for us to fear, we chose to fear love?"

"I...I don't think I love him, Alaric."

"Do we all get one?" Mal's mischievous voice came from behind me, and I unravelled myself from Alaric.

Thora's smaller form stood between the two brothers, clad in all black Adriatian leathers, looking like a warrior. She twirled around to show me, and I couldn't help but laugh a little at the pink clip holding her hair back. "Besides the squeaking when I move around, the rest of me is deadly," she said, taking a fighting stance.

Alaric sighed. "Kid, could cause for my sudden death be enough to convince you to stay back."

"But so is your smoking, drinking and many other unhealthy habits I've seen you partake in," Thora said as a matter of fact.

The old man sighed and turned to me. "She is your sister after all, didn't know what I expected. Take care of her."

"Come," Kilian said, reaching a hand for me. "We need to be there before sunrise."

It felt strange to hold him again. To hold him outside of our guise—our pretend.

The fading was quick and this time I didn't even feel it. Thora, however, swayed on her feet, dizzy. Mal wrapped an arm around her waist, helping her straighten. "There, there, little bird."

There was no lake where we were, only miles and miles of black sand, grey fog and ashen redwood tree crowns peeking above the cloud of magic that disguised the lake.

"The fog," Kilian said, "is similar to a craft veil, but not entirely so. It will not mess with your mind to lure you. But chase you through your fears."

"What would that mean?" Thora asked.

"Whatever you fear will manifest itself."

My little sister looked around and murmured to herself, "Badgers."

Mal turned his attention to her. "What?"

She shivered a little. "They terrify me. The other night I dreamed that one made a nest in my skull. Read it in a book once, they like hollow places and hide in large animal carcasses."

Mal huffed and gave me an incredulous look. "Let us all pray it is badgers that try to chase us away."

She shot him a glare while mounting an arrow on her bow. "It could be worse. I could be afraid of women that I don't pay to fuck."

Kilian snorted and ducked his head behind my shoulder a little to hide his chuckles.

Mal didn't look offended. At least the massive stupid grin he had while looking at my sister did not indicate so. "If you keep whacking your sharp tongue at me I might just bite it."

Thora stuck her tongue out at him, and he quickly grabbed her jaw, pushing her tongue back on her mouth with a finger. "Careful, Princess."

"Do I stop this, or do you stop this?" Kilian asked, staring at the bickering two.

I shrugged. "Let them play while they can."

The forest was all sorts of odd from the outside but when we entered, it looked all normal, minus the grey fog that smelled like yeast.

A screech sounded in the distance and we all lifted our weapons, readying for whatever the veil was going to brew.

"Shit," Mal bit out and Thora let an arrow loose toward where he was staring.

"What?" I asked, looking around till I noticed the human head rising from a puddle of mudd.

Ever so slow, the long-haired woman with a gnarly, bony face, pulled herself up on all fours and let out a high-pitched bawl that almost made my ears bleed. Something else peeked from behind the treeline ahead—another one. And another. And another dozen. Two dozen. Three—

We were surrounded. A throng of humans crawled on all fours towards us, tilting their heads to study us but not getting close or even attacking.

I took a step forward and one shot from the trees in my direction, howling like a banshee before Kilian slashed his black steel through it. The woman turned to a puddle of black tar. "The hells."

I lifted a hand up, feeling the electricity skittering around my fingers and shooting bolts of it toward the creatures. It took no more than a minute for them all to melt and turn to black tar. "That was…easy."

Mal shrugged though he was shaking a bit. "Henah probably didn't count for a guardian to go through here."

"I am not a—" A hand wrapped around my leg and dragged me down. My whole body lit with electricity and the gnarly woman rising from a puddle of tar turned back to liquid.

One by one, bodies rose from the ground again, creeping around us, doubling as it seemed so.

Kilian's magic had turned the whole place into a black cloud, but the gnarly creatures tore right through it.

"It's the mist," I shouted. "Magic is useless." No matter how many times we slashed through them, no matter how many times I zapped them with magic, they continuously rose, doubling and tripling till the forest began shrinking.

"Whose fear is this?" Kilian asked, slashing body after body.

A hand grabbed Thora's hair and tugged. My sister didn't scream, but a heart shattering sob left her mouth before she unsheathed a dagger and slashed it through her hair, cutting more than half its length. Ice had crawled around her, and it began spreading all over the forest coating the mist ashy white and the trees with a layer of frost.

Mal's hands dug on the ground, his body enveloped in a black phantom fire that littered the humid air with a thick taste of magic, and every crawling body stopped in their tracks—frozen still, some mid-air and others from breaking through the earth. The Eldritch Commander breathed hard and heavy, his eyes entirely black.

He had stopped them. With magic.

Why was he able—

Mal stood and ran, kneeling before her, reaching a hand out for me to stop from nearing them. "Eyes open, bird, eyes open, let me see them. Don't disappear inside your head again. Come on."

What...what did he mean?

Her forest eyes were tearless, but she sniffled and quivered. "Is my hair ugly?"

"No," Mal said, breathless, shaking his head and touching the tip of his fingers to the ends of her hair that ended just past her shoulders. "No, not ugly at all. Your face on the other hand."

It looked like she forgot all that had happened and started violently slapping him all around. "Blessed idiot."

He threw his head back, laughing. "Blessed idiot?"

"Rora?" Thin streaks of black began peeking from underneath her leathers and over her neck. "Your seal."

She stood and touched a hand to her skin, jerking a little when she saw her hands coated with spidery, black lines. "I can feel it."

"As we practised, Thora," Kilian said and my sister shut her eyes, inhaling controlled breaths till the seal began sliding and disappearing from her face and hands.

We all looked around and saw the real damage she'd made to the forest. For miles and miles, you could only see ice and frost, even the murky black mist had turned an ashen grey almost resembling snow.

Mal let out a low whistle. "The dire wolf indeed."

"Told you," my sister murmured, eyeing the rest of her long hair on the muddy ground.

"How did you do that?" Kilian asked, narrowing his attention on Mal. "They weren't dead, brother."

Mal's body stilled. "It isn't only the dead that I can command, Kil. Anything that has any fragment of life in it, I can control. Spirits, animal, flower. Everything that lives—humans too."

First time I'd seen Kilian so worried. "You've never told me."

"I've never told anyone. If I spoke it out loud, I was sure our father would rise from hells to come and have me command a whole army of the living. I don't want to feel it, brother, the dead don't feel, but the living do. I don't just control their emotion, I feel all of their emotions as mine. All of them."

"I would have never told him," Kilian said and the pain in his voice broke my heart. "I would have never told anyone, Mal. You know that."

The younger brother nodded. "I know, Kil."

The four of us were breathless by the time we reached the lake Astrid shore.

Kilian kneeled before me, inspecting a cut on my leg. Untucking his shirt, he tore the ends of it and tied it around the slash. When he stood at full height, his hands roamed my face. "Did they hurt you anywhere else?"

I shook my head. "I don't think so." My fingers went to the little bleeding cut on his cheek. "You?"

He kissed my palm. "Nothing beside that."

Reaching into his pocket, he retrieved two pairs of ear plugs. After putting a pair on me, he put the other set on his. His lips moved, but I couldn't hear anything.

I shook my head to signal him that I couldn't hear and he nodded. As long as we couldn't hear, we were safe from the call of the nereids.

The surface of the water eddied. And beneath the glassy surface something stirred—coming in our direction. Shadows of a long form became more and more visible the closer it came. A fin broke the murked grey surface, curving as the nereid reached us. Her white head peeked out of the water, porcelain skin and violet eyes—the thing was ghastly looking yet the most stunning thing I'd ever seen. She opened her mouth to speak, but something made her seal her lips closed again. She regarded me curiously, crawling on the sandbank to reach us closer. Her white hair was long to the back, covering most of her naked torso while a lilac fishtail managed to cover the rest. Or not? Would that mean it was naked?

She lifted a long lithe finger and then pointed to the grey sand before scribbling something on it.

A hand on my dagger, I kneeled to get a better look and made out a little drawing of wings. She pointed from them to me. "You know?" I didn't hear myself ask, but the words did leave my lips.

The nereid nodded. She scribbled on the sand again, this time a crescent moon and pointed to Kilian before bowing to us with a hand to her chest.

"Where is the sceptre piece?" I asked, hoping that I'd hit the stroke of luck with this whole guardian thing.

She recoiled a bit, sinking back into the water, distress painting her delicate features. Lifting a finger, she pointed to the middle of the lake.

"Is it in the water?"

She shook her head and made a strange hand gesture cupping her hands together and then opening them repeatedly before pointing to the middle of the lake again.

Kilian kneeled beside me and drew something else on the sand.

The nereid crawled to land again and studied the rune Kilian had drawn. She drew something else back and Kilian's eyes widened.

This silence was ruining the last strands of my sanity. "What?" I mouthed as exaggeratedly as I could.

"Portal," he mouthed back. "Isjord."

Another portal? Would there be another *Ybris* in there? Turning to the girl, I asked, "Could you take us there?"

She backed away again, looking between the four of us, before heaving what looked like a sigh. She swam further inside the lake and waved a hand, signalling for us to follow her.

The water was frosted, more than the normal type of cold that I was used to. Kilian followed suit and Mal helped Thora in before jumping in himself and splashing the rest of us in the process.

We swam the distance to the centre of the lake. The more we stood there in the water, the more I could feel a tug of magic weighing down my limbs—as if my magic was being called and asked to run while being sucked in a vortex at the same time.

I took off the earplugs and listened for that vibration in the air—a strange call to my senses.

"Snow," Thora said, breathing heavily. "Is it...is it just me?"

"No, I can feel it, too." I looked below us and right as I did so, something wrapped around my leg and tugged me under water.

I heard my name being called and shouted over the surface and then another scream—Thora's. The water splashed near me, and a hand brushed mine. Immediately, I grabbed onto it and held it tight, while I pulled a dagger from my thigh baldric, crouched and waved it near my foot till I felt it meet something soft before slashing the blade through it. Whatever was pulling Thora under, tugged me along as well. Not for long because Thora blasted a wave of wind and formed an air pocket around us.

"I can't see," she coughed and sputtered, hugging me tightly.

"Just hold me," I said, looking around as if *I* could see anything. My magic was useless in water, unless I wanted to electrocute or freeze everyone in it.

Something drummed against the air shield and Thora jerked in my hold. It drummed again, but this time, I felt something warm crawl around us. "Kilian?" I rested a hand on the shield and then felt something on the other side rest against it. "Thora, pull it back. Pull back the shield."

"But—"

Wrapping my arm tightly around her, I said, "I'm never letting you go. Never again. Pull it back."

We both sucked a deep breath and waited for water to surround us. Immediately, strong arms were wrapped around me and another pair over my other side—Mal.

Bright light filtered the thicket of water from below us, casting brightness to our grim surroundings and the men holding us.

Thora jerked in my hold again when dozens of nereids surrounded us, all holding a safe distance from us.

Kilian pointed his head to the floor of the lake, over a massive crafter circle and then signalled something to his brother. Mal grabbed Thora's hand and Kilian mine, and we swam toward it.

We'd not reached halfway down when a flash of light flickered to the point of blindness and then...we were no longer surrounded by the weight of water.

The ground below our feet was solid and there was air entering my lungs. It took me a moment to shake the dizziness, the ringing in my ears and the white cast on my sight. And when everything sharpened in sight, I stumbled a step back.

Piles of gold, diamonds, rubies, emeralds, sapphires, shimmering pearls and gilded weapons of all sorts rose like tall hills toward a sky that wasn't quite a sky but a twirling blue and white vortex resembling a whirlpool—the sky looked like a water surface.

I'd been so distracted that I'd not noticed that there was no one beside me. "Thora!" I shouted. "Kilian, Mal!" The sound of my voice echoed around the large maze of treasures surrounding me and then returned back to me.

My feet carried me to a sprint, I kept straight, no twisting or turning into the corridors formed along the treasures. Everything was the same and endless—gold and more gold.

"Why do you rush, young treasure?" an old slithery voice called from my side, and I stopped. Half man, half something else, the creature was vile looking. Instead of feet, he had tentacles and instead of hair, long strands of seaweed curled almost down to his back. There was a layer of pearlescent scales on his skin and his sharp teeth jutted out of his mouth. He studied me intently and frowned. "That cringe will wrinkle your pretty young face."

"You've not taken your own advice," I said, backing a step and clutching both my daggers tightly, electricity skittering from them. Thank hells I could still call my magic.

"For Ithicea," he said, leery blue eyes widening. "You're Nubil's."

"I'm not anyone's."

"You possess lightning, that makes you Nubil's."

"You possess great ugliness, does that make you Golgotha's?"

He blinked stunned for a moment before nodding to himself. "You've got a great point, but you are so rude about an old man's feelings."

"Where am I?"

"My home."

"Where is your home?"

"A pocket between realms."

"Which realm, exactly?"

"Numen and Akkamel. A home of mine. A place where I store my treasures," he said, his mouth twitched and widened. Was he grinning? "As you can tell."

"Akkamel as in the heaven of Akkamel?"

He nodded.

What in the hells. If this was his home, that meant—

"You're...Roto?" This was the god of waters?

He winked at me and did that grinning thing again before exaggerating a bow. "A pleasure, Caelum guardian."

"And the sceptre? You guard it here?"

"You're quick to the point. But, yes, it is here."

I extended a hand to him, and he wrinkled his brows at the action. "Give it."

He looked offended. Perhaps? I don't know, but his brows did a weird motion. "It is not in my power, young treasure. You have to complete the quest."

"Gods be damned, what quest?"

He gapped and put a hand to his chest. That was...offended, perhaps? "To unearth a long, lost treasure of truth from the pool of ocean inside you. Will you prevail to it or lose to its depths?"

I looked around, searching for the others, and he laughed. "I have the rest. The rest passed the test and are waiting to leave my lands. Only you remain. Pass it and I will give you the sceptre. Fail it and there will be a consequence."

He disappeared like smoke and water began rising from the floor and it soon reached up to my neck. Once it enveloped me above my height, its colour changed to a deep navy and every source of light vanished, leaving me in the middle of the dark depths. A vortex sucked me under and dropped me hard on a hard stone floor. I coughed my lungs out, sputtering a kilogram of water out of my stomach while searching my surroundings only to find nothing. I was in a small empty grey room the shape of a box with no light yet somehow it was bright enough for me to see all of its space.

A rustle of chains made me swirl around and clutch my daggers tight. I ran and kneeled before him. "Kilian, what are you doing here? That thing said you were at the portal. Fucking gods and their lies." I tugged on the chains he was wrapped in, but the metal didn't budge. The more I pulled, the more they tightened around him—the more he groaned in pain. Even the cloth over his mouth was tightly stuck to his face. Sweat beaded on my temples from how hard I was trying to free him. Was this the test? To find a way to break him free?

A numbness began settling at the tip of my fingers and it slowly spread all over my body, reining control of all of my movement. "What in the hells?" Panic struck me when I rose to my feet and struck Kilian hard across his face. What—what? "Kilian?"

Before he had a chance to reply or even move, I kicked him hard in the stomach, over and over and over till blood began staining the cloth over his mouth.

I tried to will my muscles back. Tried to command my body to stop, but nothing happened—only struck him harder.

"Stop!" I shouted when I raised two daggers up and nailed them deep in his flesh. And then again, and again. "Stop, stop, stop!" I roared, willing every fraction of my magic to pull open. Nothing. Nothing came out as I kicked and stabbed him, over and over. Nothing happened as I watched him bleed in front of me. "Please, please, please, stop. I can't. I can't do it. Just stop it. Don't. Please, don't make me kill him," I begged, and suddenly my body was mine again.

I kneeled before him, reaching a shaking hand to check his pulse. "Kilian?"

He didn't answer. Something else did, the cold, slimy voice was laced with amusement as he said, "You have finally done it. You kept your promise. The Night King is indeed dead by your hand."

No. This was a game. A veil. I'd seen him die in the Isjordian temple too. It had to be the same. "Kilian?"

Blood pooled beneath his body, spreading all over the grey floor, soaking my knees and I felt bile rise to my throat. "No, please, no." It couldn't be real.

"Wasn't this what you wanted? Isn't this your most inner truth—to want him dead?"

"No," I whispered, too afraid to even touch his bleeding body. "No."

"If I grant you a wish and a wish alone. What would it be?" He tilted his head to the side. "You can wish for the sceptre."

I didn't even have to think about it. "Bring him back."

A gust of water sloshed in the room and suddenly, I was submerged in water before surfacing in between the treasure labyrinth.

The ground beneath my palms was unsteady and the world spun furiously.

Empty. I felt empty.

Two strong hands cupped my face. I recognised them—they had held me so many times. "It's okay," he said, pulling me to his chest. "Whatever you did there, it is okay. It is okay, my love, it was not real. Whatever you chose was not real."

"You failed," the man said, clicking his tongue. "What a shame. Finicky you guardians. So much thinking with your heart and so little with your brains. Truly makes the distinction between us gods and you. But lucky me, I get to keep you."

Kilian tensed and held me tighter. "What did you choose?"

Surrendered, I rested my forehead on his chest, feeling his heartbeat beneath my palm.

The warm taste of his magic surrounded us, and the old god stumbled a few steps back, hissing at the mist of black pouring out of Kilian. "How dare, you human filth!" he roared, and the grounds shook, gold and diamond began raining down on us.

Kilian smirked and a blast of absolute darkness sent the god of waters flying back and screaming in what I'd assume to be pain—if gods could even feel pain.

He got me to my feet and clutched my hand tight before dragging me through the endless mazes of gold. "Thora and Mal are waiting for us at the portal," he said as gold, diamonds, and rubies flashed from the corners of my eyes.

"Why did you come back?"

He glanced at me over the shoulder as we took a turn "You didn't just ask me that."

The ground beneath shook and the sound of a hoard of hooves chased behind us, growing closer and closer. My senses vibrated from the danger, yet I somehow felt safe.

A bright white light flashed somewhere in the distance and my body hummed in remembrance. The sceptre piece.

I pulled my hand from his. "Go there first. I'm getting the sceptre."

"No," he gritted out, grabbing my hand again. "This is the last fucking time I get close to losing you. Next time will only be my death."

I shook my hand free from him and sprinted the opposite way. "Go!" I shouted over my shoulder. "Keep my sister safe. You owe me."

I didn't turn back to see if he was following. If I turned, I would have run after him and damned the sceptre.

Though I couldn't see where it was, I felt its presence pull and call to me. Reaching my hand forward, I called back to it, reciting those cursed words that made my magic shiver and crawl out of its depths. *"Hur ma'hazur kahaz." Kneel before the power.* Before I'd finished saying the last syllable, the silver rod tore from between a pile of coins and right into my grip. And then I ran back—the fastest I could till Kilian came in sight, breathing hard and laboured from exhausting this physical mana to draw magic in this pocket realm. A few strange bodies lay on the ground, slain to ashes by his magic.

The moment he spotted me, he turned and shouted at Mal and Thora, "Go!"

Mal dragged my reluctant sister out and into the portal, stepping safely back into Adriata and relief lifted from my chest.

"There you are," the god of waters growled. Dozens of pale creatures with fins and scales, almost resembling humans, stood behind him. "You belong to the god of waters. You will become a guardian of Akkamel, you will guard my realm along with my other guardians." His eyes gleamed. "You've become my most precious treasure."

Kilian raised a palm toward him. Blisters and sparks of night tore the sea air surrounding us and the water surface skies suddenly began murking and splattering with a grey that slowly grew to a deep black.

The creatures of Roto shrieked, backing away from Kilian and he signalled his head for me to run to him.

Roto studied him almost with curiosity. "Maybe I'll keep you, godling. You're strange for a human."

"Not human, an Aura," Kilian growled and unleashed a wave of darkness over the lands of Roto. Gold turned grey and dull, diamonds no longer clear but murking with shadows, rubies turned burgundy, and the creatures screeched and blasted to dust.

Roto hid under a shield of water and raised a hand toward the portal. "Maybe I'll keep you both since you are so reluctant to leave one another."

Our escape began shrinking and Kilian rose another hand toward it. Holding Roto back and keeping the portal from closing. "Run!" he shouted. A vortex of night swirling around him and coating the surroundings. Tentacles of darkness clung to the portal, pulling and tugging on its circumference to hold it open.

"Come," I said, extending a hand as I brushed past him, but he didn't take it.

He kneeled to the ground, arms spread wide, his body shaking as he poured gales of magic onto our surroundings to hold the gates open while keeping Roto back. "Go!"

"Not without you," I shouted back, slowing my steps as darkness blistering around us, making everything hard to see, his figure blurring too.

"I will be right behind, I promise."

Promise.

Mal grabbed my hand through the portal before pulling me through the gates.

Once I stepped out onto the black fog, a loud thud, like the crash of two storms, reverberated into the space.

It took me a long moment to catch my breath and steady my burning legs. "What was that noise?" I asked, turning to spin around to my sister and Mal. Except no one stood behind me and I was alone in the midst of the enshrouding dark that felt nothing like the dark I'd grown to like. "Kilian?"

Black mist blurred all the space around me. It was so dark—darker than the dark itself. Cold, too. My darkness was warm.

"Kilian?" I pushed my feet with no destination, I could be spinning in circles and I wouldn't know. "Kilian?" He'd promised to be right behind us. Kilian Castemont held all his promises. Kilian Castemont had held my promise for almost fifteen years.

My feet suddenly met muddy waters. The lake. The portal was on the lake, yes. He should be somewhere near here. "Kilian?"

A haunting tune drifted in the air, growing louder and eerier. The song of nereids was meant to be sweet and alluring, inviting. Yet what I heard chilled my soul and almost made my eyes well up. The mist parted and cleared ahead, and I ran through it and the lake shores, but not for long. I halted at what I saw laying ahead. A body floated on the wide black lake that was finally being touched by the shy rays of morning.

I rushed to him, dropping to my knees to hoist him up from the water. "Kilian?" My fingers trembled as I raised them to his neck. Be alive. Be alive. A sob raked my body, almost dizzying me. He was so cold. So pale.

"Kilian?" My hand fell and I frantically moved it over his chest searching for a heartbeat that I couldn't find. "Please. Please. Please. Please."

Nothing.

Utter nothingness.

I felt the hot streak off tears pour over my cheeks. No. It couldn't be. He couldn't— "Kil?" Not again, please. "Please, I can't do it again. I give up. I give up. Don't make me see this again."

Silence. Why did he feel so real in my arms?

"Darling?" I whispered.

Nothing.

More of the nothingness. Not until colourful heads of the nereids rose from the lake, that grieving tune growing louder. "Shut up! Shut up!" When lightning cracked through the day sky that had turned grey and thunderous, they backed away and lowered their heads, looking at me with pity.

Why were they looking at me like that?

"Answer me, please," I begged, cradling him close. I hugged his wet body, tightly, begging to feel his heat. Why was he so cold? Why did it feel real? Why did it feel like this was no game of craft and magic? "Please. Please. If you take him from me." A sob tore from me. "If you take him from me, I will hunt the heavens. I will hunt you all!" I shouted at the skies. "Don't take him from me, please!" More tears, more silence. No heartbeat. "I will burn you all!" I screamed and the dull throbbing in my chest grew beyond painful.

My cries echoed through the empty graveyard of dark and no one heard me. No one had ever heard me. Not gods. Not even him. No one heard me because Kilian's heart still made no sound. I held him faded in my arms, rocking the two of us as madness took over me. As a fierce heartache pierced my ribs. "Not him," I said, tracing a hand over his cold face. "Gods, please not him."

The water around me stirred and then splatters flew all over us as Mal and Thora broke through the black fog to us.

My sister put a hand over her mouth and tears streamed down her face at what she saw.

"What do I do?" I whispered. "He won't answer me." It hurt. It hurt so much.

Mal kneeled before us, his face ashen as he reached a shaking hand to Kilian. "Brother?" He grabbed Kilian's arm. "Brother? Kil?" he called desperately before stumbling a step back and then another till his limbs weakened and he collapsed to the ground.

It hurt so much. "Please," I whispered the plea again, running my fingers over his face. And when the answer was silence, I leaned to place a kiss on his forehead. "Kilian, please. I wanted you to hear it. I wanted you to hear me tell you how much I love you. Kil, please. I love you." I titled my head to the skies, rage simmering in me. Burning and spilling. Pouring in thunder and freezing the lake. "You will wait for me and you will welcome my fire." Lightning flashed with fury, and I lit the skies with brightness till the loud echo of thunder shook the ground. "I will burn you all! I will burn all your heavens," I cried, rocking the two of us in the water. "I swear it. I swear it!" Thunder rolled over us, skies flashing violently, pouring and grieving. "I swear it."

This...this...no, they couldn't...they couldn't do this. This was not happening. It couldn't be. This was my fault. I did this. I had done this. "Forgive me. Forgive me, please, come back and forgive me."

My senses were so dulled that when I felt a little movement it didn't register. It didn't register when his lids cracked open, staring at me. Not when he groaned in pain. Not when he frowned at me. Not when he caught a stray tear slipping down my cheek. "Why do you cry, my love?"

Mal gathered his face in his hands and cried out. His sobs broke my heart and ripped me apart once more.

Kilian blinked slow, still in a strange glassy haze. "Hi," I whispered.

A smile. "Hi."

I broke. Thousands of pieces that were never to repair again. How could a heart repair from being that broken? I hugged him tight to me, tears falling loose. I hugged him and cried till my voice grew hoarse and my throat hurt. "I was...I...was—" My words wouldn't come out. "I was going to burn them all."

His hand moved over my hair to soothe me as if I was the one that needed soothing. "I'm sure you would have."

At that moment everything felt right. He felt right. This was right. I lowered my lips to his and kissed him. He was still so cold—he was never this cold. I pulled back to stare at him, to stare at his beautiful face. And then I kissed him again. Senseless. Breathless. Utterly consumed. I kissed him like he was my lifeline. And he kissed me back like I was his. I was his and he was mine how it had always been. How it would always be. Always.

When I pulled back, panic set in me. Rock hard panic. I'd almost lost him. I couldn't lose him. I didn't want to lose him.

He must have sensed my thoughts because he cupped my cheeks and pulled my gaze to his. "It is alright, my love. It didn't happen. We are still in the dark, it can stay in it again. Whatever happened can stay in it."

For the first time, he'd read me wrong and for the first time the dark wasn't all that dark altogether. I'd seen darker terror less than moments ago. For the first time, I didn't want to deny myself him or us.

"It's alright," he repeated, resting his forehead on mine.

It wasn't alright. There was no such thing as alright. "Your heart stopped," I whispered, running my hand over his chest and sighing with relief when the steady beat thrummed under my touch.

His hand slid over mine. "It beats, my love."

I cupped his face, searching for answers to my insanity in his stare. "But it wasn't, Kil. It wasn't."

A small smile lifted in his lips. "What did you just call me?"

"Answer me. Where did you go?"

His expression fell. "Nowhere."

"Liar."

"I am."

"Tell me."

He leaned to kiss the tip of my nose. "Love, there is nothing to tell. Call me that again."

"Not until you tell me."

He chuckled a little, attempting to sit upright. "I'll have to cherish that then."

His attention went to Mal and Thora. My sister had pulled him out of the water and they both sat on the shore facing one another. Her mouth moved quickly, and he only listened, staring at her and her alone. He still wore the expression of someone who'd seen death, he still had tears fall from his russet eyes—tears that Thora slowly brushed away all while talking and talking to him. She'd always been like that. Always the grounding we never had.

Kilian made to stand and I rounded an arm around his waist to help him up. "Love, I am not injured," he said, unwrapping my arm and leaving a kiss on my palm before lacing our hands together.

"I missed you calling me that," I murmured to myself, and he slowly turned to me with a frown.

"What did you just say?"

"If that had been me, you would have thrown me over your shoulder."

When he smiled at me, I rose on my tip toes and kissed him again.

"What was that for?" he whispered over my mouth.

"Pretty," I said, leaving another kiss on his lips. "Smile."

And when he frowned, my black heart tore again.

Thora stood from where she had sat with Mal and grabbed the sceptre piece that I'd dropped on the lake shore. "Can we please go now?"

We nodded and I tightened my grip around his hand. "Talk to Mal."

"I will," he said, stealing a glance at his devastated brother.

The fog grew back denser the further away we moved from the lake, pulling back in place as if we'd never even stepped there. Though I was glad to leave the creeping place where I'd made some of the memories that would turn to nightmares for years to come, something in it pulled my attention back.

Unable to resist the call to my magic, I glanced over my shoulder, searching the black mist till my eyes landed on a tall figure clad in piercing white cloths with pale glistening skin, the bluest of eyes and long, straight white hair that bellowed in the air even though there was no wind. There was no man I'd ever seen with his beauty besides Kilian. His sight was otherworldly. At first, I thought the ancient fog or the shock was still playing games with my sanity. Until the man smirked and crossed an arm to his chest before bowing to me and vanishing out of sight between a gust of wind.

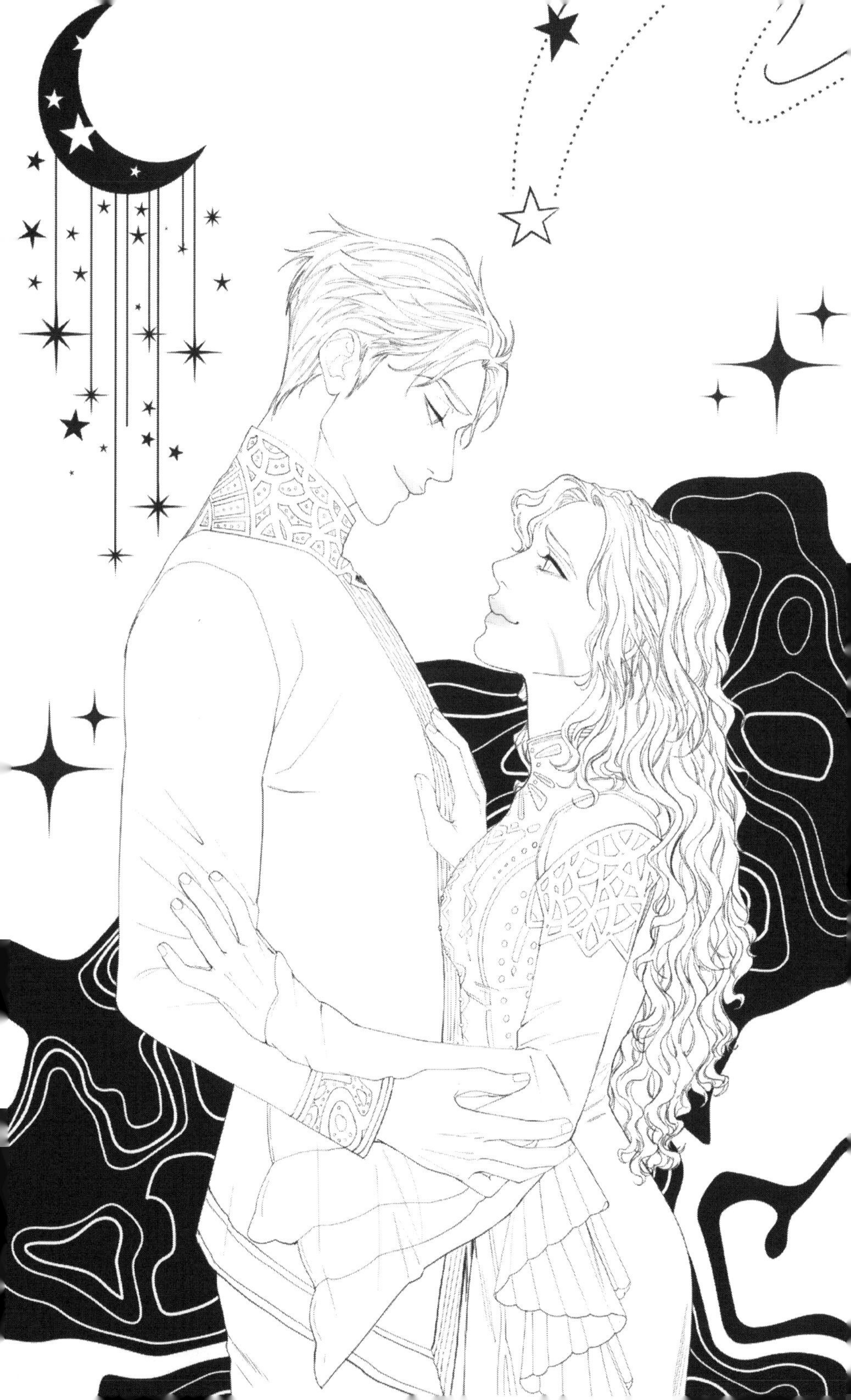

Chapter Forty

Electrum

Kilian

Cicadas serenaded the world as if they didn't know their only spectator tonight was I. The gardens were littered with joyous flower folk, night spirits and fireflies dancing excitedly at the lack of human interruption.

Despite their call to join the joy the blessed night brought upon this land and its creatures, I couldn't rejoice. Not when I couldn't think of anything but the last look of the woman who made my heartbeat pulse, made it want to stop altogether.

"You were right," Snow's soft voice came from behind me. "The Adriatian night sky is something of a wonder."

It took me a moment to process that the sound was not of my imagination. I spun around in my seat to see her approach me. She wore red and gold. The bright ruby fabric floated in the air at the touch of the spring breeze permeating the gardens and the gilded jewellery glistened under the white moonlight. She was divine in every sense, but today, she looked more than otherworldly. Tonight, she'd become a true god after claiming Myrdur from her father's reign—after she'd set the land and its suffering souls free from him. Tonight, Olympia celebrated her and their blessing.

"What are you doing here, my love?" I asked, lowering my tumbler on the ground. "Did the festivities end early?"

She nodded and came to me, perching herself in my lap and wrapping her hands around my neck. "Mine never started. Why didn't you come? What is a pretty queen without her pretty king?"

I wanted to take those words for more than what they were. I wanted to wrap my hands around her and pull her close to me. "I know where I am not wanted."

Her brows bunched together, and she searched for something in my eyes. Those golden rings pacing rapidly before she lowered her fiery red mouth on mine.

She kissed me and I couldn't get enough of her. Why did she kiss me?

"Would you like to hear a story?" she asked, weaving a hand through my hair and brushing it away from my eyes.

I nodded and she let out a soft sigh before turning her attention above us, toward the endless starry skies. "When I was younger, Eren let me play with him and a few of his friends. Hide and seek. I made it my goal to be the last one found so I went and hid where I knew no one could find me—in the winter garden maze." She looked down at her bare feet that wiggled from under the long fabric of her dress. "As you probably might have guessed, I did go barefooted. Except, this time I spent not minutes outside, but half a day. My mother found me almost frozen. I hadn't seen her in weeks." Her voice shivered a little and I damned all gods and clutched her tight to me. "But she came for me, worried and upset. My feet were pretty bad after standing on the frosted ground for so long, so they brought leeches to get the dried blood out. It was the most disgusting and uncomfortable thing I'd ever done as a six-year-old, but I loved every minute of it because my mother stood by me and looked after me. It wasn't long, though, till she was gone again. So, I fled for the gardens one more time, hid and stayed in the cold till I almost blacked out and she found me, again. She stayed and looked after me this time, too. But then I did it again and again till she got tired of my trick and called me out on it." She looked at me. "I was a horrible child."

My insides ripped apart. "You deserve to be loved more than just when you are in pain. Nothing about that makes you horrible."

She nodded and cleared her throat. "I tried to explain myself to her. That I wasn't being disobedient like everyone called me to be. I told her that I missed her so fiercely my heart hurt. That I couldn't explain to her why I was doing what I did. She taught me a new term that day. Heartache. That is what she told what I felt was. An ache so fierce for someone you love. She told me someone could become your heartache. It manifests itself like a sickness."

"You miss her."

"I do, my heartache." Her words were a whisper, so light and feathery and magnificent that I thought I might have made them up till she said, "And I miss you. I miss you so much, even when I have you near me. You make my heart hurt so fiercely." She rested her forehead on mine. "I love you. I've loved you and I love you. And I've done it so horribly—I've loved you so horribly. I love you, Kil. So much."

If I didn't hear it again, I'll think I imagined them.

Tears began streaking down her cheeks. "Say something." Her eyes searched for mine. "Please."

I wiped her tears away. "Say it again."

She frowned. "Say something or please?"

I laughed. "That you love me."

"I love you," she repeated.

"Again."

"I love you."

Gods. I never knew till now that I'd been holding my breath since the day I'd met her. I didn't know I hadn't breathed since then because now I actually felt my lungs fill with air. "Since when?" I had to know. I had to know that she was not saying it prompted by yesterday's panic.

"Why am I being investigated?"

"Since when?"

She hiccupped. "A while."

"How long a while?"

She rolled her eyes. "Long."

"Did you just roll your eyes at me?"

"So?"

"Say it again."

Her brows pulled together. "You want me to say *so*?"

My smile was uncontained. "That you love me."

She kissed me. Her soft lips nudging mine, the taste of cherries made me want to devour her. Kissing Snow was like the first breath out of water and drowning at the same time. If she wanted me to drown, I'd drown.

I'd promised to devour her yet she devoured me—wholly.

"I love you." She recited the word in every language and then in Darsan.

I pulled back a little. "You learned it in Darsan too? Now I can get it up for you in the bedroom."

She threw her head back in a bubbly laughter. And all I wished was to make her laugh like that for the rest of my life. "I learnt more than just that. I bet you wouldn't be able to get it down for a while," she said fully in Darsan, and my eyes shot wide.

"You terrify me woman."

"Good. Great. Brilliant," she said, planting small pecks all over my face. The memory made me laugh and she pulled back to look at me with that round stare she always gave. "It still undoes me." She stood up from my lap and straddled me on the bench. "You undo me," she whispered, trailing kisses down my neck, her hands travelling over the buttons of my jacket, slowly popping them open before peeling it off me. "Your smiles, your laugh," she murmured, kissing her way up to my lips. "Your scent, your eyes. Your words."

"Go on," I said, helping her take off my shirt.

Those pretty red lips curled into a wicked smile. She slowly stood, pushed my knees apart and kneeled before me.

"Never kneel before anyone."

"I've only ever kneeled before my king. No one else," she said, kissing a trail over my stomach, her tongue darting to lick a path to my neck. "I once asked you if you imagined making me scream or silencing me. I'd still like to know that answer." Her delicate fingers worked through my belt and then the fly till she had me on her hand, stroking me slowly. She looked up at me, batting those lashes innocently before leaving a little kiss on the tip and my cock jumped to attention. She smiled before licking up my shaft, my whole body springing with pleasure. Like that, she teased me with little kisses, licks, gentle strokes and smiles till I was breathless and panting.

I groaned, dropping my head back. "Suck, woman."

She slid me between her lips, taking as much of me in her mouth as she could and wrapping her hand around the rest. She sucked me once before pulling me out of her tongue almost all the way through to take a breath. The second time, her throat relaxed, taking me a bit deeper, the sensation blinding as she sucked and stroked me at the same time.

"Love," I hummed, letting pleasure work itself over my body and my head dropped back. My hips buckled and my hand shot into her hair, restraint was bordering on snapping.

Her free hand slid on top of mine and she pulled back to say, "Don't hold back, fuck my mouth how you want to."

If there was any restraint in me at all, it had snapped right there. I slid both hands through her hair and thrust up in her mouth. "Fuck." Her throat opened up for me, taking me deeper and deeper with each thrust. Her lashes rolled up at me and I read amusement on her glittering eyes. "Don't look at me like that, love."

She moaned around my cock, the vibrations shot straight to my balls, and they tightened, release racing through my body and my hips thrust up faster.

The way she looked at me as I held her there, her little gags and whimpers, my cock disappearing between her red lips and smeared with that fiery lipstick—this...I wanted to fucking paint this. "I wanted to finish inside your cunt, love."

I made to pull back, but she hooked her arms around me, holding me to her mouth, sucking me deeper, my cock bumping against her throat.

Tugging on her hair, I pulled her head back a little and came on her tongue. Fuck. Gods. And all heavens.

Sliding off her mouth and grabbing her chin, I angled her face to the ground. "Spit."

She raised a brow and then swallowed. Fucking swallowed, licking her lips as she did so.

Fuck.

Her grin was victorious. "So?"

I hooked my hands under her shoulders and lifted her up on my lap. "I forgot the question."

She giggled, running the tip of her tongue over her lip. "Never done that before." My brows rose when her cheeks flushed red. She quickly added, "But I know how to adapt well in sticky situations."

That made me laugh. With my thumb, I rubbed a bit of the smudged lipstick that had bled in the corners of her lips and then kissed her. "Are you real?" I asked, still feeling too anxious that this was a reverie created by my mind.

"If you think about it, if this wasn't real," she said, slinging her arms around my neck. "It would mean that you imagined silencing me."

"I like making you scream too."

She sighed. "Later. Let's go back to the ball. I promised Thora I'd return with you."

"Love," I said carefully. "You told me you loved me, sucked me, my cock is still out for that matter, and now you want to take me dancing?"

She shrugged and reached to put me in my britches before buttoning my fly. "Could have gone worse. I could have made you dance first." She stood, brushed a hand over her hair and gave me a beaming smile. "How do I look?"

"Magnificent."

She held my hand tight while tugging me between the horde of people filling every space of the ballroom celebrating the claim of Myrdur.

"I brought him," she said to Thora who jumped upright from her seat.

"Did she threaten you?" Nia asked, amused, sipping her drink. Her smile began to wear off the more she looked at me. "Oh."

Thora's expression turned worried as she threw jerky glances between us. "What? What is it? What did you see? Did she really threaten him?" She stopped and narrowed her forest green eyes on me and then nodded to herself. "Oh."

"*Oh* what?"

She tapped a finger to the corner of my lip. "Nice colour. Goes well with your skin tone."

"It does," Albius said, slowly making his way to us along with Alastair. He had a sombre smile on his face, but sadness in his shadows. He bowed to the two of us. "Less so than the colour of love you both wear. I still remember him hiding behind trees to spy on you."

"You knew?" Snow asked, eyes wide.

The old man chuckled. "Who do you think let him in Arynth to spy on you when you came over?"

Snow gaped a little. I liked how she found it hard to believe that we'd met long ago. "At the meeting in Arynth, you knew he was the Night King since then? Is that why you never said anything?"

He nodded. "I suppose it worked well that I did not meddle with fate."

Alastair laughed, patting his shoulder. "You did well, Albius. You did very well. The young fight what they feel so hard, but they feel so fiercely." The old man extended a hand to Nia. "Come, little hen, give your old papa a dance. Though you will have to be on your own two feet, I don't know if I can carry you the same as when you were little."

Nia grinned bright and took his hand. "You can still spin me, papa."

My brother stalked from the balcony where he was quietly watching us from and dragged Thora to the dance floor. Both glaring at each other, words spoken through clenched teeth as they slowly spun to the soft sound of music.

He'd not said a word at me. Not one. Not after our conversation after Lake Astrid. Not after I'd told him all the truth.

"Dance with me?" I asked Snow and she gave me a bright nod.

She was tightly pressed to me as I swayed the both of us slowly despite the cheery jig and the jumping people surrounding us. Her golden eyes dazzled, amazed as they landed on everyone in the room. The more she looked, the brighter her smile became, the louder her heartbeat.

When her eyes turned watery and her smile died, I lifted her face to mine. "Don't let me lose you again."

"I'm terrified," she confessed, and my heart clenched.

I pressed my lips to her because I could, because my heart had torn from all the times that I'd not been able to. "So am I."

"Will it go away?"

"As long as I am with you, love of mine, never be afraid. Even if danger prevails, even if your father wages war, even when there is time to fear, do not fear. Never fear. Because there is no rock, no mountain, no sea that I will not cross or tear through to come to you. You are not alone. Never alone. Never again. Tell me," I said, kissing her—kissing her because I could. "Tell me that you know that. That even in the worst of times you will not be afraid. Tell me."

"I will not. I will not be afraid."

I kissed her again. "Tell me that you know I will always be with you and if I am not, I will find a way."

"I know."

"Tell me that you know how much I love you."

"I know."

"Tell me," I whispered over her lips. "Tell me you love me."

"I love you, Kil."

My smile could not be contained. "Then marry me, love of mine."

She blinked stunned for a moment. "We already are. I never tore the paper."

My face hurt from happiness. "Before the gods. I want to bear the mark of our union. To heaven or to hells, I want to part along with you and when you do. I will not stay in this realm a second longer than you and I want to be with you in all our lifetimes."

"You're an Obscur and gods know what I am." She shook her head. "They won't bless us."

I kissed her red lips. They knew—gods knew better than to deny us. "Do you trust me?"

"I do."

"Then marry me."

"Alright."

"Tonight."

Her eyes almost popped out of their sockets. "Tonight?"

"If I have to wait one other day—"

She shook her head. "I won't make you wait anymore."

That made me smile. "Good. Let's gather everyone in the moon gardens."

She nodded. "I could wear something white, too."

"No," I said, shaking my head. "Red—I want you in red. You are fire, woman."

She chuckled, backing away and diving into the crowd while I faded to Amaris to find Atlas.

Everyone had clustered in the moon gardens, confused as an overly excited Atlas and Penelope led them to sit down on the cushions they had laid down on the grass.

As if they knew my joy, the stars had taken the front seat and sprinkled the skies with their presence from corner to corner. The moon also stood proudly full and radiant.

Snow arrived moments later, her hair unbound and spilling over her shoulders, a red silk and lace dress floated around her. She glistened—glistened like the first snow, like the northern star on a summer sunset. So majestic and divine. Even though the tarp of the moon goddess hung above us carrying one of her finest works, what stood before me was unmatched. I was born an adorer of night, but I'd forever live and die as her worshipper.

"You're staring," she said, reaching a hand to my face. "Hard. Are you leering at me?"

"I'm debating. I've never been one to pray, but it must be this newfound religion of mine. Do I go down on my knees or do I kiss a prayer away? How do I show my faith that I needed saving and that she has saved me?"

Her eyes rounded—they turned to my shining suns and there was suddenly so much light amidst all the dark. "Tell her that you love her. It is what saved her."

I rested my forehead against hers and breathed an unrestricted breath. "I love you, Snow."

"And I love you, Kil."

"Are we to know why we are being called all secretly in here?" Mal asked, his glances jumping between Snow and I.

Alaric suddenly stood from his seat and took one short look at us and then Atlas before he said, "You want to get married."

"You what?" Driada and Eren both asked at once, the rest were still grasping what was happening.

"We want to get married," Snow said, clutching my hand tighter.

Alaric's eyes filled with tears. "You love the boy?"

She nodded. "I love the boy very much so."

My heart threatened to burst out of my chest.

The older man beamed despite the tears pouring out of his eyes. He turned to my brother. "Did you hear that, boyo? She said *very much so*."

"You heard that too, huh?" My brother said, crossing his arms. "Thought the younger one struck me too hard in the head a moment ago."

Thora was too overwhelmed to even pay attention to my brother, she jumped from her seat and flew in her sister's arms, hugging her tight.

And so did Nia, shedding heavy tears for her friend. "I knew it," she said, holding Snow tightly. "I knew it. I've always known it. I am so happy, Snow."

"So am I," her friend whispered back. "I am happy, Nia."

Cai stood at her side, extending a reluctant hand to her head and then pulling her to him. They didn't say a word. I don't think they needed to. It was how it had always been with them. But he did bring a foil wrapped candy and handed it to her. "Samira makes them."

Snow gaped, taking the candy from him. "Why are you telling me this now?"

"Because I never knew how to make you happy any other way. This was my only trick to bring you out of whatever room you locked yourself in."

"Cai—"

He patted her cheek and turned to me. "I only had one. But maybe she has learned to share."

Snow unravelled the sweet and popped it on her mouth. "Let's not go that far."

Night was serene overhead and the garden a pool of sweet scents and fireflies. All sorts of magical folk had gathered to witness our union, littering our clothes with glitter and silently whispering sugar and sweet spice about Snow's beauty and their excitement at what had never been witnessed before—the joining of two different Aura.

Snow and I knelt facing one another in the middle of the white flowers that had fully bloomed under the starry skies. It almost…almost felt like the cruellest dream I could have ever dreamt of. The girl I'd loved for almost fifteen years stood before me. And she loved me back. Her eyes gleamed—they shone so bright. They shone looking at me. They shone round and full, beady and warm, they shone for me like they shone for no other. They shone how I'd always dreamed they would shine.

Atlas lowered a bowl of water between us with shaky hands, managing to spill most of it on the grass. "The mirror of gods."

Snow squirmed where she sat and swallowed nervously staring at the reflective surface of the water.

"Remember," I said, holding her hands tightly in mine. "For all we care, we have already blessed us."

Her thumbs smoothed over my skin. "We have."

Atlas lit a sage garni, the bitter scent spreading in the wind and the white smoke forming circles around us. "The messenger of gods." If the smoke wavered, we would be blessed and if it disappeared, gods would have sealed their disapproval.

"We gather tonight to seek your blessing," Atlas spoke loud and clear without stuttering and my chest boosted with pride. He was doing better these days. "To unite Kilian Henrik Castemont, born of Henah and Snowlin Edlynne Castemont, born of Krig and Nubil."

Snow smiled at him, and the young priest blushed red to the tip of his hair. "Will you vow to one another, will you vow to live, to prosper, to love. To join a soul and live this life and all the next as one?"

"I vow," I said.

"I vow," Snow repeated.

Atlas raised his palms to the skies, the markings of gods painted on his palms glowed gold when they were touched by moonlight. The wind picked up, swaying the moonflower, her obsidian hair billowing around her, blending in with the marvel of night. "I call to unite these two souls as one, to live and part this lifetime and all the next—together. I call for this union to be marked as one, to be marked for eternity as one soul made of two." Atlas raised the sage garni between and all around us to leave a visible mark from the smoke. "I call for your blessing."

Every heartbeat was loud in the air as they all held their breath. Waiting.

A gust of wind blew the smoke away, letting it disappear through the night and Snow's hand loosened in my hold. Her face fell and something mellow slipped in her stare—sadness.

The ground suddenly shook around us and something poked the ground where we stood, pushing to the surface. One by one, dozens of stems of white roses bloomed around us.

"What—" Snow didn't get to finish her thought because the sky brightened by light. The sun stood by the moon, not facing each other—standing by one another. And then flakes of snow brushed upon our skin, blowing lightly in the spring wind. Torches around the garden blew alit one by the other and songbirds flew overhead us, warbling a sweet tune that sent the magical folk spinning with excitement and joy. It was something of a dream.

"Mother? Sam?" Snow called looking behind me and everyone turned, gasping.

Two figures stood behind us, half fading in the night. Serene and Sam watched us from the distance, a bright teary smile on each of their faces. The gift from the god of death.

Everyone spun round, a mix of tears and unbridled happiness echoing between them.

"By the approval of gods, I call you married," Atlas said. "You might seal your bond with a kiss."

I cupped my wife's face and kissed her—unhurriedly. We had all the time in the world, so in that moment I tasted her softness and warmth—I tasted the sweetness of the lily perfume and the salt from her tears.

All of a sudden, the night was night again and the wind was no longer cold, but warm and gentle. Her loved ones no longer stood behind us and the torches had blown off. The only remainder of what had happened stood around us in aromatic white petals and the golden bands of crawling thorns around our ring fingers.

"And blessed you are," Alaric said, breaking our reverie and everyone clapped after him, howling and cheering as loud as they could, waking every sleeping soul in Amaris and in the skies above.

"I've never had that happen before," Atlas commented, looking still astounded.

Snow blinked stunned at the roses around us. "It has to be because I threatened to burn their heavens," she said with a wince. "They know I know I can now."

I raised a brow at her. "So, you don't think they've blessed us because we are in love?"

Her mouth parted open. "No."

"No?"

"I mean, yes."

I cocked my head back looking down at her. "Hm?"

She grinned brightly and jumped in my arms, toppling us both back on the grass, hugging me tightly to her. "You're forever mine. In this life and all the next." She pulled back and kissed me, hungrily. "Secured your pretty buttocks a gracious spot in hells. At least you will always be warm. Right by the pits."

That made me chuckle. "It is better for your pores, too. At least I'll hear no complaints."

A throat cleared beside us and Snow, though reluctantly, pulled away. Alaric pointed his chin to my hands on her hips. "Would you please hold my kid a bit more respectfully."

Snow sneered and gave him a lethal look. "You should see all the other respectful positions–" I quickly put a hand over her mouth, holding her from making Alaric my deathly enemy.

"Will do."

He nodded his thanks and clasped my snickering brother's shoulder. "Take us to Taren? I have a feeling none of us are wanted around anymore."

Mal gave me a smug look and winked. "Gladly."

After everyone passed their congratulations, they all reluctantly left, one by one.

"That would be my cue too," Atlas said, folding Astrum liber and standing on wobbly legs. He must have been scared.

Snow grabbed his wrist. "Thank you, Atlas."

Atlas blushed but he nodded. "Nothing to be thankful for, my queen. This was an honour."

She gave him a playful grin. "I'm alright with you calling me mama."

The young priest sighed. "My childhood mistakes precede me."

Snow shrugged. "If you felt safe enough to give him that name, then it was not a mistake. We make our own families, young Atlas, we are not born in them. Blood is blood as piss is piss, just another overrated body fluid."

I clasped his shoulder. "It made me very proud when you called me that. I've always told you not to feel embarrassed."

His cheeks flushed and he bowed to her then me. "I wish you both the very best."

"Good night, Atlas."

He blinked at her for a moment. "Uh, good...night, I suppose."

Not a second after he'd left, she jumped on my arms, toppling the both of us to the ground again.

Her mouth had tortured me all the way to our room, kisses, tongue and teeth, till my cock had strained so tight against my britches it was aching.

"My little kitten," I said, running a knuckle along her cheek as I backed us into the room. "What does my wife want?"

"You know what I want."

"Do you want your husband to fuck you."

She nodded.

"Remember that one promise, love?" I asked, pushing her against a wall.

"Vaguely."

This woman. I took her mouth in mine, begging for a taste of her. And now that she was all mine and all for me to taste. I'd found the fountain of starvation and only needed to be fed from it. My hand slid between us to cup between her legs, my fingers circling her cunt. "Fuck, love, you've soaked your pretty laces."

She moaned when I flicked her swollen nub and pinched it between my fingers. "I...I don't want to play."

My brows hiked up. "No?"

She grinded her hips against mine. "Fuck me, will you?" Her lips parted in a gasp when I drew my hand and slapped her between the legs. "Please, I meant, please."

"Is your cunt begging for me?" She nodded, and my fingers played with the seam of her underwear before I tugged to tear them away. "Is it weeping for me?" She nodded again and jerked a little when I slid two fingers down her entrance. "My cock gets a little harder when you tell me the truth." My mouth pulled onto a grin and she rolled her eyes. Another whack. "The only time you're going to roll them again is when I'm inside you," I said, undoing my britches with a hand, palming my cock and sliding inside her wet cunt.

She sucked a breath, her head lolling back, and I groaned when her warm muscles tightened around me, pulling me in further. I'd take my time with her, but she was wet enough to take me easily so I didn't hold back.

She tightened her arms around my neck and I pulled out, thrusting deep again. When her moans and whimpers of approval filled the room, I started fucking her. Faster and harder, pounding into her till the sound of our joining grew louder and louder.

So. Fucking. Beautiful.

And all mine.

All. Mine.

In this life and every life after this one.

My hand slipped to her breast and up her neck, my fingers wrapping around her slender throat as I lowered my mouth to hers while thrusting into her. Her heartbeats pounded against my chest and my own thundered in my ears as I made her mine. Our limbs had meshed together, every touch had grown demanding and rough, teeth dug onto my neck, she marked me as I marked her.

I kissed her because I could. She whimpered in my mouth, her chest stuttering, nails digging on my back. "Kilian, harder," Her thighs tightened around me for a moment, squeezing, and my name on her mouth turned to a chant full of command, adjure, anguish and exalt all at once. Magic skittered around me and I guided a thin tendril of shadows around her body and over the apex of her thighs to graze that sensitive bundle of nerves and her body jerked a little in my hold.

Her sweet moans were delicious. I tasted them around my tongue and ate all of those vowels. I was so hungry for them that I plunged my cock inside of her relentlessly only so I could hear them grow louder and fuller. I fucked her through her own release, riding out her pleasure while my own erupted and spilled inside of her. Fucking euphoric. She felt so good wrapped around my cock, pulsing with pleasure around me as I filled her insides with my come. "My hellcat is so polite and quiet when I fill her cunt. Maybe I should stay buried in you all the time."

Her pretty hair had matted to her face, sweat droplets beading to her temples while she breathed like the thunder raging outside. She bit that lower plump lip and flashed me a smile. "I've not got much room to speak."

"I'll go slower next time. Curious what you have to say while I fuck you."

"I'll prepare a speech," she said, wiggling her hips and I hissed when my cock slipped a bit deeper inside her.

I kissed that sassy mouth. "It better be an ode to my cock."

She laughed all the way to the bathroom, trying to make verses of all sorts of madness about it. My girl was no poet and that was for sure.

After I'd soaked the two of us in the bath, told her all sorts of stories she wanted to hear about me, fed her and stared at her for a long, long eternity that never seemed to be long enough, I took her again and then she rode me long and slow a third time.

We laid there for a moment after, her fingers on my hair, mine tracing along her skin.

"I want to keep you, Kil."
"I'm afraid you're stuck with me till forever."

CHAPTER FORTY-ONE

Siderus

Snowlin

It was bright and warm. Mostly inside of me in that cold place I called a heart. Or perhaps because a massive man had hugged me to his chest so tight that I was starting to sweat.

I'd stared at the gold tattoo on my ring finger for the past hour—half stunned and half grinning. We'd been blessed. Even heavens and gods had approved of us being together despite all that was against us.

Kilian traced his finger over my stomach as if he was scribbling words.

I half turned to him. "What does that mean?"

He left about a dozen kisses on my face. "Names."

"Whose?"

His grin was stupidly ridiculous. "Of all the babies I'm going to put in you."

Oh. The thought made my toes curl. Would we ever be able to have a family of our own? With what we were? "Will you feed them to me?"

He chuckled and leaned to whisper in my ear. "If you keep swallowing me, yes."

I kicked my elbow back, hitting him on the stomach and he groaned as if I'd actually hurt him. "There were a few. How many exactly are you expecting us to have."

"Eight."

I spun round fast. "You want me to give birth to eight children?"

He slid his fingers in my hair, silver irises taking in every bit of me. "We can adopt."

I chewed on my lip and he pulled the bleeding flesh from my teeth with his thumb. "Tell me. Don't leave me in the dark. Tell me everything that worries you."

"I'd be a terrible mother. I wouldn't want a child to grow as I did. But you," I said, touching the tips of my fingers to his face, "you'd be an amazing father. I'd want to have those eight children just so they could grow to be loved by you."

"We have all the time in the world, Snow, for you to figure out how I see you and how others know you to be. We have all the time in the world for me to show you what you have never seen and known about yourself. If you only were able to see what I see. Perhaps you'd fall in love with yourself, too. I want you to fall in love with yourself, too. To love this person that you are as I do, as your family does. Terrible is a word I wish you would never use for the woman who is the most magnificent to me." He dropped a kiss to my lips and stood. "Let's go feed you some proper food. If your stomach growls at me one more time I will growl back at it."

I kicked my foot on his shoulder and he chuckled.

The second he turned his back to me, I gasped, a hand slapping over my mouth. "Kil?"

Confused, he turned to me, a worried expression painted on his beautiful face. "What's the matter, my love?"

Fear filled my stomach and I almost felt sick. "Why do you bear the mark of Keres?"

He glanced at his shoulder, over at the little black mark of the death guardian, and then went utterly still.

"Answer me," I said, standing and crawling onto his lap. I shook my head, it couldn't be—I had to be wrong. "You did die." A tear slipped from my eye and then another. "You did die." Oh gods. Oh gods. No. Every feel on my body was seized from panic—thick panic that rendered me without air.

"I am here now," he said, leaning in to kiss my tears away.

"This is all my fault," I pushed away from him, crawling away from him. "This is all my fault." Walls were suddenly too close and closing in on me and I couldn't breathe. Not until I was back in his arms and he straightened my spinning world.

He cradled me in his chest. "Shhh. Love, Snow, open your eyes." After kissing me dizzy, he murmured, "Am I not here?"

"You are."

"Does anything else matter?"

"Kil—"

"Does anything matter, my heart?"

"No. No, it doesn't." It did. It did. But I was too thankful to have him here than to question anymore. He had died. Kilian had died.

Kilian clutched my hand tight as we made our way to the castle's back gardens.

"You know, I won't vanish if you hold me a little less tight."

"You might just do so," he said, yet there was not an ounce of amusement in his voice.

"Already clinging to you?" Mal asked, leaning back in his chair and munching on an apple, narrowing his eyes on us as we sat down on the table. He'd been quiet since lake Asterin—his brother was worried beyond the usual level of constant worry he had for him.

"Must be strange for you, Malik," my sister said, chewing on a piece of toast while reading some sort of poetry. "To hold a woman's hand. The only place you've had a woman's hand wrapped around is probably your—"

"Rora," Eren called, eyes wide on our little sister. He sighed, rubbing a hand over his eyes. "Not another one of you."

Driada put the back of her hand to her mouth and laughed herself to tears.

"Never a dull moment with you Skygards," Mal said. "But yes, you are quite correct. The more the merrier."

My sister cringed. "You make me gag."

Mal chewed slowly. "If you ask nicely about it."

I'd erupted in chuckles, but the frown on my husband's brows and Thora's glare made me straighten my reaction.

"So," Mal asked, "how are the happy married couple? Besides being tired, obviously, as it oddly seems you two are quite refreshed. Has my brother lost his vigour at his old age?"

Kilian stared pure frost into him, but the younger brother was unbothered.

"If you tell me, I will tell you," I said.

He glanced at his mother and then Thora before giving me a stupid grin. "Well played."

Driada laughed again, but this time it turned to a rough cough that almost tore her ribs.

My sister shot from her seat as did I. She took a tissue and cleaned the blood dripping from her mouth before resting a palm on her chest till her breathing grew back to normal. "Better?"

"Much," Driada said, patting her hand and giving us all a little smile as if to disperse our worry. "Please eat, don't let me ruin your meal."

The necklace I'd given her had paled to a dull grey colour. That had never happened before. She was not getting better. I could practically feel Kilian's ache as though it was my own, the way his attention went downcast broke my heart even more.

Mal's face was grim when pushed to his feet to leave. My sister wrapped a hand around his wrist, stopping him. "Sit, Malik. You haven't finished yet."

They weren't looking at one another as if they were purposefully trying not to.

His hand slipped through my sister's, and I swear they both flinched just a little. I don't know what was happening between the two, how they trusted one another or why Mal sat down and continued to eat his meal after my sister had told him so. But it was something between the two of them.

And everyone else on the table, despite their curiosity, thought so too.

The Autumn Queen awaited in the middle of Kilian's garden, her attention cast at the blanket of colour that spring had blessed the bushes with. She bowed her head to us, her eyes lingering over the gold band tattooed around my ring finger. "My congratulations," she said, bringing a small seed from her pocket. "A wedding gift."

I blinked between her and the tiny thing. "This is why they sing you songs of generosity."

Her reaction was as blank as a sheet of paper when she dropped the seed on the soil and rested a palm over it. Within seconds, a small green sprout broke between the ground and raised upward for several feet. Its stem thickened, several branches jutted along sprouting leaves and white flowers till the tree stood tall as though it had been there for decades.

"Lemon flower," I said, raising a hand to a branch heavy with them.

She nodded. "It will stay as such forever. Whether it's winter or spring, it will always have the white bloom."

Kilian seemed confused looking at the tree. "Why this particular one?"

"In Hanai, that time you got injured, she told me it is her favourite."

When his eyes found mine, a smile stretched on his lips. "Hanai, huh?"

"Before," I said, and his smile morphed into a massive grin. Moriko cleared her throat. "I come bearing bad news."

CHAPTER FORTY-TWO

Salum

Snowlin

We all stood over the Dardanes map.

"Around four dozen Crafters," Elias said. "That has been counted within Tenebrose walls alone. No one is permitted anywhere near the castle. Servants say the Crafter quarters are being loaded with all sorts. Potions, herbs, furniture, weapons." He moved his finger toward Modr where the northern war camps were stationed. "Freya sent news that spies have reported beast sightings. *Endless* beast sightings."

"The Crafters are helping him create them quicker than Melanthe would have on her own," Kilian said, tapping a finger on the table. "How is Silas able to control them?"

Elias brought something from his pocket—a whistle? "Paid a soldier a gold limb for that. He said Moregan kept one on her every time she brought along one of them to her expeditions. Their guess and mine is on that."

"*Ouht*," Visha said in Borsich. "It's how we train Canes and Wraths. An old Crafter had studied the call of a queen songbird to her flock and mimicked it to fit with other species. Like the call of an alfa—it's called *ouht*."

"Smart," Mal murmured. "How do we learn it? I mean, it's not like we have the weapons to fight them. Except for Snow and Kilian."

"And us," Eren said. "Mine and Thora's magic is still divine. It can kill them. We might not be Silas's weapon, but we can still be made a weapon."

"You haven't used your magic in ten years, Eren, you mean *I* am still a weapon," Thora said, staring ahead onto the height of Taren, and the room tensed a little.

"The times call for it to be used, Rora. I will use it."

Our sister looked over her shoulder at him, blinking slowly, but did not say anything, only turned toward the open balcony, looking down at the tall fall—unafraid.

"We have unblessed metal," Oryn said from the far corner of the room. "We would only need a smith and the heart of a sphinx."

Kilian ran a hand through his eyes. "Silas has a heart. Our best chance at finding one big enough to supply an army is in an underground market. But I still highly doubt one would sell it. No coin is worth the power one has."

"We could steal his," Nia said and winced. "I've hid and studied that castle for three moons. I know every corner of it."

"Too dangerous," both Kilian and I said at once.

"Besides," Eren said, "father would be an idiot to keep it anywhere near castle grounds. He probably stashed everything far from Tenebrose. And considering he does not trust any lord in his court, I'd say none are in Isjord at all."

"You're right," Kilian said. "He would be keeping it where his smiths are."

Elias nodded. "Possibly in one of the war camps since the metal was being delivered there."

I asked, "Which war camp?"

"Seraphim."

"Makes sense," Kilian agreed.

"If we can't attack it, what if we sneak a spy inside the camps?" Cai asked.

Elias shook his head. "Impossible for even a captain to get closer than three miles. Patrols are like hound dogs everywhere. Veils surround each and every tent. And you wouldn't be able to get a proper verification to go inside it."

"Renick," I said, "he'll get it for us. Select a soldier, Elias, instruct him and I will get the proper verification."

"What do we do about Eldmoor?" Nia asked. "If Urinthia is working with Silas, this is a lost war."

Visha stood to her feet. "My mother would never aid Silas. And I say that with conviction."

"She is certainly doing something for Silas, V," Elias said. "Would Red Coven allow so many of your sisters and brothers to help him create the very same monsters that your god punished you once for?"

"No," the Crafter admitted, eyes lowering on the map. "They'd be banished from Eldmoor for generations." Her fingers fumbled with her beaded bracelets. "What if we send someone to make contact with her? Not spy her. Offer her a bargain. My mother would never say no to one without considering first. It is in our primal instincts to hear the terms before refusing it."

Nia nodded. "I will go. I've spent the past three months in Asra, studying Red Coven and the veil around it. I know the people, the streets, the way around the veil and where I've planted the blue gyre to weaken it—it should have taken some effect by now."

"Too dangerous," Kilian and I said at the same time and my friend frowned at us.

Cai shook his head. "Even if you make it in, the chances that the witches will entertain what you have to say before turning you into a caged bird are very slim."

"Then I will go with her," Mal said. "Urinthia knows me and so does most of Red Coven. And I know Eldmoor."

"Then what?" Cai asked, leaning his hip on the table. "We convince the Grand Maiden not to work with Silas? As if that is something someone can do."

"Urinthia and I have worked with one another for years," Kilian said. "My father helped her take the position fourteen years ago. She will have enough reason to listen to what we have to say."

My friend raised a brow at all of us. "And what deal do we offer her?"

My attention went to Visha who had gathered herself tight on the top chair and remained quiet. "You can use me," she said quietly. "Bargain me for her attention. Make a deal for my return for her support against Silas."

"No," I said. "That is not up for discussion."

"How about," Penelope started, standing from where she'd been sitting quietly for the past three hours. "You bargain a secret. My father's secret. Me."

"No," all of us said in unison and the little carrot jerked a step back from surprise.

"You are a Delcour by blood and by right," I said. "That means—"

"You'd be taking my position as Grand Maiden and fulfilling the bargain of the dark god," Visha finished.

"Not unless I accept it," she said bravely. "Tell Urinthia that I will meet with her. Not that I would accept it. She cannot force me—I've read about it. One must swear a sacred oath to become Grand Maiden that not only by blood but by choice I swear to be so. The deal and our meeting will grant us some talking ground with her."

My mouth parted a little. "Talking ground? When have you started learning all of this?"

She raised her chin proudly. "You forget how much time I spend with old, wicked you. I have picked up a thing or two from the master bargainer herself."

"Alright, little carrot."

"It is set," Nia said, nodding. "Mal and I will head to Eldmoor."

Kilian had fallen asleep again in my arms, his head pressed to my chest, his grip around me so tight I was almost struggling to take a full breath. I liked being held, but I liked holding him even more. So much was happening around us, so much we had to take care of and barely any time to see one another. But he'd been so tired—so, so tired, he'd fallen asleep almost immediately.

Slowly, I slipped through his hold and rose to my feet. Planting a kiss on his forehead before gathering a robe and heading to the rooftop where I could feel a low hum of a heartbeat coming from.

Alaric sat at the edge of the wide terrace inhaling and exhaling a white puff of smoke. The moment he spotted me, he threw the tin of cigarettes down the height of the castle and dusted his jacket. A tinkle resonated on the valley below where his tin had hit rock and he winced.

"Too late, old man, you stink of cloves," I said, settling beside him. Only then I noticed the redness in his eyes and what he held in his palm—Sam's sunstone necklace.

He closed his fist and sighed. "Thought there would be no better time to wait for a sunrise than now."

I gathered myself tight, leaning to rest my chin on my knees, staring at the thin bronze strip of sunlight rising over the Taren mountains. "I wish he was here."

"He is," he said, looking down at the necklace, a stream of tears chasing down his beard. "I feel him in the breeze sometimes. Maybe I am growing insane, maybe what I feel comes with ageing, but I swear it, kid, I always feel him close by."

"Why can't I feel him?" I murmured. "Does he hate me, Ric?"

"He hated no one, let alone you." The old man bumped his knuckles to my chin. "You had the man wrapped around your fingers. He adored you."

"He died because of me."

"He died for you. For a better world."

"He might have died for nothing."

"You are doing the right thing, kid."

"I am not," I said truthfully, finally bearing the weight of my own decision out in the open. "Not to the girl from thirteen years ago that lost everything that night. For thirteen long years I kept her alive with thoughts of destruction and retaliation. I fed her with violence and blood when she wanted nothing but starve away. She still wants that, Ric. I think I have to let her die so I can live with the decision I've made. I have to bury her so I can't see her suffer for denying her that revenge."

Alaric grabbed my hand when I stood. "Watch the sunrise with me."

"I can't. Though I love and am loved, there is still hate in my heart. And it might never go away." I looked over the rising sunset and smiled at the surface of magenta and coral. "You're beautiful as always, Sam."

When I returned to our bedroom, Kilian stirred awake a little and blinked heavy sleep off his lids. "What is it, love of mine?" he asked, resting a gentle hand on my cheek.

Instead of telling him, I buried my face in the crook of his shoulder, inhaling the scent of spring on him. "I missed you." Perhaps I didn't need to bury her at all. Perhaps I'd bruised her back in that lake enough that she had died on her own.

He lifted my face and stared at me with those all-knowing eyes of his. "Have I lost you again?"

"No, you've found me. You always have found me."

"Then tell me. Make it my ache, too. I don't wish to feel anything different from you."

I shook my head. "It will pass. I am sure it will pass."

He knew what I meant. He knew what every word of mine meant. "Forgive me."

"It is not your fault."

"It has always been my fault. Always." He kissed me slowly, tasting me, savouring me. "Always. It will always be."

"I came into that garden, not you."

"But it is I who fell for you."

My smile was bright and his own mimicked mine. "My silver eyed boy."

"My little miss who has become my missus. I always hoped you remembered the moment where you became my all."

"I remember." I realised that the world was all too pale for all the colour I felt for this man. The world was too hollow for the way he'd stuffed my heart so tightly with emotion I didn't even know I could feel. The world was all too dim for how bright it got when he looked at me, when he smiled at me. And the world was all too cold for how warm he felt against me, how warm he made it inside of me.

Perhaps I didn't have to bury her. Perhaps she had buried herself underneath all that he'd gifted me. Perhaps that girl had needed to feel all and all of this. Perhaps she'd wanted it but denied herself.

His fingers were gentle on my face. "You're gone again."

"I'm right here."

Part V
Night

CHAPTER FORTY-THREE

Carmen

Snowlin

There was an odd calm in Myrdur after I'd claimed the bargain with my father—after I'd claimed oath on the land as mine and belonging back to Olympia. The breeze brushing past my skin was soft and sweet. It smelled of apple and rain and the softest scent of peace. The Fogling had not been seen anywhere anymore and I liked to think that their tormented souls had finally found peace and left the land for the heavens as had the spirits that used to roam the ruins.

Cai leaned down and plucked something from the ground. A tiny anemone that had sprouted on every rock, valley, and field lately. His smile was huge and ridiculous, and I could practically see the future he was dreaming of flashing on his emerald stare.

Life was beginning to grow back in old Olympia and not a foot of Isjordian soldiers had stepped ever since I'd gotten the sceptre from Valda. Had my father given up on the sceptre? Was he going to open war the good old way? He had the favour after all. It was in his blood to be war itself. But then, so was I. And this haunting silence was louder than any raging storm.

Eren stepped beside Cai and took the purple flower from him, studying the delicate thing and my friend's reaction. "You give your happiness to the strangest things there are."

He turned to my brother, grabbed his jaw and kissed him. And silly me thought it would stop there. When he began backing him to the wall and sneaking a hand down his waist, I dashed. That was something I could have lived without seeing.

Albius stood on a broken terrace, overlooking the city. "The regret that I will carry beyond my death," he sighed, full of anguish. "We could have stopped your father that night. We could have at least tried. But we let him march into Olympia, steal your mother and ruin one of the greatest kingdoms the realm had seen." He turned to me, regarding me as he always did—with the greatest respect anyone had ever given me. "Fate works in strange dishonest ways. It doesn't always favour us, but we try and make the best of it. You are the best of this rotten fate. I have faith you will make great efforts to restore some goodness in Isjord's own fate."

The thoughts crossing my mind right now were nothing short of violent and bloodied. No flower had ever bloomed beneath my feet. I intended to plant no garden in Isjord—not one with flowers at least. "You always thought that even though you knew my intentions to never be as such."

"I had faith, Elding queen. I always had faith." He smiled to himself. "I had it even after my own faith, Creda, died. My wife wanted me to live long after her. She made me make an oath that I would not follow after her. I made an oath that I would stay and see Isjord, our land, become what it always should have been—a wintery heaven." He took my hands in his. "Do this old man a favour and let me unite with my loved one."

"I can't make a promise." Not when I was planning to turn Isjord into a wintery hell.

He shook his head. "I wish for no promise, pumpkin. They always end up disappointing one or the other. But I do wish your skies would shine as they are shining now. When you find a reason to glow, you will never want to be dull." He patted my hand and took a deep breath, overlooking the distance toward the Hollow Sea cliffs. "Your father has been quiet. It is not a good sign when he is quiet. A snake always strikes when the prey is at rest."

"The bargain," I said. "I will not hesitate to use it." And I was not speaking about his allegiance in court. When I called our bargain, I'd do more damage than hurting my father. Each one that had bargained with me had signed off more than their life and loyalty. If I was going to be fire, I might as well burn my brightest.

He nodded, touching a shaky hand to his arm. "The walls would have come down one way or another. By peace or by fire, they would have all come down one day."

And perhaps Albius had been right.

Kilian and Thora were already there when I arrived at the Highwall tower. Both of them stood next to one another, arms crossed, a glacial look in their faces as they stared down at the woman sitting before them.

My husband stirred from his frozen state and turned to round me in his arms for a brief moment before pressing a kiss to my lips. It was brief and quick, but it was all I needed—all that my soul needed to spring with life. "She showed at the gates, asking to see you. She said you two know one another."

Know?

The woman raised her eyes at me and bowed her head. "We meet again," she said with a soft voice. "Snowlin."

Disdain crawled up my features. "I've always known, Macaria, that you'd be smart enough to face death without death searching for you." She had not aged a day. Her plum hair was still long and straight, her eyes the darkest of black. Macaria. Urinthia's second in command. And Penelope's grandmother—the woman that Donovan, Urinthia's father, had cheated on his wife with and birthed him a bastard son with the name Lysander. The 102nd Grand Maiden was a lot of things, just not one to hold grudges and waste talent. Talent that this one had plenty in her bag. The violet witch. The one who could see so far in your future, she could predict death and victories. The same one who had foreseen my father's success in Olympia and prompted him to attack with confidence. Some said she'd made a deal with a death godling in hells and fed him living souls every equinox. Others dared to make assumptions that she was a lovechild of hells beast and that she fed on living souls to foresee without consequence. But right now, she looked like she'd seen better days. "An odd choice of fashion for someone who has come to die."

Her hands shook and she laced them together on her lap. Fear was the last thing I thought I'd see from her. Not when she'd come to me herself. "I need your help."

That made me laugh a little. "That is a little melodramatic even for you."

Her onyx stare shivered. "Last night, Red Coven was attacked, and our Grand Maiden was taken hostage. By your father."

It took me a moment to gather what she had revealed. "Why would my father do that?"

"Because he is certain that the sceptre pieces are almost ready to assemble, and for that, he will need a Grand Maiden's magic to do so."

I scoffed. "He is delusional by default. Your Grand Maiden will be briefly returned to you, I assure you."

She steeled a look at me. "Because you have the three other sceptre pieces?"

What?

Kilian stepped forward, his jaw ticking. "And how would you come to assume that, witch?"

"I know everything. I foresee it all. Urinthia saw it all, too." Her gaze drifted all guilt to the ground. When had this poison ivy turned to a wall flower? "Months ago, Urinthia performed a celestial craft, possessing the body of an Umbra to steal the Esmeray diaries in her astral form."

"That was you?" I asked, suddenly struck with all the answers. The odd Canes and how they had been able to get the book despite the veil.

She nodded. "You had to know what you are. To know what you are able to do and retrieve the sceptre pieces. We thought you would be able to read about your ancestor and figure out how to defeat Aurora. Perhaps even destroy the sceptre itself."

Ice crawled over my hands. "Always the unnecessary scheming and plotting with you witches. Couldn't you just have told me rather than make me chase circles for months?"

She shrunk back at the sight of my magic. "Not with your father looming and looking for every opportunity to get hold of her. We haven't stepped once outside our coven for two years now. We've lost...we've lost many of our own trying to keep Silas away from Urinthia. And we lost even more when they began pledging to Melanthe and chose to serve your father. There is a new revolution within our kind." Her mouth twisted. "They think of her as some sort of a death god."

Thora shot to her feet again. "Why would Silas need the Grand Maiden's magic for the sceptre?"

"To assemble it all together," Macaria said. "Five hundred years ago, the 49th Grand Maiden and her daughter used a certain craft to divide the sceptre. The sceptre's magic was holy and heavenly, it took her many tries to manage and dissemble it and it takes an even more complicated one to reassemble it. She combined an *anima accissor* weapon along with her magic to cut it and by the same sort of weapon shall it be forged. One that takes weeks to months to years to craft and there are not many smiths who are willing or capable of completing such a weapon. The elements are rare too. Unblessed metal mined without magic, the heart—"

"The heart of an Aitan Sphinx," Kilian said, running a hand through his hair. "And he found that in Solarya. He already has all he needs to craft one. Probably already had a smith moulding one, too."

The witch nodded. "The eight elder Crafter's left pieces of hidden keys all over the hiding places to make the assembling even more challenging. The Sphinx, the diaries, the Grand Maiden. Finding the pieces was never the hard part, assembling them was. This is where it gets worse." She swallowed hard. "The sceptre cannot be wielded by just anyone. Kegan did not lose control of it. He could not control it to begin with, so Aurora's own anger took charge back then."

"You're not making sense."

"You," she said, looking at me like *I* was some sort of a death god. "Your bloodline was asked to wield the sceptre. Only the Elding could command Aurora. Humans are mercurial by their definition. And Fader hates that about us more than anything so he asked Zephyr, Nubil's second, after he descended in Numen to be with his wife to pass this ability to all his generations. Only the divine can control the divine."

Hells. "Then how would father wield the sceptre?"

"By becoming divine." Hells.

"Almost," Macaria said, unhooking a pouch from her belt and bringing a folded piece of paper from it. She smoother the edges and pointed down at an old, faded drawing of what looked like some sort of armour. "Kegan and Silas have not been the only greedy kings in this realm. Eons ago, another Krigborn king that you all might know by the name of Tenebrose, drew this. An *anima accissor* armour that would mimic the divine. One that would trick the sceptre's power. Fortunately, he died before he could assemble all the pieces to complete. But your father already has all of them."

To say that I'd been stunned into stupor was an understatement. How...how long had father been planning this for? Then came the realisation. Bitter and burning. "This...this is why father had us. Why he ruined Olympia. He wanted someone to wield the sceptre. He ruined my kingdom so there would be no more Elding to wield the sceptre."

When Macaria nodded, my sight coated red. It blurred with fury. And then burned with rage. I was sure I was breathing out fire. "He never intended to use us in the first place. He only wanted to bend us to his will." The way he'd acted when I'd returned to Isjord—had this been why, had he thought he could still use me?

Thora rested a hand on mine. "It is okay, Snow. We are okay."

"We are not, Rora. Not until I had his bleeding heart on my hand."

Kilian took the paper. "Who knew of this? Who knew to provide Silas with this much information?"

Macaria thought about it for a little and shook her head. "The only person who knew of the Aitan Sphinx, the Ahmes Lore, and the joining of the rod was the Grand Maiden. But Urinthia's only crime to this world is bringing that bitch back from the dead."

My mouth parted half from surprise and half from disappointment. Urinthia was the one to bring Melanthe back from the dead?

"My mother pulled Melanthe from Caligo?" Visha asked, entering the tower room. Her pulse was rapid, she seemed affected by the news—more affected than us. And the most affected I'd seen her.

Macaria jumped to her feet and Kilian lifted his sword to her throat. "Not another move."

"V-Visha?" the violet witch asked, teary eyed and reaching a trembling hand to my witch. "Is this where you have been, sweet child? For Celesteel, you look well."

Visha didn't falter though the news had shaken her plenty. "Answer me, Macaria. Did my mother bring Melanthe back?"

Macaria nodded. "It was her. Yes, it was her. Silas, he...he offered her a bargain."

"A bargain for what?" I asked.

Tears began pouring out of Macaria's onyx eyes as she raised them to my witch again full of beseech. "It was all for you, sweet Visha. Do not blame her. Your mother did all this for you. Because she loves you. We all do."

"Speak!" Visha bellowed and the walls shook a little. My witch was terrified. Horror painting her freckled face.

What had my father offered to make Urinthia Delcour shake the foundations of all she believed in?

"Silas offered her a babe in exchange for helping bring her back," Macaria revealed. "An *Ybris* babe of Delcour blood—an heir. One that would fulfil the fate of the next Grand Maiden without dying. One that could survive in the outer realms. One whose magic would be unending and would not die in the Otherworld. One that could travel between realms without dying. Melanthe's babe."

Visha put a trembling hand to her mouth while all of us were stunned in total shock.

Hells. What on seven bloody hells? Father...no, Urinthia had agreed to that? This was worse than I thought. "Why Melanthe? Of all the witches he could have had, why her?"

"Two prime Crafters need to join the sceptre. Melanthe's little sister would never be powerful enough and he'd found out Visha had disappeared. If he were to raise Aurora, there was no other choice but to bring Melanthe back."

"My mother was going to let Silas ruin a whole realm for selfishness?"

Macaria's face twisted with emotion. "She did not know his intentions and she was desperate."

Visha breathed out a shaky sigh and clutched on a table to steady herself.

"Does Melanthe know what my father intends to use her for?" I asked. I had not known how much more the veil of my father's lies had hidden. How he had planned so much right under everyone's sight. Had I underestimated him? Had I always underestimated him? Had I belittled his cruelty? His wit?

Macaria shook her head. "No one does, except us two and now you."

"So my father would use Melanthe to do his bidding and then rip the child out of her womb?"

"I'm sure you've seen worse been done, Night Queen," Macaria said with no remorse. "I'm sure you've done worse yourself."

"Missing my point, witch," I bit out. "Melanthe is his secret weapon in all of this. If he is betraying her—"

"She will do nothing. Because that is what fools in love do."

No. No. "Melanthe would not allow her child to be made a hock." Then thoughts struck me harder than steel. Father and her were cut from the same cloth. They complement one another not only in loyalty but in thoughts. "Unless it was what she wanted."

"To make her princess of hells," Visha finished, shutting her eyes tightly. "Silas's connection to the outer realms. Another divine child."

"Melanthe's sister, she said something dragged her out of Caligo," Kilian said deep in thought, smoothing a hand over my back—his calm grounding me from panic and ire. "If Urinthia held the portal open, who found her inside the Otherworld?"

"A beast. Silas's beast."

Of course. It all made sense. "How would it be able to cross to the Otherworld unscathed?"

"Because it cannot die. He is cursed to live forever."

"He?" I asked. "How do you know it is a *he*? Why would such a thing be cursed to live forever." It was Demir without doubt.

Macaria picked on the skin of her thumb nervously. "Because he is Vas, son of Zoltan, lover of Aurora. The one Fader cursed to live beyond moons and suns, days and nights, till the forever. Cursed to see his lover live a life unlived and to never love again. He gave him immortality and a lone life. A fate worse than death."

We'd stunned. All of us.

Demir was Vas?

All this time—

"How?" Visha asked, stunned at the secret they'd kept from her too.

"Vas was trapped in Nephthys along with the sceptre," Macaria explained, as I'd predicted. Her lover was the punishment Eamon had spoken about. "It is how the gods had ordered it. Facing one another. For him to see her, feel her but never reach her. When the daughter of Kegan retrieved the sceptre, she freed him without knowing what or who he was. At the time, he had been weak, unable to retrieve his lover from the girl and then Kegan. His happiness was short-lived when the Elding kings of that time gathered every Aura in the kingdom to trap Aurora before it was too late. Ever since, Vas has lived countless lives, searching to assemble the sceptre. Trying to find where the elder Crafters had hidden them. We...we tried to find him, we'd heard of his movement around Numengarth, but we idiotically thought it harmless. He was just a man then. What could he have done?"

"Man?" I asked. "How was he just a man when he is that now?"

Macaria lowered her eyes to the ground full of guilt and Visha crumbled to the floor, shaking her head. "No, no, no. Do not tell me, Macaria. Do not tell me."

The older witch said, "We kept vials of Caligo beasts' blood from the Ater battles. One night, several years ago, they were all stolen from us. Without the cast of craft, they are useless. In any other pair of hands, they would be useless. But he is not just any hand. He is touched by godly magic. We'd not heard anything, not even years later. Not until one of our Crafters had spotted the beast in Solarya, shortly before their sceptre piece was found. Vas had consumed the blood and along with his immortality, he became invincible, too."

"Father did not need the Ahmes Lore at all, did he?" Thora asked.

Macaria nodded. "It was suspected that Vas would be able to access the gates without the help of the codes. Besides the dark magic he possesses, he is made of godly magic—magic of the most powerful god in existence."

My hand went to Kilian's chest. It all made sense. Why the thing possessed dark magic, why it could retrieve the Octa virga pieces unscathed, why it could go through the heavenly gates.

Kilian's hand slid over mine and he leaned in to whisper. "You're worrying me, my heart. Nothing...nothing will happen."

My next breath was a bit easier. "Because my husband is not to be messed with?"

He kissed my cheek. "Because you will always have someone. Always. You're not running from this on your own anymore."

"If Urinthia has disappeared," Thora said, narrowing her eyes on the floor. "Why hasn't Mal and Nia returned from Eldmoor?"

Kilian and I exchanged a look. "Larg," my husband ordered. "Send word to them to return." He leaned in my ear and whispered, "It's nothing, my love. Breathe."

"Demir," I said, every thought assaulting my brain all at once. "He knows, father knows about me and my magic. Father knew the whole time I'd been there. He knew."

Everyone turned to me and Kilian held me tightly against him.

"Demir knew the whole time," I said, attempting to grasp and recall every moment that I'd spent with Aurora's human lover. "They all knew. Father was playing with me."

The game ahead blurred, suddenly the pieces shifting around and in the midst of chaos, the king had swapped with the rook—he'd castled away from my sight.

CHAPTER FORTY-FOUR

Furor

Snowlin

Kilian had travelled down to Lyra again. More unblessed ships had delivered metal this morning and he'd gone to oversee the delivery himself and hide any suspicion that might travel back to Silas through spies. We'd sent our own spies in search of a sphinx's heart, searching every underground market there was in the continent while Alaric had taken the task to find the smith through his connections in Fernfoss. If one could find the smith, it would be him.

Larg, Visha and Oryn sat beside me as we mapped down where Nia and Mal had last travelled to before we went to Eldmoor to search for them. Macaria vowed to help, and she was searching her lands along with us, allowing us access to any part of Eldmoor without restriction.

Something was crawling inside of me, a sense of panic, similar to what Nia had described to feel when she sensed me through her magic. Cai had called me paranoid twice in the last hour before he left for Myrdur. And my ears burned so he was probably still rattling to his soldiers about my paranoia.

Visha squinted in concentration, at least she was trying to, but I knew where her mind was flying off. From the way she still picked the skin on her nails, she was dreading her mother's plan. "The trace craft is not working."

"They could be under a veil," Oryn said, studying the map. "Or they could be hiding themselves from being detected from any veil. There is no right way to assume this. Only hope that their skills and magic have not failed them. Prince Malik is almost skilled as a death godling, and Nia is witty, she will adeptly get herself out of trouble."

No. Nothing was sitting right. "Nia would have returned immediately after finding out Urinthia was taken by Silas. I gave her an order. She has never disobeyed an order I've given as her queen."

The meeting room doors swung open, the two Adriatian guards breathed heavily. "Highwall—the beast is reaching Highwall."

Pulling my hood and veil up, I backed toward the balcony. "Signal for Amaris to take cover. Meet you two at the towers." Then I bolted right before the massive metallic gates sealing us to safety.

Soldiers poured from the steps all rushing toward me.

"My queen," they bowed in unison. "Three units are approaching south, about a dozen each."

Three units?

"Send someone to Kirkwall and alert Sebastian to delay them as much as he can," I ordered, still confused. What was father hoping to do with three dozen men? Tickle me till I surrendered?

A soldier stepped forward. "We did, my queen. Half an hour ago when our spies sent news of their approach. They couldn't find the Kirkwall Lord anywhere."

Was Bash back in Olympia? "What about Albius, have you sent someone to notify him?"

The same soldier nodded. "No news from Albius either."

Something was up. Every sense in my body hummed with anticipation. A strange magnetic pull was itching me toward the gates, like I was being lured to fall for a trap.

Soldiers rushed from all over, taking position on the terrace, their bows aimed down.

Nesrin brushed past us with one of her squadrons and shot me a strange look, her mouth curving upward as she strutted all grace, leading her soldiers further down south of the wall. Why was she all chirpy for?

"Gather everyone down here—armed," I ordered and then bolted to the roof of a tower overlooking the Zone of Peace gates.

From beyond our border, a thick storm of frost was raging over the winter lands of Krig, blurring details and hiding any movements. Though nothing was visible, I felt the heartbeats, more than three dozen of them, and then...that creeping sense brushed my fingertips like a breeze.

He was close. Demir...no, Vas was close.

A spark of red light flickered beside me, before a portal drew open from which Visha and Oryn came out from.

Visha bowed her head. "Snow—"

"Red Coven has a second and a third for a reason," I said, interrupting her. "Macaria will take your mother's position till she returns to it. You will not be forced to claim that spot. Not for her sake, not for the babe's sake.

That is on your mother and Melanthe. We are all making our fates, Visha. It's difficult to stick to instructions when they are all wrong."

"It is my duty."

"Your duties changed when you took oath under my rule. When I promised that I would shield you from your fate. Are you telling me to break my oath?"

She took a full breath and I saw relief settle in her features. "Thank you."

Oryn stood overlooking the distance behind the Highwall. "They come to bargain," he said gravely. "Careful."

The young general waved a hand up at us and flashed his pearly whites. "Come down here, Your Majesty," he shouted. "We've got a lot to discuss."

I turned to Visha and Oryn. Swallowing the crippling anxiousness that crawled from dark pits of memory I said, "Father is never this confident. Father never negotiates. I never negotiate—never with him. If I give an order, whether to die or to let me die, both of you obey without question. Understood?"

Both nodded and descended the Highwall tower toward the gates alongside me.

Wearing the face I always wore before danger, I ordered the gates open—my smile sturdy, my gaze unwavering. Two of the strongest Crafters in this realm stood beside me while the heavy metal gates groaned as soldiers pulled them open for us to go through the Zone of Peace.

Demir and a visibly pregnant Melanthe stood right where Visha's veil cut off. The Crafter studied the magic with a frown while Demir traced a finger over the invisible layer. Both were glazed in a thick coat of magic—protection magic. Were they that scared?

Melanthe almost bumped on the veil when she spotted who stood beside me. "Visha?"

"Aunt," my Crafter said boredly.

Demir fashioned an exaggerated curtsey. "Your Majesty."

"Village boy," I said, giving him a saccharine smile.

He lifted both hands as if in surrender and laughed. "Got me there."

I tilted my head to the side and gave him a version of my own amusement. "Perhaps Vas is more familiar to you? I am very accommodating, do let me know what you wish to be called." It annoyed me how long I'd taken to piece this one out.

His smile died down and he put his hands in his pockets as though we were completely at his mercy and it amused him. "What gave me away?"

"You stink like a fisherman. I suppose old smells are hard to get rid of."

"I was no fisherman," he snarled.

Indeed, pride was so easy to injure. Men held onto it like those three hairs on their chin that refused to grow into a beard but were insistent that it would someday grow into one. "No matter what beast you slayed, Vas, fish is fish. And no one is held on a pedestal for taking out creatures in their own home just because you want to trample all over it." My gaze dropped all over him. "Whatever did she see in you?"

He tensed.

"I suppose pity is a primal instinct for the heavenly." Twas not for me, but then, was I truly of heavens? "Like nursing a street dog."

Demir's face twisted. "Aurora is fire, she knows no pity, but she does have a heart for all."

"Was, knew and did. Past tense."

"She is alive."

"Not really."

"We know you have the three sceptre pieces," Melanthe said without missing a beat.

I linked my hands behind me. "Pray tell, what sceptre pieces?" Of course they knew.

"You're not all that funny," Melanthe sneered, wearing a gloriously pleased grin.

"You're the biggest joke in this realm, how could I ever match up to you?" My eyes dropped to her swollen stomach. "Stepmother."

Demir giggled and tapped his nose with a finger. "Come on, Princess, the scent of your magic was everywhere in Isjord. The same scent I felt in Hanai. Why do you think I took you to the Islines for? We were struggling with that one for a year and you got it for us in a day."

What?

The tower grew cold, air frosting around us and whatever dead lingered in the air, screeched and ran out of it.

For us.

No...no, I hadn't walked myself back into my father's trap.

He tilted his head back, all too calm and in control—control that was slipping through my fingers despite how long I'd spent with Kilian training it. "When I proposed to Silas that we let you collect the piece for us, he was hesitant, but he had not seen your power the way that I had. And besides," he said, his attention going behind me, "you were not alone. We'd heard from our...resources that you were working with the Night King. The two most powerful magical beings in this realm, the lone Obscur and the last

Elding, searching for the sceptre piece side by side could never fail." He let out a sigh and clicked his fingers. "The Myrdur attacks, the soldier you caught presumably told you about Valda Acme as I'd instructed him? I sent the whole lot for bait and you really took it. But then, you were desperate for answers."

I bristled.

Why was the grip slipping from my hands?

If father had wanted me to get the sceptre...that meant he had leverage against me.

"I was punished, you see." He startled me with a dark laugh. "Some called me blessed when Fader cursed me with immortality. Cursed me to live as long as them, to never die, to never love, to see the only one I ever loved chained and tortured."

"For your own lies and selfishness."

"We were in love," he growled like this was all my fault somehow.

I rolled my eyes. "For a day."

"It meant everything to me."

"The false sense of likeness is not love, Demir. Just because you both see the same shapes in the stars does not mean you are in love. You were greedy for greatness, and she was greedy for the human feel the divine are so fascinated with. You saw her like a trophy, and she saw you like a pet. You both sacrificed one another for a lie."

"It wasn't a lie!" he shouted, his skin fluttering with green scales like a reptile, and I felt that sense of chilling air flutter around me again.

"Is this what you do to the one you love? Make her my father's slave?" I gave him a polite smile. "Come, dear, admit it. All you want is to prove yourself among the gods. You. Are. Desperate. You seeked exalt and power, and when you got denied the highest form of it, you became petty. Poor, poor you."

Demir shook his head. "We are this realm's salvation from the stench of the divine. Once this land becomes ours, no god will ever dictate our living and then I will aim to bring down their lands next. Aurora will be free. She'll be free to live with me. We will both have defied gods and won."

My whole body shook from laughter. I laughed so hard that my belly hurt and my jaw was sore. "Pathetic little dog, you dream so big. Did all that immortality feed on your brains?"

"Don't underestimate your father, child," Silas's voice boomed around the tower, and I froze. "I thought by now you'd know better." One of the soldiers behind them pulled off his hood and revealed my father's face.

He stepped forward, eyeing me top to bottom as if he was seeing me for the first time. "I've never given you credit before. You did everything so efficiently. Just like I'd taught you. But to hide this, what you are. I have to give it to you, you've outdone efficiency. I should have known the moment I stared into those eyes that you were going to be what I planned for you to be." His eyes flashed all twisted malice. "No matter the fire in the gold, you were frost itself."

"It was a team effort," I said and watched my father's doubts tick on his temple. "Yes, father. All three of us had magic. Uncle did sort of guess when he sent news to the Adriatians thirteen years ago and welcomed them through your front gates."

His features were steel. Oh, might Silas, to be betrayed by the one his heart held most dear. "Now that is a poorly thought lie."

"By your brother," I clarified. "A poorly thought out lie by the man who had been betraying you more than just occasionally." I clicked my fingers and pointed a finger at him and his jaw ticked just a little. "Reminding me to hand you his bones. I am quite finished with his body. Alas, it's missing his head."

He glanced around a little, at Visha and Oryn and then back at the entirety of Highwall. And then he laughed. Laughed hard enough to send every sense in my body charging from the alarm. "I am proud, young rose. So proud." The words made something rumble in my chest. He shook his head and pointed a finger back at me. I was past flinching, but I felt the weight of that judgement. "Though you've disappointed me a little. Such greatness to have such a strange weakness when I worked hard to rip it off of you. You were almost perfect. Almost, my child. But I didn't want you to be perfect anymore anyway." His mouth was pulled in such a vile smile. "Have you forgotten how dangerous it is to have something worth losing?" He clicked his tongue all discontented and I felt ten again. Small and powerless. It felt as if I was his to wield. It almost made me want punishment—for disappointing him.

It was slipping away from me—control skidded between my fingers and all that Kilian had worked hard to teach me slid at the furthest back in my mind. Lightning broke the skies and hit the Isjordian earth, casting my father a sinister crown of light. I'd broken a promise. Without knowing, I'd broken a promise I'd made to Kilian. Blood soaked my gloves as I tried to regain command of my mind and body.

The day darkened. Not from me—not from thunder and storm. It darkened with night. The heavy scent of spring bloom and cool taste of night air filled the space around us. A gust of black winds swirled out of thin air and blasted while Kilian tore through it. Soaked from rain, his face was cast in shadows, the white and grey of his eyes gone and now veiled black.

Relief.

Pure relief settled in me. The world had stopped spinning.

"Brave," Kilian growled, slowly walking to me. With every step he took, the ground beneath charred and lit in a trail of black fire. "To come so close to my lands. And threatened my queen, Silas Krigborn."

Father sneered. "Mighty Night King made a puppet of my daughter's."

"Mighty Winter King made an oaf by his own insanity." Kilian stepped closer to the veil, almost going through it. And I was praying for his saintly patience to return to his body. "Get the hells out my lands. Stay the hells out of my kingdom."

My father sneered but held his composure somehow. "Then won't she miss her little...friends? Won't you miss your brother?"

Ice coated my veins when Melanthe waved a glowing red hand and nine bodies stood on their knees beside her.

No...no.

My vision had blurred, fear rippled through my bones as I took in all the faces before me. Freya, Ibe, Ivar, Albius, Sebastian, Celdric and...and—

I met the pair of strong russet eyes that showed no fear and then honey soft ones which I'd stared at for ten years stained with tears. Mal and Nia stood in my father's line—they stood as his prisoners.

A cry crawled up my throat, images of Sam tortured and lured me to lose control.

"The sceptre pieces and your life for theirs," Demir said with a wicked grin.

Kilian's hand grew tighter around mine and he pulled me behind him, shielding my body with his. "You don't want to do this, Silas."

My father simpered, folding his arms across his chest. "Does that mean you've made your choice? Her over your brother?" He laughed—laughed harder than I'd ever heard him laugh before and in that moment, I knew—we had lost.

I knew the moment I saw their faces that we had lost.

Sebastian and Celdric raised a chained fist to their chests. "*Signe oşh toc etter sben ys zguh.*" *We will rise between sky and clouds*, they both shouted and bowed their heads.

I tried to take a step toward them, but Kilian wrapped a strong hand around my arm, stopping me.

No.

No.

Permission—they'd surrendered their lives.

Then Nia and Mal did the same. And so did Albius, and Freya and Ibe. A silent sob wracked my chest.

No.

No.

Melanthe gathered her palm in a fist and squeezed. Everyone heaved for air and shook from the magic clinging to their bodies. "Decide quickly."

My trembling lips pulled to a snarl. "I'm going to rip that child out of your womb and let you watch as I feed it to rats. Piece by piece" Thunder struck behind her and her face twitched just a little. The stuttering laughter climbing up my throat was quivering poison. "Little sister will find that mercy, won't she? I'd save her from being the bride of hells."

Her hand loosened just a little and the hold of her magic slipped.

Demir pulled a dagger out of his baldric and grabbed Sebastian, tugging on his hair and resting the blade to his neck. "I've missed breakfast, I'd like to not miss lunch. Be quick."

My friend didn't falter, didn't waver, didn't blink. But I did. And when blood began gushing down where Demir's dagger nicked skin, fear swallowed me whole.

I'd lose if I surrendered to my father.

I'd lose if I surrendered them to my father.

I'd lost both ways.

And if I would lose, I would make sure to lose the best way I could. My brain began surging with solutions, it worked through thousands of outcomes—and there was only one that made the most sense. My smile was easy. "You know what I'm going to do to that lover of yours, Vas? I'm going to rip out every feather and make you a nice little blanket with it."

Every corner of the tower filled with that creeping sense that triggered each fibre in my body. His skin began turning a glistening green and that scent of rot and unusual magic heightened in the air. "You cannot kill what cannot be killed."

"No, but I'll have so much fun trying."

He pulled away from Sebastian—his expression was victorious. "You've made your choice."

Kilian took a step forward. "I'll come instead of her."

I grabbed his arm, but he would not budge—he stood before me like a shield. What was he doing? He couldn't do this to me. He wouldn't do this to me. He knew what it would do to me. "No. You want me, right?" I asked, attempting to rein calm over my rage. "Insurance in case your little armour does not work and you're not able to wield the sceptre."

My father's face reddened with ire and his narrowed attention bounced between Kilian and I. "Since you're so well aware."

"Visha," I said, without turning to her. "Get the sceptre pieces." I was only a small part of the plan to bring my father down. And if they lost me...they'd still know how to bring him down. My kingdom already had a king, and I knew he would put all his might in protecting it.

Every head lifted and turned to me with terror and panic.

Kilian's body went still as ice and when he turned to me, the look on his face was painted with pain of the most heart wracking sort. "You will not. You will not do this." His attention went to Visha who backed out of the gates obeying my order without hesitation. "Love, please. Please. Take this decision with me." His hands cupped my face. "Please. Take it with me. Let's make it together."

There was no decision to make. And he knew. He knew I'd give my life for those people. I rested my forehead on his chest, feeling him against me, letting his scent of spring soothe me. "I love you," I said, holding him tightly. "I love you so much, Kil."

"Please," he murmured into my hair. "Please. He will hurt you. I cannot let him hurt you again. Not anymore."

"He's already hurt me." Pulling away a little, I reached for my sword and handed it to him. "*Anima*," I whispered, "*accissor*. The smith who did this sword was from Modr. Find him." Courage shook me as I tried to remember everything. "Strike a deal with the unblessed for more metal. I will find the sphinx's heart. Take care of our family. Take care of Olympia. Take care of you."

He shut his eyes tightly and shook his head—he knew there was no convincing me otherwise. "You will return to me. You will return to me," he repeated as if to convince himself more than me. He held my face and kissed me. "I will come for you. I've waited for fifteen years, and I will not wait for a day more. I will come to get you."

I knew he would. "Keep our homes safe."

His face twisted with pain. "You're my home. I just found you and I'm losing you again."

My chest hurt—everything hurt.

Visha returned, her face was stolid and unafraid. As if she'd known. Perhaps she had. Perhaps she'd seen it all. "Remember, my queen. Nothing in the trace of our miserable fate is unmeant and unplanned. You're Nubil's second, the heavens are on your side. Use what your father does not know and will never understand about you."

I took the sceptre pieces from her, bright white light flashing when they met my skin and all magic in my body began drumming against the seal. A loud symphony of power and control surged through every corner of my body. *Kneel before the power* flashed over the metal. It was not a call of obedience. Not a call for me to kneel to. Not one competing against mine, but one complementing mine. One that searched for a master not a slave.

Kneel before—

Hells.

The Elding could control the sceptre. The Elding had defeated and locked Aurora. Only the divine could control the divine.

Kneel before the power.

I'd found Aurora's weakness.

Though my body had seized with fear, my mind still did not fail me. "When have you known me not to use a good opportunity. And this time, he's inviting me inside his lair himself." Looking up at her, I said, "If they do anything funny—attack. To kill, Visha."

She nodded. "Yes, Your Majesty."

Kilian's face was steel beaten with rage and sorrow, and I prayed that this wasn't the last I remembered of him.

"Don't mourn me, darling. Till my last breath, I will try to return to you." With that, I began retreating toward the edge of the veil. So little time. We'd had so little to celebrate what we'd found. I'd barely tasted it before it was ripped away from me.

I was not alone. I'd never be alone again.

I was not...alone. And...and I'd never be alone again.

I was going to be my father's weapon again.

I was going to be his to wield again.

Chapter Forty-Five

Sanguis

Kilian

I watched as my wife faced her father, a look full of threat and promises creased her golden stare as she aimed it scathingly toward him. "Let them go. And you shall have me and the sceptre pieces."

Her. Have her. I was letting him have her again. To hurt her again.

He nodded to his soldiers and they all pushed the Lords and Nia forward, holding my brother back. Snow didn't take another single step. "Him, too."

"Guarantee for any petty trick of yours," Silas said. "He'll join the rest when you are in my hold."

Snow shot Visha a look over her shoulder and stepped toward them.

Oryn's grip on me tightened when she reached outside of the veil, holding me back. Holding me up from crumbling to the ground. No, I wasn't going to lose her again. Not when I'd just barely found her. "She'll return, my king. You will see her return."

The two Crafters raised their glowing palms ahead, waiting for an unwanted move from Silas and I rose darkness all around us, scorching earth and melting ice. Clouds of black mist crashed against their shields, crawling over them and their soldiers flinched back. Demir…no, Vas hissed and took a step back, shooting a look at Melanthe who raised a hand to solidify the protection around them.

Dark magic against dark magic. The more mine raised, the more hers faltered and she struggled to keep up with it. She was fed from death, but I was made from it.

I stood there, helplessly watching as Snow crossed the threshold of safety. I watched as Nia and the rest brushed past Snow to our side—to safety.

"Show them hells," Nia whispered through tears as their hands grazed one another's and linked tight for a moment.

Something shifted in the air, the further Snow made it to their side and the more the others made it to ours, the harder it stirred. The scent of mint and magic grew heavy and thin bands of red almost resembling strings appeared around Nia's and the other's necks tied to Melanthe's extended hand. The witch had a wicked smile pasted on her face as she tugged her hand back, the thin, red bands of magic snapping.

It all happened so quickly. Too quick. As if time itself froze and then sped up.

One moment the red bands were around their necks, and the next...gone. Leaving behind a deep slash on their throats. On everyone's throat.

Blood.

Blood and death.

The wind turned quiet and soft again as nine bodies dropped to the ground.

"Snow!" My brother howled, tugging on his bounds like mad, eyes veiled black as he tried to summon magic against the veil surrounding him, bony limbs breaking earth but struggling to rise.

I ran, darkness and night roaring as I crossed our veil of protection in her direction.

Snow turned, but not quick enough to realise her father had played us because red, phantom chains rose from the ground, slithering around her limbs and neck, a Crafter's circle taking shape beneath her—trapping her in place.

Every lord and lady lay slain on the cold ground. Nia, too.

Snow's blood curdling scream drowned by thunder and hail. She fought the veil around her, drumming her fists in the invisible layer as tears spilled from her horrified stare.

Visha's magic howled and shot in crimson flames toward Melanthe while mine girthed soldier after soldier and every beast around us, turning them all to dust.

Oryn crossed the veil, too, aiming for her father.

Darkness shot from every corner reaching for Snow—reaching to catch her while I ran toward Nia.

Just before it grazed the tip of her fingers...she disappeared. One moment she was there, the next she was gone. All of them were gone, my brother, too.

She was gone.

Gone.

Both were gone.

"Take the injured to healers!" I shouted the order, gathering Nia in my arms, shedding my shirt and wrapping it around her neck that spilled a stream of blood. "Don't. Don't do this to us, Helenia Drava."

Her eyes peel open for one fragment of a second before she went completely limp in my arms again.

"My chambers!" Visha shouted and opened a portal for us to go through.

Time slipped from my fingers as I laid Nia down on Visha's marble table and clutched her cold hand in mine. *Don't, please.*

Healers flooded around us as Visha gave command after command. Hands tugged on my arms, on my wrists, on my shoulders, but I didn't move. "Come on, Nia. Come on, you can do this."

White magic glowed around us, casting Nia in gilt and vivid crimson. My own magic surrounded her, feeding her own mana, helping her body fight it through.

Her wet eyes peeled open just slightly, a tear sliding past them. *My pocket*, she mouthed.

Immediately, I reach for her pocket, fishing out what seemed like a pendant. I didn't understand.

"Snow's mother," she hoarsely whispered, a trace of blood spilling from her mouth. "I got it back for her. I found it. Mal helped me get it for her."

I wiped the blood away from her cheek and felt every string in my heart pull and snap. The edges of the pendant cut onto my skin as I clutched it tightly in my hand. "You will give it to her yourself, you hear me?"

"Tell her that I love her. So much...Kil—" With one last touch of a faint smile, her eyes drooped shut and her body went slack.

"Nia? Nia!"

Craft shot in red flames around us and I looked up at Visha whose body shook while her magic poured in gales, keeping Nia's soul from—

No. No. No.

She can't...she can't.

The doors pushed open and someone slid beside me. "Helenia?" Moriko's hand shook as she reached to touch her lover's face. "My *ahana*." The queen's unwavering stare was filled with tears when she turned to me, searching for the answer I could not give her.

The healers pulled away, feeling life leave her body as I was. Fury rising in me, coating the room with magic I didn't intend to use. "Don't you fucking dare!" I shouted, grabbing their hands and putting it back on Nia's body. "Till you've exhausted the last drop of your mana, you will try." I ran a shaking hand over my eyes. "Please. Please. Just try. Keep trying. She's suffered so much more, she will make it through this."

Visha's eyes flooded with hopelessness and tears as her bonds to Nia's body grew twice as strong to fight away the god of death. "Do it," she cried. "Do as he says."

The amount of blood pooling around Nia made me dizzy with sickening worry. The shadow of crimson suddenly became too vile to my eye and made my stomach turn. She had to live. She had to live and see happiness. She wanted happiness and she'd found some. She had to live through it.

She had to.

She had to.

Moriko pressed her lips to Nia's forehead. "We made too many promises, my beautiful Helenia. And perhaps not nearly enough. I love you, my *ahana*, come back to me."

Tears meshed with blood. Fear numbed by grief. The last string of white pain pouring out of Nia quivered and then faded like smoke in the wind.

No. No. No.

"She is not." I backed away, bumping into Cai's frozen state.

He shook at the sight of his friend, his face pale and white from fear. "Why is she not breathing, Kilian?" Slowly, he made toward her, his knees giving away before her and a heart-wracking sob vibrated through his chest. "Nia?" He crawled to her, reaching for her. "Nia?"

No.

No.

The pendant slipped from my hold, clattering to the ground. Fierce ache tore through my ribs. My heart was being pulled out of my chest again. My pulse slowed and slowed in my ears, piercing silence and rattle of death drumming in the air. And it was the last thing I heard before Alastair came in.

Abandoning his walking stick to the wall, he limped to Nia's body, resting a hand on her face. "Oh, kid. Sweet kid." With a shaky hand, he took off his dragon larch beads and put them around her neck. "I don't have much wealth beside you, little hen, and those beads that my wife left me. Now all my riches are in one place."

The air sung outside—a low, warm hum of life mottled with death.

A song of sorrow.

Death waited outside our window, a gnarly beast of shadows, but he was not waiting for Nia.

Alastair rested his hands on her shoulders, signalling his head to Visha and turning to me one last time, a bright smile on his face despite the tears staining his cheeks. "Tell the kids that I was happy. Tell her that I was happy."

By peace or by fire

Malik

Blood. So much blood. My sight was coated in crimson, too.
I took steps. I was sure I was taking steps and that I was moving but there was nothing. I saw nothing. Only the sound of chains tied to my hand and feet was heard in the corridors along with heavy stomps of the soldiers accompanying me toward the Tenebrosc dungeons.

The air vibrated.

Everyone halted, looking around at the picture frames quivering on the wall. The ground started shaking beneath my feet, and for a moment I thought I might have imagined it before a heavy blast shook the castle grounds.

Frames, statues and chandeliers crashed to the floor, walls cracking and tearing from the force of the earthquake, windows shattering in the air to dust. Panicked screams accompanied the sound of the crashing.

Three minutes. For three long minutes, hells seemed to have taken over land.

A sharp noise rang in my ear, pieces of glass stuck to my skin and another on my head. My chest rattled with every difficult breath I took. The heavy shouts of soldiers were only over exaggerated mimes. Nothing—I could hear nothing.

The whole corridor poured with soldiers and servants all running, panicked and terrified. Orders were shouted, eyes grew wider, and their faces terror stricken.

Like a trickle of wind, a little laugh permeated the corridors, leaking from somewhere further down inside it. Everybody halted and turned in its direction, listening as it grew and grew till it turned to a loud cackle.

"The walls," a soldier shouted, running from the opposite end of the corridor. "They're all down. All city walls are down. They've...they've exploded."

The laughter had stopped and turned to a low hum—the hum of a melody I recognised.

Everyone stopped, went silent and spun around in its direction, listening as they shadows of terror blurred all sight ahead.

"Under the moon and forest amid, blood was paid and bid," a sweet whisper trickled down to us, sending a slithering gooseflesh raise on my neck. "For the forest had no kin, the poppies grew as such within."

The skies lit alive with a rumble so deep, the land below trembled, too.

Acknowledgments

My dear readers, this book came to life because of your support. These past eight months, since the release of Winter Gods and Serpents, I have struggled a lot with general health and mental health. There were several instances where I considered dropping this writing path and not writing this sequel, but you have all made me pull through with your support on social media, with the love you've given my characters and this story, with the patience you've had waiting for this second book.

Lizzy, my dearest sister, who has been my rock through all of this, there are no words to express how grateful I am to have you in my life.

Neta, bestie, I love you.

If you have enjoyed Spring Guardians and Songbirds, please consider leaving a review on Amazon and Goodreads as it would help tremendously.

Season Warriors and Wolves coming this winter.

About Author

Wendy Heiss is an indie author debuting with a new adult fantasy trilogy. Winter Gods & Serpents is the first book in The Auran Chronicles, releasing autumn 2021. She has graduated with honours in Forensics Science in the United Kingdom, but literature has been one of her passions since she could manage to read and write. Despite being severely tempted to ride the Agatha Christie route to crime novels, she chose to follow the Tolkien path to fantasy. She forwent fingerprint powder for ball pen ink, inevitably forgoing her parents' hope for a good life and becoming what they always feared…a figuratively starving artist.

Any whom and how, she likes cats, coffee, particularly that cr*p from instant sachets. Claims to despise mafia romance from the pits of her gall bladder but will probably end up writing one herself to try and outwrite the greatest line in history: Are you alright baby girl.

Also, fried sweet potatoes, she can definitely eat some of those without claiming to be allergic to yet another vegetable. On that last note before straying too far from a simple bio, please read her book and more to come.

Dictionary

Aura-Magical humans veiled with god alike power. Each god gifted the lands chosen by them with fragments of their own resembling magic.

Dark Crafter-Magical human, different from Auras, they draw mana to power their magic from the ream of Caligo or otherwise known as other world or the heaven of dead.

Grand Maiden-Ruler of Eldmoor, head dark crafter

Ybris-Hybrid Aura, a child of two different Auras.

Eudemon-Creatures of Golgotha, god of demons. They rest in sea of the dark after their realm, Dissiri, fell.

Mid world-A spirit pane, between the living and the heavens. Crowded by trapped, revengeful or fearful souls.

Astrum liber-Holy book of Adriata, believers and followers of goddess Henah.

Caelus liber-Holy book of all gods. A dictate of laws, rules and principles.

Eirlys book-Holy book of Isjord, believers and followers of god Krig.

Hodr-Heaven of god Krig.

Cynth-Heaven of Henah, the moon.

Caligo-Heaven of Celesteel, the other world, realm of the dead and of hells.

Hemera-Heaven of goddess Cyra, the sun.

Mankai-Heaven of goddess Plantae.

Empyrea-Heaven of Adan.

Caelum-Heaven of Nubil

Neith-Heaven of Dyurin

Kemeri-Language of Hanai

Darsan-Language of Adriata

Dahaara- Steel tongued

Borsich-Language of Eldmoor

Calgnan-Language of Olympia

Zgahna-Calgnan for magic mist, sense beyond sense between magic and human awareness.

Alaar-Darsan for magic mist

Tahuma-Language of Solarya

Old Ysolt-Language of Isjord, no longer spoken in main land winter kingdom. Only used by Isline Krigborn's.

Karndu-Language of Seraphim

Laoghrikrease-Language of the unblessed, spoken main land Vrammethen and Islands of Comnhall

Anima Accisor-Soul Killer